BOLLINGEN SERIES LXXII

Eugene Onegin

A NOVEL IN VERSE BY Aleksandr Pushkin

TRANSLATED FROM THE RUSSIAN, WITH

A COMMENTARY, BY Vladimir Nabokov

PAPERBACK EDITION

IN TWO VOLUMES

II

———

Commentary and Index

———

Bollingen Series LXXII

Princeton University Press

*Contents**

VOLUME II

Commentary, Part 1

(Volume 2 of 1975 Edition)

* The pagination of the 1975 edition has been retained for this paperback edition.

Commentary, Part 2

(Volume 3 of 1975 Edition)

Index

(Volume 4 of 1975 Edition)

NOTE OF ACKNOWLEDGMENT

The publishers acknowledge permission for the use in the Commentary of quotations as follows: to Random House, New York, for passages from Babette Deutsch's translation of *Eugene Onegin* in *The Works of Alexander Pushkin*, ed. A. Yarmolinsky, copyright 1936 by Random House, Inc.; to the Pushkin Press, London, for passages from Oliver Elton's translation of *Evgeny Onegin*, 1937; to the University of California Press, Berkeley, for passages from Dorothea Prall Radin's and George Z. Patrick's translation of *Eugene Onegin*, copyright 1937 by the Regents of the University of California Press; to Macmillan and Co., London, for passages from Henry Spalding's translation of *Eugene Onéguine*, 1881; and to Mr. Edmund Wilson for a passage translated in his *The Triple Thinkers*, revised edition, Oxford University Press, New York, 1948, and J. Lehmann, London, 1952.

COMMENTARY TO *EUGENE ONEGIN*

PART 1

Foreword

The following commentary consists of a series of notes to the whole of *EO*, including rejected stanzas and variants preserved in Pushkin's cahiers as well as projected continuations. Among these comments, the reader will find remarks on various textual, lexical, biographical, and local matters. Numerous instances of Pushkin's creative indebtedness are pointed out, and an attempt has been made, by a discussion of the actual melody of this or that line, to explain the enchantment of his poetry. Most of my notes are the result of original research, or amplify and continue research done by others, but in some cases they reflect a background of anonymous knowledge shared by all Russian lovers of Pushkin.

The four "English," "metrical" "translations" mentioned in my notes and unfortunately available to students are *Eugene Onéguine*, tr. Lt.-Col. Henry Spalding (London, 1881); *Eugene Onegin*, tr. Babette Deutsch, in *The Works of Alexander Pushkin*, ed. A. Yarmolinsky (New York, 1936 and 1943); *Evgeny Onegin*, tr. Oliver Elton (London 1937; also published serially in *The Slavonic Review*, Jan., 1936–Jan., 1938); and *Eugene Onegin*, tr. Dorothea Prall Radin and George Z. Patrick (Berkeley, Cal., 1937).

Commentary

Even worse are two rhymed versions, which, like grotesque satellites, accompanied the appearance of the first edition of this work; one is Walter Arndt's (a Dutton Paperback, New York, 1963, two printings), a paraphrase, in burlesque English, with preposterous mistranslations, some of which I discussed in *The New York Review of Books*, April 30, 1964; and the other Eugene M. Kayden's product (The Antioch Press, Yellow Springs, Ohio, 1964), of which the less said the better.

V. N.

Preliminaries

Pétri de vanité . . . : The corrections in PB 8 and the ini-
tials "A. P." replacing it in PD 129 lead us to suppose
that the quotation is a spurious one—at least in its final
aphoristic form. It would be idle to speculate if that
"private letter" ever existed, and if it did to wonder who
was its author; but for those who like to look for the
actual models of fictional characters and who search for
"real life" in the dead ends of art, I have prepared a
little line of sterile inquiry in One : XLVI : 5–7.

The idea of tipping a flippant tale with a philosophical
epigraph is obviously borrowed from Byron. For the first
two cantos of *Childe Harold's Pilgrimage, a Romaunt*
(London, 1812), Byron sent R. C. Dallas (Sept. 16, 1811)
a motto beginning: "L'univers est une espèce de livre,
dont on n'a lu que la première page," etc., from Louis
Charles Fougeret de Monbron's *Le Cosmopolite* (London,
1750), p. 1.*

The oblique epigraph was a great favorite with Eng-
lish writers; it aimed at suggesting introspective associa-

---

*A later edition, 1752, presumably printed in Amsterdam, has
the added subtitle, *ou le Citoyen du monde.*

5

Commentary

tions; and, of course, Walter Scott is remembered as a most gifted fabricator of mottoes.

Pétri in a metaphorical sense (possessed with, steeped in, consisting of) was not uncommonly used by Pushkin's French models. La Bruyère, in *Les Caractères ou les mœurs de ce siècle* (1688), uses *pétri* (spelled in the first editions *paistri* and *paitri*) in par. 15 of "De la société et de la conversation" ("Ils sont comme pétris de phrases") and in par. 58 of "Des biens de fortune" ("âmes sales, pétries de boue"). Voltaire, in Epistle XLI (1733), says that the poems of Jean Baptiste Rousseau are "pétris d'erreurs, et de haine, et d'ennui," and in Canto III (1767) of *La Guerre civile de Genève* he refers to Jean Jacques Rousseau as a "sombre énergumène . . . pétri d'orgeuil," which is practically Pushkin's term.

In *Mémoires d'outre-tombe* (1849–50), Chateaubriand defines himself as "aventureux et ordonné, passionné et méthodique . . . androgyne bizarre pétri des sangs divers de ma mère et de mon père" (written 1822, rev. 1846); and I find *pétri* at least once in that author's *René* (1802 and 1805): "Mon cœur est naturellement pétri d'ennui et de misère."

In Russian literature the next *pétri* (half a century after Pushkin's) occurs, with a literal sense, in the famous French phrase spoken by the repulsive homunculus in Anna Karenin's fateful dream (*Anna Karenin*, pt. IV, ch. 3).

The master motto contains, I suggest, a possible reminiscence of a passage in Nicolas de Malebranche, *De la Recherche de la vérité* (1674–75; edn. seen, 1712), vol. I, bk. II, pt. III, ch. 5:

Ceux qui se louent se . . . [mettent] au-dessus des autres. . . . Mais c'est une vanité encore plus extravagante . . . de décrire ses défauts. . . . Montaigne me paroît encore plus fier et plus vain quand il se blâme que lorsqu'il se loue, parce que c'est un orgueil insupportable que de tirer vanité de ses défauts. . . . J'aime mieux un homme qui cache ses crimes avec honte qu'un autre qui les publie avec effronterie.

I also suggest that this epigraph contains, if not a direct allusion to Jean Jacques Rousseau and his influence on education, at least a possible echo of current discussions on the subject. Its rhythm is not unlike the quotation from Rousseau in Pushkin's n. 6 (to One : XXIV : 12). In a pamphlet published early in 1791 (*A Letter to a Member* [Menonville] *of the National Assembly; in answer to some objections to his book on French affairs*), Edmund Burke, that "diffuse and ingenious" orator (as Gibbon calls him), thus speaks of Rousseau: "We have had the . . . founder of the philosophy of vanity in England . . . [who] entertained no principle . . . but vanity. With this vice he was possessed to a degree little short of madness. It is from the same deranged eccentric vanity . . ." But let me rather continue in the French translation (*Lettre de M. Burke, à un membre de l'Assemblée Nationale de France*, Paris, 1811), which Pushkin might have seen: "Ce fut cette . . . extravagante vanité qui [le] détermina . . . à publier une extravagante confession de ses faiblesses . . . et à chercher un nouveau genre de gloire, en mettant au jour ses vices bas et obscurs"; and further, in the original: "Through him [Rousseau] they [the rulers of revolutionary France] infuse into their youth an unfashioned, indelicate, sour, gloomy, ferocious medley of pedantry and lewdness."

Pushkin's library contained a cut copy of *Réflexions sur la révolution de France*, "par Edmond Burke" (Paris, 1823), which is an anonymous translation of *Reflections on the Revolution in France* (London, 1790), the "book on French affairs" referred to in the 1791 pamphlet.

It would be vain, however, to seek in those publications the source of the Burke epigraph in PB 8 (see under

"Dropped Mottoes," below). I have traced it to Burke's *Thoughts and Details on Scarcity; originally presented to the Right Hon. William Pitt in the month of November, 1795.* The passage where it occurs (my italics) reads:

> If the price of the corn should not compensate the price of labour . . . the very destruction of agriculture itself . . . is to be apprehended. *Nothing is such an enemy to accuracy of judgment as a coarse discrimination,* a want of such classification and distribution as the subject admits of. Increase the rate of wages to the labourer, say the regulators . . .

I cannot imagine Pushkin, who, at the time, had no English (and was as indifferent to blights in England as he was to grasshoppers in Russia), reading Squire Burke on his turnips and pease. Presumably he came across the quotation in somebody's scrapbook and planned to use it in allusion, perhaps, to readers who do not "discriminate" between an author and his characters *—an idea that recurs in One : LVI, where Pushkin describes himself as anxious to mark the difference between author and protagonist, lest he be accused of imitating Byron, who portrayed himself in his characters. It is to be noted that Byron is said by his biographers to have enjoyed sending (from Venice) defamatory paragraphs about himself to the Parisian and Viennese newspapers in the hope that the British press might copy them, and that he was called (by the Duc de Broglie) *un fanfaron du vice*—which brings us back to the master motto.

DROPPED MOTTOES

The fair copy of Chapter One (listed as PB 8 and termed "The Autograph" in Acad 1937), which was prepared by Pushkin in Odessa not earlier than October, 1823,

---

*Or to grandees who forget that an impecunious poet may be as noble-born as they (see vol. 3, p. 306).

and before January, 1824, differs in several details from the first edition of the chapter (Feb. 16, 1825). This fair copy is headed by a master motto written on the cover, namely, ll. 252–53 of Evgeniy Baratïnski's poem *The Feasts* (later Pushkin planned to use them as a motto to Four, judging by the fair copy of that canto); then comes the title, *Evgeniy Onegin,* and, under this, another motto: "Nothing is such an ennemy [sic] to accuracy of judgment as a coarse discrimination. Burke." (See above, "Master Motto.") Under this appears "Odessa MDCCC-XXIII." This is followed by two chapter mottoes:

> O'er life thus glides young ardor:
> to live it hurries and to feel it hastes . . .*

(Pushkin at first wrote "hastes," *speshít,* instead of "glides," *skol'zít*); and

Pas entièrement exempt de vanité il avait encore de cette espèce d'orgueil qui fait avouer avec la même indifférence les bonnes comme les mauvaises actions, suite d'un sentiment de supériorité peut-être imaginaire.

> Tiré d'une lettre particulière

Pushkin first wrote "encore plus d'orgueil et de ce genre" and "suite d'un sentiment de supériorité sur les autres."

A thirty-page transcript (termed *Kopiya* in Acad 1937) of Chapter One made by a copyist in the autumn of 1824, corrected by Pushkin, and sent with Lev Pushkin to Petersburg, omits Baratïnski and Burke. It is headed by a dedication written on the cover in the poet's hand:

> Inscribed to Brother
> Lev Sergeevich
> Pushkin

Then comes the autograph title:

> *Evgeniy Onegin*
> A Novel in Verse
> The work of A. P. . . . . .

---

*These are ll. 75–76 from Pyotr Vyazemski's poem *The First Snow* (1819), discussed in my note to One: motto.

Commentary

In the French motto that follows, the three initial words ("Pas entièrement exempt") are crossed out by Pushkin; he replaced them by the one word *Pétri* (in pencil, according to V. Sreznevski's description of this MS in *P. i ego sovr.*, II [1904], 3).

The motto from Vyazemski is omitted and does not appear in either the 1825 edition or the 1829 reprint; it heads One in the 1833 and 1837 editions.

DROPPED INTRODUCTIONS

Pushkin prefaced Chapter One, when published separately (1st edn., Feb. 16, 1825; 2nd edn., late March, 1829), with a dedication to his brother and with the following lines (pp. vii–viii), which were meant to suggest the aloofness of an editor and which were not reprinted by him in the complete editions of the novel:

Here is the beginning of a long poem [*bol'shogo stihotvoreniya*], which probably will not be finished.

Several cantos [*pesen*] or chapters [*glav*] of *Eugene Onegin* are now ready. Written as they are under the influence of favorable circumstances, they bear the imprint of that gaiety* which marked the first works of the author of *Ruslan and Lyudmila* [1820].

The first chapter [*glava*] presents a certain unity. It contains the description of a St. Petersburg young man's fashionable life [*svetskoy zhizni*] at the end of 1819 [sts.

---

*Actually, by mid-February, 1825, Pushkin had ready only three chapters (and about half of Four). None of these is particularly gay. We should remember that in 1820 he had been ordered by the government to remain domiciled in southern Russia until further notice and that at the end of July, 1824, he had been expelled from Odessa to Mihaylovskoe, the familial countryseat in northwestern Russia; the indolence of his life in Kishinev (where *EO* was begun in May, 1823) and Odessa and the not-too-dull retirement of Mihaylovskoe are the "favorable" circumstances mentioned here.

Pesen is the gen. pl. of *pesnya* or *pesn'* (song, canto), and *glav* is the gen. pl. of *glava* (head, chapter).

xv–xxxvii] and recalls *Beppo,** somber Byron's humorous production.

No doubt farsighted critics will notice the lack of plan. Everyone is free to judge the plan of an entire novel after reading the first chapter of the latter [*onogo*]. Critics will also deplore the antipoetical nature of the main character, who tends somewhat to resemble the Caucasian Captive [the hero of Pushkin's romantic poem of the same title published in 1822], as well as certain strophes written in the depressing manner of the latest elegies "wherein the feeling of dejection engulfs all other feelings." † We crave permission, however, to draw our readers' attention to merits rare in a satirical writer: the absence of insulting personal remarks and the observance of strict decorum in the humorous description of mores.

In the MS of this introduction, written in 1824 (Cahier 2370, ff. 10ʳ, 11ʳ), with a charming drawing of Onegin's profile above the abbreviated title (*Predislovie k Evg. Oneg.*), the second sentence of the fourth paragraph begins: "One will be right in condemning the nature of the main character, remindful of *Ch* H" (sic; ‡ altered from *Adol'f*, a reference to Benjamin Constant's *Adolphe*); and the following two paragraphs replace paragraph five:

The status of editor allows us neither to praise nor to blame this new work. Our views may seem partial; but we crave permission to draw the attention of the esteemed

---

*The allusion is to *Beppo* (1818) or, rather, to *Beppo, nouvelle vénitienne*, in the French version of Byron's works. A. Pichot, in his introduction (vol. II, 1820; repr. in vol. IV, 1822), says: "Comme Don Juan, Beppo est un *hoax* continuel: le poète semble se jouer de toutes les règles de son art. . . . Cependant, au milieu des digressions continuelles, le sujet marche toujours."

†From Wilhelm Küchelbecker's critical essay "On the Tendency of Our Poetry, Especially Lyrical, in the Last Decade," *Mnemosyne* (*Mnemozina*), pt. II (1824), pp. 29–44. See also n. to Four : XXXII : 1.

‡A Russian *Ch* and a Latin H. As further noted: *Childe Harold* is *Chayl'd Garól'd* in Russian and was pronounced *Shild-Aróld* in French.

public and of Messrs. the Reviewers to a merit as yet new in a satirical writer: the observance of strict decorum in the humorous description of mores. Juvenal, Catullus, Petronius, Voltaire, and Byron far from seldom failed to retain due respect toward readers and toward the fair sex. It is said that our ladies are beginning to read Russian [instead of French]. We boldly offer them a work wherein they will find, beneath a light veil of satirical gaiety, observations both true and entertaining.

Another merit, almost as important, and doing considerable honor to our Author's mildness of heart, is the total absence of insulting personal remarks; for [*ibo*] one should not attribute this solely to the fatherly watchfulness of our censorship, custodian of morals [and] of the tranquillity of the state, protecting citizens with no less solicitude from the attack of "naïve slander" [and] of derisive levity . . .

(The last sentence is incomplete.)

In the 1825 and 1829 editions of One, the preface was followed (pp. xi–xxii) by a curtain raiser or *Vorspiel* in freely rhymed iambic tetrameters (ending in an emphatic sentence in prose) entitled *Conversation of Bookseller with Poet* (*Razgovor knigoprodavtsa s poetom*). It was completed Sept. 26, 1824, at Mihaylovskoe, and republished as a separate poem (i.e., not associated with *EO*, with which indeed it has little to do) in our poet's first collection of poems (1826; it appeared Dec. 28, 1825). In a letter of Dec. 4, 1824, Pushkin had asked his brother Lev to have the piece dated 1823 in print— with the purpose, perhaps, of preventing anyone from identifying certain lines in it (e.g., 144–59) with the author's experiences in Odessa during the early summer of 1824, when he had his affair with Countess Elizaveta Vorontsov. In translating this piece (which contains some admirable lines but is, on the whole, one of Pushkin's least successful poems), I have preserved the measure (and even a few docile rhymes here and there), except in the case of ll. 97–100, which absolutely refused

to turn into English tetrameters without loss or padding
of sense and have therefore been abandoned to prose.

Conversation of Bookseller with Poet

BOOKSELLER *

1   Versets for you are mere amusement
     you just have to sit down a bit.
     Fame has already managed everywhere
     to spread the pleasantest of news:
     'Tis rumored, a long poem's ready,
     a new fruit of the mind's devices.
     Decide, then; I await your word.
     Name your own price for it.
     The versets of the pet of the Muses and Graces
10   we shall at once replace by rubles
     and into a bunch of ready banknotes
     transform your little leaves of paper.
     Why have you sighed so deeply,
     may I learn?

POET

            I was far away.
     I was remembering the time
     when in the opulence of hope,
     a carefree poet, I would write
     from inspiration, not for pay.
     I saw again the cliffs' retreats
20   and the obscure roof of seclusion
     where to Imagination's feast,
     time was, I used to call the Muse.
     There sweeter would my voice resound,
     there longer brilliant visions,
     in loveliness ineffable,†

---

*Pushkin has a footnote here (1825, 1829, p. x): "Let us observe
for the edification of the squeamish custodians of decency that
the Bookseller and the Poet are fictitious persons. The former's
compliments are but social urbanity, a pretense necessary in a
conversation, if not in a magazine."

†*S neiz 'yasnímoyu krasóy*, "with ineffable beauty." The same
term is employed in connection with Lenski's vision of Olga,
EO, Six : xx : 7–8.

swirled, flew above me
in hours of nighttime inspiration.
All would excite the tender mind:*
a blooming mead, the moon's effulgence,
30 the storm's noise in a moldering chapel,
an old crone's wondrous legend.
A kind of demon would preside
over my games, my leisure;
he after me flew everywhere;
to me he whispered sounds sublime,
and with a grievous flaming sickness
my head was filled;
within it, wondrous dreams were born,
into eurythmic measures flowed
40 together my obedient words
and with a ringing rhyme were closed.
In Harmony my rivals were
the sough of woods, or raging whirlwind,
or the oriole's live strain,
or the sea's muffled noise at night,
or purl of gently streaming river.
Then, in the silence of my toil
I was not prepared to share
flaming transports with the crowd;
50 and the sweet favors of the Muse
debase I did not by a shameful trade.
I was their miserly protector.
Exactly thus, in muted pride,
from eyes of the bigoted rabble
the favors of his youthful mistress
does a foreboding lover hide.

BOOKSELLER

But fame for you replaced
joys of a secret reverie:
you've been snapped up by eager hands,
60 whereas the dusty cumulations
of moldy prose and verse

---

*Chateaubriand, in *René*, had a similar intonation: "Qu'il
falloit peu de chose à ma rêverie: une feuille séchée . . . une
cabane dont la fumée s'élevoit dans la cîme dépouillée des
arbres . . . une roche ecartée, un étang désert . . ." (ed.
Armand Weil [Paris, 1935], pp. 44–45).

await in vain their readers
and fame's fickle reward.

POET

Blest he who in himself concealed
the high creations of the soul
and from men as from tombs
never awaited recompense for feeling.
Blest who in silence was a poet,
who unwreathed with the thorn of fame,
70 forgotten by the despicable rabble,
quitted the world without a name.
E'en more than dreams of hope deceitful,
what's fame? Is it a reader's whisper?
Base ignorance's persecution?
Or a fool's admiration?

BOOKSELLER

Lord Byron held the same opinion;*
Zhukovski used to say the same;†
but the world learned of, and bought up,
their sweet-toned works.
80 And verily your lot is enviable:
the poet punishes, the poet crowns;
villains with levin of eternal darts

---

*Byron went to Pope, and Pushkin went to Pichot. Pope (*An Essay on Man*, ep. IV, 237–38) has:
"What's Fame? a fancy'd life in others breath,
  A thing beyond us, ev'n before our death."
Byron (*Don Juan*), I, CCXVIII, 1–2, 7–8) has:
"What is the end of Fame? 'tis but to fill
  A certain portion of uncertain paper:

  .   .   .   .

To have, when the original is dust,
  A name, a wretched picture and worse bust."
Pichot's wretched version (a fourth monument) turns Byron's first two lines into: "A quoi aboutit la gloire? à remplir peut-être une petite page de papier." See also in Lamartine's *Harmonies* the passage "Qu'est-ce que la gloire? Un vain son répété," etc. Pushkin himself used the formula in a long poem of the same period as the *Conversation*, his frankly Byronic *The Gypsies* (ll. 219–23). I quote it in n. to One : VIII : 10–14.
†The reference presumably is to Vasiliy Zhukovski's ballad *Svetlana*, l. 259: "Fame, we have been taught, is smoke."

he smites in far posterity;
heroes he comforts.
Onto the throne of Cytherea with Corinna*
he elevates his mistress.
Praise is for you a tiresome din,
but hearts of women ask for fame:
for them write. To their ears
90   the flattery of Anacreon is pleasing:
In young years roses are to us
dearer than bays of Helicon.

POET

Conceited daydreams,
pleasures of frenzied youth!
I also 'midst the storm of noisy life
sought the attention of the fair.
Charming eyes read
me with a smile of love;
magic lips whispered
100 my sweet sounds to me.
But 'tis enough. To them his freedom
the dreamer immolates no more:
let them by Shálikov† be sung,
nature's amiable darling.
To me what are they? Now in backwoods
my life sweeps on in silence.
The moaning of the faithful lyre
will not touch their light, giddy souls.
Unclean is their imagination,

---

*The "mistress" of the Roman poet Ovid, whom he celebrated
in his elegies (*Amores*), c. 16–1 B.C.

†Why Pushkin thought fit to pay this Gallic compliment
(*lyublezniy baloven' prirodi*, Fr. "aimable favori de la nature")
to the lackadaisical poetaster, Prince Pyotr Shalikov (1768–
1852), editor of the *Ladies' Journal* (*Damskiy zhurnal*, Fr.
Journal des dames), is not clear—unless it was simply prompted
by the professions of rapturous admiration for Pushkin that
Shalikov made in his magazine. Anyway, Pushkin replaced
"Shalikov" by *yunosha* (the young man) when this *Conversa-
tion* appeared in his first collection of poems (1826). The sudden
innomination and juvenescence greatly puzzled the elderly
journalist, it is said. The draft has *Bátyushkov* instead, a
reference to the poet Konstantin Batyushkov (1787–1855).

110   it does not understand us:
to them God's token, Inspiration,
is alien and preposterous.
When to my mind, against my will,
there comes a line they have instilled,
at once I redden,* my heart aches,
I am ashamed of my idols.
To what, unfortunate, did I aspire?
Before whom my proud mind debase?
Whom with the rapture of pure thoughts
120   did I not shrink from deifying?

BOOKSELLER

I love your anger. That's your poet!
The reasons of your bitterness
I cannot know. But some exceptions
for winsome ladies don't you make?
Can it be true that none is worth
the inspiration or the passions†
and won't appropriate your songs
to her almighty loveliness?
You do not speak?

POET

    Why should a poet
130   disturb the grievous slumber of the heart?
Remembrance he torments in vain;
and then? What is it to the world?
To all I am a stranger. Does my soul
preserve an image unforgettable?
Did I know ecstasy of love?
With a prolonged heartache exhausted,
in stillness did I hide my tears?
Where was the one of whom the eyes‡
like heaven used to smile on me?
140   All life is it one night or two?
    .   .   .   . §

---

*Altered to "I trepidate" (*ya sodragayus'*) in the 1826 collection.
†Cf. One : XXXIV : 11–12.
‡"Of whom the eyes," *kotóroy óchi*—a clumsy turn.
§The dots are Pushkin's pause, not an omission.

And then? My tiresome moan of love,
my words would seem
a lunatic's wild babble.
Afar, one heart would understand them,
and even so—with a sad shudder.
Fate once for all has so decided.
Ah, thoughts of *her* a wilted soul's
youth might revive,
and dreams of whilom poetry
150 would be again stirred up in swarms.
Alone she would have comprehended
my hazy verse;
she'd in my heart alone have flamed
like love's pure lamp.
Alas, of no avail are wishes:
she has rejected exorcisms,
complaints, the heartache of my lot;*
unbosomings of earthly transports
she, a divinity, needs not.

BOOKSELLER

160 To sum up: having tired of love,
grown bored with rumor's prattle,
a priori, you have repudiated
your inspired lyre.
Now that you've left the noisy world,
the Muses, and volatile Fashion,
what will your choice be?

POET

Freedom.

BOOKSELLER

Fine. Here is my advice to you.
Hark to a useful truth:
our time's a huckster. In this iron time
170 where there's no money there's no freedom.
What's fame? A gaudy patch
upon the songster's threadbare rags.

---

*Poems (1826) gives "soul" for "lot."

What we need is gold, gold, and gold;
accumulate gold to the last!
I see beforehand your objection,
but then I know you gentlemen:
your work to you is valuable
while, set upon the flame of toil,
Fancy boils, bubbles.
180   It cools, and then
you are fed up with your own composition.
Allow me to say simply this:
not salable is inspiration,
but one can sell a manuscript.
Why then delay? Already come to me
impatient readers;
around my shop reviewers prowl;
followed by scrawny songsters;
one for a satire food is seeking,
190   another for the soul, or quill.
That lyre of yours, quite frankly speaking,
much good is going to fulfill.

POET

You are perfectly right. Here, take my manuscript.
Let us come to terms.

PREFATORY PIECE

Rhyme sequence: ababececdiidofof (here as elsewhere
the vowels stand for feminines). Meter: iambic tetram-
eter. The story of the publication of this piece (composed
Dec. 29, 1827, after three chapters of *EO* had already
come out and six had been finished) is rather curious.

The first edition of Chapter One (printing completed
Feb. 7, 1825, on sale nine days later) was inscribed by
Pushkin to his brother Lev (*Posvyashcheno bratu L'vu
Sergeevichu Pushkinu*). Lev Pushkin (1805–52), on
leaving Mihaylovskoe in the first week of November,
1824, had taken an apograph of Chapter One to St.
Petersburg to have it published there with the assistance
of Pletnyov (see below). Lev Pushkin was an enthusiastic
literary factotum; but he was negligent in money

19

matters, and, even worse, he circulated his brother's MS poems, reciting them at parties and allowing them to be transcribed by admirers. He had a marvelous memory and much artistic acumen. The exile in Mihaylovskoe began to grumble in the summer of 1825 and exploded the following spring. Baratïnski did his best to exculpate "Lyovushka" (diminutive of Lev), but Pushkin's relations with his dissipated young brother never regained their initial warmth.

Much more diligent was Pyotr Pletnyov (1792–1862), a gentle scholar, ecstatically devoted to talent and poetry. In the 1820's he taught history and literature to young ladies and cadets at various schools; in 1826 he gave lessons at the Imperial Palace; from 1832 on he was professor of Russian literature at the Petersburg University and in 1840 wound up as its president (*rektor*).

Pushkin wrote to Pletnyov, from Mihaylovskoe to Petersburg, at the end of October, 1824; the draft of this letter (Cahier 2370, f. 34^r) reads:

> You published once my uncle.
> The author of *The Dangerous Neighbor*
> was very worthy of it,
> although the late Beséda
> spared not his countenance. *
> Now, chum, do publish ⟨me⟩,
> ⟨the fruit⟩ of my frivolous labors;
> but in the name of Phoebus, my Pletnyóv,
> when will you be *your* publisher?

Lightheartedly and joyfully, I rely upon you in relation to my *Onegin*! Summon my Areopagus—you, Zh[ukov-ski], Gned[ich], and Delvig—from you [four] I await judgment and with submissiveness shall accept its decision. I regret that Bara[tïnski] is not among you; it is said he is writing [a long poem].

The first reference in these versicles (iambic tetram-

---

* *Works* 1949 (II, 225) has instead "did not even take notice of him."

eters) is to Vasiliy Pushkin (a minor poet, 1767–1830), Aleksandr Pushkin's paternal uncle. His best work was the satirical poem mentioned here, *The Dangerous Neighbor* (*Opasnïy sosed*, 1811), the disreputable hero of which, Buyanov, was to appear in *EO* (see nn. to Five : XXVI : 9, and XXXIX : 12) as our poet's "first cousin" and the first pretendant to Tatiana's hand (Seven : XXVI : 2). The next reference is to the literary feud between the Moderns, or Westernizers (the Arzamas group), and the Ancients, or Slavonizers (the Beseda group), a feud that had no effect whatever on the course of Russian literature and was marked by execrable taste on both sides (see n. to Eight : XIV : 13). Pletnyov had supervised the publication of Vasiliy Pushkin's poems (*Stihotvoreniya*, St. Petersburg, 1822), *not* including, of course, *The Dangerous Neighbor*.

Pletnyov's participation came about in the following way: in 1821 Vyazemski, writing from the province of Moscow to his Petersburg correspondent, Aleksandr Turgenev, had urged the latter to arrange the publication by subscription of Vasiliy Pushkin's poems. Turgenev procrastinated, saying (Nov. 1, 1821) that since he had "no time to plant the flowers of literature when there were so many weeds to be pulled out elsewhere" he had entrusted the task to Pletnyov. Pletnyov received five hundred rubles for his pains; but only at the end of April, 1822 (a delay that almost drove poor Vasiliy Pushkin insane), had enough subscribers been rounded up—mainly through kindly Vyazemski's efforts—to start printing the book. I cannot discover what financial arrangements Pletnyov had with Aleksandr Pushkin, but there is a genuinely unmercenary ring to the delight with which he undertook the publication of *EO*, Chapter One, charmingly characterizing it in a letter to the author, of Jan. 22, 1825, as "the pocket speculum of Petersburg's young set."

Pushkinists accuse Pletnyov of having been a poor proofreader and of not having done enough for Pushkin's posthumous fame. He was, however, the poet's first biographer (*Sovremennik*, X [1838]).

The Prefatory Piece first appeared in the separate edition (c. Feb. 1, 1828) of Four and Five, with the dedication "Petru Aleksandrovichu Pletnyovu" and the date "December 29, 1827"; although it introduces only these two chapters, its wording implies the whole set of five chapters. A friendship prompting such an inscription is likely to remain unclouded, even after losing its first careless glow, and there is reason to believe that Pushkin was doing his utmost to make amends for having hurt Pletnyov's feelings (see below); but, in general, dedications have a way of becoming a burden to all concerned. In the first complete edition of *EO* (Mar. 23, 1833) the piece was relegated—somewhat pathetically—to the end of the book (pp. 268–69), among the notes, with n. 23 reading: "Chapters Four and Five came out with the following dedication" (under this, a reprint of the piece). Then, after a sojourn in this purgatory, the piece was shifted again to the front of the novel, where it occupied two unnumbered pages (vii and viii), before p. 1 in the second complete, and final, 16° edition (January, 1837), without any trace of the inscription to Pletnyov. Its vicissitudes did not end here. If we may judge by a specimen of the rare 1837 edition in the Bayard L. Kilgour, Jr., Collection, No. 688, Houghton Library, Harvard University, some copies must have had the fourth leaf with the Prefatory Piece misplaced between pp. 204 (ending on Seven : II : 9) and 205.

Pletnyov wrote very poor verse. In a dreadful little elegy, clumsy and coy but otherwise harmless, which appeared in Aleksandr Voeykov's magazine *Son of the Fatherland* (*Sïn otechestva*, viii [1821]), Pletnyov described—in the first person!—what purported to be the nostalgic emotions of the poet Batyushkov (whom he did not know personally) in Rome. Thirty-four-year-old Konstantin Batyushkov, who had recently entered the first stage of the thirty-four-year-long madness that was to last till his death in 1855, took exception to the "elegy" much more strongly than he would, had he been sane. The unfortunate incident, which was particularly distressing in view of Pletnyov's passionate admiration for Batyushkov, was harshly commented upon by Pushkin in his correspondence. To Pletnyov's "corpse-pale" style he alluded rather brutally in a letter of Sept. 4, 1822, to Lev Pushkin, who showed it "by mistake" to good Pletnyov; in reply, the latter at once addressed to Pushkin a very poor but very touching poem (beginning "Your caustic censure does not anger me"), in which he expresses the doubt that he, Pletnyov, would ever be able to say about his fellow poets, to whom "the brotherhood of art" united him:

> "Part in their fame I'm given, and I'll live
> in the immortality of those I cherish."
> Vain hopes! Perhaps, with all my love
> for poetry, with deep woe in my soul,
> under the tempest of menacing days
> earthward I'll bend like a lone poplar.

From Petersburg, Pletnyov sent his poem to Pushkin in Kishinev sometime in the autumn of 1822, and Pushkin, in his reply (December?), of which only the draft has reached us, did his best to soothe the distressed lover of the Muses and attributed his "flippant sentence" about Pletnyov's style to "the so-called hyp [*handra*], to which I am subject." "Do not think, however," Pushkin continues in his draft, "that I am not capable of appreciating your indubitable talent. . . . Whenever I am completely myself, your harmony, your poetical accuracy, the nobility of expression, the grace, the purity,

the finish of your verses, captivate me as much as does
the poetry of my favorites."

Pushkin's Prefatory Piece is but a versified extension
of these well-meant but mendacious blandishments—
and for fifteen years that albatross hung about our poet's
neck.

*

Not only is the Prefatory Piece a good-natured inscrip-
tion to a friend who has to be soothed, and not only does
it adumbrate some of the novel's moods and themes; it
also prefigures three constructional devices that the
author will use throughout *EO*: (1) the participial line;
(2) the definitional line; and (3) the tabulation device.

The opening participial lines of the Prefatory Piece,
as sometimes happens with Pushkin, seem to float along-
side the context; their points of attachment are ambig-
uous. These verses may be understood as: "Since I do
not plan to entertain the world and since my main
concern is the opinion of my friends, I would have liked
to offer you something better than this"; but the sub-
ordinate clauses may be also connected with the main
clause in another way: "I wish I were concerned only
with the opinion of my friends; *then* I might have offered
you something better."

The quatrain is followed by definitional phrases and
sets of listed items grading into what I have called
"tabulation": "My gift ought to have been more worthy
of you and your fine soul. Your soul consists of (1) a holy
dream, (2) vivid clear poetry, (3) high thoughts, and
(4) simplicity. But no matter—accept this collection of
pied chapters, which are [here follows a definition of the
gift]: (1) half droll, (2) half woeful, (3) plebeian (or
'realistic'), and (4) ideal. This gift is also the casual
product of [here follows the tabulation]: (1) insomnia,
(2) light inspirations, (3) unripe and withered years,

(4) the cold observations of the mind, and (5) the mourn-
ful memoranda of the heart."

*

1 The device of beginning a dedication or an address with
a negative formula is a common one. In England it goes
back to the seventeenth century. James Thomson's
epistolary dedication of his *Summer* (1727) to the Right
Honorable Mr. Dodington (George Bubb Dodington,
Baron Melcombe, 1691–1762) starts on a similar note:
"It is not my purpose . . ."

3, 5 / *zalóg* / *dushí prekrásnoy*: Fr. *gage . . . d'une belle
âme*, common lyrical Gallicisms of the day. "Vous verrez
quelle belle âme est ce Zhukovski," wrote Pushkin to
Praskovia Osipov on July 29, 1825.

6 / [full of a holy] dream: Some editors have been tempted
to accept as a final correction a curious misprint in the
1837 edition that fuses the epithet in *svyatóy ispólnennoy
mechtí* into *svyatoispólnennoy* ("holiful"—an impossible
compound). I suspect that a proofreader (Pushkin him-
self?), having noticed a previous misprint, *svyatoi
ispolnennoy*, put in the diacritical sign (see "Method of
Transliteration," ñ) so roughly that it encroached upon
the last letter of the first word that it should have crested,
seeming to indicate, instead, that the space should be
closed up.

10 / take / *primí*: *Prinyat'* is usually "to accept"; it in-
cludes the idea of "to take" (*vzyat'*), which is dominant
in the present passage.

11–17 Cf. James Beattie (1735–1803), Letter XIII, to Dr.
Blacklock, Sept. 22, 1766: "Not long ago I began a poem
[*The Minstrel*, 1771, 1774] in the style and stanza of
Spenser, in which I propose to give full scope to my
imagination, and be either droll or pathetic, descriptive

or sentimental, tender or satirical, as the humour strikes
me" (in Sir William Forbes, *An Account of the Life and
Writings of James Beattie* [2nd edn., Edinburgh, 1807],
I, 113).

Byron quotes this in his preface to the first two cantos
(February, 1812) of *Childe Harold*, and it fits in rather
well with Pushkin's program. Pichot's version (1822)
goes: ". . . en passant tour à tour du ton plaisant au
pathétique, du descriptif au sentimental, et du tendre
au satirique, selon le caprice de mon humeur" (*Œuvres
de Lord Byron* [1822], vol. II).

15, 17 / [of] years . . . [of] remarks [or "marks"] / *let . . .*
zamet: An improved echo of Baratïnski's rather lame
lines in his poem *The Feasts* (*Pirï*, 1821; see Three :
XXX : 1), ll. 252–53:

> Collections of the flaming marks
> of the rich life of youthful years . . .
>
> *Sobrán'e plámennïh zamét*
> *Bogátoy zhízni yúnïh lét . . .*

There is a still more curious, though fainter, echo
here—namely, of two lines (7–8) of a 23-line dedicatory
piece (*To Friends*) by Batyushkov, prefacing pt. II
(October, 1817) of his collection *Essays* [*Opïtï*] *in Verse
and Prose*:

> [Find here] the story of my passions,
> the errors of the mind and heart . . .
>
> *Istóriyu moíh strastéy,*
> *Umá i sérdtsa zabluzhdén'ya . . .*

Chapter One

K. Vyazemskiy: Prince (*knyaz'*) Pyotr Vyazemski (1792–
1878), a minor poet, was disastrously influenced by the
French poetaster Pierre Jean Béranger; otherwise he was
a verbal virtuoso, a fine prose stylist, a brilliant (though
by no means always reliable) memoirist, critic, and wit.
Pushkin was very fond of him and vied with him in scat-
ological metaphors (see their letters). He was Karamzin's
ward, Reason's godchild, Romanticism's champion, and
an Irishman on his mother's side (O'Reilly).

Vyazemski, who was the first correspondent Pushkin in-
formed (Nov. 4, 1823) of his writing *EO*, plays a curiously
pleasing part in it: he presides at its opening (the epi-
graph is l. 76 of his *The First Snow*; see also Five : III,
where Vyazemski is linked with Baratïnski); enlivens
with a pun Tatiana's journey to Moscow (see Pushkin's
n. 42 and my n. to Seven : XXXIV : 1, on McEve); and
then, as the author's proxy, comes to Tatiana's rescue in
Moscow, during one of her dullest society chores (see
n. to Seven : XLIX : 10).

The First Snow (*Pervïy sneg*, written 1816–19, pub.
1822*) consists of 105 iambic hexameters, freely rhymed.

---

*In *Literary News* (*Novosti literaturï*), the supplement of the
Russian Disabled Soldier (*Russkiy invalid*), no. 9, pp. 173–76.

Let spring be welcomed by the "spoiled child" of the South, where "the shade is more fragrant, the waves are more eloquent"; I am the "sullen son" of the North, "well used [*obíklïy*] to blizzards," and I "welcome the first snow"—this is the gist of its beginning. There follows a description of naked autumn, and then comes the magic of winter: "Burning blue skies . . . dales under brilliant carpets . . . the pine tree's somber emerald powdered with silver . . . the blue glass of the frozen pond." These images are repeated by Pushkin, in sharper outline, in 1826 (*EO*, Five : I) and especially in 1829 (*Winter Morning*, a short poem in iambic tetrameter). This takes care of the first third of Vyazemski's piece. There follows a description of bold skaters celebrating the expected return of winter (cf. *EO*, Four : XLII, late 1825); then there is a glimpse of a hare hunt ("the impatient eye interrogates the tracks") and another of a rosy-cheeked lady abloom in the frost (both images are echoed in Pushkin's descriptive poem in Alexandrines, *Winter*, 1829). A sleigh ride (alluded to in *EO*, Five : III : 5–11) is then compared (ll. 75–76) to the passing of youth:

> O'er life thus glides young ardor:
> to live it hurries and to feel it hastes . . .

(The poem is, I repeat, in iambic hexameter, but anything longer than eight or ten syllables would force the translator to pad these two lines. The first line was criticized by Shishkov—see n. to Eight : XIV : 13—as being too Gallic: "ainsi glisse la jeune ardeur"; the second, Pushkin used for his chapter motto.)

Vyazemski goes on to say (I metaphrase in prose):

Happy years! . . . But what am I saying [the pseudoclassical Gallicism, "que dis-je"]? . . . Love betrays us . . . the soul's losses live in the soul's memory, and it is with this remembered anguish that I promise always to welcome—not you, handsome spring [*krasívaya vesná*], but you,

O Winter's firstling, brilliant and morose,
first snow, the virgin fabric of our fields [ll. 104–05].

The poem is sumptuously and somewhat archaically worded, and replete with certain Vyazemskian idiosyncrasies that make his diction immediately recognizable amid the rather drab language of Pushkin's contemporaneous imitators (although actually Vyazemski's poetical power was inferior to that of, say, Baratínski). One seems to be looking through a magnifying but not very clear glass. It will be noted that Pushkin went to the last, philosophical part of the poem for his epigraph, but had in mind the central, pictorial part when alluding to the same poem in Five : III (see n. to Five : III : 6).

Vyazemski, from Moscow, had sent to Pushkin, at Kishinev, a copy of *The First Snow* (which Pushkin had known since April, 1820, in MS) only a couple of months before the first stanza of *EO* was composed.

I

1 / My uncle has most honest principles / *Moy dyádya sámïh chéstnïh právil*: Grammatically, "my uncle [is a person] of most honest [honorable] rules."

This is not a very auspicious beginning from the translator's point of view, and a few factual matters have to be brought to the reader's attention before we proceed.

In 1823 Pushkin had no rivals in the camp of the Moderns (there is a tremendous gap between him and, say, Zhukovski, Batyushkov, and Baratínski, a group of minor poets endowed with more or less equal talent, insensibly grading into the next category, the frankly second-rate group of Vyazemski, Kozlov, Yazïkov, etc.); but c.1820 he did have at least one in the camp of the Ancients: this was Ivan Krïlov (1769–1844), the great fabulist.

In a very curious piece of prose (Cahier 2370, ff. 46ʳ, 47ʳ), an "imagined conversation" between the author and the tsar (Alexander I, r. 1801–25), jotted down by our poet in the winter of 1824, during his enforced seclusion at Mihaylovskoe (Aug. 9, 1824, to Sept. 4, 1826), there occurs the phrase, spoken by the author: "*Onegin* [Chapter One] is being printed. I shall have the honor of sending two copies to Ivan Krïlov for your Majesty's library" (since 1810 Krïlov had been holding a sinecure at the public library of St. Petersburg). The opening line of *EO* is (as is known, I notice, to Russian commentators) an echo of l. 4 of Krïlov's fable *The Ass and the Boor* (*Osyol i muzhik*), written in 1818 and published in 1819 (*Basni*, bk. VI, p. 77). Pushkin, early in 1819, in Petersburg, had heard the portly poet recite it himself, with prodigious humor and gusto, at the house of Aleksey Olenin (1763–1843), the well-known patron of the arts. At this memorable party, complete with parlor games, twenty-year-old Pushkin hardly noticed Olenin's daughter, Annette (1808–88), whom he was to court so passionately, and so unfortunately, in 1828 (see n. to Eight : XXVIa : vars.), but did notice Mrs. Olenin's niece, Anna Kern (Cairn), née Poltoratski (1800–79), to whom at a second meeting (in the Pskovan countryside July, 1825) he was to dedicate the famous short poem beginning, "I recollect a wondrous moment," which he presented to her enclosed in an uncut copy of the separate edition of Chapter One of *EO* (see n. to Five : XXXII : 11) in exchange for a sprig of heliotrope from her bosom.

Line 4 of Krïlov's fable goes: "The donkey had most honest principles"; grammatically: "the donkey was [a creature] of most honest [honorable] rules." When told by the countryman to patrol the vegetable garden, he did not touch a cabbage leaf; indeed, he galloped about so vigilantly that he ruined the whole place, for which he was cudgeled by its owner: asininity should not accept grave tasks, but he errs, too, who gives an ass a watchman's job.

1–2 For these two lines to make sense, the comma must be replaced by a colon; otherwise, the most painstaking translator will go astray. Thus, the usually careful Turgenev-Viardot prose translation (1863) opens with the bungle: "Dès qu'il tombe sérieusement malade, mon oncle professe les principes les plus moraux."

1–5 The first five lines of One are tantalizingly opaque. I submit that it was, in fact, our poet's purpose to have his tale start opaquely and then gradually disengage itself from the initial vagueness.

In the first week of May, 1820, twenty-five-year-old Eugene Onegin receives a letter from his uncle's steward telling him of the old man's being at death's door (see XLII). He forthwith leaves St. Petersburg for his uncle's countryseat, which lies south of that city. On the basis of certain viatic data (discussed in my notes to the journey the Larins make in Seven : XXXV and XXXVII), I situate the cluster of four estates ("Onegino," "Larino," Krasnogorie, and Zaretski's seat) between parallels 56 and 57 (the latitude of Petersburg, Alaska). In other words, I would locate the manor that Eugene inherits the moment he gets there at the junction of the former provinces of Tver and Smolensk, some two hundred miles W of Moscow, thus about midway between Moscow and the Pushkin countryseat Mihaylovskoe (province of Pskov, district of Opochka), and some 250 miles S of St. Petersburg, a distance that Eugene, by bribing coachmen and post innmasters and changing horses every ten miles or so, might cover in a day or two.

We are introduced to him as he bowls along. The first stanza expresses the mists and wisps of his drowsy cerebration: "My uncle . . . man of principle . . . Krïlov's

donkey of principle . . . *un parfait honnête homme* . . . a
perfect gentleman, but, after all, a fool . . . commands
respect only now, when he has sickened not in jest . . .
il ne pouvait trouver mieux! . . . this is all he could devise
in the way of universal esteem . . . too late . . . good
lesson to others . . . I, too, may end up thus. . . ."

Thus flows, I imagine, the inner monologue through
Onegin's brain; it forms a specific pool of sense in the
second part of the stanza. The bedside ordeal evoked by
Onegin with such passive disgust will be spared him:
his most proper man of an uncle is even more of an
honnête homme, or *honnête âne*, than his cynical nephew
thinks. Those precepts of conduct include an unobtrusive
departure. As we are going to learn from one of the most
rollicking strophes ever written on death (One : LIII),
Uncle Sava (the MS name, which, I think, is his) will
not allow himself any time to enjoy the esteem that, in
these immemorial dramas of heritance, has been won
for him by a literary tradition going back at least to
Rome.

Here and there in the course of these very first lines
odd echoes are aroused in the mind of the reader, who
recalls "my uncle . . . a man of honor and rectitude" in
ch. 21 of Sterne's *The Life and Opinions of Tristram
Shandy, Gentleman* (1759; which Pushkin had read in
a French version made "par une société de gens de
lettres," in Paris, 1818), or XXVI, 7, of *Beppo* (1818), "a
woman of the strictest principle" (which Pichot, 1820,
translates "une personne ayant des principes très-
sévères"), or the stanza opener in I, XXXV, of *Don Juan*
(1819), "Yet José was an honorable man" (which Pichot,
1820, translates "C'était un brave homme que don
Jose"), or the similarity in position and intonation of
Don Juan, I, LXVII, 4, "And certainly this course was
much the best" (translated by Pichot "c'était ce qu'elle
avait de mieux à faire"). The pursuit of reminiscences

may become a form of insanity on the scholiast's part; but there can be no doubt that, despite Pushkin's having in 1820–25 practically no English, his poetical genius managed somehow to distinguish in Pichot, roughly disguised as Lord Byron, through Pichot's platitudes and Pichot's paraphrases, not Pichot's falsetto but Byron's baritone. For a fuller account of Pushkin's knowledge of Byron and of Pushkin's inability to master the rudiments of the English language, see my notes to One : XXXVIII.

It is curious to compare the following sets:

Evgeniy Onegin, One : I : 1–5 (1823)

Moy dyádya sámïh chéstnïh právil:
Kogdá ne v shútku zanemóg,
On uvazhát' sebyá zastávil,
I lúchshe vídumat' ne móg.
Egó primér drugím naúka . . .

Moya Rodoslovnaya, Octet VI, ll. 41–45 (1830)

Upryámstva dúh nam vsém podgádil:
V rodnyú svoyú neukrotím,
S Petróm moy práshchur ne poládil
I bïl za tó povéshen ím.
Egó primér bud' nám naúkoy . . .

My Pedigree

A stubborn strain has always let us down:
indomitable, after all his kin,
my grandsire did not hit it off with Peter,
and in result was hanged by him.
To us let his example be a lesson . . .

My Pedigree, an 84-line piece in iambic tetrameter, with alternate rhymes, consists of eight octets and a postscriptum of five quatrains; it was composed by Pushkin on Oct. 16 and Dec. 3, 1830, soon after he had completed the first draft of *EO*, Eight. Its composition

Commentary

was provoked by Fadey Bulgarin's coarse article in the *Northern Bee* (*Severnaya pchela*), in which that critic made fun of Pushkin's keen interest in his Russian "six-hundred-year-old" nobility and in his Ethiopian descent (see App. I). The intonations of ll. 41–45 bear a weird resemblance to *EO*, One : 1 : 1–5, with an analogous feminine rhyme in the second and fourth lines (*EO*: *právil–zastávil*; *Pedigree*: *podgádil–poládil*) and an almost identical fifth line.

Why did our poet choose, in *My Pedigree*, to imitate Béranger's vulgar *Le Vilain* (1815), with its refrain, "Je suis vilain et très vilain"? This can only be explained by Pushkin's habit of borrowing from mediocrities to amuse his genius.

6 / what a bore / *kakáya skúka*: Or "how borish," as a London macaroni might have said half a century before.

14 It is rather amusing that the first stanzas of both *EO* and *Don Juan* close with an invocation of the devil. Pichot (1820 and 1823) has: "Envoyé au diable un peu avant son temps" ("Sent to the Devil somewhat ere his time"—*Don Juan*, I, I, 8).

Pushkin wrote his first stanza May 9, 1823, by which time he must already have seen the French version of the first two cantos of *Don Juan*, in the 1820 edition. He had certainly seen it by the time he left Odessa in the summer of 1824.

1–5 A canceled draft (2369, f. 4ᵛ) reads:

> My uncle has most honest principles.
> He nothing better could invent:
> he has made one respect him
> when taken ill in earnest.
> To me, too, his example is a lesson ...

The same simple theme occurs in Byron's *Don Juan*, can. I (written Sept. 6–Nov. 1, 1818), CXXV, 1–3:

> Sweet is a legacy, and passing sweet
>   The unexpected death of some old lady,
> Or gentleman of seventy years complete . . .

(Pichot, 1823: "Il est doux de recevoir un héritage, et c'est un bonheur suprême d'apprendre la mort inattendue de quelque vieille douairière, ou d'un vieux cousin de soixante-dix ans accomplis . . .")

A MS variant (unknown to Pichot or Pushkin) of the end of the octave reads:*

> Who've made us wait—God knows how long already,
> For an entailed estate, or country-seat,
>   Wishing them not exactly damned, but dead—he
> Knows nought of grief, who has not so been worried—
> 'Tis strange old people don't like to be buried.

II

1 Cf. the beginning of *Melmoth the Wanderer*, by C. R. Maturin, 1820 (see n. to Three : XII : 9): "In the autumn of 1816 John Melmoth, a student in Trinity College, Dublin, quitted it to attend a dying uncle in whom his hopes for independency chiefly rested." This "solitary passenger in the mail" is "sole heir to his uncle's property." Pushkin read *Melmoth*, "par Mathurin," in the "free" French version by Jean Cohen (Paris, 1821), who caused four generations of French writers to misspell the original author's name when quoting him.

2 The young blade is driving "with posters" or "behind post horses" (*na pochtovïh*). Note the accents: *pochtováya (loshad')*, "post horse," but *pochtóvaya proza*, "postal

*Byron, *Works*, ed. E. H. Coleridge (1903), VI, 49, n. i, ll. 4–8.

prose" (Three : XXVI : 14). However, further on (Seven : XXXV : 11) Pushkin shifts the accent to the second syllable in speaking of posters.

3 A vivid vibration of *v*'s (*Vsevíshney vóleyu Zevésa*) somewhat redeems the painful Gallic cliché (*par le suprême vouloir*). Pushkin had already used this mock-heroic formula in 1815, in a madrigal to Baroness Maria Delvig, a schoolmate's sister (*vsevíshney blágost'yu Zevésa*, "by the most lofty grace of Zeus"). The opulent-looking rhyme *povésa* (scapegrace)–*Zevésa* (of Zeus) is merely a borrowing from Vasiliy Maykov's long poem *Elisey* (1771; see n. to Eight : Ia : 3), where it occurs in can. I, ll. 525–26. The borrowing was more obvious and more amusing in 1823 than it is now, when *Elisey* is remembered only by a few scholars.

5 / *Druz'yá Lyudmíli i Ruslána*: Reference to his own writings is used by Pushkin thematically throughout *EO*. The allusion here is to his first long work, *Ruslan and Lyudmila*, a mock epic in six cantos (*Ruslan i Lyudmila: Poema v shesti pesnyah*, St. Petersburg, [Aug. 10], 1820). This spirited fairy tale, bubbling along in freely rhymed iambic tetrameters, deals with the adventures of pleasantly Gallicized knights, damsels, and enchanters in a cardboard Kiev. Its debt to French poetry and to French imitations of Italian romances is overwhelmingly greater than the influence upon it of Russian folklore, but the purity of its diction and the verve of its colloquial modulations make of it, historically, the first Russian masterpiece in the narrative genre.

8 / *Pozvol'te poznakómit' vás*: Lexically: "let me acquaint you with," but in English that would imply a matter rather than a person, and Pushkin is speaking of a person.

9 / Onegin / *Onégin, Onyégin* (old orthography): The name
is derived from that of a Russian river, the Onéga, flow-
ing from Lacha Lake to Onega Bay, White Sea; and
there is an Onega Lake in the province of Olonets.

13 / promenaded / *gulyál: Gulyat'* has not only the sense
of "to stroll," "to saunter," but also "to go on a spree."
From June, 1817, when he graduated from the Lyceum,
to the beginning of May, 1820, Pushkin led a rake's
life in Petersburg (interrupted, in 1817 and 1819, by
two summer sojourns at his mother's country estate,
Mihaylovskoe, province of Pskov). See n. to One : LV : 12.

14 Pushkin often alludes to personal and political matters
in geographical, seasonal, and meteorological terms.

Bessarabia, of Pushkin's n. 1, is the region between
the rivers Dnestr (or Dniester) and Prut, with forts
Hotin (or Khotin), Akkerman, Izmail, etc., and the main
town of Kishinev. If Hotin in a sense is the cradle of the
Russian iambic tetrameter (see App. II, "Notes on Pros-
ody"), Kishinev is the birthplace of the greatest poem
written in that meter. After beginning his novel there on
May 9, 1823, Pushkin revised and completed the first
stanzas nineteen days later. Acad 1937 publishes (p. 2) a
facsimile of the draft of the first two stanzas (Cahier 2369,
f. 4ᵛ). At the top of the page our poet put two dates sepa-
rated by a full stop, with the first numeral overwritten
and thickened by several emphatic strokes of the pen, and
the second date underlined:

9 May. *28 May* night.

When composing these two stanzas, he synchronized
retrospectively his expulsion from the "North," exactly
three years before, with Onegin's departure for the
country. They will meet again briefly, late in "1823,"
in Odessa, after a separation of three and a half years.

On Apr. 30, 1823, a few days before Pushkin had begun *EO* in Bessarabia, Vyazemski in Moscow wrote to Aleksandr Turgenev in Petersburg: "I have recently had a letter from Pushkin, the Arabian devil [*bes Arabskiy*]"—a pun on *bessarabskiy*, "the Bessarabian." The epithet should have been, of course, *arapskiy*, from *arap* ("Blackamoor," an allusion to Pushkin's Ethiopian blood), and not *arabskiy*, from *arab* ("Arab").

III

1 / Having served / *Sluzhív*: I have followed bald grammar here in rendering what sounds to a modern ear like a perfective form similar to *prosluzhív* instead of the protracted *sluzhá*, "serving." Although this may be splitting dyed hairs, I cannot help suggesting that perhaps what Pushkin really meant was not that Onegin's late father made debts *after* retiring from the civil service (as the perfective leads one to assume), but that he had *simultaneously* served, contracted debts, *and* given balls.

1 / excellently, nobly / *otlíchno, blagoródno*: A comma separates the two words in the draft (2369, f. 5ʳ) and in the fair copy (PB 8). The 1833 and 1837 editions also give *otlichno, blagorodno*. But the 1825 and 1829 editions omit the comma, and modern editors cannot resist the temptation of following N. Lerner,* who recognized the humor of the archaic formula (*otlichno blagorodno*, "right honorably," as used, for instance, in official documents of the time) resulting from the absence of a comma and pointed out that the good gentleman apparently did not take bribes (as some other bureaucrats did), hence his debts. Acad 1937 compromises by joining the two words with a hyphen.

***Pushkinologicheskie etyudï*, essays in the collection *Zven'ya* (1935), V, 60–62.

4 / *promotálsya*: Cf. the French verb *escamoter*, "to scamble away" something.

In a MS note of 1835 Pushkin carefully computed that Byron's father squandered, at twenty-five rubles to the pound sterling, 587,500 rubles in two years. This was about the sum Pushkin's friend Vyazemski gambled away in his twenties and about three times the sum Pushkin owed various creditors at the time of his death (1837).

For old Onegin's financial operations see also VII : 13–14.

5 / Eugene / *Evgéniy* (rhymes with "Allegheny"): Onegin's Christian name, first mentioned here, will be easy for Pushkin to rhyme with nouns ending in *-éniy* (gen. pl. of nouns ending in *-énie*, corresponding to the English "-ation" in general meaning). It also rhymes with *geniy*, "genius." The surname *Onegin* has no rhyme in Russian, and rhymes only with "vague in," "plaguin'," and "Fagin" in English.

6–14 The names of Pushkin's house tutors, three successive Frenchmen in the first decade of his life, were Monfort (or Montfort or Count de Montfort), Rousselot, and Chedel. He had also a Russian teacher with a German name, Schiller. His sister had at one time (before 1809) an English governess, a Miss or Mrs. Bailey, apparently a relation of John Bailey, lecturer in English at Moscow University; but if she gave Pushkin a few lessons, these were completely forgotten by 1820. A Greek Catholic deacon, Father Aleksandr Belikov, taught him arithmetic. At one time, before Pushkin was enrolled at the Litsey or Lyceum (founded by Alexander I Aug. 12, 1810, and opened Oct. 19, 1811, at Tsarskoe Selo; see nn. to Eight : I), there had been a plan to have him enter a Jesuit boarding school in St. Petersburg; Vyazemski and a number of other distinguished Russians had been educated there. In 1815 the school was accused of striv-

ing to lure its students from the Greek faith to the
Roman one, instead of sticking to the teaching of Virgil
and Racine. The Jesuits were expelled from St. Peters-
burg and Moscow in December, 1815, and from the rest
of Russia five years later.

At the close of the eighteenth century, during the
years of change and bloodshed in their country, many
bewildered people left France to be miscast as governesses
and domestic tutors in the wilds of Russia. Russian
noblemen, most of them Greek Catholics, in their
legitimate eagerness to have their children acquire a
modish smattering of French culture, thought nothing
of engaging a Jesuit priest as *uchitel'* (tutor). These
indigent "outchitels" (Fr.) often had a rough time. Ac-
cording to Pushkin (in a letter to his fiancée dated Sept.
30, 1830), whose creative imagination worked wonders
with family tradition, his paternal grandfather, Lev
(1723–90), a quick-tempered squire (as given to brutal
jealousy, in fact, as was Pushkin's maternal great-grand-
father, Abram Gannibal), suspecting the French tutor
in his household, an Abbé Nicole, of being his wife's
lover, unceremoniously hanged him in the backyard of
the Pushkin manor, Boldino.

In Pushkin's day French governesses of gentle birth
were referred to in Russian as *Madám* (even if unmar-
ried) or *Mamzél'*. Cf. in his short story *The Miss Turned
Peasant* (*Barïshnya-Krest'yanka*): "His daughter had an
English *Madam* [governess]—Miss Jackson, a prim
spinster of forty."

The conjecture that "l'Abbé" may have been meant
as a surname is defeated by a canceled reading in the
draft (2369, f. 5ʳ): "*mos'e* l'abbé" (monsieur l'abbé).

8 / *rezóv no míl*: Cf. Byron's *Don Juan*, I, L, 1–3:

> . . . he was a charming child . . .
> Although in infancy a little wild . . .

Pichot (1823) feebly translates: "le fils d'Inèz était un aimable enfant . . . [qui] avait été un peu espiègle dans son enfance . . ."

It is curious that the predicative *rezóv*, with the accent shifted to the last syllable, makes the epithet stronger than the basic adjectival form, *rézvïy*, which ordinarily means "frisky," "frolicsome," "gamesome," "sportive," "spry" (the last I have used for rendering the arch-seeming but really quite innocent intonation of the words *Olga rézvaya*, as used by Onegin in speaking of Lenski's fiancée in Four : XLVIII : 2).

9 / *Frantsúz ubógoy*: The adjective *ubogoy** combines the ideas of destitution, humbleness, shabbiness, and mediocrity.

11 / in play [or "in jest"] / *shutyá*: His devices do not seem to have been as shrewd as those of Benjamin Constant's tutor, who taught Greek to his pupil by the simple method of suggesting they invent together a new language.

14 / Létniy Sad: Le Jardin d'Eté, a public park on the Neva embankment, with avenues of crow-haunted shade trees (imported elms and oaks) and noseless statues of Greek deities (made in Italy); there, a hundred years later, I, too, was walked by a tutor.

VARIANTS

1 Canceled draft (2369, f. 5^r):

> His father, a rich widower . . .

---

*The correct form is, of course, *ubogiy*, but to render a more euphonious old-fashioned pronunciation, as well as for reasons of rhyme (see also Two : VI : 5–6), poets of the time not seldom substituted an *o* (sounded rather like "uh") for the unaccented *i* (or *ï*) in the masculine endings of adjectives.

9 The tutor was at first (drafts, 2369, f. 5^r) a "noble Swiss," then a "very strict Swiss," then a "very dignified Swiss," and finally (in the fair copy) a "very clever Swiss."

13 The draft (2369, f. 5^r) reads:

> fed him sometimes preserves . . .

These altered from "bonbons" and "ice cream," and corrected in the fair copy to:

> talked to him about Paris . . .

13–14 Canceled draft (2369, f. 5^r):

> and when about sixteen, my friend
> saw his whole course of studies end.

In the margin of this page, with the drafts of III and IV, Pushkin wrote:

> Evgeniy Onegin
> a poem in

IV

1 A French cliché; cf. Jacques Delille, *Epître sur la ressource contre la culture des arts et des lettres* (1761):

Dans l'age turbulent des passions humaines
Lorsqu'un fleuve de feu bouillonne dans nos veines . . .

Bouillonne, Russian *kipít*, is met several times later (e.g., One : XXXIII : 8: *kipyáshchey mládosti moéy*, "of my ebullient youth").

Onegin was born in 1795 and completed his studies not later than 1811–12, about the time Pushkin was beginning his at the newly founded Lyceum. Between him and Pushkin there was a difference of four years.

Clues to these dates are found in Four : IX : 13; Eight : XII : 11; and the Introduction to the separate edition of Chapter One.

4 / *prognáli so dvorá*: "Driven off the premises," "kicked out of the house." The closest meaning of *dvor* in this context is "dwelling place," the old "stead."

6 Liberal French fashions, such as haircuts à la Titus, (short, with flattened strands), appeared in Russia immediately after the lifting of various preposterous restrictions dealing with dress and appearance that had been inflicted on his subjects by Tsar Paul (who was strangled by a group of exasperated courtiers on a March night in 1801).

In 1812–13 European dandies wore their hair rather short, in ragged locks, which were "composed into a studied negligence by the labour of two hours," as W. M. Praed says of a later exquisite's head ("On Hair-Dressing," in *The Etonian*, I [1820], 212).

7 / London Dandy: To this last word, printed in English, Pushkin appended his n. 2: "Dandy, *frant* [fop]." In the draft of his notes for the 1833 edition he added the definition "un merveilleux."

The word "dandy," which was born on the Scottish border c. 1775, was in vogue in London from 1810 to 1820 and meant "an exquisite," "a swell" ("*swell kids* of the Metropolis," as Egan curiously puts it in bk. II, ch. 1, of the work mentioned below). Pichot, in a footnote to his "translation" (1820) of Byron's *Beppo*, LII, inexactly says of "un Dandy": "Petit-maître anglais."

Pierce Egan, in his *Life in London* (1821), bk. I, ch. 3, thus describes the pedigree of a London dandy:

The DANDY was got by *Vanity* out of *Affectation*—his dam, *Petit-Maître* or *Maccaroni*—his grand-dam, *Fribble*

—his great-grand-dam, *Bronze*—his great-great-grand-dam, *Coxcomb*—and his earliest ancestor, FOP.

Beau Brummell's dandy days in London lasted from 1800 to 1816, but he was still living elegantly in Calais in Onegin's time. His biographer, Captain William Jesse, writing in London in the 1840's, when the term "dandy" had been replaced by "tiger," makes the following remark: *

If, as I apprehend, glaring extravaganzas in dress—such, for instance, as excessive padding, trowsers containing cloth enough for a coat besides, shirt-collars sawing off the wearer's ears and the corners threatening to put out his eyes . . . constitute dandyism, Brummell most assuredly was no dandy. He was a *beau*. . . . His chief aim was to avoid anything marked.

Onegin, too, was a beau, not a dandy. (See also n. to One : XXVII : 14.)

8 / he saw the World / *uvidel svét*: *Svet*, in this sense, is *le monde, le beau monde, le grand monde* (*bol'shoy svet*), "the world of Fashion," "the Gay World," "the Great World," "High Life," "High Society"—a bouquet of synonyms.

Cf. Pope: "My only Son, I'd have him see the World: | His French is pure . . ." (*Imitation of Horace*, bk. II, ep. II).

Cf. Byron: "Don Juan saw that Microcosm on stilts, | Yclept the Great World . . ." (*Don Juan*, XII, LVI, 1–2).

Cf. Egan: "The advantages resulting from 'seeing the World'. . . excited the curiosity of our Hero" (*Life in London*, bk. II, ch. 3).

10 / write: The text has "wrote" (*pisál*), a slight solecism, which the English past tense would unduly magnify.

---

* *The Life of George Brummell, Esq., Commonly Called Beau Brummell* (London, 1844), I, 58–59.

12 / unconstrainedly; v : 9 / without constraint; v : 7 and
11 / learned: Repetition of epithets in close proximity
is characteristic of Russian nineteenth-century litera-
ture, with its comparatively small vocabulary and youth-
ful contempt for the elegancies of synonymization.

14 / *Chto ón umyón i óchen' míl*: *Mil*, which Pushkin
had already used in the preceding stanza ("boisterous
but charming"), is the French *gentil*: "Le monde
décida qu'il était spirituel et très gentil."

VARIANT

8 Draft (2369, f. 5^r):

    no later than at sixteen years . . .

(The "sixteen" is altered from "seventeen.")

V

1–2 / *Mï vsé uchílis' ponemnógu* | *Chemú-nibud' i kák-
nibúd'*: See App. II, "Notes on Prosody": § 13, Rhyme,
for an analysis of the stress accents in the second line.

    A paraphrase of these two lines, which are difficult to
translate without either impoverishing or enriching the
sense, would be: "We all rambled through our studies,
which were random in matter and in manner," or
simply: "We learned any old thing in any old way."

    The whole description of Onegin's desultory educa-
tion (One : III–VII) is similar, in flippant tone, to Byron's
Don Juan, I, XXXVIII–LIII, especially LIII, 5–6: "I think
I picked up too, as well as most, | Knowledge of matters
—but no matter *what*." Pichot (1820): "Je crois bien
que c'est là que j'appris aussi, comme tout le monde,
certaines choses—peu importe."

    Pushkin's text also bears a bizarre resemblance to a

passage, which he could not have known at the time, in Ulric Guttinguer's mediocre *Arthur* (1836):* "Je finissais négligemment une éducation très negligée" (pt. I, ch. 3).

Arthur, incidentally, is one of Onegin's cousins who, like Chaadaev (see n. to One : XXV : 5), found a cure for his spleen in the Roman Catholic faith.

7 / a learned fellow but a pedant: One variety of pedant is the person who likes to perorate, to air, if not to preach, his opinions, with great thoroughness and precision of detail.

The term (Ital. *pedante*, used by Montaigne c. 1580, *un pedante*) originally meant "teacher" (and is probably allied to "pedagogue"); the type was satirized in farces. Shakespeare used it in this sense, and it was so used in eighteenth-century Russia by Denis Fonvizin and others (also in the verbal form *pedantstvovat'*, to preach and to prate). In the nineteenth century it appears with various connotations as "one who knows books better than life," etc., or "one who lays excessive stress upon trifling details" (*OED*). It is also applicable to persons who flaunt their esoteric learning, or apply a pet theory in a grotesque way, without discrimination. Scholarship without humility or humor is a basic type of pedantry.

Mathurin Régnier (1573–1613) thus described *un pédant* (*Satire* X):

Il me parle Latin, il allegue, il discourt

. . . .

[dit] qu'Epicure est ivrogne, Hypocrate un bourreau, Que Virgile est passable . . .

(See n. to One : VI : 8.)

---

*Pt. I consists of "Mémoires"; pt. II, of "Religion et Solitude," the last a pious discourse more or less coinciding with the fragmentary first edition entitled *Arthur, ou Religion et Solitude, troisième partie* (Rouen and Paris, 1834).

Malebranche, early in the eighteenth century, in the same passage that I quote in my note to the Master Motto, has the following to say about a pedant (for him Montaigne was a pedant!):

L'air du monde et l'air cavalier soutenus par quelque érudition . . . deux vers d'Horace . . . petits contes. . . . Pédants [sont] ceux qui, pour faire parade de leur fausse science, citent à tort et à travers toutes sortes d'auteurs . . . parlent simplement pour parler et pour se faire admirer des sots . . . [sont] vains et fiers, de grande mémoire et de peu de jugement . . . d'une imagination vigoureuse et spacieuse, mais volage et déreglée.

On the whole, Addison's definition (*The Spectator*, no. 105, June 30, 1711) is the closest to Pushkin's idea of superficially educated Onegin:

A Man that has been brought up among Books, and is able to talk of nothing else, is . . . what we call a Pedant. But, methinks, we should enlarge the Title, and give it every one that does not know how to think out of his Profession and particular way of Life.
What is a greater Pedant than a meer man of the Town? Bar him the Play-houses, a Catalogue of the reigning Beauties, and an Account of a few fashionable Distempers that have befallen him, and you strike him dumb.

See Hazlitt's subtle defense of pedantry in *The Round Table* (1817), no. 22, "On Pedantry": "He who is not in some measure a pedant, though he may be a wise, cannot be a very happy man," etc.

"The vacant scull of a pedant," says William Shenstone, "generally furnishes out a throne and temple of vanity" (*Essays on Men and Manners*, in *Works* [London, 1765], II, 230).

Yet another variety of pedant is one who deceives people with samples of "scholarship." The scholiast who is overabundant and overexact in his references may well be absurd; but he who, in his anxiety to impress with sheer number, neither bothers to verify the items he copies out (or has others copy out for him) nor cares if his source, or his science, errs is a fraud. Compare, in this connection, Pushkin's short poem in iambic tetrameter, *A Good Man* (*Dobrïy chelovek*, c. 1819):

> You're right: unbearable is learned Thyrsis,
> a pedant self-important and abstruse:
> he gravely judges everything,
> of everything he knows a little.
> I love you, neighbor Pachomius:
> you're merely stupid, and thank God for that.

An appreciation of the fun of *EO*, v : 7 also depends on the reader's realizing that those solemn and self-sufficient worthies (universal and omnipresent characters, of course) who were deemed "stern judges" by the world of fashion were actually so ignorant that a flippant display of light wit on the part of a modern young man, or his profound silence, struck them as a deliberate show of unduly exact knowledge.

It has been suggested (see note in the Paris edition of 1937) that the "but" (*no*) is a typographical error for "not" (*ne*); this does not explain why Pushkin retained the "but" through the next three editions.

In his usual effort to make of Onegin a paragon of progressive virtue, N. Brodski (*Evgeniy Onegin* [1950], pp. 42–44) attempts to prove by the forced cards of specious quotation that in Pushkin's day, as well as in Fonvizin's, *pedánt* meant an honest man and a political rebel. See variant.

8 / the happy talent / *schástlivïy talánt*: A Gallicism. See, for example, in Voltaire's poem *Le Pauvre Diable*:

> J'ai de l'esprit alors, et tous mes vers
> Ont, comme moi, l'heureux talent de plaire;
> Je suis aimé des dames que je sers.

9 See n. to One : IV : 12.

14 / the fire of unexpected epigrams: Another Gallicism. Cf. *le feu d'une saillie.*

1–4 A first draft of the first four lines reads (2369, f. 5ᵛ):

> Despite the verdict of stern critics
> he was, of course, no pedant;
> many considered that in Eugene
> more than one talent lay concealed.

5–8 Tomashevski (Acad 1937) quotes the draft (2369, f. 6ᵛ):

> My friend was burning with impatience
> forever to get rid of study:
> the hum and glitter of high life
> had long attracted his young mind.

A fair-copy variant of the second half of the stanza reads:

> It was suspected he had talent;
> and Eugene could, in point of fact,
> join in a pleasant conversation—
> and sometimes in learned discussions—
> on Monsieur Marmontel,
> on Carbonari, on Parny,
> on General Jomini.

The life of these allusions has somewhat faded by now. An Italian secret society aiming at establishing a republic, a French emperor's Swiss-born general's becoming a Russian emperor's aide-de-camp—these were no doubt likely topics in the teens of the century, though their coincidence is not necessarily typical. Baron Henri Jomini (1779–1869), who switched his allegiance from Napoleon to Alexander I in 1813, was popular in Russian military schools. His main work on military science, in eight volumes, is *Traité des grandes opérations militaires contenant l'histoire critique des campagnes de Frédéric II, comparées à celles de l'empereur Napoléon; avec un recueil des principes généraux de l'art de la guerre* (Paris, 1811–16). According to him, the fundamental principle of this "art" "consiste à opérer avec la plus grande masse de ses forces un effort combiné sur le point décisif" (VIII, 681).

Marmontel's *Contes moraux* (see n. to Five : XXIII : 10) was widely read; but the good-natured irony of this combination of names is no longer obvious, and Pushkin showed foresight in canceling a local pattern of tenuous associations. As to Evariste Désiré Desforges, Chevalier de Parny (1753–1814), it was not his lyrical strain that might have interested Eugene, but rather the diverting (though somewhat protracted) blasphemies of *La Guerre des dieux* (see n. to Three : XXIX : 13, 14). The audacities of one age become the platitudes of the next, and some twenty years later it was the barracks-room *esprit fort*, M. Bovary *père*, and the crass Philistine Homais, who thought highly of "naughty" Evariste.

8–14 A draft of the last seven lines reads (2369, f. 6ʳ):

> In him the ladies perceived talent,
> and he indeed with them was able
> to have a learned conversation,
> and even a virile discussion
> on Byron, on Manuel,
> on Carbonari, on Parny,
> on General Jomini.

Other canceled variants on the same folio read (l. 12):

> on Mirabeau, on Marmontel . . .
> on Bergami, on Manuel . . .
> on Benjamin, on Manuel . . .

and (l. 13):

> on magnetism, on Parny . . .

The English poet's name appears here as *Beyron*, a popular Russian (more exactly, Baltic) mispronunciation of the time instead of the correct *Bayron*. (Thus the title of Zhukovski's translation of *The Prisoner of*

Chillon reads in the 1822 edition: *Shil'onskiy Uznik, poema lorda Beyrona.*) The other persons are: Jacques Antoine Manuel (1775–1827), French politician and orator; Honoré Gabriel Victor Riquetti, Count de Mirabeau (1749–91), French orator and revolutionist; Bartolommeo Bergami, favorite of Queen Caroline (1768–1821), wife of the Regent (George IV), the reference being to the apocryphal *Mémoires de Monsieur le Baron Pergami* (Paris, 1820), widely read in an anonymous translation from the Italian; and, finally, Henri Benjamin Constant de Rebecque (1767–1830), French orator and writer.

VI

1–4 This can be construed as (1) "since Latin is obsolete, no wonder Onegin could only make out epigraphs," etc. (and in this case, *tak*, which I have translated as "still," would mean "so" or "consequently"); or as (2) "although Latin is obsolete, yet he could make out epigraphs," etc. The first reading seems pointless to me. The knowledge Onegin had of Latin tags, however meager, is placed in contrast to, rather than seen as a result of, the initial situation; the second, and to me correct, reading contains an element of humor: "Latin is obsolete; but would you believe that he actually was able to decipher trite mottoes and discuss Juvenal [in a French version]!" The irony is echoed by VIII : 1–2:

> All Eugene knew besides
> I have no leisure to recount.

One of the epigraphs he could decipher heads Two.

3 / *On znál dovól'no po-latíne:* Should be *latíni.*

5 / descant on Juvenal / *Potolkovát' ob Yuvenále:* Pushkin had used the same verb as a rhyme (imperfective, third person singular, *tolkovál*) to *Yuvenál* in his first pub-

lished poem, *To a Rhyming Friend* (*K drugu stihotvortsu*, 1814).

La Harpe, writing in 1787, in *Lycée, ou Cours de littérature ancienne et moderne*,* quotes Juvenal's translator, Jean Joseph Dusaulx: "[Juvenal] écrivait dans un siècle détestable [c. A.D. 100]. Le caractère romain était tellement dégradé que personne n'osait proférer le mot de liberté," etc.

Jean François de La Harpe (1739–1803), the celebrated French critic, whose *Cours de littérature* was young Pushkin's textbook at the Tsarskoe Selo Lyceum, should not be confused with Frédéric César de La Harpe (1754–1838), Swiss statesman and Russian general, who was the tutor of the Grand Duke Alexander, later Tsar Alexander I.

Byron, writing to Francis Hodgson, Sept. 9, 1811 (at the time that Onegin was completing his studies), says: "I have been reading *Juvenal*. . . . The Tenth Sat^e . . . is the finest recipe for making one miserable with his life. . . ."

Satire x begins, in a French version (with the Latin *en regard*) by Père Tarteron, "de la compagnie de Jésus" (new edn., Paris, 1729), which Onegin's tutor might have had him read: "De tous les hommes qui sont au monde . . . peu de gens sçavent discerner le vrai bien d'avec le vrai mal." In this satire occurs the famous phrase about the people being content with bread and circuses (ll. 80–81) and the one about a despot's seldom dying a bloodless death (l. 113). Well known to Pushkin was the passage about the misery and ridicule of old age (ll. 188–229). The satire ends with an injunction to be virtuous and to let the gods determine what is good for us (ll. 311–31).

6 / *vale*: Pushkin, writing to Gnedich, May 13, 1823, closes

*(Paris, 1799–1805), II, 140–41; (Paris, 1825–26), III, 190.

his letter with "Vale, sed delenda est censura" (which does not suggest that his or Onegin's use of *vale* was a "revolutionary gesture," as Soviet commentators might think); and to Delvig, in November, 1828, "Vale et mihi favere, as Evgeniy Onegin would say." It was a French epistolary fashion of the eighteenth century (e.g., Voltaire closed a letter to Cideville in 1731 with "Vale, et tuum ama Voltairium").

8 / two lines from the *Aeneid:* For example, "Una salus victis, sperare nullam salutem"—"Le seul salut des vaincus est de n'attendre aucun salut" (*Aeneid*, II, 354, with a comfortable French position for *nullam* after, instead of before, *sperare*); or the common Russian mistake of quoting the following as a discrete verse: "sed duris genuit te cautibus horrens Caucasus"— "l'affreux Caucase t'engendra dans ses plus durs rochers" (Dido to Aeneas, IV, 366–67, Charpentier's version), which Jean Regnault de Segrais "translated":

> Et le Caucase affreux t'engendrant en courroux;
> Te fit l'âme et le cœur plus durs que ses cailloux.

There is some family resemblance in these stanzas to Samuel Butler's *Hudibras* (1663), pt. I, can. I, ll. 136–37:

> And as occasion serv'd, would quote;
> No matter whether right or wrong . . .

VARIANTS

In rough drafts (2369, f. 6^r) there are allusions to Onegin's not being able to understand *Tatsíta, Líviya, Fédra* (all in the genitive), to his not being able to decline *tabula* and *aquila*, and to his being able to quote "three lines from Catullus." The references are to the following.

Cornelius Tacitus, Roman historian, died in the beginning of the second century; Titus Livius, or Livy,

Roman historian, died in the beginning of the first century; Phaedrus, Roman fabulist, flourished in the first century; and Gaius Valerius Catullus, Roman poet, died c. 54 B.C.

5–7 A fragment (2369, f. 6ᵛ) related to this or the preceding stanza reads:

> he'd sit down at the clavichord
> and play but chords on it
> with ⟨careless⟩ . . .

This was later assigned, in a moodier vein, to Lenski on the eve of his duel (Six : XIX : 5–6).

9–10 In a canceled draft (2369, f. 6ʳ), the sextet began:

> He knew German literature
> from the book of Madame de Staël . . .

meaning that the little knowledge Onegin (or Pushkin, for that matter) had of it was derived from Mme de Staël's *De l'Allemagne* (3 vols., Paris, 1810; this first edition was confiscated by Napoleon's police, and only a few copies survived its destruction; a second edition was brought out in London in 1813). For other notes on this work see Two : VI : 8–9.

VII

3–4 / *Ne móg on yámba ot horéya,* | *Kak mÍ ni bÍlis', otlichÍt'* : Pushkin will refer to this theme again in Eight : XXXVIII.
    For a discussion of Russian metrical feet, see App. II, "Notes on Prosody."

5 / Homer, Theocritus: Onegin knew Homer, no doubt, from the same French adaptation by the archcriminal

P. J. Bitaubé (12 vols., 1787–88) in which Pushkin, as a boy, had read *L'Iliade d'Homer* and *L'Odyssée d'Homer*.

The Greek poet Theocritus, born in Syracuse (fl. 284–280 or 274–270 B.C.), was imitated by Virgil (70–19 B.C.) and other Latin poets; and both were imitated by West European lyricists, especially in the three centuries preceding the nineteenth.

In Pushkin's day Theocritus seems to have been known mainly for his pastoral pieces, although his best works are undoubtedly *Idyls* II and XV.

French writers, before the Romantic revival, paradoxically and ridiculously accused Theocritus of affectation and of giving his Sicilian goatherds more grace of expression than French peasants of 1650 or 1750 had. Actually, the criticism is more applicable to insipid Virgil and his pale pederasts; those of Theocritus have certainly a higher color, and the poetry, though minor, is often rich and picturesque.

What was Onegin's quarrel with Homer and Theocritus? We may guess that he accused Theocritus of being too "sweet" and Homer of being too "extravagant." He may also have considered the whole matter of poetry not serious enough for mature men. A general notion of these poets he obtained from execrable French rhymed versions. In modern times we have of course P. E. Legrand's admirable prose translations of Theocritus (*Bucoliques grecs* [Paris, 1925], vol. I). Victorian translators managed to expurgate, twist, or veil Theocritus in such a way as to conceal completely from gentle readers that lads rather than lassies were pursued by his pastoral characters. The "slight liberties" that such scholars as Andrew Lang admit taking with "passages which are offensive to Western morality" are far more immoral than the liberties Comatas ever took with Lacon.

Onegin's (and Pushkin's) knowledge of Theocritus was based no doubt on such paltry French "translations" and "imitations" as, for example, *Les Idylles de Théocrite*, by M. P. G. de Chabanon (Paris, 1777), or another prose version of the same by J. B. Gail (Paris, 1798). Neither is readable.

5–7 / dispraised Homer . . . but . . . was a deep economist: I find the following in William Hazlitt (*Table Talk*, 1821–22):

> A man is a political economist: Good: but . . . let him not impose the same pedantic humour as a duty or a mark of taste on others. . . . A man . . . declares without preface or ceremony his contempt for poetry. Are we therefore to conclude him a greater genius than Homer?

Pyotr Bartenev (1829–1912), who had it from Chaadaev, says, in *Stories about Pushkin* (1851–1860; collected in 1925), that Pushkin began to study English as early as 1818, in St. Petersburg, and for this purpose borrowed from Chaadaev (who had some English) *Table Talk* by "Hazlite." But I do not believe that our poet's interest in English was awakened before 1828; and, anyway, *Table Talk* had not yet appeared (possibly Chaadaev meant Hazlitt's *The Round Table*, 1817).

Cf. Stendhal: "Je lis Smith avec un très grand plaisir" (*Journal*, 1805).

And it will be recalled that Theresa, the maiden in Goethe's *Wilhelm Meister* (1821), was a passionate political economist.

The verse:

> and was a deep economist

has again an unpleasant resemblance to *Hudibras* (see n. to One : VI : 8), pt. I, can. I, l. 127 (long rhyme):

> Beside he was a shrewd *Philósopher* . . .

6 / Adam Smith; 12 / simple product / *prostóy prodúkt*:
Primal product, *matière première*, raw produce, *produit
net*—these and other terms have danced through my
mind; I am satisfied, however, that I know as little
about economics as Pushkin did, although Prof. A.
Kunitsïn *had* lectured at the Lyceum on Adam Smith
(Scottish economist, 1723–90).

Smith, however, in his *Recherches sur la nature et les
causes de la richesse des nations* (Kunitsïn had a choice
of four French translations: by an anonymous "M,"
1778; by the Abbé J. L. Blavet, 1781; by J. A. Roucher,
1790–91; and by Germain Garnier, 1802), considered
le travail the source of that *richesse*. "Labour alone . . .
is [the] real price [of all commodities]; money is their
nominal price only."

It is apparently to the physiocratic school, before
Smith, that we must turn to rationalize Pushkin's ironic
stanza. *The Encyclopaedia Britannica* (11th edn., 1910–
11) has supplied me with some information on the
subject (XXI, 549):

Only those labours are truly "productive" which add to
the quantity of raw materials available for the purposes
of man; and the real annual addition to the wealth of the
community consists of the excess of the mass of agricultural
products (including, of course, metals) over their cost of
production. On the amount of this *produit net*

—sung by J. F. Ducis, c. 1785, in *Mon Produit net,* * and
close to Pushkin's *prostóy produkt*, "simple product"—

depends the well-being of the community and the pos-
sibility of its advance in civilization.

See also François Quesnay (1694–1774), in his *Physio-
cratie* (1768): "La terre est la source unique de la richesse
et l'agriculture est la seule industrie qui donne un
produit net en sus des frais de production."

---

*Ten tetrameters, reprinted in *Almanach des Muses* (1808),
p. 259, ending: "Ton produit net?—Je suis heureux."

Cf. the *Edinburgh Review* (XXXII [July, 1819], 73):
"It is obviously by the amount of the *nett* profit and rent
of a country, and not, as Dr. Smith seems to have sup-
posed [in *Wealth of Nations*], by the amount of its gross
revenue, that its power is to be estimated, and its capacity
of happiness determined."

See also David Ricardo (1772–1823), English econ-
omist: "It was the endeavour of Bonaparte to prevent
the exportation of the raw produce of Russia . . . which
produced the astonishing efforts of the people of that
country against [his] . . . powerful force" (*Essay on . . .
the Profits of Stock* [1815], p. 29).

7 / economist / *ekonóm*: Russians today say *ekonomíst*, and
this is the form of the word Karamzin used in a letter to
Dmitriev, Apr. 8, 1818.

VARIANTS

1–5 Draft (2369, f. 6ʳ):

⟨Confucius⟩, the Chinese sage,
teaches that youth we should respect
⟨from errors guarding it⟩
⟨not hastening to condemn it⟩
⟨alone it holds out hope⟩ . . .

Pushkin's knowledge of Confucius (K'ung Fu-tzŭ,
c. 551–479 B.C.) came from such works as Nicolas Gabriel
(Le) Cleri, *Yu le Grand et Confucius, histoire chinoise*
(Soissons, 1769), and Pierre Charles Levesque, *Con-
fucius, Pensées morales* (Paris, 1782), commonly found
in Russian libraries of the time.

2 Canceled drafts (2369, f. 6ʳ):

with verses to harass his mind

and

not to spare Life for Rhyme . . .

5 Instead of "Homer," drafts read (2369, f. 6ʳ⁻ᵛ): *Virgíl'ya*
(gen. of *Virgíliy*; also in fair copy), *Bióna* (gen. of *Bion*;
Greek poet, fl. c. 100 B.C.), and *Tibúlla* (gen. of *Tibull*;
Albius Tibullus, Roman poet of the first century B.C.).

13–14 Canceled draft (2369, f. 7ʳ):

> With him his father argued half an hour—
> —and sold his forests [as before].

VIII

4 / than all the arts / *vséh naúk*; 9 / the art / *naúka: Naúka*
usually means "knowledge," "learning," "science," but
here the title of Ovid's work gives the translator his cue.

10 / *Nazon*: The Roman poet Ovid, Publius Ovidius Naso
(43 B.C.–?A.D. 17). Pushkin's knowledge of him was
mainly derived from *Œuvres complèttes d'Ovide*, trans-
lated into French by J. J. Le Franc de Pompignan
(Paris, 1799).

10–14 These lines echo the following dialogue referring to
Ovid in Pushkin's *The Gypsies* (*Tsïganï*), a Byronic
poem begun in winter, 1823, in Odessa and finished
Oct. 10, 1824, in Mihaylovskoe; published anonymously
in early May, 1827, in Moscow (ll. 181–223):

THE OLD MAN

> There is a legend in our midst:
> once by some king was sent
> to us in banishment a native of the South
> (I used to know but have forgotten
> his baffling name).
> In years he was already old
> but young and lively in unrancored spirit.
> He had the sublime gift of song,
> and a voice like the sound of waters.
> And everyone grew fond of him,

and on the Danube's banks he dwelt,
doing no harm to anybody,
with stories captivating people.
He comprehended nothing
and was as weak and timid as a child.
Strangers for him
fishes and beasts would catch with nets.
When froze the rapid river
and winter cyclones raged,
they covered with a furry hide
the old and holy man.
But he to hardships of a poor existence
never was able to grow used.
He wandered, shrunken, pale:
he said a wrathful god
was for a crime chastising him.
He waited for release to come
and went on yearning, hapless one,
while roaming on the Danube's banks,
and bitter tears he shed,
remembering his distant city,
and on his deathbed he desired
that to his native South be carried
his yearning bones—
even by death, in this strange land,
unrested guests.

ALEKO

So this is the fate of your sons,
O Rome, O resonant empire!
Poet of love, poet of gods,
tell me: what kind of thing is fame?
a tombal rumbling, a praise-giving voice,
a sound that runs from race to race—
or in the shelter of a smoky tent
the tale of a wild gypsy!

13 Moldavia included Bessarabia, where this was written
(see also vol. 3, p. 155). Pushkin's note appended to the
separate edition of One (1825), but omitted from the
complete editions of the novel, reads:

The contention that Ovid was banished to what is now
Akkerman [Romanian Cetatea Albă, SW of Odessa,

Russia] is baseless. In his elegies *Ex Ponto,* he clearly
indicates that the place of his residence is the town of
Tomi at the very mouth of the Danube. Just as incorrect
is the view of Voltaire, who supposed that the reason for
Ovid's banishment was the secret favors accorded him by
Julia, daughter of Augustus. Ovid was about fifty at the
time [this seemed senility to Pushkin at half that age],
and the depraved Julia had been herself banished by her
jealous sire ten years before. Other conjectures on the
part of scholars are mere guesswork. The poet kept his
word—and his secret died with him: "Alterius facti culpa
silenda mihi" ["About my other faults I should better be
silent"; the quotation is from *Tristia,* bk. II].—Author's
Note.

"Son exil," says La Harpe (*Cours de littérature*
[1825], III, 235), "est un mystère sur lequel la curiosité
s'est épuisée en conjectures inutiles."

Pushkin makes a singular mistake in his reference to
Voltaire. The latter said nothing of the sort. What he
did say was:

Le crime d'Ovide était incontestablement d'avoir vu
quelque chose d'honteux dans la famille d'Octave. . . .
Les doctes n'ont pas décidé s'il [Ovide] avait vu Auguste
avec un jeune garçon . . . [ou] quelque écuyer entre les
bras de l'impératrice . . . [ou] Auguste occupé avec sa fille
ou sa petite-fille. . . . Il est de la plus grande probabilité
qu'Ovide surprit Auguste dans un inceste.

(I quote from *Œuvres de Voltaire,* new edn. "avec des
notes et des observations critiques" by C. Palissot de
Montenoy, in *Mélanges de littérature, d'histoire et de
philosophie* [Paris, 1792], II, 239.)

13 / in the wild depth of steppes / *v glushí stepéy*: The noun
glush' and its adjectival form, *gluhoy,* are pet words of
Pushkin's. *Gluhoy:* "deaf," "muffled," "stifled,"
"deadened"; *gluhoy zvuk,* "a dead sound"; *gluhoy ston,*
"a hollow groan." In speaking of vegetation, it means

"thick-set," "close," "matted," "dense." *Glush'*: "forest depth," "deep retirement," "stagnant depth," "provincial remoteness," "gloomy seclusion"; "back settlement," "back country," "boondocks," "outback"; *v glushi*, "in the backwood," "in the sticks," "deep in the country," Fr. *au fin fond* (with connotations of density and dullness). See also for the use of *glush'*, Two : IV : 5; Three : Tatiana's Letter : 19; Seven : XXVII : 14; Eight : V : 2[3]; Eight : XX : 4.

IX

Canceled in fair copy (PB 8):

> The fervor of the heart torments us early.
> Enchanting fiction:
> not nature teaches us love,
> 4 but Staël or Chateaubriand.
> We thirst to learn life in advance—
> we learn it from a novel.
> We have learned everything; meantime
> 8 nothing have we enjoyed.
> Anticipating nature's voice,
> we only injure happiness,
> and too late, too late after it
> 12 young ardor flies.
> Onegin had experienced this—
> but then how women he had come to know!

12 / young ardor: Another echo of *The First Snow* (l. 75), Vyazemski's poem from which the chapter motto came (see n. to One : motto).

VARIANT

2–4 Draft (2369, f. 8ᵛ):

> And, says Chateaubriand,
> not nature teaches us love,
> but the first nasty novel [*pákostnïy román*].

The epithet *pakostnïy* connotes "lewdness."

X

3 / shake one's belief / *Razuverýát'*: There is no exact
equivalent in English. The verb means to unpersuade,
to unconvince, to dispel or change another's belief, to
make one stop believing something. The verb, moreover,
is in the imperfective. *Ona dumala, chto on eyo lyubit,
ya dolgo razuveryal eyo*: "She thought he loved her; I
spent a long time convincing her that she was mistaken."

XI

2–14 / amaze . . . alarm . . . amuse . . . catch . . . con-
quer . . .: Cf. one of Pierce Egan's "amorous heroes,"
Old Evergreen, who "deceived . . . decoyed . . . entreated
. . . persuaded . . . inveigled . . . cajoled . . . tricked . . .
amused . . . played with . . . cheated . . . deluded . . .
seduced . . . betrayed . . . debauched . . . duped . . .
frightened . . . coaxed" (*Life in London* [1821], bk. II,
ch. 1; a French translation by "S. M." is mentioned by
Pichot in his notes to *Don Juan* [1824], vol. VII).
 Or Pierre Bernard (Gentil-Bernard, 1710–75), *L'Art
d'aimer*, can. II:

> Pour mieux séduire apprends à te contraindre;
> L'amour permet l'art que l'on met à feindre
>
> .   .   .   .
>
> Fuis, mais reviens; fuis encor, mais regarde . . .

11 / *vdrug*: The brevity of the Russian adverb allows it to
be used much more frequently than any of its English
equivalents such as "suddenly," "all at once," "all of a
sudden," "in a trice," and so on. The same applies to
uzhe, uzh, "already."

14 / quietness: The word *tishiná* is a great favorite with
Russian poets, who use it as a *cheville* (that is, a phrase
or word that is rhyme-ready and gap-filling), since any-

thing can happen "in the stillness," "in the silence." The rhyme -*ná* collects a tremendous number of welcome words, such as *oná* ("she"), *zhená* ("wife"), *luná* ("moon"), *volná* ("wave"), *vesná* ("springtime"), *sná* ("of the dream"), *okná* ("of the window"), *polná* ("is full," fem.), *vlyublená* ("is in love," fem.), and many others, without which no poet of 1820–30 could have existed.

14 / lessons: Love lessons, no doubt; but the involuntary association established thereby in the reader's mind with the later, loveless lecture in the seclusion of an avenue (Four : XII–XVI) is unfortunate. The entire stanza is on the verge of light verse, with a derivative eighteenth-century tang about it.

VARIANTS

13–14 Draft (2369, f. 7ᵛ):

> How well he knew, alone with her—
> —but it is time I modest were.

Canceled draft (ibid.):

> How he would act alone with her,
> to this I'd better not refer.

XII

9–10 / sly spouse, Faublas' disciple: Faublas is the hero of the once famous, now hardly readable, novel by Jean Baptiste Louvet de Couvrai or de Couvray (1760–97).

Louvet's novel is generally, and incorrectly, referred to as the *Amours du Chevalier de Faublas*. According to Modzalevski (1910), p. 276, Pushkin's library contained

a copy of *Vie du Chevalier de Faublas*, by Louvet de
Coupevray [sic] (Paris, 1813). Actually, the novel came
out as follows: 1787, *Une Année de la vie du Chevalier
de Faublas* (5 parts); 1788, *Six Semaines de la vie du
Chevalier de Faublas* (8 parts); 1790, *Fin des amours du
Chevalier de Faublas* (6 parts).

The Marquis de B. and the Count de Lignolle, the two
betrayed husbands in this picaresque, easygoing, ami-
able, but essentially inept novel hovering mostly on the
fringe of farce (with an unexpected "romantic" ending
—flashing swords, thunderbolts, madness, and mutilated
mistresses), are naïve nonentities, so that the sixteen-
year-old Faublas, disguised as a damsel, has no difficulty
in slipping into their young wives' beds. When a third
personage, the Count de Rosambert (a rake and Faublas'
abettor), marries at last, he ruefully discovers that his
bride has already been deflowered by his friend; not one
of these gentlemen can be called a sly husband. The
suprúg lukávïy, époux malin, would presumably be one
who, having read *Faublas*, befriends his wife's admirers,
either to keep an eye on them or to use their courtships
for concealing his own intrigues.

Every time a French novel crops up in the course of
EO, Brodski dutifully (but always vaguely, as is the wont
of Russian commentators) alludes to Russian transla-
tions of it. He forgets, however, that the Onegins and
the Larins of 1820 read these books in French, whereas
the grotesque, barbarous, monstrously stilted Russian
versions were read only by the lower classes.

12 / cornuto / *rogonósetz*: A cornuted, or horned, husband;
cornus, cuckold; *encorné, cocu.*

A. Lupus, in the commentary to his German version
of *EO* (1899), p. 60, cites an amusing epigram by
Lessing:

Einmal wechselt im Jahr der Edelhirsch seine Geweihe,

Doch dein Mann, O Clarissa, der wechselt sie monatlich
  vielmals. *

The earliest notice of the use of horns as symbolical
of a husband's dishonor is, according to C. Forbes (in
Notes and Queries, 1st ser., II [1850], 90), to be found
in the *Oneirocritica* of Artemidorus, who lived during
the reign of the Roman emperor Hadrian (A.D. 117–38).

VARIANT

10 Canceled draft (2369, f. 8^r):

> Who all his life had spent with rakes . ..

XIII, XIV

These two stanzas were omitted. After stanza XII in the
1837 edition, the Roman numerals are followed by
three lines of dots.

XIII

Draft (2369, f. 8^{r-v}):

> How well he could a humble widow's
>   pious gaze lure
>   and with her, modest and confused,
> 4 start, blushing, a conspiracy,
>   captivate her with tender ⟨inexperience⟩
>   ⟨. . . .⟩ a stanch devotion
>   of love which in the world is not,
> 8 and with the fervidness of innocent years!
>   How well he could with any lady
>   discuss Platonic love,
>   and play dolls with a little goose,
> 12 and with an unexpected epigram
>   perturb her—and at last
>   snatch the triumphal crown!

---

*Once a year does the stag change his antlers,
 Yet, O Clarissa, your husband changes them many times
  monthly.

XIV

Draft (2369, ff. 8ʳ, 7ᵛ, 8ᵛ):

> Thus the maidservant's frisky pet,
> guard of the garner, whiskered tom,
> leaves the stove ledge to stalk a mouse,
> 4 stretches, walks on, walks on,
> his eyes half closed, approaches,
> curls up, lumplike, plays with his tail,
> prepares the claws of cunning paws—
> 8 and, all at once, he scrabs the poor thing up.
> Thus, the rapacious wolf, oppressed with hunger,
> comes out of the dense depth of woods
> and prowls near the unwatchful dogs,
> 12 around the inexperienced flock.
> All sleeps. And sudden the ferocious thief
> rushes a lamb away into the thick fir forest.

14 / thick fir forest / *dremúchiy bór*: In this old formula, the epithet, derived from "slumber," conveys a sense of impenetrable lichened gloom.

XV

5 / here . . . elsewhere / *Tam . . . tám*: "There, a ball will be; there, a children's fete." The "there" does not necessarily refer to any of the three houses mentioned in the preceding line. In fact, the addition of two more invitations, making five in all, yields the best sense.

5 / a children's fete / *détskiy prázdnik*: There is an allusion to these *fêtes d'enfants* in Lermontov's novel *Princess Ligovski* (1836), ch. 5, where the mother of the hero "used to give children's soirees [*detskie vechera*] for her little daughter. These were attended also by grown-up young ladies and overripe maidens." When the children went to bed, the dancing was continued by the adults.

67

9–12 Cf. N. J. L. Gilbert, *Satire* II, *Mon Apologie* (1778):

> Tous les jours dans Paris, en habit de matin,
> Monsieur promène à pied son ennui libertin.

10 / bolivar: This was a silk hat, slightly funnelform, with a wide, upturned brim, especially fashionable in Paris and Petersburg in 1819. Russian commentators from P. Bartenev to M. Tsyavlovski give an incorrect description of it. Albert Dauzat, *Dictionnaire étymologique* (Paris, 1938), says of it "à la mode chez les libéraux" (since it was named after the South American liberator, Simón Bolívar, 1783–1830). Lupus, in the commentary to his German version of *EO*, pp. 46–47, notes that as late as 1883 the Parisian *Figaro*'s special correspondent (reporting on the coronation of Alexander III) loosely described the top hats of Russian coachmen as "une sorte de chapeaux Bolivar." Larousse (*Grand Dictionnaire universel du XIXe siècle*) quotes Scribe (c. 1820): "Les avoués maintenant ont des fracs à l'anglaise et des bolivars."

11 / boulevard: The Nevski Boulevard (part of the Nevski Avenue), a shaded walk for pedestrians, still flourished in Pushkin's youth. It consisted of several rows of anemic lindens and ran from the Moyka Canal ESE to the Fontanka Canal, along the middle line of the Nevskiy Prospekt (Neva Prospect, *Nevskaya pershpektiva* or *prospektiva*, in the eighteenth century; "the Perspective" of English travelers in the 1830's; "la Perspective de Nevsky" in official French, or, colloquially, "le Nevsky"; the Nevski or Nevskiy Avenue in correct English). In 1820, about the time Pushkin was banned from the city for seven years, most of the trees were cut down, leaving a mere five hundred (to improve—in an Age of Improvement—the broad and stately flow of the *prospekt*). The Nevski "boulevard" was so well forgotten

by the end of the century that Pushkinists of the time
sent Eugene for his afternoon stroll to the Admiralteyskiy
Boulevard (immediately NW of the Nevski) instead.
This, however, was also a fashionable promenade, con-
sisting, in Alexander I's reign, of three avenues of
linden trees, and there is no special reason to debar
Onegin from access to it, except that strollers may have
used it more often in summer than in winter. He might
easily have walked to Talon's (instead of taking a
hackney sleigh) either from the Admiralteyskiy Boule-
vard (two blocks) or from the Moyka.

12 / unconfined / *na prostóre*: "In free space," "in the
open." See n. to Eight : IX : 8.

13 / Bréguet: An elegant repeater made by the celebrated
French watchmaker, Abraham Louis Bréguet (1747–
1823). On a spring being touched at any time, a Bréguet
watch struck the hour and the minute. Cf. Pope's
". . . And the press'd Watch return'd a silver Sound"
(*The Rape of the Lock*, I, 18).

At this point, H. Dupont, in his French version of *EO*
(1847), is suddenly moved to comment: "Son large
bolivar, son [sic] bréguet . . . Nous conservons, par
respect pour l'original, ces expressions étrangères qui ne
sont pas de bon goût en français. On dit à Paris ma
montre et mon chapeau." Fastidious Dupont also pulls
such boners (in his translation of Two : III and VI) as
"l'almanach de l'an VIII" and "Lensky, âme vraiment
Goethienne." So much for *le bon goût*.

Actually, Pushkin's Bréguet and bolivar (see n. to
One : x) are Gallicisms: *une Bréguet* (but *un bolivar*).
See Larousse, *Dictionnaire . . . du XIXe siècle*: "*Maître
Pastreni tira de son gousset une magnifique Bréguet . . .*
(Alexandre Dumas); *Mais qu'on se dépêche, il est huit
heures à ma Bréguet* (Siraudin)."

Commentary

5 Draft (2369 f. 9ʳ):

Ball at the count's, fete at the prince's . . .

In the fair copy, the hosts are transposed.

14 Draft (2369, f. 9ʳ⁻ᵛ): Our poet wavered between having Onegin's repeater "chime six times" or "ring five o'clock."

XVI

1–3 / sleigh . . . frostdust: In 1819, the first snow fell on Oct. 5, and the Neva froze ten days later. In 1824 the river was still free on Nov. 7.

2 / Way, way! / *Padí! padí!*: Rhyming with the French *pardi* and meaning "go," "move," "look out," "away with you"; this *padi* or *podi* used to be the crack coachman's traditional warning cry, aimed mainly at foot passengers. Some amusing variations are listed by Leo Tolstoy in his autobiographical sketch, *The History of Yesterday* (this "yesterday" being Mar. 25, 1851).

3–4 / *Moróznoy píl'yu serebrítsya* / *Egó bobróvïy vorotník*: Braving inversions and obsoletes, I have preferred an exact rendering (allowed by the intransitive use of "to silver") to the more elegant but less accurate: "the powder of the frost besilvers his beaver collar."
    This is the fur collar of the deep-caped, ample-sleeved *shinel'* of Alexander I's era, which was a cross between a civilian greatcoat (or box coat) and an army cloak of the period; a glorified capote or, quite exactly, a furred carrick—the English homecoming from France of *une*

karrick (derived from Garrick—the English actor David Garrick, 1717–79, whose name, curiously enough, came from Garric—a Huguenot family).

A collar of beaverskin cost two hundred rubles in 1820, with the ruble then worth three English shillings.

In the 1830's, the *Nikolaevskaya* (from the Tsar's name) *shinel'*, as worn, for instance, by officials in the civil service, might be without fur, or lined with cheaper fur (see Bashmachkin's dream cloak in Gogol's *The Carrick* or *The Overcoat*). This caped greatcoat should not be confused with the later army *shinel'*, which was, and still is, a capeless long military overcoat with a strap in the back and a spinal fold.

According to Charles Philippe Reiff's *Etymological Lexicon* (*Dictionnaire russe-français . . . ou dictionnaire étymologique de la langue russe*, St. Petersburg, 1836), the word *shinel'* comes from "chenille, tissu de soie velouté." Littré, under *chenille*, says: "Autrefois, un habillement négligé que les hommes portaient avant de faire leur toilette."

5 / Talon: Early in 1825 Pierre Talon warned his customers through the gazettes that he was leaving Nevski Avenue (he had had his restaurant at what is now No. 15) for his native France.

5–6 / *ón uvéren* / he is certain . . . [Kavérin]: The unexpected mating by rhyme of a masculine surname (replaced by asterisks in the 1825–37 edns.) with a predicative adjective (*uvéren–Kavérin*—a rhyme young Pushkin used also, c. 1817, in an epigram, *Works* 1936, I, 198) surprises the Russian ear and eye most delightfully. As in French orthometry, the punctilious spangle of the *consonne d'appui* (reckoned tawdry in English) increases the acrobatic brilliance of the Russian rhyme.

Pyotr Kaverin (1794–1855), hussar, man about town,

and former Göttingen student (1810–11), of whom Pushkin says (c. 1817) in an inscription to his portrait:

> In him there always boils the heat of punch and war;
> a warrior fierce he was in fields of Mars;
> 'mid friends, stanch friend; tormentor of the fair;
> and everywhere hussar!

A brief message in Pushkin's hand (MS unseen, date uncertain: 1820 or 1836) reads: "Mille pardon, mon cher Kaverine, si je vous fais faux bon—une circonstance imprevue me force à partir de suite." I transcribe from Lerner's "Dopolneniya k pis'mam Pushkina" in the Brockhaus-Efron edition of Pushkin's works (1915), VI, 608, and am not sure who exactly is responsible for these homey mistakes in the French. Tsyavlovski (Acad 1938, p. 451) has *pardons* and *imprévue* but retains the *bon* (*bond*).

In 1817 Pushkin had addressed a poem of sixteen lines to the *lyubeznïy* (amiable) Kaverin, advising him to go on leading a happy, thoroughly dissipated life and to despise "the envious murmur of the rabble" (*i chérni prezíráy revnívoe roptán'e*; compare these rippling *r*'s with Four : XIX : 4–6), and assured him that one could combine a lofty mind with crazy ventures. Kaverin was able to stow away at one meal four bottles of champagne, one after the other, and leave the restaurant at a casual stroll.

It was Kaverin who is said to have suggested to Pushkin one of the images in his *Ode to Liberty* (namely, the colorful allusion to the murder of Paul I), which was probably composed in December, 1817, and partly written down in Nikolay Turgenev's St. Petersburg flat. (See n. to Ten : XII : 3.)

7–14 (and see var. : 10–11; XVII : 1–2; XXXVII : 8–9): The reader will be amused to compare Onegin's diet with the dinner, a "tumult of fish, flesh, and fowl, | And vegetables, all in masquerade," described by Byron in octaves LXII–LXXXIV of *Don Juan*, can. XV, where LXXI ends with: "But I have dined, and must forego, alas! | The chaste description even of a 'bécasse.' " Compared to the Talon menu, the fare in *Don Juan* is more profuse and more specific, with borrowings from Louis Eustache Ude's *The French Cook* (1813) and an Englishman's awful stress accent on the first syllable of French words (*bécasse* is an exception).

8 / of comet wine / *vina kométi*: Fr. *vin de la comète*, champagne of the comet year, an allusion to the comet of 1811, which was also a wonderful vintage year. This anonymous but spectacular comet was first seen by Honoré Flaugergues in Viviers Mar. 25, 1811. Then on Aug. 21, 1811, Alexis Bouvard in Paris saw it. Astronomers in St. Petersburg observed it Sept. 6, 1811 (these dates are N.S.). It haunted European skies till Aug. 17, 1812, according to Friedrich Wilhelm August Argelander (*Untersuchungen über die Bahn des grossen Cometen vom Jahre 1811*, Königsberg, 1823).

9 / Rost beef *okrovavlénnïy*: A Gallicism (not a misprint), *rost-beef sanglant*, which comes, with the chef's compliments, from Parny (*Goddam!*, can. 1; see n. to One : XXXVII : 6–10).

10 / truffles: These delicious fungi were appreciated to a degree that we, in a palateless age of artificial flavors, might hardly credit. There is the well-known anecdote (well told in William Cooke's *Memoirs of Samuel Foote, Esq., with a Collection of His Genuine Bon-mots, Anecdotes, Opinions, etc.*, London, 1805) about the poet Samuel Boyse (1708–49), who "was so miserably poor . . . that he was obliged to lie in bed for want of clothes; and when a friend . . . sent him a guinea, he instantly

laid out a crown of it for mushrooms and truffles, to garnish a slice of roast beef."

Joseph Berchoux (1765–1839) has sung truffles in *La Gastronomie* (1800), penultimate (third) canto:

> Du sol périgourdin la truffe vous est chère.

12 / *Strázburga piróg: Pâté de foie gras*. James Forbes, writing in 1803 (*Letters from France* [London, 1806], I, 395–96), quotes from the *Almanach des gourmands*:

> . . . At Strasburg are manufactured those admirable pâtés that form the greatest luxury of an *entremet*. To procure these livers of a sufficient size the [goose] must for a considerable time become a living sacrifice. Crammed with food, deprived of all liquid, and nailed by the feet to a board . . . The punishment . . . would be intolerable, if the animal was not cheered . . . by . . . the prospect [of her liver] larded with truffles, and encrusted in a scientific paste, [spreading] through the medium of Mons. Corcellet . . . the glory of her name.

Bulwer-Lytton, perhaps availing himself of the same French source, has a similar passage in *Pelham* (1828), ch. 22.

Cf. Pushkin's poem *To* [Mihail] *Shcherbinin* (1819), ll. 7–8:

> . . . and Strasbourg's rich pie,
> with fragrant wine . . .

The goose-liver pie should not be, but frequently is, confused with the *foie gras* paste (Russ. *pashtet*) that comes in terrines. The pie was *un vrai gibraltar* (as Brillat-Savarin describes it somewhere) that had to be attacked and "cut into by a carving knife" (as Brummell says in a letter).

14 Everybody remembers the kindly lines (685–87) in James Thomson's *Summer* (1727):

> . . . thou best anana, thou the pride
> Of vegetable life, beyond whate'er
> The poets imag'd in the golden age.

Of less repute is a short poem by William Cowper, *The Pineapple and the Bee* (1779). Throughout the nineteenth century this fruit was deemed in Russia a symbol of high living.

VARIANTS

3 Canceled draft (2369, f. 9ᵛ):

> With flying snow . . .

10–11 A more colorful fair-copy cancellation (*Rukopisi*, 1937) reads:

> double *bécasse* and vinaigrette
> and truffles, luxury of youthful years . . .

The first term, *dvoynóy bekás* (now *dupel'*), refers not to a woodcock but to a great snipe (Fr. *bécassine double*), broiled or roasted. Vinaigrette is a dish of vegetables seasoned with oil and vinegar. Pushkin sent his brother this change, and the latter transferred it to the transcript he had taken to St. Petersburg. The transcript went later to the brothers Turgenev (Aleksandr and Nikolay) and from their collection finally found its way to the Pushkinskiy Dom.

10–12 Canceled drafts (2369, f. 9ᵛ):

> 10   a *vol-au-vent* and vinaigrette
> 10   a hazel grouse and a double *bécasse* [*bekás*]
> 11   and you, fragrant pineapple [*ananás*]
>
> 10   . . . [*bekás*],
> 11   and my Onegin in an hour [*chás*]
> 12   forsakes the animated feast . . .

Vol-au-vent. An ethereal crust filled with braised white of chicken and cut-up mushrooms (*vol-au-vent de volaille aux champignons*) or with oysters poached in white wine (*vol-au-vent d'huîtres*); and there are several other varieties, all delicious.

XVII

3–4 The performance started at half past six, and of the two imperial theaters of the time (1819) presumably the Bolshoy Kamennïy, in the Kolomna quarter, is meant. Ballets were combined in various ways with operas and tragedies.

It will be noticed how dependent this vapid day is on timepieces. "Those who have the least value for their time have usually the greatest number of watches and are the most anxious about the exactness of their going" (Maria Edgeworth, *Ennui* [1809], ch. 1).

5 / unkind / *zloy*: Also, "wicked," "evil," "vicious," "malignant," "bad." It enjoys the distinction of being the only monosyllabic adjective in Russian. (See Vol. 3, p. 492.)

6 / *Nepostoyánnïy obozhátel*': *Volage adorateur* (as used, for example, by Racine in *Phèdre* [1677], II, i).

7 / enchanting actresses: Cf. Stendhal, *Le Rouge et le noir* (1831), ch. 24:

"Ah ça, mon cher [dit le prince Korasoff à Julien Sorel] . . . seriez-vous amoureux de quelque petite actrice?" Les Russes copient les mœurs françaises, mais toujours à cinquante ans de distance. Ils en sont maintenant [in 1830] au siècle de Louis XV.

So are Stendhal's Russians of 1830: they belong to the eighteenth-century literary type of traveling Muscovite.

How euphemistic is our poet's account here of gay times in the Petersburg of his and Onegin's youth may be gathered from a ribald letter Pushkin wrote to another profligate (Pavel Mansurov, b. 1795, thus Onegin's coeval) from Petersburg to Novgorod, Oct. 27, 1819, about mutual friends and young actresses, with various priapic details (curiously intermixed with flippant political cracks):

. . . We have not forgotten you; at 7:30 every night at the theater we celebrate your memory with applause and sighs. Good old Pavel, we say, what may he be doing now in Great Novgorod? He envies us, and sheds tears—from a certain lower orifice, no doubt—in memory of Kr[ïlova, a young ballerina]. . . .

. . . Let us set aside the elegiac, my friend. Turning to the historical, let me talk to you about our pals [a venereological survey follows]. I too am developing a nice little case. [Nikita] Vsevolozhski gambles, the chalk dust twists, the money pours in! The Sosnitska [an actress] and Prince Shahovskoy [the playwright] keep getting fatter and sillier, and, although I am not enamored with them, I still applauded him for his poor comedy and her for her mediocre acting.

[Yakov] Tolstoy is ill—I shall not tell his complaint—I have too much pox in this letter as it is. The Green Lamp [an association of rakes and *frondeurs*] seems to be in need of snuffing and to be going out, which is a pity since there is still oil, mainly the champagne of our friend [Vsevolozhski, at whose house the club met]. Are you writing to me, my confrere, will you write to me, my sweet lad [*holosen'koy*; this lisping endearment has no homosexual implications]? Talk to me about yourself and about military settlements. All this I need because I love you and hate despotism. . . .

Young liberals of 1819 severely condemned the military settlements (*voennïe poseleniya*). These were established in 1817 to reduce the cost of keeping the huge army in times of peace and were directed by Alexander I's military adviser, Count Aleksey Arakcheev (1769–1834). They were formed of governmental peasants (i.e., serfs belonging not to private landowners but to the state). Such settlements were established in the bleak marshes of Novgorod and in the wild steppes of Herson (Kherson). Each village consisted of one company (228 men). The settlers were obliged to combine army service and agriculture, under conditions of the strictest discipline, with harsh punishment for the least misdemeanor. The idea of these "military settlements" greatly appealed to Alexander's mystical and methodical mind. He saw them, in their perfect form, as a solid band of villages, consisting of permanent recruits, a Chinese wall of *chair à canon* traversing the whole of Russia from north to south. Neither he nor Arakcheev could understand why this beautiful idea repelled some of Russia's most distinguished generals. Military settlements were a dim foreglimpse of the considerably more efficient and extensive Soviet labor camps established in 1920 by Lenin and still thriving (1973).

8 / *Pochyótnïy grazhdanín kulís*: After some deliberation with my literary conscience, I decided that "freeman of the greenroom" was sufficiently correct (and, in fact, blended more delicately with the relevant associations in English) and had the advantage of better harmony with Pushkin's neat style in this stanza; after which, I went back to literalism.

9 / *Onégin poletél k teátru*: Onegin has made off for the theater but does not fly fast enough: his fellow hero, Pushkin, outstrips him, and has been at the theater for three stanzas (XVIII, XIX, XX) when Onegin arrives there (XXI). The Pursuit Theme, with its alternate phases of overtaking and lagging behind, will last till XXXVI.

12 / *Fedru, Kleopatru* [acc. of *Fedra, Kleopatra*]: I presume that the first refers to J. B. Lemoyne's three-act opera *Phèdre* (1786), based on Racine's *tragédie* and

produced in St. Petersburg Dec. 18, 1818, with a libretto
by Pyotr Semyonov adapted from that of F. B. Hoffman
and additional music by Steibelt. The role of Fedra was
sung by Sandunova.*

Prevented as I am by a barbarous regime from travel-
ing to Leningrad to examine old playbills in its libraries,
I cannot say for sure what "Cleopatra" Pushkin had in
view. Presumably, it was played by the French company
that performed at the Bolshoy three times a week in
1819 (fide Arapov). A French company—the same one?
—gave performances from Oct. 4, 1819, on, at the
Malïy Teatr, on Nevski Avenue.† Corneille has a
Syrian queen of that name in his wretched *Rodogune*
(1644); there have been several operas and tragedies
devoted to the more famous Egyptian; I doubt that the
opera *Cleopatra e Cesare*, composed for the inauguration
of the Berlin Opera House (Dec. 7, 1742) by my ancestor
Karl Heinrich Graun (1701–51) and founded by G. G.
Bottarelli on Corneille's miserable *La Mort de Pompée*
(1643), was ever performed in St. Petersburg; but an-
other opera, *La Morte di Cleopatra* by S. Nasolini (1791),
text by A. S. Sografi, which was performed (according
to Alfred Loewenberg's admirable *Annals of Opera*,
Cambridge and New York, 1943) in London (1806) and
in Paris (1813), may have come to Petersburg. Another,
stronger, contender is the opera *Cleopatra* written by
Domenico Cimarosa (while court composer to Catherine
II) with a libretto by Ferdinando Moretti. It was first
performed at the Court Opera, St. Petersburg, Oct. 7,
1789 (*Grove's Dictionary of Music and Musicians*,
5th ed. 1955, Vol. II). A "ballet historique en trois
actes" by J. P. Aumer, entitled *Cléopâtre*, with music

*See Pimen Arapov, *Letopis' russkogo teatra* (Annals of the
Russian Theater), St. Petersburg, 1861.
†Fide Tsyavlovski, *Letopis' zhizni Pushkina* (Annals of the Life
of Pushkin; Moscow, 1951), I, 739.

by R. Kreutzer, was performed in Paris Mar. 8, 1809. Alexis Piron (*Œuvres complettes* [1776], VIII, 105, epistle "Au Comte de Vence sur une estampe de Cléopâtre") says: "J'en ai vu plus d'une au théâtre," and adds in a footnote: "La Demoiselle Clairon jouait alors une Cléopâtre dont on ne se souvient plus." I have not read Jodelle's *Cléopâtre captive* (1553), and all I care to know about Marmontel's *Cléopâtre* (1750) is that its first-night audience joined in the hissing emitted by a very efficient mechanical asp, with Bièvre quipping: "Je suis de l'avis de l'aspic."

Voltaire never wrote any play on Cleopatra. The legend that the "Cleopatra" in *EO* is a reference to *Kleopatra, tragediya Vol'tera* stems from M. Gofman's error in his notes to the Narodnaya Biblioteka edn. of *EO* (1919) and goes through Brodski's commentaries (Mir edn. of *EO*, 1932) to D. Chizhevski's careless compilation (Harvard University Press, 1953), although attention to these "nonexisting ballets based on nonexisting tragedies" was drawn as early as 1934 by Tomashevski (*Lit. nasl.*, XVI–XVIII, 1110).

13 / call out Moëna / *Moinu* [acc. of *Moina*]: Pronounced Mo-eena (rhyming with "arena"). The heroine of V. Ozerov's insipid tragedy, *Fingal* (St. Petersburg, Dec. 8, 1805), derived from the French version of Macpherson's prose poem. The role was "created" by the great actress Ekaterina Semyonova (1786–1849) and was later graced by her rival, Aleksandra Kolosova (1802–80). Pushkin has some curious "remarks" on these two players in his notes (posthumously published) on the Russian theater, written in the beginning of 1820.

For the Ossianic strain in Russian literature see my n. to Two : XVI : 10–11.

VARIANTS

1–3 Draft (2369, f. 10ʳ):

> Onegin drinks, is noisy, but again
> ⟨under the finger hissing⟩ his Bréguet
> ⟨informs him⟩ that [a play] by Shahovskoy . . .

The "hissing" is a first-rate image, unfortunately deleted. For the playwright Shahovskoy, see my n. to XVIII : 4–10.

10 A cancellation in the fair copy and in the transcript reads:

> where everybody, breathing liberty [*vól'nost'yu*]...

The change to *krítikoy* is probably a concession to censorship. Tomashevski says that in Pushkin's fair copy it is inserted in a strange hand. The transcript has it in Lev Pushkin's hand.

XVIII

Stanzas XVIII and XIX were added in autumn, 1824, at Mihaylovskoe about a year after the chapter was finished. The drafts are in Cahier 2370, f. 20^r, after the last stanza of Three (f. 20^r, dated Oct. 2, 1824).

1–4 I have kept the somewhat ill-balanced syntax whereby the verb that Fonvizin shares with Knyazhnin is suspended between two definitional clauses.

The epithet *pereímchivïy*, which so melodically occupies divisions 2nd to 6th of l. 4, is impossible to render by an English adjective that, if turned back into Russian, would find its exact counterpart *only* in the word used by Pushkin (the proof of accuracy). *Pereimchivïy* combines the significations of "imitational," "adaptorial," and "appropriative," and these three adjectives are rendered respectively by *podrazhátel'nïy*, *prisposóbchivïy*, and *prisvóychivïy*.

3 / Fonvízin: Denis Fonvizin (1745–92), author of a primitive but racy and amusing comedy *The Minor* (*Nedorosl'*, produced Sept. 24, 1782). In its temporary slant, as a satire directed by an eighteenth-century liberal's honest pen against cruelty, smugness, and ignorance, it has lost

most of its freshness; but the flavor of its idiom and the force of its lusty characterizations endure.

Fonvizin is also the author of some excellent verses, such as his fable in fifty-two Alexandrines about a scheming fox (*Lisitsa koznodey*), and of a boldly satirical (in keeping with the style of Empress Catherine herself at the time) *Universal Court Grammar* (1783).

In his superficial but admirably written *Letters from France* (1777–78), Fonvizin reveals very clearly the mixture of fierce nationalism and incomplete liberalism that persistently distinguished the most advanced Russian political thinkers from his times to those of the Decembrists. "In examining the condition of the French nation," says he in a letter from Aachen to Pyotr Panin, Sept. 18/29, 1778, "I learned to distinguish legal liberty from real liberty. Our nation does not possess the former, but in many respects enjoys the latter. On the other hand, the French, who possess the right of liberty, live in essential slavery," etc. He was unpleasantly struck by "the lack of military discipline," when, at the theater in Montpellier, the sentinel assigned to the town governor's box "got bored with standing at his post, moved away from the door, took a chair, and, having placed it beside all the people of rank sitting in the box, sat him down, still holding his musket." Upon Fonvizin's expressing his surprise to the commanding officer, the latter placidly replied, "C'est qu'il est curieux de voir la comédie."

4–10 / Knyazhnín . . . Ózerov . . . Katénin . . . Shahovskóy: A foursome of mediocrities.

Yakov Knyazhnin (1742–91), author of tragedies and comedies awkwardly imitated from more or less worthless French models. I have tried his *Vadim of Novgorod* (1789), but even Voltaire is more readable.

Vladislav Ozerov (1769–1816). "Very mediocre" (as Pushkin himself remarked in the margin of Vyazemski's

biography of Ozerov); author of five tragedies in the
stilted and sentimental manner of his Frenchified era:
Yaropolk i Oleg (1798), *Oedipus in Athens* (*Edip v
Afinah*, 1804), *Fingal* (1805), *Dmitri Donskoy* (1807),
and *Polyxena* (*Poliksena*, 1809). The writing of a sixth,
Medea (*Medeya*), was interrupted (its MS is now lost)
by the poor man's going mad. This fatal insanity was
brought on, it is said, by the intrigues of literary foes
(among them, Shahovskoy).

Pavel Katenin (1792–1853). Much overrated by his
friend Pushkin—who overrated also *le grand* (Pierre)
Corneille, whose bombastic and platitudinous *Cid* (1637)
Katenin "translated" into Russian (1822). In the draft
of a poem referring to a theatrical feud (eighteen lines
composed in 1821, published posthumously, 1931),
Pushkin had already found the formula (ll. 16–17):

> And for her [Semyonova] . . .
> . . . .
> youthful Katénin will revive
> Aeschylus' majestic genius . . .

Prince Aleksandr Shahovskoy (1777–1846), yet an-
other bibliographic burden. Theatrical director and
prolific author of various paltry imitations from the
French, mainly comedies, such as *A Lesson to Coquettes,
or, The Lipetsk Waters* (produced Sept. 23, 1815), in
which he, a follower of the Archaic School, caricatures
Zhukovski in the ballad-maker Fialkin (Mr. Violette),
as ten years before he had mocked Karamzin's senti-
mentality in the farce *The New Sterne* (*Noviy Stern*).
The Lipetsk Waters (a reference to the mineral springs
of Lipetsk in the province of Tambov) was the play that
provoked the younger generation of writers to form the
group Arzamas (see n. to Eight : XIV : 13).

By winter, 1819, however—Onegin's time—"caustic"
Shahovskoy had already given up so-called "classicism"
and assumed a so-called "pro-romanticist" position, but

this had no effect whatever on his wretched writings. He is remembered by students of prosody as having been the first to write a Russian comedy (*Do Not Listen If You Do Not Like It*, Sept. 23, 1818) in "free iambics" (that is, freely rhymed lines of varying length), previously used in fables by Krïlov, a measure in which the only great Russian comedy in verse, *Woe from Wit*, was to be written by Aleksandr Griboedov (finished 1824). Pushkin in his Lyceum diary, late in 1815, correctly described Shahovskoy as "tasteless" and "mediocre."

In 1824, Bulgarin's publication *The Russian Thalia* announced that it would publish excerpts from a dramatic adaptation by Shahovskoy of Pushkin's long poem *The Fountain of Bahchisaray* and from Shahovskoy's "Magicheskaya trilogiya," *Finn*, based on passages from *Ruslan and Lyudmila*. This *Finn* was performed in St. Petersburg Nov. 3, 1824.

I am not quite sure if the unexpected and unjustified compliment paid to Shahovskoy in this stanza (composed, with the next, a year after the canto had been finished) is not connected with an awareness of these coming events.

5–7 Cf. Voltaire, *L'Anti-Giton, à Mademoiselle* [*Adrienne*] *Lecouvreur* (the French actress; 1714):

> Quand, sous le nom de Phèdre, ou de Monime,*
> Vous partagez entre Racine & vous
> De notre encens le tribut légitime

—imperfectly quoted by Lerner, *Zven'ya* (1935), no. 5, p. 65. *L'Anti-Giton* attacks the homosexual Marquis de Courcillon, son of the memoirist Philippe de Courcillon, Marquis de Dangeau.

12 Charles Louis Didelot (1767–1837), French dancer and

---

*Heroine of Racine's *Mithridate*.

choreographer. From 1801 on he was *baletmeyster* in St. Petersburg, and was dubbed "the Byron of the Ballet" for his "romantic" fancy.

13–14 / *kulís* / of coulisses / *neslís'* / swept along: A poor rhyme, despite the *consonne d'appui.*

XIX

1 / *Moi bogíni   Chtó vï? Gdé vï?*: One of the rare cases in which the situation is reversed, and four Russian words ("What you? Where you?") demand twice as many English ones in translation.

The split rhyme *gdé vï–dévï* is very beautiful. (See App. II.) In English poetry the analogy is of course not the macaronic and Byronic "gay dens"–"maidens," but rather the pristine use of "know it"–"poet" or "sonnet"–"on it," both of which by now have become trite and drab.

XX

3 / in the top gallery / *V rayké*: *Rayók*, "little paradise," a Gallicism, the cant term for the top gallery in a theater. Eric Patridge, in his *A Dictionary of Slang and Unconventional English* (1951), gives 1864 as the first appearance in England of "paradise" as the gallery of a theater and adds: "always felt to be French; obsolete by 1910." There is no doubt that it is merely an adaptation of the Parisian *paradis* (a region of plebeian beatitude and infernal heat) mentioned by many eighteenth-century topicists (e.g., Voltaire). By an odd coincidence, the occupants of the highest seats in London theaters were called (around 1810) "gallery gods" (John S.

Commentary

Farmer and W. E. Henley, *Slang and Its Analogues*, 1893).

5–14 Dunyasha Istomina (the first name is a diminutive of Eudocia, Avdotiya; 1799–1848), a very gifted and comely *pantomimnaya tantsovshchitsa*, "pantomimic ballerina," a pupil of Didelot (see n. to XVIII : 12). She made her debut Aug. 30, 1815, in a "pastoral ballet," *Acis et Galathée* (music by C. Cavos, scenario by Didelot). Arapov, in his fascinating *Letopis'* (pp. 237–38), says of her:

She was of middle stature, a brunette, with a lovely countenance and a very shapely figure; her black eyes, replete with fire, were shaded by long lashes that lent a special character to her face; she had great strength in her legs, aplomb on the stage, and, at the same time, grace, lightness, rapidity. She amazed one with her pirouette [gyration on one toe], and her elevation [elevation proper, which is the ability to rise into the air], and *ballon* [which is the ability to remain there for a miraculous moment].

The closest I am able to get to the specific performance Pushkin may have had in mind here is Didelot's two-act ballet, *The Caliph of Bagdad*, music by Ferdinando Antonolini, given Jan. 12, 1820 (at least a fortnight too late), in which the role of Zetulba was danced by Istomina. It was, however, not new, being the second performance (the first took place Aug. 30, 1818, with Lihutina as Zetulba). Other dates are inconclusive. Arapov says that all the ballerinas participated in a "grand divertissement," Didelot's *Sea Victory*, music by Antonolini, given July 20, 1819, as an afterpiece, with the first part of *Rusalka* (see nn. to Two : XII : 14 and Five : XVII : 5). The "dragons" or "serpents" (*zmei*) and canceled "bears" mentioned further (XXII : 1 and n. to XXII : 1–4) suggest another *ballet magique* staged by Didelot, belonging this time to the *genre chinois*, namely, the four-act entertainment, *Hen-Zi and Tao* (Beauty and the Beast), music by Antonolini, but the date of the first performance (Aug. 30, 1819) is also too early, and I have reason to believe that Istomina did not dance that particular night. It was repeated Oct. 30 and Nov. 21. On one of these two dates, Pushkin was late in attending the performance; he had just returned from a visit to Tsarskoe. There, a bear had broken his chain and had scampered along an avenue in the park where he might have molested Tsar Alexander, had the latter happened to be passing by. Pushkin quipped: "When at last one good fellow turns up, he is only a bear." (See also XXII : vars. 1–2.)

Pushkin was vegetating in Kishinev when in Petersburg, at the Bolshoy Kamenniy, Istomina danced the Cherkes girl in a ballet derived by Didelot from the long poem *The Caucasian Captive*, written by Pushkin in 1820–21. This choreographic pantomime (*The Caucasian Captive, or, The Shade of the Bride*, music by Cavos), complete with Circassian games, combats, and a soaring ghost, was much applauded at its first performance on Jan. 15, 1823. A fortnight later (and a little more than three months before starting *EO*), Pushkin, from Kishinev, wrote to his brother Lev in St. Petersburg, clamoring for details of the staging and of the dancing of the Cherkeshenka, Istomina, "whom once upon a time I used to court like the Caucasian captive." If, as the sleuths of prototypism believe, the ugly duckling Maria Raevski, who at thirteen was acquainted with Pushkin in the Caucasus, did really provide him, behind Pichot's back, with a "model" for a (not very specific or original) Oriental heroine, then the later replacement of one girl by another, earlier, one should interest them.

This stanza (One : XX), composed in Odessa, was no doubt dictated by Pushkin's desire to thank a talented dancer for her part as the Cherkes girl and for her coming

appearance as Lyudmila. And merely to maintain
that Tatiana is superior to lewd Helen of Troy will our
poet, in November, 1826, facetiously concede (Five :
XXXVII : 7–11) that Homer's Cypris is superior to "my
Istomina."

By arriving only in the next stanza, Onegin has missed
Istomina's number, but seven cantos later he will be
told what exactly he missed when (as described in
Eight : XXXV : 9, 12–13) he reads, during the winter of
1824, the Russian magazines for that year. In Bulgarin's
Literary Leaflets, IV (Feb. 18, 1824), he then may find
these ten lines—the very first passage ever published of
Pushkin's novel (One : XX : 5–14), said by the editor
to have been "dictated from memory by a traveler,"
perhaps by Onegin himself, who had just been in
Odessa; or, more verisimilarly, he may open Bulgarin's
"almanac" *The Russian Thalia for 1825* (published
mid-December, 1824) and find therein the same ten
lines reprinted as a legend to Fyodor Yordan's portrait
of a rather plump-looking Istomina (she danced in St.
Petersburg Dec. 8, 1824, in the first performance of a
"magico-heroic" ballet in five acts based by Didelot on
Ruslan and Lyudmila), as well as the first passages ever
to be published of Griboedov's *Woe from Wit*. (See nn.
to Eight : XXXV : 7–8.)

Istomina was only eighteen in autumn, 1817, when
her soft charm, her dark hair, and her rosy beauty were
the cause of a famous duel in St. Petersburg. On Nov. 5
of that year, after a tiff with her young protector, Count
Sheremetev, she was induced by Griboedov to have a cup
of tea at the apartment he shared with Count Zavadovski
(in whom prototypists recognize a character mentioned
in *Woe from Wit*, IV, iv:

> . . . First, Prince Grigoriy, a unique
>   Side-splitting freak:
> Lifelong with Englishmen, all's English about him;

Like them, he through his teeth will speak
And wear his hair cut short and trim.)

Zavadovski was passionately in love with her. Shere-
metev sought the advice of Yakubovich, the celebrated
daredevil (he had already dispatched a dozen brave men),
who suggested a *partie carrée*. Both Zavadovski and
Griboedov, naturally enough, were eager to take on
Yakubovich; after some deliberations, Zavadovski was
paired off with Sheremetev, and Griboedov with Yaku-
bovich. The duel started with the Zavadovski-Shereme-
tev encounter on the Volkov Field in the early afternoon
of Nov. 12 (Onegin probably was still in bed). The
weapons were Lepage pistols, the distance in paces was
6 + 6 + 6 (see nn. to Six : XXIX–XXX); a Dr. Yon (John)
and Onegin's friend Kaverin were the seconds. Shere-
metev fired first—and his shot ripped off a piece of
Zavadovski's surtout collar. "Ah, il en voulait à ma vie!
À la barrière!" cried Count Zavadovski (unconsciously
paraphrasing Count de Rosambert's exclamation in *Fin
des amours de Faublas*, when, in a different sort of duel,
his enemy's bullet clips a lock of his hair: "C'est à ma cer-
velle qu'il en veut!")—and, at six paces, shot Sheremetev
through the breast. In his ire and agony, the poor fellow
flapped and plunged all over the snow like a large fish.
"Vot tebe i repka [Well, that's the end of *your* little
turnip]," said Kaverin to him, sadly and colloquially.
Sheremetev's death delayed the Yakubovich-Griboedov
meeting; it took place a year later (Oct. 23, 1818) in
Tiflis; the great marksman, knowing how much the
great writer liked to play the piano, neatly wounded him
in the palm of the left hand, crippling the fifth digit;
it did not prevent Griboedov from going on with his
musical improvising, but some ten years later this con-
tracted finger provided the sole means of identifying his
body, horribly mutilated by a Persian mob in an anti-
Russian riot at Teheran, where he was envoy. On June

11, 1829, when traveling south from Georgia, through Armenia, on his way to Erzerum, Pushkin, who had known Griboedov since 1817, chanced to meet, at a turn of the road, the cart drawn by two bullocks that was carrying Griboedov's body to Tiflis. Istomina married the second-rate actor Pavel Ekunin and died of cholera in 1848.

VARIANT

8 The fair copy, instead of "stands Istomina," *stoít Istómina*, reads "runs Istomina," *bezhít Istómina*, which, though lacking the subtle alliteration, produces a more vivid effect: gaining impetus for the take-off.

XXI

Onegin's general behavior in this and other stanzas may be compared to that ironically described by an anonymous author in the magazine *Son of the Fatherland* (*Sïn otechestva*), XX (1817), 17–24:

When entering high society, make it your first rule to esteem no one. . . . Be sure never to be surprised; display cold indifference to everything. . . . Make an appearance everywhere, but only for a moment. To every gathering take with you abstraction, boredom; at the theater, yawn, don't pay any attention [to the performance]. . . . In general, make it clear that you don't care for women and despise them. . . . Pretend that you recognize neither kith nor kin. . . . In general be wary of all attachment: it may ensnare you, may unite your lot to a being with whom you shall have to share everything: joy and sorrow. This will lead to obligations. . . . Obligations are the lot of simple minds—you aspire toward higher achievements.

In curious correlation to this, I cannot forbear quoting a rigmarole à la Voltaire (with an injection of symbolic romanticism) in Stendhal's much overrated *Le Rouge et le noir*, ch. 37:

À Londres, [Julien Sorel] connut enfin la haute fatuité. Il s'était lié avec de jeunes seigneurs russes [called further "les dandys ses amis"] qui l'initièrent.

—Vous êtes prédestiné, mon cher Sorel, lui disaient-ils, vous avez naturellement cette mine froide et à *mille lieues de la sensation présente,* que nous cherchons tant à nous donner.

—Vous n'avez pas compris votre siècle, lui disait le prince Korasoff: *faites toujours le contraire de ce qu'on attend de vous.* . . .

1, 4, 5, 7–9 This is the stanza with the maximum number of lines scudded on the second foot. The bilingual reader should consult the original. As elsewhere (see n. to Four : XLVI : 11–14) the use of this variation coincides with the sense conveyed. No other rhythm could better render Onegin's laborious progress and the moodiness of his survey of the house.

2, 5 / toes . . . tiers: In "My Remarks on the Russian Theater" (*Moi zamechaniya ob russkom teatre*), Pushkin wrote in 1820: "Before the beginning of an opera, tragedy, or ballet, a young blade circulates along all ten rows of stalls, walks on everybody's feet, converses with all the people he knows or does not know." Note the Gallic turn of the sentence.

The Bolshoy Kamennïy Teatr had five tiers.

3 / *Dvoynóy lornét*: Throughout the novel Pushkin uses "lorgnette" in two senses—in the general sense of an eyeglass, or eyeglasses, modishly perched on a long handle, which a dandy used as elegantly and expertly as a belle her fan, and in the specific sense of "opera glass," Fr. *lorgnette double,* "binocle," which I presume is the meaning here.

In Maykov's *Elisey* (1771), can. I, l. 559, Hermes disguises himself as a police corporal by making a mustache out of his own dark wings, and, in another impersona-

Commentary

tion, can. III, l. 278, transforms himself into a *petit-maître* (*petimetr*, fopling). In ll. 282–83:

Hermes had now a cane, Hermes had a lorgnette:
Through it he with hauteur gazed at the girls he met.

This is the "quizzing glass" of eighteenth-century beaux.

In Griboedov's *Woe from Wit*, III, viii (in which Chatski's day in Moscow is synchronous with Onegin's day in St. Petersburg, winter, 1819–20), the young Countess Hryumin directs her "double lorgnette" at Chatski; in this case it is certainly not a binocle, but quizzing glasses, i.e., eyeglasses attached to a stem.

Toward mid-century and later, when vulgarity and sloppiness pervaded the Russian novel (excepting, of course, Turgenev and Tolstoy), one finds sometimes *dvoynoy lornet* used for pince-nez!*

5 / has scanned / *okínul vzórom*: "Has scanned with the gaze"—which is tautological in English.

14 / *No i Didló mne nadoél*: The "romantic writer" mentioned in Pushkin's n. 5 appended to Onegin's alliterative yawn is identified in a canceled draft (2370, f. 82^r), where the sentence begins, "Pushkin himself used to say."

VARIANTS

10 In two canceled drafts (2369, f. 10^v) our poet had Onegin survey from the orchestra seats various "Natashas known to him," and "his Anyutas, Natashas, and Annettes" (the reading of the third name is doubtful, according to Tomashevski). The next generation would have called these young ladies "Claras" or "Camelias."

13 Canceled draft (2369, f. 10^v):

---

*Owing to a confusion of *lorgnette* with *lorgnon*.

Alone Lih[útina] is sweet . . .

Lihutina (1802–75), one of Didelot's most charming pupils, made a brilliant debut May 23, 1817, in the ballet *Acis et Galathée*, dancing Galatea (as Istomina had at her first appearance; see n. to One : XX : 5–14). The performance was repeated June 12, 1817. Lihutina died, forgotten, some six decades later, without ever learning that the melody of her name lay preserved in a MS line. This line may have been a reference to her appearance Aug. 28, 1819, in a Didelot ballet that graced Boïeldieu's opera *Le Petit Chaperon rouge* (*Krasnaya shapochka*).

XXII

1–4 Translators have had a good deal of trouble with the first quatrain.

Lt.-Col. Spalding (1881):

> Snakes, satyrs, loves with many a shout
> Across the stage still madly sweep,
> Whilst the tired serving-men without
> Wrapped in their sheepskins soundly sleep.

Clive Phillipps-Wolley (1904 [1883]):

> Still cupids, demons, dragons, monkeys
> Upon the boards loud revel kept,
> Within the porch the weary flunkeys
> Still curled up in their shubas slept.

Babette Deutsch (1936):

> The imps and cupids, quick as monkeys,
> Upon the boards still flutter free,
> While in the lobby sleepy flunkeys
> Are guarding fur-coats faithfully.

Oliver Elton (1937):

> Loves, serpents, demons still are leaping
> Upon the stage, with wild uproar;
> Still are the weary lackeys sleeping,
> Wrapt in their mantles, at the door.

Dorothea Prall Radin (1937):

> But still the cupids, snakes, and devils
> Career about and scream and roar;
> The tired lackeys in their sheepskins
> Still doze before the entrance door.

None of these translators understood that the lackeys, an idle and drowsy tribe, while guarding their masters' coats, sprawled fast asleep *upon* those comfortable heaps of furs. The coachmen were less fortunate.

Incidentally, Pushkin first (draft, 2369, f. 10ᵛ) had "bears" instead of "amors"—which might assist one when tracing a connection in the poet's mind between the theater and Tatiana's dream (Five), with its "shaggy footman."

Those *amours, diables et dragons*, romping in a Didelot ballet at St. Petersburg in 1819, had been the stock characters of the Parisian Opéra a hundred years earlier. They are mentioned, for instance, in a song by C. F. Panard, *Description de l'Opéra* (to Dufresny's and Ragot de Grandval's tune *Réveillez-vous, belle endormie*), *Œuvres* (Paris, 1763).

5–6 This intonation (technically belonging to the Tabulation Device) inaugurates a series of fateful echoes that will follow each other through Tatiana's dream (in Five), the name-day party (ibid.), and her Moscow impressions (in Seven):

One : XXII : 5–6:

> *Eshchyó ne perestáli tópat',*
> *Smorkát'sya, káshlyat', shíkat', hlópat'* . . .

> still people have not ceased to stamp,
> blow noses, cough, hiss, clap . . .

Five : XVII : 7–8:

> *Lay, hóhot, pén'e, svist i hlóp,*
> *Lyudskáya mólv' i kónskiy tóp* . . .

Barks, laughs, singing, whistling, and claps,
parle of man and stamp of steed!

Five : XXV : 11–14:

> *Lay mósek, chmókan'e devíts,*
> *Shum, hóhot, dávka u poróga,*
> *Poklóni, shárkan'e gostéy,*
> *Kormílits krík i plách detéy.*

the bark of pugs, girls' smacking kisses,
noise, laughter, a crush at the threshold,
the bows, the scraping of the guests,
wet nurses' shouts, and children's cry.

Seven : LIII : 1:

> *Shum, hóhot, begotnyá, poklóni . . .*
> Noise, laughter, scampering, bows . . .

Also to be marked are:
Six : XXXIX : 11:

> *Pil, él, skuchál, tolstél, hirél . . .*

[would have] drunk, eaten, moped, got fat, decayed . . .

Seven : LI : 2–4:

> *Tam tesnotá, volnén'e, zhár,*
> *Muzíki gróhot, svéch blistán'e,*
> *Mel'kán'e, víhor' bístrih pár . . .*

the crush there, the excitement, heat,
the music's crash, the tapers' blaze,
the flicker, whirl of rapid pairs . . .

The last two examples grade into the inventory technique, the many long listings of impressions, things, people, authors, and so forth, of which Seven : XXXVIII is the most striking example.

Analogous intonations are found elsewhere in Pushkin, but nowhere so conspicuously as in his long poem *Poltava* (Oct. 3–16, 1828), pt. III, ll. 243–46:

> *Shved, rússkiy—kólet, rúbit, rézhet.*
> *Boy barabánnïy, klíki, skrézhet,*
> *Grom púshek, tópot, rzhán'e, stón,*
> *I smért' i ád so vséh storón.*

> Swede, Russian—stabbing, hacking, slashing.
> The beat of drums, the cries, the gnashing,
> the roar of cannons, stamping, neighing, groans,
> and death and hell on every side.

7 / outside and inside / *snarúzhi i vnutrí*: "Without and within."

It is wildly unlikely that James Russell Lowell had read *Eugene Onegin* in Russian, or in a literal MS translation, when he wrote his poem in nine quatrains *Without and Within* (in the volume entitled *Under the Willows and Other Poems*, 1868), which begins:

> My coachman, in the moonlight there,
> Looks through the side-light of the door;
> I hear him and his brethren swear . . .

and goes on to describe "the ungyved prance with which his freezing feet he warms"; but the coincidence is charming, and one can well imagine a parallelist's exultation, had Lowell been born in 1770 and been translated by Pichot in 1820.

12 The old English term "to beat goose" tempts one here, meaning as it does to beat one's palms together with a swinging motion of the arms, alternately in front of one's chest and behind one's back; this is exactly what these coachmen, gentlemen's serfs, were doing as they stood, dressed in their well-padded, but not necessarily frost-proof, overcoats, blue, brown, green, of a Santa Claus cut, around those bonfires in front of the theater.

The Englishman Thomas Raikes (1777–1848), who visited Petersburg ten years later (1829–30), mentions in his *Journal* the "large bonfires . . . lighted near the principal theatres for the preservation of coachmen and servants." Still later the fires were replaced by "street stoves."

14 The beau of the times "invariably went home to change . . . after the opera, previously to attending . . . either ball or supper" (see Captain Jesse's *Brummell*, II, 58).

By Sept. 5, 1823, in Odessa, Pushkin had finished this first part of One, excepting two stanzas (XVIII and XIX), inserted a year later.

VARIANTS

1–2 Drafts (2369, f. 10^v):

1   Still bears, gods, serpents
1   Still Chinamen, gods, serpents
2   in the fourth act make noise

In the fair copy and transcript the "gods" become "devils."

10 Draft (2369, f. 10^v):

in their bright harnesses . . .

XXIII

Alongside the heavily corrected draft of this stanza (2369, f. 11^r; reproduced by A. Efros, *Risunki poeta* [Moscow, 1933], p. 121), in the left-hand margin, Pushkin drew the profiles of Countess Vorontsov, Aleksandr Raevski, and, lower down, against the last lines, Count Vorontsov. Judging by the presence of these drawings, I should not date the stanza before mid-October, 1823—unless Pushkin had glimpsed the Countess immediately upon her arrival in Odessa from Belaya Tserkov, in September, when she was in the last stage of pregnancy. (See n. to One : XXXIII : 1.)

Commentary

1 / Shall I: A Gallic turn; cf. *dirai-je*.

2 / secluded cabinet: A dressing room; a masculine boudoir. Cf. Parny's "Voici le cabinet charmant | Où les Grâces font leur toilette" (*Le Cabinet de toilette*, in *Poésies érotiques*, bk. III, 1778).

4 / is dressed, undressed, and dressed again / *Odét, razdét i vnóv' odét*: The original bears an uncanny resemblance to l. 70 of Samuel Butler's *Hudibras* (pt. I, can. I, 1663):

> Confute, change hands, and still confute.

The French rhymed version—

> Change la thèse, et puis réfute.

—*Hudibras*, "poëme écrit dans le tems des Troubles d'Angleterre" (London, 1757), by John Towneley (1697–1782), was a rare book by 1800. Pushkin probably saw Towneley's tour de force in Jombert's edition, ". . . poême . . . écrit pendant les guerres civiles d'Angleterre" (3 vols., London and Paris, 1819), with the English *en regard*.

It may be argued that, given the mock-heroic manner, one element must automatically lead to another in the same series, producing here a quadruple coincidence (stylistic formula, meter, rhythm cut, and sound of words). See, for example, ll. 52–53 in *Les Journées de Tancarville* (1807) by Pierre Antoine Lebrun:

> Le lièvre qui, plein de vitesse,
> S'enfuit, écoute, et puis s'enfuit . . .

5–8 In *Le Mondain* (1736), Voltaire has (ll. 20–27): "Tout sert au luxe, aux plaisirs. . . . | Voyez-vous pas ces agiles vaisseaux | Qui . . . de Londres . . . | S'en vont chercher, par un heureux échange, | De nouveaux biens," and Byron, in *Don Juan*, X (1823), XLV, when steering his hero into Empress Catherine's arms, refers to the com-

mercial treaty between England and Russia and to "the
Baltic's navigation, | Hides, train-oil, tallow." But, un-
less the passage had been quoted in French or Russian
periodicals, Pushkin could not have known can. X at
the time, as it was not reviewed even in English journals
until Sept.–Oct., 1823, and came to Russia in Pichot's
version not before the end of 1824 (". . . la navigation
sur la Baltique . . . les fourrures, l'huile de pêche, le
suif . . .").

6 | *Lóndon shchepetíl'nïy*: This epithet would mean merely
"meticulous" today, but in Pushkin's time it still re-
tained its eighteenth-century flavor of "pertaining to
fashionable bagatelles." A dealer in such wares would
stand midway between a French *bijoutier* or *orfèvre* and
an English "haberdasher."

See *Shcheptetíl'nik* (1765), *The Trinklet Dealer*, a one-
act comedy not devoid of talent—and, in fact, charming
when compared to the trash appearing in Russia at the
time—by the little-known playwright Vladimir Lukin
(1737–94), who imitated Pierre Claude Nivelle de la
Chaussée (1692–1754). The imported (from France)
fancy articles mentioned in the play are spyglasses,
Sèvres china, snuffboxes, bronze statuettes of cupids,
silk masks, wedding rings, repeaters, and other baubles
(*bezdelitsï, bezdelki, bezdelushki, bezdelyushki*).

11–13 Cases of adjacent position of a second-foot scudder,
or Slow line, and a first-and-third-foot scudder, or Fast
Flow, occur not infrequently throughout *EO*; but the
occurrence of a Slow line between two Fast Flows is very
rare. In fact, the present passage seems to be the only
one in *EO* containing this magnificent modulation:

> *Izobretáet dlya zabáv,*
> *Dlya róskoshi, dlya négi módnoy—*
> *Vsyo ukrashálo kabinét*

which can be rhythmically duplicated as:

> does manufacture for delights,
> for luxury, for modish pleasure—
> all decorated the retreat

and schematically represented (with o denoting a scud-
less foot and x a scudded one*) thus:

$$\begin{array}{cccc} \text{x} & \text{o} & \text{x} & \text{o} \\ \text{o} & \text{x} & \text{o} & \text{o} \\ \text{x} & \text{o} & \text{x} & \text{o} \end{array}$$

It is amusing to find among English verses (in which
the first-and-third scudder is so much rarer than in
Russian) a similar pattern; cf. Emerson's *Threnody*,
ll. 19–21:

> And by his cóuntenance repáy
> The fávor of the lóving Dáy,
> Has disappéared from the Day's éye.

XXIV

1 / *Yantár' na trúbkah Tsaregráda*: Russian poets used the
euphonious *Tsar'grad* (see also *Onegin's Journey*, XXVI :
4) to designate Constantinople, a city that Russian pa-
triotic groups (such as the Slavophiles) were bent on
taking from Islam and giving over to Greek Catholicism
as represented by "Holy Rus'." The fashionable smoking
implements mentioned here, long Turkish pipes, with
amber mouthpieces and various ornaments, are the
South-Russian *chubuks*, and the "gem-adorned chi-
bouques" of Byron (who carelessly used a French tran-
scription of the local word in his *The Bride of Abydos*
[1813], I, 233). In rendering Pushkin's rather clumsy
line it was difficult to resist the pretty paraphrase:

> ambered chibouks from Istanbul . . .

---

*See App. II, "Notes on Prosody," §3, The Scud.

1–8 Pope (also following French models but transcending
them, thanks to English richness of imagery and
originality of diction) describes (1714) a lady's dressing
room in more sophisticated detail (*The Rape of the Lock,*
I, 133–38):

> This Casket *India*'s glowing Gems unlocks,
> And all *Arabia* breathes from yonder Box.
> The Tortoise here and Elephant unite,
> Transform'd to *Combs*, the speckled, and the white.
> Here Files of Pins extend their shining Rows,
> Puffs, Powders, Patches, Bibles, Billet-doux.

Pope was little known in nineteenth-century Russia,
where his name was pronounced with the *o* as in "pop"
and with the closing vowel sounded, so that Pope prac-
tically rhymed with "poppy." At the time of writing
One (1823), Pushkin knew "the English Boileau" in
French versions. His *Œuvres complettes* had been brought
out by Joseph de La Porte (Paris, 1779), and there
existed several versions of *The Rape of the Lock, La
Boucle de cheveux enlevée*—by Marthe, Countess de
Caylus (1728), P. F. Guyot-Desfontaines (1738),
Marmontel (1746), Alexandre Des Moulins (1801),
E. T. M. Ourry (1802), and others.

*

Among the articles of George Bryan Brummell, the
notorious man of fashion (when the effects of the Broken
Beau were sold at public auction after he left London for
Calais in May, 1816), his biographer, Capt. William
Jesse (*Life*, vol. I, ch. 24), mentions "a mahogany-
framed sliding cheval dressing-glass on casters, with
two brass arms for one light each" and various articles
of virtu such as Sèvres ware and a letter scale with an
ormolu Cupid in the act of "weighing a heart." Later,
in Caen, the seedy but incorrigible virtuoso dissipated
large sums in the purchase of bronzes such as a paper

weight of "marble, surmounted by a small bronze eagle," said to have belonged to Napoleon.

*

The boredom of reading through the English, German, Polish, etc., "translations" of our poem was much too great even to be contemplated, but I find in my files copies of the following atrocious, incredibly "expanded," and abominably vulgar versions of this stanza.

Alexander Puschkin, Dichtungen, tr. Dr. Robert Lippert (vol. I, Leipzig, 1840):

> Hier Bernstein auf den Türkenpfeifen,
> Porz'lan und Bronzen überall,
> Und in geschliffenem Krystall
> Odeurs, den Schwindel abzuwehren,
> Gerade, sowie krumme Scheeren,
> Stahlfeilen, Kämmchen, feine Seifen
> Und Bürsten dreissig an der Zahl,
> Sowohl für Nägel als für Zähne.

Alexander Puschkin's poetische Werke, tr. Friedrich Bodenstedt (vol. II, Berlin, 1854):

> Gold, Porzellan und Bronze blitzen
> Auf seinen Tischen überall,
> An Türkenpfeifen Bernsteinspitzen,
> Und Wohlgerüche in Krystall.
> Krumme und grade Scheeren, Schwämme,
> Stahlfeilen, klein' und grosse Kämme,
> Zahllose Bürsten jeder Art
> Für Nägel, Zähne, Kopf und Bart.

Eugén Onégin, "Roman in Versen," tr. Dr. Alexis Lupus (1st can., rev. edn., Leipzig and St. Petersburg, 1899):

> Auf Stambul's Pfeifen Bernsteinspitzen,
> Porz'llan und Bronze überall,
> Und Taschentücher anzuspritzen,
> Odeurs in böhmischem Krystall;
> In eleganten Necessairen
> Gerade so wie krumme Scheeren,

> Und Bürsten dreissigerlei Art
> Für Zähne, Nägel, Haar und Bart.

A Polish translation by Julian Tuwim (Warsaw, 1954)
grapples with the awful difficulty of finding masculine
rhymes in Polish (there are none among words of more
than one syllable):

> Cybuchow carogradzkich jantar
> Fajense, braz na tkanin tle
> I—rozkosz zmyslow, skarb galanta
> Perfumy w szlifowanym szkle . . .

The prize for grotesque achievement goes, however,
to an earlier Polish version: *Eugenjusz Oniegin,* tr.
L. Belmont (1902), ed. Dr. Waclaw Lednicki (Kraków,
1925):

> Bursztyn na fajkach Carogradu;
> tu porcelana, ówdzie bronz,
> w krysztale rznietym won ogrodu,
> ekstrakty kwiatow—fiolet, pons . . .

These violet and corn-poppy extracts are superior in
circus value to Lippert's smelling salts and soaps,
Bodenstedt's sponges and beard brushes, and Lupus'
smart toilet sets.

The performance of the English team is on the whole
considerably soberer, even when it errs. Spalding (1881),
7–8: ". . . lo! brushes | Both for the nails and for the
tushes"; Elton (Jan., 1936), 5: ". . . little files of steel
for scraping"; Deutsch (1936), 3: ". . . And, for the
senses' sweet confusion"; Radin (1937), 2: ". . . Bronzes
and porcelain *en masse.*"

4 / perfumes / *duhí*: The Russian word is always in the
plural; perhaps only one kind of perfume would be used
by a genuine beau.

10 / *vázhnïy Grím*: In reference to things this epithet
signifies "important," but in reference to people it

passes through a whole prism of merging meanings, related to office (important, high-ranking), position (influential), demeanor (grave, dignified), and general appearance (important-looking, imposing). A similar difficulty attends the exact rendering of *vazhnïy general* in Seven : LIV : 4.

12 / the eloquent crackbrain: Epithetically, midway between Voltaire's coarse definition of Rousseau as "un charlatan déclamateur" (Epilogue to *La Guerre civile de Genève*, 1768) and Byron's romantic conception of "the self-torturing sophist, wild Rousseau . . . who from Woe | Wrung overwhelming eloquence" (*Childe Harold*, III, LXXVII).

Pushkin's n. 6 to these lines is a quotation from *Les Confessions de Jean-Jacques Rousseau* (Geneva, 1781 and 1789), referring to Frédéric Melchior Grimm (1723–1807), French encyclopedist of German descent. The passage is in pt. II, bk. IX, written in 1770 and treating of 1757, and begins:

Aussi fat qu'il étoit vain [compare intonation to that of Master Motto], avec ses gros yeux troubles et sa figure dégingandée [ill-favored], il avoit des prétentions près des femmes . . . il se mit à faire le beau; sa toilette devint une grande affaire; tout le monde sut . . .

XXV

5 / Chadaev: Replaced by asterisks in the first edition. Correctly pronounced "Chadáev," generally spelled "Chaadaev," and sometimes "Chedaev." Colonel Pyotr Chaadaev (1793–1856) was in Onegin's day a strange and brilliant personality, fop and philosopher, a man of mercy and wit, and an influential freethinker—to be later engulfed in organized mysticism. Denis Davïdov, in a striking poem, *A Contemporary Song* (1836), which

prefigures Nekrasov's satirical style, refers to Chaadaev contemptuously as "the little abbé." Chaadaev is the author of *Lettres philosophiques*, written in French and begun in the early 1820's. One of these was published in Russian in the review *Telescope*, XXXIV (1836), upon which the author was officially declared insane. The first edition of the *Lettres*, in *Œuvres choisies de Tchadaïef*, was published by Ivan Gagarin, a Jesuit, in Paris, 1862.

12 / Venus: I suppose Pushkin is thinking here of *Venus in Her Dressing Room* (also known as *The Toilette of Venus*), by Francesco Albano or Albani (1578–1660), a mediocre painter of maudlin mythologies (his extraordinary fame seems to have rested on conventionally eulogistic allusions to him in French eighteenth-century poetry—see n. to Five : XL : 3).

VARIANT

1–8 In the draft (2369, f. 11ᵛ), a rejected variant stands thus:

> All over Europe in our time
> among civilized people
> no one considers burdensome
> the tender finish of his nails.
> And nowadays the warrior and the courtier,
> ⟨the poet⟩ and the daring liberal,
> and the sweet-voiced diplomatist
> are ready . . .

XXVI

1–4 Alongside the draft (2369, f. 12ᵛ; Efros, p. 125), in the left-hand margin, Pushkin drew the Roman-nose profile of Amalia Riznich. (See n. to One : LIV.)

4 / his attire: I imagine he wore to that particular ball (winter, 1819) not simply a black *frac* but (following

London rather than Paris), a brass-buttoned, velvet-collared, sky-blue coat—with skirts enclosing the thighs—over a very close-fitting white waistcoat; quite certainly, his Bréguet repeater, with a dangling fob seal, was carried in the right front pocket of the trousers; these, I imagine were blue pantaloons (also termed "tights"—nankeen tights with three buttons at the ankle) strapped over varnished *escarpins*. There were thirty-two styles of tying a cravat.

7 | *pantaloni̇̈, frak, zhilet*: An obviously French listing—*pantalon, frac, gilet.*

Ten years earlier, in his poem *The Monk*, young Pushkin followed Karamzin and other writers in using, for the upper garment clothing the legs, the Russian word *shtani̇̈* (*frak s shtanami . . . zhilet*), which initially had meant any kind of linen underwear for the legs (today *podshtanniki* or *kal'soni̇̈*, Fr. *caleçon*) but by the end of the eighteenth century had stood for "smallclothes," i.e., knee breeches, reaching only to the top of the stockinged calf. In my youth, before the era of Soviet provincialization, *pantaloni̇̈* and *shtani̇̈* meant simply trousers, while the synonym *bryuki* was regarded in St. Petersburg as a dreadful vulgarism, on a par with the lower-class variant *zhiletka* for *zhilet* (waistcoat).

In the course of a rather comical examination of Friedrich Engels' tussle with the Russian language (as reflected in his German MS notes to the meaning of words in the first thirty-three stanzas of *EO*), M. P. Alekseev remarks (collection *Pushkin, issledovaniya i materiali̇̈*, [Leningrad, 1956], p. 89n.) that, although it is true that the words *pantaloni̇̈, frak, zhilet* are absent from the *Slovar' Akademii Rossiyskoy* (6 vols., St. Petersburg, 1789–94), they had been already incorporated in Yanovski's *Noviy slovotolkovatel', raspolozhenniy po alfavitu* (St. Petersburg, 1803–04, 1806).

14 / the Academic Dictionary / *Akademicheskiy Slovar'*: A
note (6) appended by Pushkin here, in the separate edi-
tion to Chapter One (1825), reads:

One cannot but regret that our writers too seldom con-
sult the dictionary of the Russian Academy.* It will
remain an everlasting monument to the solicitudinous
will of Catherine and to the enlightened labors of Lo-
monosov's successors, strict and trustworthy guardians
of our native tongue. Here is what Karamzin† says in his
speech [before the Rossiyskaya Akademiya, Dec. 5, 1818]:
"The Russian Academy marked the very beginning of its
existence by a work of the utmost importance to the lan-
guage; indispensable to authors, indispensable to any-
body who desires to present his ideas with clarity, who
desires to comprehend himself and others. The complete
dictionary, published by the Academy, belongs to the
number of those phenomena by means of which Russia
astonishes attentive foreigners: our destiny, certainly a
fortunate one in all regards, is characterized by a kind
of extraordinary velocity: we mature not in the course of
centuries, but in the course of decades. Italy, England,
Germany were already famous for many great writers,
while not yet possessing a dictionary; we have had
religious, spiritual books, we have had writers in verse
and in prose, but only a single true classic—Lomonosov—
and we have produced a system of the language that may
vie with the celebrated works of the Academies of
Florence and Paris. Catherine the Great [Empress of
Russia, 1762–96]—who of us even in the most flourishing
age of Alexander I [r. 1801–25] can pronounce her
name without a deep feeling of love and gratitude? [a
very Gallic oratorical formula]—Catherine, loving the
glory of Russia as her own, loving the glory of victory as
well as the peaceful glory of Reason [Fr. *raison*, Russ.
razum], accepted this fortunate fruit of the Academy's
labors with that flattering benevolence with which she

---

*This *Slovar' Akademii Rossiyskoy* was in Pushkin's library;
see Modzalevski, "Biblioteka A. S. Pushkina," *P. i ego sovr.*,
III, 9–10 (1909), 94.
†Reformer of the language, Gallicist, essayist, novelist, poet,
and historian, Pushkin's precursor in literary style, Nikolay
Karamzin (1766–1826).

knew how to reward all that was praiseworthy, a
benevolence that has remained for you, gentlemen, an
unforgettable, most precious recollection."

[signed] The Author's Note.

(Pushkin evolved a subtle interplay between the
"authorial" and the "editorial" in his notes: literary
masquerades were fashionable among Romantic writers.)

XXVII

The series of nineteen stanzas from XVIII to XXXVI may be
termed The Pursuit. In XXVII Pushkin overtakes his
fellow hero and reaches the lighted mansion first. Now
Onegin drives up, but Pushkin is already inside. In this
stanza XXVII, I have attempted to render exactly the
Russian perfective aspects (under other circumstances
sufficiently well expressed by the English present) so as
to preserve intact the significant structural transition
from one character to another at this point, after which
Pushkin, the conventional libertine (XXIX) and the in-
spired preterist (XXX–XXXIV, ending on the initial flippant
note), takes over so thoroughly that the troublesome
time element in the description of Onegin's night is
juggled away (since he is not shown wenching and
gaming, the reader has to assume that seven or eight
hours are spent by Onegin at the ball) by means of a
beautiful lyrical digression, and Pushkin, after lagging
behind at the ball (as he had lagged in Onegin's dressing
room before it), must again overtake Onegin on his drive
home (XXXV)—only to fall behind again while the ex-
hausted beau goes to sleep (XXXVI). The pursuit that
Pushkin started upon in XVIII–XX, when, on the wings
of a lyrical digression, he arrives at the opera house
before Onegin (XXI–XXII), is now over.

If the reader has understood the mechanism of this pur-
suit he has grasped the basic structure of Chapter One.

3, 7 / in a hack coach / *v yamskóy karéte* / twin lamps of
coupés / *Dvoyníe fonari karét*: The Russian word for any
kind of four-wheeled close carriage, with an outside box
in front for the coachman—be it a road coach of the
berlin type, or a chariot of the eighteenth century (with
its two footmen behind), or a post chaise, or the sober
functional brougham of modern times—is *kareta* (Pol.
kareta, It. *carretta*, Eng. chariot, Fr. *carrosse*). The
English were always highly precise in their application
of carriage terms; and the difficulty of establishing what
specific vehicle a Russian means in this or that case under
the generic term of *kareta* is augmented by the difficulty
of matching the actual variety of Continental carriage
with its nearest English counterpart. Pictures of English
post chaises are very close to those of the Russian
dorozhnaya (road) *kareta*.

In Onegin's time the ornate and heavy chariot was
already giving way in cities to the *carrosse-coupé* (Fr.),
the cut chariot, the coupé. The passenger part of the
chariot was, in lateral view, a more or less symmetrical
affair (easily derived from the fairy-tale pumpkin) with
a door between its two windows, distal and proximal.
The passenger part of the cut chariot lost its proximal
third, retaining the door and the distal window. The
form of the very light coupé called brougham was pre-
served in the first electric automobiles just as the outline
of the passenger part of the chariot was multiplied in the
lateral view of the first railway carriage: I have not seen
any notice taken before of the curious prudishness with
which conventional man disguises transitions from one
form to another.

There was no disgrace in Russia for a young man of
fashion in not keeping his own horses and chariot.
Pushkin's friend Prince Pyotr Vyazemski did not bother
to buy a coach during a protracted stay in St. Petersburg.
The same was true of London. In Lady Morgan's

Passages from My Autobiography (1859; begun in 1818), Lady Cork notes that "some right honourables of my acquaintance go in hacks" (p. 49).

6–11 Cf. Baratïnski's *The Ball* (begun February, 1825; finished September, 1828; pub. 1828), a story in verse consisting—in the autograph fair copy—of 658 iambic tetrameters in forty-seven stanzas of fourteen lines with rhymes abbaceceddifif (ll. 15–18):

> . . . In a long array,
> besilvered by the moon,
> coupés stand parked . . .
> before a house sumptuous and ancient.

The separate edition of *EO*, One, appeared Feb. 16, 1825. Baratïnski by the end of February had written forty-six lines. Of these, ll. 15–19 came out in the *Moscow Telegraph*, 1827.

9 / rainbows / *rádugi*: My own sixty-year-old remembrance is not so much of prismatic colors cast upon snowdrifts by the two lateral lanterns of a brougham as of iridescent spicules around blurry street lights coming through its frost-foliated windows and breaking along the rim of the glass.

10 / with lampions / *plóshkami*: Cuplike or potlike vessels of glass (often colored—red, green, blue, yellow) containing oil with a wick, used for illuminations.

14 / of modish quizzes / *módnïh chudakóv*: Eccentric men of fashion, *hommes à la mode*. I suspect that my translation is overnice, and that Pushkin tautologically used two words ("fashionable dandies") to render one, namely, "fashionables," "elegants," "exquisites," "extravagants," "fantastics," *merveilleux* (from *merveille*, "marvel," Russ. *chudo*), which does suggest some freak-

ish strain—whereas the trivial *modnik* would have implied conformity. *Chudak* (which I have rendered by "quizz," a modish English word of the time) also means "an odd fellow," "an eccentric," *un original*; and it is in this sense that Pushkin applies it elsewhere to Onegin: Two : IV : 14, "most dangerous eccentric" (reported speech); Five : XXXI : 6, "odd chap" (colloquial); Six : XLII : 11, "begloomed eccentric"; Seven : XXIV : 6, "sad and dangerous eccentric" (as fancied by Tatiana); Eight : VIII : 2, "play the eccentric"; Eight : XL : 4, "my unreformed eccentric" (jocose).

Chudak has no feminine (the dreadful Moscow vulgarism *chudachka* belongs, of course, to a different word level); but just as *chudak*, an "odd fellow," graded into "a fashionable" in Pushkin's day, so might the feminine noun *prichudnitsa*, coming from *prichuda* (caprice, whim, megrim, fad) and meaning *une capricieuse*, be made to mean *une merveilleuse*, i.e., an extravagantly fashionable woman, a capricious belle, an odd female, a spoiled beauty (One : XLII : 1 and Three : XXIII : 2).

VARIANT

1–4 Amalia Riznich in profile, wearing bonnet and shawl, is sketched alongside a first draft (2369, f. 20ʳ; Efros, p. 129):

> But let us save our pages.
> To work! Let's hasten to the ball
> whither ⟨. . . .⟩ of the city
> Onegin too has sped.

XXVIII

4 / *Rasprávil volosá rukóy*: Idiom: "has arranged his hair with his hand." The process here is not necessarily one of smoothing down; on the contrary, a studied rufflement

might be the purpose (see n. to IV : 6). Miss Deutsch has the ridiculous interpolation: "... with his narrow | White hand he swiftly smoothed his hair ..."

5 / has entered / *Voshyól*: The intonation of listed actions in the beginning of this stanza is the same as in XVI : 5–7.

7 / crowd / *Tolpa*: Frequently used in *EO*. In several instances I have preferred "throng" to "crowd." The image of a ball, a dinner, a rout, or any other convocation is consistently linked up in *EO* with that of a close-packed (*tesnïy*) throng, a crush, a squeeze, Fr. *la presse* (*tesnota*); see l. 8 and n. to One : XXX : 6. In English memoirs of the time one often finds such phrases as "at her squeeze," "the squeeze was great," "a rout-compressed company"; Pushkin's *tolpa*, *tesnota*, and *tesnïy* are in the same key. In a metaphorical sense, *tolpa* is frequently used by Pushkin to mean "the common herd."

9 / cavalier guard's / *kavalergárda*: Or *chevalier garde*'s.

9 / spurs: Pushkin's MS note about this (2370, f. 82^r) reads:

Inexact. Cavaliers, as well as hussars, of the guard wore court dress and low shoes for balls. A judicious remark, but the notion lends something poetical to the description. I refer to the opinion of A. I. V.

This is Anna Ivanovna Vulf (Netty Vulf), of whom Pushkin saw a lot at the Osipovs' countryseat, Trigorskoe, near Mihaylovskoe, when this note was made (early in 1826, about a year after One had been published; see also n. to Five : XXXII : 11).

It is not quite clear to which part of the note the word "opinion" should be applied.

Cf. quatrains VIII and IX of Denis Davïdov's trochaic ten-stanzaed *Song of an Old Hussar* (1817):

And what now? In the high world
even (ugh!) hussars you see
wearing court dress and low shoes
waltzing on the parquetry.

They've more brains, 'tis said, than we,
but from each of them what's heard?
"Jomini" and "Jomini"—
and of gin not half a word.

(For Jomini, see n. to One : v : vars. 1–4.)

11 The adjective "captivating," *plenítel'nïy*, easily fills the middle of the iambic tetrameter with third-scud music. *Plenít'*, "to captivate," and its derivatives are typical pet words of the romantic poetry of the time. Sometimes one can use "enthralled" to relieve the monotony of "captivated," a deadish epithet in English. Two near synonyms: *obol'stitel'nïy*, "enravishing," and *ocharovatel'nïy*, "enchanting." At the lowest level of "attraction," we have *prelestnïy*, "charming"; *lyubeznïy*, Fr. *aimable*; and *milïy*, "dear," "sweet," "nice," "winsome" (see n. to Three : XXVII : 6, 12).

11–12 / upon their captivating tracks | flit flaming glances: The literal sense is trivial enough, but mark the supple alliterations: *Po íh plenítel'nïm sledám | Letáyut plámennïe vzórï.* Here, as so often in *EO*, a miracle of phrasing turns water into wine.

14 An eighteenth-century Gallicism, *femmes à la mode*, rendered in the English literature of the time as "fashionable women," "ladies of fashion," "modish wives," or even "Modern Ladies." The "jealous whispering" (in the fair copy it reads "perfidious" instead of "jealous") is not quite clear but presumably signifies that some *modnïe zhyonï* were berating their lovers for attentions to other *modnïe zhyonï* or perhaps not *modnïe zhyonï*

(termed in l. 10 "winsome ladies," *milïe damï*, amiable dames).

Cf. Coleridge, *Lines Composed in a Concert-Room*:

> Hark! the deep buzz of Vanity and Hate!
>   Scornful, yet envious, with self-torturing sneer
> My lady eyes some maid of humbler state . . .

Brodski (1950), p. 90, misinterprets the obvious Europeanism of *modnïe zhyonï*, takes "modish" to mean "adulterous," and goes on to rant sociologically: "Pushkin by means of this putative image . . . stresses the dissolution . . . of society," etc.

A rhymed tale by Dmitriev, *The Fashionable Woman* (*Modnaya zhena*, 1792), a poor imitation of La Fontaine's style in his *Contes*, is as much an echo of the frivolous European fictions of the eighteenth century as is Pushkin's casual image here.

VARIANT

2 / Fair copy:

> the bell has rung; he like an arrow . . .

This is corrected to the published text in Pushkin's letter to his brother of Oct. 18, 1824.

XXIX

9 / most strictly / *postrózhe*: This is not the simple comparative (which is *strozhe*, "more strictly"), but a kind of iterative form of the comparative grading into the superlative by implying a strongly sustained repetition of the action it enjoins to perform.

12 / *izbávi, Bózhe*: Idiom: "God [vocative] spare," "God deliver." Another similar term is *upasi Bozhe*, "God forfend."

XXX

6 / the crush / *tesnotú*: A word constantly recurring in descriptions of balls and routs. The squeeze, the close throng, Fr. *la presse.* (See n. to XXVIII : 7.)

8–14 / little feet / *nózhki* [Fr. *petits pieds*]: This is the beginning of the famous pedal digression (written in Odessa, begun not before mid-August, 1823), one of the wonders of the work. The theme goes on through five stanzas (XXX–XXXIV), and its last nostalgic vibrations are:

One : LIX : 6–8 (Pushkin mentions the pen drawings of feminine feet in the margin of his manuscripts).

Five : XIV : 6–7 (Pushkin describes with erotic tenderness Tatiana's losing her slipper in the snow of her dream).

Five : XL (Pushkin, about to describe a provincial ball, recalls the digression of One : XXX–XXXIV, to which the invocation of a Petersburg ball had led).

Seven : L (Pushkin clinches the lyrical circle by alluding to the terpsichorean spectacle with which the whole thing started, One : XX, Istomina's volitations, the prelude to the digression One : XXX–XXXIV).

The associative sense of the Russian *nozhki* (conjuring up a pair of small, elegant, high-instepped, slender-ankled lady's feet) is a shade tenderer than the French *petits pieds*; it has not the stodginess of the English "foot," large or small, or the mawkishness of the German *Füsschen.*

Neither Ovid, nor Brantôme, nor Casanova has put much grace or originality into his favorable comment on feminine feet. Among the tenderer French poets, Vincent Voiture sang ". . . deux pieds gentils et bien faits" (*A la reine Anne d'Autriche*, 1644); and other quotations might be added; but on the whole, there do not seem to have been too many tender references to *petits pieds* prior to the Romantic era (Hugo, Musset).

Byron has a trite reference to the belles of Cádiz in *Don Juan*, II, v and vi: ". . . Their very walk would make your bosom swell" and ". . . their feet and ankles —well, | Thank Heaven I've got no metaphor quite ready . . ."

English versionists of *EO* have not been happy: bluff Spalding has "Three pairs of handsome female feet," and entomologically minded Miss Radin mentions "Six pretty feet"; Elton speaks of "Three pairs of feet, in womankind" and of "*one* pair, long kept in mind"; and Miss Deutsch has not only the "little feet" but throws in some "lovely limbs," and has the heart beat "When two feet tripped toward their lover."

For the plain translator, the difficulty of exactly following Pushkin's text is enhanced by his using the nondiminutive *nógi* (e.g., One : XXX : 10) in the same breath as the diminutive (*nózhki*). Taken out of context, and considering that *noga* may mean both foot and the entire leg, XXX : 10 might seem to be an invocation of graceful feminine legs. But a little further, in XXXIII, the *nogi* certainly means feet, and this, as well as current fashions of dress, and the vignettes Pushkin penned in the margins of his MS, decides the issue in favor of ankle, instep, and toe against calf, shin, and thigh.

*

Cf. P. P., "A Word with Blackwood in His Own Way," *London Magazine and Review* (Mar. 1, 1825), pp. 413–14:

. . . All persons who have an atom of taste, or a sense of proportion, will agree that the French women shine in their feet and ankles, and truth compels me to confess that . . . generally speaking, the foot is not an admirable feature of the British female person. . . . Even in London there are not more than two or three artists to be found who can make a lady's shoe.

The passion for a pretty instep that Pushkin shared with Goethe would have been called "foot-fetishism" by a modern student of the psychology of sex.

The Count in *Wahlverwandtschaften* (1809), pt. I, ch. 11, thus describes the charm of Charlotte O.'s foot:

Ein schöner Fuss ist eine grosse Gabe der Natur. . . . Ich habe sie heute im Gehen beobachtet; noch immer möchte man ihren Schuh küssen und die zwar etwas barbarische, aber doch tief gefühlte Ehrenbezeugung der Sarmaten wiederholen, die sich nichts Besseres kennen, als aus dem Schuh einer geliebten und verehrten Person ihre Gesundheit zu trinken.

12–14 In the transcript (and in the 1825 edn.), where the lines read:

> . . . Doleful, grown cool,
> even at present in my sleep
> they disturb my heart

Pushkin, without altering them, made a footnote: "An unforgivable Gallicism." This is corrected in the errata affixed to Six (1828).

Pushkin may have recalled such Gallic constructions as André Chénier's "Ainsi, triste et captif, ma lyre toutefois | S'éveillait . . ." (*La Jeune Captive*, 1794).

VARIANTS

7–9 In canceled drafts (2369, f. 14^r), the "waltz and *écossaise*" are fondly recalled, and "all Petrograd" more logically replaces "all Russia."

XXXI

14 In *Autumn Morning*, a short pentametric poem of 1816, Pushkin had (ll. 10–12):

> . . . upon the green of meads,
> I did not find the scarcely visible
> prints left by her fair foot . . .

Commentary

See also Lenski looking for Olga's footprints on a mead in Two : XXIc, variant of 12–14.

XXXII

3–4 Cf. *Le Joli-pied* of Nicolas Edme Restif de la Bretonne, a mediocre but entertaining writer of the eighteenth century (1734–1806):

> Saintepallaie avait un goût particulier, et tous les charmes ne faisaient pas sur lui une égale impression . . . une taille svelte et légère, une belle main flattait son goût: mais le charme auquel il était le plus sensible . . . c'était un joli pied: rien dans la nature ne lui paraissait audessus de ce charme séduisant, qui semble en effet annoncer la délicatesse et la perfection de tous les autres appas.

7 / with token beauty / *uslóvnoyu krasóy*: Although *uslovnïy* means "conditional" or "conventional," the only possible sense here must turn on the idea of *un signe convenu*, with the emphasis on the sign, the emblem, the cipher, the code of beauty, the secret language of those narrow little feet. (See n. to XXXIV : 14.)

Cf. Shakespeare, *Troilus and Cressida*, IV, v, 55:

> There's language in her eye, her cheek, her lip,
> Nay, her foot speaks . . .

8 / willful swarm / *svoevól'nïy róy*: A common Gallicism, *essaim*, with *svoevol'nïy*, "self-willed," echoing alliteratively such cliché epithets as *volage*, *frivole*, *folâtre*.

Cf. La Harpe writing in 1799 on Jean Antoine Roucher (1745–94, author of didactic poems; died on the scaffold with André Chénier) and his *Les Mois*: "[le] défaut dominant dans ses vers . . . c'est le retour fréquent des mots parasites [tels que] 'essaims' . . . termes communs trop souvent répétés" (*Cours de littérature* [1825 edn.], X, 454). The term *mots parasites* was first employed in a poem by J. B. Rousseau.

A few examples will suffice:

Parny, in *Poésies érotiques*, bk. III (1778), *Souvenir*: "L'essaim des voluptés."

Antoine Bertin, in *Elégie* II, *à Catilie* (1785): "tendre essaim des Désirs."

Ducis, in *Epître à l'amitié* (1786): ". . . des plaisirs le dangereux essaim."

J. B. L. Gresset, *Vert-vert* (1734; a poem—greatly admired by Pushkin—in four small cantos, about a renegade parrot which had been the pet of a nunnery): "Au printemps de ses jours | L'essaim des folâtres amours . . ."*

For years, Pushkin, not to speak of the minor poets of his day, could not get rid of these Wounds, Charms, and Ardors, of these clusters of cupids coming from their porcelain beehives in the eighteenth-century West. Gresset was a gifted poet, but his idiom was the same as that of the whole *essaim* of the *folâtres* poets of his time.

Yuriy Tïnyanov ("Pushkin i Kyuhelbeker," an essay that should be taken with a lick of salt, in *Lit. nasl.*, nos. 16–18 (1934), pp. 321–78) suggests that Pushkin first read Gresset in 1815, when Küchelbecker's mother sent two volumes of that poet to her son, Pushkin's Lyceum comrade.

Incidentally, the variations in the spelling of the name of Gresset's parrot are amusing. My copy has the following title: *Les Œuvres de Gresset, Enrichies de la Critique de Vairvert | Comédie en I acte* (Amsterdam, 1748). In the table of contents the title is *Vert-Vert*. In the half title (p. 9) and in the poem itself it is "Ver-Vert," and in the critique in comedy form appended to the volume, "Vairvert."

---

*See also Pope, *Imitation of Horace*, bk. IV, ode I:
        "Thither, the . . . Lyres
        Shall call the . . . young Desires."

9 / Elvina: I suspect this is a natural child of Macpherson's
Malvina. It occurs in French imitations of the Ossian
poems (e.g., *Elvina, prêtresse de Vesta*, by Philidor R.,
Almanach des Grâces [1804], p. 129).

11–14; XXXIII : 1–4 In the last lines of XXXII, after the
poet's invoking pretty ankles under the long cloth of
tables, there comes that rare event, a run of several
(namely four) second-foot scudders, which acts as a
kind of brake, a pulling up, an impetus-storing retard-
ment before the rush of Fast and Fast Flow lines in the
next stanza. To reproduce this effect, the passage can
be paraphrased thus:

> In spríngtime on the túrf of méads,
> In wínter on the íron fénder,
> On glóssiness of bállroom flóor,
> On gránite of the rócky shóre.
>
> The séa, the témpest that was rúmbling . . .
> Oh, the temptátion to compéte
> With bíllows túrbulently túmbling
> And lýing dówn to kíss her féet!

Moreover, there are as many as four first-foot scudders
in the rest of the stanza, a very rare event.

XXXIII

The search for a historically real lady, whose foot the glass
shoe of this stanza would fit, has taxed the ingeniousness
or revealed the simplicity of numerous Pushkinists. At
least four "prototypes" have been named and defended
with considerable heat. Let us examine first a particu-
larly specious candidate, Maria Raevski.

The last week of May, 1820, saw the realization of a
pleasant plan that had been devised at least a month
before. General Nikolay Raevski, hero of the Napoleonic
wars, traveling with one of his two sons and two of his

four daughters from Kiev to Pyatigorsk (N. Caucasus), passed through Ekaterinoslav (now Dnepropetrovsk) and picked up Pushkin, who had been sent there from St. Petersburg a fortnight before to join the chancery of another kindly general, Ivan Inzov. General Raevski's party consisted of his son Nikolay, a close friend of Pushkin; little Maria, aged thirteen and a half; little Sofia, aged twelve; a Russian nurse, an English governess (Miss Matten), a Tatar *dame de compagnie* (the mysterious Anna, of whom further), a physician (Dr. Rudïkovski), and a French tutor (Fournier). The elder son, Aleksandr, whom Pushkin had not yet met, was expecting the travelers at Pyatigorsk, while Mme Raevski and the two elder daughters (Ekaterina and Elena) were to welcome the party in August at Gurzuf (S. Crimea).

The very first lap of the journey from Ekaterinoslav to Taganrog easily cured the ague caught by our poet on the Dnepr. One morning, May 30, between Sambek and Taganrog, the five occupants of one of the two huge berlins or dormeuse-chariots, namely, the two little girls, the old nurse, the governess, and the lady companion, caught a glimpse of the white-capped sea on their right and tumbled out to admire the surf. Young Pushkin quietly emerged from the third coach, a calash.

In her remarkably banal and naïve memoirs (*Mémoires de la Princesse Marie Volkonsky*, "préface et appendices par l'éditeur prince Michel Wolkonsky," St. Petersburg, 1904), the former Maria Raevski thus describes (p. 19), some twenty years later, this scene:

Ne me doutant pas que le poète nous suivait, je m'amusais à courir après la vague et à la fuir quand elle venait sur moi; elle finit par me baigner les pieds. . . . Pouchkine trouva ce tableau si gracieux qu'il en fit de charmants vers *

---

*She quotes them below, not mentioning that they represent *EO*, One: XXXVII: 2–6.

poétisant un jeu d'enfant; je n'avais que quinze ans alors . . .

The last statement is certainly wrong: Maria Raevski was only thirteen and a half, having been born Dec. 25, 1806, O.S. (see A. Venevitinov, *Russkaya starina*, XII [1875], 822); she died Aug. 10 (O.S.?), 1863 ("agée de 56 ans"; see M. Volkonski's preface to the *Mémoires*, p. x).

After a summer sojourn at the Caucasian spas, where Pushkin fell under the cynical spell of Aleksandr Raevski, our travelers, leaving Aleksandr in the Caucasus, crossed over to the Crimea and reached Gurzuf at dawn on Aug. 19, 1820. Pushkin saw Maria Raevski occasionally in the course of the next four years. Of course, no commentator should ignore our poet's marginal drawings; thus, in the draft of Two : IXa, alongside ll. 6–14, where Lenski is said not to glorify "voluptuous snares . . . exhaling shameful delectation, as one whose avid soul [pursues] the images of former pleasures and to the world in fateful songs madly uncovers them," Pushkin in late October or early November, 1823, in Odessa, left a pen drawing of a bonneted female profile easily determinable as that of Maria Raevski (now almost seventeen years old); above it he sketched his own head, cropped as it was at the time. * If One : XXXIII does refer after all to *these* wave-wooed feet then the recollection *is* marked by "delectation" and *does* divulge "former pleasures" (the drawings representing Maria Raevski are to be found in Cahier 2369, ff. 26ᵛ, 27ᵛ, 28ʳ, and 30ᵛ; see my nn. to Two : IXa).

She married at eighteen (January, 1825). Her husband, Prince Sergey Volkonski, a prominent Decembrist of the "Southern" group, was arrested when the St.

---

*After which he let his hair grow, so that it was like Lenski's by the time he journeyed from Odessa to Mihaylovskoe in the summer of 1824.

Petersburg insurrection of Dec. 14, 1825, failed. His heroic young wife followed him into his remote Siberian exile—and there, rather bathetically, fell in love with another man, also a Decembrist. The heroic part of her life has been chanted by Nekrasov in a long jogging poem, unworthy of his real genius, the painfully mediocre *Russian Women* (1873; MS title *Dekabristki*), which has always been a favorite with such readers as are more interested in social intent than in artistic accomplishment. The only lines I ever liked therein are from another, more melodious, section, in a passage related to the hobbies of the Decembrists:

> a collection of butterflies, plants of Chitá,
> and views of that rigorous region.

After November, 1823, Pushkin saw her again on Dec. 26, 1826, in Moscow (at the house of her sister-in-law, Princess Zinaida Volkonski), on the eve of her departure for Siberia to join her husband at Blagatski Mine, Nerchinsk, 4000 miles away. On Oct. 27, 1828, at Malinniki, province of Tver, Pushkin wrote the famous dedication of his narrative poem *Poltava*, and it is thought that this dedication (sixteen iambic tetrameters rhymed abab) is addressed to Maria Volkonski:

> To you—but will the obscure Muse's voice touch your ear?
> Will you, with your modest soul, understand
> 4   the aspiration of my heart?
> Or will the poet's dedication,
> as formerly his love,
> in front of you without response
> 8   pass, unacknowledged once again?
> Do recognize at least the measures
> that pleasing were to you of yore
> and think that in the days of separation
> 12   in my unstable fate,
> your woeful wilderness,
> the last sound of your words,

> are the one treasure, shrine,
> the one love of my soul.

The draft and the fair copy are headed with the words, written in English, "I love this sweet name" (the heroine of *Poltava* is called Maria). One would like to see for oneself this draft (Cahier 2371, f. 70ʳ), where a canceled variant of l. 13 is said to read (see Bondi, Acad 1948, V, 324):

> *Sibíri hládnaya pustínya*
> Siberia's cold wilderness . . .

It is on this alone that the supposition that *Poltava* was dedicated to Maria Volkonski rests. The reader will note the curious resemblance between lines 11–16 of the *Poltava* dedication and lines 9–14 of *EO*, Seven : XXXVI (composed a year earlier), where it is Moscow, the dowager empress of Russian cities, that is addressed by our poet in commemoration of the end of his provincial exile.

Another candidate for the lady of One : XXXIII is Maria Raevski's elder sister, the twenty-two-year-old Ekaterina (who was to marry Mihail Orlov, a lesser Decembrist, in 1821). While the rest of the family traveled, she, her sister Elena, and their mother were dwelling in a rented palazzo near the Tatar village of Gurzuf on the beautiful southern shore of the Crimea, whose romantic rocks and turfy terraces, dark cypresses and pale minarets, picturesque hovels and pine-covered steeps are surmounted by the jagged stone brow of the high plateau, which from the sea looks like a mountain ridge but degenerates, as soon as you get up there, into a grassy plain gently sloping north. It was at Gurzuf that our poet made the acquaintance of Ekaterina Raevski when a navy brig brought him there from Feodosia on Aug. 19, 1820, with Nikolay Raevski, Sr., Nikolay Raevski, Jr., and the two little girls, Maria and Sofia. Additional details relating to the voyage will be found in my notes to *Onegin's*

Journey : XVI, in which, a decade later, Pushkin was to recall a love at first sight in the following rather poor lines:

> Beauteous are you, shores of the Tauris,
> when one sees you from the ship
> by the light of morning Cypris,
> 4 as for the first time I saw you.
> . . . .
> 10 And there. . .
> What ardency awoke in me!
> With what a magic yearning
> my flaming bosom was compressed!
> But, Muse, forget the past!

She was a splendid-looking, goddesslike, proud young woman, and is thus briefly referred to in stanza XVII of *Onegin's Journey*, where the surf, and the rocks, and romantic ideals are evoked. To her Pushkin probably dedicated the elegy beginning "Sparser becomes the clouds' volatile range" (Alexandrine couplets, 1820), wherein a young maiden, a very Venus in beauty, is alluded to as trying to distinguish in the dusk the planet Venus (which, as noted by N. Kusnetsov, in the publication *Mirovedenie* [1923], pp. 88–89, could not have been seen at that time and place, August, 1820, the Crimea) and calling it by her own name—humorously confusing, perhaps, *katharos* and *Kypris*, Kitty R. and Kythereia (she was something of a bluestocking).

During his three-week stay at Gurzuf, Pushkin may have heard from Katerina ("K"—see his appendix to *Bahchisarayskiy fontan*, 1822) the Tatar legend of the Fountain of Bahchisaray, which he eventually visited with her brother Nikolay about Sept. 5, 1820, on the way north; but whether the Black Sea waves ever kissed her feet is another question.

At this point (before taking leave of the Raevski sisters and welcoming a third candidate, Elizaveta Vorontsov) the actual genesis of One : XXXIII must be discussed.

Certain curious fragments written by our poet not later than 1822, in Kishinev, at least one year before he began *EO*, include a few verses that he used about June 10, 1824, in Odessa for making One : XXXIII. These fragments are in Cahier 2366, which is preserved (or at least was preserved in 1937) in the Lenin Library in Moscow. They have been described by V. Yakushkin, * Tsyavlovski, † and G. Vinokur. ‡ According to Yakushkin, the cahier contains forty-three folios numbered by hand, with many folios torn out before the beginning of the numeration. According to Tsyavlovski, a number of folios are also torn out after f. 13.

The jottings in Cahier 2366 now to be considered belong to a poem, *Tauris* (*Tavrida*), of which a few fragments forming in all about one hundred lines (in iambic tetrameter, freely rhymed) are known to Tomashevski (see the easily accessible, complete, but also unscholarly 1949 edition of Pushkin's works, II, 106). Its title, date of composition (1822), and motto ("Gieb meine Jugend mir zurück," from the prologue to *Faust*, "Vorspiel auf dem Theater," last line of ninth speech [c. 1790], a quotation frequently found in scrapbooks, commonplace books, and table books of Pushkin's time) are written out calligraphically on f. 13^r, probably in preparation or anticipation of a fair copy later canceled.

On f. 13^v we find a not very legible, incomplete note in prose: "My passions calm down, quiet reigns in my soul, hate, repentance [or "despair"?]—all vanishes, love anim—," and this seems to adumbrate the theme

---

*"Rukopisi A. S. Pushkina, hranyashchiesya v Rumyantzovskom Muzee v Moskve" (Pushkin's MSS, Preserved in the Rumyantsov Museum, Moscow), *Russkaya starina*, XLII (1884), 331–32.
† *Rukoyu Pushkina* (1935), pp. 293–94, and Acad 1947, II¹, 256–57.
‡ "Slovo i stih v *Evgenii Onegine*" (*EO*: Word and Verse), in *Pushkin* (Publications of the Chernïshevski Institute of History, Philosophy, and Literature, Moscow, 1941), ed. A. Egolin, pp. 155–213. See also *Works* 1960, I (1959), 513–14.

of a fragment of *Tavrida*, represented by a rough draft
on both sides of f. 16:

> You are with me again, Delight!
> Stilled ⟨in the soul⟩ is gloomy thoughts'
> monotonous agitation!
> The senses are revived, the mind is clear.
> With some mollitude unknown [*neizvéstnoy*],
> some melancholy I am filled.
> The animated plains.
> the hills of Tauris—region charming [*preléstniy*]
> I visit ⟨you again⟩,
> drink languorously the voluptuous air,
> I seem to hear nearby the voice
> of happiness lost long ago.
>
> Happy region, where glisten waters
> as they caress the sumptuous shores,
> and where, with nature's bright luxuriance
> the hills, the meadows are illumed;
> where frowning vaults of rocks . . .

The arbitrary rhyme pattern is ababeccedidi ababa.

Going back to f. 13ᵛ, we find there a strange spatter
of dates (presumably jotted down after our poet canceled
the fair copy of *Tavrida*):

1811	1812	1813	1814	1815	1816	1817
	1818	1818	1819	1820		

The first series would seem to refer to Pushkin's years
of schooling in Tsarskoe, 1811–17, and the second to his
years of dissipation in St. Petersburg (with the winter
of 1817–18 counted separately?).

This is followed on the same page by four irregular
columns of dates covering nineteen years, of which at
least nine were yet to come:

1821		1814	
1822			
22			
	22		16 avr
22			1822
	22	1815	

	22		1816	1820
	1822			1823
		1828	1817	1824
	22		1819	
	1822		1830	
	1822		24 31	
	33			

Soothsayers affirm that a person cannot help writing the future date of his death in a hand that slightly differs from that in which he writes any other past or future date. Pushkin, whose concern with the fatidic was almost morbid, may have been trying here, on this Apr. 16, 1822, to find out if his "22" was in some way different from the other dates he jotted down. The date "16 avr[il] 1822" can be taken, I think, to refer to the actual writing of a fragment from *Tavrida* that follows. Was this on the eve of Pushkin's duel with Zubov? (See n. to Six : xxix–xxx.) Incidentally: a mistake on the part of Yakushkin, who read the French *avr* as a Russian *avg*, has misled a number of compilers into having Pushkin write *EO*, One : xxxiii, or its prototype, on "Aug. 16"!

The dates are followed at the bottom of the same page (f. 13ᵛ) by twelve lines of verse, of which the last five are the models of *EO*, One : xxxiii : 7–10 and 12:

> After her on the slope of mountains
> I went along a road unknown [*neizvéstnoy*],
> and my shy gaze observed
> the prints of her foot charming [*preléstnoy*].
> Why dared I not its prints [*sledóv*]
> touch with hot lips,
> besprinkling them with burning [tears]?
>
> No, never midst the stormy days
> of my tumultuous youth
> did I long ⟨with such⟩ agitation
> to kiss the lips of young Circes,
> and the breasts full of languishment . . .

The rhyme scheme is babacee ddidi.

It is to be noted that insofar as the fragment obviously refers to the unfinished *Tavrida*, this Crimean mountain trail (presumably above the village of Gurzuf) has nothing to do with the "graceful games" of a child on the Taganrog strand some 300 miles to the northeast, in another part of Russia. Thus it is not a recollection of the specific event Maria Volkonski describes in her memoirs; this glass shoe does not fit her foot; it may fit Ekaterina's, but that is a mere guess based on our knowledge of Pushkin's infatuation with her during his three-week stay at Gurzuf. The really important fact is that, as we shall see presently (for we must interrupt the history of One : XXXIII in order to introduce a third lady), Pushkin derived part of an *EO* stanza from the fragment at the bottom of f. 13^v and transformed a Crimean mountainside into an Odessa seashore.

We can now turn to the lady who particularly occupied our poet's thoughts in 1824. This third candidate for the part of the Lady of the Sea is Countess Elizaveta (Elise) Vorontsov, or Woronzoff as the name was transcribed at the time (following a dreadful Germanic eighteenth-century mode), the handsome, Polish-born wife of the Governor General of Novorossiya, to whose chancery in Odessa Pushkin was attached. The affair between Pushkin and Countess Vorontsov (née Countess Branitski, 1792–1880) does not seem to have gone very far, and its actual course was brief. She came to Odessa (from Belaya Tserkov, "Whitechurch," the Branitski estate in the province of Kiev) on Sept. 6, 1823 (after Pushkin had been in Odessa for about two months). She was in the last month of pregnancy; amorous intrigues in those days used to ignore such trifles, but it would seem that Pushkin's interest in her was kindled only in November of that year. The most passionate period of Pushkin's courtship lasted from then to mid-June, 1824, with the demoniac connivance of her lover, Aleksandr

Raevski, who is said to have used his friend Pushkin as a lightning rod to deflect the betrayed husband's thunder —which must have been of a rather muffled kind, since Vorontsov had amours of his own. Her profile is sketched by our poet in the margin of drafts beginning with One : XXIII (see my notes to that stanza), and crops up again near the end of Two : XXIII (see note) and the beginning of Two : XXIV. She left for the Crimea on a yacht cruise June 14, 1824, and did not return to Odessa until July 25. A week later (July 31) Pushkin left for Mihaylovskoe. (See vol. 3, p. 303.) They corresponded throughout the autumn of that year, after which our poet plunged into a series of more or less unsavory intrigues with various ladies of the Osipov-Vulf clan. (See n. to Five : XXXII : 11.)

We have a curious letter* written by Princess Vera Vyazemski on July 11, 1824, to her husband (Pyotr Vyazemski, the poet, Pushkin's close friend) from Odessa, where she had arrived from Moscow, with her children, on June 7. She describes in rather vivid French a scene on the rocky beach. The event could have taken place only in the second week of June, 1824, or say about June 10. That day Vera Vyazemski, Elizaveta Vorontsov, and Pushkin went to wait at close range for the ninth billow in the crescendo series of the surf and while dodging the breakers got drenched by the spray. Vera Vyazemski was Pushkin's confidante, and his admiration for the Countess' pretty ankles in pretty retreat could not have escaped her notice. I suggest that Pushkin told Vera Vyazemski he would commemorate the promenade by means of an *EO* stanza. Except for XXXIII, the pedal digression in One had been written several months before (with the stanzas arranged in a different order), but now it occurred to our poet that in an old cahier of 1822 he

---

*See *Ostaf'evskiy arhiv Knyazey Vyazemskih*, ed. V. Saitov and V. Sheffer (St. Petersburg, 1899–1913), V, 2 (1913), 119–23.

had certain lines that might be used for an *EO* stanza.
Soon after the promenade, and the promise, not later
than June 13, he examined the fragment "Behind her
on the slope of mountains," etc., written on f. 13ᵛ of
his Kishinev Cahier 2366. This fragment I have already
quoted. Our poet decided to rework this. On the same
page (f. 13ᵛ) there is a rapid note in French written in
his 1824 hand among the jottings of 1822:

> Strophe 4 croisés, 4 de suite, 1.2.1 et deux.

This is the formula of the *EO* type of stanza (four lines
rhyming alternately, two consecutive couplets, four lines
with enclosed rhyme, and a closing couplet). This for-
mula he decided to apply to the fragment. The first four
lines (rhyming baba) could be dismissed, since a marine
scene was to replace the montane one. The lines that
followed were:

> Why dared I not its prints [*sledóv*]
> touch with hot lips [*ustámi*],
> besprinkling them with burning [obviously "tears,"
>   *slezámi*] . . .

Sledov is left without a rhyme, and there is a working
gap of probably three lines before the fragment con-
tinues:

> No, never midst the stormy days [*dnéy*]
> of my tumultuous youth [*yúnosti moéy*]
> did I long ⟨with such⟩ agitation [*volnén'em*]
> to kiss the lips of young Circes [*Tsirtséy*],
> and the breasts full of languishment
>   [*tomlén'em*] . . .

Pushkin found a blank space on f. 17ᵛ of the same two-
year-old cahier and started combining the old lines with
a new set having a typical *EO* intonation. I suggest that
the "You recollect" (in place of the final "I recollect")
is addressed to Vera Vyazemski, who had watched with
our poet the waves falling at her (Elizaveta Vorontsov's)
feet:

You recollect the sea before a tempest [*grozóyu*]?
How I envied the waves [*volnám*]
running in turbulent succession [*cheredóyu*]
⟨with love to fall down⟩ at her feet [*nogám*]
and how I wished with the waves [*volnámi*]
to touch her feet with my lips [*ustámi*].
No, never midst ⟨the stormy days [*dnéy*]⟩
of ⟨my⟩ ebullient youth [*mládosti moéy*]
did I long ⟨with such agitation [*volnén'em*]⟩
⟨to kiss the lips of young Circes [*Tsirtséy*]⟩
⟨and the breasts full of languishment [*tomlén'em*]⟩
no, never [line unfinished] . . .

The deletion of "with love to fall down" (*past'*) "with
such agitation" (*volnén'em*—which clashed with *vol-
námi*), and "breasts full of languishment" (rhyming
with *volnén'em*) is explained by the improvements and
readjustments of the final text. The rest of the deletions
are evidently due to the trouble Pushkin had in getting
rid of a superfluity of rhyme words. Either the rhyme
dney–moéy or the rhyme word *Tsirtséy* had to go. We
know that finally Pushkin replaced "Circes" by "Ar-
midas," inserted a new line (the "roses of flaming
cheeks," *lanít*, to rhyme with *Armíd*), and found the
closing couplet (obsessively repeating the *ey–ey* rhyme).

At this time (second week of June, 1824) our poet was
in the midst of Chapter Three, so that when he went on
working at what is now One : XXXIII, it got written down
after Three : XXIX in his Odessa Cahier 2370 (f. 4^r), with
the variants (ll. 10–11, 13–14):

no, no, of love the fondest gift [*dar*],
of kisses the languorous heat [*zhar*] . . .

and:

no, never did all the poison of passions [*strastéy*]
thus rive my soul [*dushí moéy*].

On or before June 13, 1824, our poet reworked the
stanza on a scrap of paper (with abbreviations of words,

according to Tomashevski, Acad 1937, p. 550, but apparently in its final form, if I understand my source correctly), which scrap he inadvertently used on June 13 for a letter to his brother in Petersburg. This letter, with One : XXXIII on the back of it, is preserved (1937) at the Lenin Library, Moscow (MS. 1254, f. 24ᵛ). Later, Tomashevski suggested (*Pushkin* [Moscow and Leningrad, 1956], I, 493n) that this might have been jotted down on the back of "the unsealed but refolded" letter to Lev Pushkin, *after* the brothers had been reunited at Mihaylovskoe in the autumn of 1824. I am unable to unravel this skein of conjectures without having examined the MS. Anyway, Tsyavlovski errs when stating (*Letopis' zhizni . . . Pushkina* [Moscow, 1951], I, 516) that the stanza was composed in the fall of 1824; it was merely rewritten at the time Pushkin was preparing Chapter One of *EO* for publication. I suggest that only then, in the latter part of October, did Pushkin send to his confidante Vera Vyazemski "the strophe that [he] owed [her]." The draft of this letter (of which a passage beginning "Tout ce qui me rappelle la mer" will be found below) is in Cahier 2370, f. 34ʳ, beneath the draft of the letter to Pletnyov accompanying the apograph of Chapter One, which our poet sent to Petersburg with Lev Pushkin (see my notes to the Prefatory Piece).

In this half-French, half-Russian letter to Vera Vyazemski (end of October, 1824, from Mihaylovskoe to Odessa), Pushkin writes:

. . . Tout ce qui me rappelle la mer m'attriste—le bruit d'une fontaine me fait mal à la lettre—je crois qu'un beau ciel me ferait pleurer de rage; but, thank God, the sky here is dun-colored, and the moon is exactly like a small turnip [*repka*]. A l'égard de mes voisins je n'ai eu que la peine de les rebuter d'abord; ils ne m'excédent pas —je jouis parmi eux de la réputation d'Onéguihe—et voilà je suis prophète en mon pays. Soit. Pour toute ressource je vois souvent une bonne vieille voisine—j'écoute

ses conversations patriarcales. Ses filles assez mauvaises
sous tous les rapports [i.e., in looks, manners, and morals]
me jouent du Rossini que j'ai fait venir. Je suis dans la
meilleure position possible pour achever mon roman
poétique, mais l'ennui est une froide muse—et mon
poème n'avance guère—voilà pourtant une strophe que
je vous dois—montrez là au Prince Pierre. Dites lui de
ne pas juger du tout par cet enchantillon . . .

The "assez mauvaises" is obviously a diplomatic move,
since a warm friendship, apart from amorous relations,
existed between the Osipovs and Pushkin.

It is interesting to place alongside this a letter Pushkin
received a little earlier from Aleksandria, near Belaya
Tserkov, the Vorontsov estate, from Aleksandr Raevski,
written Aug. 21, 1824: he had left Odessa some ten days
after Pushkin's departure for Mihaylovskoe. The code
name for Elizaveta Vorontsov was "Tatiana"—Push-
kin's heroine.

Je remets à une autre lettre le plaisir de vous parler des
faits et gestes de nos belles compatriotes; présentement je
vous parlerai de Tatiana. Elle a pris une vive part à votre
malheur, elle me charge de vous le dire, c'est de son aveu
que je vous l'écris, son âme douce et bonne n'a vu dans le
moment que l'injustice dont vous étiez la victime; elle
me l'a exprimé avec la sensibilité et la grâce du caractère
de Tatiana.

Surely, Tatiana's epistle must have been known to
Raevski, and thus must have been composed before
Pushkin left Odessa.

There is yet a fourth candidate, according to one
D. Darski, whose idea was discussed, and dismissed, on
a dismally cold evening in Moscow, Dec. 21, 1922, by
the Obshchestvo Lyubiteley Rossiyskoy Slovesnosti,
Society of Lovers of Russian Letters, heroically meeting
amidst the gloom and famine of Lenin's reign. Darski
assigned the little feet of stanzas XXXI and XXXIII to the
kompan'onka (*dame de compagnie*) of the two Raevski

girls, the aforementioned Tatar lady, Anna Ivanovna (surname unknown).

My final impression is that if the pair of feet chanted in XXXIII does belong to any particular person, one foot should be assigned to Ekaterina Raevski and the other to Elizaveta Vorontsov. In other words, a Crimean impression belonging to August, 1820, and the resulting verses (presumably composed Apr. 16, 1822) were transmuted in the second week of June, 1824, into an *Onegin* stanza related to an Odessa romance.

Incidentally, that seashore sport was a fashionable ritual of the day. "Un des premiers plaisirs que j'aie goûtés," says Chateaubriand, writing in 1846 (*Mémoires d'outre-tombe*, ed. Maurice Levaillant [Paris, 1948], pt. I, bk. I, ch. 7), "était de lutter contre les orages, de me jouer avec les vagues qui se retiraient devant moi, ou couraient après moi sur la rive."

3–4 / running in turbulent succession with love to lie down at her feet: Readers who know Russian will discern a complex of beautifully onomatopoeic alliterations in the original here: *Begúshchim búrnoy cheredóyu | S lyubóv'yu léch' k eyó nogám.*

Cf. Ben Jonson, *The Poetaster*, IV, vi (Julia's parting with Ovid):

> . . . I kneel beneath thee in my prostrate love
> And kiss the happy sands that kiss thy feet.

Cf. Thomas Moore, *The Loves of the Angels*, ll. 1697–1702:

> He saw, upon the golden sand
> Of the sea-shore a maiden stand,
> Before whose feet the expiring waves
>   Flung their last tribute with a sigh—
> As, in the East, exhausted slaves
>   Lay down the far-brought gift, and die.

Commentary

(This I find quoted in a review of Moore's *Loves of the Angels* and Byron's *Heaven and Earth* in the *Edinburgh Review*, XXXVIII [Feb., 1823], 38; on p. 31, Byron's poetry is said to be "sometimes a deadly Upas" [*Antiaris toxicaria*, Leschenault de La Tour, 1810]. Curiously enough, a paraphrase of "exhausted slaves | Lay down the far-brought gift, and die" appears in Pushkin's poem *The Upas* [*Anchar*], penultimate stanza. See n. to L: 10–11.)

References to feet-kissing waves abound in English poetry; one more example will suffice. In Byron's enthusiastic description (1816) of Clarens (*Childe Harold*, III, C: "Clarens! by heavenly feet thy paths are trod"), where Undying Love is confusingly identified with the emotions that Rousseau's Julie and Saint-Preux left behind them to permeate Switzerland at low elevations, there occur the lines (CI, 5–6):

> . . . the bowed Waters meet him [Love], and adore,
> Kissing his feet with murmurs . . .

Feet and waves are blended also by Lamartine in *Le Lac* (September, 1817):

> Ainsi le vent jetait l'écume de tes ondes
> Sur ses pieds adorés

and by Hugo in *Tristesse d'Olympio* (1837):

> D'autres femmes viendront, baigneuses indiscrètes,
> Troubler le flot sacré qu'ont touché tes pieds nus!

*

As known to Russian commentators, the literary reminiscence here (resulting, I suggest, in one of those deliberate artistic parodies of which *EO* offers several examples in the first quatrains of its stanzas) is a passage from *Dushen'ka*:

> Pursuing her, the billows there
> keep jostling jealously each other,

and breaking from the throng in haste
seek to fall humbly at her feet.

This *Sweet Psyche* or *Little Psyche* is a long poem in
iambic lines of various length, which its author, Ippolit
Bogdanovich (1743–1803), kept improving upon in the
course of its several editions (1783–99) after its first
"Book" appeared in 1778 under the title *Sweet Psyche's
Adventures* (*Dushen'kinï pohozhdeniya*). It is in the
frivolous French style of the day and treats pleasantly of
Psyche's and Cupid's amors, following La Fontaine's
romance. The airiness of its tetrametric passages and its
glancing mother-of-pearl wit are foregleams of young
Pushkin's art; it is a significant stage in the development
of Russian poetry; its naïve colloquial melodies also
influenced Pushkin's direct predecessors, Karamzin,
Batyushkov, and Zhukovski. I think that Griboedov's
technique also owes it something. It was overrated in its
time and then underrated in the dull era of civic
criticism inaugurated by the famous but talentless
Vissarion Belinski. (See also n. to Three : XXIX : 8.)

Cf. "L'onde, pour [Vénus] toucher, à longs flots s'entre-
pousse; | Et d'une égale ardeur chaque flot à son tour |
S'en vient baiser les pieds de la mère d'Amour," the last
lines of the second rhymed interpolation in bk. I of *Les
Amours de Psiché et de Cupidon* (1669), by Jean de La
Fontaine (1621–95), who took its *conduite* and its "fable"
from French adaptations of the *Metamorphoses*, also
known as *The Golden Ass* (bks. IV–VI), of Lucius
Apuleius (b. c. A.D. 123), whose burlesque he tempered
with *badineries galantes* and pedestrian common sense
dear to his age of *bienséance*, *goût*, and *raison*—that
impotent trinity. (I notice after writing this note that
G. Lozinski briefly refers to the same reminiscence in his
notes to the 1937 Paris edition of *EO*.)

The theme exploited by La Fontaine and Bogdano-
vich is the allegoric episode of Psyche and her lover

Cupid, son of Venus, in bks. IV–VI of the *Metamorphoses* (11 bks.). In bk. IV of that feeble romance there is a glimpse of gentle waves advancing toward Venus, who with rosy feet touches them as she boards her sea chariot among bobbing mermen and mermaids.

5–6 / How much I longed then with the waves | to touch the dear feet with my lips! | *Kak yá zhelál togdá s volnámi* | *Kosnút'sya milïh nóg ustámi!*: "Comme je désirais alors avec les vagues effleurer ses chers pieds de mes lèvres!"

In a compilatory *biographie romancée*, tritely written and teeming with errors (*Pouchkine*, 2 vols., Paris, 1946), Henri Troyat writes (I, 240) in regard to the incident: "Séduit par l'image de cette enfant de quinze ans jouant avec les flots, Pouchkine écrivit une poésie sentimentale à son intention:

> . . . Je désirais comme les vagues
> Effleurer vos pieds de mes lèvres."

It is odd that Princess Maria Volkonski, who quotes the Russian original in her French memoirs, forgot that this was a passage from *EO* (One, XXXIII : 5–6); much odder is the fact that Troyat does not know this. But that Miss Deutsch, who had actually translated *EO* (1936), did not recognize the quotation and rendered* Troyat's version as:

> How happy were the waves that were caressing
> The darling feet my lips should have been pressing!

would be completely incomprehensible, had one not discerned here a kind of poetic justice; for Miss Deutsch's version of One : XXXIII is a paraphrastic mutilation so far removed from the original that even she could not

---

*In an abridged English translation, in 1 vol., of Troyat's book, *Pushkin. A Biography*, tr. Randolph T. Weaver, with verse translations by Babette Deutsch, p. 131.

identify it with the (slightly garbled) quotation in Troyat. Her 1936 "translation" reads:

> The billows covered them with kisses,
> My lips were envious of their blisses!

The other paraphrasts have:

> How like the billow I desired
> To kiss the feet which I admired!
>
> —Matter-of-fact Lt.-Col. Spalding

> And those dear feet aroused my longing
> To kiss them, like the billows thronging!
>
> —Solecistic Prof. Elton

> I would have found it ah! how sweet,
> As did the waves, to kiss her feet.
>
> —Helpless Miss Radin

6 / **dear feet** / *mílïh nog* [gen.]: Since so much has been written on the subject of their particular ownership, I must go into some more details concerning the matter.

In the extraordinary lines, among his greatest, that Pushkin added in 1824, four years after its publication, to the beginning of *Ruslan and Lyudmila*—

> *Tam lés i dól vidéniy pólnï;*
> *Tam o zaré prihlínut vólnï*
> *Na brég peschánïy i pustóy*

> There wood and dale are full of visions;
> there at sunrise the waves come plashing
> upon the empty sandy shore

—these waves give birth to thirty handsome knights who emerge one after the other from the limpid waters. Here, in xxx–xxxiv of *EO*, One, while the echoes of the stage-wonderland from the preceding digression (xviii–xx) still ring in his ears, and while Istomina (xx : 8–14) still dances in his mind's eye, the reader witnesses another magic performance, a succession of magical sea waves (xxxiii) and the birth of several feminine phantoms whose delicate feet are alone perceived.

There has been a tendency among prototypists to concentrate on one lady in the Mystery of the Feet. Actually, Pushkin speaks of several in the course of XXX–XXXIV and confirms this multiplicity in Five : XL : 7, where he recalls his Chapter One digression on "the little feet of ladies known to me":

A. The lady of stanza XXXI, who was brought up in Oriental luxury, had never lived in the North of Russia, and was loved by our poet in the beginning of his Southern peregrinations.

B. A generalized and overlapping lady in stanza XXXII, addressed as "Elvina" (which is a poetical synonym of "Malvina," "Elvira," and "Elmina") and imagined in various surroundings and attitudes.

C. A lady on a seashore: stanza XXXIII.

D. A lady with whom the poet went riding (possibly in Kishinev or Kamenka): stanza XXXIV.

This makes at least four persons, whose presumable or possible existence in "real life" is of no interest whatsoever.

8 / of my ebullient youth / *Kipyáshchey mládosti moéy*: A widespread French cliché, the Russian versions of which appear with irritating frequency in the verses of Pushkin and his constellation. It is the "fervid young age" of Latin poets.

See Voltaire, *Précis de l'Ecclésiaste* (written 1756, pub. 1759), l. 1: "Dans ma bouillante jeunesse . . ."; or, in a collective sense, Montaigne, *Essais*, bk. III, ch. 5, "Sur des vers de Virgile" (written 1586, pub. 1588): "Cette verte et bouillante jeunesse . . ."

10 / Armidas: The French lexicon definition of *Armide* is: "Nom donné par autonomase à une femme qui réunit l'art de séduire à la beauté et aux grâces."

The sensual image in ll. 8–12 is easily traced to French versions of Tasso's *Gerusalemme liberata* (1581): "Armide . . . est couchée sur le gazon; Renaud est couché dans ses bras. Son voile ne couvre plus l'albâtre de son sein . . . elle languit d'amour: sur ses joues enflammées brille une sueur voluptueuse qui l'embellit encore" (Prince Charles François Lebrun's version, *La Jérusalem délivrée* [1774], XVI).

XXXIV

8 / the ache / *toská*: No single word in English renders all the shades of *toska*. At its deepest and most painful, it is a sensation of great spiritual anguish, often without any specific cause. At less morbid levels it is a dull ache of the soul, a longing with nothing to long for, a sick pining, a vague restlessness, mental throes, yearning. In particular cases it may be the desire for somebody or something specific, nostalgia, lovesickness. At the lowest level it grades into ennui, boredom, *skuka*. The adjective *tosklivïy* is translatable as "dismal," "dreary." (See also n. to Three : VII : 10.)

9 / *nadménnïh*: Although literally this means "proud ones" or "arrogant ones" (accus.), the term is obviously a stylish imitation of the sound and sense of the French *inhumaines, beautés inhumaines*, "pitiless belles," "the cruel fair," so often met with in eighteenth-century madrigals.

11–12 Tomashevski (Acad 1937, p. 262) says that these two lines are found in Cahier 2366, f. 34ᵛ.

14 / deceptive / *Obmánchivï*: One would be tempted to use the formula "as false as fair," but "false," in the context, would have been *izménchivï* (fickle). Furthermore, the translator should bear in mind that the "deception"

really regards the nonfulfillment of anatomical promises (see XXXII)—a bit of sly lewdness with which our poet gets away here in the best manner of his French models.

In the draft (2369, f. 14^v), stanza XXXII comes after what is now XXXIV, which follows XXXI.

3 In the fair copy a cancellation reads:

> I hold the reins, I grasp the stirrup . . .

XXXV

1 / And my Onegin?: Cf. Byron in *Beppo*, XXI, "But to my story," and in *Childe Harold*, II, XVI, "But where is Harold?"

2 / to bed: "The other night there was a ball at the K.'s," writes a young lady in the "epistolary novel" that Pushkin began in 1829 (experimenting with an archaic form). "The dance lasted till five in the morning." Onegin stayed even longer.

3–4 / *A Peterbúrg neugomónnïy* | *Uzh barabánom probuzhdyón*: Mark the beautiful, very Pushkinian, sequence of two double-scud lines with strikingly apt alliterations. These depend on the repetition of stressed and unstressed *u* and *bu*, pronounced as the short *oo* in "book," and on the interplay between *o* and *n*. An approximate transference of melody, with a *t* keynote, would be: "The indefatigable city | is stimulated by the drum." It was an indefatigable city of 377,800 inhabitants.

5 / *Vstayót kupéts, idyót raznóshchik*: My version of this line is on the brink of abhorred paraphrase. But somehow I disliked the falsely literal:

> Rises the merchant, goes [comes, walks] the hawker . . .

7 / Okhta: * East of the city, on the eastern bank of the Neva
along a south-north stretch called in Finnish Okha. The
Okhtan girl is carrying a milk jug; the snow "sings"
underfoot (as Walter Scott says somewhere of creaking
snow).

Although this is not a reminiscence on the part of our
poet, it is curious to compare Pushkin's St. Petersburg
morning with John Gay's London morning in *Trivia:
or, the Art of Walking the Streets of London* (1716),
which has a milkmaid chalking her gain on doors, the
"vellum thunder" of a drum, hawkers, rolling coaches,
opening shops, and so forth.

9 / *Prosnúlsya útra shúm priyátnïy*: An analogous line oc-
curs in *Poltava* (1828), pt. II, l. 318: *razdálsya útra
shúm igrívïy*, "morn's frisky hubbub has resounded."
Compare these epithets with those used by English poets,
e.g., Milton's "the busy hum of men" and John Dyer's
"the Noise of busy Man."

Generally speaking, the sense of *shum* implies a more
sustained and uniform auditory effect than the English
"noise." It is also a shade more remote and confused. It
is at heart more of a swoosh than a racket. All its forms
—*shum* (n.), *shumnïy* (adj.), *shumyashchiy* (part.),
shumet' (v.)—are beautifully onomatopoeic, which
"noisy" and "to noise" are not. *Shum* acquires a number
of nuances in connection with various subjects: *shum
goroda*, "the hum of the city," "the tumult of the
town"; *shum lesov*, "the murmur of woods"; *shum-
yashchiy les*, "the soughing of forests"; *shumnïy ruchey*,
"the dinning stream"; *shumyashchee more*, "the sound-

---

*As a rule, I use *h* (strongly aspirated) to denote the Russian
letter generally transliterated *kh*, since otherwise the English-
speaking reader is likely to pronounce it as a plain *k*, saying
"Chekov" instead of "Chehov" (and "Krúshchev" instead of
"Hrushchyóv"); but in some geographical names I have
resigned myself to the *kh* for the sake of easy identification.

ing sea," the rote, the thud, and the roar of the surf
on the shore—"the surgy murmurs of the lonely sea,"
as Keats has it in *Endymion*, l. 121. *Shum* may also mean
"commotion," "clamor," and so forth. The verb *shumet'*
is poorly rendered by "to be noisy," "to clatter." (See
also n. to One : XXXVII : 2.)

12 / a punctual German / *Némets akurátnïy*: *Akuratnïy*, or
akkuratnïy (which is of the same origin as "accurate"),
a Polonism of the eighteenth century, means more than
"punctual" usually implies; it has additional connota-
tions of tidiness and method, virtues that are not typical
of Russians. Pushkin, rather cynically, expects here a
guffaw from the gallery, if one may judge by a passage
in his letter to Gnedich (May 13, 1823, from Kishinev
to St. Petersburg) in which he refers to a one-act comedy
in verse, *The Waverer* (*Nereshitel'nïy*, performed for
the first time on July 20, 1820), by the third-rate play-
wright Nikolay Hmelnitski, who adapted it from the
French (presumably from *L'Irrésolu* of Philippe
Néricault Destouches):

> Well do I know the measure of the public's comprehen-
> sion, taste, and culture. . . . Once, I remember Hmelnitski
> was reading to me his *Nereshitel'nïy*. When I heard the line:
>
> . . . and one must own, Germans are punctual [*akuratnï*] . . .
>
> I said to him: Mind my words, at this verse everybody
> will applaud and roar with laughter. Yet what is there
> witty or funny about it? I should very much like to know
> if my prediction came true.

13 / *V bumázhnom kolpaké*: Not only some translators of
EO, but Russian commentators as well, have understood
bumazhnïy as "made of paper"! Actually, the locution
bumazhnïy kolpak is an attempt on Pushkin's part to
render the French term *bonnet de coton*, house-cap of
cotton. The word calpac, or calpack, or kalpak, repre-

sented in English dictionaries, has Oriental implications. I have used it to render the Russian *kolpak* in Five : XVII : 4.

14 / *vasisdas*: A French word (Academically admitted in 1798), *vasistas*, meaning a small spy-window or transom with a mobile screen or grate; here the loaves were passed out; believed to come from the German *was ist das*, "what is it?" (a derivation as fanciful as that of "haberdasher" from *habt ihr dass*); occurs in the form *vagistas* in vulgar French.

Pushkin wavered between spelling it *Wass ist das* and *vas-isdas*, settling for the second spelling in his fair copy (*Rukopisi*, 1937).

Lupus, in his notes to his German version of *EO* (1899), observes (p. 80) that, in their ground-floor shops, German bakers of St. Petersburg had a lower windowpane replaced by a brass plaque that, at the customer's knock, could be lowered like a small drawbridge, forming a counter for the transaction.

In *Al'bom Pushkinskoy yubileynoy vïstavki* (Album of the Pushkin Anniversary Exhibition), ed. L. Maykov and B. Modzalevski (Moscow, 1899), I find, on pl. 19, a cartoon, an aquarelle painted about 1815 by Pushkin's schoolmate, A. Illichevski, now in the Pushkinskiy Dom, that shows a group of Lyceum students, with vulgar antics, annoying a German baker; he and his wife are depicted at their first-floor window, in dignified wrath, with the baker wearing a striped house-cap.

VARIANT

9–12 Draft (2369, f. 15ʳ):

Morn's anxious hubbub has awoken

. . . .
. . . . . .

and the baker, a careful German
in house-cap...

XXXVI

Here ends the description of Onegin's day, winter, 1819, which, interrupted by digressions, occupies only thirteen stanzas (XV–XVII, XX–XXV, XXVII–XXVIII, XXXV–XXXVI).

See, in Modzalevski's biography of Yakov Tolstoy (*Russkaya starina,* XCIX [1899], 586–614; C [1899], 175–99), the amusing parallel between Onegin's day and Yakov Tolstoy's quatrains (devoid of any talent), in rather archaic iambic tetrameter, with a dash of journalistic jauntiness foreshadowing mid-century satire, *Epistle to an Inhabitant of Petersburg* (*Poslanie k Peterburgskomu zhitelyu,* in Tolstoy's collection of execrable verses, *Moyo prazdnoye vremya, My Spare Time* [May?], 1821), where the following lines—which I will not bother to iambize—occur:

You awake about ten and by noon have completed your toilet; meanwhile, a billet inviting you to a ball is already lying in the vestibule . . . You hurry out as if forced to do so, and pace the boulevard . . . But dinnertime is near . . . Then it is time to go to the theater, to the ballet . . . and five minutes later . . . you are directing your lorgnette at the ladies in the boxes . . . You drive home, give your little figure [*figúrke,* a dreadful Germanism] the best *ton,* and lo, there you are skipping in the mazurka . . . At dawn your day is finished . . . and tomorrow you repeat it all over again, you, victim of fashion.

Less than three years before Pushkin wrote Chapter One, this Yakov Tolstoy (1791–1867, military man and poetaster), whom he had met at semiliterary parties in Petersburg (meetings of the liberal Green Lamp Club, which is invariably mentioned, along with the dinner club Arzamas, by every historian of literature, though they have no importance whatsoever in relation to the development of Pushkin's talent; but a group is always impressive to historians of literature), naïvely begged Pushkin in a rhymed epistle to teach him to rid himself

of his Germanic rhythms and write just as elegantly as
the author of *Ruslan*. It would seem that Pushkin in
Chapter One deliberately gave the poor rhymester a
demonstration based on the latter's own theme.

*

Cf. "Hints for a Reform, particularly of the Gaming
Clubs," by a Member of Parliament (1784; quoted by
Andrew Steinmetz, *The Gaming Table* [London, 1870],
I, 116), on the day of a young London "fashionable":

He rises just time enough to ride to Kensington Gardens;
returns to dress; dines late; and then attends the party of
gamblers, as he had done the night before. . . . Such do
we find the present fashionable style of life, from "his
Grace" to the "Ensign" in the Guards.

(Cf. also Two : XXX : 13–14.)

A paper by V. Rezanov on "Voltaire's Influence on
Pushkin"* led me to look up Voltaire's satire *Le Mondain*
(1736), which depicts the "train des jours d'un honnête
homme" (l. 64) and contains such Oneginesque lines as
(ll. 65–66, 89, 91, 99, 105–07):

Entrez chez lui; la foule des beaux arts,
Enfants du goût, se montre à vos regards. . . .
Il court au bain . . .
. . . il vole au rendez-vous . . .
Il va siffler quelque opéra nouveau . . .
Le vin d'Aï, dont la mousse pressée,
De la bouteille avec force élancée
Comme un éclair fait voler son bouchon . . .

(See also n. to One : XXIII : 5–8.)

In vol. XIV (1785) of Voltaire's complete works
(1785–89), this *Le Mondain* (pp. 103–26) consists of an
Avertissement des éditeurs; the thing itself (pp. 111–15),
in abominably pedestrian verses, like all Voltaire's
verses; some curious notes to it (including the famous

---

*"K voprosu o vliyanii Vol'tera na Pushkina," *P. i ego sovr.*,
IX, 36 (1923), 71–77.

explanation of the author's flight to Sans Souci); two epistles; a *Défense du mondain ou l'apologie du luxe*, and a final doggerel *Sur l'usage de la vie*.

8 / and next day same as yesterday: Cf. La Bruyère, *Les Caractères* (1688): "Il [Narcisse] fera demain ce qu'il fait aujourd'hui et ce qu'il fit hier" (description of a young man's day, "De la Ville," par. 12).

XXXVII

2 / the social hum / *svéta shum*: An old French cliché, *le bruit, le tumulte, le fracas du monde*, a standardized echo of Rome and her poets. I have gone to English formulas, e.g., Byron's "the gay World's hum" (*Don Juan*, XIII, XIII, 4). This is different from the actual buzzing and thudding of town life as described in a recent stanza (see my n. to XXXV : 9).

6–10 Cf. Parny, *Goddam!* (in four cantos, "par un French-Dog"), composed in Frimaire (rime month), year XII (October–November, 1804), can. I:

> Le Gnome Spleen, noir enfant de la Terre
> Dont le pouvoir asservit l'Angleterre,
>
> . . . .
> . . . le sanglant rost-beef,
> Les froids bons mots . . .
>
> . . . .
> Le jus d'Aï . . .
> Et ces messieurs, ivres des vins de France,
> Hurlent un toast à la mort des Français.

For "spleen," see nn. to next stanza.

8 / beefsteaks: The European beefsteak used to be a small, thick, dark, ruddy, juicy, soft, special cut of tenderloin steak, with a generous edge of amber fat on the knife-side. It had little, if anything, in common with our American "steaks"—the tasteless meat of restless cattle. The nearest approach to it is a *filet mignon.*

Pushkin wrote the word in Latin script, but it had long been Russianized (see, for instance, *Sïn otechestva,* 1814, p. 128) as *bifsteks,* singular; later, through German influence, to become *bifshteks.* A serving in Pushkin's time cost a quarter of a ruble, whereas a yearly sub-scription to a weekly magazine cost thirty rubles.

9 / *Shampánskoy* [instead of *shampánskogo*] *oblivát' butílkoy:* I have preserved Pushkin's bad grammar here. The meaning is "wash down with champagne."

In 1818, according to Nikolay Polevoy (*Moscow Tele-graph,* pt. 34, no. 14 [1830], p. 229), 158,804 bottles of champagne were imported from France, to the tune of 1,228,579 rubles; and 374,678 bottles in 1824.

14 / strife, saber and lead / *brán', i sáblyu, i svinéts:* This is an irritatingly vague line. What exactly did Onegin fall out of love with? *Bran',* implying as it does, warfare, might lead one to suppose that about 1815 Onegin, like many other exquisites of the time, had been on active duty in the army; it is, however, much more probable that the reference is to single combat, as suggested by a MS reading; but (in evaluating Onegin's later behavior, Six) it would have been highly important to be told in plainer terms of Onegin's dueling experience.

Sablyu i svinets, "saber and lead," is a Gallicism: *le sabre et le plomb,* "broadsword and pistol ball." An Irishman of 1800 would have said "the hilt and the muzzle."

Commentary

Sir Jonah Barrington, in *Personal Sketches of His Own Times* (1827), II, 6–7, writes:

About the year 1777, the *Fire-eaters* [duelers] were in great repute in Ireland. No young fellow could finish his education till he had exchanged shots with some of his acquaintances. The first two questions always asked as to a young man's respectability . . . were: "What family is he of?" [and] "Did he ever blaze?"

Twenty-seven rules of a MS code of honor accepted at Clonmell are given on pp. 10–14. (See also nn. to Six : XXIX–XXX, on duels.)

One wonders if the derivation of the Fr. *blasé* is not connected somehow with this sense of "to blaze."

Pushkin is mentioned as one of the "nobles seigneurs . . . qui . . . appelaient près d'eux pour s'exercer avec lui dans cet art qu'ils aimaient" the famous scriming master A. Grisier, who sojourned in Russia in the reign of Nicholas I ("Notice sur [Augustin] Grisier," by Roger de Beauvoir, in *Les Armes et le duel*, by A. Grisier, Paris, 1847).

VARIANTS

8 The draft (2369, f. 16ᵛ) reads:

> *bif-sték* ⟨*i*⟩ ⟨*tryúfel'nïy*⟩ *piróg* . . .

12–14 A direct allusion to Onegin's former duels is found in the draft (2369, f. 16ᵛ) and the fair copy:

> and though he was a fiery scapegrace,
> he tired at last of offering [to those he challenged]
> saber or lead.

XXXVIII

1–2 / A malady, the cause of which | 'tis high time were discovered: To this quest Russian critics applied themselves with tremendous zeal, accumulating in the course of a dozen decades one of the most boring masses of comments known to civilized man. Even a special term for Onegin's distemper has been invented (*Oneginstvo,* "Oneginism"); and thousands of pages have been devoted to him as a "type" of something or other (e.g., of a "superfluous man" or a metaphysical "dandy," etc.). Brodski (1950), standing on the soapbox that had been provided a hundred years ago by Belinski, Herzen, and many others, diagnosed Onegin's "sickness" as the result of "tsarist despotism."

Thus a character borrowed from books but brilliantly recomposed by a great poet to whom life and library were one, placed by that poet within a brilliantly reconstructed environment, and played with by that poet in a succession of compositional patterns—lyrical impersonations, tomfooleries of genius, literary parodies, and so on—is treated by Russian pedants as a sociological and historical phenomenon typical of Alexander I's regime (alas, this tendency to generalize and vulgarize the unique fancy of an individual genius has also its advocates in the United States).

3 / English "spleen" [and see XVI : 9 / roast beef; XXXVII : 8 / beefsteaks]: The diet that Pushkin gives Onegin is conducive to the latter's hyp; for I think we should admit here a curious reminiscence leading us back to Karamzin's *Letters of a Russian Traveler,* where, in a letter from London, undated (summer, 1790), the following (even then far from original) thought occurs:

Roast beef, beefsteaks are the staple foods of the English. This is why their blood thickens; this is why they become phlegmatic, melancholic, unbearable to their own selves, and not infrequently suicidal. [This is the] physical cause of their [spleen]. . . .

3–4 *Handrá,* "chondria," and spleen, "hyp," illustrate a neat division of linguistic labor on the part of two

nations, both famed for ennui, the English choosing
"hypo" and the Russian "chondria." There is, of
course, nothing especially local or time-significant
about hypochondria (in the initial large sense; and ex-
cluding the American connotation of *maladie imagi-
naire*). The spleen in England and ennui in France came
into fashion about the middle of the seventeenth century,
and throughout the next hundred years French inn-
keepers and Swiss mountain folk kept begging hypish
Englishmen not to commit suicide on their premises or
in their precipices—a drastic measure to which the
endemic and more benign ennui did not lead. The
theme itself, even if we strictly limit ourselves to literary
phenomena, is much too boring to be treated at length
in these notes; but a few examples have to be given in
order to prove that ennui was by 1820 a seasoned cliché
of characterization that Pushkin could play with at
leisure, on the flowered brink of parody, by transforming
West-European formulas into virgin Russian. French
literature of the eighteenth and early nineteenth cen-
turies is full of restless young characters suffering from
the spleen. It was a convenient device to keep one's
hero on the move. Byron endowed it with a new thrill;
René, Adolphe, Oberman, and their cosufferers received
a transfusion of daemon blood.

In various works that I have glanced through in con-
nection with my *Onegin*, I have found the following
authors referring to the subject of this note:

Voltaire, in his *Pucelle d'Orléans* (1755), VIII: "[Sire
Christophe Arondel, of the *altière* and *indifférente* soul]
Parfait Anglais, voyageant sans dessein . . . parcourait
tristement l'Italie; | Et se sentant fort sujet à l'ennui, |
Il amenait sa maîtresse [Lady Judith Rosamore] avec
lui . . ." (intonations that, incidentally, were to be
curiously echoed a hundred years later in Alfred de
Musset's famous reference to Byron and "sa Guiccioli"—

rhyming with *lui*); and in Voltaire's *La Guerre civile de Genève*, III (1767), there is a similar gentleman, "milord Abington," who "voyageait [in Switzerland] tout excédé d'ennui, | Uniquement pour sortir de chez lui; | Lequel avait, pour charmer sa tristesse, | Trois chiens courans, du punch, et sa maîtresse."

James Boswell, in *The Hypochondriack*, no. 1 (*The London Magazine*, October, 1777):

I flatter myself that *The Hypochondriack* may be agreeably received as a periodical essayist in England, where the malady known by the denomination of melancholy, hypochondria, spleen, or vapours, has been long supposed almost universal.

Further, no. V (February, 1778), he draws a distinction between Melancholy and Hypochondria, defining the first as "gravely dismal" and the second as "fantastically wretched." And of course the malady grades at various points into the classical sense given to it in essays on hypochondriasis and hysteria by medical men. In France, La Fontaine had used the noun *hypocondre* (*Fables*, bk. II, no. XVIII: "Chatte métamorphosée en femme") in the sense of "madly extravagant," which coincides with the first part of Boswell's definition only.

La Harpe's *Lycée* (1799; quoted from 1825 edn., V, 261):

Je ne sais si même en Angleterre, où l'on connait une maladie endémique qui est le dégoût de la vie, on parlerait ainsi [as Seneca does] de la passion de la mort; et le spleen n'était pas connu à Rome.

See also n. to XXXVII : 6–10, Parny's "Spleen, noir . . . ," and the *chyórnïy* (black) *splin* in Six : XV : 3 (in nn. to Six : XV–XVI).

Nodier, writing to a friend (Goy) in 1799:

Je ne suis plus capable d'éprouver aucune sensation vive. . . . A vingt ans j'ai tout vu, tout connu . . . épuisé la lie

de toutes les douleurs. . . . Je me suis aperçu à vingt ans
que le bonheur n'était pas fait pour moi.

Stendhal, 1801 (at eighteen): ". . . ma maladie habi-
tuelle est l'ennui" (*Journal*).

Chateaubriand's René (1802) perceived himself ex-
isting only "par un profond sentiment d'ennui."

Mme de Krüdener (1803): "Quelle est donc cette
terrible maladie, cette langueur . . . ennui insuppor-
table . . . mal affreux . . ." (Gustave de Linar brooding
in *Valérie*).

Senancour, *Oberman* (1804), Letter LXXV:

Dès que je sortis de cette enfance que l'on regrette,
j'imaginai, je sentis une vie réelle; mais je n'ai trouvé
que des sensations fantastiques: je voyais des êtres, il n'y
a que des ombres: je voulais de l'harmonie, je ne trouvais
que des contraires. Alors je devins sombre et profond; le
vide creusa mon cœur; des besoins sans bornes me con-
sumèrent dans le silence, et l'ennui de la vie fut mon seul
sentiment dans l'âge où l'on commence à vivre.

Pushkin had not read *Oberman* when composing *Onegin*;
he acquired a copy of the first edition only when the
Delorme epigraph (1829, from the first paragraph of
Oberman's Letter XLV) and a second edition (1833) had
made the incomparably charming *Oberman* famous at
last. Lermontov imitates the *Oberman* intonations (given
above) in *A Hero of Our Time* (1840), Pechorin's
journal, "June 3."

Pushkin's critical acumen is curiously absent in the
extravagant praise he bestows in a published article
(*Literaturnaya gazeta*, XXXII [1831], 458–61; see
Acad 1936, V, 598) on Sainte-Beuve's derivative and
mediocre *Vie, poésies et pensées de Joseph Delorme* (1829).
He found therein unusual talent and considered that
"never, in any language, has naked spleen expressed
itself with such dry precision"—an epithet that is

singularly inappropriate in regard to Sainte-Beuve's florid platitudes.*

Chateaubriand, 1837 (*Mémoires d'outre-tombe*, ed. Levaillant, pt. II, bk. I, ch. 11):

Une famille de Renés-poètes et de Renés-prosateurs a pullulé; on n'a plus entendu bourdonner que des phrases lamentables et décousues . . . il n'y a pas de grimaud . . . qui, à seize ans, n'ait épuisé la vie . . . qui, dans l'abîme de ses pensées, ne se soit livré au "vague de ses passions."

Finally—Byron, *Don Juan*, XIII, CI, 5–8:

> For *ennui* is a growth of English root,
>   Though nameless in our language:—we retort
> The fact for words, and let the French translate
> That awful yawn which sleep can not abate.

(The last line is a good one, with a first-rate imitation of a yawn at the end.)

Pichot's n. 40 to this passage reads: "*Ennui* est devenu un mot anglais à la longue. Nos voisins ont les mots *blue devils*, *spleen*, etc., etc."

Byron and Pichot had been forestalled by Maria Edgeworth and her translator, Mme E. de Bon: "For this complaint [ennui] there is no precise English name; but alas! the foreign term is now naturalized in England." (Maria Edgeworth, *Ennui or the Memoirs of the Earl of Glenthorn* [written in 1804, pub. London, 1809], ch. 1. This "Tale of Fashionable Life," hinging on a change at nurse, appeared in French in 1812, but was not very popular on the Continent.)

G. Fonsegrive has thus described *ennui* in *La Grande*

---

*Incidentally, in one of those *Delorme* poems—namely, in one inscribed to Musset—there occurs the most ludicrous piece of imagery I have ever found in French romantic verse:
>   ". . . je valsais . . .
> Entourant ma beauté de mon bras amoureux,
> Sa main sur mon épaule, et dans ma main sa taille;
> Ses beaux seins suspendus à mon cœur qui tressaille
> Comme à l'arbre ses fruits . . ."

Encyclopédie, vol. XV (c. 1885), and his definition
(which I translate) applies to the splenetic moods of all
fictional characters allied to Onegin:

> "Ennui" is a sensation of sadness, anxious and confused,
> derived from a feeling of lassitude and impotency. . . .
>
> After having enjoyed a pleasure, the soul that reflects
> is surprised at finding pleasure so vapid. . . .
>
> When this discrepancy between hope and reality . . .
> has been registered several times . . . the soul sees therein
> a natural law. . . . This is René's state of mind.
>
> The profession of Epicureanism engenders ennui.

Judged by a number of early-nineteenth-century
English and French novels that I have perused, the four
main outlets or cures for ennui found by the characters
suffering from it were: (1) making a nuisance of oneself;
(2) committing suicide; (3) joining some well-organized
religious group; and (4) quietly submitting to the situa-
tion.

The vocabulary of ennui also includes *skuka* ("bore-
dom," "tedium," "dullness") and *toska* (a preying
misery, a gnawing mental ache), which, according to his
prosodic needs, Pushkin often uses as synonyms of
handra.

9 / Childe Harold: The hero of Byron's "romaunt" (1812),
along whose brow "oft-times in his maddest mirthful
mood | Strange pangs would flash" (I, VIII), whom
"none did love" (IX), whose "early youth [had been]
misspent in maddest whim" (XXVII), who has "moping
fits" (XXVIII), who is bid to loath his present state by a
"weariness which springs | From all [he] meets"—the
"settled, ceaseless gloom | The fabled Hebrew Wanderer
bore" (inserted tetrameters, after LXXXIV), and so
forth.

In a canceled draft of this verse (2369, f. 16ᵛ) the

name of Byron's man is replaced by that of Benjamin Constant's man, Adolphe.

Pichot and de Salle, when referring to this work in the table of contents prefixed to vol. I of the *Œuvres de Lord Byron* (1819), spelled its title "Childe-Arold." In the fourth French edition the poem appeared in vol. II (1822) as *Childe-Harold*, "poème romantique" (which explains, incidentally, why Pushkin, in a celebrated letter from Odessa to Moscow, in spring, 1824, termed his *EO* "the motley strophes of a romantic poem," *romanticheskoy poemï*). In alluding to *Childe Harold*, later French practice was not only to hyphenize the two words, but to omit the *e* in the first, e.g., Béranger, 1833, in a note to couplets inscribed to Chateaubriand: ". . . le chantre de Child-Harold est de la famille de René."

Cf. the end of One : XXXVIII with Byron's I, VI, in the French version: "Or Childe-Harold avait le cœur malade d'ennui. . . . Il allait errer seul, et dans une triste rêverie."

The aggregate result of French pronunciation and custom, some knowledge of the English *ch*, Russian transcription from a mixture of English and French, and, last but not least, the printers' carelessness caused the name Childe Harold (of which the absurd but accepted Russian transliteration is *Chayl'd Garol'd*) to undergo a number of mutations in the various editions of *EO* during Pushkin's lifetime:

Child-Harold (Fr.), One : XXXVIII : 9—1825, 1829 (thus also in the draft, 2369, f. 16^v);

Child-Horald (Fr.), One : XXXVIII : 9—1833, 1837;

Chil'd Garol'd (Russ.), Four : XLIV : 1—1828, 1833, 1837 (with a hyphen in the draft, 2370, f. 77^v, and in both fair copies);

Chel'd Garol'd (Russ.), n. 4—1825;

Chil'd Garol'd (Russ.), n. 4—1829;

Chal'd Garol'd (Russ.), n. 5—1833;
Chal'd Garal'd (Russ.), n. 5—1837.

The last four consecutive varieties occur in Pushkin's note to One : XXI : 14. In the draft of the note, this is abbreviated "*Ch* H," as if by using the Russian letter *Ch* Pushkin was reminding himself to pronounce the English correctly and not in the French manner (*sh*).

Garol'd in Russian, as of course Harold in French, is accented on the ultima. The hyphen is derived from the French manner of linking first names (e.g., Charles-Henri). Actually, of course, "Childe" is an archaic term denoting a youth of tender birth, especially a budding knight.

See also my n. to Four : XLIV : 1.

Russian commentators keep overlooking the significant fact that in Pushkin's day Russian writers knew the literatures of England, Germany, and Italy, as well as the works of the ancients, not from original texts but from the stupendous exertions of French paraphrasts. The ignoble Russian adaptations of popular European novels were read only by the lower classes, whereas the admirable melodies of Zhukovski's versions of English and German poems won such triumphs for Russian letters as to make negligible the loss Schiller or Gray suffered in adaptation. The gentleman author, the St. Petersburg fashionable, the ennuied hussar, the civilized squire, the provincial miss in her linden-shaded château of painted wood—all read Shakespeare and Sterne, Richardson and Scott, Moore and Byron, as well as the German novelists (Goethe, August Lafontaine) and Italian romancers (Ariosto, Tasso), in French versions, and French versions only.

The first French translator of Byron seems to have been Léon Thiessé (*Zuleika et Sélim, ou la Vierge d'Abydos*, Paris, 1816), but his version was little read. Fragments of the four cantos of *Childe Harold*, as well as passages from *The Prisoner of Chillon*, *The Corsair*, and *The Giaour*, appeared anonymously in *La Bibliothèque universelle de Genève*, series *Littérature*, vols. V–VI (1817), vols. VII and IX (1818), and vol. XI (1819). It is to these versions (which Byron himself, whose French was limited, preferred to Pichot's!) that, for example, Vyazemski refers in a letter of Oct. 11, 1819, to A. Turgenev in Petersburg: "I am permanently immersed in the surf of poetry, reading and rereading Lord Byron—in miserable French excerpts, of course." In France, about the same time, Lamartine and Alfred de Vigny were depending on the same Geneva source.

By 1820, eager Russian readers had already at their disposal the first four volumes of Pichot's and de Salle's first edition (1819) of Byron's works in French, and it is in these prose versions, pale and distorted shadows of the original, that Pushkin read for the first time (possibly during the journey from Petersburg to Pyatigorsk, and certainly at Pyatigorsk, with the Raevski brothers, in the summer of 1820; see nn. to XXXIII) *Le Corsaire*, *Manfred*, and the first two cantos of *Le Pèlerinage de Childe-Harold*. Visions of the Raevski girls (who had learned their English from a governess) teaching, in bowers and grots, the language of Byron to a studious albeit love-stricken Pushkin are the mild hallucinations of Russian editors. It should be noted that while turning the entire poetic production of Byron into easy French prose, Pichot not only made no attempt to be accurate, but methodically transposed the text into the most hackneyed, and thus most "readable," French of the previous age.

In that first edition of Byron's *Œuvres* the translators, Amédée Pichot and Eusèbe de Salle, remained anonymous. In the second, they used the joint pseudonym "A. E. de Chastopalli," which is an (imperfect) anagram of their names and by a bizarre coincidence resembles the

Commentary

Russian word for "six-fingered" (*shestipalïy*). In the course of the third edition, A. P. and E. D. S. quarreled (see Pichot's note, VI, 241), and beginning with vol. VIII (1821), Pichot became alone responsible for the translation. Here is a brief description of the four editions of this monumental and mediocre product, all brought out in Paris by Ladvocat (for additional bibliographic details, see the Bibliothèque Nationale catalogue and the list of French translations in Edmond Estève's *Byron et le Romantisme français* [Paris, 1907], pp. 526–33):

(1) *Œuvres de lord Byron*, "traduits de l'anglais," 10 vols., Paris, 1819–21 (*Le Corsaire, Lara*, and *Adieu* are in vol. I, 1819; *Le Siège de Corinthe, Parisina, Le Vampire, Mazeppa*, and short pieces are in vol. II, 1819; *La Fiancée d'Abydos* and *Manfred* are in vol. III, 1819; the first two cantos of *Le Pèlerinage de Childe-Harold* are in vol. IV, 1819; the third canto of *Childe-Harold, Le Giaour*, and *Le Prisonnier de Chillon* are in vol. V, 1820; the first two cantos of *Don Juan* are in vol. VI, 1820; the fourth canto of *Childe-Harold* is in vol. VII, 1820; *Beppo* and short pieces are in vol. VIII, 1820; four acts of *Marino Faliero* are in vol. IX, 1820; the fifth act of *Marino Faliero*, short pieces, and *Les Poètes anglais et les Critiques écossais* are in vol. X, 1821).

(2) *Œuvres complètes de lord Byron*, tr. A. E. de Chastopalli (first 3 vols.) and A. P. (last 2 vols.), 5 vols., 1820–22 (vol. II, 1820, includes *Le Giaour*, the first two cantos of *Don Juan*, and *Beppo*; vol. III, 1820, contains *Childe-Harold* and *Le Vampire*; the latter was dropped in later editions).

(3) *Œuvres complètes de lord Byron*, tr. A. P. and E. D. S. (first 7 vols.) and A. P. only (last 3 vols.), 1821–22.

(4) *Œuvres de lord Byron*, "4ᵉ édition entièrement revue et corrigée," tr. "A. P. . . . t," with an introduction by Charles Nodier, 8 vols., 1822–25 (the first 5 vols.

came out in 1822, with *Childe-Harold* in vol. II; the first five cantos of *Don Juan* are in vol. VI, 1823, and the rest in vol. VII, 1824).

For my notes in the commentary I have consulted edns. 2 and 4.

According to a letter of November, 1824, written by Pushkin, in Mihaylovskoe, to Vyazemski, in Moscow, our poet when he "read the first two cantos [of *Don Juan*] immediately said to [Nikolay] Raevski that it was Byron's masterpiece, and was greatly pleased to learn later that this opinion was shared by W. Scott" (Scott's remarks, made in the *Edinburgh Weekly Journal*, May 19, 1824, had been quoted in Russian periodicals).

These first two cantos of Pichot's *Don Juan* appeared in vol. VI, 1820, and Pushkin read them, and the last two cantos of *Le Pèlerinage*, for the first time between January, 1821, and May, 1823, either at Kamenka (province of Kiev) or in Kishinev. Afterward, not later than autumn, 1824, he found the two cantos of *Don Juan*, which he knew already, and three more cantos of the stuff, in vol. VI of Pichot's 4th edn. (1823).

In the same letter to Vyazemski of November, 1824, from Mihaylovskoe to Moscow, the passage preceding the one already quoted reads: "What a marvel—*Don Juan*! I know only the first five cantos."

Finally, in December, 1825, at Mihaylovskoe, through the good offices of his friends Annette Vulf and Anna Kern, Pushkin obtained from Riga (the gateway to the literary West) the remaining eleven cantos of *Don Juan*, in Pichot's vol. VII (1824).

It may be useful at this point to give a few examples in chronological order illustrating our poet's tussle with the English language. They are based mainly on the MS texts collected in *Rukoyu Pushkina* (In Pushkin's Hand) by Lev Modzalevski, Tsyavlovski, and Zenger (Moscow, 1935).

For some quaint reason, it often happened, among fashionable Russian families of the early 1800's, that, whereas children of both sexes were taught French, only the girls were taught English. Pushkin's sister Olga had at one time a Miss or Mrs. Bailey or Baillie for English governess, but it is quite certain that, when in 1820 our poet left St. Petersburg for his fertile Southern exile, he had no English. Like most Russians, Pushkin was a poor linguist: even the fluent French he had learned as a child lacked personal tang and, judging by his letters, remained throughout his life limited to a brilliant command of eighteenth-century ready-made phrases. When he tried to teach himself English (as he did at various odd moments from the early 1820's to 1836), he never went beyond the beginner's stage. From a letter of June, 1824 (to Vyazemski from Odessa), we find that he still pronounced the "Childe" of *Childe Harold* as "chilled," which is only one step removed from the French pronunciation.

In 1821 or 1822, Pushkin, attempting to translate without a crib the first fourteen lines of Byron's *The Giaour* into French (the choice of the "into" language is characteristic), renders "the Athenian's grave" as "la grève d'Athènes"—"the strand of Athens," a schoolboy's howler. In Pushkin's magic Russian this came out as *prah Afin*, "the dust of Athens."

In 1833, when attempting, with the help of an English-French dictionary, a literal translation into Russian of the beginning of Wordsworth's *The Excursion*, Pushkin fails to understand such simple phrases as "brooding clouds," "twilight of its own," "side-long eye," and "baffled" (Cahier 2374, f. 31$^{\text{r-v}}$).

In 1835, while compiling a note based on *Mémoires de lord Byron* (ed. Thomas Moore, tr. Mme Louise Sw[anton]-Belloc, Paris, 1830), he still writes "mistriss" for "Mrs.," in the dreadful French manner, just as he had ten years before in a draft of *EO*, Two : xxɪb : 1.

In 1836, he still does not know the simplest forms of English and renders l. 14 of Byron's *To Ianthe*, "guileless beyond . . . imagining," in Russian prose as (if we English it back) "not false to the imagination," and "hourly brightening" as "a minute's gleam."

No wonder that only a few pages, in several places at random, are cut in his copy of P. J. Pollock's *Cours de langue anglaise . . .* (St. Petersburg, 1817).*

11 / boston / *bostón*: Not the dance, but the card game, a member of the whist family. This "Russian boston" differs only slightly (diamonds, for instance, not hearts, are the top color) from the ordinary boston. It is a variation of the Fontainebleau boston.

12 One is obliged to go all the length of an English Alexandrine to render a Russian tetrameter exactly! Truly, a rare, paradoxical case.

13 / *Nichtó ne trógalo egó*: A Gallicism (*rien ne le touchait*) that as late as 1860 was still being criticized even by some Westernizers. Today the formula is completely at home in the Russian language.

VARIANTS

3 Draft (2369, f. 16ᵛ):

a paltry imitation of the spleen . . .

9 Draft (ibid.), canceled:

But like Adolphe, gloomy and languid . . .

---

*According to "Biblioteka A. S. Pushkina," a bibliographic description of Pushkin's library by Boris Modzalevski, in *P. i ego sovr.*, III, 9–10 (1909), 312.

XXXIX, XL, XLI

Nothing in Pushkin's manuscripts has been found that might lend itself to an insertion under these stanza headings. In the fair copy, XLII immediately follows XXXVIII. It is not unthinkable that this gap is a fictitious one, with some musical value—the artifice of a wistful pause, the imitation of a missed heartbeat, the mirage of an emotional horizon, false asterisks of false suspense.

XLII

6 / Say and Bentham: The inimitable Brodski hints that the "bourgeois liberalism" of Jean Baptiste Say's *Traité d'économie politique* (1803) and the "oracular babble" (teste Marx) of the learned jurist Jeremy Bentham (1748–1832) could not satisfy Onegin's subconscious Bolshevism. A delightful notion.

Pushkin (later) had in his library *Œuvres de J. Bentham, jurisconsulte anglais* (Brussels, 1829–31, 3 vols., uncut). He also had Say's *Petit Volume contenant quelques aperçus des hommes et de la société* (2nd edn., Paris, 1818).

9 / *neporóchnï*: "Immaculate," "stainless," "sinless"—all these are possible renderings of this vague epithet.

13 / so inaccessible: Playing the scholiast, Pushkin in his n. 7 refers the reader to Mme de Staël's *Dix Ans* [or *Années*] *d'exil*. I have perused, in that posthumous work (1818), its last ten chapters, wherein de Staël, a poor observer, describes her visit to Russia in 1812 (she arrived in July) that so curiously synchronized with Napoleon's less happy venture. The passage to which no doubt Pushkin alludes occurs in pt. II, ch. 19; the lady is speaking of a fashionable St. Petersburg boarding

school for girls: "La beauté de leurs traits n'avoit rien
de frappant, mais leur grâce étoit extraordinaire; ce sont
des filles de l'Orient, avec toute la décence que les
mœurs chrétiennes ont introduite parmi les femmes."
The *décence* and *mœurs chrétiennes* must have greatly
amused Pushkin, who had no illusions about the morals
of his fair coevals. Thus the irony describes a full circle.

VARIANT

9–12 The first edition of the chapter gives:

> Moreover, they're so stately,
> so sinless, so intelligent,
> so full of piety,
> preserve so chastely morals . . .

XLIII

1 The "young beauties," *krasótki molodíe,* are courtesans,
whom dashing rakes whirl away in light open carriages.
This type of carriage came to England, through many
stages of transliteration, as a *droitzschka,* but by the
1830's became in London a "drosker" or "drosky," al-
most reverting to its native form, *drozhki.*

   Pushkin, in the fair copies, wavered between *krasotki,*
"little beauties," and *geterï,* "hetaerae," or, in the dis-
gusting London idiom of the day, Cyprians. In Russian
there was no polite term for these girls (many of whom
hailed from Riga and Warsaw). Eighteenth-century
writers, including Karamzin, had tried to render *filles
de joie* by the impossible *nimfï radosti,* "nymphs of joy."

3 / *drózhki udalíe:* A difficult epithet to render. It ranges
from such ideas as "at a spanking pace," "with a rakish
air," "in dashing style," etc., to connotations of pluck,
luck, bold unconcern, and the sort of gallant vitality that
is associated with highway robbers and buccaneers. The

onomatopoeic value of the initial *u* (beautifully accented
in the noun *údal'*), suggestive of war whoops, ululation,
a whistling wind, or a moan of passion, and the coinci-
dence of the *d*, *a*, *l* with the Russian word for *le lointain*
(not merely distance, but the romance of distance, misty
remoteness), add a singing note to the virility of *údal'*,
udalóy, *událïy*. A little further (XLVIII : 12), Pushkin
uses *udaláya* as a stock epithet (bold, brave) for *pesnya*,
"song."

4 / over the Petersburgan pavement / *Po Peterburgskoy
mostovoy*: Pronounced *pa peterbúrskoy mastovóy*. Mark
the double scud in this line and the spanking *pa pe*
repetition that the verse is attacked with. Pushkin em-
ployed the same device in his long poem *The Bronze
Horseman: a Petersburg Tale* (1833), pt. II, l. 188,
where the animated statue of Tsar Peter, with a pon-
derous reverberation, gallops (I again give the *o* its
positional value)

> *pa patryasyónnoy mastovóy.*
> over the shaken pavement.

Here the two rapid identical *pa*'s, detonating the line,
make it still more sonorous (in keeping with the beat of
the bronze hoofs).

Some streets in St. Petersburg were cobbled, others
macadamized. Pavements consisting of hexagonal blocks
of pinewood fitted like joiner's work were introduced
about 1830.

6 / Apostate from the turbulent delights / *Otstúpnik búrnïh
naslazhdéniy*: A somewhat similar term was applied by
our poet (at the end of August, 1820, in Gurzuf, Crimea)
to the anonymous Russian gentleman, hero of *The Cau-
casian Captive*, *otstupnik sveta*, "apostate from the *grand
monde*," who, having found treachery in the hearts of

friends, having recognized the madness of love dreams, and (ll. 75–76)

> Weary to be the wonted victim
> of vain pursuits he long despised

traveled to the distant Caucasus (vicinity of Pyatigorsk —the only Caucasian region Pushkin then knew) in a Byronic search for inner "liberty," and found captivity instead. He is a vague and naïve prototype of Onegin.

13–14 With this little professional aside, the second main character of Chapter One, Pushkin, now re-enters; he, rather than Onegin, criticizes contemporaneous literature in XLIV; and from XLV to the last (LX) stanza of the chapter, with the exception of LI–LV (and even here Pushkin's voice is heard in the first two stanzas), he will predominate.

XLIV

2 / by emptiness of soul / *dushévnoy pustotóy*: Cf. "my existence [is] a dreary void," Byron's letter to R. C. Dallas, Sept. 7, 1811.

4 A commonplace formula of the time. Cf. Matthew Lewis, *The Monk* (1796), ch. 9: "Unable to bear this state of incertitude, [Ambrosio] endeavored to divert it by substituting the thoughts of others to his own."

7 / deceit / *obmán*: This is not the enchanting *obman* (illusion) of Tatiana's favorite novels, but the cheap imposture of fashionable philosophies and party politics.

VARIANT

14 In the draft (2369, f. 17ᵛ), Pushkin hesitated between "pink" and "green" taffeta.

XLV

This and the next stanza are transposed in the 1825 edition of Chapter One.

2 / vain pursuits: The word *suetá*, as used here, implies a combination of fuss, bustle, worldliness, vanity, and idle show. Nowadays it is mainly employed in the first sense, except in the locution *sueta suet* (Lat. *vanitas vanitatum*). Pushkin and other Russian poets of his time had a romantic predilection for that meaning of *sueta* which corresponds to Wordsworth's "fever of the world" and Coleridge's "stir and turmoil of the world." The adjective based on the first sense is *suetlivïy* (fussing), and the one based on the fourth sense is *suetnïy* (vain, vacuous, frivolous).

3 In the draft (2369, f. 17ᵛ), just beneath this line, Pushkin sketched in ink his own, slightly simian, profile, with the long upper lip, sharp nose, and upcurved nostril (somewhat like a written *h* or an upside-down written 7) that he gave himself as key feature in his autoportraits. The collar of his cambric shirt, English fashion, is highly starched and looks like winkers, its points projecting upward in front with a wide gap between. His hair is short. Similar drawings (says Efros, p. 232) are found on ff. 36ʳ and 36ᵛ of the same cahier (drafts of Two : XXVII and XXIX–XXX).

4 / traits / *chertí*: A Gallicism, *ses traits*, his features, his "lines."

5 / to dreams the involuntary addiction / *Mechtám nevól'-naya predánnost'* [note the archaic accent on -*dán*, instead of the modern *pré*-]: Cf. Seven : XXII : 12 / to dreaming measurelessly given / *Mechtán'yu prédannoy bezmérno*.

Onegin's reverism is supposed to be egocentric and sterile in contrast to Lenski's warm *Schwärmerei* (see n. to Two : XIII : 5–7). What exactly were Onegin's dreams in 1820 we neither know nor care (Russian commentators have hoped they were on "politico-economical subjects"); but that there must have been some rich and fantastic tinge to them is belatedly suggested by one of the greatest and most artistic stanzas in the entire romance, namely, Eight : XXXVII, where Onegin broods over his entire past.

6 / oddity / *stránnost*: "Strangeness"; *stránnïy*, "strange"; this is exactly the French *bizarrerie, bizarre,* so persistently employed by French novelists of the late eighteenth and early nineteenth centuries to characterize their attractively freakish heroes. Pushkin uses the same epithet for both Onegin and Lenski (cf. Two : VI : 11–12; this would be in French "un tempérament ardent et assez bizarre").

To summarize: the "young scapegrace" of stanza II is now clearly portrayed. An attractive fellow, who—although opposed to poetry and lacking all creative capacity —actually depends more upon "dreams" (fanciful interpretations of life, thwarted ideals, doomed ambitions) than upon reason; uniquely bizarre—although this oddity is never to be fully revealed to the reader in direct description or otherwise; endowed with a cutting cold wit—probably of a higher and maturer type than that revealed by the brutal vulgarity of his speech to Lenski in Three : V; gloomy, brooding, disenchanted (rather than embittered); still young, but vastly experienced in "passions"; a sensitive, independent young man, rejected or on the point of being rejected by Fortune and Mankind.

Pushkin at the period of his life within which he retrospectively inserted a meeting with his creature

Commentary

(represented as persecuted by vague forces of which the
clearest are heartless mistresses and old-fashioned people
critical of Romanticist trends) had got into trouble with
the political police over some of his antidespotist (*not*
prorevolutionary, as is popularly believed), widely cir-
culated manuscript verses and was soon (early in May,
1820) to be expelled to a Southern province.

This stanza XLV is one of the most important ones of
the chapter. This is how twenty-four-year-old Pushkin
(born 1799) saw his twenty-four-year-old hero (born
1795). Not only is it a summary of Onegin's nature (all
later clues to it in the novel—which it will take Onegin
five years to live through, 1820–25, and Pushkin eight
years to write, 1823–31—will be either modulated rep-
etitions or a slow, dreamlike disintegration of direct
meaning). It is also the point where Onegin comes into
contact with the other main character of the chapter—
Pushkin, the character who has been gradually built up
by means of the previous sustained digressions or brief
interpolations—nostalgic yearnings, sensuous enchant-
ments, bitter memories, professional remarks, and
genial banter:

II : 5–14; V : 1–4; VIII : 12–14 (in the light of the
author's n. 1); XVIII, XIX, XX (Pushkin overtakes his hero
and comes to the theater first, as he will come first to the
ball in XXVII); author's n. 5 to XXI : 13–14; XXVI (to which
have led asides in the three previous stanzas); XXVII (cf.
XX); XXX, XXXI, XXXII, XXXIII, XXXIV (the ballroom and
nostalgic "little feet" digression developing the nostalgic
ballet theme of XIX, XX); XLII (and author's n. 7 to it);
XLIII : 12–14.

Pushkin now meets Onegin on equal terms and estab-
lishes similarities before drawing the line of demarcation
later in XLV, XLVI, XLVII. He will listen with Onegin to
the sounds of the night (XLVIII); will launch upon a third
nostalgic digression ("beyond the seas," XLIX, L); will

part with Onegin (LI : 1–4); will recall his introduction
of his hero in II (LII : 11); will dissociate himself from
Onegin (LV, LVI)—and, by implication, from Byron (who
despite preambulatory reservations did Byronize his
mental men); and will wind up the chapter with a few
professional observations (LVII, LVIII, LIX, LX).

8 The specific ill-humor of the younger man (the fair copy
reads even more familiarly, *ya bíl serdít*, "I was cross")
is compared to his friend's generic gloom. Here are
the main shades of Onegin's Anglo-French moodiness
throughout the romaunt:

ugryúmïy	sullen
mráchnïy	gloomy
súmrachnïy	somber
pásmurnïy	clouded
tumánnïy	bemisted

This set should not be confused with the states of
meditativeness that Onegin shares with other people in
the world of our book, which are designated by the
epithets:

toskúyushchïy	fretting, pining, yearning
zadúmchivïy	pensive
mechtátel'nïy	daydreaming, musing, given to reverie
razséyannïy	distrait, abstracted, absent-minded

A third set of epithets, denoting despondency, is also
employed in regard to Onegin, but is especially lavishly
applied to the more poetical characters of the novel,
Pushkin, Lenski, and Tatiana:

grústnïy	melancholy
pechál'nïy	sad
unílïy	glum, dejected

XLVI

This preceded XLV in the edition of 1825. The error was corrected in the separate edition of Chapter Six (1828), errata.

1–2 / He who has lived and thought . . . ; 13 / banter blent
. . . bile: Cf. Chamfort, *Maximes et pensées*, in *Œuvres de Chamfort* "recueillies et publiées par un de ses amis [Pierre Louis Ginguiné]" (Paris, 1795), IV, 21: "La meilleure Philosophie, relativement au monde, est d'allier, à son égard, le sarcasme de la gaîté avec l'indulgence du mépris." (See also n. to Eight : XXXV : 4.)

Under the draft of the last lines of the stanza Pushkin drew the figure of a demon in a dark cave and other diableries (2369, f. 18ʳ).

1–9 There is a touch of the reported-speech style in 1–7 and of retrospective irony in 8–9. Onegin's speech is full of the pseudophilosophic clichés of his times. Cf.: ". . . we have both seen the world too widely and too well not to contemn in our souls the imaginary consequences of literary people" (Sir Walter Scott, *Journal*, entry of Nov. 22, 1825, on Thomas Moore).

XLVIa

A drafted fragment (2369, f. 29ᵛ, where there is also the drafted Two : XVIa) may refer to a false start after One : XLVI:

> It saddened me, oppressed me, pained me,
> but having overcome me in the strife,
> involuntarily he linked me
> 4   to his mysterious fate;
> I started looking with his eyes,
> with his sad speeches
> my words would sound in unison . . .

5–7 / *Ya stál vzirát' egó ochámi, | S egó pechál'nïmi rechámi | Moí slová zvucháli v lád*: This contains a marvelous fourfold alliteration based on the *cha* sound, which, with Pushkin, so often shimmers in passages of intense emotion, the two most famous being *óchi ocharúyut* ("eyes will enchant") in *Talisman* (1827) and *ochéy ocharován'e . . . proshchál'naya krasá* in *Autumn* (1833). To a Russian's ear the sound *ch*, which occurs in many beautiful words (such as *chúdo*, "marvel"; *chárï*, "charms"; *chúvstvo*, "feeling"; *chu*, "hark"), is associated with the "chug-chug" of the nightingale's song.

Another charming alliteration on the letter *ch* occurs in *The Fountain of Bahchisaray* (ll. 493–96), where it is both emotional and onomatopoeic:

> *Est' nádpis': édkimi godámi*
> *Eshchyó ne sgládilas' oná.*
> *Za chúzhdïmi eyó chertámi*
> *Zhurchít vo mrámore vodá . . .*

> There's an inscription: by the acid years
> 'tis not obliterated yet.
> Beyond its alien characters,
> within the marble, water purls . . .

Baratïnski has a somewhat similar, and even more sustained, alliteration in his *The Ball* (1827), ll. 171–74:

> *Sledí muchítel'nïh strastéy,*
> *Sledí pechál'nïh razmïshléniy*
> *Nosíl on na chelé; v ocháh*
> *Bezpéchnost' mráchnaya dïshála . . .*

> the traces of tormenting passions,
> the traces of sad meditations
> he wore upon his forehead; in his eyes
> there breathed a gloomy heedlessness . . .

(*Bezpechnost' mrachnaya*—a typical Baratïnskian tight knot of twisted meaning.)

Commentators have compared One: XLVIa with

Pushkin's short poem *The Demon* (1823), in its first draft especially, where the "tempter" has been identified with Aleksandr Raevski (whom our poet had first met in Pyatigorsk during the summer of 1820), son of General Nikolay Raevski, who courted Countess Elizaveta Vorontsov in Odessa; the assumption is that during Pushkin's sojourn there (1823–24) Raevski had his less experienced friend make love to the Countess in order to divert the husband's suspicions from himself. (See also n. to One : XXXIII : 1.)

It may be assumed that in messages exchanged between Pushkin and Eliza Vorontsov at that time remarks were passed, by Pushkin or his correspondent, criticizing or condoning Raevski's cynical ways—and the next step is to conjure up the origin of the Master Motto; but this is mere *biographie romancée*.

For a translation of *The Demon* and additional Raevskiana, see commentary to Eight : XII : 7.

XLVII

1–3 The publication *Literaturnïy arhiv*, I (1938), reproduces (facing p. 76) a beautiful engraved chart from Pushkin's library showing the Neva's melting and freezing dates for 106 years (*Hronologicheskoe izobrazhenie vskrïtiya i zamerzaniya reki Nevï v S. Peterburge s* 1718 *po* 1824 *god*). In 1820, the ice broke up on Apr. 5, about a week earlier than the average date and some three weeks later than the earliest records. April and the beginning of May (except May 1, which was cold and wet, according to an observation in *Otechestvennïe zapiski*, II [1820]) were warm, but there was an abrupt drop in the temperature on May 13; and on June 7 Karamzin wrote from Petersburg, in a letter to Dmitriev, "This year, we cannot boast of our summer: we have not seen fair days yet."

Onegin left Petersburg about the time Pushkin did
(May 9, 1820); their summer-night, or rather spring-
night, walks on the Neva embankment could not have
taken place later than the first week in May (O.S.);
about May 20 (N.S.; unless, of course, there is a vague
backcast to June, 1819). In that latitude (60° N) at that
time of the year the sun sets at 8:30 P.M. and rises at
3:15 A.M., with evening twilight ending not long before
midnight, and with morning twilight beginning about
half an hour after. These are the famous "white" nights
(which are at their shortest in June: sunset 9:15 P.M.,
sunrise 2:30 A.M.), when the sky remains "limpid and
luminous," although moonless.

3 Gnedich's piece, to which Pushkin refers in his n. 8, is
The Fishermen, a long-winded and monotonous eclogue
in unrhymed amphibrachic pentameters involving two
shepherds who fish from the banks of one of the Neva
islands (presumably Krestovski Island). The quoted
lines come from the first edition of pt. II (1822, in the
magazine *Sïn otechestva,* VIII), which differs slightly
from Gnedich's final text of 1831. This prolix quotation
was no doubt prompted by the fact that our poet was
grateful to Gnedich for supervising the publication of
Ruslan and Lyudmila in 1821.

4–6 A very pretty example of Pichot's influence sneaking
past Byron's is furnished by a line in this magically
modulated stanza, where Pushkin describes his and
Onegin's strolls along the Palace Quay, in a reverie of
retrospection and regret.
  Cf. *Childe Harold,* II, XXIV:

> Thus bending o'er the vessel's laving side,
> To gaze on Dian's wave-reflected sphere,
> The Soul forgets her schemes of Hope and Pride,
> And flies unconscious o'er each backward year . . .

Commentary

The French version (Pichot's 1822 edn.) is a wretched paraphrase:

Penchés sur les flancs arrondis du vaisseau pour contempler le disque de Diane, qui se réfléchit dans le miroir de l'Océan [hence Pushkin's "glass of the waters," *vod . . . steklo*], nous oublions nos espérances et notre orgueil: notre âme se retrace insensiblement le souvenir du passé.

Mark this curious and significant case: a reminiscence tainted by the influence of a hack coming between two poets.

XLVIII

1–4 The allusion is to a stilted mediocrity, the poetaster Mihail Muravyov (1757–1807). See Pushkin's n. 9.

2 / granite: The granite of the parapet. In the stanza Onegin and Pushkin are on the south bank of the Neva, on the stretch called the Palace Quay, and stand facing the Petropavlovskaya Krepost', the SS. Peter and Paul Citadel, a fortress used as a prison for political offenders on the so-called Petersburg Island, on the north side of the 500-meter-wide Neva.

In a letter to his brother Lev (November, 1824), when preparing the first edition of One, our poet wrote (from Mihaylovskoe to Petersburg): "Brother, here is [the idea of a] picture for *Onegin*. Find a skillful and prompt illustrator. Even if the picture be altered, see that . . . the scene remains the same. . . . I need it absolutely."

In *Pushkin v izobrazitel'nom iskusstve*, ed. A. Slonimski and E. Gollerbah (Leningrad, 1937), I find a good reproduction of that pencil sketch (MB MS. 1254 f. 25^r). It represents the two persons referred to in the stanza leaning upon the Neva's parapet, with numerals from 1 to 4 affixed by Pushkin to the various items. No. 1, "Pushkin" seen from behind, apparently con-

templating the river: he is a shortish man wearing a
Bolivar top hat (from under which shoulder-length locks
come down in a dense dark stream, corkscrewing at the
ends—he had shaved his head in the summer of 1819,
at Mihaylovskoe, after a severe illness, of which the less
said the better, and had worn a brown curly wig until
his hair grew long again), the tapering pantaloons of
the times, and an hourglass-shaped, long-skirted frock
coat with two back-waist buttons. He is leaning at ease
with his left elbow on the parapet, feet crossed, the left
one nonchalantly toed. No. 2, Onegin in profile, simi-
larly dressed, minus the romantic curls. His pose is
much more constrained than the poet's, as if he had
just taken a big stiff step in order to lean perfunctorily
on the parapet. No. 3, a sailing boat of sorts on the Neva.
No. 4, a rough outline of the Peter and Paul fortress.
Under this sketch, Pushkin scribbled in the same rapid
pencil: "1. [Pushkin should be made] good-looking
[*horosh*], 2. [Onegin] should lean on the granite, 3. boat,
4. fortress."

The 1825 edition, however, appeared without the
picture. It was redrawn eventually by the miserably bad
artist, Aleksandr Notbek or Nothbeck, and was one of a
series of *EO* illustrations, six engravings, published in
January, 1829 (in the *Nevski Almanac*, ed. Egor
Aladyin). The boat has been deprived of its sail; some
foliage and part of the wrought-iron railings of a park,
the Letniy Sad, have been added along one margin;
Onegin wears an ample fur carrick; he stands barely
touching the parapet with the palm of his hand; his
friend Pushkin now blandly faces the spectator with his
arms crossed on his chest.

In mid-March, 1829, Pushkin reacted to this little
monstrosity with an amusing epigram:

> Here, after crossing Bridge Kokushkin,
> With bottom on the granite propped,

> Stands Aleksandr Sergeich Pushkin;
> Near M'sieur Onegin he has stopped.
>
> Ignoring with a look superior
> The fateful Power's citadel,
> On it he turns a proud posterior:
> My dear chap, poison not the well!

The place name in the first line is that of a bridge across the Catherine Canal. It is curious to note that in the initial sketch Pushkin gave himself long dark hair, which immediately makes us think of Lenski, whose only physical characteristics are the epithet "handsome" and those curls. One would like to hear Onegin saying to Lenski in Chapter Two: "You know, you remind me a little of young Pushkin, whom I used to see in Petersburg."

At the same time (1829) Pushkin dedicated some licentious lines to an even worse daub by the miserable Notbek in the same series: "Tatiana writing to Onegin." This represents a portly female in a clinging night dress, with one fat breast completely bare; she sits sideways in a chair, facing the spectator, her laced feet crossed, her hand with a quill pen stretched toward a very formal-looking table, with a curtained bed behind it. I have wavered whether to quote these lines. Here they are, for what they are worth:

> Through her chemise a nipple blackens;
> Delightful sight: one titty shows.
> Tatiana holds a crumpled paper,
> For she's beset with stomach throes.
>
> So that is why she got up early
> With the pale moonlight still about,
> And tore up for a wiping purpose
> The *Nevski Almanac*, no doubt.

The funniest picture, however, is the one with which Notbek illustrates Six : XLI (referring to the transient amazon who stops to read the epitaph on Lenski's grave). It depicts an enormous female calmly sitting on a horse as on a bench, with both her legs dangling down one flank of her slender microcephalous white steed, near a formidable marble mausoleum. The whole series of six illustrations reminds one of the artwork produced by inmates of lunatic asylums.

5 / 'Twas stillness all / *Vsyo bílo tího*: I wished to find some way to render the Russian "all was still" iambically, without either overaccenting the "was" or prefacing the phrase by an "and" not found in the text. James Thomson, whose idiom corresponds so nicely to that of Pushkin and other Russian poets writing a century after him, obliged me with the formula: " 'Tis silence all" (*The Seasons: Spring*, l. 161). It is rendered "Tout est tranquille" in a French version (J. Poulin's?), *Les Saisons* (1802).

8 / *Mil'ónnoy*: This street runs from the Palace Square to the Field of Mars, parallel to, and south of, the embankment, from which it is separated by a row of palaces and with which it is connected by transverse little streets some hundred meters long.

9 See below, pp. 181–2.

10 / *Plilá*: I have used the literal translation of the verb, which is archaic in English, in order to link up stylistically the boat with the gondola in the next stanza, as Pushkin does.

12 / horn / *Rozhók*: I think that this means a French horn, not the shepherd's flute or flageolet, as some (basing themselves on a canceled draft, 2369, f. 18ᵛ, reading *svirel'*—"flute" or "pipe") have suggested, and cer-

Commentary

tainly not a whole orchestra—"the orchestral diversions of the Russian nobility," as Brodski grotesquely glosses. Had Pushkin in 1823 known Senancour's novel, one might have suspected that these sounds came from the moonlit Swiss lake on which Oberman's valet "donnait du cor" (with "deux femmes allemandes chantant à l'unisson") in one rowboat, while Oberman mused, alone, in another (*Oberman*, Letter LXI).

The epithet *udaloy* (see n. to XLIII : 2), used by Pushkin for "song" (*pésnya udaláya*), is a telltale echo of the adjective to "oarsmen" in Derzhavin's ode *Felitsa* (composed in 1782, pub. 1783), which contains the following lines (st. IX):

> Ili nad Névskimi bregámi
> Ya téshus' po nochám rogámi
> I grébley udalíh grebtsóv.

> Or else above the Neva's banks
> I relish in the night the horns
> and rowing of the oarsmen bold.

This music on the waters has been assigned by solemn commentators* to the kind of slave orchestra so wittily described by Mme de Staël in reference to Dmitri Narïshkin's musicians, each of whom could draw only one note from his instrument. People said on seeing them: "[There goes] le *sol*, le *mi* ou le *ré* de Narischkin" (*Dix Ans d'exil*, pt. II, ch. 18). This orchestra had existed in the Narïshkin family since 1754. Actually, Pushkin refers to less formal merrymaking; but the impact of de Staël's observation was so overwhelming throughout the world that in mid-century we find Leigh Hunt referring in *Table Talk* to a man converted into a crotchet, and Major W. Cornwallis Harris, in his *Highlands of Aethiopia* (London, 1844), stating (III, 288)

---

*See, for example, G. Gukovski, *Hrestomatiya po russkoy literature XVIII veka* (Kiev, 1937), p. 173n.

that an Abyssinian piper in the royal band is "like the Russian, master . . . of [only] one note."

A rare print, c. 1770, showing a horn band (fourteen men and a conductor) is reproduced in M. Pïlyaev's *Starïy Peterburg* (St. Petersburg, 1889), p. 75.

The confusion in the minds of commentators is no doubt enhanced by a passage in the diary of Anton Delvig's cousin Andrey (*Polveka russkoy zhizni. Vospominaniya [barona] A[ndreya] I[vanovicha] Del'viga*, 1820–1870 [Moscow and Leningrad, 1930], I, 146–47):

During the summer of 1830 the Delvigs [the poet and his wife] dwelled on the bank of the Neva, close to the Krestovski ferry. . . . We listened to the splendid horn music of Dmitri Narïshkin, [whose orchestra of slave musicians] played on the river immediately opposite the summer house occupied by the Delvigs.

9–14 and XLIX If the horn may be felt to have a faint local touch about it, the allusions to gondoliers and Tasso's octaves belong, on the other hand, to the tritest commonplaces of Romanticism, and it is a pity Pushkin used so much talent, verbal ingenuity, and lyrical intensity to render in Russian a theme that had been sung to death in England and France. The fact that it leads to the perfectly original and adorable nostalgic digression in One : L spites its banality but does not condone it.

The Romantic formula—

Rowboat + river or lake + musician (or vocalist)

—which, from the *Julie* of Rousseau (the most notorious of the earlier offenders) to passages in Senancour, Byron, Lamartine, and others, continually haunts the poetry and fiction of the time, evolved this special mutation—

Gondola + Brenta + Tasso's octaves

—and this had a most powerful fascination for the Romanticists, in both its positive and negative subvariations (gondolier sings Tasso; gondolier no longer sings Tasso).

Commentary

It would be tedious to list, even briefly, the many tributes this theme received, but a few of the more obvious ones will be found in the course of the following notes.

14 / the strain of Torquato's octaves / *Napév Torkvátovïh oktáv*: The Italian octave rhymes aeaeaeii.

Apart from French prose versions of *Gerusalemme liberata* (1581), by Torquato Tasso (1544–95), whose handsome witch Armida lures and lulls knights amid the indolent delights of an enchanted garden, the main source of a Russian poet's information regarding *Torkvatovï oktavï* was, in 1823, Rossini's opera (*melodramma eroico*) *Tancredi* (1st performance, Venice, 1813), founded on Tasso's poem, or rather on Voltaire's worthless tragedy *Tancrède* (1760); this opera was performed in St. Petersburg in the autumn of 1817 and later.

References to gondoliers singing Tasso are innumerable. Here are some that come to mind:

J. J. Rousseau (under "Barcarolles," in his *Dictionnaire de musique*, 1767) speaks of hearing them when he was in Venice (summer of 1744).

A sentence in Mme de Staël's *De l'Allemagne* (pt. II, ch. 11): "Les stances du Tasse sont chantées par les gondoliers de Venise."

French versions of such passages in Byron as (1819): "'Tis sweet to hear | At midnight . . . | The song and oar of Adria's gondolier" (*Don Juan*, I, cxxi, which Pichot in 1820 paraphrases à la Lamartine: "Il est doux, à l'heure de minuit . . . d'entendre les mouvements cadencés de la rame, et les chants lointains du gondolier de l'Adriatique"); or "In Venice Tasso's echoes are no more | And silent rows the songless Gondolier" (*Childe Harold*, IV, III, 1818).

The last is vulgarly echoed in 1823 by the inept

Casimir Delavigne's "O Venise . . . tes guerriers | . . .
ont perdu leur audace | Plus vite que tes gondoliers |
N'ont oublié les vers du Tasse" (*Messéniennes*, bk. II,
no. v, *Le Voyageur*, ll. 29–32) and paraphrased with
grim satisfaction in 1845 by Chateaubriand (who bore
Byron a grudge for his never mentioning René, the
Pilgrim's prototype): "Les échos du Lido ne le [Byron's
name] répètent plus . . . il en est de même à Londres,
où sa mémoire périt" (*Mémoires d'outre-tombe*, ed.
Levaillant, pt. I, bk. XII, ch. 4).

Pushkin was loath to part with the theme. In a frag-
ment he wrote probably in 1827 ("Who knows the
land"), Torquato's octaves "are repeated even now by
Adria's waves," and in the same year, in September, he
translated into Russian Alexandrines Chénier's poem:

Près des bords où Venise est reine de la mer,
Le Gondolier nocturne, au retour de Vesper,
D'un aviron léger bat la vague aplanie,
Chante Renaud, Tancrède, et la belle Herminie.*

(*Œuvres posthumes d' André Chénier*, "augmentées
d'une notice historique par M. H[enri] de Latouche,
revues, corrigées, et mises en ordre par D. Ch[arles]
Robert" [Paris, 1826], pp. 257–58.) The model of the
poem (written probably in 1789, in England) is, accord-
ing to L. Becq de Fouquières in his *édition critique* of
Chénier (Paris, 1872, p. 427), a sonnet by Giovanni
Battista Felice Zappi (1667–1719).

Finally, in 1829, accepting as it were the Pilgrim's
melancholy statement, Pushkin in the course of an un-
finished elegy lists various remote lands where he might
seek to forget a "cruel mistress" (Russ. *nadmennaya*,
Fr. *l'inhumaine*) and evokes Venice, where "the noc-
turnal boatman does not sing Tasso."

---

*"Chantant . . . Erminie," in Chénier, *Œuvres*, "texte établi
et annoté" Gérard Walter (Paris, 1940), p. 509.

Actually, it would seem that Pushkin disliked Tasso (according to Mihayl Pogodin in a letter of May 11, 1831, to Stepan Shevïryov, who had "translated" a few octaves).

In a short poem (*Venetsianskaya noch'*, *fantaziya*, 1824), dedicated to Pletnyov, the gentle blind poet Ivan Kozlov (1779–1840) had all these formulas too—Brenta, the besilvering moon, gondolas, and Torquato's octaves (see my n. to Eight : XXXVIII : 12).

Kozlov had taught himself to read English and to write it. Here is a poem he composed in that language, *To Countess Fiequelmont* (c. 1830):

> In desert blush'd a rose; its bloom,
> So sweetly bright, to desert smiled;
> Thus are by thee my heavy gloom
> And broken heart from pain e'er wiled.
> Let, O let Heaven smile on thee
> Still more beloved, and still more smiling.
> Be ever bless'd—but ever be
> The angel all my work beguiling.

In a charming piece on Venice in *Curiosities of Literature*, Isaac D'Israeli (I quote from the 4th edn., London, 1798; incidentally, Pushkin had the 1835 Paris edn. in his library), the author alludes to what the Italian dramatist Carlo Goldoni (1707–93) has to say in his autobiography about a gondolier who took him back to Venice: he turned the prow of his gondola toward the city, singing all the way the twenty-sixth stanza of canto XVI of the *Gerusalemme* ("Fine alfin posto al vagheggiar . . ."—"At length her toilette o'er . . ."). D'Israeli continues (II, 144–47):

There are always two concerned, who alternately sing [Tasso's] strophes. We know the melody eventually by Rousseau, to whose songs it is printed. . . . I entered a gondola by moonlight; one singer placed himself forwards, and the other aft . . . their sounds were hoarse and screaming . . . [but at a great distance, the vocal performance is] inexpressibly charming, as it only fulfils its design in the sentiment of remoteness [as Pushkin heard it—from Pichot's gondola, across a wilderness of liberty].

The music of Albion's lyre (see next stanza) in a Gallic transposition was, however, not the sole medium; Pushkin had also read the novels he supplied Tatiana with in Three : IX–XII. Valérie, Countess de M., and her husband's secretary, Gustave de Linar, in Mme de Krüdener's novel *Valérie* (1803; for more details on this work see n. to Three : IX : 8) realize the romantic dream of the age: they drift on the Brenta in a gondola—and listen to the "chant de quelque marinier" in the distance.

XLIX

See also n. to XLVIII : 9–14.

1–2 *Adriatícheskie vólnï,* | *O, Brénta! nét, uvízhu vás*: The rhythms and instrumentation here are divine. The sounds *v, to, tov, tav* of the flowing line that closes the preceding stanza (*napév Torkvátovïh oktáv*) now swell into the rush and rote of *Adriatícheskie vólnï,* a double-scudded line, rich in echoes of previous alliterations; and then, in a glorious run-on, comes the sunburst of *O, Brenta!* with its last, apotheotic *ta,* and the rise of *net,* which is perhaps better rendered here by "yet" than by "no" or "nay."

And here starts a marvelous digression, which in a way had been promised by the breakers in One : XXXIII, where the evoked surf of the Black Sea had already hinted at some nostalgic exotic remoteness. Adria's waves and the brilliantly vibrating Brenta are of course loci of literature, as in Byron's *Childe Harold,* where "gently flows | The deep-dyed Brenta" (IV, XXVIII); but how heart-rending, how tender, their transfiguration! Pushkin had never been abroad (and this is why a blunder in

185

the Spalding and Deutsch versions that causes the poet to revisit Venice is so misleading). In a curious poem, the great poet Vladislav Hodasevich (1886–1939), a century later, described the kind of therapeutic shock he experienced when, upon visiting the real Brenta, he found it to be a *rízhaya rechonka*, a rust-colored, mean little stream.

5 / to Apollo's nephews / *dlya vnúkov Apollóna*: A Gallicism (and a Latinism in French): *neveux*, Lat. *nepotes*, "grandchildren," "descendants." In the sixteenth and seventeenth centuries the English "nephew" was often employed in this sense.

Cf. in the anonymous and mysterious Kievan epic, *Slovo o polku Igoreve* (1187?, 1787?), the apostrophe *veshchey Boyane, Velesov' vnuche* ("vatic Boyan, nepote of Veles"—where Boyan is supposed to be an ancient bard, and Veles a kind of Russian Apollo). See *The Song of Igor's Campaign*, tr. V. Nabokov (New York, 1960), l. 66. (See also n. to Two : XVI : 10–11.)

6 / the proud lyre of Albion: The reference is to Byron's poetry as transposed by Pichot into French prose.

9 / sensuousness / *négoy*: *Nega*, with its emphasis on otiose euphoria and associations with softness, luxuriousness (*iznezhennost'*), tenderness (*nezhnost'*), is not exactly synonymous with *sladostrastie*, "sweet passion," *volupté*, "volupty," where the erotic element predominates. In using *nega*, Pushkin and his constellation were trying to render the French poetical formulas *paresse voluptueuse*, *mollesse*, *molles délices*, etc., which the English Arcadians had already turned into "soft delights." Elsewhere I have rendered *nega* by the archaic but very exact "mollitude."

12 The "mysterious gondola" (the draft has "mystic," in
the sense of "secrecy") glides straight out of Pichot's
version (1820) of Byron's *Beppo,* XIX: "quand on est
dedans, personne ne peut voir ni entendre ce qui s'y
fait ou ce qu'on y dit." Byron's motto to *Beppo* is from
As You Like It (IV, i); Rosalind's words, ". . . you have
swam in a gondola," suggested to me the wording of
XLIX : 12.

4 Draft (2369, f. 19ʳ):

your merry voice . . .

A canceled draft (ibid.) reads:

your limpid [*prozráchnïy*] voice . . .

L

This stanza is of such special importance, and a correct
translation of it presents such special difficulties, that in
order to attain absolute accuracy (while preserving a
semblance of the iambic meter), I have found myself
obliged to cripple the rhythm. I could have easily said:
"beneath the heavens of my Africa," but Pushkin uses
nébo, not *nebesá;* and "Afric's sky" was too hideous to
envisage. Another tangle of difficulties attends the
rendering of the third line: *Brozhú nad mórem, zhdu
pogódï.* The preposition *nad,* though grammatically
"above," means little more than "near" or "by" or
"along" when used in connection with a body of water
(cf. below, Four: XXXV : 11, *nad ózerom moím,* "along
my lake," i.e., along its banks). I have kept "above"
only because Pushkin might have said *u mórya,* "by the
sea," but did not, having perhaps in mind the elevation
of the Odessa seashore. The Russian word for "weather,"
pogóda, when used (as here) without an adjective, fre-

quently implies (especially in southern Russia) favorable qualification: "propitious weather," "weather suitable for some kind of purpose." This sense is obsolete in English (the *OED* gives a few examples of it in the fifteenth century); in modern English usage, adverse weather is pessimistically suggested by the bare noun (and, similarly, *pogoda* in northern central Russia tends to mean not simply "weather" but "foul weather," despite the existence of the negative *nepogoda*). The English locution closest to *pogoda* in the sense employed here by Pushkin would have been "wind and weather"; but that "wind" is the flatus of a paraphrase unsuitable to my purpose. The harassed translator has to bear in mind that Pushkin's verse *Brozhú nad mórem, zhdu pogódï* is based on the common saying: *sidet' u morya i zhdat' pogodï*, "to sit by the sea and wait for (suitable) weather," meaning "to wait inertly for circumstances to improve."

And, finally, one cannot afford to overlook the well-known fact that here, as in other poems, Pushkin makes an allusion to his political plight in meteorological terms.

*

"I beckon to the sails of ships . . . 'Tis time to leave the dreary shore . . . 'mid the meridian swell . . . [to] sigh . . . for somber Russia," etc.: These themes, so beautifully expressed here in Russian and animated with such authentic emotion, are, technically, Romantic European commonplaces of the time. Pierre Lebrun, Byronizing in *Le Voyage de Grèce*, can. III, chaunts thus:

> J'irai, loin de ce bord que je ne veux plus voir,
> Chercher . . . quelqu'île fortunée.
> . . . .
> Vaisseau, vaisseau que j'aperçoi

. . . .
. . . écoute, écoute!

. . . .
Et pourtant je l'aimais [ce bord]! . . .

. . . .
Je regretterai ses collines;
Je les verrai dans mon sommeil.

*

Here are five rhymed English "translations" of this
stanza:

Spalding (1881):

> When will my hour of freedom come!
> Time, I invoke thee! favouring gales
> Awaiting, on the shore I roam
> And beckon to the passing sails.
> Upon the highway of the sea
> When shall I wing my passage free
> On waves by tempests curdled o'er!
> 'Tis time to quit this weary shore
> So uncongenial to my mind,
> To dream upon the sunny strand
> Of Africa, ancestral land,
> Of dreary Russia left behind,
> Wherein I felt love's fatal dart,
> Wherein I buried left my heart.

Phillipps-Wolley (1904 [1883]):

> When will my hour of freedom come?
> 'Tis time! 'Tis time! My beckoning hand
> Implores each sail, when e'er I roam
> Waiting fair weather on the strand.
> When shall I set my homing sail,
> And through the waves before the gale
> Their shattered crests about me toss
> Unstayed o'er troubled ocean cross
> Touch homeland and be free?
> 'Tis time the dreary land to flee
> To me ungenial, and my verse.
> 'Tis time to rest where south seas swell

> 'Neath native Afric's skies, to dwell
> In peace, and Russia's cloud-land curse
> Where, wrecked by grief, to love a slave,
> My heart has found itself a grave.

(Note the length.)

Elton (January, 1936, *Slavonic Review*):

> High time, high time for me to reckon
> On freedom; comes she at my cry?
> I wait for weather, and I beckon
> The sails, and haunt the sea.—Shall I
> Never with storm-fringed waves be warring,
> Or travel swift and freely, sharing
> The trackless freedom of the sea?
> This element displeases me,
> This dry dull shore; I must be flying;
> For my own skies are African;
> And there, mid Southern surge, I can
> Bide, over sombre Russia sighing,
> —Russia, where once I suffered, where
> I loved: my heart is buried there.

Deutsch (1936):

> 'Tis time to loose me from my tether;
> I call on freedom—naught avails:
> I pace the beach, await good weather,
> And beckon to the passing sails.
> When, wrapped in storm, shall I be battling
> The billows, while the shrouds are rattling,
> And roam the sea's expanse, unpent,
> Quit of the shore's dull element?
> 'Tis time to seek the southern surges
> Beneath my Afric's sunny sky,
> And, there at home, for Russia sigh,
> Lamenting in new songs and dirges
> The land that knew my love, my pain,
> Where long my buried heart has lain.

Radin (1937):

> Oh, will it come, my hour of freedom?
> For it is time to hear my cry.

I wait fair winds upon the seashore
And hail the vessels sailing by.
When shall I start my own free course?
When, under storm clouds, shall I force
My way across the battling sea
And leave a land so harsh to me?
And when at last I leave it, then
By the warm seas beneath the sky
Of sunny Africa I'll sigh
For gloomy Russia once again,
Where I had learned to love and weep
And where my heart lies buried deep.

4 / *Manyú vetríla korabléy*: According to Bartenev, who had it from A. Rosset in the 1850's, Pushkin used to call (in 1824?) Countess Eliza Vorontsov "la princesse Belvetrille," because in Odessa, looking at the sea, she liked to repeat two lines from Zhukovski:

> *Ne beléet* [shows white] *li vetrílo* [sail],
> *Ne plïvút li korablí.*

These are from Zhukovski's ballad *Achilles* (1814), which consists of 208 trochaic tetrameters with rhymes abab; ll. 89–92:

> From the shore with mournful air
> you will look: in the blank distance
> does a sail show white,
> are ships swimming [to harbor].

Bartenev misquotes this; and, furthermore, one cannot help wondering if the reference is not to Countess Vorontsov but to Princess Vyazemski.

5 / Under the cope of storms / *Pod rízoy búr'*: The *riza*, suggesting to a modern reader rich vestments (festive or ecclesiastic garb), is the iris spot of the line, but it is not Pushkin's find. Cf. a line from Mihail Heraskov's poem *Vladimir* (1785), which describes the Christianization of Russia in the tenth century:

There Pósvist, wrapped around in storms as in a cope . . .

In rococo Russian, Posvist is the Slavic or pseudo-Slavic god of the whistling wind, a neoclassical *nepos* of Stribo (who is mentioned in *Slovo o polku Igoreve*), the strepitant god of atmospheric disturbance, son of Perun, who is the Slavic Jove.

11 / beneath the sky of my Africa / *Pod nébom Áfriki moéy*: A similar intonation occurs in connection with Pushkin's *Anchar* (Nov. 9, 1828), nine tetrametric quatrains—namely, in a canceled line (5), "the nature of my Africa" replaced in the final text by "the nature of the thirsting plain," which "generated on a day of wrath" the Antiaris or upas tree, a Malayan plant, visualized by Pushkin as growing in generalized tropical surroundings. The poem is based on a French translation by Pichot of a monologue in Colman the Younger's musical drama *The Law of Java*, first produced in London May 11, 1822.

In an epistle to Nikolay Yazïkov (Sept. 20, 1824, forty-nine lines in iambic tetrameter), Pushkin invites him to Mihaylovskoe, where our poet's dark-skinned ancestor had retired from life at court and where (ll. 31–33)

> Beneath the screen of linden walks
> he thought in years of chilly age
> about his distant Africa . . .

—a process that directly reverses that in *EO*, One : L.

For a detailed discussion of Pushkin's African descent, see App. I, "Abram Gannibal."

LI

4 / for a long time: Three and a half years. Within the chronology of the novel the rambles of its two main characters, Pushkin and Onegin, along the Neva take place in the "summer" (XLVII : 1) of 1820. The first

week in May is the latest period we can choose when adjusting "fiction" to "life." After having been denounced (by one Karazin, a littérateur) on Apr. 2, 1820, as a seditious epigrammatist, the real Pushkin left Petersburg for seven years in the beginning of May, 1820, thus exactly three years before he began *EO* (see also n. to Four : XIX : 5). Traveling post, he covered a thousand miles in twelve days, stayed for a few days in Ekaterinoslav (Dnepropetrovsk), where he had been assigned to General Inzov's Regional Office, and set out with the Raevski family for Pyatigorsk on May 28. Although planning a trip to the Crimea as early as mid-April, he does not seem to have been then *in meditatione fugae*, as he was to be in October, 1823, when composing this stanza. He stayed at the N. Caucasian spas from June to August, 1820, spent the second part of August and the beginning of September in Gurzuf, Crimea (which Onegin was to visit three years later), thence proceeded to Kishinev (whither the Ekaterinoslav office, from which he was absent on sick leave, had meanwhile migrated), lived in Kishinev from Sept. 21, 1820, to about July, 1823, and clinched his Southern period of banishment with a year's stay in Odessa (where he was attached to the bureau of the Governor General), leaving for his Northern place of exile (till 1826), the Pushkin countryseat Mihaylovskoe, in the province of Pskov, July 31, 1824. The fragments of *Onegin's Journey* published during Pushkin's lifetime end with the first line of a fading-out stanza, "And so I lived then in Odessa . . ." The intonation promises what we do learn from posthumously published remnants of the canceled continuation of the *Journey*—that Onegin and Pushkin meet again, in 1823, in Odessa, whence both set out for the North in 1824, Pushkin for Mihaylovskoe and Onegin for St. Petersburg (see also n. to *Onegin's Journey*, XXX : 13).

Commentary

8 | *U kázhdogo svoy úm i tólk*: Fr. *chacun à son goût*. Apart from the usual difficulty of translating the unqualified *tolk* (notion, understanding, judgment, interpretation, etc.), there is an additional obscurity here. Does it mean that each of the creditors had his own views, or is this a transitional phrase introducing Onegin's individual attitude toward the matter?

LII

The wording of this stanza is awkward in the original. Derivations from "prepare" are repeated twice (after having been used once in the preceding stanza), and there are two "already's" (*uzh*). In l. 3 the *prí smerti v postéle* (from *postelya*, not *postel'*) is the dissolution of a Gallicism, *sur son lit de mort*, "on his deathbed" (which had long ago entered Russian as *na smertnom odre*). It would have taken a minute to iron out all these creases by means of an English paraphrase, but I preferred to render them faithfully, even if this entailed a good deal of fumbling and fussing.

7 | drove | *poskakál*: "Translators" have had great difficulties with the verb *skakat'*, which occurs several times throughout the novel. It means literally "to drive at a gallop": see, for example, Thomas Raikes, *A Visit to St. Petersburg in the Winter of 1829–30* [Nov. 26, 1829– Mar. 25, 1830, N.S.] (London, 1838): "The four post-horses were harnessed to the carriage abreast: they went at a hand-gallop all the way, and we got over eight or nine wersts [a verst is equal to 0.6629 mile, or 1.067 kilometers] every hour" (Letter IV, from Mittau, Nov. 28, 1829); and his *Journal* (entry of Friday, Aug. 17, 1838):

Went on a party to Elnbogen, which is distant about eight miles [from Karlsbad], and famous for its romantic scenery. Count de Witt, who has twenty horses here, brought from Russia, supplied three carriages. We travelled at the Russian pace, full gallop, and reached our point in half an hour.

But employed in a general sense as here and elsewhere in the novel, the verb *skakat'*, although presupposing a certain velocity of motion, means merely to drive in a carriage—unless the traveler be definitely stated to be riding on horseback, when the verb would mean to go at a gallop or fast canter.

11 / and with this I began my novel: The circle is now complete (I–LII–I). It encompasses fifty-two stanzas. Within this circle, Eugene drives on the smaller, concentric one of his daily rounds (XV–XXXVI). The propelling force that spins the wheels of the chapter is the digressive spirit, Pushkin's participation, a succession of lyrical explosions. As Sterne said of his *Tristram Shandy* (vol. I, ch. 22), ". . . my work is digressive, and it is progressive, too. . . . Digressions, incontestably, are the sun-shine— they are the life, the soul of reading." Pushkin added the internal combustion.

The next stanza (LIII) will continue the story begun in I–II. It will go on for another stanza (LIV)—and that is all there will be in the way of direct narrative in One (five stanzas: I–II, LII–LIV).

12 / manor / *derevnya*: In this sense *derevnya* (which otherwise may mean "village" or "countryside," *campagne*) means manor, countryseat, place in the country, domain, demesne, estate—and not "village," as "translators" have it here and throughout the novel (a village, or villages, might be in serf-owning days the most important part of the country estate, but that is beside the point). Pushkin himself in his correspondence, when writing in French, was prone to use the glaring Rus-

Commentary

sism *mon village* (e.g., letter to Anna Kern, July 25, 1825: ". . . ce que j'ai de mieux à faire au fond de mon triste village, est de tâcher de ne plus penser à vous") instead of the correct *mon bien* or *ma propriété* or *ma campagne* (terms he and his fellow squires used elsewhere). Tatiana also uses "village" poetically in her epistle (Three), where the Pushkin–Anna Kern situation is as it were reversed (see also n. to Two : 1 : 1).

11 Canceled draft (2369, f. 19ᵛ):

> *Priéhali! skazál Iván.*
> Ivan said: Here we are!

Apparently the coachman says this.

12 Canceled draft (ibid.):

> but having ridden more than one day . . .

Meaning: more than two hundred miles, with posters, which *could* be done in one day and night.

1–7 In this stanza, in which Pushkin treats the theme of death with a kind of thumping joviality, very different from the lyrical eschatologics of the next, Lenskian, chapter, the Russian-speaking reader will enjoy the amusing sets of alliterations in ll. 1–7, enhanced by the ponderous double sag (‿ ⏑́ ‿ – ‿ – ‿ ⏑́) in ll. 4 and 5—a rare rhythm, and exceptionally rare in consecutive lines:

> *Nashyól on pólon dvór uslúgi;*
> *K pokóyniku so vséh storón*
> *S'ezzhális' nédrugi i drúgi,*
> *Ohótniki do pohorón.*
> *Pokóynika pohoroníli.*
> *Popí i gósti éli, píli,*
> *I pósle vázhno razoshlís'* . . .

The alliterative elements in these lines are:

ól, ól;
pó, po, po, po, po, po, pó;
ohó, oho, oho;
li, li.

These recurrent sounds run through the following words:

nashyól (found), *pólon* (full);

pólon, k pokóyniku (to the dead man), *pohorón* (of funerals), *pokóynika pohoroníli* (l. 5), *popí* (the priests), *pósle* (afterward);

ohótniki do pohorón (l. 4), *pohoroníli;*

éli (ate), *píli* (drank).

The components of *pohoroníli* seem to have gone on a spree.

One question in connection with this passage has bothered me since childhood. How could it be that Onegin's country neighbors, the Larins, did not attend the funeral and the burial feast, of which such a definite echo seems to occur in Tatiana's dream (Five : XVI : 3–4), when she hears a clamor of voices and a clinking of glasses *Kak na bol'shíh pohoronáh*, as at some big funeral?

8 / had been sensibly engaged / *délom zanyalís'*: In this common locution, *delo* means anything worth while in implied contrast to *bezdel'e,* "idleness," "doing nothing."

10 / *Zavódov, vód, lesóv, zemél'*: *Vodï, lesa* sounds like the "Eaux et forêts" of French officialdom. The word closing the line makes a rather lame ending: the whole hobbles after the parts. *Zavodov, vod* is marked by a somewhat too conspicuous alliteration. *Zavod* has many meanings; "works" or "workshops" seems the amplest here, but that still leaves out a few possibilities. The *zavodï* belonging to a wealthy landowner of the time might in-

clude any kind of manufactory or mill, as well as a stud, a fish hatchery, a distillery, a brickyard, and the like.

LIV

A charmingly drawn figure in the left margin is identified by Efros (who, on p. 133 of *Risunki poeta*, reproduces the draft 2369, f. 20ʳ) as Amalia Riznich (1803–25) in shawl and bonnet. Her attitude, the position of her hands, suggest to shrewd Efros the quietude of pregnancy (a son was born to her in the beginning of 1824). The same commentator identifies a handsome profile in the right margin as that of her husband, Ivan Riznich (b. 1792).

3 / the coolness of the somber park / *Prohláda súmrachnoy dubróvï*: Wherever possible, I translate *dubrova* (also spelled *dubrava*) as park and *roshcha* as grove. *Dubrova* is hardly ever used today. It has a poetical, stylized, pseudo-archaic, artificial ring.

In a *dubrova* deciduous trees (though not necessarily *dub*, "oak") predominate—as evergreens do in a *bor*.

In Pushkin's time, and earlier, *dubrova* was used in the sense of both "public park" and, less happily, private park—the stately alleys of trees on a gentleman's country estate. It was also used loosely in the sense of "small wood." An oak wood would be *dubnyak*, not *dubrova*.

4 / the bubbling of the quiet brook / *Zhurchán'e tíhogo ruch'yá*: Cf. Philippe Desportes (1546–1606), *Prière au sommeil*: "[un petit ruisseau] doux-coulant"—to which the established Russian epithet *tihostruynïy* (gentle-streaming) is close, though not as close as *tihotechnïy* would have been.

See also André Chénier, *La Retraite*:

> Il ne veut que l'ombre et le frais,
> Que le silence des forêts,
> Que le bruit d'un ruisseau paisible . . .

Mark this demure rill on Onegin's estate. Many are the bubbling, babbling, brawling, purling, gurgling, chattering, warbling, murmuring brooks, streams, rills, and rillets running through the bosquets of western European poetry, with their sources in (Virgil's) Arcadia, in Sicily, and in Rome, and their most maudlin meanders in the topiary poetry of the Italian, French, and English sixteenth, seventeenth, and eighteenth centuries; and there is invariably the cool shade of foliage near by.

It is with this literary landscape, imported mainly from France or through France, that in *EO* Pushkin replaces a specific description of summer in northwestern Russia, whereas his winters (as will be seen further) belong to the arctic order of such as were described by his predecessors and contemporaries in Russia, but are selected and arranged by him with incomparably greater art and talent.

Actually, the theme goes back not so much to Virgil's elegiac landscape, nor to Horace and his Sabine farm, as to the rococo Arcadias of later Mediterranean poets, the kind of idealized surroundings, turfy and thornless, that would tempt a knight-errant to take off his armor. A famous offender was Ariosto in his dreary *Orlando furioso* (1532). In 1826, Pushkin transposed into Russian several octaves (C–CXII) of *Roland furieux*, can. XXIII. The Comte de Tressan's prose version of octave C (where every couple of words is a cliché) goes:

. . . Le paladin [Roland, Comte d'Angers] arriva sur le rivage agréable d'une belle fontaine qui serpentoit dans une prairie émaillée de fleurs; de grands arbres dont le

Commentary

faîte s'unissoit en berceaux ombrageoient cette fontaine, et le zéphir qui pénétroit leur feuillage tempéroit la chaleur sur ses bords tranquilles.

Our poet boiled this down to five iambic tetrameters with rhymes ababa:

> Before the knight gleam, more pellucid
> than glass, the waters of a brook.
> Nature with amiable flowers
> its shady margin has decked out
> and planted it about with trees.

We shall recognize the "brook meandering through a meadow" in the landscape around Lenski's tomb (Seven), with a shepherd imported from Ariosto's octave CI.

Specifically the bodies of water mentioned in the novel are:

1. A brook or brooklet running through a meadow, and through a linden bosquet, from a spring located immediately west of Fairhill (Krasnogorie; see Six : IV : 3–4), Lenski's estate and the village on that estate; at this fountainhead he will be buried (dead duelists and suicides not being admitted to the consecrated earth of a cemetery).

2. A continuation of that brook through a neighboring valley, where it joins a river.

3. On the way to this river, it passes in the back of the Larin garden and park (near the linden alley where Tatiana is to be sermonized by Onegin) and, after turning around a hill (the one from which Tatiana will descry Onegin's manor), runs through groves belonging to Onegin.

4. The brook—an emblem of separation in Tatiana's mind—undergoes a curious transformation in her dream, becoming a swollen torrent that, however, is simultaneously perceived as the prototypical idyllic rill.

5. The anonymous river into which the brook flows consists of two stretches; one is the Larin river seen from the Larin house.

6. The other bend of this river is the local "Hellespont" where Onegin goes for swims; it shines at the foot of a hill on a slope of which his manor stands.

The river (*reka*, *rechka*) running through Onegin's estate is clearly indicated in the following passages:

Two : 1 :	7	[Onegin's house] stood above a river [*réchkoyu*]...
Four : XXXVII :	7	[Onegin] proceeded [*réke*]
	8	to the river that ran below the hill.
Seven : V :	5	with my wayward Muse
	6	let's go to hear the murmur of a park
	7	above a nameless river [*rekóy*]
	8	... where my Eugene ...
	10	... dwelt in the winter
	11	in the vicinity of youthful Tanya...
Seven : XV :	8	long did Tatiana walk alone
	9	... And suddenly before her
	10	sees from a hill a manor house,
	11	a village, a grove below hill,
	12	... above a bright river [*rekóyu*].
Seven : XX :	4	[As seen from the window of Onegin's study] The grove sleeps
	5	above the misted river [*rekóyu*] ...

Connected with this river, or perhaps synonymous with it, are streams (*strui*, shafts of water) pertaining to a brook (*ruchey*) running through Onegin's estate:

One : LIV :	3	the coolness of the somber park,
	4	the bubbling of the quiet brook [*ruch'yá*]...
Four : XXXIX :	2	the sylvan shade, the purl of streams [*strúy*] ...

The streamlets (*struyki*, small shafts of water) of Onegin's brook reach Krasnogorie and Lenski's grave:

Six : XL : 5   There is a spot: left of the village
         6   where [Lenski] dwelt
         8   [there] have meandered streamlets
              [*strúyki*]
         9   of the neighboring valley's brook
              [*ruch'yá*].
      13   there, by the brook [*ruch'yá*] . . .
      14   a simple monument is set.

These streamlets (or other runlets coming from a fount, *klyuch*) fall into a river:

Seven : VI : 2   let us go thither [to Lenski's grave]
              where a rill [*rucheyók*],
          3   winding, by way of a green meadow, runs
          4   through a lime bosquet to the river
              [*reké*].
          7   . . . the gurgle of the fount [*góvor
              klyuchevóy*] is heard.

This river (*rechka*, *potok*), or another river, runs through the Larins' estate.

Three : XXXII : 10   [As the sun rises] the stream [*potók*]
             11   starts silvering.
   Seven : XV : 1   . . . Waters [*vodï*]
          2   streamed [*struílis'*] quietly.
          4   [Fishermen's fire flamed] across the
              river [*rekóy*].

As in the case of Onegin's river, the Larins' river is supplemented, or replaced, by a brook or brooks:

Three : XXXVIII : 13   [Tatiana flees] across the flower
              plots to the brook [*ruch'yú*] . . .
   Seven : XXIX : 1   Her walks last longer.
          2   At present, here a hillock, there a
              brook [*ruchéy*],
          3   stop [Tatiana].

Seven : LIII : 10   [In Moscow she recalls] that
                          secluded nook
              11   . . . a bright brooklet [*rucheyók*],
              13   . . . the gloam of linden avenues . . .

In Tatiana's dream this brook (which in a generalized
form—"by the old limes, by the small brook"—appears
in Three : XIV : 4, where our poet plans an idyllic novel
in prose) undergoes strange transformations:

Five : XI : 7   a churning, dark, and hoary
            8   torrent [*poték*] . . .
Five : XII : 2   Tatiana murmurs at the brook
                     [*ruchéy*] . . .
            13   [she] worked her way across the
                     brook [*ruchéy*] . . .

We suspect that the same waters that connect the
three country places are those which (now frozen) per-
tain to the mill (*mel'nitsa*) mentioned in Six : XII : 11
and XXV : 10, near which Lenski is dispatched in his
duel with Onegin. There is also an "ice-clad river"
(*rechka*) shining in Four : XLII : 6, which is made level
with its banks by snow in Seven : XXX : 5, in fitting
Russian conclusion to a Mediterranean theme.

One : LIV : 4–5; Three : XIV : 4; and Four : XXXIX : 2
are especially typical illustrations of the "eaux-et-
forêts" cliché. Pushkin took a perverse pleasure, it
would seem, in finding various elegant Russian versions
of this commonplace, already stylized to death through
the centuries. It would be pedantic to list the innumer-
able examples of this "shady wood-murmuring brook"
symbiosis in western European poetry; a few examples
are given in my n. to Four : XXXIV.

5–8 Cf. Voltaire, *La Bégeule* (1772):

      Le lendemain lui parut un peu fade;
      Le lendemain fut triste et fatiguant;
      Le lendemain lui fut insupportable.

11 / cards . . . verses: Pushkin refrained from describing
Onegin the gambler, and in the next chapter discarded
a magnificent digression on his own passion for banking
games. (See nn. to Two : XVII : a–d.) The "verses" al-
lude to the table books of fashionable ladies described
in Four : XXVII–XXX.

12 / The hyp was waiting for him on the watch: Cf. Jacques
Delille, *L'Homme des champs, ou les Géorgiques
françoises* (1800), can. I, ll. 41–46:

> Ce riche qui, d'avance usant tous ses plaisirs,
>
> . . . .
>
> S'écrie à son lever: "Que la ville m'ennuie!
> Volons aux champs; c'est là qu'on jouit de la vie,
> Qu'on est heureux." Il part, vole, arrive; l'ennui
> Le reçoit à la grille et se traîne avec lui.

LV

As a poet, Pushkin does not show any genuine knowledge
of the Russian countryside (as Turgenev and Tolstoy
were to show fifteen years after our poet's death).
Stylistically, he remains true to the eighteenth-century
concepts of generalized "nature," and either avoids
specific features and subjective details of landscape al-
together or serves them up with a self-conscious smile
as something that might perplex or amuse an ordinary
reader. (I am not speaking here of grotesque selections
of country-life characteristics slanted for the purpose of
humor or social satire—any journalist can do *that*.) On
the other hand, as an individual, Pushkin not only was
fond of villatic seclusion, but actually needed it, espe-
cially in autumn, for creative work. It may be useful to
the reader if at this point I sum up what is known of
Pushkin's country sojourns.

As a boy, Pushkin spent half a dozen summers at Zaharino (or Zaharovo), his maternal grandmother's estate (acquired by Maria Gannibal in November, 1804, and sold in January, 1811), in the province of Moscow, district of Zvenigorod.

Pushkin's nine sojourns in Mihaylovskoe (see below, LV : 12), province of Pskov, district of Opochka, were:

Autumn and winter, 1799, in his first year of life.

Mid-June to end of August, 1817, soon after graduation from the Lyceum.

Mid-July to mid-August, 1819.

Aug. 9, 1824, to Sept. 4, 1826—by order of the government.

Early November to mid-December, 1826.

Late July to second week of October, 1827.

May 8 to 12, 1835 (visits Trigorskoe on business).

Second week of September to mid-October, 1835.

Second week of April, 1836 (burial of his mother).

In the autumn of 1830, his last bachelor year, he spent three exceptionally fertile months (September through November) at Boldino, the paternal estate in the southeastern corner of the province of Nizhni-Novgorod, district of Lukoyanov, and stayed there again for two months of work in October–November, 1833. There was a third, and last, visit from mid-September to mid-October, 1834. (See also n. to Eight : XVII : 3.)

Other country places associated with Pushkin's literary occupations are the Davïdovs' estate, Kamenka, in the province of Kiev, where Pushkin sojourned in the winter of 1820–21, and the lands belonging to the Vulf family in the province of Tver, district of Staritsa (Malinniki, Pavlovskoe, etc.), where Pushkin stayed four times (a fortnight in February, 1827; from last week of October to first week of December, 1828; Jan. 7–16, 1829; and mid-October to first week of November, 1829).

Commentary

1–2 In a letter to Vyazemski, Mar. 27, 1816, from Tsarskoe
Selo, Pushkin thus complains of the scholastic seclusion
at the Lyceum:

> Happy who in the tumult of the town
> dreams of seclusion;
> who only at a distance sees
> a wilderness, a little garden,
> a country house, hills with hushed woods,
> a valley with a sprightly rivulet,
> and even—a shepherd with his flock . . .

Cf. Ducis: "J'étais né pour les champs" (*Epître à
Gérard*) or "C'est pour l'ombre et les champs que le
ciel m'a fait naître" (*Vers d'un homme qui se retire à la
campagne*).

2–4 *The Country* (*Derevnya*, 1819), a sixty-one-line poem
by Pushkin in free iambics, contains the following
related lines:

> The oracles of ages, you I question!
> In this majestic solitude
> your gladdening voice is more distinct
> . . . .
> and your creative thoughts
> ripen in the soul's depth.

6 / by a wasteful lake / *nad ózerom pustínnïm*: The epithet
I have used is somewhat archaic, but is textually closer
than "desolate" or "lonely."

7 / and *far niente* is my rule / *I "fár niénte" móy zakón*:
Cf. François de Bernis (1715–94), *Epître sur la paresse*:
". . . Goûter voluptueusement | Le doux plaisir de ne
rien faire," or Louis de Fontanes (1757–1821), *Ode*
(1812): "Je lis, je dors, tout soin s'efface, | Je ne fais
rien et le jour passe | . . . je goûte ainsi la volupté,"
and a hundred other passages in a score of other *petits*

poètes. The use of the Italian words *far niente* (which are given four syllables here as if they were Latin) is really a Gallicism (see, for example, *Journal des Goncourt*, entry Oct. 26, 1856: "un farniente sans la conscience de lui-même, sans le remords").

8 / *Ya kázhdïm útrom probuzhdyón*: The reader's ear is likely to comprehend this weak line as a current solecism for *ya kazhdoe utro probuzhdayus'*, "I every morning wake up."

12 / former years: The summers of 1817 and 1819, when our poet visited his mother's country place, Mihaylovskoe (pronounced "me-high-loves-coy-eh"), which he wrote in French Michailovsk, Michailovsky, Michailovskoy, and Michailovsko. This Mihaylovskoe (also known locally as Zuyovo), situated in the province of Pskov, district of Opochka, twenty-six miles from that town, 120 miles from Novorzhev, 285 miles SW of St. Petersburg, and 460 miles W of Moscow, belonged to Abram Gannibal and then to his son Osip (Pushkin's maternal grandfather), after whose death, in 1806, it went to Nadezhda Pushkin. According to the land survey of 1786, the estate comprised about 5500 acres, of which one sixth was heavily timbered (mostly with pine), and several scattered hamlets with some two hundred slaves of both sexes.

The manor house (as described in 1838) was a very modest affair of wood on a stone foundation, one-storied, fifty-six feet long by forty-five and a half broad, with two porches, one balcony, twenty doors, fourteen windows, and six Dutch stoves. It was surrounded by lilac bushes. There were four habitable outbuildings, one with a bagnio, and a three-thousand-foot-long park with fir alleys and a linden avenue. From the garden terrace one could see the fourteen-foot-wide river Sorot (Sorot'), winding its way through lush meadows, with a lake on either side of it: the small Malinets Lake and the very large Luchanovo Lake. The reader will find the river mentioned in the last stanza of *Onegin's Journey* (and there is a reflection of it in Four : XXXVII), and Luchanovo Lake figures in Four : XXXV and is mentioned in a poem that I cite in my notes to the first stanza of Chapter Two.

13 / in the [shade] / *v teni*: There is a clerical error here: *v tishi*, "in the stillness," which does not rhyme in Russian with *dni*, "days," in both separate editions of the chapter and in the complete 1833 and 1837 editions. The draft (2369, f. 20ᵛ) has *v seni*, "in the shelter," corrected from *v teni*. A later correction in the fair copy has *v teni* (in Pushkin's hand), whereas the transcript has *v tishi* (in Lev Pushkin's hand).

LVI

1 / Flowers, love, the country: The intonation is the banal one of similar enumerations of *objets charmants* in minor French poetry. Cf. J. B. Rousseau, *Odes*, III, VII:

> Des objets si charmants, un séjour si tranquille,
> La verdure, les fleurs, les ruisseaux, les beaux jours . . .

2 / ye fields! / *Polya!*: *Champs*, employed in a pseudo-Latin sense (countryside, champaign, *campagne*), a painful Gallic cliché. *Aller aux champs* meant in the seventeenth century "to go to the country," *aller à la campagne*. See, for example, Etienne Martin de Pinchesne (1616–1705), *Les Géorgiques de Virgile*, II:

> Champs, agréables champs, vos bois et vos fontaines
> Règleront désormais mes plaisirs et mes peines;
> Je cueillerai vos fleurs, vivrai de votre fruit,
> Content d'être éloigné de la gloire et du bruit.

Praise of the countryside was by 1820 probably the most worn commonplace of poetry. From the great Horace's *Epistles* to Delille's rational trash, the theme had undergone a conventional crystallization and an artistic dissolution. Even the powerful melody of André Chénier at the end of the eighteenth century failed to give new life to the theme:

> Quand pourrai-je habiter un champ qui soit à moi?
> Et, villageois tranquille, ayant pour tout emploi
> Dormir et ne rien faire, inutile poète,
> Goûter le doux oubli d'une vie inquiète?
> Vous savez si toujours, dès mes plus jeunes ans,
> Mes rustiques souhaits m'ont porté vers les champs . . .
> —*Elégies* (ed. Walter), II, ll. 19–24

> Mes rêves nonchalants, l'oisiveté, la paix,
> A l'ombre, au bord des eaux, le sommeil pur et frais.
> —*Epîtres* (ed. Walter), IV, 2, to Abel de Fondat, ll. 5–6

See also nn. to Four : XXXIV : 1–4.

Pushkin's *rustiques souhaits* were to be realized, somewhat unexpectedly for him, in the following August (1824).

See also Guillaume Amfrye de Chaulieu (1639–1720), who begins his *Des Louanges de la vie champêtre* thus:

> Désert, aimable solitude,
> Séjour du calme et de la paix,
>
> . . . .
>
> C'est toi qui me rends à moi-même;
> Tu calmes mon cœur agité;
> Et de ma seule oisiveté
> Tu me fais un bonheur extrême.

In Russian, the theme had already been illustrated as early as 1752 (when Russian metrical verses were not yet twenty years old) by Vasiliy Trediakovski in his *Strophes in Praise of Country Life* (*Strofï pohval'nïe poselyanskomu zhitiyu*; an imitation of Horace in alternately rhymed trochaic pentameters—a meter to be

beautifully used in the nineteenth century by Lermontov
and in the twentieth by Blok), in which the Arcadian
décor is given in ll. 37–40:

> Meantime rapidly the river flows,
> sweetly little birds sing in the woods,
> shepherds blow their vibrant little horns,
> springs from hills pour forth a sonant stream.

3–4 / the difference between Onegin and myself; 10–11 /
[I have not] scrawled my portrait like Byron: Cf. Byron,
Childe Harold, can. IV, dedication to John Hobhouse,
Jan. 2, 1818:

> . . . I had become weary of drawing a line which every one
> seemed determined not to perceive . . . it was in vain that
> I asserted, and imagined that I had drawn, a distinction
> between the author and the pilgrim; and the very anxiety
> to preserve this difference, and disappointment at finding
> it unavailing, so far crushed my efforts in the composition,
> that I determined to abandon it altogether—and have
> done so [in the last canto].

In a letter (rough draft) to Nikolay Raevski, Jr., in
July, 1825, Mihaylovskoe, while in the middle of com-
posing *Boris Godunov*, Pushkin wrote:

> La vraisemblance des situations et la vérité du dialogue
> . . . voilà la véritable règle de la tragédie. . . . Quel homme
> que ce Sch[ekspir]. . . . Comme Byron le tragique est
> mesquin devant lui . . . ce Byron . . . a partagé entre ses
> personnages tels ou tels traits de son caractère: son orgueil
> à l'un, sa haine à l'autre, sa mélancolie au troisième . . .
> ce n'est pas là de la tragédie. . . . Lisez Sch[ekspir]. . . .

(This is a French eighteenth-century way of spelling
Shakespeare; see, for example, La Harpe, in his satire
L'Ombre de Duclos, 1773. There were other spellings:
Ducis, in his *Epistle*, 1780, to the Curé [Lemaire] of
Rocquencourt near Versailles, reveals himself as a fer-
vent admirer of "Sakespir.")

7 | of complicated | *Zamïslovátoy*: The epithet has no exact English equivalent. "Abstruse," "deep," "mazy-witted"—these and similar meanings are, ironically, implied.

LVII

Pushkin expresses here his concept of the workings of the poet's mind, in four stages:

1. Direct perception of a "dear object" or event.

2. The hot, silent shock of irrational rapture accompanying the evocation of that impression in one's fancies or actual dreams.

3. The preservation of the image.

4. The later, cooler touch of creative art, as identified with rationally controlled inspiration, verbal transmutation, and a new harmony.

2 | fancifying | *mechtátel'noy*: The word *mechta*, with its derivations, is the main heroine of the Russian romantic vocabulary. Its recurrence forces the translator to use the word "dream" over and over; even if he varies it where possible with "waking dream," "daydream," "fancy," and "reverie" (the last a maudlin and moribund vocable in English), still the process is somewhat of a strain. The combination of sounds in *mechtá* blending the mellow *m* with the kissing *ch* and the musical *ta*; the natural rhyming of the *tá* (feminine singular) or *tï* (gen. sing. and nom. pl.) with words meaning "beauty" (*krasotá*) and "flowers" (*tsvetï*), and "thou" (*tï*); and the numerous shades of meaning, from "chimera" to "ambition," that it serves to convey, make of it the hardest-working member of the romantic team. The term in fact had been overworked by the poets of the nineteenth century until it lost all meaning and all grace in the easy lines of poetasters and the fiction of lady

writers. Pushkin greatly favors not only *mechta* but all
its derivatives such as *mechtanie*, or *mechtan'e* ("day-
dreaming"), *mechtat'* (to indulge in reverie), *mechtatel'*
("reverist," "dreamer"), and *mechtatel'nïy* ("dreamy,"
"meditative"), which is close to *zadumchivïy* ("pen-
sive"), another Pushkin philologism.

8–9 / a maiden of the mountains . . . as well as captives
of the Salgir's banks: The two references are: (1) to the
Cherkes maiden in *The Caucasian Captive*, "a tale"
(*Kavkazskiy Plennik, povest'*), begun in August, 1820,
finished in spring, 1821, published in 1822, last week
of August; and (2) to the harem captives in *The Fountain
of Bahchisaray* (*Bahchisarayskiy fontan*), written in
the first part of 1822, published Mar. 10, 1824, with an
interesting foreword by Vyazemski. *

These poems, twin torrents of iambic tetrameters,
unstanzaed, belong distinctly to Pushkin's youthful
Orientalia. The rudimentary bibliography that our poet
outlines in One : LVII will be amplified by him in the
first stanzas of Eight, when he tours his works and
identifies his Muse with their heroines.

According to B. Nedzelski (see Brodski, 1949), Salgir—
pronounced to rhyme with "gear"—is a name applied
by the Tatars to *any* river in the Crimea; here it stands
obviously for Churyuk (Churuk) River, near the Tatar
town of Bahchisaray (Bakhchisarai), central Crimea,
former residence of the Crimean Khans (1518–1783),
afterward a tourist showplace. It may be, however, that
Pushkin confused the Churyuk with the true Salghir
River that flows in another part of the Crimea, crossing
its eastern portion from the vicinity of Ayan northward
to Simferopol.

---

* "Conversation between the Editor and the Classicist." It attacks
the review *Blagonamerennïy*.

LVIII

2 / with a touching caress / *Umil'noy láskoy*: The same
epithet is used in Two : XXXV : 10, and connotes *atten-
drissement*, softheartedness, a state of being touched by
something that pleasantly affects one's sensibility. It has
no exact English equivalent. Pushkin uses it practically
as a synonym of *umilyonnïy*, Fr. *attendri*, experiencing
umilen'e, although, to be quite exact, *umil'nïy* denotes
the way something or somebody looks when provoking
or experiencing *umilen'e*.

5 / Faith: This was the best I could do in trying to render
the archaic emphasis of the asseverative interjection *i*.
It can be compared to the French *ma foi*.

8 / Happy who / *Blazhén, kto*: It is hardly necessary to re-
mind the reader that all these "happy he," "blessed he,"
"blest he," and so forth, stem (through the French,
heureux qui) from the *felix qui* or *beatus ille qui* of the
ancient poets (e.g., Horace, *Epodes*, II, 1).

LIX

6–8 This was written Oct. 22, 1823, in Odessa, and seven
months later Pushkin drew in ink, in the left-hand
margin of the draft of Three : XXIX (2370, f. 2ʳ; Efros,
p. 197), alongside ll. 6–8—

> to me will Gallicisms remain
> as sweet as the sins of past youth,
> as Bogdanovich's verse

—a charming pair of feminine feet, crossed, stretched
out from under an elegant skirt, white-stockinged, in
pointed black patent-leather slippers with interlaced
ribbons on the instep. They are assigned by Efros to
Countess Elizaveta Vorontsov, whose portrait (minus

feet) is sketched above and among the rhymes of XXIX, in the same MS, right-hand part of the text. Her shapely neck lacks, however, the necklace. The date of the draft of Three : XXIX is May 22, 1824, which heads (2370, f. 1^r) the first rough draft of Pushkin's famous letter (ending just above Eliza Vorontsov's profile, f. 2^r) to Aleksandr Kaznacheev (1788–1880), director of Count Vorontsov's chancellery, a good friendly man. In this letter Pushkin claims that any actual work as clerk on the staff of the General Governor of New Russia would interfere with his considerably more remunerative literary occupations. He desires to remain formally attached to the office but, in view of the fact that he suffers from "aneurysms" (this is, *sensu stricto*, a permanent, abnormal, blood-filled dilatation of an artery resulting from disease of the vessel wall; Pushkin's complaint was actually varicosis of the legs, as diagnosed at the end of September, 1825, in Pskov, after our poet had vainly tried to use his "fatal aneurysm" as a pretext to obtain permission for a journey abroad), asks "to be left in peace for the short period of a life that will surely not last long" (thus ends the 1824 letter on f. 2^r, with the word "surely" half lost in Eliza Vorontsov's hairdo).

S. Vengerov, in his edition of Pushkin's works, III (1909), 247, was the first to reproduce the drawings of feminine feet from Pushkin's drafts of *EO* (then in the Rumyantsov Museum). He published three such sketches in a row. I identify the middle one as the pair I have just described from Efros' reproduction, p. 197 (2370, f. 2^r). The first in the row depicts a feminine left foot in profile, sheathed in a kind of close-fitting riding boot, with its sharp toe resting on the support of a triangular stirrup. If Vengerov's casual mention of "Cahier 2369, f. 1^v" refers to it and not to the third vignette, this would suggest assigning it to some lady in Kishinev, in the spring of 1823. The third vignette, which may come from "Cahier 2370, f. 8," following the drafts related to Three : XXII, is obviously the limb of a ballerina, standing on the point of a toe, with a curved instep and a muscular calf.

14 This has the humorously ominous tang of Gresset's ". . . Et par vingt chants endormir les lecteurs" (*Vertvert*, I, 19; see n. to One : XXXII : 7–8). Byron promised to have "twelve, or twenty-four" cantos in *Don Juan* (II, CCXVI, 5), but he died after beginning the seventeenth.

LX

2 This gives an additional touch of life to the chapter, since by a feat of style it implies that Onegin had somehow ("meantime") evolved a strong personality while the author was fussing over the (unknown) hero of *another* epic (promised in LIX : 14), belonging to a long-winded genre and a priori a bore.

3–4 / my novel's first chapter: This novel's.

6 / inconsistencies: Hardly an allusion to chronological flaws; perhaps a reference to Onegin's dual nature—dry and romantic, chilly and ardent, superficial and penetrating.

8 / censorship its due: Meaning that some passages may have to be deleted.

9 / reviewers: "Messrs. the Monthly Reviewers!" as Sterne would have said.

11–12 An obvious imitation of the well-known passage in Horace, *Epistles*, I, XX. It was often paraphrased in the

eighteenth century. Thus Lewis, in his "Preface" to
The Monk:

> Now, then, your venturous course pursue,
> Go, my delight! dear book, adieu!

Newborn, *novorozhdyónnoe*, is in this context a
Gallicism. Cf. Gilbert, *Le Dix-huitième Siècle* (1775),
l. 391: "Officieux lecteur de ces vers nouveaux nés . . ."

14 / false interpretations / *Krivíe tólki*: This seems to be the
best sense. In a less specifc context, the phrase might
also be "false rumors" or "idle talk."

The preconception that, because the first chapter of
EO has some superficial affinity with *Beppo*, Pushkin
was to be regarded as a disciple of Byron led to his being
compared by his first readers to the "Russian Byron,"
Ivan Kozlov, a popular mediocrity; and, quirkishly
enough, the comparison was not always in Pushkin's
favor. On Apr. 22, 1825, Vyazemski in a letter to
Aleksandr Turgenev remarked in connection with the
publication of Kozlov's poem *The Monk* (*Chernets*; the
tetrametric story of a young monk with a grim past):
"Let me tell this in your ear—there is in *Chernets* more
feeling, more thought than in Pushkin's poems." And
on the very same day, Yazïkov wrote to his brother about
the same *Chernets*, which he had not yet read: "God grant
that *Chernets* be a better poem than *Onegin*!" Why God
should be expected to grant this is not too clear, but
when Chapter Two of *Onegin* came out, Yazïkov had at
least the pleasure of finding it "no better than the first
canto—mere rhymed prose."

Under this stanza Pushkin wrote in French:

October 22
1823
Odessa

Chapter Two

O rus! O Rus'!: The first ("O countryside!") is from
Horace, *Satires*, II, VI:

… O countryside, when shall I behold you ["O rus, quando
ego te aspiciam"] and when shall I be allowed, now with
books of the ancients, now with slumber and hours of
idleness, to taste sweet forgetfulness of the ills of life?

(This theme is taken up again by our poet in Four :
XXXIX : 1, to which see nn.)

The second, *Rus'*, is the old form, and lyrical abbrevi-
tion, of Russia, *Rossiya*.

I find the following in Stendhal's diary for 1837: "En
1799 … le parti aristocrate attendait les Russes à Gre-
noble [Suvorov was in Switzerland]; ils s'écriaient: O
Rus, quando ego te aspiciam! …" (*Journal*, Paris, 1888
edn., App. VII). Stendhal chose the same motto ("O rus,
quando ego te aspiciam!") for ch. 31, "Les Plaisirs de la
campagne," of his novel *Le Rouge et le noir* (1831).

L. Grossman, *Etyudï o Pushkine* (Moscow, 1923), p.
53, has found the same pun in an edition (1799) of
Bievriana. The collection I have consulted, *Bievriana,
ou Jeux de mots de M. de Bièvre* (François Georges Maré-
chal, Marquis de Bièvre, 1747–89), ed. Albéric Deville

217

(Paris, 1800), does not contain it. In the various collections of this type many of the bons mots attributed to Bièvre concern events that happened after his death.

In a draft possibly referring to Onegin's Album (see its fourteenth entry in nn. to Seven : XXII alt.), the *Bievriana* anecdotes are correctly termed *ploshchadnïe* (common, ignoble, of the market place).

I

From Pushkin's famous piece *The Country* (*Derevnya*; see n. to One : LV : 2–4), a poem consisting of two parts (an idyllic description of Mihaylovskoe, which he visited that summer, and an eloquent denunciation of serfdom), the following terms are echoed in *EO*, Two: "nook," "retreat," "streams," "grainfields," "scattered cots," "roaming cattle," and so forth. In the second part of the poem the "friend of mankind" foreshadows the "friend of innocent delights," and harsh words are hurled at philandering squires. In later years, however, Pushkin was not above walloping a male slave or impregnating a female one (see n. to Four : XXXIX : 1–4).

1 / *Derévnya, gde skuchál Evgéniy*: "La campagne où s'ennuyait Eugène." The Russian *derevnya* and the French *campagne* both include the notions of "countryside" and "countryseat." The word *derevnya* has three senses, and the translator should know which not to choose: (1) *Derevnya*, in the general sense of countryside, rural life as opposed to the town; *v derevne*, "in the country," *à la campagne*. (2) *Derevnya* in the sense of a village or hamlet; synonyms: *selo, sel'tso*. (3) *Derevnya* in the sense of estate, place in the country, countryseat, manor, demesne, land; synonyms: *pomest'e, imen'e*; example: *Derevnya Pushkina v Pskovskoy Gubernii bïla men'she Oneginskoy derevni* (Pushkin's country place in

the province of Pskov was smaller than Onegin's place). *Derevnya* might include more than one village in the days when a village with all its souls belonged to the landowner. Instead of the correct *ma campagne* or *ma propriété*, a Russian squire might use in French the Russism *mon village*. (See also n. to One : LII : 12.)

2 / *nook* / *ugolók*: Lat. *angulus mundi* (Propertius, IV, IX, 65) and *terrarum angulus* (Horace, *Odes*, II, VI, 13–14); Fr. *petit coin de terre*.

Horace's small domain (*parva rura*, "small fields") nestled in a natural amphitheater among the Sabine hills, thirty miles from Rome. Pushkin draws upon his own rural recollections of 1819 for the end of One and the beginning of Two, but it should be noted that Onegin's manor is not in the province of Pskov, and not in the province of Tver, but in Arcadia.

Pushkin was to repeat the *petit coin* formula twelve years later in his admirable elegy in blank verse beginning . . . *Vnov' ya posetil* . . . , dedicated to Mihaylovskoe (Sept. 26, 1835):

> [Mihaylovskoe!] I've revisited [*Vnóv' ya posetíl*]
> That little corner of the earth where I
> Spent as an exile two unnoticed years.

The bracketed "Mihaylovskoe" is, I suggest, the word, omitted by Pushkin, that most logically fills the first five divisions of the opening line.

The question of the influence of Wordsworth on *Mihaylovskoe Revisited*, as we might entitle the piece, is far too complicated to be discussed here, but in connection with *angulus* I may quote the following from *The Excursion* (1814), I, "The Wanderer," ll. 470–73:

> . . . we die, my Friend,
> Nor we alone, but that which each man loved
> And prized in his peculiar nook of earth
> Dies with him, or is changed . . .

Commentary

3 / *drúg nevínnïh naslazhdéniy*: An appreciative dweller would have been, for instance, the Abbé (Pierre) de Villiers (1648–1728). See his stanzas *Eloges de la solitude* (at Torigny, near Sens):

I

Dans le fond d'un vallon rustique,
Entre deux champêtres coteaux,
De toute part entourés d'eaux,
S'élève un bâtiment antique:
Des prés s'étendent d'un côté,
De l'autre avec art est planté
Un bois percé de vingt allées . . .

II

C'est là l'aimable solitude
Où d'un tranquille et doux loisir
Je goûte l'innocent plaisir,
Libre de toute inquiétude . . .

VIII

Ici, pour l'Auteur de mon être
Tout sollicité mon amour . . .

And see J. B. Rousseau, *Cantata* III:

Heureux qui de vos doux plaisirs
Goûte la douceur toujours pure!

8 / variegated / *pestréli*: Or "showed their varied hues." Elsewhere I have used the epithet "motley" to translate this word, which in its intransitive verbal form has no English mate.

10 / one could glimpse hamlets / *Mel'káli syóla*: Another difficult intransitive. "Scattered villages were glimpsed." The suggestion of glancing light in *mel'kat'* has been lost in most applications, so that "villages glinted" would have too sparkling an effect. Modern editions ar-

bitrarily have a comma or semicolon after *syola* and no punctuation after *tam*, "there."

12–14 *Impénétrables voûtes, dômes touffus, larges ombrages, épaisse verdure, abris, retraite, dryades*, etc., are the amiable clichés of eighteenth-century French poesy (as used, for example, by Fontanes in his *La Forêt de Navarre*, 1780, in whose *dédales* the poet wandered "tel jadis à Windsor Pope s'est égaré"), here, in Pushkin, reduced to a neat miniature.

VARIANTS

1–4 Canceled draft (2369, f. 23ʳ):

> The country place where Eugene moped
> was an empty region.
> For irreproachable delights
> it seemed created.

6 Canceled draft (ibid.):

> protected by two gardens . . .

II

1 / castle / *zámok*: This is a commonly used Russian translation of the French *château*. Chizhevski's explication of Pushkin's use of the word ("perhaps under the influence of the Baltic provinces near by"—what influence? near what?) is a typical example of the comic naïvetés in his running, or rather stumbling, commentary to *EO* (see n. to Two : XXX : 3).

1–3 There is a surplus of predicative forms in the original. The colon does not really do away with the solecism: *postróen . . . próchen* instead of *postróen . . . próchno*, "built comfortably."

4 / ancientry / *starínï*: In a work where "novelty" (*novizna*)
and "fashion" (*moda*) are constantly referred to, their
juxtaposition with the old, the dismoded, the old times,
is inevitable. Moreover, *stariná* belongs to the rhymes
on *-ná* group, for which Pushkin had a special predilec-
tion.

4–7 The descriptive formulas in this stanza were common
to the European novel of the time, whether the locale
was Muscovy or Northamptonshire. A case in point is
the description of James Rushworth's house (in Jane
Austen's *Mansfield Park* [1814]—a novel little known
in Russia: see my n. to Three : Tatiana's Letter : 61),
which consisted of "a number of rooms, all lofty . . .
amply furnished in the taste of fifty years back, with
shining floors [and] rich damask. . . . [The] larger part
[of the pictures] were family portraits" (vol. I, ch. 9).

7 Pushkin had first written "of tsars the portraits"; but
dlya tsenzurï, "for reasons of censorship" (tsars were
not to be mentioned in so offhand a way), he altered the
line to *portrétï dédov*, "portraits of grandsires."
His MS footnote in both fair copies reads:

Dl[ya] tsenz[urï]: portrétï prédkov.
For censorship: portraits of forebears.

14 / modish / *módnïh*: Perhaps the epithet "modern"
would do better here.

VARIANTS

5 Canceled draft (2369, f. 24^{v}):
        The sumptuous chambers glitter.

7–8 Canceled draft (ibid.):
        but very little cared for this
        the miserly old uncle . . .

III

11 / *eau-de-pomme* / *yablochnaya voda*: "Apple water,"
an apple decoction, ciderkin. The French term, of which
the Russian is a literal translation, occurs constantly in
medical prescriptions of the eighteenth century. Other
readers understand this to mean *yablochnaya voditsa*
or *yablochnaya vodka*, "applejack," kept in corked or
otherwise closed jugs. Cf. the lingonberry decoction,
brusníchnaya vodá, mentioned in Three : III : 8 and
IV : 13.

12 / calendar / *kalendár*': I derive my conception of
kalendar' from a passage in the first chapter of Pushkin's
novel *The Captain's Daughter*, begun ten years later
(Jan. 23, 1833):

By the window Father was reading the Court Calendar
[*Pridvorniÿ Kalendar*'], annually received by him. This
book always had a strong influence upon him: never did
he reread it without a special sense of participation, and
its perusal always produced in him a remarkable agitation
of the bile. . . .

It should be noted, however, that the yearly *Bruce's
Calendar*, a kind of *Farmer's Almanack* (see my n. to
Two : XLI : var. 7), might have been in the present
case just as obvious a book, except that a landowner
might have been supposed to use a newer edition of it.

VARIANTS

In a canceled draft (2369, f. 25ʳ), the room is identified as
kabinét, a "study"; the "housekeeper" is replaced by a
"steward," the room is furnished with "large arm-
chairs, a table of oak" (l. 5), and when Onegin opens
the cupboards he finds "liqueurs, sugar," in one, "tea"
in the other (l. 11). In this draft III comes after V.

IV

6–7 / *corvée* . . . quitrent / *bárshchinï* . . . *Obrókom*: *Bar-shchina*: unpaid labor due from a serf to his owner; *obrok*: a kind of quitrent paid by the serf in commutation of his *corvée* or in consideration of being allowed to ply a trade elsewhere.

Civilized squires in the first half of the nineteenth century did what they could to lighten the lot of the slave—often against their own interests, which a Marxist would hardly believe. They were none too numerous, but humanity prevailed in the long run, and the serfs were officially liberated in 1861.

In their prime, various people—poets, potentates, and others—are anxious to improve the world, later to become serene conservatives or seedy despots. Onegin, under Pushkin's amused supervision, makes his little oblation to compassionate and venturous youth—and cynical neighbors smile (IV : 12), knowing this fad will not last.

Brodski makes a tremendous fuss over the matter, devoting four pages to macabre discussions of such questions as: "How come that *dvoryanin* [nobleman] Onegin was carrying out a non-*dvoryanski* program?" He answers it, too.

8 *Muzhík*, "peasant," in all editions 1825–37. In the draft (2369, f. 24^v), *i Nébo*, "Heaven," and *ráb*, "slave": "the slave blest Heaven." In canceled drafts, *naród*, "the people," and *muzhík*. In the fair copy, *i ráb sud'bú* (fate) *blagoslovíl* (blest).

11 / neighbor / *soséd*: Here and throughout the romance (e.g., Eight : XVIII : 4), *sosed*, "neighbor," tends to mean "country neighbor," "local landowner," "fellow squire," and in two cases simply "squire" (Five : XXXV : 6; Six : XXXV : 4). Its adaptive iambic form and the ease

with which it can be rhymed make of it one of those verse words that slip nicely into place, hence its rather monotonous recurrence.

5 The draft (2369, f. 24ᵛ) reads:

> Of freedom ⟨eremitic sower⟩
> *Svobódï* ⟨*séyatel' pustínnïy*⟩,

which Pushkin used for a short poem written soon afterward (Odessa, Nov., 1823):

> Of freedom eremitic sower,
> early I went, before the star.
> With a hand pure and guiltless
> into the enslaved furrows
> I cast the vivifying seed;
> but all I did was lose my time,
> well-meaning thoughts and labors.
>
> Graze, placid peoples!
> What are to herds the gifts of liberty?
> They have to be slaughtered or shorn.
> Their heirdom is from race to race
> a yoke with jinglers and the whip.

V

6 / one heard / *Zaslíshat*: The meaning of the transitive verb *zaslïshat'* (used in the text in the third person plural) is, in terms of hearing, equivalent to what "to descry" or "to espy" means in terms of seeing.

6 / shandrydans / *drógi*: The word *drogi* used here may mean either "antiquated carriages" in a general sense or, as I think it does here, a specific homemade vehicle of simple, sturdy construction, without springs, which a Russian squire would employ much as an English squire might his shooting brake or dogcart.

7 / by such behavior / *Postúpkom . . . takím*: Basically, *postupok* is almost synonymous with *deystvie*, which is "act" or "action"; but contextually (i.e., given the reiteration of the action) it is closer to *povedenie*, which is "behavior" or "conduct."

10 / Freemason / *farmazón*: Eighteenth-century liberal thought had sought refuge in masonic organizations. A provincial squire would regard a Freemason as a revolutionary. Masonic lodges were forbidden in Russia in the spring of 1822 (see also, in my introd., "The Genesis of *EO*," vol. 1, pp. 61–62).

A canceled draft (2369, f. 24^r) reads "a liberal," *liberál*, instead of *farmazón*; it is restored in the first fair copy of the canto.

The term *farmazón* (a vulgarism of the time for *frankmasón* or *masón*) is derived from the French *francmaçon* and was used in the sense of "arrogant freethinker."

10–11 / *p'yót odnó stakánom krásnoe vinó*: The implication is presumably that Onegin prefers a beaker of foreign wine to a jigger of national, right-thinking vodka. However, it is possible to understand the word *odno* as meaning not "only" but "straight"

> he's a Freemason, drinks red wine
> unwatered in tumblerfuls.

But in those days the one to dilute his drink would have been the jaded beau from St. Petersburg rather than the provincial tippler. It would seem that Onegin has graduated, like Pushkin, from champagne to Bordeaux (see Four : XLVI).

In the eighteenth and early nineteenth centuries, ripe gentlemen watered their wine. Anthologically, Pushkin advocated it in stylized little pieces of 1833 and 1835 (*Yúnosha skrómno pirúy*, "Youth, feast modestly,"

Chtó zhe súho v cháshe dnó, "Why is the bottom dry in the cup"); and, biographically, added seltzer to his champagne, as Byron did to his hock. According to a remark of Wellington's (1821) reported by Samuel Rogers in his *Recollections* (1856), Louis XVIII mixed water with his champagne.

14 Provincial fogies deem Onegin a freak; actually, his brand of eccentricity (Byronic moodiness, the metaphysical cult of Napoleon, French clichés, English clothes, an attitude of "revolt"—derived from "*Volt*-aire" rather than from "*Revol*ution"—and so forth) is itself characteristic of a certain set, to the conventions of which he conforms as closely as the Philistines he despises do to those of their own, larger, group. Of late, Soviet idealists have considerably idealized Onegin's ideology. And this is the only reason why, in this note, I have gone out of my way to discuss him as if he were a "real" person.

One wonders if at the back of Pushkin's prismatic mind there did not lurk the remarkable story of the Decembrist Ivan Yakushkin's attempts in 1819 to improve the condition of his peasants on his estate (province of Smolensk). (Yakushkin had perhaps told it to Pushkin in 1821.) Yakushkin says in his memoirs (1853–55, in *Izbrannïe . . . proizvedeniya dekabristov*, ed. I. Shchipanov, Leningrad, 1951, I, 115–17) that his neighbors deemed him "an eccentric" (*chudak*), which is the term applied to Onegin. (See also n. to Ten : XVI.)

VI

5 / Lenski: The third main male character in the novel. In the present stanzas eighteen-year-old Lenski strikes up a closer friendship with twenty-five-year-old Onegin than twenty-year-old Pushkin had in Chapter One; but

on the other hand, the naïve enthusiast, who more than replaces Pushkin in Onegin's affection, differs more from Onegin than Pushkin, who is at least as experienced and disillusioned as he. Both Lenski and Pushkin know more about poetry than Onegin does; but Pushkin was at eighteen (in 1817) an incomparably better poet than Lenski is now (in "1820"), despite their sharing of the mŏdish influence of the French elegy, Frenchified "Ossian," and Zhukovski's and Mme de Staël's versions of German poets. Onegin will develop a protective attitude toward Lenski, with alternate fits of condescension and raillery; Onegin and Pushkin meet on equal terms despite the difference in age; and if Onegin is Pushkin's master in Byronic gloom, Pushkin can teach him a number of additional things about women, not found in Ovid.

The name Lenski (derived from that of a river in eastern Siberia) had been used before. In the first edition (April, 1779) of the epic *Rossiada*, by Mihail Heraskov (1733–1807), a monstrously boring accumulation of pseudoclassical platitudes (but considered immortal by his coevals), one of Tsar Ivan's counselors is a villain called Lenski. In the one-act comedy *Feigned Infidelity* (*Pritvornaya nevernost'*), adapted from Nicolas Thomas Barthe's *Les Fausses infidélités* (1768) by Griboedov and Andrey Zhandr or Gendre (1789–1873), first performed Feb. 11, 1818, there lurks a Lenski among the Russian names that replace the French (this Lenski, a merry young man, and a friend of his make fun of an old fop by having their sweethearts feign love for him).

6 / Göttingenian: Göttingen University (in the town of that name, province of Hannover, NW Germany) is pleasingly alluded to in a letter from the poet Batyushkov to Aleksandr Turgenev (a Göttingen graduate), Sept. 10, 1818, from Moscow to St. Petersburg:

What is Sverchok* doing? Has he finished his long poem
[*Ruslan and Lyudmila*]? It would not be bad to lock him
up at Göttingen and for some three years feed him milk
soup and logic. . . . However great his talent, he will
squander it if— But let our muses and our oraisons pre-
serve him.

Aleksandr Turgenev (1784–1845) had been instru-
mental in enrolling Pushkin in the Lyceum in 1811, and
it was he who accompanied Pushkin's coffin from Peters-
burg to Svyatïe Gorï (province of Pskov) in February,
1837.

It is amusing to note that the fictional Vladimir Lenski
is the second Göttingen student to be Onegin's friend:
the first was Kaverin (One : XVI : 6; see n.), who, in
terms of historical reality, finished his studies there at
seventeen, Lenski's age.

Tïnyanov (see n. to Two : VIII : 9–14, vars.) has seen
in the Lenski of Two a portrait of Küchelbecker, who,
in 1820, had visited Germany. I object to the proto-
typical quest as blurring the authentic, always atypical
methods of genius.

The adverb *pryámo* (really, directly, genuinely,
frankly) qualifying *gettingénskoy* is a weak afterthought.
Both separate editions of Two (1826, 1830) have *dushóy*
(in soul) *filíster gettingénskiy* instead of the final *s
dushóyu* (with soul) *pryámo gettingénskoy*. In review-
ing Two, Bulgarin pointed out in his *Northern Bee*,
CXXXII (1826), that *Philister* was student cant for
"townsman," an outsider as opposed to a collegian,
whereas Pushkin (who, incidentally, makes the same
mistake in a letter of May 7, 1826, to Aleksey Vulf, a
Dorpat student) had in mind the word *Bursch*, or
Schwärmer, applied to students. Had Pushkin been pre-

---

*"Cricket"—the nickname of dissolute nineteen-year-old
Pushkin as member of the literary goose-dinner club Arzamas,
founded in 1815.

pared to take the advice of that critic, he might have simply altered the line to *Dushóyu shvérmer gettingén-skiy*: but then Bulgarin's exultation would have been unbearable. It is a pity our poet did not, at least, revert to his draft (2369, f. 25ᵛ) and first fair copy: . . . *shkól'-nik* (scholar, schoolboy) *gettingénskoy*. (*Gettingenskoy* is the older form of the nominative masculine ending and happens to coincide with the instrumental feminine ending.)

7 / full / *pólnom*: The adjective *pólnïy*, "full," "complete," is often used by poets to fill the middle of the line (as here) or to close it. The feminine predicative form, *polná*, is an easy rhyme, and the masculine predicative form is the only rhyme to *voln* ("of the waves") and *chyoln* ("skiff"). *Polnaya luna* is the full-orbed moon.

8–9 / Kant's votary . . . misty Germany: Apart from translations and adaptations from German writers by Zhukovski and others, it was Mme de Staël's *De l'Allemagne* (a very mediocre work, which she completed in collaboration with the well-meaning but *talentlos* August Wilhelm Schlegel in 1810) that was almost entirely responsible for Pushkin's knowledge of German literature (see One : VI : var. 9–10). Such passages therein (vol. X of the complete edition of her works, 1820–21) as "Les Allemands . . . se plaisent dans les ténèbres" (pt. II, ch. 1), "[ils] peignent les sentimens comme les idées, à travers des nuages" (pt. II, ch. 2), "[et ne font] que rêver la gloire et la liberté" (ibid.) (cf. Two : VI : 11, *vol'nol-yubívïe mechtí*, "liberty-loving dreams"), as well as the *sentiments exaltés* (cf. Two : IX : 12, *vozvíshennïe chúv-stva*) that she attributes to Wieland's poetry (pt. II, ch. 4) or the *enthousiasme vague* of her Klopstock (pt. II, ch. 5), are the stuff of which Lenski's mentality is formed by his maker. As will be seen further, however, Lenski's own poetry and vocabulary owe French minor poetry at least as much as they do French or Russian versions of Schiller.

What Lenski derived from Kant may be found in the same *De l'Allemagne* (pt. III, ch. 6: *Œuvres*, vol. XI): "[Kant] assigne [au sentiment] le premier rang de la nature humaine . . . le sentiment du juste et de l'injuste est, selon lui, la loi primitive du cœur, comme l'espace et le temps celle de l'intelligence." And further: ". . . [De l']application du sentiment de l'infini aux beaux-arts, doit naître l'idéal, c'est-à-dire le beau, considéré . . . comme l'image réalisée de ce que notre âme se représente." The noun "ideal" will be the last word of the last poem upon which poor Lenski will fall asleep for the last time before his duel in Chapter Six. Curiously enough, it is also the main component in the last stanza of the last canto of *EO*.

11 / *vol'nolyubívïe*: Pushkin, who had used this artificial epithet before (*To Chaadaev*, 1821, l. 82), observed in a letter to Nikolay Grech (Sept. 21, 1821, Kishinev) that it rendered well the French *libéral*. The rhyme *plodí—mechtï* ("fruits"–"dreams") is poor.

13 / an always enthusiastic speech / *vostorzhennaya*: "Transported" would seem closer, but is a deadish epithet. Cf. Rousseau, *Julie*, Seconde Préface: ". . . une diction toujours dans les nues." Compare Three : XI : 10.

14 It was in those days no mark of effeminacy in a stripling to wear his hair down upon his shoulders.

VARIANTS

2–3 Canceled draft (2369, f. 25ᵛ):

> another squire ⟨arrived⟩—
> Vladímir Hólmskoy . . .

Commentary

It seems clear that Pushkin altered this surname to *Lénskoy* (spelling it subsequently *Lenskiy*, "Lenski") to have it rhyme with the adjectival *gettingénskoy* (thus l. 6 ends in the draft).

6–8 Canceled drafts (2369, f. 25ᵛ) read:

> 6 a lock-headed schoolboy from Göttingen [*shkól'nik gettingénskoy*] . . .
> 6 in soul a reverist [*mechtátel'*] from Göttingen . . .

8–12 Draft 2369, f. 25ᵛ:

> vociferous [*krikún*], a rebel [*myatézhnik*], and a poet, he from free Germany
> ⟨brought⟩ the fruits of learning:
> fame-loving dreams,
> a spirit impetuous, really noble.

In this draft Pushkin toyed with "slightly liberal dreams" (*nemnógo vól'nïe mechtí*) and "imprudent dreams."

In the first fair copy *myatézhnik* is prudently changed to *krasávets*, "a handsome chap."

VII

Here Pushkin commences his special treatment of the Lenski theme. It consists in describing the nature of that young and mediocre poet in the idiom Lenski himself uses in his elegies (a sample is given in Six), an idiom now blurred by the drift of unfocused words, now naïvely stilted in the pseudoclassical manner of minor French songsters. Even the closest translation is prone to touch up with some applied sense the ambiguous *flou* of Pushkin's remarkable impersonation.

This stanza (see "The Publication of *EO*", vol. 1, p. 74) was the first stanza of *EO* ever to be published by Pushkin (in Delvig's *Northern Flowers* for 1825, end of December, 1824). I suspect that the reason our poet chose these passages (from VII–X) for preliminary publication is that he did not mind drawing his friends' attention (in VIII) to the fact that none had done much to break the vessel of *his* slanderers (see my n. to Four : XIX : 5).

VARIANTS

4 A canceled draft (2369, f. 25ᵛ) reads:

> and with the welcome of Parnassian maids.

This proves that Lenski was true to his betrothed and dallied only with the Muses.

9–14 The first fair copy reads:

> He knew both work and inspiration
> and the refreshment of repose,
> and toward *something* a young life's
> indescribable urge;
> of stormy passions the wild feast,
> and tears, and the heart's peace.

VIII

5–6 / friends . . . fetters: There is an echo here of the story of Damon and Pythias (the latter obtaining three days to arrange his affairs before his execution; the former pledging his life for his friend's return) as told by Schiller in his ballad *Die Bürgschaft* (1799), of which there were several French versions.

VARIANTS

9–14 The expunged lines (10–14) are supplied in two variants.

First fair copy (PB 9):

> that there were some chosen by fate,
> whose life—heaven's best gift—
> and heat of thoughts incorruptible,
> and genius of power over minds,
> were dedicated to the good of mankind
> and valorously equaled fame.

Second fair copy (from the Turgenev brothers' archives):

> that there were some chosen by fate,
> the holy friends of men,
> that their immortal family
> with overwhelming rays
> someday would illumine us
> and with felicity endow the world.

The censor may have perceived in 10–14 of either fair copy a political implication, hence the deletion. Actually, as Tïnyanov (1934) has shown, the passage is a subtle allusion to a very Schillerian poem by Küchelbecker (*The Poets*, 1820) on the mythical origin of poets. Man initially was immortal and happy, but the fleeting phantoms of carnal pleasure seduced him. In result "he suffers in his delights and grieves when surfeited." So the gods delegate to our world certain beings composed of celestial essence whom in their incarnation we call poets. The idiom of the Küchelbecker poem with its terms "chosen ones," "immortal bliss," "race of mortals," and so forth is obviously imitated by Pushkin.

IX

1 / Indignation, compassion / *Negodován'e, sozhalén'e*: My English hardly scans, but I did not care to transpose the order of the words.

1–2 Keats, whom Pushkin did not know, begins a sonnet (*Addressed to Haydon*, composed 1816) with a strikingly similar intonation:

> Highmindedness, a jealousy for good . . .

Such coincidences baffle and thwart similarity chasers, source hunters, relentless pursuers of parallel passages.

2 Perhaps I should have translated *blago* as "what is right" (instead of "Good," which would be *dobro*), to have it correspond to the philosophic *blago* in Six : XXI : 10, to which see notes.

5–6 / on earth . . . Goethe / *na svéte* . . . *Géte*: This dreadful rhyme (with the German poet's name, in a slovenly Russian pronunciation, made to sound almost like "gaiety") was, oddly enough, repeated in 1827 by Zhukovski, in a poem inscribed to Goethe, of which the fourth of six quatrains reads:

> In a remote boreal world [*svéte*],
> I lived because I loved your muse;
> and thus for me my genius Goethe [*Géte*]
> was what gave life to life itself.

Pushkin had even less German than he had English, and only very vaguely knew German literature. He was immune to its influence and hostile to its trends. The little he had read of it was either in French versions (which quickened Schiller but asphyxiated Goethe) or in Russian adaptations: Zhukovski's treatment of Schiller's "Thecla" theme, for instance, is, in art and harmony, far superior to its model; but gentle Zhukovski made (in 1818, *Lesnoy tsar'*) a miserable hash of Goethe's hallucinatory *Erlkönig* (as Lermontov was to do, in 1840, *Gornïe vershinï*, of the marvelous *Über allen Gipfeln*). On the other hand, there are readers who prefer Pushkin's *Scene from Faust* (1825) to the whole of Goethe's

Faust, in which they distinguish a queer strain of triviality impairing the pounding of its profundities.

A somewhat Lenskian figure, the minor poet Dmitri Venevitinov (he committed suicide in 1827, at the age of twenty-one), had, I think, more talent than Lenski, but the same naïve urge to seek spiritual guides and masters. With other young men, he ardently flocked to the altars of German "romantic philosophy" (whose fumes were to mingle so paradoxically with those of Slavophilism, one of the most tedious creeds ever thought of), adoring Schelling and Kant, as the young men of the next generation were to adore Hegel, sinking thence to Feuerbach.

Although still ready to talk about "Schiller, glory, and love" with his mistier young friends (see in his 1825 poem commemorating the Lyceum anniversary, Oct. 19, the stanza addressed to Küchelbecker), and although professing a boundless admiration for Goethe, whom he placed above Voltaire and Byron, next to Shakespeare (Pierre Letourneur's Shakespeare, of course), Pushkin was never very specific on the subject of *le Cygne de Weimar*. In a faintly ridiculous poem (*To Pushkin*, 1826) Venevitinov vainly pleaded with him to address an ode to Goethe: "And believe me, in the seclusion of gloomy old age, he may hear your voice, and perhaps, charmed by it, in a last glow of inspiration, the swan will respond . . . and, soaring heavenward with that last song, may name you, O Pushkin."

9–10 / *I múz vozvíshennïh iskússtva* | . . . *ón ne postídíl*: I am not quite sure that there is not a violent inversion here, making the meaning: "and he did not disgrace the art of the exalted Muses" (*i on ne postídil iskusstva vozvïshennïh muz*).

13–14 It would seem that here, when conceiving the image

of Lenski, Pushkin had a higher opinion of him than in
Six : XXI–XXIII, where Lenski's verses, as quoted and
described, hardly can be called "the surgings [*porívï*,
Fr. *les élans*] of a virgin fancy," but are deliberately
made by Pushkin to conform to Russian derivations from
French rhymed platitudes of the times.

IXa, b, c, d

An interesting variant sequence of four stanzas meant to
follow IX is canceled in the first fair copy (a, b, c) and
represented (d) in a draft (2369, f. 31^v):

IXa

He did not sing corrupt amusement,
did not sing scornful Circes;
he shrank from outraging morality
4 with his elected lyre.
A votary of true felicity,
the snares of volupty he did not glorify,
breathing disgraceful mollitude,
8 as one whose avid soul,
the victim of pernicious errors,
the pitiful victim of passions,
in its misery pursues
12 the pictures of past pleasures
and to the world in fateful songs
reveals them in his folly.

a: 5–7 Note the frightful jumble of definitional clauses:
"A votary . . . he," etc., "did not glorify," etc., while in
the act of "breathing," etc.

a: 8–10; XI : 12–14; XIVa : 8–14; and XVIIb : 9–12: Alongside
the draft of these lines (2369, ff. 26^v, 27^v, 28^r, 30^v), in
the left-hand margins, Pushkin made sketches of Maria
Raevski's profile: short nose, heavyish jaw, and curly
strands of dark hair escaping from under an elaborate

bonnet. The time is late October or early November, 1823; the place, Odessa. She is not quite seventeen. It is much too cold to race the surf. Her profile is beside that of beautiful Amalia Riznich in the draft of xviib : 9–12, f. 30ᵛ. (Reproductions of these four autographs have been published by Efros in his useful, albeit sadly unscholarly, *Risunki poeta*, pp. 145, 149, 153, 157.)

ixb

Bards of blind pleasure,
in vain your wanton days'
impressions you transmit
4 to us in vivid elegies;
in vain the maiden furtively,
harking to sounds of a sweet lyre,
directs at you her tender gaze,
8 not daring to begin a conversation;
in vain does giddy youth,
over the brimming bowl, in garlands,
recall at banquets
12 of verses the effeminate sweetness
—or in the ear of modest maids
whisper them, overcoming shyness;

ixc

unfortunates, judge for yourselves
what trade is yours;
by means of empty sounds, of words,
4 you sow debauchery's evil.
Before the tribunal of Pallas
you get no crown, you get no prize,
but dearer is to you, I know myself,
8 a tear blent halfwise with a smile.
For feminine fame you were born,
worthless to you is rumor's judgment,
I pity you . . . and you are dear to me.
12 For you proud Lenski was no mate:
his verse a mother would, of course,
tell her daughter to read.

c: 9–10 / *Vï rozhdení dlya slávï zhénskoy*, | *Dlya vás nichtózhen súd molví*: The idea somewhat obscurely expressed here is the juxtaposition of popularity and a good name: "Yours is the fame that depends on a feminine audience; otherwise, reputation means nothing to you."

c: 13–14 / *Egó stihí konéchno mát'* | *Veléla b dócheri chitát'*: In the draft of this stanza (2369, f. 27ʳ) Pushkin appended a footnote to the last two lines:

"[La mère] en prescrira la lecture à sa fille." Piron. This verse has become a proverb. It should be noted that apart from his *Métrom[anie]*, Piron is good only in such poems as are impossible even to be hinted at without offending propriety.

In *La Métromanie*, by Alexis Piron (1689–1773), a comedy first performed in 1733, Damis, a young poet enthusiastically dedicated to his art, explains to an unconvinced uncle that he will conquer Paris merely by his writings (act III, sc. 7):

Je veux que la vertu plus que l'esprit y brille.
La mère en prescrira la lecture à sa fille;
Et j'ai, grâce à vos soins, le cœur fait de façon,
À monter aisément ma lyre sur ce ton.

Dmitriev has a couplet similar to IXC : 13–14 among his *Legends to Portraits*, namely the lines assigned (c. 1800) to Mihail Muravyov, tutor of the Grand Dukes Constantine and Nicholas:

He earns the highest tribute: to her daughter
The mother says that read his works she ought to.

Pushkin's 13–14 echo a little grudge that he bore against those who three years earlier had criticized *Ruslan and Lyudmila* from the point of view of its morals: the *konechno*, "certainly," in regard to Lenski's absolutely chaste poesy implies a stress on *his* verse, which in *his* case maidens might read in contrast to the author's *not* presentable works.

Dmitriev, in a letter to Vyazemski, soon after *Ruslan and Lyudmila* had appeared, remarked (in French) that mothers would surely forbid daughters to read it. And eight years later, at the end of a witty preface (dated Feb. 12, 1828) to the second edition of *Ruslan*, Pushkin alluded to Dmitriev's remark thus: "A first-rate national writer crowned with bays greeted this effort of a young poet with the following verse: Mother tells daughter to ignore [Russ. idiom: "to spit on"] this tale."

The Piron quotation had been done to death by 1824, when Yazïkov, with his usual display of bad taste, used that hackneyed line as a motto for his collection of poems.

In his *Curiosités littéraires* (Paris, 1845), Ludovic Lalanne says (p. 279):

Nous ne pouvons dire l'espèce d'agacement que nous éprouvons à la lecture . . . du vers suivant, que l'on a modifié si souvent en le prenant pour épigraphe, qu'il est assez difficile de retrouver sa forme primitive:

La mère	⎫		permettra	⎫			sa fille
L'époux	⎬	en ⎰	défendra	⎬	la lecture à ⎰		sa femme
Le père	⎭		prescrira	⎭			son fils.

IXd

But the good youth who is prepared
a high deed to accomplish,
in austere pride will not
4 verses unclean declaim;
nor will the just man, worn away,
to chains condemned unjustly,
on his last night, in prison,
8 before a lamp that dozes in the dark,
let fall in eremitic stillness
his eyes upon your scroll,
and your licentious line upon the wall
12 will not write with his guiltless hand

in mute and sorrowful greeting
meant for a prisoner ⟨of future years⟩.

Tomashevski (Acad 1937, p. 282) finds another place for ixd, namely, immediately before XVIII. I use his latest recension (*Works* 1957, p. 517).

d: 9, 12 The rhyme *pustínnoy* (eremitic) and *bezvínnoy* (guiltless) echoes that in the beginning of the poem quoted in connection with Two : IV : var. 5.

X

2 / clear / *yasná*: The Russian word has connotations of limpidity, purity, and serenity that its English counterpart does not reveal quite so lucidly (i.e., in regard to the "thoughts" and the "sleep" in the comparisons). On the other hand, we learn later that Lenski's crowning achievement, the last elegy he composed, was even more obscure than the "dim remoteness" mentioned here. The "clarity" obviously refers to his nature rather than to his art.

8–9 / *I néchto, i tumánnu dál'*: The line would go in French as "Je ne sais quoi de vague, et le lointain brumeux."

Cf. Chateaubriand's note on "le vague de ses passions," "the haze of his emotions," which I quote in my n. to One : XXXVIII : 3–4. See also my nn. to Four : XXXII.

An additional touch of vagueness is beautifully given by using the stylized and archaic contraction *tumánnu* instead of *tumánnuyu*, all this modulated in the sighing key of the second-foot scud (see App. II, "Notes on Prosody"). A wonderful line in a wonderful stanza.

8 *Dal'*—"distance," "remoteness," "the faraway," Fr. *le lointain*; a far range, reach, or stretch; a long view, a vista; the mystery of distant space—a great favorite with Russian romanticists, has poetical connotations that are absent in English and rhymes well with associative words such as *zhal'* ("pity"), *pechal'* ("sadness"), and *hrustal'* ("crystal"). The derivative *otdalenie* is Fr. *l'éloignement*, which has no exact equivalent in English; and there is also *udalyat'sya*, Fr. *s'éloigner*, "move away," which Lenski uses in his elegy, Six : XXI : 3.

11 / bosom of the stillness / *lóno tishiní*: The French *sein*, a word that in the trite parlance of eighteenth-century French poesy and prose is used for "womb" (and technically *lono* is "womb") in such phrases as "l'enfant que je porte dans mon sein." Even busy bees were said by poets to carry honey in their *sein*.

The "lap," "womb," or "bosom of the stillness," *lóno tishiní*, is a common Gallicism: *le sein du repos*. Its English equivalent would be James Beattie's "When in the lap of Peace reclin'd . . ." (*Retirement*, 1758, l. 35). A perfect French model is Charles Pierre Colardeau (1732–76), *Vers pour mettre au bas d'une statue*:

> . . . cette jeune beauté . . .
> Rêveuse au sein de la tranquillité . . .

or Mme Bourdic-Viot, *Epître à la campagne* (*Almanach des Muses* for 1801, p. 195):

> Au sein de la tranquillité,
> Loin du tumulte de la ville . . .

Numerous other French examples might be listed.

This *lóno tishiní* haunted the verses of Pushkin's contemporaries long after Lenski's death. Yazïkov (whose elegies are referred to in the same breath as Lenski's in Four : XXXI) uses it in his poem *Trigorskoe* (Mme Osipov's countryseat; see *Onegin's Journey*, last stanzas), and it is found in Aleksandr Polezhaev's *A Ballad* (*Romans*, 1831). Curiously enough, Pushkin himself uses it in Seven : II : 8, *na lóne sél'skoy* [rural] *tishiní*, in a romantic evocation of spring's languors. It will be noted, however, that in Two : X : 11 the phrase is in the accusative; an odd estuary for Lenski's tears.

As with most Gallicisms in *EO*, the otherwise inexact and very mediocre, but in regard to clichés idiomatic, Dupont translates the locution correctly, whereas the ambitious, hard-working, and on the whole much more accurate Turgenev-Viardot team produces the artificial "sur le sein de la placidité."

13–14 As young Pushkin had sung, at seventeen, in his senior year at the Lyceum (*Enjoyment*, 1816, ll. 1–2):

> The bloom of life, hardly expanded,
> must fade in dull captivity.

Here is the beginning of the "bloom-doom" theme that will go through Four : XXVII (Lenski's contributions to Olga's album: a dove, a tombstone), will find complete expression in Lenski's last elegy ("Whither, ah! whither are ye fled, my springtime's golden days," Six : XXI–XXII; see nn.), will link up with Pushkin's 1816 elegy Lenski's death in Six : XXXI : 12–13 ("The storm has blown; the beauteous bloom has withered"), and will culminate in the synthesis of Six : XLIV : 7–8, where the wreath of the author's youth has "withered."

Note that Two : X : 14 nicely matches One : XXIII : 14.

VARIANTS

8–9 The draft (2369, f. 27ʳ) and first fair copy read:

> and the romantic faraway,
> and dying roses.

The "dying," *umiráyushchie*, was altered to "fading," *uvyadáyushchie*, in the 1825 publication, but this clashed with another line in the stanza.

13–14 The draft (2369, f. 27ʳ) has, according to Tomashev-
ski, *Works* 1949:

> and the groves' shade where he would meet
> his everlasting true Ideal.

XI

1 / wilderness / *pustínya*: In monastic language, the re-
treat of an eremite. It might also be translated "desert"
or "desart," which in the sixteenth century often meant
a wild forest or any wild desolate place. Cf. French *désert*
in such locutions as *mes déserts*, *beau désert*, etc.

See, for instance, Chaulieu, who begins his *Des
Louanges de la vie champêtre* with "Désert, aimable
solitude." (See One : LVI : 2.)

See also Eight : XLIV : 1.

In the preceding stanza (X : 5) the word *pustïni*,
"deserts," is employed in the sense of vast empty spaces.
In this stanza, *pustïnya* is practically synonymous with
glush' or *zaholust'e*, meaning a remote, sparsely popu-
lated place, a provincial hole, backwoods, forlorn place,
neck of the woods, backwater. (See n. to One : VIII : 14.)

3 / *Gospód sosédstvennïh seléniy*: This merely means "of
the local landowners," except that there is a slight
Gallic flavor of *ces messieurs* in *gospod* (gen. pl. of
gospodin) as used with ironic ceremony here.

It is never easy to decide between "village" and
"manor" whenever *selenie* (habitation, rural commu-
nity, homestall) is used. The French *manoir* meant both
"village" and "domain." The "masters of villages"
make a worse combination than the clumsy *gospoda
seleniy*.

7 / liquor: The unqualified singular here means hard
liquor, rye, gin, vodka; and, moreover, the making of

vino is implied; hence "distilleries." The plural (*vina*) always means "wines."

VARIANTS

1–2 A false start canceled in the draft (2369, f. 27ᵛ) reads:

> More often, though, with angry satire
> his numbers would be animated . . .

This variant is interesting in the light of Six : XXXVIII. Pushkin wavered between making Lenski a feeble elegiac minstrel and having him be a violent political poet.

14 / much / *Gorázdo*: "Still" (*eshchyó*) in the first edition of the chapter.

XII

2 / a suitor / *zheníh*: The whole passage rings false since we have been led to presume that Lenski avoided his fellow squires. Moreover (in the light of XXI), everybody surely knew that Lenski was in love with Olga. The transition to Onegin (what does this "But" mean?) in the beginning of XIII is very lame. It would seem that at this point Pushkin had not yet evolved the plan of having an Olga Larin exist.

5 / half-Russian / *polurússkogo* [acc.]: A jocular allusion to Lenski's having been educated abroad.

6 / drops in / *Vzoydyót*: An old-fashioned provincialism for *zaydyot*.

11 / "Dunya, mark!": Transposed into English, this diminutive of Avdotia (Eudocia) corresponds to Annie, Dotty, or Edie. The peremptory "mark!"—i.e., "take notice of this eligible bachelor!"—is only a peg below the nudge Tatiana will be given in Seven : LIV.

Commentary

12 / the guitar (that, too) is brought / *prinósyat i gitáru*:
I can find no better way of expressing the positional value
of this *i*.

14. As Pushkin's note reads: "From the first part of *Dnieper
Rusalka*" (a *rusalka* is a female water sprite, a water
nymph, a hydriad, a riparian mermaid, and, in the strict
sense, differs from the maritime mermaid in having
legs).

The tune is that of Hulda's aria from the once popular
comic opera ("Ein romantisches komisches Volksmär-
chen mit Gesang nach einer Sage der Vorzeit," in three
acts, first performed in Vienna, Jan. 11, 1798), *Das
Donauweibchen*, by Ferdinand Kauer (1751–1831)—
whom, in retaliation, the nixie caused to lose most of his
manuscripts in the Danube flood of 1830.

For some unknown reason, the author of an otherwise
excellent paper on the source of an unfinished drama by
Pushkin* does not give the composer's name at all, con-
fuses "opera" with "play," and calls the author of its
book "Gensler" (here, in reverse transliteration) instead
of Karl Friedrich Hensler (1759–1825)—and it is funny
to follow uninformed but wary compiler Brodski's ma-
neuvers (1950), p. 139, to circumnavigate the issue
without revealing his ignorance.

The complete couplet, sung by Lesta, Hulda's counter-
part, in the Krasnopolski adaptation of the first part of
the opera under the title *Dneprovskaya Rusalka* (first
performed Oct. 26, 1803, in St. Petersburg; published
1804), the sheet music of which was everywhere at
home—on the pianoforte of a provincial miss, in the
attic of an amorous clerk, and on the window sill of a

_____

*Ivan Zhdanov, "Rusalka Pushkina i Das Donauweibchen
Genslera," in *Pamyati Pushkina* (Zapiski istoriko-filologiches-
kogo fakul'teta imperatorskogo S.-Peterburgskogo universiteta
LVII; St. Petersburg, 1900), pp. 139–78.

whorehouse (as mentioned in Vasiliy Pushkin's poem *Opasnïy sosed* [1811], l. 101)—runs: "Come to me in my golden castle, come, O my prince, my dear"; in Russian: *Pridí v chertóg ko mné zlatóy, pridí, o knyáz' tï móy dragóy*; or in the no less trashy German original: "In meinem Schlosse ist's gar fein, komm, Ritter, kehre bei mir ein" (act I, sc. 4).

Curiously enough, the *Dneprovskaya Rusalka* not only served Pushkin as a working base for his unfinished drama, labeled by later editors *Rusalka*, "The Hydriad" (he worked at it at various times between 1826 and 1831), but also affected some details in Tatiana's dream in *EO* (see n. to Five : XVII : 5).

I note that Pushkin's library contained a copy of *Rusalka*, "Opera komicheskaya v tryoh deystviyah," in three parts, adapted from the German by Nikolay Krasnopolski, with music by Kauer, Cavos, and Davïdov (St. Petersburg, 1804).

Pushkin had a strange leaning toward borrowing from ludicrous sources. Tomashevski* shows that from Rossini's *Gazza ladra*, act I, sc. 8, Pushkin lifted a situation for the frontier scene in *Boris Godunov*, in which the fugitive deliberately misreads aloud his own description in a sheriff's warrant.

I find, from Loewenberg's *Annals of Opera*, various French encyclopedias, and other sources, that Gioacchino Antonio Rossini's opera *La Gazza ladra* (libretto by G. Gherardini, founded on *La Pie voleuse*, 1815, a melodrama by J. M. T. Baudouin d'Aubigny, or Daubigny, and L. C. Caigniez) was first performed May 31, 1817, at La Scala, Milan, had its first Russian performance in St. Petersburg, Feb. 7, 1821, N.S. (in a translation by I. Svichinski), and was given in Odessa (during Pushkin's stay there) in 1823–24, by an Italian company.

---

*"Pushkin i ital'yanskaya opera," *P. i ego sovr.*, VIII, 31–32 (1927), 50.

Commentary

14 Canceled draft (2369, f. 27^v):
  "I'm Cupid, if you want to know."

XIII

1–2 Perhaps we should understand that while courting
  Olga metaphysically, as a heavenly ideal of love, Lenski
  thinks he is not thinking of mundane marriage. But the
  plans his parents and Dmitri Larin had laid for him
  have not died with them as automatically as Lenski
  seems to think here and in XXXVII. By the end of the
  summer he will be formally engaged.

4 / close / *pokoróche*: This curious Russian form, giving a
  conditional slant to the comparative *koroche* of *korotkiy*
  (adj. "short," "close"), implies here the idea of "as close
  as circumstances might permit."

5 / They got together / *Oní soshlís'*: This is ambiguous:
  soytis' may mean either "to meet" or "to become closely
  united." (The rest of the stanza is, then, either a de-
  velopment or a recapitulation.)

5–7 Actually, Lenski's temperament, that philosophic mel-
  ancholy which Margery Bailey, in reference to Thom-
  son's *Seasons* (see the Introduction, p. 78, to her edition
  [1928] of Boswell's *The Hypochondriack*), nicely de-
  fines as "a sort of gusty, expansive sympathy with the
  distant woes of others" resulting in "a mystic love of
  mankind, nature, God, fame, virtue, one's country,
  etc.," is but a variety of the same Melancholy Madness
  that takes the form of Byronic ennui and Russian
  "chondria" in Onegin (see also X : 7, etc.).

  The "wave and stone" are replaced by "dawn and
  midnight" in both fair copies.

13–14 No, Pushkin was not the "first": Cf. ". . . le dés-
œuvrement rendant les hommes assez liants, il [Lord
Bomston] me [St.-Preux] rechercha" (Rousseau, *Julie*,
pt. I, Letter XLV).

14 / *Ot délat' néchego—druz'yá*: *Ot* is "from," *delat'* is
"to do," *nechego* is "nothing," and *druz'ya* is "friends."
Three days after Pushkin had completed Chapter Two,
Dec. 8, 1823, and more than a month after he had com-
posed XIII (on, or before, Nov. 1), he used the same ex-
pression in a note addressed to Küchelbecker (see n. to
Four : XXXII : 1) under the following circumstances. On
Dec. 11, 1823, Vasiliy Tumanski (1800–60), a pallid ele-
giac poet, wrote from Odessa, where he was Pushkin's
coworker under Vorontsov, a long letter on literary mat-
ters (obviously composed in collaboration with Pushkin).
It begins: "Thank you, my friend Wilhelm, for remem-
bering me: I was always sure that you loved me from the
heart and not *ot delat' nechego* [out of do-nothingness]."
Here in the MS an asterisk leads to a twin asterisk and
footnote at the bottom of the page, both in Pushkin's
hand. The note reads: "Citation de mon nouveau poème.
Suum cuique" ("To each his own").

XIV

9 / More tolerant: To the modern reader *terpimee* would
seem preferable here to Pushkin's *snosnée*, which would
be taken to mean "more tolerable." (Cf. Four : XXXIII : 7,
where the word is used in the ordinary sense.)

12 Commentators have regarded this as reported speech; I
think they are right.

13–14 *Iníh on óchen' otlichál,* | *I vchúzhe chúvstvo uvazhál*:
Again the enchanting alliteration on *ch*, for which Push-

kin, in emotional passages, had a particular predilection.

In connection with this stanza, the ascetical Brodski (1950), p. 140, suddenly says that, through Onegin, Pushkin denounced the way of life of the young noblemen of his day, such as "parties, dances, restaurants, the ballet, and other pleasures"!

14 / though estranged from it / *vchúzhe*: *Vchuzhe* is an adverb that has no mate in English. The implications are "as one who is strange to the issue," "as an impartial observer," "neutrally," "detachedly," "from outside," "while remaining uninvolved," and so forth.

VARIANTS

The first fair copy contains the following variants, of which the second is canceled:

XIVa

```
 8 To sacrifice oneself is funny;
   to have enthusiastic sentiments
   is pardonable at sixteen;
   he who's full of them is a poet—
12 or wishes to display his art
   before the credulous crowd:
   so what are we? O Lord. . . .
```

(See n. to XXXVIII : 4–14.)

XIVb

```
  Eugene, however, was more tolerant:
  he simply did not care for people,
  and to direct the rudder of opinions
4 did not find a great need,
  did not promote friends unto spies,
  although he did consider that "Good," "Laws,"
  "Love for one's Country," "Rights,"
```

8 were but conventional words.
He understood Necessity,
and one moment of his own peace
would not have sacrificed for anybody;
12 but he respected in others: resolution,
of persecuted fame the beauty,
talent, and rectitude of heart.

b: 5 The meaning of this rather unexpected line is, "Onegin did not spread rumors about his friends, accusing them of being secret agents of the government—of prying, for example, into the activities of clandestine groups" (see also *Onegin's Journey*, VIII : 12, given in my nn.).

b: 6–13 Draft (2369, f. 28ᵛ):

did not consider that "Good," "Laws,"
"Love for one's Country," "Rights,"
8 are ⟨only⟩ for an ode sonorous words,
but understood Necessity
.   .   .   .
.   .   .   .
12   . . . the destitution
of persecuted talent . . .

XV

2–5 / conversation . . . mind . . . gaze . . . all this: An adumbration of the stylistic form of introductory description used more fully in relation to Olga in XXIII : 1–8. See n. to XXIII : 5–8.

13–14 The meaning is: "Let us ascribe to the fever of youth its heat and rant—and condone them." The lines are built around a stale Gallicism. See, for example, Claude Joseph Dorat (1734–80), *A Monsieur Hume*:

. . . les tendres erreurs,
Et le délire du bel âge . . .

XVI

There seems to be a reminiscence here, leading us back to the source of the chapter's motto, Horace, *Satires*, II, VI, namely to ll. 71–76, where the host and his guests at the rural board discuss whether people find happiness in riches or virtue, what makes friends—usefulness or uprightness—and what is the nature of good.

Pushkin's dormitory discussions with Küchelbecker at the Lyceum are no doubt in the background of this stanza. In fact, it would seem that Pushkin was much obsessed by personal memories of Küchelbecker, which threatened to make of the invented relationship between invented Onegin and invented Lenski a parody of a relationship between two other persons on different levels of time, Pushkin as he was at the end of 1823 and the remembered Küchelbecker of 1815–17.

According to Tïnyanov (*Lit. nasl.*, 1934), young Küchelbecker's favorite book had been a work by a Swiss follower of Rousseau, François Rudolphe (Franz Rudolf) Weiss, *Principes philosophiques, politiques et moraux* (1785), on which Küchelbecker at the Lyceum had based a MS encyclopedia for his private use. The dangerous prejudices listed in Weiss are: idolatry, sacrificial rites, religious persecution.

The pacts (*dogovórï*) and the effects of sciences and arts (*plodí naúk*, "fruits of studies, of learning") are obvious references to Rousseau—to his *Contrat social* (1762) and his *Si le rétablissement des sciences et des arts a contribué à épurer les mœurs* (1750).

The incredible Brodski (1950), pp. 143–45 (who spells the title of Rousseau's work *Contrat sociale*), suggests that the *plodï nauk* that the progressive squires Onegin and Lenski discuss (in 1820) were the attainments of technology, such as new agricultural machines, and remarks that people who had been abroad were appalled by the reactionary mentality of ordinary Russian squires, who discussed haymaking, gin, and hounds!

The incredulous reader is reminded that Brodski's book is "A Manual for the Use of High-School Teachers," published by the State Scholastic and Pedagogical Publishing Department of the Ministry of Education of the USSR, Moscow, 1950.

10 The untranslatable Russian *mézhdu tém* (or *mezh tém*) is the French *cependant*, a kind of abstraction of our "meantime."

10–11 [Lenski] recited, in a trance . . . fragments of Nordic poems / *Otrívki sévernïh poém*: Where had he found those fragments? The answer is: in Mme de Staël's *De l'Allemagne*:

Sur le rocher de la mousse antique, asseyons-nous, ô bardes!

> —Klopstock, *Hermann, chanté par les bardes*
> (*De l'Allemagne*, pt. II, ch. 12)

. . . les morts vont vite, les morts vont vite. . . . Ah! laisse en paix les morts!

> —Bürger, *Lenore* (ibid., pt. II, ch. 13)

Il est, pour les mortels, des jours mystérieux
Où, des liens du corps notre âme dégagée,
Au sein de l'avenir est tout à coup plongée,
Et saisit, je ne sais par quel heureux effort,
Le droit inattendu d'interroger le sort.
La nuit qui précéda la sanglante journée,
Qui du héros du Nord trancha la destinée . . .

> —Schiller, *Walstein* (sic), act II, "translated"
> by Constant (ibid., pt. II, ch. 18; note the
> ridiculous *cheville* of "heureux effort")

Coupe dorée! tu me rappelles les nuits bruyantes de ma jeunesse.

> —Goethe, *Faust* (ibid., pt. II, ch. 23)

That these were the "Nordic poems" recited by Lenski
is clear from yet another passage in the same work (pt.
II, ch. 13):

Ce qui caractérise les poètes du Nord [c'est] la mélancolie
et la méditation. . . . La source inépuisable des effets
poétiques en Allemagne [c'est] la terreur: les revenans
et les sorciers plaisent au peuple comme aux hommes
éclairés . . . une disposition qu'inspirent . . . les longues
nuits des climats septentrionaux. . . . Shakespeare a tiré
des effets prodigieux des spectres et de la magie, et la
poésie ne sauroit être populaire [= national] quand elle
méprise ce qui exerce un empire irréfléchi sur l'imagi-
nation.

He also recited, no doubt, bits from *Ossian, fils de
Fingal,* "barde du troisième siècle, poésies galliques,
traduites sur l'anglais de M. Macpherson, par M. Le
Tourneur," Paris, 1777 (or, more probably, the *nouvelle
édition* of the same, "ornée de belles gravures," which
have to be seen to be believed, of 1805). The "anglais de
Monsieur Macpherson" is the edition of 1765, in two
volumes, of the *Works of Ossian,* which in its turn is a
snowball accumulation of *Fragments of Antient Poetry
collected in the Highlands of Scotland, and translated
from the Galic of Erse Language* (Edinburgh, 1760)
and two other installments, *Fingal,* "an ancient epic
poem" in six books, published in 1762, and *Temora,*
another "ancient epic poem," in eight books, 1763.

James Macpherson's famous fraud is a mass of more or
less rhythmic, primitively worded English prose, which
can be easily translated into French, German, or Russian.
The recitative coagulates here and there into short iam-
bic lines with tetrameter-trimeter alternations of the
ballad type in some passages—e.g., in *Fingal,* bk. III:
"The wind was in her loose dark hair, her rosy cheeks
had tears"; but this, of course, was lost in the French
paraphrastic prose that popularized Ossian on the Con-
tinent.

The kings of Morven, their blue shields beneath the mountain mist upon a haunted heath, the hypnotic repetitions of vaguely meaningful epithets, the resounding, crag-echoed names, the blurred outlines of fabulous events, all this permeated romantic minds with its nebulous magic so unlike the flat classical backdrop colonnades of the Age of Taste and Reason.

Macpherson's lucubrations had as tremendous an impact upon Russian literature as upon that of other nations.

Ryno, son of Fingal, Malvina, daughter of Toscar, and Ullin, chief of Fingal's bards, found their way into incongruous adaptations and are used by Zhukovski as mere evocative names ("Rino, the highland chief," and "Malvina," daughter of Ullin) in his rather comical version of Campbell's second-rate ballad, *Lord Ullin's Daughter.*

In *Ruslan and Lyudmila*, "a tale of times of old" and "of deeds of old" (Ossianic phrases), Ossian's father Fingal (or the Irish Finn mac Cumhail) becomes *Fin* the Hermit (a Finn), and Moina (the daughter of Reuthamir and mother of Carthon) becomes the maiden sorceress *Naina*, while Reuthamir becomes *Ratmir*, a young Hazaran (Persian-speaking Mongol from Afghanistan).

XVIa

Cahier 2369, f. 29ᵛ, contains the following interesting draft, which ties up nicely with Eight : XXXV : 7–14:

> Proceeding from important subjects,
> the conversation [. . .] touched
> also on Russian poets now and then.
> 4 With a sigh and downcast gaze,
> Vladimir listened while Eugene
> . . . ⟨of our crowned works⟩
> ⟨Parnassus⟩ . . . ⟨praiseworthy⟩
> 8 ⟨mercilessly⟩ denounced.

Commentary

Apparently this was to be followed by some lines (found, in the same cahier, eleven pages further) in which Zhukovski, with the epithets "holy" and "Parnassian wonder-worker," is dismissed by Onegin as having become merely a "courtier," whereas Krïlov is said to be "stricken with paralysis."* Pushkin wisely refrained from letting Onegin make these sarcastic remarks—which, moreover, had already become petulant platitudes in literary circles.

See also One : XLVIa in my nn.

XVII

1 / passions / *strasti*: *Les passions*. Byron played constantly on these strident strings. Violent, conflicting, high-wrought emotions, with a singular knack of becoming abstract from sheer emphasis, like a shrill sound vibrating itself into silence. The two young men are imagined discussing such burning themes as love, jealousy, fate, gambling, rebelling. The dangerous passions listed by Weiss (above, n. to XVI) are: laziness in boyhood, sexual love and vanity in adolescence, ambition and vengefulness at the adult stage, avarice and self-indulgence in old age.

14 / deuce: Any two-spot card; the humble slave of luck, which, however, may turn traitor; here used synecdochically for any banking game such as faro or stuss.

These seventeen stanzas were finished by Nov. 3, 1823, in Odessa.

---

*See T. Zenger, "Novïe tekstï Pushkina," in *Pushkin, rodonachal'nik novoy russkoy literaturï*, a collection edited by D. Blagoy and V. Kirpotin (Moscow and Leningrad, 1941), pp. 44–45.

XVIIa, b, c, d

After XVI we have a batch of extremely interesting stanzas in the fair copy. The established XVII branches off, after 4, into a description of moods that (in conjunction with the beautiful and mysterious two stanzas, Eight : XXXVI–XXXVII—where imagination holds a faro bank) give an additional dimension to the otherwise rather flat character of Onegin; and this description, in its turn (following as it were the cue of XVII : 14), slips into an admirable digression on gaming.

The first fair copy contains the following canceled continuation:

XVIIa

4 Onegin spoke of them
as of acquaintances who had betrayed,
had long been sleeping the grave's sleep,
and now had left no trace;
8 but there would burst, at times,
out of his mouth such sounds,
such a deep wondrous moan,
that it would seem to Lenski
12 to be the mark of unstilled anguish,
and truly: there were passions here,
to hide them was a task of no avail.

XVIIb

What feelings had not seethed
in his tormented breast?
How long ago, for how long, had they been
    subdued?
4 They will wake up—just wait.
Happy who knew their agitation,
surgings, sweetness, intoxication—
and finally detached himself from them;
8 happier he who did not know them;
who cooled with separation love,
with tattle, enmity; at times
yawned with his friends and wife,

12 by jealous anguish undisturbed;
   as for myself, unto my lot
   there fell a flaming passion

XVIIc

—passion for banking! neither gifts of freedom,
nor Phoebus, nor fame, nor feasts
in years agone could have diverted
4 me from a game of cards.
Pensive, all night till daybreak,
I used to be prepared in former years
to question fate's disposal:
8 would the jack come up on the left?
Liturgic chimes would sound already;
amidst torn decks
the weary dealer would be nodding;
12 whereas with furrowed brow, peppy and pale,
hopeful, closing my eyes,
upon the third ace I would set.

XVIId

And I, a modest hermit, now
with no faith in the covetous dream,
no longer bet on a dark card,
4 having remarked a dread *ruté*.
I now have left the chalk in peace,
the fateful word *atánde*
does not come to my tongue.
8 I'm also disaccustomed of the rhyme.
What will you? Between you and me,
of all this I am weary.
One of these days, I'll try, friends,
12 to take up blank verse—
although "quinze-et-le-va"
still has great claims on me.

To understand stanzas XVIIc and d, as well as other
passages in Pushkin (see especially his great story "The
Queen of Spades," of which translators, including the
usually careful Bernard Guerney, have made such a
mess), it is necessary for the reader to have a clear con-
cept of the banking game. In Pushkin's day, the fashion-

able banking game (*bank*) was a German variation of pharo, called *Stoss* (Russ. *shtos*) or stuss, the latest mutation in a specific group of games whose evolution since the seventeenth century followed the sequence: lansquenet, bassette (basset, barbacole, or hoca), pharo (pharaon, faro). We are not concerned here with variational distinctions, and what follows is a general description of the *bank* of Pushkin's time.

The player or "punter" chose a card from his pack, put it down on the green or blue cloth of the card table, and set his stake, generally in coin or paper money, upon it. The dealer or "banker" ("he that holds the bank"), also called "tailleur" ("talliere" or "tallier" in basset), unsealed a fresh pack and proceeded to turn the cards up from its top, one by one, the first card on his right hand, the second on his left, and so on, alternately, until the whole pack was dealt out. The process was termed in English "to tally," and in Russian *metat'*, a verb connotatively evoking a rapid sustained flicker, although, actually—and especially if the punters were several—the dealer might have to stop drawing cards fairly often— for instance, when anybody said *atande* (Fr. *attendez*), asking for the opportunity to make or reconsider a bet. The banker won when a card equal in points to that on which the stake had been set came up on his right hand, but lost when it was dealt to the left. This left-hand card, the card for the punter, was called *carte anglaise*, and if it won for him at the first deal, it was said to win "sonica" (or "simply," "at once"); this happened twice (in "The Queen of Spades") when Herman punted, or, in other words, he twice guessed the second card from the top of the dealer's deck, and this would have happened a third time had he not produced, by a sinister blunder, the wrong card (he "mispulled," or "misdrew," *obdyornulsya*)—a queen instead of the ace he thought he had taken from his deck.

A "dark" card was the Russian term for a card that the punter chose from his deck and did not show the dealer until its equivalent turned up in the latter's deck.

When a doublet occurred—two cards of the same denomination turning up in the same coup (i.e., within one turn)—the punter lost half his stake at faro, the whole of it in stuss. If, having won the event, a punter chose to venture his stake *and* gains, he let his money lie and cocked (or "crooked") his card at one corner, and this was called a "parolet" or "paroli." If he wished to venture his gains only, he made a bridge (or a bend, *un pli*) of his card, and this was called a "pay" or "paix" (or "parolet-paix," if he had just gained a parolet). A "sept-et-le-va," or, in Russian, *setel'va* (or, as Pope spelled it, "septleva"—in his charming eclogue *The Basset-table*, 1751), succeeded the gaining of a parolet, by which the punter, being entitled to thrice his stake, risked the whole again and, cocking his card a second time, tried to win sevenfold; if he was fortunate, he could bend a third corner, venturing for fifteen times his stake, and this fateful attempt was called "quinze-et-le-va" (transliterated into Russian as *kenzel'va*). (The next pleasant possibility for the punter would be "trente-et-le-va," which in Susanna Centlivre's dull comedy *The Basset-Table* [London, 1706] appears as "Trante et leva," and is rendered *trantel'va* in Russian.)

In the concluding couplet of XVIId—

> although "quinze-et-le-va"
> still has great claims on me

—the last line, *Bol'shíe na menyá pravá*, is a Gallicism: *a de grands droits* (see, for example, Voltaire's *La Pucelle*, VIII, l. 30, and his note, of 1782, to X: "l'épopée a de grands droits").

In the description of a faro game in ch. XXII of *Candide* the lady of the house, sitting next to the dealer, watches

sharply "tous les parolis, tous les sept-et-le-va de cam-
pagne [i.e., improper augmentation of stakes with no
winnings to back them], dont chaque joueur cornait ses
cartes" (cocked his cards); "elle les faisait décorner avec
une attention sévère, mais polie . . ." Pushkin, in the
opening scene of his novella *The Shot* (*Vïstrel*, written
in the autumn of 1830), has Silvio, the banker at a faro
table, observe in a somewhat similar way that the punt-
ers do not, by mistake, cock a card when they are not
entitled to do so.

Editors invariably print the terminal of l. 13 as
quinze elle va (see *Works* 1936, p. 431; Tomashevski,
Acad 1937, p. 282; *Works* 1949, p. 519), instead of
quinze et le va; possibly this is Pushkin's mistake, but
it should be checked by those who have access to the MS.
According to Tomashevski, the draft (2369, f. 31ʳ) gives
the variant reading *sept il va*, which again is an error for
sept et le va.

If the basic stake ("what goes") is, say, one dollar,
then:

first win: $1 + 1 = 2$ (*un et le va*)
second win: $2 + 2 = 4$ (*trois et le va*)
third win: $4 + 4 = 8$ (*sept et le va*)
fourth win: $8 + 8 = 16$ (*quinze et le va*)

and so on.

*

The cancellation of these magnificent stanzas is of
psychological interest. At one time Pushkin hesitated
whether to make himself or Onegin the pale and ener-
getic gambler depicted here. (We know that Onegin did
play; see One : LIV and Eight : XXXVII.) This very chap-
ter, in which he describes himself as a humble hermit
no longer addicted to the gaming table, was actually lost
by him at cards, despite his quibbling assertion (see be-
low) to the contrary. Early in 1828, he published, in Bul-

Commentary

garin's review *The Northern Bee*, a little poem in iambic
tetrameter, *Epistle to V.* (Ivan Velikopolski, 1797–1868,
author of *To Erastus, A Satire on Gamesters*), in which,
after praising V. for his sound morals and the good advice
he gave, Pushkin had the following sarcastic conclusion
(I give it in prose):

A neighbor of mine, having in the throes of a noble thirst,
swilled down a bumper of Castilian water, wrote—as you
did—a wicked satire on gamesters and with much anima-
tion recited it to his friend. The latter, in reply, took a
deck of cards, silently shuffled it, gave it him to cut, and
the moralistic author punted, alas, all night. Are you ac-
quainted with that gay dog? A session with him I would
deem most festive. With him I am ready not to sleep all
night and until the blaze of noon read his moral epistle and
write down his losings.

Velikopolski, a kindly fellow who later helped Gogol
financially, mildly retaliated by composing at once, in
the same meter, a little poem in which he said that the
moralist in question remembered very well his sessions
with Pushkin when "*Onegin*, Chapter Two, humbly
slid down [= was lost] on an ace." (Incidentally, it is
quite clear that Velikopolski had read the stanzas on the
passion for play that Pushkin omitted when publishing
Chapter Two separately in 1826.) From Petersburg, in
April, 1828, Pushkin wrote to Velikopolski in Moscow:

Bulgarin has shown me the very amiable stanzas you ad-
dress to me in answer to my pleasantry. He told me that
the censor refused to pass them (as a "personality") with-
out my consent. Sorry—but I cannot give it. . . . Do you
want to quarrel with me in earnest and make me, your
peace-loving friend, include some inimical stanzas in
Chapter Eight of *Onegin*? *Nota bene*: I did not lose Chap-
ter Two to you; what I did was to pay you my debt with its
published copies, exactly as you paid me your debts with
parental diamonds and the thirty-five volumes of the
Encyclopédie. What if I publish this well-meaning ob-
jection?

All this does not make very pretty reading.

Pushkin preferred keeping bank to punting and went on gaming very deep till the end of his life.

In *A Portion of the Journal kept by Thomas Raikes, Esq., From 1831 to 1847*: "comprising reminiscences of social and political life in London and Paris during that period" (4 vols., London, 1856–57, with a misleading preface), there is the following entry (III, 129), under Tuesday, Feb. 28, N.S., 1837, on which date the news of Pushkin's duel (Feb. 8, N.S.) and death (Feb. 10, N.S.) reached Paris, where Raikes was then living:

I find the following note in page 141 of my journal when in Russia [winter, 1829–30]: "I met last night [Dec. 23, 1829, N.S.; thus Dec. 11, O.S.] at Baron Rehausen's the Byron of Russia; his name is Pouschkin, the celebrated and almost the only poet in Russia. . . . In his person and manners I could observe nothing remarkable except a want of attention to cleanliness, which is sometimes the failing of men of genius, and an undisguised propensity to gambling; indeed the only notable expression which dropped from him during the evening was this, 'J'aimerois mieux mourir que ne pas jouer.' "

(I am indebted to Miss Filippa Rolf, of Lund, Sweden, for kindly identifying for me Raikes' host as Baron Johan Gotthard von Rehausen, 1802–54, secretary of the Swedish legation in St. Petersburg.)

The passage is somewhat differently worded by Raikes in *A Visit to St. Petersburg* (see n. to One : LII : 7).* This work is in the form of letters (to "My dear ——"); and Letter IX, dated Petersburg, Dec. 24, 1829, N.S., starts:

I met last night at Baron Rehausen's the Byron of Russia; his name is Pouschkin, the celebrated, and, at the same time, the *only* poet in this country. . . . I could observe nothing remarkable in his person or manners; he was slovenly in his appearance, which is sometimes the failing

---

*First mentioned in connection with Pushkin by S. Glinka, in *P. i ego sovr.*, VIII, 31–32 (1927), 109–10.

of men of talent, and avowed openly his predilection for gambling; the only notable expression—[etc.]

In connection with our poet's appearance, which Raikes, a professed dandy, was not alone in criticizing, there is a coincidental note by Pushkin himself referring to more or less the same period. It is an autobiographical fragment (starting with: "My fate is settled, I am going to marry . . .") written apparently about May 13, 1830, a week after he had been accepted by Natalia Goncharov, and contains the following observation: "I dress negligently, when visiting people, but with all possible care when dining in a restaurant where I read either a new novel or a magazine" (Acad 1936, V, 358).

Pushkin started to compose Chapter Eight Dec. 24, 1829, O.S., and it is tempting to see Raikes (whom our poet met again at a rout on Feb. 16, 1830) in the "far-flung traveler, a brilliant London jackanapes" of Eight : XXIIIb : 9–10, and in the "far-flung traveler, an overstarched jackanapes" of Eight : XXVI : 9–10 (although, as I point out in my nn. to these verses, we also discern therein other, earlier, impressions going back to Odessa, 1823–24). The epithet "overstarched" refers, I suppose, to an Englishman's stiffly starched neck-cloth. The frontispiece of Raikes' *Journal* shows him from top hat to elegant toe in peripatetic profile—a rather corpulent gentleman with strangely thin legs, in a shortish frock coat and tight checked trousers.

Tom Raikes (1777–1848) was, of course, an expert in gaming-table matters:

Upon one occasion [1814, in a London club], Jack Bouverie, brother of Lady Heytesbury, was losing large sums [at macao], and became very irritable: Raikes, with bad taste, laughed at Bouverie, and attempted to amuse us with some of his stale jokes; upon which, Bouverie threw his play-bowl, with the few counters it contained, at Raikes's head; unfortunately it struck him, and made

the City dandy angry, but no serious results followed this
open insult.
> —Captain (Rees Howell) Gronow, a stale
> joker in his own right, in *Reminiscences*
> (London, 1862), p. 80

c Before striking out this stanza, Pushkin started to change
the first person to "Onegin" and "he." In l. 2, "Phoebus"
was deleted, and in l. 3 "ladies" was substituted for
"feasts." In the draft (2369, f. 30ᵛ), "the gifts of liberty"
(ll. 1–2) was "the love for liberty" and "fame" (l. 3) was
replaced by "friendship." In l. 1 "passion for banking
games!" was changed to "O cards!" and then to the
synecdochical "O deuce!" Another curious variant (ll.
1–4) was communicated by Sobolevski to Bartenev and
to Longinov, who published it in *Sovremennik*, VII
(July, 1856). It was composed, with the rest of the
stanzas on gaming, at Odessa in the winter of 1823; but
Pushkin liked to repeat aloud in later years, at cards, on
walks, any resonant line that he had composed at one
time or another; Sobolevski could not have heard these
verses before 1826, which is the year he and Pushkin
struck up a warm friendship in Moscow:

> O deuce! Neither the gifts of freedom,
> nor Phoebus, nor Olga, nor feasts
> in days agone could have Onegin
> diverted from a game of cards.

"Olga" is of course not the fictional Olga Larin, who
appears for the first time only in XXI (2369, f. 34ʳ) and
apparently had not yet been devised, but most probably
the notorious Petersburg courtesan, Olenka Masson (b.
1796), daughter of a Swiss historian and a Russian
noblewoman. Our poet met Mlle Masson in 1816 and
saw her again in 1826, judging by dates in the draft of a
madrigal beginning "Olga, though godchild of Cypris."

d: 3–4 / [I] no longer bet on a dark card, having remarked

a dread *ruté* [a hostile run] / *Uzhé ne stávlyu kártï tyómnoy,* | *Zamétya gróznoe ruté*: This is a good example of Pushkin's poetical syntax. He does not mean to say, "Now that luck is against me, I do not bet any more on a dark card, I do not gamble"; what he means is, "I do not gamble any more, I do not bet on a dark [undisclosed] card as I used to when luck was against me" (cf. the beginning of the Prefatory Piece).

The word Pushkin has here is *ruté*, which I have rendered as "run." I have seen it written *routé* (*jouer le routé*). It seems to be connected with the English "rut" taken in the sense of "sustained course." Russian gamesters used it to denote a run, a run of luck, a great run, a ride, a trend, a streak, a series, when the same card wins several times running. *Igrat' na rute* meant to keep staking on the same lucky card. In this stanza the great run is in the dealer's favor (hence "hostile," *gróznoe*), and by a blind or random selection of his card, or by not showing it till it had won or lost, the punter sought to interrupt such an adverse sequence. In a first draft, Pushkin had *táynoe*, "secret," instead of "hostile."

The term also occurs (ll. 192–97) in an excellent poem by Krïlov (229 freely rhymed tetrameters) addressed *To Luck* (first published in the *St. Petersburg Mercury*, 1793, pt. IV, pp. 96–108):

> And through thy furtherance, in town
> Jack Sixpip with a little knowledge
> of the light art of faro dealing,
> for every ruble herds in flocks of them;
> there is before him a *ruté*; wealth's mother
> is hardly cocked before she fades.

XVIII

4–5 The established reading is "their willfulness or surg-
ings" (*Ih svoevól'stvo, il' porívï*), but I feel sure that
the *il'* is a misprint for a second *ih*: "their willfulness,
their surgings."

11 / disabled soldier / *invalíd*: A military invalid.

11–14 The MS of a forty-four-line tetrametric poem Push-
kin addressed in September, 1821, to "[Nikolay] Alek-
seev," a good friend of Pushkin's in Kishinev, dealing
with the same theme as does Two : XVIII, contains among
other discarded lines the following:

> Far from the bayonet and drum
> exactly thus an old disabled soldier [*invalíd*]
> meets youthful uhlans
> and speaks to them of battles.

Pushkin's (discarded) note to this stanza (in the draft
of notes for the 1833 edition, PD 172):

> Et je ressemble au vieux guerrier
> Qui rencontre ses frères d'armes
> Et leur parle encore du métier.

Pushkin does not mention the author of these lines,
and either he or his transcribers (I have not seen the
autograph) err in writing "encore," which does not
scan. I have traced the quotation to the beginning of
Parny's *Coup d'oeil sur Cythère* (1787; entitled in the
edition of 1802 *Radotage à mes amis*):

> Salut, ô mes jeunes amis!
> Je bénis l'heureuse journée
> Et la rencontre fortunée
> Qui chez moi vous ont réunis.
> De vos amours quelles nouvelles?

> Car je m'intéresse aux amours.
> Avez-vous trouvé des cruelles?
> Vénus vous rit-elle toujours?
> J'ai pris congé de tous ses charmes,
> Et je ressemble au vieux guerrier,
> Qui rencontre ses frères d'armes,
> Et leur parle encor du métier.

The idea is not new. Cf. Ronsard's Sonnet XL, from *Pour Hélène* [de Surgères], 1578 (Ronsard, *Œuvres complètes*, ed. Gustave Cohen [2 vols., Paris, 1950], I, 258), ll. 1–5:

> Comme un vieil combatant . . .
> . . . .
> Regarde en s'esbatant l'Olympique jeunesse
> Pleine d'un sang boüillant aux joustes escrimer,
> Ainsi je regardois [les champions] du jeune
> Dieu d'aimer . . .

and a sonnet from his *Œuvres*, 1560, dedicated to Prince Charles, Cardinal of Lorraine (ed. Cohen, II, 885), l. 9:

> Maintenant je ressemble au vieil cheval guerrier . . .

13 / mustached braves / *usachéy*: *Usachi*, "mustaches," a Gallicism.

13–14 / *Rasskázam yúnïh usachéy*, | *Zabítïy v hízhine svoéy*: The masculine singular ending of *zabítïy*, "forgotten," attaches it easily to l. 11; not so in English.

XIX

5 / *V lyubví schitáyas' invalídom*: Spalding paraphrases:

> Deeming himself a veteran scarred
> In love's campaigns . . .

14 / to us: To Pushkin, Onegin, and the novel's third protagonist, the Reader, all three, men of the world.

XX

1, 9 / our years / *náshi léta;* / long years / *dólgie letá*: The shift in accent (analogous to *gódï, godá,* also meaning years) is curious. I do not know whether in the earlier line Pushkin meant "in our age" or "at our age."

12 / studies / *naúki*: A more general term than "sciences" since it includes all varieties of knowledge. See also introductory n. to XVI.

14 / virgin fire: This and the other epithets characterizing Lenski were current ones. See, for example, the description of Allan Clare in Charles Lamb's *Rosamund Gray* (1798), ch. 4: ". . . at the sight of Rosamund Gray his first fire was kindled" and "his temper had a sweet and noble frankness in it, which bespake him yet a virgin from the world."

VARIANT

6–14 Draft (2369, f. 33ᵛ):

> one object, one desire,
> one woe, one love,
> 8 torrents of tears, and tears again.
> Neither long years of separation,
> nor foreign beauties,
> nor hours given to the Muses,
> 12 nor distance, nor cold studies,
> in the world's noise or in the stillness,
> had changed his soul.

A canceled draft (ibid.) reads (l. 10):

> nor the glances of foreign maids . . .

XXI

3 / tender / *umilyónnïy*: The French *attendri*, "enten-
dered," "intenerated," "in a melting mood," "soft-
eyed," "moved."

3–4 / *On bíl svidétel' umilyónnïy | Eyó mladéncheskih za-
báv*: The phrase is blatantly Gallic: "Il fut le témoin at-
tendri de ses ébats enfantins." The curious accord of
zabáv (frolics, amusements, games) and Fr. *ébats* is
rather pleasing and on a par with the *nadménnïh*
(haughty) and Fr. *inhumaines* of One : XXXIV : 9.

7–8 My translation is awkward but accurate.

9–14 Cf. Parny, *Poésies érotiques*, bk. IV, Elegy IX:

> Belle de ta seule candeur,
> Tu semblois une fleur nouvelle
> Qui, loin du Zéphyr corrupteur,
> Sous l'ombrage qui la recèle,
> S'épanouit avec lenteur.

11 / under the eyes / *V glazáh*: A Gallicism (*aux yeux*) that
has thrived. See, half a century later, Tolstoy's *Anna
Karenin*, pt. I, ch. 6: *v glazah rodnïh* ("in the eyes of
[her] kinfolk").

12–14 Butterflies as a rule do not care for the sweet-smelling
white bells of the conval lily, *Convallaria majalis* L., the
landïsh of the Russians, the *muguet* of the French, the
"mugget" of old rural England, the "Lily of the Vale"
of Thomson (*Spring*, l. 447) and the "valley-lilly" of
Keats (*Endymion*, bk. I, l. 157), a beautiful but poisonous
plant, that, although used by poets to adorn pastoral
landscapes, is, in fact, lethal to lambs.

In another, canceled, metaphor related to the same

maiden (in XXIa), Pushkin no doubt has in mind the same flower when hinting it may perish under the scythe (his initial plan being, perhaps, to have Olga more thoroughly courted by Onegin than she is in the final text).

In a marginal note left by our poet in his copy of Batyushkov's *Essays in Verse and Prose* (pt. II, p. 33, *Convalescence*, 1808), Pushkin correctly criticizes his predecessor for having used in connection with the death of a lily of the valley the harvester's sickle instead of the mower's scythe (for this note see *Works* 1949, VII, 573; date unknown, probably 1825–30).

It will be noted that in Six : XVII : 9–10, the lily of the valley becomes a conventional lily upon which a generalized but entomologically not impossible caterpillar feeds.

VARIANTS

Three variants of XXI are canceled in the first fair copy.

XXIa

Who, then, was she whose eyes
he, without art, attracted,
to whom he days and nights,
4 and meditations of the heart devoted?
The younger daughter of poor neighbors.
Far from the harmful pastimes of the capital,
full of innocent charm,
8 under the eyes of her parents, she
bloomed like a hidden lily of the valley
which is unknown in the dense grass
either to butterflies or bee—
12 a blossom that perhaps is doomed
without yet having dried the dew,
to the sweep of the fatal scythe.

Commentary

a: 1 / Who, then, was she / *Kto zh tá bïlá*: At the top of the margin of this stanza (2369, f. 34ᵛ), written in November or early December, 1823, in Odessa, Pushkin made an ink sketch (above other faces) of the profile (dark glasses, high coat collar) of Griboedov, the playwright, author of *Woe from Wit* (*Gore ot uma*), which was circulated in MS 1823–25, staged in 1831, and published in 1833, the same year as the first complete edition of *EO*. Pushkin had seen Griboedov some four years before. At the bottom of the margin, Pushkin drew his own likeness in the guise of a turbaned and plumed Negro courier of sorts.

a: 2 / without art / *bez ikússtva*: A Gallicism, *sans art*. Cf. Jean Desmarets de Saint-Sorlin (1596–1676), *Promenades de Richelieu*:

> Je ne vois qu'à regret ces couleurs différentes
> Dont l'Automne sans art peint les feuilles mourantes.

a: 2–4 / art . . . heart: One of those very rare cases when the jinni of a literal translation presents one with a set of ready rhymes. A little judicious touching up may even produce the right meter: "Who, then, was she, the girl whose gaze | he charmed without a trace of art, | to whom he gave his nights and days, | the meditations of his heart?" The incorruptible translator should resist such temptations.

a: 12–14 / doomed . . . to . . . the fatal scythe: One wonders if Olga's destiny as we know it was quite clearly seen by Pushkin at this point. (See n. to XXI : 12–14.) I suggest that at this point Olga was a combination of Olga and Tatiana, an only daughter whom (in automatic literary result) the villain, Onegin, was to seduce. We witness in this set of variants a process of biological differentiation. In my n. to XXIb : 13–14, I explain our poet's attempt to replace "Olga" in that stanza by "Tatiana." That in his mind's eye Tatiana had dark hair is suggested by his also substituting in XXIb the word "silk" for "gold" (l. 11).

XXIb

Neither a goose of English breed
nor a wayward mam'selle—
in Russia by fashion's decree
4 up to now indispensable—
came to harm winsome Olga.
Fadeevna with debile hand
had rocked her cradle,
8 she it was who made her bed,
she it was who looked after her,
"Bová" to her narrated,
combed the silk of her curls,
12 taught her to pray "Have mercy upon me,"
at morn poured out the tea,
and spoiled her on occasion.

b The rather unexpected attack on the learning of Western languages (which even the most foolish and flighty governess might help a provincial Russian girl to master) was wisely abandoned by Pushkin. In the final text, the Larin girls read and write French with considerably more ease than Russian, a fact that implies the recent presence of a French governess in the family.

The three different patronymics that at various stages of his draft Pushkin applies to the nurse (the patronymic instead of the Christian name is used in the case of faithful household plebeians whose age entitles them to respect) all begin with an *F*: Fadeevna, Filipievna, Filatievna (daughter of Faddey, Thaddeus; of Filip, Philip; of Filat, Philetus; see Pushkin's n. 13 to XXIV : 2).

273

The story-telling old nurse is of course an ancient thematic device. In Maria Edgeworth's *Ennui* (1809), she is Irish and her tales are of the Irish Black Beard and the ghost of King O'Donoghue.

b: 1–2 Canceled draft (2369, f. 34ᵛ):

> Neither a Mistress of the English breed
> nor a wayward Madame . . .

Thus, according to Tomashevski (Acad 1937), p. 287n. I am sure, however, without seeing this autograph, that Pushkin wrote "Mistriss," *à la française*, a corrupt form of "Mistress," met with in England in the seventeenth century and retained in France well into the nineteenth century.

b: 10 / Bová: *Anglice*, Bevis. In Russian fairy tales Prince Bevis (Bova Korolevich) is the son of Gvidon and grandson of Saltan. His prototype is Buovo (or Bueve) d'Antona of fourteenth-century Italian romance (*I Reali di Francia*).

b: 13–14 First fair copy:

> and in the evening would undress
> her and her elder sister.

Subsequently, after settling in his draft of Two : XXIV (see my n. to it) the name of Olga's sister, Pushkin returned to the fair copy of XXIb and in the same fair copy started to substitute "Tatiana" for "Olga" but did not go beyond l. 5, and struck out the whole stanza.

XXIc

(From 1–8 as in the established text.)

> Thus a sweet friend in Olga
> Vladimir grew to see;

was dull without her at an early age;
12 and often on the matted mead
without dear Olga, mongst the blooms
sought nothing but her traces.

XXII

4 | *Egó tsevnítsï*: Poets begin with this Arcadian instrument, graduate to the lyre or lute, and end by relying on the free reeds of their own vocal cords—which closes the circle with a Hegelian clasp.

5 | golden games: Childhood being the golden age of life, the frolics of infants are golden, too.

All this does not mean much in the text; nor is it meant to mean much—or to mean whatever it would mean in a modern account of childhood. We are deep in Lenski's Gallic (rather than Germanic) word-world of *flamme, volupté, rêve, ombrage, jeux*, and so forth.

5–8 It would be a mistake to regard Lenski, the lyrical lover, as "a typical product of his time" (as if time can exist apart from its "products"). Let us recall the sweets of "lovely melancholy": "Fountain heads, and pathless Groves, | Places which pale passion loves: | Moon-light walks . . . | A mid-night Bell, a parting groan" (Fletcher, *The Nice Valour*, act III, sc. 1), and suchlike seventeenth-century *fadaises* going back to the nauseating "student-shepherds" of early Italian and Spanish bucolic fiction.

6 | groves: Pushkin economically gave Lenski, XXI and XXII, lines he had himself attempted to use in his youth. Cf. the rough draft of a short poem thought to have been composed in 1819:

> In the shade of enthralling woods
> I'd been the tender witness

> of her infant amusements
>
> . . . .
>
> and thought of her inspirited
> the first sound of my Panpipes.

I generally try to render *dubráva* by "park" (which it certainly is in several instances throughout *EO*), but sometimes the "park" insensibly shades into "wood" (*les*) or "grove" (*roshcha*). Here, moreover, the plural form in the elegy of 1819 gives a definite clue to the meaning of the singular in the stanza of 1823.

XXIII

1–2 Pushkin did not know, and probably had not even heard of, Andrew Marvell (1621–78), who in many ways has such affinities with him. Cf. Marvell's *An Epitaph upon* —— (pub. 1681), l. 17: "Modest as morn; as Mid-day bright . . ." and *My Peggy Is a Young Thing* (*The Gentle Shepherd*, 1725) of Allan Ramsay (1686–1758), l. 4: "Fair as the day, and always gay."

The intonation in Pushkin's first line is the same as in *Le Sermon inutile* of Ponce Denis (Ecouchard) Lebrun (1729–1807), *Œuvres* (Paris, 1811), bk. II, Ode VII:

> Toujours prude, toujours boudeuse . . .

3 / naïve / *prostodúshna*: Cf. X : 3. Pushkin uses this term *prostodushnïy, -naya, -no* (which means, grammatically, "simple-souled" in the sense of "simplehearted") more than once to translate the French *naïf, naïve, naïvement*. The phrase "naïve as a poet's life" is not particularly good in English, but "openhearted," or "guileless," or "candid" would have been less accurate. Though Lenski's naïveté persists to the end of his life (and even well into the realm of posthumous metaphor and Arcadian sepulchers), that of Olga turns out to be not unmixed with a kind of coyish and hard guile.

Speaking of poets, Chateaubriand says through *René*

(ed. Armand Weil [Paris, 1935], p. 28): "Leur vie est à
la fois naïve et sublime . . . ils ont des idées merveil-
leuses de la mort." The comparison of the "naïve" life
of a poet with Olga's nature has its counterpart in the
comparison of Lenski's poetry to the "naïve maid's
thoughts" of X : 3, which is preceded in VII : 14 by a
faint echo of "idées merveilleuses."

5–6 The prototype of both Pushkin's Olga and Baratïnski's
Eda is the Arcadian maid, e.g., in Batyushkov's *My
Guardian Spirit* (1815):

> I recollect the azure eyes,
> I recollect the golden locks
> . . . .
> of my incomparable shepherdess . . .

5–8 / eyes . . . smile . . . waist—everything in Olga . . .:
This listing-and-summing-up device is a parody not only
of matter but of manner. Pushkin interrupts himself as
if almost carried away by Lenski's style and by the flow
of the sentence, which deliberately mimics the conven-
tional rhetorical figures of similar descriptions in the
European novel of his day, with its patter of clauses end-
ing in the enthusiastic gasp of "everything . . ."

Cf. "Sa taille . . . ses regards . . . tout exprime en
elle . . ." (description of Delphine d'Albémar in Mme de
Staël's insipid novel of that name [1802], pt. I, Letter
XXI, from Léonce de Mondoville to his bosom friend
Barton, literary nephew of Lord Bomston [in *Julie*];
see also n. to Three : X : 3); Nodier's "Sa taille . . . sa
tête . . . ses cheveux . . . son teint . . . son regard . . .
tout en elle donnait l'idée . . ." (description of Antonia
de Monlyon in Nodier's lurid but not quite negligible
novel, *Jean Sbogar* [1818], ch. 1; see also n. to Three :
XII : 11); and finally Balzac's "Le laisser-aller de son
corps . . . l'abandon de ses jambes, l'insouciance de sa

pose, ses mouvements pleins de lassitude, tout révélait
une femme . . ." (description of the Marquise d'Aigle-
mont in the much overrated vulgar novelette, *La Femme
de trente ans*, ch. 3; *Scènes de la vie privée*, 1831–34).

6 / locks / *lókonï*: I fear I have taken the line of least re-
sistance in translating *lókonï* as "locks" and *kúdri* as
"curls" (see VI : 14). Actually, it might be demonstrated
that the notion of a maiden's "curls" is closer to *lókonï*,
whereas "locks" connotes *kúdri*, especially when speak-
ing of men.

7 / waist / *stan*: Fr. *taille*, which comprises waist and torso.

8 / but any novel: Cf. Piron, *Rosine*:

> Ne détaillons pas davantage
> Un portrait qui court les romans.

That a prose translation is not always closer than a
metrical version with rhymes tagged on is nicely ex-
emplified by a sequence of hilarious blunders in the
English "translation" of some fragments of *EO* supplied
by an anonymous writer (William Richard Morfill, au-
thor of several worthless works on Russia) in an article
on Pushkin (*The Westminster and Foreign Quarterly
Review*, CXIX [1883], 420–51). This is how he under-
stood the allusion to "any novel," *lyuboy roman* (confus-
ing *lyuboy*, "any," with *lyubovnïy*, "amorous," and
roman, "novel," with *roman*, "love affair") in XXIII : 8:

> . . . Eyes blue as heaven,
> A smile, flaxen hair,
> Harmony of motion and voice and figure,
> 8 All these are in Olga. She was
> A living love-story.
> There you will find the portrait of the sweet girl.
> Well, I was some time in love with her myself,
> 12 But it ended in nothing.

Despite his not knowing the simplest Russian terms and constructions, this critic has the temerity to dismiss Spalding's version of *EO* (1881) with a few contemptuous words (pp. 443–44). I was led to this article by a footnote in an essay by M. Alekseev, "I. S. Turgenev— propagandist russkoy literaturï na zapade,"* in which, however, there are two mistakes: the date of the Spalding version is not "1888," and Morfill did not give "a detailed analysis" of it, but limited himself to six examples of awkward English.

14 / take up / *Zanyát'sya*: One of those simple terms which are the despair of a translator. *Zanyát'sya* here is really the French *m'occuper de*, but to render this by "occupy myself" or "get busy on" would not be exact. I have wavered between "turn to" and "take up."

VARIANT

13–14 First fair copy:

> And I take a new pencil
> her sister to depict.

Between the draft of these lines and the beginning of XXIV ("Her sister was called ⟨Natasha⟩ Tatiana"), Cahier 2369, f. 35ʳ, there is a large drawing of Eliza Vorontsov in bonnet and shawl.

XXIV

1 / Her sister was called Tatiana / *Eyó sestrá zvalás' Tat'yána*: Trisyllabic, with a moist medial *t*, and the accented *a* sounded as "ah." In Pushkin's day the name was considered lowly (*prostonarodnoe*).

The Russian forms of the Greek names mentioned in

---

*In *Trudï otdela novoy russkoy literaturï*, I (Akademiya nauk SSSR, Institut Literaturï; Moscow and Leningrad, 1948), 53.

Pushkin's n. 13 are Agafon, Filat, Fedora, and Fyokla.

In his draft of notes for the 1833 edition (PD 172), Pushkin has, moreover, the names Agofokleya and Fevroniya (Russianized to Havron'ya).

In his draft of this stanza (2369, f. 35ʳ) Pushkin toyed with the name Natasha (the diminutive of Natalia), instead of Tatiana, for his heroine. This was five years before he first met his future wife, Natalia Goncharov. Natasha (as also Parasha, Masha, etc.) has considerably fewer rhyming possibilities (*násha*, "our"; *vásha*, "your"; *kásha*, "porridge"; *chásha*, "cup," and a few more) than Tatiana. The name had been tried before in fiction (Karamzin's *Natalia, boyarskaya doch'*, "the boyar's daughter," for instance). Pushkin used Natasha in his *The Bridegroom, a Folk Tale* (*Zhenih, prostonarodnaya skazka*) in 1825 (see Five: Tatiana's dream), and at the end of the same year in *Count Nulin*, for its charming heroine, a Russian Lucrece, who boxes the ears of a transient Tarquin (while quietly cuckolding her husband, a landed gentleman, with his twenty-three-year-old neighbor).

Tatiana, as a "type" (that pet of Russian critics), is the mother and grandmother of a number of female characters in the works of numerous Russian writers, from Turgenev to Chehov. Literary evolution transformed the Russian Héloïse—Pushkin's combination of Tatiana Larin and Princess N.—into the "national type" of Russian woman, ardent and pure, dreamy and straightforward, a stanch companion, a heroic wife—and, in historical reality, this image became associated with revolutionary aspirations that produced during the subsequent years at least two generations of noble-born, delicate-looking, highly intellectual, but incredibly hardy young Russian women who were ready to give their lives to save the people from the oppression of the state. In actual contact with peasants and workers, many disappointments came the way of these pure Tatianalike souls: they were neither understood nor trusted by the common people they tried to teach and enlighten. Tatiana faded out of Russian literature, and Russian life, just before the revolution of November, 1917, the leadership of which was taken over by matter-of-fact, heavily booted men. In Soviet literature, the image of Tatiana has been superseded by that of her sister Olga, now grown buxom, ruddy-cheeked, noisily cheerful. Olga is the good girl of Soviet fiction; she is the one who straightens things out at the factory, discovers sabotage, makes speeches, and radiates perfect health.

This business of "types" may be quite entertaining if approached in the right spirit.

9–10 / very little taste | we have even in our names / *vkúsa óchen' málo* | *U nás i v náshih imenáh*: Since *i* can be either "even" or "and," this can be understood also as: "there is very little taste in us and in our names." But the first reading is better.

14 / affectation: "I do not like," Pushkin wrote to Vyazemski (end of November, 1823), "to see in our primevally wild language any traces of European affectation and French refinement. Coarseness and simplicity suit it better."

In *EO*, however, Pushkin did not retain the "Biblical outspokenness" that he preached.

VARIANTS

10 Second fair copy:

in our attires and in our names . . .

13–14 The draft (2369, f. 35^r) reads:

I might have proved it instantly,
but not with this concerned are we.

XXV

2 After this negative introduction Pushkin does not, as the intonation would lead one to expect, use a subordinate clause beginning with "but" to accumulate compensative items (stylistically, these come only in Eight : XIV and XV). Cf. the anon. *The Modern Wife* (London, ·1769), I, 219–20 (Capt. Westbury to Sir Harry):

> She [Juliet, youngest daughter of Lady Betty Percy] was not handsome, but possessed in a high degree that *je ne sais quoi* which is even more captivating than a too regular beauty. . . . I was charmed . . . with her good sense, her unaffected manner, so free from levity, coquetry, or airs.

8 / a strangeling / *dévochkoy chuzhóy* [instr. after "seemed"]: A strange lassie, a little waif, a little foundling girl.

The theme of unsocial children of either sex was a commonplace of Romanticism. Thus, Charles Lamb's Rosamund Gray: "From a child she was remarkably shy and thoughtful . . ." (*Rosamund Gray*, ch. 1).

14 / sat silent by the window; Three : V : 3–4 / silent . . . sat down by the window; Three : XXXVII : 9 / Tatiana stood before the window; Five : I : 6 / Tatiana from the window saw; Seven : XLIII : 10 / Tanya sits down beside the window; Eight : XXXVII : 13–14 / and by the window sits *she*: Her selenotropic soul is constantly turned toward a romantic remoteness; the window becomes an emblem of yearning and solitude. Onegin's last evocation of Tatiana (Eight : XXXVII : 13–14) is very elegantly connected with his first vision of her (Three : V : 3–4).

VARIANTS

4–6 A canceled draft (2369, f. 35^v) presupposes another beginning:

> You can, my friends,
> imagine her [. . . . .]
> but only with black eyes . . .

The words Pushkin left out are almost certainly *i sámi,* "also yourselves," rhyming with *glazámi,* "eyes" (instr.).

14 Draft (ibid.) reads "with a book," instead of "in silence."

XXVI

14–XXVII : 1 This is another rare instance of one stanza flowing into another.

XXVII

2 The idiom is *v rúki ne bralá,* "in hands did not take."

6 / grisly / *stráshnïe*: The 1837 edn. has *stránnïe,* "strange," which makes little sense and is presumably a misprint. Earlier editions give *strashnïe.*

7 Depending on rhythm and rhyme, Pushkin uses *temnota* (as here), *t'ma,* or *potyomki* for "darkness." Other substitutes are *sumrak, mrak,* and *mgla.* The last, in its exact sense, is murkier and foggier than the not unfrequently pleasurable and poetical glooms conveyed by the nouns *sumrak* and *mrak.* The adjectives *tyomnïy* ("dark"), *sumrachnïy* ("somber"), and *mrachnïy* ("gloomy") are frequent throughout Pushkin's works. By some Russians *sumrak* is felt to be lighter than *mrak,* perhaps being influenced by *sumerki,* "twilight."

12 / *gorélki*: The Scottish and English barla-breikis (barley-bracks, barlibrakes, barleybreaks, with "barley" meaning a cry of truce) does not differ essentially from the Russian *gorelki,* both being country games of tig, tag,

Commentary

or tick. *Gorelki* is of pagan origin, and in Pushkin's time
was still associated among peasant folk with Maying.
The word itself comes from *goret'*, "to burn," taken in
the special sense of being "it" in the game. A curious dif-
ference between barleybreaks and *gorelki* is that in the
former the tigger, or tagger, is stationed "in hell," where
he "burns" as a sinner, whereas in the latter he "burns"
with vernal desires and amorous fire under the glossy
birches on the burnished knoll. (It is interesting to note
that in a canceled draft, 2369, f. 36ʳ, l. 12 reads: "in
spring played not at barleybreaks.")

In certain old rustic variants of *gorelki* the "burning
one" represents a burning stump, *goryashchiy pen'* (a
stump being in Russian a symbol of "oneness " "mate-
lessness" a lone unit, a materialized "I"). The deriva-
tion of *pen'* is obscure, but I suspect it should be sought
among the ancestry of pin, pinnacle, pen (a pointed hill),
and peg. Vladimir Dahl's *Dictionary* (*Tolkovïy slovar'
zhivogo velikorusskogo yazïka*, 3rd edn., 1903) gives the
following dialogue between the "it" and the paired
players, chanted before the "break" begins:

"I, the stump, am burning, burning."—"Wherefore
burning?"—"I want a girl."—"What girl?"—"A young
one."—"And do you love her?"—"I do."—"Will you
buy her a pair of fancy shoes [*cherevichki*]?"—"I will."

In *gorelki* as played by little Olga and her little girl
friends whom the nurse brings together on the lilac-
bordered oblong lawn, a much tamer version is in use.
After the paired players have queued behind a single
one, the latter chants:

> Burn, burn bright,
> Let me keep alight,
> Look at the sky,
> Up there birds fly,
> Little bells jingle . . .
> Here they go!

At this point the hindermost pair of players separates, each running forward on either side of the "burning" one, away from him (or her), whereupon he sets out in pursuit. Eventually, with his tagged captive, he takes his stand in the queue, while the uncaught player becomes "it."

I find this ancient game alluded to by Thomas Dekker in *The Honest Whore* (1604) pt. I, act v, sc. 2: "We'll run at barley-break first, and you shall be in hell" (meaning "you shall be the tagger"); and by Allan Ramsay in *The Tea-Table Miscellany*, in the song entitled *The Invitation* (1750 edn., p. 407), st. 2, which starts:

> See where the nymph, with all her train,
> Comes skipping through the park amain,
> And in this grove she means to stay,
> At barley-breaks to sport and play . . .

*

Elton assembles "in the big meadow . . . romping girls and boys," Spalding calls it "a gay rout" of "young people," Miss Radin explains Tatiana's not joining in the game because "it seemed so boisterous yet so tame," and Miss Deutsch has the little girls not only tag each other but "roam the woods" while "Tatyana stayed at home, | By solitude nowise dejected." And all this is supposed to be *Eugene Onegin*.

XXVIII

2 / to prevene / *Preduprezhdát'*: I chose to use this obsolete verb in order to stress the fact that the Russian word (a translation of the French *prévenir* or *devancer*) is obsolete, too.

This stanza is a particularly delightful one, a melody and a miniature, in Pushkin's happiest vein of stylization. Without transcending the classical limits of eighteenth-century achromatic detail, he still manages to give depth and air to the picture.

To forestall the dawn as Tatiana did was a romantic act. See, for instance, in Pierre Lebrun's *La Promenade matinale aux bois de Ville-d'Avray* (1814), the verse:

> J'éprouve de la joie à devancer l'aurore . . .

6–8 There is a lovely alliteration on *v* and *t* in l. 6:

> *I véstnik útra, véter véet . . .*

In the next line I have put up with an indifferent inversion to render the expressive delaying note based on the scudding of the second foot:

> *I vskhódit postepénno den'.*

And, of course, I have felt bound to imitate the wonderful way l. 8 leaves the octave to join the sextet.

Whatever accuracy I have achieved in this stanza, I owe to the ruthless and triumphant elimination of rhyme. Its conservation was one of the things that led a predecessor of mine (Miss Deutsch, 1936) to string the following versicles supposedly representing the passage given above (XXVIII : 1–8):

> Tatyana might be found romancing
> Upon her balcony alone
> Just as the stars had left off dancing,
> When dawn's first ray had barely shown;
> When the cool messenger of morning,
> The wind, would enter, gently warning
> That day would soon be on the march,
> And wake the birds in beech and larch.

The sins of omission are too simple to be noted; but there is one sin of commission that is typical of this particular version of *EO*, in which all kinds of images and details are bountifully added to Pushkin. What, for instance, are those birds and trees doing here: "And wake the birds in beech and larch"? Why this and not, for instance: "And take in words to bleach and starch" or any other kind of nonsense? The charming point is that beeches and larches, not being endemic in west central Russia, are the very last trees that Pushkin would imagine growing in the Larins' park.

XXIX

1–4 / novels . . . of Richardson and of Rousseau; 5–12 / Her father . . . : See my nn. to the more detailed description, in Three : IX–X, of the "secret" library Tatiana enjoys—reading these books in the original French or in French "translations"—in the years 1819–20, just after a French governess (who had certainly been living in the Larin household, despite XXIb) had left and not long before Dmitri Larin died. These are "sentimental" novels by Rousseau, Mme Cottin, Mme Krüdener, Goethe, Richardson, and Mme de Staël; and in Three : XII (see nn.) Pushkin cites in contrast to them a list of more "romantic" works (into which, from a modern point of view, the first list insensibly grades) by Byron, Maturin, and their French follower, Nodier, works that nowadays, *nïnche* (i.e., in 1824, the time of Pushkin's writing Three), trouble the sleep of a teenage girl (*otrokovítsï*). This second, fashionable, reading list is essentially Onegin's in 1819–20, as implied retrospectively by allusions in Seven : XXII, at which point (summer, 1821, in the chronology of the novel) Tatiana catches up with him in her reading.

The literary evolution is from Lord Bomston to Lord Byron.

3 / *Oná vlyublyálasya v obmáni*: This might be rendered also: "she fell in love with the deceptions," but I am certain that "fictions" or "illusions" comes closer to

Pushkin's meaning. Cf. Gilbert's satire against Voltaire, *Le Dix-huitième Siècle* (1775):

> Sous le voile enchanteur d'aimables fictions . . .

And I notice that Aleksey Vulf, in his famous journal (Nov. 1, 1828),* uses *obman* to render the French *illusion*.

8–9 / *On, ne chitáya nikogdá,* | *Ih pochitál*: This punnish alliteration, once you have noticed it, spoils both lines for you.

VARIANT

1–4 A first draft (2369, f. 36ᵛ) reads, in conjunction with the last lines of XXVII (XXVIII was composed after the chapter was finished):

> More to her liking was to read.
> In this none hindered her,
> and the longer the novel dragged
> the more it pleased her.

XXX

3 / Grandison: Prof. Chizhevski (Čiževsky) of Harvard, in his commentary to *Evgenij Onegin* (Cambridge, Mass., 1953), makes the following incredible statement (p. 230):

> Grandison, the hero of *Clarissa Harlowe* [wrong novel] is familiar to the mother only as the nickname of a Moscow sergeant [mistranslation]! . . . The development of old Larina from a sensitive girl into a strict mistress [ambiguous] was a familiar experience for both men [very ambiguous] and women in Russia.

3–4 / *Grandisóna . . . Lovlásu*: The noblehearted Sir Charles Grandison and the scoundrel and gentleman, Lovelace

---

*In *P. i ego sovr.*, VI, 21–22 (1915), 23.

(*Lovlas* rhymes in Russian with *Foblás*, Fr. Faublas), are, as Pushkin's n. 14 says, "the heroes of two famous novels." These are, of course, the epistolary novels (1753–54 and 1747–48, respectively) by Samuel Richardson (1689–1761): *The History of Sir Charles Grandison*, in 7 vols.; and *Clarissa; or, The History of a Young Lady*, "Comprehending the Most Important Concerns of Private Life, and Particularly Shewing, the Distresses that May Attend the Misconduct Both of Parents and Children, in Relation to Marriage," in 8 vols.

I have consulted an 1810 edn. of these two works. In his preface to *Grandison*, Richardson thus defines Clarissa, the heroine of his earlier "collection":

A young lady . . . is seen involved in such variety of deep distresses, as lead her to an untimely death; affording a warning to parents against forcing the inclination of their children in the most important article of their lives. . . . The heroine, however, as a truly *Christian heroine*, proves superior to her trials; and her heart, always excellent, refined and exalted by every one of them, rejoices in the approach of a happy eternity.

And Grandison:

. . . Grandison, the example of a man acting uniformly well through a variety of trying scenes, because all his actions are regulated by one steady principle: a man of religion and virtue; of liveliness and spirit; accomplished and agreeable; happy in himself, and a blessing to others.

7 / would often talk / *Tverdíla chásto*: It is not possible to find an exact and constant equivalent. *Tverdit'* means "to dwell upon," "to iterate," "to repeat over and over again," but "often iterated to her [things] about them" will not do. The verb was widely used in verse as a mere disyllable variant of *govorit'*, "to talk," with only a very slight stress on reiteration. "To harangue," "to harp," "to declaim," and so on, would be much too strong in the context.

Commentary

8–9 | *V to vrémya bíl eshchyó zheníh | Eyó suprúg; no
po nevóle*: This is very awkwardly and incorrectly ex-
pressed in Russian; an elegant paraphrasian, pruning
his author, would render it: "To Larin in those days
already | she was engaged, but by compulsion."

13–14 | *that* Grandison was . . . an Ensign in the Guards:
Gvárdii serzhánt (abolished in 1798) corresponded to
the rank of sublieutenant in the Army, as distinguished
from the Guards, which possessed special privileges in
relation to officers' advancement; according to Tsar
Peter's regulation of 1722 (*tabel' o rangah*), a rank in the
Guard was two rungs higher than the homonymous one
in the Army. Another point worth making is that the
officer's rank of *gvardii serzhant* had more glamour to
it than practical signification and, being a sort of ab-
stract steppingstone for subsequent rapid advancement,
did not imply immediate service when a youth was en-
tered therein. It will be also recalled that Pyotr Grinyov,
the "first person" of Pushkin's charming short novel
The Captain's Daughter (1836), at his birth, in 1757,
was registered by his father (through the kindness of a
titled kinsman) as *gvardii serzhant* (in the Semyonovskiy
regiment), and was formally "considered on leave until
[he] had completed [his] education," i.e., the casual
schooling he received at home under the direction of a
crapulous French tutor. The boy was sixteen when his
father decided he should start to serve—in the Army
("to become a warrior") and not in the Guard ("to be-
come a rake"), as had been planned originally.

At society balls, the dashing *gvardii serzhant* of
Catherine's reign (1762–96) was replaced in Alexander's
times (1801–25) by the somewhat languid elegance of
the *arhivnïy yunosha* (applied to young men in the fash-
ionable Moscow Archives of the Foreign Department;
see n. to Seven : XLIX : 1), who, in his turn, gave way in

the thirties, under Nicholas I, to the *kamer-yunker* (junior gentleman of the chamber), as F. Vigel notes (c. 1830) in his nasty but clever memoirs (*Zapiski*).

Tatiana—Praskovia Larin's elder daughter—was born in 1803. When the dashing young gamester courted Pachette, the latter could hardly have been more than sixteen or eighteen. All things considered, I think she must have been born about 1785 and thus, though termed a "nice old lady" by her maker (Three : IV : 12), was in her late thirties in 1820. She and her maiden cousin, Princess Alina (pronounced Aleena, Russian form of the French Aline, which was used as a fashionable diminutive of Aleksandra), will be reunited in Seven.

Some analogy may be found in English life of the time. Thus, Captain Gronow, in his crude and clumsy memoirs, *Reminiscences* (p. 1): "After leaving Eton, I received [in 1812] an Ensign's commission in the First Guards . . . [and] joined in . . . 1813."

*

At this point Turgenev-Viardot, in their French version of *EO* (1863), have the following muddled footnote: "Comme il n'y avait alors qu'un seul colonel dans la garde, qui était l'empereur [or the empress], et que les simples soldats étaient gentilhommes, le grade de sergent équivalait à celui de colonel [à celui de lieutenant?]."

VARIANTS

9–10 Canceled draft (2369, f. 36ᵛ):

> . . . she shone
> among the beauties of those times . . .

13–14 Draft (ibid.):

> her Lovelace was a mighty dandy,
> an Ensign of Catherine's reign.

XXX–XXXI

In the margins of the draft (2369, f. 37ʳ), written not earlier than the end of November and not later than Dec. 8, 1823, in Odessa, Pushkin made two interesting drawings in ink (see Efros, *Risunki poeta*, p. 185).

Right-hand margin, alongside XXX : 11–12 and XXXI : 1–6, Countess Elizaveta Vorontsov, dorsal view: simple elegant low-necked dress; string of diamonds visible across the nape.

Left-hand margin, alongside XXXI : 11–14, Pushkin's stylized profile: no sideburns; hair curly.

In his remarkable drawings of people, Pushkin would find a key trait, a graphic constant, and repeat it throughout several likenesses of a given person. Thus the clue to his own profile is the sharp curve of the nostril (so that the outline of the pointed nose looks like a rapid cursive *h* or an upside-down 7 in script) above a long, simian upperlip, and the clue to the profile of Ekaterina Ushakov (1809–72; Pushkin's intermittent Moscow love— spring, 1827; spring, 1829—who married, c. 1840, a Dmitri Naumov) is a special downward dash, the cirrus of a smile, added at the wick to the pretty contour of her lips. Elizaveta Vorontsov is characterized by her shapely neck, sometimes with a dotted-line necklace around it. Her shoulders and neck appear also, with no head or body, in Cahier 2369, f. 42ʳ, right-hand margin, beneath a draft of the poem beginning "The stirless sentinel drowsed . . ." (see n. to Ten : I : 1) and above the line "perhaps—flattering hope!" of Two : XL : 5 (reproduced by Efros, p. 189).

XXXI

4 Lexically: "the maiden they vehiculated to the wedding crown."

8–9 / *Rvalás' i plákala snachála*: The verb *rvat'sya* (which comes from *rvat'*, "to tear") is saturated with far more expressive force than any one English verb can convey. It is not just "to fling oneself about," but implies the violent agitation of a person who is restrained by others while indulging in a passion of grief, seeking an issue in desperate writhings and other wild motions. When Maria Kochubey's mother, in Pushkin's marvelous narrative poem *Poltava*, tells her daughter to do her utmost in order to have Mazepa spare Kochubey, she says: *Rvis'*, *trebuy* . . . The second imperative means "demand," while *rvis'* connotes all the body expressions of grieving and raving, including wringing one's hands, tearing one's hair, and so forth.

14. The passage quoted in Pushkin's n. 15 is from *René*, a little beyond one third of the story (ed. Weil, p. 41):

> Est-ce ma faute, si je trouve partout les bornes, si ce qui est fini n'a pour moi aucune valeur? Cependant je sens que j'aime la monotonie des sentimens de la vie, et si j'avois encore la folie de croire au bonheur, je le chercherois dans l'habitude.

See also Voltaire, *Le Fanatisme, ou Mahomet le prophète*, act IV, sc. 1: "La nature à mes yeux n'est rien que l'habitude." See another "substitute for happiness" in Eight: Onegin's Letter : 20–21.

XXXIa, XXXIb

After XXXI Pushkin began a stanza (XXXIa) thus (draft, 2369, f. 37ʳ):

> They were accustomed to have meals together,
> to call together on their neighbors,
> attend ⟨on feast days Mass⟩,
> 4 snore all night long and in the daytime yawn;
> in a barouche to tour the farming,
> ⟨. . . in the bathhouse on Saturdays⟩,
> pickle mushrooms and watermelons.

a: 5 I have translated *linéyka* "barouche," since one of the

Commentary

meanings conforms to the notion of a comfortable, low-slung, old-fashioned vehicle of that kind, well cushioned and snugly hooded, a bedroom on wheels at its luxurious best. However, the same word *lineyka* was employed in the Russian 1820's to designate a carriage that, curiously enough, was closely allied to the Irish jaunting car —namely, to the outside-car variety of that species, with passengers seated back to back on its lateral seats, which held at least three on each side.

Robert Lyall, *Travels in Russia, the Krimea, the Caucasus, and Georgia* (London, 1825), I, 22, describes the *lineyka* as "a kind of long half-open double-seated carriage, in which a dozen or more persons can sit."

a: 7 Another cancellation of l. 7 reads:

> pickle white mushrooms . . .

What Russians call "white mushrooms," *belïe gribï,* are boletes belonging to the species *Boletus edulis,* a succulent toadstool with a thick white stem and a tawny cap, which, fried or pickled, are much prized by European gourmets. For a more detailed account of the Russians' love and understanding of mushrooms, see pp. 43–44 of my *Speak, Memory* (New York, 1966).

*

In the drafts of xxxIa and xxxIb (2369, f. 37^r and 38^v), Larin was unsympathetically portrayed.

a: 13–14 The draft (f. 37^r) has:

> . . . rather stingy,
> ⟨exceeding⟩ kind and very stupid.

See also below, b: 2.

b: 1–3 The draft (f. 38^v) has:

> Her spouse—his name was Dmitri Larin—
> a gin distiller and a genial host [*I vinokúr i hlebosól*],
> well, in a word, a truly Russian *bárin.*

b: 2 The canceled draft (f. 38ᵛ) reads:
> a dunce, a fat and genial host . . .

b: 3 The word *barin* comes from *boyarin* (boyar; *Webster's New International Dictionary* has a pithy note on the subject). In a superior-versus-inferior context it means "master"; but otherwise, as here, it has the connotations of "squire," "gentleman," and—to squeeze out the last associative drop—"easygoing, genuine, old-fashioned nobleman."

Incidentally, Pyotr Gannibal, our poet's granduncle and country neighbor, was, like the MS Larin, a passionate distiller of gin, *vodka*.

XXXII

5 / *mezh délom i dosúgom:* An idiomatic expression, which I have closely mimicked.

7 The 1826 edn. gives "like Mrs. Prostakov," and this was changed to *edinovlástno,* "monocratically," in the errata appended to the 1828 edn. of Six and in the text of the 1833 and 1837 editions. Modern editors substitute *samoderzhavno,* "autocratically," assuming that this imperial epithet was canceled in MS because of censorship considerations.

11 / "shaved foreheads" / *brîla lbî:* Among her serfs she chose recruits for the army: those deemed fit for military service had their front hair snipped for easy recognition.

XXXIII

2 / albums: "*Album* . . . le livre dans lequel, selon les bienveillans usages de l'Allemagne, chacun se fait donner une marque de souvenir par ses amis." Definition

given by Mme de Staël, in *De l'Allemagne*, pt. II, ch. 23 (*Œuvres*, vol. X, 1820). See also Four : XXVII–XXXI.

3 / would call Praskóvia "Polína": Praskovia or Paraskovia, a common Russian feminine name with diminutives Parasha and Pasha. In her Frenchified youth Mme Larin (whose name, incidentally, was Praskovia) would address Praskovia (or Paraskovia) not as Pasha, but as Polina (pron. Poleena; cf. "Alina," XXX : 5 and n. to XXX : 13–14), from the French Pauline. Even Russian diminutives were Frenchified, and Pasha Larin is called Pachette by her fashionable Moscow cousin (see Seven : XLI : 1).

4. The Moscow way, especially on the part of women, of intoning syllables in speech so as to produce a kind of musical drawl is again referred to in Seven : XLVI : 13.

6–7 She nasalized the Russian *n*, in, say, *solntse*, "sun," as if it were a French *n* in, say, *son* (*son-tse*).

Lerner (*Zven'ya*, no. 5 [1935], p. 65) notes that, in reading the line *I Rússkiy N kak N Frantsúzskiy*, a good reader of Pushkin's day would read the first *N* as *Násh*, which was the old name for that letter in the Russian alphabet. The second *N* is, of course, pronounced "én" (as in "ken").

14 / quilted chamber robe . . . mobcap / *Na váte shláfor . . . chepéts*: *Shlafor* comes from the German *Schlafrock*, Fr. *robe de chambre*, "dressing gown"; *na vate* means lined with cotton wool (Fr. *ouatée*). *Chepets* is a frilled or goffered cap worn by matrons. At its ornamental best, it merges with the English concept of "bonnet" (cf. Three : XXVIII : 4).

VARIANT

In the first fair copy, this stanza is absent from the main

text of the chapter and is added at the end in the following charming form:

> In albums she would write in blood,
> after the mode of Ryazan maidens,
> call Paraskóvia "Polína"
> 4 and speak in singsong tones;
> a very tight corset she wore,
> and Russian *Nash* as a French *N*
> knew how to nasalize
> 8 (among the fashionables this was done);
> before a ball she liked
> to learn a complicated *pas*,
> her father she would call *papá* [Fr.],
> 12 knew how to snap her fan,
> and her Grandison
> loved above all.

L. 11 at first read:

> her father she would call *mon cher papa* . . .

The allusion in l. 2 is to the province of Ryazan, south of Moscow, between Moscow and Tambov.

XXXIV

2 / *zatéi*: *Zateya* is a favorite word with Pushkin. It has many shades of meaning: "project," "device," "enterprise," "whim," "fancy," "trick," and so forth.

7 / kindly group / *dóbraya sem'yá*: These goodmen will have undergone a strange transformation for the worse by the time our poet reaches Chapter Five. He never quite made up his mind whether to satirize or praise (grotesque or fundamentally sound?) old-fashioned provincialism and (vacuous or broad-minded?) St. Petersburg society (which at one point—namely, in Eight: XXIIIa, b—he attempted to reconcile, as he did Slavisms and Gallicisms in his style).

14 / away / *so dvorá*: This idiomatic term means "off the premises," "from the place," "leaving the grounds."

7–8 The draft (2369, f. 38ᵛ) reads:

> an amiable group of neighbors,
> the pope, the pope's wife, and the police captain.

"Pope," *pop*, familiar name for a Russian priest; "police captain," *ispravnik*, head of the district police.

This is a good couplet, and artistically much better than the lame final text; but no doubt Pushkin felt that he was going too far in playing down the social status of Tatiana's parents, who after all belonged to the nobility and would not limit their acquaintance to rural priests and policemen. Old Larin had a high rank in the Army and was a gentleman, and, if we judge by the title of her unmarried Moscow cousin, his wife, Pauline Larin, may have been—for all we know—née Princess Shcherbatski, paternal grandaunt of Tolstoy's Dolly Oblonski. Soviet commentators miss these fine points.

3 / during fat Butterweek / *na máslyanitse zhírnoy*: The epithet corresponds to that of Mardi Gras (Shrove Tuesday, last day of carnival, or Shrovetide, but second day of Lent in Russia). The Russian *maslyanitsa* lasts from Monday to Quinquagesima Sunday (Shrove Sunday), and next day (Shrove Monday) the Russian *Velikiy Post* (Great Fast) begins. Germans living in Russia used to translate the term *maslyanitsa* as *die Butterwoche* (*maslo* means "butter"), while Russians jocosely called Shrove Monday and Shrove Tuesday (the first days of Great Lent) *nemetskaya* (German) *maslyanitsa*.

It was formerly the custom in England for the people to confess their sins to the priest on Shrove Tuesday and afterward to eat pancakes and make merry. The Russian festive food, *blini* (pl. of *blin*), are light, fluffy, raised pancakes of yeasted dough, very thin and delicate in comparison with our American variety. Having folded the tawny, brown-speckled *blin* and speared it with his fork, a Russian eater would dip it in melted butter and consume it with pressed (black) or fresh (gray) caviar and a dab of sour cream, repeating this performance as many as forty times at a sitting. The *blin* is related to the flawn, French *flan*, and to the Jewish-American blintz.

5–11 In the fair copy this passage (omitted in the lifetime editions) reads:

> They fasted twice a year;
> loved whirligigs,
> dish-divination songs, the choral dance.
> 8 on Trinity Day, when the people,
> yawning, attended the thanksgiving service,
> upon a bunch of giltcups touchingly
> they shed two or three tearlets . . .

5 / *goveli*: Fasted and went to church in preparation for the sacrament.

6 / *kruglïe kacheli*: In *A Thousand Souls* (*Tïsyacha dush*, 1858), by the minor novelist Aleksey Pisemski (1820–81), one of these "round" (*kruglïe* or *krugovïe*) swings is mentioned (in the description of the front yard of a landowner, a Prince Ivan Ramenski) as carrying the steward of the manor and the two daughters of a priest while being revolved by a neatherd, his chest pressed against the shaft.

7 / dish-divination songs: See n. to Five : VIII : 5–8. The choral dance, *horovód*, is a simple, garlandlike walk-dance, performed here by the serf girls.

Commentary

10 / upon a bunch of giltcups / *puchók zarí*: There are sev-
eral plants to which the name *zarya* or *zorya* is applied
in Russia. Dahl's *Dictionary* lists six. Among these, the
least likely is lovage of the carrot family; however, all
translators automatically hit upon it, without bothering
to find out if this southern European apiaceous herb
(*Levisticum officinale*) occurs endemically in north-
western Russia (where the Larins lived); it does not; and
none of the other plants that are, or have been, desig-
nated as "lovage" in England coincides with any *zarya*
in Russia. Among the other flowers that go under the
latter name, sneezewort and wild angelica have some
claims to be used in the Whitsuntide ritual; and there is
a *Conioselinum* (hemlock parsley) species whose very ob-
scurity appeals to the pedant; but the most obvious *zarya*
with definite connotations of spring is of course *Ranun-
culus acris*, the meadow buttercup, also called crazy,
craisey, giltcup, goldcup, and kingcup. (In western
Europe the flower connected with Whitsuntide used to
be the clove pink, *Dianthus caryophyllus*.)

Two customs have become hopelessly entangled in
the dutiful commentaries mechanically accumulated by
Pushkinists in regard to the hapless *puchok zari*.

On Trinity Day rural churches in Russia are decorated
with birch-tree branches, and in some districts the tra-
dition is that a person must shed as many tears for his
sins as there are dewdrops on the branch he carries, if
he has no flowers. The well-to-do classes, and indeed
many poor people, bring, however, a bouquet of flowers
with them to church. * In the province of Pskov, those
bunches of flowers were used subsequently—in pro-
longation of the pagan part of the rite—to brush lightly
(*obmetat'*) the grave of one's parents, in order to clear
(*prochishchat'*) their eyes. This is mentioned by Ivan

*The reader may find additional particulars in William Walsh's
Curiosities of Popular Customs (London, 1898), p. 1002.

Snegiryov—without the faintest allusion to his source—
in his *Russian Popular Festivities and Superstitious
Rites.* * Only the first custom—the "dews of sins" (of
which the Larins had only three little ones or so)—is
alluded to in *EO.* The second custom was mentioned by
Pushkin in conversation with Snegiryov.

Lerner† quotes an entry under Sept. 18, 1826, in the
diary kept during 1825–27 by this Professor Snegiryov,
ethnographer, censor, and fogy:

Went to see A. Pushkin, who had brought [i.e., from
Mihaylovskoe to Moscow] his piece *Onegin,* Chapter Two,
to show it to me in my capacity of censor. He agreed with
my remarks and deleted or altered several verses.‡ He
told me that in certain localities there is the custom of
brushing the coffins of one's parents with Whitsuntide
flowers.

A similar detail is mentioned by Pavel Melnikov (pseud.
Andrey Pecherski) in his ethnographical novel *In the
Woods* (*V lesah,* 1868–75), pt. III, ch. 1, wherein he
describes some curious blends of pagan tradition and
Christian ritual existing among Russian peasants in the
woodlands of the Kostroma and Nizhni-Novgorod prov-
inces.

10 / *umil'no*: I think Pushkin used this adverb here in the
sense of *umilyonno,* "tenderheartedly," "in a melting
mood"; it generally means "sweetly" or "touchingly"
(i.e., touching the observer). See n. to Two : XXI : 3.

***Russkie prostonarodnïe prazdniki i severnïe obryadï,* I (Mos-
cow, 1837), 185.
†"Zametka o Pushkine," in *P. i ego sovr.,* IV, 16 (1913), 47.
‡The deletions were VIII : 10–14, requested because these lines
might be misapplied to the Decembrists, and XXXV : 5–11, de-
leted because such homely and perhaps "satirical" descriptions
of churchgoing were taboo; among the alterations were II : 7,
IV : 8, VI : 9, and, possibly, the "O Rus' " of the motto, which,
however, was re-established in the list of errata appended to
the 1828 edn. of Six and in the text of the 1830 reprint of Two.

Commentary

11 / two or three tearlets / *slyózki trí*: In Russian the posi-
tion of three (*tri*) after the tearlets (*slyozki*) gives the
sense of "two or three." The odd number ("some three
little tears") causes the image to limp a little. One recalls
Keats writing to his brother and sister-in-law, Apr. 21,
1819, in reference to the "kisses four" in *La Belle Dame
Sans Merci*, which he was sending them: "I was obliged
to choose an even number that both eyes might have fair
play."

12 / *Im kvás kak vózduh bíl potrében*: Cf. Tredyakovski,
Strophes in Praise of Country Life (see my n. to One :
LVI : 2), ll. 87–88:

> *Vsyó zh v domú, v chyom vsyá egó potréba,*
> *V prázdnik pívo p'yót, a kvás vsegdá.*

> all that's requisite to him is homemade;
> beer he drinks on holidays, kvas always.

Kvas is the national soft drink (sometimes mildly fer-
mented), usually made of leavened rye dough or rye
bread with malt. There are other varieties in which
honey or fruit is used.

*

The stanza was written, in the draft, after XLI (and after
the first fair copy had been completed), on f. 43ʳ of
Cahier 2369. In this draft the "round swings" (l. 6) are
"country swings."

XXXVI

1 / And thus they both declined / *I ták oní staréli óba*: The
logical intonation here is of the same long-drawn,
dreamy kind as in a series culminating in *Oná egó ne
podïmáet* (Eight : XLII : 1), discussed further (this won-
derful stanza XXXVI inaugurates the series with a tuning-

302

key note, repeated three times within the stanza—ll. 1, 5, and 9: *I ták oní staréli óba; On úmer v chás pered obédom; On bíl prostóy i dóbrïy bárin*).

There is a protracted, imperfective sense to the Russian *staret'*, "to be growing old," "to be getting along in years," that is impossible to convey quite exactly in English. The perfective aspect would be *postaret'*, "to become old." The obvious translation of XXXVI : 1, "And thus both aged," lacks somehow the emotional tone of "growing old," *staret'*.

4 / new crown: This is the second crown—the aura of a good man's death; the first is the wedding crown held over a bridegroom's head by his *shafer* (best man).

12 / Dmitri Lárin [rhyming with "áre in"]: In the first fair copy, Pushkin tried and rejected several other Christian names, "Antoniy," "Sergiy," and, possibly, "Sava" (Acad 1937 has this with a question mark).

The name Larin exists. Sometime in the 1840's, in Moscow, the writer Aleksandr Veltman (Weldmann; 1800–60) ran into an old acquaintance of his, Ilya Larin. He was "a character," a crackpot and a bum who had roamed all over Russia and, a quarter of a century before, in Kishinev, had amused Pushkin with his antics and drinking parties—incidentally presenting the poet with a name for his squire (perhaps a subliminal link may be distinguished here connecting Larin, Pushkin's court fool, and the Yorick of the next lines). In the course of the conversation, Larin asked Veltman, "Do you remember Pushkin? He was a good soul. Where is he, do you know?" "Long dead," answered Veltman. "Really? Poor fellow. And what about Vladimir Petrovich" (whoever that was), "what is *he* doing?"*

I suggest that, apart from all this, Pushkin's choice

---

*Quoted by Lerner, *Zven'ya*, no. 5 (1935), p. 70.

of the name Larin for his static squire may have been prompted by its resemblance to *lares*, thus evoking an atmosphere of somnolent old-world existence under the protection of quiet household gods.

13 / Brigadier: A military rank of the fifth class, according to the official tabulation (*tabel' o rangah*). It was established by Peter I and abolished by Paul I, thus leaving a blank in the scale. A brigadier commanded a brigade of two or three regiments. Standing midway between "colonel" (rank 6) and "major general" (rank 4), this rank corresponded to "captain-commodore" in the Navy, and to "state councilor" in the civil service. It seems to have been a shade less important than the rank of brigadier general in the U. S. Army.

XXXVII

1 / *Svoim penátam vozvrashchyónnïy*: The same locution makes up l. 181 of Baratïnski's narrative poem of 1510 iambic tetrameters, *The Concubine* (*Nalozhnitsa*), completed by the fall of 1830 and published in 1831. (The title of its final text, 1835, is *The Gypsy Girl, Tsïganka*.)

6 / Poor Yorick: Brodski (1950), referring to Pushkin's n. 16, glosses: "By referring to Sterne . . . Pushkin subtly discloses his ironic attitude to Lenski's applying the name of an English fool to Brigadier Larin."

Alas, poor Brodski! Pushkin's note comes straight from F. Guizot's and Amédée Pichot's revised edition of Letourneur's translation of *Hamlet*, in Pushkin's possession (*Œuvres complètes de Shakespeare*, vol. I, Paris, 1821), in which a note, pp. 386–87, reads: "Alas, poor Yorick! Tout le monde se souvient et du chapitre de Sterne, où il cite ce passage d'Hamlet, et comment dans le Voyage Sentimental [translated by J. P. Frénais,

1769], il s'est, à ce propos, donné à lui-même le nom d'Yorick."

The title of Pierre Prime Félicien Letourneur's initial version is *Hamlet, Prince de Dannemarck* "par Shakespeare, traduit de l'anglois, par M. Le Tourneur, dédié au Roi." Paris, 1779.

The actual passage in Sterne's *Tristram Shandy* (vol. I, end of ch. 12) reads:

> He [Parson Yorick] lies buried in the corner of his church-yard . . . under a plain marble slab, which his friend Eugenius, by leave of his executors, laid upon his grave, with no more than these three words of inscription serving both for his epitaph and elegy: "Alas, poor Yorick!"
>
> Ten times a day has Yorick's ghost the consolation to hear his monumental inscription . . . not a passenger goes by without stopping to cast a look upon it—and sighing as he walks on, "Alas, poor Yorick!"

Pushkin's knowledge of Sterne was based on French versions such as *La Vie et les opinions de Tristram Shandy*, in 4 vols., the first two by Frénais, 1776, and the rest mainly by de Bonnay, 1785. More than a year before beginning *EO*, in a letter of Jan. 2, 1822, from Kishinev to Moscow, he criticizes as trashy orientalizations Moore's *Lalla Rookh* (in Pichot's prose), saying that the entire thing "is not worth ten lines of *Tristram Shandy*."

9 / Ochákov: At the time, and later, the name of this fortified Moldavian town, and Russian port, some forty miles east of Odessa, was spelled "Oczakow" in the British press. The fortress was stormed by Suvorov's troops in 1788, during the Turkish campaign, and became Russian by the treaty of 1791. Larin must have married at thirty-five, say, in 1797, and died between 1817 and 1820.

Commentary

14 / *nadgróbnïy madrigál*: This epitaphic or monumental
or funerary madrigaletto dashed off by Lenski has puz-
zled some commentators. Actually, the noun is em-
ployed here not in the modern sense of "compliment"
(as it is in Five : XLIV : 7 and Eight : XXXV : 12), but in
an older one going back to the French sixteenth century:
poets of Ronsard's time used "madrigal" as a technical
term for a hybrid form of poem, often elegiac in gist,
that had a sonnetlike sequence of rhymes but more than
fourteen lines.

XXXVIII

4–14 In a sermon "Sur la mort," preached at the Louvre on
Wednesday, Mar. 22, 1662, Bossuet says:

> Cette recrue continuelle du genre humain, je veux dire
> les enfants qui naissent, à mesure qu'ils croissent et
> qu'ils avancent, semblent nous pousser de l'épaule, et
> nous dire: Retirez-vous, c'est maintenant notre tour.
> Ainsi comme nous en voyons passer d'autres devant nous,
> d'autres nous verront passer, qui doivent à leurs suc-
> cesseurs le même spectacle. O Dieu! encore une fois,
> qu'est-ce que nous?

I have been led to this source by a vague reference in
Lozinski's edition of *EO* (1937). I note that the last sen-
tence of the passage quoted is paraphrased by Pushkin in
Two : XIVa : 14 (*Chto zh mí takóe!* . . . *bózhe móy.* . . .
"so what are we? O Lord. . . .").

5 / harvest / *zhátvoy* [instr.]: A venerable French cliché. The
metaphors "la mort fait sa moisson," "le temps moissonne
les humains," "sa vie a été moissonnée," and so on, occur
in thousands of combinations in French classical literature
and vulgar journalism. It is therefore very funny to see
Russian commentators (e.g., Chizhevski) solemnly go for
their glosses to Slavic antiquities or pseudoantiquities.

10 / *volnúetsya*: Fr. *s'agite*, heaves, pulses, and sways,

like a billowy sea or grainfield; is in a state of excitement or anxiety. The verb occurs commonly in Russian and is always a little difficult to translate.

11 / crowds / *tesnít*: A misprint in the 1826 edn. alters this to the meaningless "hastes," *speshít*. (The two words look very similar in Pushkin's hand.)

13 / one fine day / *v dóbrïy chás*: "At the good hour," an idiomatic term, midway between *un beau jour* and "in due time." With an exclamation mark it means "good luck!"

VARIANT

1–2 Draft (2369, f. 39ʳ):

> Another object ⟨of dire heartache⟩
> ⟨was, too, his father's recent grave⟩ . . .

Pushkin wisely left the date and circumstances of the death of Lenski's parents to the reader's imagination. It might have been a little complicated to explain who exactly (an uncle? a guardian?) had sent fourteen-year-old Vladimir from Krasnogorie to Göttingen, or, if his father was still alive in 1817, had or had not Vladimir been summoned back *in consequence* of the old man's death? I am also not sure if a youth of seventeen could be in those days a full-fledged, independent squire, as he seems to be when introduced (see Two : VI, etc.). Perhaps his Göttingen diploma granted him a kind of majority. His age is "not quite eighteen" in May, 1820, and "eighteen" in January, 1821 (see Two : X : 14 and Six : X : 8).

XXXIX

1–4 The quatrain goes in Russian:

> *Pokámest' upiváytes' éyu,*
> *Sey lyógkoy zhízniyu, druz'yá!*

> *Eyó nichtózhnost' razuméyu,*
> *I málo k ney privyázan yá . . .*

This bears a striking resemblance to the intonations
of Derzhavin's ode *Invitation to Dinner* (*Priglashenie k
obedu,* 1795), strophe IV, ll. 1–4:

> *Druz'yám moím ya posvyashcháyu,*
> *Druz'yám i krasoté sey dén';*
> *Dostóinstvam ya tsénu znáyu,*
> *I znáyu tó, chto vék nash tén' . . .*

> To friends of mine I dedicate—
> to friends and to the fair—this day;
> of merits I well know the value
> and know that our life is a shadow . . .

8 / Pushkin *wanted* to say (but did not):

> Without a trace, however slight . . .

As usual, I prefer to be loyal to my author's mistake.

12 / my woeful lot: This personal complaint, voiced in
exile and outdated by October, 1826, when he was
pardoned and the canto was published, was the reason
Pushkin deemed it wise to date in print the separate
edition of Two (p. 5): "Pisano v 1823 godu." Under
the draft of this stanza (2369, f. 41ᵛ) Pushkin had
written the date: "8 Dekabrya 1823 nuit" (Russ. and Fr.).

XL

5 / flattering hope / *léstnaya nadézhda*: A Gallicism: *espé-
rance flatteuse*.
  The suppositions (XL and XL : var. 5–8) referring to
the destiny of his work are similar in tone to those Push-
kin makes in regard to Lenski after his death in Six—a

similarity in keeping with the fateful note running through Two, the canto dedicated to the doomed poet.

9 / my thanks / *moi blagodarén'ya*: Thus in MS and in the *Northern Flowers* for 1826, but elsewhere misprinted *moyo blagodaren'e* (sing.), which does not rhyme properly.

VARIANTS

5–8 A draft (2369, f. 42ʳ) reads:

> and this young, careless verse
> shall outlive my tempestuous life.
> May I exclaim, O friends,
> I, too, have reared a monument?

Tomashevski (Acad 1937, facing p. 300) publishes an enlarged reproduction of this. The corrected draft is at the top of the page. Beneath it, a fragment (possibly continuing this stanza, ll. 9–10, despite the final dash under l. 8) reads:

> I recognize these tokens [*priméti*],
> these presages of love . . .

That the "tokens" are related to the "monument," and that the "love" is the reader's veneration for an author, seem to be borne out by the canceled draft:

> I recognize its [*ego*] tokens,
> the tokens true of love . . .

Under this, to the bottom of the page along the left margin of the drafts (XL : 5–8 and XLI : 9–14), there are several ink sketches of male and female profiles, while the right-hand margin (above XL : 5) is graced with a man's ear and a female necklaced neck. This neck with its string of diamonds belongs to Countess Eliza Vorontsov.

*

In its canceled form, l. 8 of the draft of var. 5–8 (ibid.) reads:

> *exegi monumentum ya* . . .

Derzhavin, imitating Horace, produced in 1796 the following piece in iambic hexameters alternately rhymed (abab):

> I've set up to myself a monument,
> wondrous, eternal. Stronger 'tis than metals,
> higher than pyramids. Neither fleet thunder,
> nor whirlwinds, nor the flight of time can break it.
>
> So! I'll not wholly die; a large part of me,
> fleeing decay, will after death exist;
> my fame will grow, nor will it fade as long
> as Slavs are by the universe respected.
>
> Tidings of me will go from White to Black Sea,
> where flow Neva, Don, Volga, where Ural
> from Riphaeus flows. Tribes countless will remember
> how I, unknown, became renowned, because
>
> I was the first in the quaint Russian style
> to dare proclaim the virtues of Felitsa,
> with simpleheartedness converse of God,
> and with a smile to monarchs speak the truth.
>
> O Muse, be justly proud of your achievement
> and if by some you're scorned, scorn them yourself,
> and with a hand unforced, unhurried, crown
> your brow with dawning immortality.

In 1836, in one of the most subtle compositions in Russian literary history, Pushkin parodied Derzhavin stanza by stanza in exactly the same verse form. The first four have an ironic intonation, but under the mask of high mummery Pushkin smuggles in his private truth. They should be in quotation marks, as Burtsev pointed out some thirty years ago in a paper I no longer can trace. The last quatrain is the artist's own grave voice repudiating the mimicked boast. His last line, although ostensibly referring to reviewers, slyly implies that only fools proclaim their immortality.

Exegi monumentum

"I've set up to myself a monument
   not wrought by hands. The public path to it
   will not grow weedy. Its unyielding head
   soars higher than the Alexandrine Column.

"No, I'll not wholly die. My soul in the sacred lyre
   is to survive my dust and flee decay;
   and I'll be famed while there remains alive
   in the sublunar world at least one poet.

"Tidings of me will cross the whole great Rus,
   and name me will each tribe existing there:
   proud scion of Slavs, and Finn, and the now savage
   Tungus, and—friend of steppes—the Kalmuck.

"And to the nation long shall I be dear
   for having with my lyre evoked kind feelings,
   exalted freedom in my cruel age
   and called for mercy toward the downfallen."

To God's command, O Muse, obedient be,
   offense not dreading, and no wreath demanding;
   accept indifferently praise and slander,
   and do not contradict a fool.

The Alexandrine Column is not the Pharos of Alexandria (the great lighthouse of white marble, reputed to be four hundred feet high, that stood on the eastern point of the Pharos Island, North Africa), as a naïve reader might think; nor is it the ninety-eight-foot-high Pompey's Pillar on the highest point of Alexandria (although its beautiful polished-granite shaft does bear some resemblance to Tsar Alexander's Column). This "Alexandrine Column," now called Alexandrovski Column, erected by Nicholas I (1829–34) in the Palace Square in St. Petersburg to commemorate Alexander I's victory over Napoleon, is a single shaft of dark-red granite eighty-four feet high, exclusive of pedestal and capital.

On the summit stands an angel holding a cross in his left hand and pointing to heaven with his right. Russian sources give the height of the whole thing, with the angel, as about 125 feet. It was, when built, the tallest column in the world, exceeding Napoleon's Colonne Vendôme (1810) in Paris by more than four feet.

Pushkin had in his library a Polish poem, with its French translation: *Ode sur la colonne colossale élevée à Alexandre I à Saint-Pétersbourg le 30 Août 1834*. Pushkin's MS bears the date Aug. 21, 1836, Kamennïy Ostrov (Stone Island, north bank of Neva, St. Petersburg).

"Alexandrine" pertains here to Alexander, as it does in the word Alexandrine (twelve-syllable verse), derived from medieval French poems about Alexander the Great, king of Macedon in the fourth century before our era. The critic Pogodin, in his diary (entry of Oct. 16, 1822), noted that, according to Aleksandr Raevski, Pushkin used to call Alexandrines *imperatorskie*, "imperial" lines, in punning allusion to Tsar Alexander I.

Zhukovski, in his posthumous edition of Pushkin's poems (vol. IX, 1841), substituted "Napoleon's Column" for "Alexander's Column," and amended st. IV in such a manner as to exclude the reference to the "cruel age" and to the "downfallen" Decembrists.

Some Soviet editions replace, in l. 15, the words *v móy zhestókiy vék* ("in my cruel age" or "times") by an earlier MS variant: *vsléd Radíshchevu* ("in the wake of Radishchev"), an allusion to Aleksandr Radishchev's ode, *Liberty* (*Vol'nost'*; written c. 1783), and to Pushkin's own ode, *Vol'nost'* (written 1817). See comm. to fragments of Ten, vol. 3, pp. 336–45.

L. 20 ("and do not contradict a fool"): cf. in comm. to Seven, following vars. to XXI–XXII, "Onegin's Album": III : 4:

> and don't argue with a fool . . .

6 Canceled draft (2369, f. 41ᵛ):

> a dunce will point out ex cathedra . . .

XLI

Pushkin started to copy out the following stanza (in PB) from his draft (2369, ff. 41ᵛ and 42ʳ), but did not go beyond l. 8 and struck out what he had written. The lines given here in pointed brackets represent the canceled first fair copy, and ll. 9–14 are from the draft:

⟨But possibly, and this is even
more verisimilar a hundred [times],
all torn, covered with dust and soot,
4 my story not read to the end,
banned by the housemaid from the dressing room,
will finish belowstairs its shameful span,
like last year's calendar
8 or a dilapidated primer.⟩
Well, what? In drawing room or vestibule
readers are equally ⟨plebeian [*chern*]⟩;
over a book their rights are equal;
12 not I the first, not I the last
shall hear their judgment over me,
captious, stern, and obtuse.

This beautiful stanza (canceled by the poet for unknown reasons) affords an admirable example of Pushkin's genius for extracting meaningful and noble music out of the most trivial words; in fact, it is exactly the contrast between their humdrum, subservient nature and the sonorities they develop within the acoustical paradise of Pushkin's tetrameter that produces the impression of noble sense. In the first line, *No mozhet bït' i eto dazhe*, the insignificant words *mozhet bït'* ("possibly" or "perhaps," which Pushkin uses with a similar intonation in Six : XXXIX : 1) and *dazhe* ("even") practically make up the line; the magic of their position in it, the *zh* alliteration, the fullness and weightiness of the sounds, raise the triviality of "perhaps" and "even" to the booming echoes of fate and metaphysical disaster. The reverberation unfolds in full in the fast-flowing *pravdopodóbnee* ("more verisimilar") and in the next highly scudded lines. See also Five : III : 1.

This is exactly opposite to the technique that Gogol employed when introducing dummy words, adverbal weeds, and prepositional debris into the stumbling patter of his automatons and larval homunculi, as, for instance, in his *The Carrick* (or *Greatcoat*).

I have discussed this device in my *Nikolai Gogol* (New Directions, 1944), a rather frivolous little book with a nightmare index (for which I am not responsible) and an unscholarly, though well-meant, hodgepodge of transliteration systems (for which I am). I take this opportunity to point out that the anecdote at the bottom of p. 8 concerns Delvig and that the aphorism at the top of p. 27 belongs to him too (and not to Pushkin, who only reports both anecdote and remark).

1–2 / But possibly, and this is even more verisimilar a hundred [times] / *No mózhet bít', i éto dázhe* | *Pravdo-podóbnee* [*v*] *sto ráz*: The *sto raz* ("a hundred times") is incorrectly replaced by *stokrát* ("a hundredfold") in some editions (following a slip on Pushkin's part in the canceled fair copy of the first eight lines); and this has misled Chizhevski (p. 233) into supposing the stanza to be incomplete.

The draft (2369, f. 41ᵛ) reads *sto raz*.

6 There are numerous allusions throughout the French seventeenth century to a poet's works being used as wrapping paper, etc. Cf. Scarron, *Roman comique* (1651–57), pt. I, ch. 8: ". . . un poète, ou plutôt un auteur, car toutes les boutiques d'épiciers du royaume étoient pleines de ses œuvres, tant en vers qu'en prose"; and

Father (Jean-Antoine) du Cerceau (c. 1670–1730), *Epître à Monsieur Etienne, Libraire*:

> Mais s'il avient, comme tout se peut faire,
> Que mes écrits, par un triste destin,
> Triste pour sûr, mais assez ordinaire,
> De la boutique aillent au magasin,
> Et que de-là, moisis dans la poussière
> Ils soient enfin livrés à la beurrière . . .

All this stems, I believe, from Horace, *Epistles*, I, xx, to his book, " . . . then when you begin to grow dirty, soiled by the hands of the crowd, you will . . . in quiet repose feed the illiterate worms," and from the end of II, i, where a book is compared to the "useless papers in which aromatic seasonings and pepper are wrapped up."

9 / *v perédney*: The same term is used in l. 6, where I have rendered "vestibule" by its Russian metonym, "below-stairs." The *perednyaya*, vestibule, with its purlieus, was the haunt of footmen, some of them great readers of tattered books. Cf. Boileau's *Epistres*, IX: "Ses vers, jetés d'abord sans tourner le feuillet, iralent dans l'antichambre amuser Pacolet" (the name of a valet).

VARIANTS

7 Corrected draft:

> like *Invalid* or *Kalendar'* . . .

The first means *The Disabled Soldier* and is the title of a periodical of the time.

A clue to the second is provided by the canceled reading: *Bryusov Kalendar'*. *Bruce's Calendar*, a kind of *Farmer's Almanack* (cf. the calendar, which is probably the Court Calendar, in III : 12), was the delight of the eighteenth and early nineteenth centuries. It was attributed to Count Yakov Bryus (James Bruce, 1670–

1735), one of Peter I's generals, who was reputed to be an alchemist. Actually, he was an excellent astronomer and mathematician. The real author of the calendar was the librarian Vasiliy Kipriyanov, an obscure scholar of lowly birth, who in 1709 (May 2) published in Moscow the first issue—mainly devoted to astronomy—of the *Calendar*, under the auspices (*pod nazreniem*) of Lieutenant-General Yakov Vilimovich [Williamovich] Bryus. A second part came out six months later, packed with ecclesiastic information, and this was followed in (June?) 1710 by a third, oracular, part ("Prognostication of seasons for every year by the planets," etc.), which made Kipriyanov's fortune. Numerous reissues and imitations followed, and parts of it were integrated in the Martin Zadeck dream book, of which further (n. to Five : XXII : 12).

Chapter Three

This is a line from *Narcisse, ou l'île de Vénus* (pub. 1768), can. II, a third-rate poem in four long cantos, by Jacques Charles Louis Clinchamp de Malfilâtre (1733–67): "Elle [the nymph Echo] était fille [and thus, inquisitive as they all are]; elle était [moreover] amoureuse | . . . Je lui pardonne [as my Tatiana should be pardoned]; Amour la fit coupable [cf. *EO*, Three : XXIV]. | Puisse le sort lui pardonner aussi!"

In Greek mythology, Echo, who pined away for love of Narcissus, who in turn pined away for love of his own reflection, is reduced to a mere woodland voice, much as Tatiana is in Seven : XXVIII, while Onegin's image ripples in the margins of the books he has read (Seven : XXII–XXIV).

In Pushkin's schoolbook, *Lycée, ou Cours de littérature ancienne et moderne* (which was also the manual of Lamartine, whose unfortunate *goût* it formed, and of Stendhal, who in an 1804 entry of his *Journal* mentions his wish to *délaharpiser* his style, which he, a descendant of Voltaire and Laclos, never succeeded in doing), La Harpe (VIII, 252) quotes two quite innocent passages from *Narcisse*, the first of which starts with the line Pushkin may have later recalled from that very page.

Although, generally speaking, Pushkin can always be relied upon for improper innuendoes, I am not certain he was aware in this case that Malfilâtre's nymph was eavesdropping—behind La Harpe's back—on a definitely salacious conversation between Venus and old Tiresias, whom Juno had afflicted with nervous impotence for slaying two dragons *in copula*.

On the title page of the fair copy of Three (PB 10) Pushkin preceded the established motto with three lines from Dante (*Inferno*, can. v):

> Ma dimmi: al tempo de' dolci sospiri,
>   A che e come concedette amore,
>   Che conoscete i dubbiosi desiri?

> But tell me: in the time of dulcet sighs
> by what, and in what manner, did love grant
> that you should know your indistinct desires?

I–II

Chapter Three opens with a dialogue—pure dialogue, i.e., without any inserted "he said," "he replied," and so forth. It occupies the first two stanzas and the first foot and a half of the third one (*Poédem*, "Let's go"). At the time (1824), this device (introductory dialogue) was relatively new in the European novel.

Having a "realistic" conversation conform—while retaining its natural flow—to a rigid poetical structure with an intricate rhyme pattern, and thus gain in vivid comedy by contrast, was, on the other hand, no novelty in Pushkin's time. Among numerous examples, a most charming sonnet of this kind is one by Bernard de La Monnoye (1641–1728), *Dialogue de deux Compères à la Messe*, imitating an Italian sonnet by Matteo Franco (1447–94):

. . . .
"Voulez-vous qu'au sortir nous déjeunions en ville?"
"Tope." "Nous en mettrons Sire Ambroise et Rolait."
"D'accord" . . .

    . . . .
"A propos, on m'a dit que le voisin Lucas
  Épouse votre . . ." "Point. J'ai découvert ses dettes" . . .

We find everything in this opening of Three—the col-
loquial intonation, the cutting of a line into two or three
répliques, the question-and-answer shuttle, the fitting
of a brief *réplique* into the first foot of a line, interruption
of speech, and even one enjambment. It is also in the
manner of some of La Fontaine's and Krïlov's fables.

Sts. I and II of Chapter Three are logically fused in one
piece, and their twenty-eight lines are broken into six-
teen ($7+9$) *répliques*, with Onegin being for the nonce
three times more talkative than Lenski: Onegin utters in
all 103 Russian words and particles to Lenski's 39. The
fond enthusiast is at first *sur ses gardes*; for sarcastic
Onegin is here certainly not the same lenient listener
who, in Two : XV, endeavored to restrain the chilling
word. Onegin taunts him here into an outburst (II : 3–5);
but then puzzles and pleases Lenski with an amiable
suggestion (reverting as it were to the tolerant mood of
Two : XV : 13–14).

This is the first time in *EO* that we actually hear an
exchange of words between Onegin and Lenski, who
have been *described* as conversing as early as Two : XV.
It would seem, incidentally, that Two : XIX should have
long satisfied the curiosity Onegin voices in Three : I–
II; actually, it appears that Onegin hears the name of
Larin for the first time only now.

I

1, 3 The rich rhyme here depends on the splitting of one of
the components: *poétï* ("poets"), *gdé tï* ("where do

you"), comparable to "poet"–"know it" or "prodige"–"dis-je."

1–7 Tomashevski publishes* one corner of a page "From Pushkin's cahier (1824)," with a nightcapped head of Voltaire sketched by our poet in the right-hand margin. It did not occur to the editors to identify the MS. The tails of seven terminal words, however, can be made out in its reproduction. It is the beginning of Chapter Three.

The whereabouts of the cahier (now in the Pushkinskiy Dom) are given as Vsesoyuznaya Biblioteka imeni Lenina (the All-Union Library "of the name" of Lenin) in Moscow. This library is also referred to as Leninskaya Biblioteka and Publichnaya Biblioteka.

To judge by Tomashevski's description of Pushkin's drafts in Acad 1937, this autograph is in Cahier 2369, f. 39^v, and is dated "8 févr. la nuit 1824."

In the margin of the draft there is a jotting referring to Countess Elizaveta Vorontsov (or, as she wrote her name, Elise Woronzoff): "soupé chez C.E.W." ("supped at C.E.W.'s").

5 / *Vot éto chúdno*: A Gallicism (*voilà une belle merveille*), which finds a kind of excuse in such Russian expressions of surprise as *chudnoe delo* ("wonderful matter"), meaning "now, that's odd."

7 / thus / *Tak*: Other editors have *Tam*, "there."

11 The comma after *prostaya*, "simple," demands the "truly" before "Russian."

VARIANTS

13–14 In the draft (2369, f. 48^v) Tomashevski reads (l. 13):
    in the reception room a tallow candle

and (ll. 13–14):

    jams, tallow candle,
    the mention of Sava Ilyich [*Pomín pro Sávu Il'ichá*].

---

*Lit. nasl., nos. 31–32 (1937), p. 29.

A strange figure, this Sava (or Savva; Sabas, a Serbian
patron saint), son of Ilya. I should have to examine
Cahier 2369 myself in order to come to some conclusion
that would satisfy me; I have only material where such
drafts of l. 14 as "and the jokes" and "the stories" are
seen to be altered to "the mention" (see above). *Pomín*
may be understood in the sense of commemorational
chitchat, and I would suggest that, perhaps, what Eugene
apprehended with disgust was Dame Larin's recalling
for his benefit the bons mots and other characteristics of
his uncle Sava. Eugene would not have known, or been
able to use with such familiarity, the names of other
landowners in the neighborhood, and he certainly is not
supposed to bear in mind that his creator toyed at the
time (see n. to Two : XXXVI : 12) with the idea of giving
the name of Sava to the late father of Lenski's sweet-
heart.

The lone candle conjured up by Onegin in his dis-
gusted visualization of a parsimonious parlor may be
contrasted with the multiple blaze in Senancour's *Ober-
man*, Letter LXV, where a pleasing light is thrown on
household practices of the time: ". . . j'aime à être assis
sur un meuble élégant à vingt pieds de distance d'un
feu de salon, à la lumière de quarante bougies."

A dazzling phrase!

II

5 / Again an eclogue / *Opyát' eklóga*: A Gallicism. "Eclogue"
is to be understood here not as a literary form (pastoral
poem, one of Virgil's bucolics, dialogue between shep-
herds, idyl, familiar ode, or just "short poem" in the
Roman sense), but in the general—French—sense of
agréments de la vie champêtre; pastoral patter.

9 / Phyllis: *Fillída*; Eng. Phyllida or Phillida (e.g., in
Izaak Walton, c. 1640) and Phillis; Fr. Philis, Phylis,

Filis, and Fillis (see, for example, the various editions, 1609, 1627, etc., of the *Stances* by Jean de Lingendes: "D'où vient que sans effort," etc.).

This is not the lovelorn Phyllis, princess of Thrace, who upon hanging herself was changed into a pink-flowering almond tree, but a generalized figure, the beloved maiden of "Arcadian" poetry, pastorals and the like, presupposing a bucolic space time within which refined shepherds and shepherdesses tend immaculate flocks amid indestructible meadow flowers and make sterile love in shady bosquets near murmuring rills. That sheep look like toads and can devastate a continent did not concern poets. The overrated Virgil was a popular exponent of the theme on the burnished threshold of an ormolu era: in his ten eclogues, which are stale imitations of the idyls of Theocritus, this or that shepherd, when not burning for some younger assistant shepherd, courts an occasional shepherdess, and one of these girls is called Phyllis. Nothing, incidentally, is more depressing than the arbitrary symbols that English commentators read into these pieces.

Subsequently the bucolic theme flourished in perfumed and beribboned forms throughout Renaissance Europe until the beginning of the last century, without anywhere producing great masterpieces, although there are echoes of it in the works of a number of great poets such as Shakespeare and La Fontaine.

10–11 / *Predmét i mísley, i perá,* | *I slyóz, i rífm et ceterá?*: To the ear of a Frenchman of 1820, Onegin's badinage would sound distinctly dated:

Antoine Bertin, *A une femme que je ne nommerai point,* 1785:

> Beauté, talens, esprit, jeunesse,
> Taille, et minois d'une déesse,
> Jambe élégante, *et cætera.*

Piron, *Rosine* (*Œuvres complettes*, 1776):

> Le sort bientôt se déclara:
> Le lot fut pour un Insulaire . . .
> Beau, bien fait, jeune, et cætera.

Gabriel Charles de Lattaignant (1697–1779; a poetaster, except for a striking piece, *Réflexions sérieuses*), *Couplets pour être mis à la suite d'une comédie intitulée les Héritiers*:

> J'appris dès mon bas âge
> Le chant, la danse *et cætera* . . .

La Harpe, *L'Ombre de Duclos*, 1773:

> Couplets badins, et tristes facéties,
> Contes rimés, lyriques inepties;
> *Flore, Zéphyr,* et jargon d'opéra,
> *Roses, baisers, boudoirs,* et cætera . . .

Pushkin himself had used the formula as early as 1816 in some tetrametric lines to his uncle, the poet Vasiliy Pushkin, wishing him and everybody a good Easter (ll. 14–15):

> . . . and lots of silver [*serebrá*]
> and gold [*zólota*] et ceterá.

12 / No / *Nétu*: Onegin uses an old-fashioned and dialect form of the denial *net*, something between "no" and "not at all."

13 / Now, if you like / *Hot' seychás*: Yet another thorn in the translator's flesh. The *hot'* connotes both "even now" and "why not now?" A correct paraphrase would be "Any time" or "Right now, for instance."

III

1 / Let's go / *Poédem*: I understand this as the end of Lenski's final *réplique*. There is a kind of interstrophic

Commentary

enjambment here, though not as strong as in Three :
XXXVIII–XXXIX and Eight : XXXIX–XL.

6 / jams: Homemade preserves—cherry, raspberry, straw-
berry, gooseberry, red and black currant (a canceled
draft has "honey jam"), to mention only the commonest
sorts—would be presented to guests in small glass dishes
on a tray ("with but one spoon for all"—var. l. 7); the
guests would transfer their helpings (by means of that
spoon) onto their respective saucers and then would eat
the jam with their teaspoons or mix it with their tea.

7 / oilcloth'd small table / *stólik . . . voshchanóy*: Not
"waxed," as a grammatical translation demands, but
"covered with a *toile cirée*."

In a poem to his schoolmate Ivan Pushchin, May 4,
1815, Pushkin had already mentioned a *stolik voshcha-
noy*—and had suggested setting a mug of beer upon it.

Dmitriev, in his satirical fantasy *Prichudnitsa* (Fr.
La Capricieuse or *L'Extravagante*; 1798), has a doctor
write out his order at the patient's bedside on a table
covered with a *voshchanka*, "oilcloth" (see also n. to
Five : XVIII : 12).

Pisemski, in his novel *A Thousand Souls*, pt. III, ch. 1,
describes a one-ruble, fourth-floor, small hotel room
"with an oilcloth'd"—*voshchyonnïy* (sic)—"table and
similar sofa."

The *Slovar' yazïka Pushkina* (vol. I, Moscow, 1956)
understands *voshchanoy* as *navoshchyonnïy*, "waxed."

8 / lingonberry: *Brusnika* is *Vaccinium vitis-idaea* Linn.,
the red bilberry—the "red whorts" of northern Eng-
land, the *lingon* of Sweden, the *Preisselbeere* of Ger-
many, and the *airelle ponctuée* of French botanists—
which grows in northern pine forests and in the moun-
tains. It is also called "cowberry" and "windberry," but

so are some of its congeners. In Scotland it goes under the names of "common cranberry" and "lingberry," both of which are misleading since it has nothing to do either with the true cranberry, *Oxycoccus oxycoccus* or *palustris* (the Russian *klyukva*), or with the capsules of "ling," heather, *Calluna*. In America it is termed "mountain cranberry" (e.g., by Thoreau in *The Maine Woods*, 1864) and "lowbush cranberry" (by Canadian fishermen), which leads to hopeless confusion with American forms of true cranberry, *Oxycoccus*. Dictionaries, and the harmful drudges who use them to translate Russian authors, confuse the lingonberry with its blue-fruit ally, *Vaccinium myrtillus* Linn. (bilberry proper, whortleberry, the "hurts" or "roundels azure" of heraldry; Russ. *chernika*); and I notice that Turgenev lets Viardot get away with the ridiculous "cassis," black currant!

The combination *brusníchnaya vodá* (or *voditsa*), *eau d'airelle rouge*, might perhaps be translated simply "redberry water" (cf. Swift's "citron water," *Journal of a Modern Lady*, 1729), had not there existed other red berries. Onegin, as will be seen further (IV : 13–14), is distrustful of Mme Larin's lingonade, fearing the action of a country brew on a city stomach. Lingonberry was extensively used in rural communities, as both berry extracts and herb decoctions, for internal ills such as kidney trouble and gastric disorders. As early as the sixteenth century the *Domostroy*, a MS set of household injunctions, lists *vodï brusnichnïe* among the contents of a goodman's cellar.

The lingonberry is as popular in Russia as are the bilberry, the cranberry, the raspberry (*malina*), the wild and cultivated strawberry (*zemlyanika*), and the wild and cultivated hautbois or green strawberry (*klubnika*—often confused by provincial Russians with the ordinary garden strawberry, *sadovaya zemlyanika, viktoriya,* etc.). Students of Russian literature will recall the beautiful new tail coat "of a lingonberry red, sparked" that Chichikov sports in Gogol's *Dead Souls*, pt. II (c. 1845).

I expect some acknowledgment for all this information from future translators of Russian classics.

Miss Deutsch serves "huckleberry syrup," and Miss Radin "A jug of huckleberry juice." Spalding skips the stanza but in the next refers to "that bilberry wine"; and Elton upsets Onegin's stomach with "bilberry-decoctions . . . in a jar" and "that liquor from bilberries."

VARIANTS

6–14 The rest of the stanza reads in the fair copy (PB 10):

> in little dishes jams are brought
> with but one spoon for all.
> 8 Other occupations and pleasures
> are lacking in the country after dinner.
> With snugly folded arms, at doors,
> the serf girls speedily have gathered
> 12 to have a look at the new neighbor;
> and in the court a crowd of menials
> criticized their steeds.

I am pretty sure Pushkin canceled the end of the stanza because of two flaws he could not correct without rewriting it: the "all" in l. 7 may refer either to the jams or to the people partaking of them. The other error is "their steeds." This should have been "Onegin's steeds," for it is clear from the context (see the master speaking to his coachman, in IV : 9) that Onegin's, not Lenski's, carriage was used for the visit; but even if it can be imagined that *Poskakáli drúgi* ("off the two friends drove"—III : 1) refers to "galloping off on horse-back" (and not to "driving off"), the phrase "their steeds" would still be wrong, since, surely, one of the two mounts was a sufficiently familiar sight at the Larins' not to be gaped at by critical domestics!

The cancellation provides a structural pause.

8–9 The draft reads (2369, f. 49ʳ):

> a big carafe [*butïl'*] of lingonade,
> a watermelon, golden peaches

with canceled "homegrown watermelon" and "a platter of golden peaches."

Recalling probably that the Larins were supposed to be comparatively "poor," Pushkin canceled the Southern fruit that wealthy Northern squires cultivated in hothouses. By 1820 ingenious horticulturists were replacing with metal pipes and hot steam the old-fashioned flues of forcing houses, and already the mandarin orange was being ripened in Edinburgh, St. Petersburg, and Riga. Peaches were found to be much hardier than it had been thought; and pineapples were amazed at what they were made to do.

IV

2 Pushkin's n. 17 refers to the misprint *Zimóy* ("in winter") for *Domóy* ("homeward").

5–6 / Onegin . . . Lenski: In Pushkin's (and Tolstoy's) day, among people of gentle birth, whether military men or literary ones, it was quite customary for friends *qui se tutoyaient* to call each other by their surnames or titles (cf. my nn. to Eight : XVII–XVIII). They would address acquaintances or old people by first name and patronymic, reserving first names for very close relatives and childhood friends.

The *Nu chtó zh* ("Well now") with which Lenski begins the conversation is the French *eh bien*.

5–14 In the second dialogue that occupies IV : 5–14 and V : 1–12, there are eight speeches, and again Onegin, with seventy-five words to his credit, is three times more loquacious than Lenski. It will be noted that in comparison to the introductory dialogue (I–III : 1), the order of emotional sequence is reversed: it starts here with Onegin chatting in a languid but fairly amiable mood and ends in cold sarcasm. Onegin lulls Lenski into a sense of false security by good-naturedly praising Dame Larin; his casual question "which was Tatiana?" is merely meant to bring on what follows: Lenski naïvely explains what Onegin surely must have learned in the course of the visit—and then the epigrammatic storm breaks. Actually, Onegin is less witty than rude, and it is a wonder hot-tempered Lenski did not challenge him to a duel there and then. This Three : v upset me so much when I first read *EO* as a boy of nine or ten that I mentally had Onegin next morning ride over to Lenski's to apologize —with the suave frankness that made the proud man's charm—for venting his spleen on the lover's lady and the poet's moon.

"Dame Larin . . . a very nice old lady," *une petite vieille très aimable*. At least "forty winters had besieged her brow," to paraphrase Shakespeare's Sonnet II. (See n. to Two : XXX : 13–14.)

8 / field / *póle*: Fr. *la campagne*.

10 / What silly country / *Kakie glúpïe mestá*: This line is curiously echoed by l. 6 (*Kakie grústnïe mestá*) of Tyutchev's famous little poem *Pesók sïpúchiy po koléni* (in iambic tetrameter, rhymed ababecec; written in 1830, published in 1837 in Pushkin's literary review *The Contemporary*, *Sovremennik*):

> The crumbly sand is knee-high.
> We're driving late. The day is darkening,
> and on the road the shadows of the pines
> into one shadow have already fused.

Blacker and denser is the deep pine wood.
What melancholy country!
Grim night like a hundred-eyed beast
looks out of every bush.

As has been pointed out by Russian critics, the image in
ll. 7–8 is an improvement upon a metaphor in Goethe's
Willkommen und Abschied: "Wo Finsternis aus dem
Gesträuche mit hundert schwarzen Augen sah."

11 / Ah, apropos: The "silly country" suggests to Onegin
its "silly people"—simple Madam Larin; hence the
"apropos."

11–14 Bodenstedt's unbelievable German "translation" of
EO has at this point:

> "Lensky! Die Larina ist schlicht,
> Aber recht hübsch für ihre Jahre;
> Doch ihr Likör, wie schlechter Rum,
> Steigt mir zu Kopfe, macht mich dumm."

A rare instance of a liqueur not only being imagined by
the translator but affecting him in the same way as it
does the imagined speaker.

VARIANTS

6–8 Draft (2369, f. 49ʳ):

> . . .—*tí skucháesh'*—
> *Vsegdá i vsyúdu; právda —no*
> *Segódnya ból'she —nét, ravnó.*

> . . . "You are bored?"
> "True, everywhere and always." "But
> tonight more?" "No, the same."

9 Onegin's coachman is "Ilyushka" in the fair copy of this
verse. Pushkin's coachman at Mihaylovskoe was named
Pyotr.

Commentary

V

1 / "Tell me, which was Tatiana?": Tatiana henceforth
will be present throughout Chapter Three save for two
digressions wherein Pushkin intrudes—to promise a
later novel in prose (XI–XIV); and to discourse: on co-
quettes as compared to Tatiana (XXIV, XXV), on letter
writing, and on feminine grammar (XXII–XXIII, XXVII–
XXX); there are, moreover, a fruit-picking song (in tro-
chaic trimeter with long terminals) and a closing
digression (XLI : 9–14).

1–12 See n. to IV : 5–14.

2–4 The reference is to Zhukovski's masterpiece, *Svetlana*
(1812), sts. II, ll. 3–4 ("silent is and sad dear Svetlana"),
and XVII, ll. 1–2 ("sat down . . . by the window"). This
is a ballad (*ballada*) consisting of twenty stanzas of four-
teen lines each, with a sonnetlike rhyme sequence
(babaceceddiffi) in two trochaic measures, tetrameter
(the eight lines with masculine rhymes b, c, d, f) and
trimeter (the six lines with feminine rhymes a, e, i). I
have often wondered if Zhukovski's adoption of this
fancy sonnet form for his stanza in *Svetlana* had not in-
fluenced Pushkin's choice of the *EO* stanza, although,
of course, owing to the trochaic skip-skip and to the in-
trusion of the feminine-ending trimeter into the mascu-
line tetrameter, the effect is quite unlike the *EO* melody.

This ballad starts with girls divining (as they do in *EO*,
Five : VIII) by means of wax (*Svetlana*, I, 8), "golden
rings, emerald eardrops" (I, 10–II, 14; see my n. to
Five : VIII), and a "mirror with candle" (IV–VI). Thanks
to these conjurations, her lover appears—and the next
nine stanzas parody the equestrian and funereal theme
of Bürger's *Lenore*. The vision proves to be a harmless
dream, and the ballad ends in delightful diurnal bathos:

the light of blissful reality dispels the chaotic nightmare as Svetlana's lover returns to her, safe and sound after a year's absence.

There are other echoes of *Svetlana* in *EO*. Thus, the last sextet of Zhukovski's ballad foretells, as it were, with its "pleasant rill's gleam on the bosom of a meadow" the Lenskian landscape (Seven : VI, especially), while various details are curiously echoed in Tatiana's dream (Five).

This was not the first time Pushkin referred to Zhukovski's maiden. In 1814, our poet had addressed an epistle of 121 lines in iambic tetrameter to his sister, Olga Pushkin, in which he wondered if she was peering into the dark distance "like a pensive Svetlana" (ll. 45–46). See also my nn. to the motto of Five; to Five : X : 6; and to Eight : IV : 7–8.

9 / *Toch'-v-tóch' v Vandíkovoy Madóne*: The first edition of the canto gives *kak u* (Fr. *comme chez*) for *toch'-v-toch'* ("just"), which necessitates the genitive (*madóni*), killing the rhyme.

According to Gofman (1923), Pushkin toyed not only with *Rafaélevoy* but also with *Perudzhínovoy* (Perugino's) before hitting on *Vandíkovoy*. Of Vandyke's (Sir Anthony van Dyck or Vandyke, 1599–1641) religious pictures (such as the *Virgin with the Rosary* in the Oratorio del Santissimo Rosario, Palermo, or the *Virgin and Child* in the Louvre, or the *Holy Family with the Partridges* in the Hermitage, St. Petersburg), none is very interesting.

Pushkin was fond of the word "madonna." Bartenev, in a notebook,* says that Pushkin, in a (lost) letter to Elizaveta Hitrovo (1783–1839), informs her, in 1830,

---

*The jottings of which are published by Tsyavlovski in *Pushkin* (Letopisi gosudarstvennogo literaturnogo muzeya), pt. I (Moscow, 1936), pp. 491–558.

that he is about to marry "a madonna with a squint and
red hair" ("j'épouse une madonne louche et rousse").
Pushkin's term of contradistinctive endearment for his
wife, "strabismic madonna" (Russ. *kosaya madonna*), is
also mentioned by other memoirists (Princess Vera
Vyazemski, according to Bartenev's notes).

10–11 | *Kruglá, krasná litsóm oná* | *Kak éta glúpaya luná*:
The old meaning of *krasnïy* is "beautiful," and I under-
stand *ona krasna litsom* as "she is fair of face," and not
as "she has a red face," which would have been *u neyo
krasnoe litso*. A *krasnoe litso* is a florid face connoting the
coarse flush of intemperance, high blood pressure, anger,
shame, and so on, and would be totally unsuited to
describe the rosy Pamela, or the rosy madonna, whom
Onegin has in mind. His rudeness is bad enough, with-
out it. The term Pushkin employs for denoting Olga's
pretty carnation is the noun *rumyanets* and the adjective
rumyanaya: in fact, in a canceled draft (above a sketched
profile of Count Vorontsov, whose epaulet hobnobs with
a draft of l. 13) we can decipher the words *rumyána i
belá*, "rosy and fair-skinned." *Krasnaya devitsa* means
"beautiful girl," and several generations of foreign cor-
respondents would be surprised to learn that Krasnaya
Ploshchad', the famous ancient square in Moscow,
means a "beautiful, festive place," and not "Red
Square."

My choice of meaning is supported by the simile of
the moon, which is here the beautiful sphere ("round
and fair") sung by poets and, indeed, is the same bright
moon with which Lenski is elegiacally enamored in
Two : XXII : 8–12. No moon appears in any of the drafts,
nor is it to be found in the fair copy; but that a variant
of the moon lines existed is suggested by a curious
passage in a letter (published in *Arhiv brat'ev Tur-
genevïh*) from Vyazemski to Aleksandr Turgenev and

Zhukovski, of Jan. 6, 1827 (nine months before the canto was published), in which he quotes Three : v : 11–12, thus:

> *Kak vásha glúpaya luná*
> *Na váshem glúpom nebosklóne*
>
> as is your stupid moon
> up in your stupid sky

—the "your" being obviously used in the plural sense (i.e., "the moon you poets sing"). This lyrical generalized moon is, of course, not tinged with any color; and, anyway, the equation of a red face and a red moon would make one see the face as being of the hue of a tomato, not of a rose. I am quite aware that in a poem of 1819 (*Rusalka*, seven tetrametric octets in the iambic measure, about a mermaid and a monk) Pushkin, in describing a summer evening with a mist on the lake, speaks in l. 14 of what seems to be a definitely ruddy moon, or half-moon, in the clouds (*I krásnïy mésyats v oblakáh*), but that is an Ossianic landscape (as, for example, in *Sul-malla of Lumon*), not the Arcadian one of *EO*, Three.

The general notion, which not only translators but good innocent Russians (including the compilers of *Slovar' yazïka Pushkina*, vol. II, Moscow, 1957) share, that *krasna litsom* is "red-faced," culminates, as it were, in a version that for sheer imbecility can hardly be matched.

In a "correct" English translation (published in New York for the Metropolitan Opera House, c. 1920) of the incredible Italian libretto of Chaykovski's silly opera *Eugene Onegin* (*Evgeniy Onegin*, "liricheskie stsenï v 3-h deystviyah, tekst po Pushkinu," Moscow, 1878, libretto by the composer and by Konstantin Shilovski [a poetaster]; first performed by the students of the Imperial College of Music in Moscow, 1879), when in

Act I "Signora Larína" is seated under a tree, "making candy" (with Olga in a tree and Tatiana in a swoon), the following lunatic scene takes place:

Oneghin (to Lenski): "Now, tell me, which is Tatiana? | . . . Her being doth not possess the lukewarmness | Of the classical Madonna. | Deep purple, by my soul, | Shining like the stupid moon." (. . . [he] rudely stares at Tatiana).

12 / sky / *nebosklón*: The noun *nebosklon* ("sky-slope," arch of the sky) had long ago lost its metaphoric character and become a mere synonym of "sky" (*nebo*), to which a Russian poet would frequently prefer it because of its better rhyming facilities.

13 / curtly / *súho*: A Gallicism, *sèchement*, *d'un ton sec*. The English "dryly" (which is the grammatical counterpart of *suho*) suggests "dry wit," etc., which, of course, has nothing to do with this.

VARIANTS

8–14 Tomashevski (Acad 1937, p. 575n.) gives two fair-copy variants, starting (ll. 8–9):

There is no thought in Olga's features
as there is none in Raphael's Madonna

thence branching and continuing (initial stage of fair copy; ll. 10–14):

Rosiness and a sinless gaze
have bored me a long time."
"Each worships his own icon,"
Vladimir answered curtly,
and our Onegin became silent

and (corrected fair copy, ll. 10–14):

Believe me, innocence is nonsense;
what's more, Pamela's sickly-sweet gaze

even in Richardson has bored me."
Vladimir answered curtly
and thenceforth the whole way was silent.

The Pamela of l. 11 is the heroine of Richardson's
Pamela; or, Virtue Rewarded, in A. F. Prévost's French
version (1741–42). (See n. to Three : IX : 10.)

va, vb, vc

The beginning of a conventional plot is represented by
the following drafts in Cahier 2369, ff. 50ʳ and 51ᵛ:

va

Lying in bed, our Eugene
was reading Byron with a skimming eye,
but the tribute of evening meditations
4 was mentally devoting to Tatiana.
⟨He⟩ woke before daybreak,
and still about Tatiana was his thought.
"Here is a new thing," he reflected.
8 "Can it be I'm in love with her?
Upon my soul, that would be famous!
What a conferment ⟨upon me indeed⟩!
We'll see." And he at once decided
12 assiduously to visit the fair neighbors
as oft as he was able—every day:
⟨for⟩ they have time and we're not slack.

vb

⟨Decided⟩—and soon Eugene was
like Lenski . . .

vc

Can it be that Onegin has indeed
⟨fallen in love⟩ . . .

a: 1–3, 7–9 When in *Graf Nulin* (composed Dec. 13–14,
1825; published Dec. 22, 1827, in *Northern Flowers* for
1828) the count goes to bed—in the house of the lady

who gives him shelter when his traveling carriage
breaks—and is brought by his French valet a decanter,
a silver glass, a cigar, a bronze candlestick, a snuffer,
an alarm clock (replaced by a chamber pot in the draft),
and an uncut novel,

> 216 Lying in bed, he Walter Scott
> scans with a skimming eye,
> but inwardly he is diverted
> . . . .
>
> 220 . . . he wonders:
> Can I have really fallen in love?
> . . . How amusing!
> My word, that would be famous.

In the draft of l. 221—"God damn! Have I fallen in
love?"—the first two words are in English. This exple-
tive crops up in French fiction and fugitive poetry of the
eighteenth century, as "Goddam" or "Goddem," when
Englishmen are portrayed. The "Walter Scott" in l. 217
is a French version of one of the Waverley novels.

VI

VARIANT

13–14 The draft (2369, f. 51ᵛ) gives:

> Of like opinion were the pope
> and his sexton himself, Antrop.

*

After Three : VI, having filled up the black ledger known
as Cahier 2369, begun (with One) in May, 1823, Push-
kin turned to the similar 2370, which starts with Three :
XXIX (May 22, 1824, Odessa), a number of preceding
leaves having been apparently destroyed. According to
Tomashevski (Acad 1937, p. 309), the drafts of twenty-
two stanzas of Three (VII–XXVIII) are lost, except for the
quatrain of IX, already jotted down in 2369, f. 50ʳ (which
contains the false start, VA), and the whole of XXV (the

Parny imitation), written in 2370, f. 12ʳ, after the next
batch, comprising Tatiana's Letter, from XXIX to XXXV
had been composed. The period of time involved in the
gap (May, 1824) was marked by Pushkin's quarrel with
the governor general, and it may be assumed that our
poet destroyed the drafts of letters or other material
written among the VII–XXVIII stanzas, the drafts of which
consequently perished, too.

VII

10 / *Sgoráya négoy i toskóy*: Both nouns belong to the
vaguely evocative type of romantic locution so frequent
in *EO* and so difficult to render by exact English words.
Nega ranges from "mollitude" (Fr. *mollesse*), i.e., soft
luxuriousness, "dulcitude," through various shades of
amorous pensiveness, *douce paresse*, and sensual tender-
ness to outright voluptuousness (Fr. *volupté*). The trans-
lator has to be careful here not to overdo in English what
Pushkin is on the point of overdoing in Russian when
he makes his maiden burn with all the French languors
of flesh and fancy.

Toska is the generic term for a feeling of physical or
metaphysical dissatisfaction, a sense of longing, a dull
anguish, a preying misery, a gnawing mental ache.
(See also n. to Three : XIV : 9–10.)

10, 12 Pushkin's three favorite words, *nega*, *toska*, and
tomlen'e, are all collected here in one bunch.

14 / *Dushá zhdalá . . . kogó-nibúd'*: This is not a particu-
larly good line, and its would-be cynical flippancy sounds
flat and conventional.

My literal translation hardly scans, a recurrent and
completely unimportant feature of a work whose only

337

Commentary

purpose is textual fidelity with just as much music as might not interfere with accuracy of sense.

VIII

7 / speaks / *Tverdít*: See n. to Two : XXX : 7.

IX

3–4 and X : 5 Cf. Mary Hays, *Memoirs of Emma Courtney* (1796), vol. I, ch. 7: ". . . the Héloise of Rousseau fell into my hands.—Ah! with what transport . . . did I peruse this dangerous, enchanting work!"

4 / illusion / *obmán*: Delusion, fiction, and, through consonance, the mist (*tuman*) of mystification, all these connotations are contained in Pushkin's philologism, *obman*. See One : IX : 2; Two : XXIX : 3.

7 / the lover of Julie Wolmar: Inexact; she was Julie d'Etange, not Wolmar, when she became the mistress of "Saint-Preux" (as her girl friend, Claire d'Orbe, nicknames the author's anonymous representative). The novel is *Julie, ou La Nouvelle Héloïse*, "lettres de deux amants, habitants d'une petite ville au pied des Alpes, recueillies et publiées par J. J. Rousseau" (Amsterdam, 1761, 6 vols.).

Julie is a *blonde cendrée* (a shade much in vogue with later conventional heroines, such as, for example, Clélia Conti in Stendhal's *La Chartreuse de Parme*, 1839), with gentle azure-blue eyes, auburn eyebrows, beautiful arms, and a dazzling complexion, the daughter of Baron d'Etange, who used to thrash her (pt. I, Letter LXIII). Saint-Preux is a private tutor, "un petit bourgeois sans fortune." Of his appearance we do not know much except that he is nearsighted ("la vue trop courte

338

pour le service," pt. I, Letter XXXIV; a device much used by later authors). His pupil deliberately gives herself to him for one night. She falls ill (smallpox). He leaves Europe and spends three or four years in a completely abstract South America. His return, Julie's married life and her death take care of the last part of the novel.

Julie marries M. de Wolmar (derived fancifully from "Waldemar"), also called Volmar in some editions, a Polish nobleman of fifty winters brought up, by inadvertence or prudence on his maker's part, "dans le culte grec," and not a Roman Catholic as most Poles; a sometime exile in Siberia; later a freethinker. One wonders what Tatiana Larin made of Rousseau's (admirable) footnotes on religious persecution and his epithets "culte ridicule" and "joug imbécile" applied to the Greek-Catholic religion to which Tatiana belonged. (There was an expurgated and mangled Russian "translation" brought out in the 1760's, but, as most commentators do not seem to realize, Tatiana read the book in French.)

Smallpox, which later was to afflict for purpose of plot or emotional interest so many handsome characters (who can forget the eye that Mme de Merteuil lost in *Les Liaisons dangereuses* of Choderlos de Laclos or the awful difficulties Dickens got into toward the end of *Bleak House* after having all but wrecked Esther Summerson's looks!), is caught by Saint-Preux from sick Julie, whose hand he kisses before starting on his *voyage autour du monde*; he comes back from it badly pockmarked, *crottu* (pt. IV, Letter VIII), but her face is spared except for some fugitive *rougeur*; he wonders if they will recognize each other; they do; and presently Saint-Preux is gorging himself on curds and whey at Julie de Wolmar's house, in a Rousseauesque world of eggs, *laitages*, vegetables, trout, and generously watered wine.

Artistically, as fiction, the novel is total trash, but it contains digressions of some historical interest, and the glimpses it affords of its author's morbid, intricate, and at the same time rather naïve mind are far from negligible.

There is a remarkable storm on Lake Geneva (pt. IV, Letter XVII), which occurs during a "promenade sur l'eau" in a rowboat, a frail bark, "un frêle bateau," manned by five oarsmen (Saint-Preux, a footman, and three local professionals), with Julie very seasick and very helpful: she "animoit [notre courage] par ses caresses compatissantes . . . nous essuyoit indistincte-ment à tous le visage, et mélant dans un vase [!] du vin avec de l'eau de peur d'ivresse [!], elle en offroit alter-nativement aux plus épuisés" (all of which implies a good deal of movement and stumbling over oars in the "frêle bateau").

The preoccupation with tipsiness is very curious throughout the novel: after Saint-Preux gets badly drunk one day and uses abominable language in her presence (pt. I, Letter LII), she enforces upon him "dans ses repas l'usage sobre du vin tempéré par le cristal des fontaines" (water). Saint-Preux, however, succumbs again in Paris, where, not realizing that his companions have led him to a brothel (as he writes Julie in detail), he mistakes white wine for water and when he regains his senses is amazed to find himself "dans un cabinet reculé, entre les bras d'une de ces créatures" (pt. II, Letter XXVI). After saving her little boy Marcellin from falling into the dangerous lake on another occasion, Julie dies very gently of shock in one of the least credible scenes of the novel. Her death is very Socratic, with long speeches, assembled guests, and a good deal of drinking—indeed, she all but gets intoxicated during those last hours.

The epistolary form of novels, so dear to the eighteenth century, seems to have been prompted by the singular notion that (as the poet Colardeau maintains in *Lettre amoureuse d'Héloïse à Abailard*, c. 1760) "L'art d'écrire

... fut sans doute inventé | Par l'amante captive et l'amant agité," or, as Pope puts this in his *Eloisa to Abelard* (1717), ll. 51–52, "Heav'n first taught letters for some wretch's aid, | Some banish'd lover, or some captive maid." It necessitates the author's providing his main characters with confidants (Laclos and Goethe ignored the letters of these stooges, it is true). Saint-Preux's bosom friend is a certain Lord Edward Bomston (who has passions of his own in Italy). In Letter III of pt. II, he offers Julie and her lover "un lieu fait pour servir d'asile à l'amour et l'innocence" in his country-seat "dans le duché d'York," where (strangely enough) "l'habitant paisible . . . conserve encore les mœurs simples . . . le bonheur des âmes pures." One wonders what Lord Bomston's tenants would have thought of all this.

It was not this nonsense that made the novel's fortune, but its romantic strain, the dramatic expletives ("Barbare!" "Fille insensée!" "Homme sauvage!"), addressed either to oneself or to one's correspondent, the fare-thee-wells, the famous first kiss in the bosquet. . . . Histories of literature have greatly exaggerated Rousseau's *sens de la nature*; he still saw *les champs* through a moral lace curtain.

Voltaire was very hard on his chief competitor: in *Epître* XCIV to the Duchesse de Choiseul (1769), he has:

[Jean-Jacques] . . . aboie à nos beautés [our fair ladies].
Il leur a préféré l'innocente faiblesse,
Les faciles appas de sa grosse suissesse,
Qui contre son amant ayant peu combattu
Se défait d'un faux germe, et garde sa vertu.
. . . .
. . . gardez-vous bien de lire
De ce grave insensé l'insipide délire.

(Cf. *EO*, One : XXIV : 12.)

La Harpe himself, author of Pushkin's school manual, though criticizing the plot and the characters, praised Rousseau's novel for its passion and eloquence, and for his giving human weaknesses the language of honesty and virtue.

It should be noted, in relation to this and the other novels Tatiana read, that their heroines—Julie (despite her premarital *fausse-couche*), Valérie, and Lotte (despite the forced kiss)—remained as faithful to their respective husbands as Princess N. (born Tatiana Larin) will be to hers, and that Clarissa refused to marry her seducer. Mark, too, the almost pathological respect and a kind of exalted filial love that the young heroes of these books have for the mature and morose spouses of the young heroines.

7–11 / Julie Wolmar, Malek-Adhel . . . de Linar . . . Werther . . . Grandison: The alliterative magic that our poet distills from these names of popular characters—or better, say, from the contrapuntal sequence of selected names—is an admirable example of an artist's finding a poetic pattern in pedestrian chaos. Tuning-forked by a lisping and languorous play on *l* (*Lyubóvnik Yúlii Volmár*, *Malék-Adél i de Linár*), the melody passes on to the moody *m*'s of *múchenik myatézhnïy*; and a comic apotheosis of brassy *o*'s (*I bespodóbnïy Grandisón*, | *Kotórïy nám navódit són*) rounds up the instrumentation of this marvelous stanza.

8 / Malek-Adhel: The hero of *Mathilde* (1805), a completely dead novel by the sensitive but talentless Sophie Cottin, née Marie Ristaud (1773–1807), widow of a Parisian banker who, "touched by her gentleness," had married her when she was "a pensive child of seventeen." Malek-Adhel is a Moslem general in the days of the Third Crusade (twelfth century), a dashing and

dazzling warrior, who in the midst of sandstorms falls in love with an English tourist, the virtuous Princess Mathilde, sister of King Richard Cœur de Lion. I skipped dozens of pages, I confess. But this is nothing compared to the boredom induced by Mme de Staël's *Delphine* (to be noticed presently) or, for that matter, to that of the luscious "historical" novels distributed among house-wives by the American book clubs of today.

8 / de Linar: This is the young man in *Valérie, ou Lettres de Gustave de Linar à Ernest de G.* (London, 1803; Paris, 1804; I have consulted an 1837 edn.), by Mme de Krüdener (Barbara Juliana, Baroness von Krüdener, née von Vietinghoff), a German lady writing in French, one of the most romanesque women of her time, novelist and influential religious mystic, born in Riga, 1764, died at Karasu-bazar, Crimea, 1824. Her first lover, about 1785, was a Russian gentleman (Aleksandr Staheev, I think) in Venice, the secretary of Baron von Krüdener, a Russian diplomat whom she had married at seventeen and to whom the lover wrote a letter of confession before his death: he shot himself, after she had been unfaithful to him—and to the baron—with another man in Copenhagen. Her novel, which she wrote in Italy and Switzerland, is to a certain extent autobiographical. She boosted it by asking at milliners for hats à la Valérie. Her exaltation completely overwhelmed Alexander I—whom she dubbed the Angel of the Lord—when they met in Heilbronn in 1815.

Young Valérie, Countess de M., presumably from Livonia, who married M. at fourteen, and met Linar at sixteen, has inherited her admirable sad old husband and her ash-blond hair from *Julie*; but, contrary to the buxom *suissesse*, Valérie is delicate, pale, fragile, and svelte, with eyes that are of a darker blue than Julie's; now excessively gay, now listless.

Gustave de Linar, her admirer whom she does not love, a dark-haired violent young Swede, is related metaphysically to Axel Fersen, the heroic, bizarre, and melancholy lover of Queen Marie Antoinette. The emblems of Linar's nature and moods are: solitude, mountains, storms, the "marchant-à-grands-pas" style of locomotion (which will have its last famous exponent in Konstantin Lyovin, of Tolstoy's *Anna Karenin*), the pressing-of-burning-brow-to-windowpane procedure (which Bazarov, of Turgenev's *Fathers and Sons*, will yet use), ennui, languor, moon, and pneumonia.

There are some pretty passages in the book—the fragrance of oranges and strong tea around Valérie, a dramatic little shawl dance, Italian nightingales, the rose in her hair, "mon âme défaillante de volupté"—and suddenly a noticed detail: "des vers luisants sur les haies de buis," or that sphinx (hawk moth) dislodged from the trunk of a cypress in an old cemetery full of plum trees in bloom. It should be marked that not only the new richness of a hazy and mellow landscape, but also the basic moods of languor, passion, and consumption are closer to Chateaubriand than to Rousseau. And those box hedges harboring lampyrid beetles are trimmed by the same gardener who clipped the "myrtle hedges . . . bower of fireflies" that edged the Leghorn lanes where, according to his widow, Shelley one summer evening heard the skylark and saw the "glow-worm golden in a dell of dew" mentioned in his famous ode.

A copy of *Valérie* (1804) preserved among Pushkin's books is said to bear several jottings (in whose hand?) on the half-title pages (such as "Hélas, un moment . . . ," "Dieu tout puissant . . . ce ravissant éclair de vie," etc.) and the name "Mlle Olga Alekseev."

9 / Werther: The hero of *Die Leiden des jungen Werthers* (Leipzig, 1774), a sentimental romance by Goethe. It

was read in French by Pushkin and Russian damsels. Several versions existed at the time: *Les Passions du jeune Werther*, by C. Aubry (Count F. W. C. von Schmettau) (Paris, 1777); *Les Souffrances du jeune Werther*, by Baron S. von Seckendorf (Erlangen, 1776); *Werther*, "traduit de l'allemand sur une nouvelle édition augmentée par l'auteur [i.e., Goethe] de douze lettres et d'une partie historique entièrement neuve," by Charles Louis Sevelinges (Paris, 1804).

A faded charm still clings about this novel, which artistically is greatly inferior to Chateaubriand's *René* and even to Constant's *Adolphe*. Werther, a young painter of sorts, retires to a secluded little burg, with grottoes, and lindens, and gurgling springs, and discovers in its vicinity Wahlheim, the perfect village. He meets Charlotte S., Lotte, "Mamsell Lottchen" (as he delightfully addresses her in the original, using a German bourgeois intonation peculiar to the period). She marries the good, stolid, honest Albert. The novel is mostly in epistolary form, consisting of letters—really monologues—addressed by Werther to a certain Wilhelm, who mercifully remains mute and invisible.

Werther weeps on every occasion, likes to romp with small children, and is passionately in love with Charlotte. They read *Ossian* together in a storm of tears. He is a prototype of Byron's heroes: "Je souffre beaucoup, car j'ai perdu ce qui faisait l'unique charme de ma vie; cet enthousiasme vivifiant et sacré qui créait des mondes autour de moi, il est éteint" (tr. Sevelinges, p. 190). ". . . Quelquefois je me dis . . . Jamais mortel ne fut tourmenté comme toi!" (ibid., p. 198).

His last days are described by "L'Editeur," i.e., Goethe. Tortured by a tragic love, haunted by melancholy, disgusted with life, Werther pistols himself. In an age that saw in novels the case history of its "sickness," Mme de Staël could say of *Werther* that it depicts "pas

seulement les souffrances de l'amour, mais les maladies
de l'imagination dans notre siècle" (*De l'Allemagne*,
pt. II, ch. 28).

10 / and the inimitable Grandison / *Ibespodóbnïy Grandisón*;
x : 3 / Clarissa / *Klarísoy* (instr.): Tatiana reads Richard-
son (see n. to Two : XXIX : 1–4) in the French version,
due to the pen of the monstrously prolific Abbé Antoine
François Prévost. His translations of *Clarissa Harlowe*
and *Sir Charles Grandison* came out in 1751 and 1755
respectively and went through several printings; pre-
sumably Tatiana had them in the same 1777 edition that
Pushkin plodded through in November, 1824, at Mihay-
lovskoe, whence he wrote to his brother: "Am reading
Clarissa; cannot endure her—such a tedious goose."

I have compared the English and the French texts,
using Prévost's 1784 editions (Amsterdam and Paris),
vols. XIX–XXIV and XXV–XXVIII of his *Œuvres choisies*
(mark *choisies*!). These sets are respectively: *Lettres
angloises, ou Histoire de Miss Clarisse Harlove* (sic)
(London, 1751), 6 vols.; and *Nouvelles Lettres angloises,
ou Histoire du chevalier Grandisson* (sic), "par l'auteur
de *Pamela* et de *Clarisse*" (Amsterdam, 1755), 4 vols.

Letourneur's version is: *Clarisse Harlowe*, "revue
par Richardson" (Geneva, 1785–86).

In France, Richardson's novels in Prévost's version
had already been criticized in the eighteenth century.
The songmaker Charles Collé (1709–83) wrote, about
1753, an ironic ballad, *Clarisse*, in which one of the
quatrains goes:

> Ce ne sera point par lettres
> Que j'écrirai ma chanson;
> Deux bonnes sur cent de piètres
> Se trouvent dans Richardson.

Chateaubriand, by far the greatest French writer of
his age, very admirably said in 1822: "Si Richardson

n'a pas de style (ce dont nous ne sommes pas juges, nous autres étrangers), il ne vivra pas, parce que l'on ne vit que par le style" (*Mémoires d'outre-tombe*, ed. Levaillant, pt. I, bk. XII, ch. 2).

Richardson had no style; but here and there some picturesque passages are not wholly negligible. Unfortunately, Prévost's method was to abridge and purify. Thus, in *Grandisson*, he carefully deleted such things as the excellent Hogarthian description of "vile, vile" Sir Hargrave's accomplice (in the attempted abduction of hysterical Harriet), a tall, big-boned, splay-footed, shabby-gowned, huge-faced, red-pimpled clergyman. And, of course, cliché-governed mistranslations (the French *bon goût* of the time) abound (such as: "une multitude de fous qui me prodiguaient leur admiration" for the pleasant liquidity of "the shoals of fools who swam after me").

VARIANT

1–5 A draft (2369, f. 50^r; see also n. following Three : VI : var. 13–14):

> With what attention now
> she ⟨reads⟩ in bed a novel;
> ⟨in dreams, with what⟩ enchantment
> appears to her Malek-Adhel!
> Her father . . .

The mention of her late father seems to lead us back to the theme of Two : XXIX : 5–12 (draft in 2369, f. 36^v).

X

1, 3 / heroine . . . Delphine / *geroínoy* (instr.) . . . *Delfínoy* (instr.): To make the instrumental case (necessary after "Imagining herself") of *geroínya* rhyme with that of *Delfína*, our poet changed the correct ending *-ney* to the nonexisting *-noy*.

3 / Clarissa: See n. to Three : IX : 10.

3 / Julie: The name was Englished, as I now realize, in my first edition, in despicable concession to rhythm.

3 / Delphine: If the moribund *Werther* and *Julie* are still readable today—in a detached mood of study, at least—Mme de Staël is not endurable under any circumstances —and I am not sure Pushkin would have inflicted her epistolary novel *Delphine* (1802), a thing of 250,000 gray words, upon his Tatiana, had he remembered that it did not even possess the pseudo-exotic book-of-the-month glamour of Cottin's preposterous *Mathilde*, let alone the emotional drive of Goethe's and Rousseau's novels.

Delphine d'Albémar is a widow of twenty-one, working her way through a love affair in 1790–92. Her admirer is a married man, Léonce de Mondoville, whom eventually she gives up because of moral obligations to his wife. When Delphine is ill, he stands "attaché aux colonnes de son lit, dans un état de contraction qui [est] plus effrayant encore que celui de son amie" (pt. IV, Letter IV). There are some robust romps in pt. IV, Letter XIX (Delphine to Mme de Lebensei): ". . . je me jetai aux genoux de Léonce . . . il . . . me replaça sur le canapé, et se prosternant à mes pieds," etc. As an artist, Staël is totally blind: "Matilde, lui dis-je en serrant ses deux mains qu'elle élevoit vers le ciel" (pt. IV, Letter XXXIV).

5 See n. to IX : 3–4.

14 / Grandison: At this point Chizhevski, in his commentary to *EO* (p. 237), is again moved to misinform the reader (see n. to Two : XXX : 3): "Grandison—the hero of Richardson's *Clarissa Harlowe*." He is also under the impression that Pushkin read these novels in Russian.

xa

There is an additional stanza in the fair copy:

> Alas, friends! The years flicker by,
> and with them one after another
> flicker the giddy fashions
> 4 in varied sequence.
> All things in nature change:
> patches and panniers were in fashion;
> the court fop and the usurer
> 8 wore powdered wigs;
> there was a time when tender poets
> in hope of glory and of praise
> would point a subtle madrigal
> 12 or witty couplets;
> there was a time when a brave general
> would serve, and be illiterate.

5 / All things in nature change / *Vsyo izmenyáetsya v priróde*: Had I not been wary of too modern a ring, I would have done this into: "Nature is in constant flux."

6 / patches and panniers were in fashion / *Lamúsh i fízhmï bïli v móde*: Tomashevski (*Works* 1957, p. 625) explains *lamush* as "a card game that went out of fashion in the beginning of the nineteenth century." I find that this game, called in France *la mouche* or *pamphile* (pam, i.e., the jack of clubs), is the English lu or loo (from the older "lanterloo," Fr. *lanturelu*, a refrain). I think, but have no means of ascertaining, that the five-card variety of loo was called in Russia, in the eighteenth century, *kvintich*. It is curious to note that loo, which Pushkin seems to consider an eighteenth-century relic in 1823, again became fashionable some four years later, judging by a police report of March, 1827, on Pushkin's card-playing. If this meaning of *lamush* is the correct one, then l. 6 should read:

> loo and hoop dresses were in fashion . . .

However, I am not at all sure that a card game is what Pushkin has in mind here. In so far as he is concerned with attires here, *la mouche* may well mean the little patch of black taffeta, Russ. *mushka*, that, beginning with the fifties of the seventeenth century, French and English ladies stuck on chin and cheek to bring out the whiteness of the complexion.

The word *fizhmï*, which I have rendered as "panniers" or "hoop dresses," comes from Ger. *Fischbein* and denotes the type of skirt that eighteenth-century ladies wore over hoops of whalebone. The vogue of hooped petticoats started in the second half of the seventeenth century. They are allied to the earlier farthingale and to the later crinoline.

10 / in hope of glory and of praise / *V nadézhde slávï i pohvál*: The lame tautology is accentuated by a contrastive recollection in the reader's mind of the line *V nadézhde slávï i dobrá* (of good) opening a later short poem by Pushkin (*Stansï*, 1826; in praise of Nicholas I).

XI

2 / *plámennïy*: A definite philologism with Pushkin and his school. The accented first syllable of this trisyllabic word easily—perhaps too easily—coincides with the second stress of the iambic tetrameter so that the ultima slips into the banal modulation in Russian verse, the third-foot scud of a three-word line (as here). Similar metrical elements are *rádostnïy* ("glad"), *trépetnïy* ("tremulous"), *dévstvennïy* ("chaste"), and so on, as well as the singular plural (and various case and gender forms) of disyllabic adjectives; for example, Three : XVI : 12: *Napévï zvúchnïe zavódit*, lit. "chants sonorous intones." *Plamennïy* is close to *pïlkiy* ("fiery," "impetuous"), another favorite of Pushkin and his school.

5 / object / *predmét*: Presumably the author's loved object —his hero.

9 / nourishing the . . . glow / *Pitáya zhár*: A common Galli-
cism. See, for instance, in Racine's dramatic eclogue
("tragédie") *Phèdre* (1677), III, i: "Vous nourrissez un
feu . . ."; and there are countless other examples.

10 / *Vsegdá vostórzhenniy geróy*: The first two words make
up the same epithet as that applied in Two : VI : 13 to
Lenski's way of talking, *Vsegdá vostórzhennuyu réch'*;
and with that verse still singing in his mind the reader
automatically lines up *vsegda* and *vostorzhenniy*. Actu-
ally, in this stanza the logic of its didactic phrasing sug-
gests that "always" refers to the next line ("was always
ready"), in conformance with the next "always," which
refers to vice being punished and virtue being rewarded.
Incidentally, in those last two lines 13–14, the two dif-
ferent shades of *bil* are very nicely rendered by "got."

<h3 style="text-align:center">XII</h3>

5 / *nebílitsi*: "Unrealities," "figments," "never-haps,"
"phantasmata."

6 / disturb the young girl's sleep / *Trevózhat són otro-
kovítsï*: A commonplace of the time; cf. Charles Sedley,
The Faro Table; or, The Gambling Mothers, "a fash-
ionable fable by the author of *The Barouche Driver and
His Wife*" (London, 1808): "Motto":

> Romantic authors have essayed to make novel reading
> useful to the rising generation: Nonsense!—Would you
> set your house on fire, merely, to play off the engines?—
> The moral, of such books, instead, of being directed
> towards its proper object, is always addressed to the girl—
> as if girls had any share in the evil complained of!

It is strange that even the careful and learned Lerner
(*Zven'ya*, V [1935], 71–73) makes the mistake of equat-
ing the *otrokovitsa* of XII with Tatiana and of assigning
to Tatiana the library of XII (on top of the eighteenth-

century novels listed in X), when actually the list in XII refers to a young girl of Pushkin's "present day," in 1824, as well as to Onegin's favorite authors in 1820. Otherwise Seven : XXII–XXIV, wherein Tatiana discovers Byron (and, through Byron, glimpses Onegin's mind), would be meaningless since she would have long known those phantasmata of the British Muse. It is true, however, that Tatiana's impressions of Onegin's demon eyes in Seven : XLI and Five : XVII–XX are decidedly more in line with Maturin than with Jean Jacques; but then Pushkin had been reading Maturin, too.

The five novels of Mrs. Radcliffe in Ballantyne's Novelist's Library (vol. X, 1824), including *A Sicilian Romance* and *The Mysteries of Udolfo*, were in Pushkin's library, but neither he, nor the *otrokovitsa*, nor Onegin, read them in English.

8 / the pensive Vampyre: The vampire superstition is mentioned in Byron's poem *The Giaour* (1813), and there is, of course, *The Vampyre, a Tale*, first published in the *New Monthly Magazine*, April, 1819, the work of Dr. John William Polidori (Byron's physician, with whom he left England forever April 25, 1816), and in July, 1819, as a novel *The Vampyre, a Tale*, "by Lord Byron. To which is added an Account of his Residence in the Island of Mitylene."

Critics were hard on the poor thing: *The British Review* (XVIII, 1819) referred to it as "a tale of disgusting horror" for which "the name of that nobleman [Lord Byron]" had "been borrowed"; and *The London Magazine* (II, 1820) called it a "miserable imposition." It was, however, translated several times into French, the first time as *Le Vampire*, "nouvelle traduite de l'anglais de Lord Byron" (Paris, 1819), by H. Faber.

9 / Melmoth, gloomy vagabond: *Melmoth, ou l'Homme*

errant, "par Mathurin [sic], traduit librement de
l'anglais" by Jean Cohen (Paris, 1821; 6 vols.). The
original, little known in Russia, was *Melmoth the Wan-
derer* (Edinburgh, 1820; 4 vols.), by Charles Robert
Maturin (an Irish clergyman), who used to compose
with a wafer pasted on his forehead, which was the sig-
nal that if any of his family entered they must not speak
to him. The book, although superior to Lewis and Mrs.
Radcliffe, is essentially second-rate, and Pushkin's high
esteem for it (in the French version) is the echo of a
French fashion.

I have already mentioned, in a note to One : II : 1,
young John Melmoth's arrival at his uncle's house. He
and his uncle are descendants of the diabolical Melmoth
the Traveler ("Where he treads, the earth is parched!
Where he breathes, the air is fire! Where he feeds, the
food is poison! Where he turns his glance, is lightning.
. . . His presence converts bread and wine into matter as
viperous as the suicide foam of the dying Judas . . .").
John discovers a moldering manuscript. What follows is
a long tale full of tales within tales—shipwrecks, mad-
houses, Spanish cloisters—and here I began to nod.

The name of the author of *Melmoth the Wanderer* is
constantly misspelled "Mathurin" (a common French
name) by French writers of the time, who followed
Cohen's lead.

Melmoth's nature is marked by pride, intellectual
glorying, "a boundless aspiration after forbidden knowl-
edge," and a sarcastic levity that make of him "a Harle-
quin of the infernal regions." Maturin used up all the
platitudes of Satanism, while remaining on the side of
the conventional angels. His hero enters into an agree-
ment with a Certain Person who grants him power over
time, space, and matter (that Lesser Trinity) under the
condition that he tempt wretches in their hour of extrem-
ity with deliverance if they exchange situations with

him. Baudelaire said of Melmoth "quoi de plus grand . . . relativement à la pauvre humanité que ce pâle et ennuyé Melmoth"; but, then, Baudelaire also admired Balzac, Sainte-Beuve, and other popular but essentially mediocre writers.

In Pushkin's n. 19 *Melmoth* is called a "work of genius." The "genius" is especially odd in view of the fact that Pushkin knew only Cohen's "free" version in French.

10 / the Wandering Jew: Fr. *le Juif errant*, Russ. *vechnïy zhid* (from the German *der ewige Jude*; otherwise the use of *zhid* is obsolete, or vulgar). This might be taken for a reference to *Ahasuerus, the Wanderer*, "a dramatic legend," in six parts (London, 1823), published anonymously by Captain Thomas Medwin (1788–1869) of the 24th Light Dragoons, who, in the following year, became famous as the note-taking author of the controversial *Journal of the Conversations of Lord Byron, Noted during a Residence with His Lordship at Pisa, in the Years 1821 and 1822* (London, 1824). Pushkin and his literary friends read—with great delectation—its French version by the indefatigable Pichot, *Les Conversations de Lord Byron, recueillies par M. Medwin, ou Mémorial d'un séjour à Pise auprès de lord Byron contenant des anecdotes curieuses sur le noble lord . . .* (Paris, 1824). I cannot discover, however, whether the note-taker's poem had appeared in a French version; if not, it could not have been known to Pushkin and his readers.

There is no reason to drag in here, as compilers of commentaries do, "an epic fragment" (1774) by Goethe (which is in a totally different vein from that implied by the stanza), or the Rev. George Croly's *Salathiel: A Story of the Past, the Present, and the Future* (the title of which Spalding, p. 264, misquotes, without knowing, moreover, that its three volumes appeared only in 1828, too late by four years for our purpose). Equally irrelevant here would have been references to Schubart's "lyric rhapsody" *Der ewige Jude* (1783), to the Sicilian's tale in Schiller's *Der Geisterseher* (1789), to Wordsworth's *Song for the Wandering Jew* (1800), and to *The Wandering Jew*, by the Rev. T. Clark (1819)—and more could be listed—since the young Franco-Russian reader could hardly have known anything about them in 1824. We are also haunted by such bibliographic spooks as the references to nonexistent authors and works in Chizhevski's notes to *EO*: there is no such person as his "Rocca de Corneliano, French poet," author of a (nonexistent) novel, *Eternal Jew* (1820), nor is there any playwright named "L. Ch. Chaignet" (Chizhevski, pp. 239, 316). There is, however, a completely insignificant work, *Histoire du Juif-errant écrite par lui-même*, published anonymously in Paris, 1820, by the writer on political, historical, and religious matters, Count Carlo Pasero de Corneliano; and there is a miserable melodrama in three acts by Louis Charles Caigniez, also spelled Caignez (1762–1842), in which the Wanderer appears as Iglouf (from *ich lauf*), first presented, without any success, on Jan. 7, 1812, at the Théâtre de la Gaîté, Paris. This Caigniez, incidentally, was also "coauthor" (with Théodore Baudouin, alias d'Aubigny, its true author) of the very successful play *La Pie voleuse, ou la Servante de Palaiseau* (Paris, April 29, 1815), on which the libretto (by D. G. Gherardini) of Rossini's opera *La Gazza ladra* (1817), a great favorite with Pushkin in his Odessa period, is founded.

The legend of Ahasverus, alias Joannes Buttadeus, who refused to help Jesus Christ on his way to Calvary and was doomed to roam forever, which Charles Schoebel (1877) connects with the legends of Cain and of Wotan, seems to have appeared first as a German popular pam-

Commentary

phlet (*Ahasverus, Erzählung von einem Juden*, etc.,
Leiden, 1602) and then in a French ballad form, as a
small book of sixteen pages printed in Bordeaux, 1609,
"jouxte la coppie imprimée en Allemagne," with the
title *Discours véritable d'un Juif errant, lequel maintient
avec parolles probables avoir esté present à voir crucifier
Jesus-Christ*. And there exists an English ballad, *The
Wandering Jew*, published by Pepys in his collection
(1700). Historically, the survival of an obscure apocry-
phon is mainly owing to its having been frequently used
as a mysterious and fatalistic excuse by dominant sects
for the persecution of an older but less fortunate one.

The Wanderer is said to have appeared for the first
time in Hamburg, in the winter of 1542, where he was
seen by a Wittenberg student, Paulus von Eitzen (later
archbishop); his next appearances were in Vienna, 1599,
Lübeck, 1601, Moscow, 1613, and so forth.*

In the romantic era the legend lost its flavor of Chris-
tian propaganda and became a more generalized symbol
connoting the peregrinations and despair of the Byronic
hero at odds with heaven and hell, with the gods and
mankind.

Pushkin's *vechnïy zhid* is a reference to the legend as
frequently alluded to in the poetry and fiction of his time.
The "fabled Hebrew Wanderer" appears in the inset
tetrametrics of Byron's *Childe Harold*, can. I, after
LXXXIV (see my n. to *EO*, One : XXXVIII : 9). And another
wanderer is mentioned in *Melmoth* (see n. to XII : 9,
above). In Lewis' *The Monk*, an inept concoction anony-
mously published in 1796, there is among the incidental
characters a mysterious stranger who hides under a band

*I have consulted for the notes given above: *Catalogue général
des livres imprimés de la Bibliothèque nationale*; Michaud's
Biographie universelle; Charles Schoebel, *La Légende du Juif-
errant* (Paris, 1877); Champfleury (Jules Fleury), *L'Imagerie
populaire* (Paris, 1886); Paul Ginisty, *Le Mélodrame* (Paris,
c. 1910), and various encyclopedias.

of velvet the burning cross upon his forehead, and he is none other than the Wandering Jew. In its Russian adaptation, this novel was attributed (as noted by Lerner, *Zven'ya*, no. 5 [1935], p. 72) to that popular lady, *slavnaya gospozha Radklif*, Ann Radcliffe (1764–1823), whose Gothic megrims, in various translations, so influenced Dostoevski—and through him the lady's ghost still troubles the sleep of English, American, and Australian adolescents.

The theme of the Wandering Jew was used by Pushkin himself, in a fragment of twenty-eight iambic tetrameters, composed probably in 1826, beginning "A lampad in a Jewish hut is palely burning in one corner," which was to be the beginning of a *Juif errant* poem (according to an entry of Feb. 19, 1827, in the diary of Franciszek Malewski, published in *Lit. nasl.*, LVIII [1952], 266); by Zhukovski, in *Stranstvuyushchiy zhid* (an initial fragment in 1831 and a tedious poem in 1851–52); and by Küchelbecker, in his remarkable *Agasver*, planned as an epic in 1832 (introduction composed Apr. 6, 1832, Sveaborg Fortress, Helsinki), then as a *dramaticheskaya misteriya*, mid-May, 1834, still in the Sveaborg Fortress, written in its final form in 1840–42, at Aksha, Siberia; and published (incomplete text) posthumously in 1878 by *Russkaya starina*, XXI, 404–62.

10 / the Corsair: *The Corsair*, a poem written in the heroic measure, which consists of three cantos, and was composed by Byron in the latter part of December, 1813 (published February, 1814). "Lone, wild, and strange" Conrad of "the lofty port, the distant mien" ("solitaire, farouche et bizarre" in Pichot's version, 1822), saves from the flames Gulnare, the harem queen (see my n. to Four : XXXVII : 9).

In the draft of a critique (1827), taking to task a certain V. Olin for his poem *Korser* (Russian transcription of the French *corsaire*; the accepted word is *korsar*), an imitation of *The Corsair*, Pushkin observes that English critics of Byron's poem saw in its hero not so much the character of its author as that of Napoleon. He had it from Pichot: "On a prétendu que lord Byron avait voulu dessiner dans son corsaire quelques traits de Napoléon" (Chastopalli's note in *Œuvres complètes de Lord Byron*, I [1820], 81).

My translation of XII : 10 does not scan iambically, but this does not matter.

11 / mysterious Sbogar: Here a short French novel of a Chateaubyronic genre is smuggled in by Pushkin among the fancies of the British Muse. This is *Jean Sbogar*, by Charles Nodier, 1818 (edition consulted: Paris, 1879). The girl is Antonia de Montlyon, born in Bretagne, now aged seventeen (see also my n. to Two : XXIII : 5–8), a pretty and sickly creature who walks "appuyée sur sa sœur": the physical disintegration of buxom Julie, through languorous and hysterical Valérie, is nearly complete in Antonia. The mysterious Jean Sbogar, a young Dalmatian with blond hair, is the chieftain of a band of brigands—"Frères du bien commun," amateur communists of sorts—who infest the wild neighborhood of Trieste, in Istria, on the Adriatic, not far from the gondoliers still singing Tasso. He is a shadowy demon of a man; we meet him, light-footed, singing and flitting from rock to rock, then "poussant un cri sauvage, douloureux, plaintif, semblable à celui d'une hyène qui a perdu ses petits," which does not happen every day. He wears an elegant hat with a white plume, and a short cloak; his face is gentle, and his hands are delicate and white. At one time he thinks nothing of disguising himself as an Armenian monk. Later he appears under the name of Lothario, not a rare name, at a reception in Venice: his emerald earrings blaze, his gaze is a torrent

of celestial light, there is on his brow "un pli bizarre et tortueux." He is interested in the redistribution of riches. But I am not an *otrokovitsa*, and at this point Sbogar ceased to disturb my sleep.

Nodier's novel was reviewed, two years after publication (on the occasion of the appearance of a miserable English version, under the title *Giovanni Sbogarro*), in *The London Magazine*, II (1820), 262–68:

A basking, panting, overpowering, yet ardent pulsation seems to beat through it. A hectical warmth, a nervous sensibility, the longings of faintness, the paroxisms of sickly imaginations. . . . It is distinguished by a soft eolian melody of which we know no other example in the French language. Mr. Nodier's is precisely what we understand by a modern romantic style: harmonious, heightened, ambitious and successful. . . . [Sbogar] is as full of sensibility as a German ballad, and talks very much in the manner of Mme de Staël. He appears and disappears, in the Magic-lanthorn style of Lord Byron's entrances and exits, and excepting that he is inclined to be chaste, might be taken for a twin-brother to the Corsair.

14 / hopeless egotism / *beznadézhnïy egoízm*: I was sorely tempted to use here the very close but not literal "gloomy vanity" that Byron himself mentions in his dedicatory letter to Moore prefixed to *The Corsair*.

XIII

11 / shall detail / *pereskazhú*: The same verb is repeated in the first line of the next stanza and grades there into its other sense, "shall retell."

14 / ancientry: The recurrence of *stariná* is very striking.

XIV

1, 9 / speeches . . . accents / *réchi . . . réchi*: There is a slight shade of difference between these two *rechi*, one didactic and the other lyrical.

9–10 / sensuousness . . aching / *négi . . . toskúyushchey* [gen.]: These formulas have been mentioned in connection with Tatiana's emotions in Three : VII : 10. *Nega* is repeated in XV : 8, where it is tinged with connotations of sweetness, dulcitude, *tendresse*.

VARIANT

12 A fair copy doubtfully reads "of fair Amalia" instead of "of a fair mistress."

XV

2 Pushkin's sympathy for his heroine is reflected further on in XXXI : 1–2, and in Four : XXIV : 13–14.

13 / everywhere, everywhere: The formula *vezdé, vezdé,* fitting two iambic feet in Russian, makes two unwieldy dactyls in English. The long tilt does its best to iambize the opening foot. My war with "everywhere" is a long one.

XVI

5 / *Pripodnyalásya grúd'*: "Risen somewhat has [her] bosom." I am not sure that the paraphrase "her bosom heaves" would not have been enough.

8 / *I v slúhe shúm, i blésk v ocháh*: Constructionally: "and in the hearing [there is] noise, and flashing [there is] in the eyes."

"Flashing" is a well-known photomatic phenomenon, typical of the slight insanity of adolescence.

9–10 Cf. Marvell, *Upon Appleton House* (pub. 1681), st. XL:

> But when the vigilant patrol
> Of stars walk round about the pole . . .

11 / nightingale: The popular European songbird, any species of the old-world genus *Luscinia.* The sweet, rich, bubbling, and whistling song of the male is often heard in the breeding season, mainly at night, and, among birds, has been to countless poets what the rose is among flowers.

14 / nurse: This literary character, which Pushkin was pleased to think portrayed his—or, more exactly, his sister's—old nurse, has already been mentioned in Two : XXIb : 6–14 (see n.) and XXVII : 9. A vibrant passage in Three : XVIII redeems her somewhat from the role of comic confidant in which technically she is cast. The person whom Pushkin called "his old nurse" in real life appears quite separately from gray Filatievna (Three : XXXIII : 6) as a character in her own stylistic right, in Four: XXXV : 3–4, where she is termed "companion of my youth."

Russian commentators are too much intoxicated with the notion of a "simple Russian woman of the people" telling old tales (alas, stemming from Italian chapbooks) to "our national poet" (as if a true poet could be "national"!) to concentrate on certain amusing points in connection with Tatiana's old nurse.

In a letter of c. Dec. 9, 1824, from Mihaylovskoe to Dmitri Shvarts, a functionary in Odessa (*chinovnik osobïh porucheniy* on Vorontsov's staff), Pushkin writes:

The storm seems to have abated; I dare peep out of my nest and make my voice heard to you [*podat' golos*], dear Dmitri Maksimovich. For four months now I have been in a remote hole up in the country: boring, but nothing to be done; there is here no sea, no meridional sky, no Italian opera. But, in compensation, neither are there any locusts, or any milords Worontsovs.* My seclusion is perfect, my idleness is solemn.† Neighbors in my vicinity are few, I am acquainted with only one family,‡ and even them I see rather seldom; I spend the whole day riding; in the evening, listen to the fairy tales of my nurse, the original of Tatiana's nurse; you saw her once, I think;§ she is my only companion, and with her alone I am not dull.

This proves decisively that Pushkin, in Odessa, before the end of July, 1824, read Chapter Three, at least as far as XX, to Shvarts. The curious part is that when composing those stanzas he had not seen his sister's old nurse since his last visit to Mihaylovskoe in the summer of 1819 (*if* she was there at the time) and was unaware in the summer of 1824 that in a month or so he was going to meet her again in the role of housekeeper (and *his* nurse).

See also my nn. to Four : XXXV : 3.

---

*Pushkin, by means of an initial *U*, stresses the English *W* sound in his Russian transliteration of the more or less established German transliteration "Woronzoff" of "Vorontsov," so as to express his contempt for the governor general's Anglomania.

†*Prazdnost' torzhestvenna*: no doubt some kind of imitative gibberish, a foreigner's mistake retained as a private joke between Pushkin and his correspondent; garbled *prazdnestvo torzhestvennoe*, a solemn public ceremony.

‡The Osipovs, whose countryseat Trigorsk, or Trigorskoe, is sung in the last stanzas of *Onegin's Journey*.

§Where? When? In Moscow c. 1810, where little Shvarts may have danced at *fêtes d'enfants* with little Olga Pushkin?

XVII

3 / The diminutive appears here for the first time in the novel, after eleven "Tatiana"s. The nurse breaks the ice, addressing the girl as "Tanya" three times in XVII, once in XVIII, and once in XXXV. Henceforth, Pushkin will call her "Tanya" thirty-three times, thus thirty-eight times in all, which is about one-third of the "Tatiana" frequency rate (see Index).

3 / I'm dull / *Mne skúchno* [*skúshno*]: "I am ennuied," as an English miss of the time would have said. Tatiana's provincial pronounciation of *ch* as *sh* (a maternal Moscovism, no doubt) allows Pushkin to rhyme *skuchno* with the *dúshno* ("stuffy") of l. 1.

4 / about old days / *o stariné*: The "ancientry" I have tried to use consistently does not ring true here.

5 / Well, what about them / *O chyóm zhe?*: The sense idiomatically compressed here is "Exactly about what [do you want to talk]?"

7 / *Starínnïh bíley*, *nebílíts*: Another rendering: "of ancient facts and fables."

12 / *Zashíblo*: "[Age] has stunned me," or "I'm blundered" —to use a provincial transitive. Cf. *otshiblo pamyat'*, "my memory is knocked off."

13 / your / *váshi*: This is the plural, implying "the past years of yourself and your likes."

XVIII

1 / Oh, come, come / *I, pólno*: An idiomatic double expletive, consisting of (1) a sharp vowel expressing reproachful astonishment or doubt and (2) an adverb meaning "that will do," "come to your senses"; the grammatical meaning of *polno* is "[it] is full."

5–6 Elton has:

> "But then thy marriage, nurse, how came it?"
> "Why, God's plain will it was to frame it."

The *cheville* is especially comic to an American's ear.

13 / my braid they unplaited: "La tresse de cheveux que portent les jeunes filles est cachée au mariage et ne se montre plus désormais," says Turgenev. "In order to retress it in two braids when the maiden becomes a married woman," says Spalding. Both are right.

A well-known song in trochaic trimeter, with the vulgar tilting of *moyú*, typical for these literary imitations of folk songs, contains the same idea:

> *Ráno moyu kósïn'ku*
> *V léntï ubirát'—*
> *Ráno moyu rúsuyu*
> *Ná dve raspletát'* . . .

> Too soon my plait
> with ribbons to deck—
> too soon my auburn [plait]
> to divide in two . . .

*

The draft of notes for the 1833 edn. reads (PD 172):

> Somebody asked an old [serf] woman: "Was it passion that brought you to the altar, Granny?" "Sure, my dear, passion," she answered. "The steward and the village bailiff were in such a passion they almost beat me to death" [when forcing her to marry the serf of their choice]. In former days weddings, as also the courts, were not often dispassionate [adds Pushkin, contributing his own pun].

XIX

1 / *I vót vvelí v sem'yú chuzhúyu*: The narrational, long-drawn, and plaintive intonation here is not unlike that of *I ták oní staréli óba* (Two : XXXVI : 1). It is one of the leitmotivs of the novel.

Vveli: idiom, "they led me into."

XX

5–7 | *luná siyála* | *I tyómnïm svétom ozaryála* | *Tatyánï blédnïe krasf*: The epithet *tyomnïm* (instr.), "dark," is in all three editions (canto edition of 1827 and complete editions of 1833 and 1837). Modern editions consider this to be a misprint for *tómnïm*, "languorous" (one of the stock epithets for moon), or else restore the *pólnïm*, "full," of the fair copies (the complete autograph in PB and the autograph of XVII–XX : 1–12 in PD). The draft is lost (see n. following var. to VI). The epithet *tomnïm* appears in the page proofs of the *Little Star* (*Zvyozdochka*) for 1826 (a collection, *al'manah*, which Bestuzhev and Rïleev were prevented from bringing out by their arrest in December, 1825)* and in Delvig's *Northern Flowers* for 1827, which appeared about Mar. 25, 1827; but it is quite possible that *this* was a misprint or somebody's well-meaning correction. The rococo conceit of the moon's light being darker than Tatiana's pale beauty is far from being inconsistent with the pastichelike strain running through the chapter.

On the other hand, the epithet *tomnïy* as applied to the moon has its counterpart in such English verses as Thomson's l. 1038 of *Spring*, "Beneath the trembling languish of her beam," and Keats' l. 127 of *The Eve of St. Agnes* (1820), "Feebly she laugheth in the languid moon."

12 | *v dlínnoy telogréyke*: Spalding has a note (p. 265) saying that this garment is called in French *chaufferette de l'âme*; the latter is a literal equivalent of the Russian *dushegreyka*, "soul warmer," which is synonymous with *telogreyka*, "body warmer."

---

*This was to continue, in a smaller form, their annual magazine the *Polar Star* (1823–25).

American and western European readers are apt to imagine a housewife's quilted jacket in a painting of the Dutch school rather than the ample warm smock or coat peculiar to certain districts of Russia.

The variety that Pushkin has here in view is presumably the well-padded cloth *shushun* (see my nn. to Four : XXXV : 3–4).

13–14 / and in the stillness everything dozed by the inspirative moon: I cannot help seeing a very subtle imitation in these lines:

> *I vsyó dremálo v tishiné*
> *Pri vdohnovítel'noy luné.*

In the last line, the adjective "inspirative," although not exactly new, sounds curiously artificial. I suggest that Pushkin remembered a compliment paid by a critic he admired to a versificator he did not, and reproduced in Russian a French epithet reputed "daring" by the standards of the Age of Taste and Reason. In one of Mme de Staël's works (*De la Littérature considerée dans ses rapports avec les institutions sociales* [3rd edn., 1818], vol. II, pt. II, ch. 7, p. 246n), so influential then, so stale now, she remarks: "*Delille, dans son poëme de l'Homme des Champs, s'est servi d'un mot nouveau, inspiratrice.*" She has in mind a passage in can. I of the four cantos that make up Delille's uncommonly dreary *L'Homme des champs* (1800):

> Que dis-je? autour de lui tandis que tout sommeille,
> La lampe inspiratrice éclaire encor sa veille.

The PB fair copy has the canceled variant:

> and all was silent; by the moon
> only a cat mewed on the window [sill]

In the *Little Star* proof and in the separate edition of Three (c. Oct. 10, 1827) these lines read:

and in the stillness everything
breathed by the inspirative moon.

In a letter of Apr. 23, 1825, our poet writes to his
brother from Mihaylovskoe to St. Petersburg: "You, my
dear fellow, do not find any sense [*tolku*] in my moon—
well, nothing to be done, just have it printed as is." The
injunction evidently refers to the transmission of XVII–
XX to Bestuzhev and Rïleev, who paid five rubles per line
for this "Night Conversation of Tatiana with Her
Nurse."

XXI

1–2 / *I sérdtsem dalekó nosílas'* | *Tat'yána, smótrya na
lunú:* "And with [her] heart far ranged Tatiana, looking
at the moon." The participle *smótrya* (instead of
smotryá) is accented on the first syllable, a jarring pro-
vincialism by 1820.

3–8 I paraphrase to render the rhythm:

> A sudden thought occurs to Tanya:
> "I want to be alone. Please, go.
> Oh, give me, nurse, a pen and paper,
> Approach that desk; remove that taper;
> Good night." And now she is alone.
> All's still. Their light the moonbeams loan.

This is the longest run of consecutive scudless lines in
EO, if we discount a similar row of six strung together
to render Lenski's feeble elegy in Six : XXI : 4–9. Ta-
tiana's flat little speech, with its deliberate concealment
of emotion, follows immediately upon a radiant sequence
of eighteen spankingly scudded lines.

9–14 The nice point here is that Eugene's image, with
which Tatiana is obsessed, does not quite coincide with
the real Eugene. She sees herself as a romantic heroine
writing to the fictional hero who has Eugene's face; but

as she goes on with her reckless epistle, the two images, fiction and reality, fuse. The letter is finished; it has been written automatically, in a trance, and now as reality asserts itself again she becomes aware that it is addressed by the real Tatiana to the real Eugene.

XXIa

The following stanza is canceled in the fair copy:

> I now should take time out
> to exculpate my Tatiana.
> A captious critic in a modish circle
> 4 will, I forsee it, argue thus:
> "Could one not have beforehand
> instilled into pensive Tatiana
> the statute of radical decencies?
> 8 Moreover, elsewhere errs the poet:
> Could it be that at the first meeting
> she with Onegin fell in love?
> And what had fascinated her?
> 12 What in his intellect, what in his speeches
> had managed in a trice to captivate her?"
> Wait, let me disagree, my friend.

XXII

10 Dante Alighieri, *Inferno*, III, 9: "Abandon hope forever, ye who enter here!"

In Pushkin's ambiguous n. 20, the *double entente* of "modest" has escaped the notice of scholars, thus sharing the fate of the naval obscenity that Jane Austen, not understanding its full implications, allows Miss Crawford to repeat (presumably, after Charles Austen) in *Mansfield Park*, vol. I, ch. 6; and of the disgusting sustained pun running through a whole line in the last stanza of the much less innocent Lord Byron's *Beppo*.

I find in Chamfort's *Maximes et pensées* (in his *Œuvres* collected by his friends [Paris, 1796], IV, 43) the following: "Je mettrais volontiers sur la porte du Paradis le vers que le Dante a mis sur celle de l'Enfer."

XXIII

A footnote in the fair copy reads:

> E 'l viso di pietosi color farsi,
> Non so se vero o falso, mi parea.
> Petr[arca]

This is the beginning of the second quatrain of Sonnet LXIX in *Rime di Francesco Petrarca in vita di Laura.* The Henry G. Bohn edition (London, 1859) gives three "translations," which prove that Petrarch did not fare any better than Pushkin. I transcribe:

> And true or false, meseem'd some signs she show'd
> As o'er her cheek soft pity's hue was thrown.
> —Anon., 1795

> Ah! then it seem'd her face wore pity's hue,
> Yet haply fancy my fond sense betray'd.
> —Nott

> And—was it fancy?—o'er that dear face gleaming
> Methought I saw Compassion's tint divine.
> —Wrottesley

1 / *Sredí poklónnikov poslúshnïh*: A very poor line. The poet saw the eccentric belles of the next line surrounded by dutiful adulation. The word *pohval* (gen. pl.) that closes l. 4—and recurs so frequently in *EO* (being easy to rhyme on)—is the *éloges* of the French; which, judging by its use as a fashionable cliché by English letter writers of the time, has no absolutely accurate counterpart in English.

10 / sound of spoken words / *zvúk rechéy*: *Rechi* is "accents" as well as the plural of *rech'*, "speech." (See also n. to XIV : 2.)

11 / more [tender] / *nezhnéy*: Thus in previous editions. The *vazhnéy* ("more important") of 1837 is a misprint.

XXIIIa

The following stanza is canceled in the fair copy:

> But you, avowed coquettes,
> I love you—though 'tis wrong.
> Smiles, caresses made to order
> 4 you dispense to everyone,
> at everyone direct a pleasant gaze.
> He to whom words are not convincing
> will be converted by a kiss;
> 8 whoever wants—is free to triumph.
> I formerly myself used to be satisfied
> merely with the gaze of your eyes.
> Now I respect you only,
> 12 but, by chill experience afflicted,
> I'm even ready to help you myself—
> yet eat for two and sleep all night.

Despite the pretty French turn of ll. 6–7, the stanza is but a patter of platitudes, and Pushkin was right in canceling it. Much later, when working on Seven, he seems to have planned to transfer this stanza to "Onegin's Album" (see comm. to Seven, following vars. to XXI–XXII, "Onegin's Album": x), but then expunged the Album, too.

XXV

According to Tomashevski (Acad 1937, p. 310), the draft of this stanza (2370, f. 12^r) is written in the same ink as the *Conversation of Bookseller with Poet*, the draft of which is near it, written Sept. 26, 1824, to which date Tomashevski also assigns this stanza, which thus was written about three months after the batches I–XXIV and XXVI–XXIX had been completed.

Apart from a possible wish to bring "tender Tatiana"

and "tender Parny" into close contact so as to prop
stylistically the otherwise somewhat irrelevant XXIX :
13–14, Pushkin, I suggest, may have been perversely
prompted to do his impish imitation by his coming across
a piece by Bulgarin, "Literary Ghosts," in the review
Literary Leaflets (*Literaturnïe listki*),* 1824 (not before
Aug. 27), pt. III, no. XVI, where the phrase occurs (spoken
by one Talantin, in whom one easily recognizes Bul-
garin's friend, Griboedov): "The imitation [on the part
of Russian poets] of Parny and Lamartine is a diploma
of bad taste."

1–6 Evariste Parny ("tender Parny," as Pushkin calls him
in Three : XXIX : 13), in the second piece (*La Main*) of
his *Tableaux*, has the following (ll. 5–12):

> On ne dit point: "La résistance
> Enflamme et fixe les désirs;
> Reculons l'instant des plaisirs
> Que suit trop souvent l'inconstance."
> Ainsi parle un amour trompeur
> Et la coquette ainsi raisonne.
> La tendre amante s'abandonne
> A l'objet qui toucha son cœur.

> One does not say: "Resistance
> inflames and fixes the desires;
> let us defer the moment of delights
> which by inconstancy too oft is followed."
> Thus speaks false love
> and the coquette thus reasons.
> The tender mistress yields
> to the object that has touched her heart.

In speaking of his forthright and tender Tatiana Larin,
Pushkin imitates Parny very closely (Three : XXV : 1–6):

*A supplement (1823–24) to his *Northern Archives* (*Severnïy
arhiv*), 1822–28 (merged in 1829 with *The Son of the Father-
land, Sïn otechestva*).

> *Kokétka súdit hladnokróvno,*
> *Tatyána lyúbit ne shutyá*
> *I predayótsya bezuslóvno*
> *Lyubví, kak míloe dityá.*
> *Ne govorít oná: Otlózhim—*
> *Lyubví mï tsénu tém umnózhim . . .*

We are completely entitled to reflect the imitation, and synchronize the two sets of terms, those of Parny and those of Pushkin, by choosing for our translation of Pushkin's lines such words among the English equivalents of *koketka sudit, predayotsya,* and *otlozhim* as suit best both Parny and Pushkin:

> The coquette reasons coolly;
> Tatiana in dead earnest loves
> and unconditionally yields
> to love like a dear child.
> She does not say: Let us defer;
> thereby we shall augment love's value . . .

xxva, xxvb

St. xxv is not represented in the fair copy (no doubt made before September, 1824), where we find canceled two other stanzas connected by means of an eloquent enjambment:

xxva

> And you who loved
> without your relatives' permission
> and kept a tender heart
> 4 for young impressions,
> heartache, hopes, and sweet mollitude,
> perhaps ⟨if⟩ you had furtively
> happened the secret seal
> 8 of a love letter to tear off,
> or timidly, into bold hands,
> a chary lock of hair relinquish,
> or even silently permitted

12 at the bitter minute of parting
   a trembling kiss of love,
   in tears, with tumult in your blood—

xxvb

   do not condemn unconditionally
   my giddy Tatiana,
   do not coolly repeat
4 the verdict of prim judges.
   And you, O "Maids without Reproach,"
   whom even vice's shadow
   frightens today as if it were a snake,
8 I give the same advice to you.
   Who knows? With flaming heartache
   you too, perchance, may be consumed,
   and Rumor's flippant tribunal tomorrow
12 will to some hero à la mode
   ascribe the triumph of another conquest:
   the god of love doth seek us out.

Mark the same rhyme on the same words (*bezuslóvno, hladnokróvno*) in b : 1 and 3 and in XXV : 3 and 1. Pushkin did well to expunge XXVa and b and replace both stanzas by his charming paraphrase from Parny (added at Mihaylovskoe, probably on Sept. 26, 1824). I am not sure I am not overdoing accuracy by translating *porók* always as "vice," in distinction from *greh*, "sin." *Porok* is an easy word to rhyme on, and seems to be here (b : 6), and elsewhere, hardly more than a synonym of "sin." To judge by the recensions, the *Dévï bez upryóka* phrase (b : 5), "virgins [or maidens] without reproach," is italicized by Pushkin. It is a commonplace Gallicism, *vierge sans reproche*—on the lines of *chevalier sans peur et sans reproche*.

XXVI

7 / expressed herself / *vïrazhálasya*; 12 / expressed itself / *iz'yasnyálasya*: Russian has two words for the verb "to express." One can be paraphrased "to put one's thoughts into words"; the other, "to make oneself clear." Cf. Fr. *s'exprimer* and *s'expliquer*.

XXVIa, XXVIb

The following two stanzas were canceled in the fair copy, and the octets of both were used later, with only minor changes (XXVIb : 1 and 3), for a sixteen-line entry in "Onegin's Album" (st. VII; see nn. to Chapter Seven, following vars. to XXI–XXII), which eventually was also canceled.

XXVIa

The treasures of our native letters
(grave minds will note)
for foreign lisping
4 we in our folly have neglected.
We love the toys of foreign Muses,
rattles of foreign idioms,
and read not our own books.
8 But where are they? Let's have 'em.
Of course, boreal sounds
caress my wonted ear;
my Slavic spirit loves them;
12 the heart's pangs with their music
are lulled to sleep. . . . But cherishes
the poet sounds alone.

XXVIb

But where, then, did we our first knowledge
and first ideas find?
Where do we put to use our trials?
4 Where do we learn earth's fate?
Not in barbarous translations,

not in belated works,
wherein the Russian mind and Russian spirit
8 rehash old stuff and lie for two.
Our poets make translations,
but there's no prose. One magazine
is filled with cloying eulogies,
12 another with banal abuse. All cause
the yawn of boredom, if not sleep.
Fine thing—the Russian Helicon!

The rather meaningless *primenyáem* ("put to use" or "apply"), in b : 3, is altered to *poveryaem* (which may be understood as "verify") in the "Album." By a strange· trick of literality, the phrase *Gde primenyáem ispïtán'ya*, if taken uncritically, turns into "Where do we apply tests"; but I can see no sense whatever in that phrase here. If *poveryaem* in the "Album" is taken to mean "we verify" instead of "we confide," it would seem that *ispïtán'ya* should be taken not in the sense of "tests" but in that of "trials," implying *our* trials, *nos épreuves*, the ordeals of our history as seen through the prism of foreign histories or of works of foreign historians. (See also my n. to Three : XXIX : 6, on Gallicisms.)

XXVII

4 | *The Well-Meaner* in their hands | *S Blagonamérennïm v rukáh*: The *Blagonamerennïy* was a monthly, then a weekly, magazine (1818–27), edited by Aleksandr Izmaylov (1799–1831), author of *Fables* (1826), who, on the occasion of a delay in publication during Butter- week, 1820, explained in verse that he:

> . . . went on a spree on holidays as Russian people do,
> forgetting wife and child—not only the review.

Pushkin's l. 4 was given an obscene twist (*blagona- merennïy fallos*) by its author and his friends in their private correspondence. (The joke was started by

Vyazemski in a letter to Pushkin of July 26, 1828.) It should also be marked that in 1822 the *Blagonamerennïy* (no. 38), in a short poem called *The Union of Poets*, had attacked Pushkin's friends Baratïnski and Delvig.

Cf. Baratïnski, *To Gnedich, Who Advised the Author to Write Satires,* in 150 Alexandrines (1823), ll. 115–16:

> The reader of [Izmaylov's] sheets is warned
> by their good editor that he likes to carouse.

5 / to [you] / *na vas*: There is an obvious misprint in the 1837 edn.: *na nas*, "to us."

6, 12 Our poet uses the epithet *mílïy* ("amiable," "sweet," "dear," "winsome," "winning," "charming," "cute") and its adverbial form, *mílo*, much too often. It is the French *gentil, gentiment.*

XXVIII

3 / seminarian in a yellow shawl / *seminarístom* [instr.] *v zhyóltoy shále*: This is a wrong locative ending. It should be *sháli*, unless Pushkin derived it from *shalya* instead of *shal'*. The word (a borrowing from the Persian) came from Germany via France, where in the beginning of the nineteenth century it was spelled *schall*.

One wonders if Pushkin committed this solecism deliberately in order to illustrate l. 6.

Shále rhymes with *na bále* (l. 1), an archaic locative. (Today, "at a ball" would be *na balu*.)

A *seminarist* is a young theologue, a student of the *seminariya* (ecclesiastical school).

VARIANTS

2 Canceled fair copy:

> or at Shishkov's upon the porch . . .

For Shishkov, see my n. to Eight : XIV : 13.

3 The shawl is "red" in the fair copy.

XXIX

This stanza was written May 22, 1824, in Odessa. It is here that Cahier 2370 starts (see n. following var. to VI), with, on f. 1^r, the draft of a letter to Kaznacheev, director of Vorontsov's chancellery (see n. to One : LIX : 6–8).

2 / delivery of words / *vïgovor rechéy* [gen. pl.]: The way of pronouncing words rather than pronunciation (*proiznoshenie*) itself, and utterance rather than accent—although both Russian terms (*vïgovor* and *proiznoshenie*) commonly merge. The translator's task is not made any lighter by the fact that the word *rechi* (nom. pl.) does not mean "speeches," "discourses," "conversations" here (as it does, for example, in Three : XIV : 2), but has the Gallic tinge of "accents," "spoken words." The verb *proizvodit'*, "produce" (l. 4), is likewise a Gallicism, *produire.*

In "My Remarks on the Russian Theater," Pushkin, in speaking of the young Russian actress Kolosova, lists her various assets—beautiful eyes, beautiful teeth, and *nezhnïy nedostatok v vïgovore* ("a soft flaw of enunciation"). And further he suggests she ought to do something about her Parisian burr (Fr. *grasseyement*), "very pleasing indoors but incongruous in a tragedy on the stage."

6 / Gallicisms: In December, 1823, Bestuzhev (in his and Rïleev's review, *Polar Star*, 1824, pp. 1–14) argued that the complete "inanition of Russian literature" in 1823 was owing to the "latent passion for Gallicisms" that had burst forth and afflicted everybody since the end of the war (1812–14). Tsyavlovski (Acad 1936, V, 630) com-

pares with *EO*, Three : xxviᴀ (and Seven : "Album" :
vii; see comm. to Seven, following vars. to xxi–xxii), a
fragment (1825) in which Pushkin expresses his reac-
tion to Bestuzhev's attack on the French influence and
queries:

> Where are our Addisons, La Harpes, Schlegels? What
> have we analyzed critically [*razobrali*]? Whose literary
> opinions have become national [*narodnïmi*, meaning
> "have been accepted as original and typical of Russian cul-
> ture"]? Whose [Russian] critical works can we use for
> reference and support? . . .

And in a letter to Vyazemski (July 13, 1825) Pushkin
writes:

> You did well to come out in defense of Gallicisms. Some-
> day we really must say aloud that metaphysical Russian
> is with us still in a barbarian state. God grant it may ac-
> quire form someday similarly to the French language, to
> that limpid, precise language of prose, i.e., to the language
> of thought.

Alongside this line and the next two Pushkin made a
drawing, which I have described in my n. to One : LIX :
6–8.

8 / Bogdanóvich's verse: Ippolit Bogdanovich, minor poet,
author of *Dushen'ka* (see my n. to One : xxxiii : 3–4) and
of translations from Voltaire and other French writers of
his time. Some influence of his is distinguishable in
Pushkin's *Ruslan and Lyudmila* (1820).

11 / Yea, yea / *ey-éy*: Bases on Matt. 5 : 37. The Russian
formula is a euphemism for *ey Bogu*, "I swear by God."
It should be noted, however, that in Russian the terms
"By God!" "My God!" "God!" etc., being influenced in
polite literature by the French *mon Dieu*, etc., do not
have the profane force of their English exact equiva-

lents. Thus *Dieu!* or *Bozhe!* is not "God!" but "Good God!" "Goodness!" "Good gracious!" and so on.

13 / tender Parny: Evariste Désiré Desforges, Chevalier de Parny (1753–1814). The words *tendre* and *tendresse* occur more often in Parny's elegies and idyls than they do in the poems of any other French poet of the time. See, for instance, *Les Serments* (*Poésies érotiques*, bk. III, 1778), ll. 16–20:

> Viens donc, ô ma belle maîtresse,
> Perdre tes soupçons dans mes bras;
> Viens t'assurer de ma tendresse,
> Et du pouvoir de tes appas.
> Aimons, ma chère Eléonore . . .

The frankly iambic modulations of ll. 18–20 should please a Russian or an English ear.

14 In the last lines of *Réponse à un jeune poête*, first published in 1809 (*Mercure*, vol. XXXVI), Parny mentions the passing of his fame:

> Pour cette France repétrie
> L'élégance est afféterie,
> La délicatesse est fadeur,
> Et mes vers une rêverie
> Sans espérance et sans lecteur.

VARIANT

9–13 Draft (2370, f. 2ʳ):

> Enough, however. Though I'm free
> to recollect this thing or that
> in my enchantment,
> the missive ⟨of youthful Tatiana⟩
> awaits translation . . .

After the draft of this stanza comes One : XXXIII.

Commentary

XXX

1 / Bard of *The Feasts* / *Pevéts Piróv*: If in the taxonomy of talent there exists a cline between minor and major poetry, Evgeniy Baratïnski (1800–44) presents such an intermediate unit of classification. His elegies are keyed to the precise point where the languor of the heart and the pang of thought meet in a would-be burst of music; but a remote door seems to shut quietly, the poem ceases to vibrate (although its words may still linger) at the very instant that we are about to surrender to it. He had deep and difficult things to say, but never quite said them. He was regarded by Pushkin with a tender and grave respect: its tonality is unique in the annals of the greater poet's literary sympathies.

Early in 1816, Baratïnski was expelled from the Corps-des-Pages (a military school for young noblemen): with a schoolmate (Hanikov) he had stolen a valuable snuffbox and five hundred rubles in bank notes from the bureau of Hanikov's uncle. After spending three years in the country, Baratïnski returned to St. Petersburg in 1819 (where he became acquainted with Pushkin) and then served in Finland, starting as a private, 1820–24. Attempts on the part of Soviet commentators to compare his fate with that of Pushkin in terms of political martyrdom are grotesque.

Baratïnski's *The Feasts* (*Pirï*; composed 1820) is an indifferent elegy, greatly influenced by the French poetry of the elegant and banal eighteenth century. In its first edition (1821), it consists of 268 iambic tetrameters freely rhymed. In gaunt Finland, where his regiment was stationed, Baratïnski nostalgically evoked friendly feasts with fellow poets in the gay Petersburg of 1819. Pushkin imitated ll. 252–53 of *The Feasts* in his Prefatory Piece (first published as a dedication of Four and Five to Pletnyov in February, 1828) and had

at one time considered promoting these two lines to a
motto for either One or Four—a promotion that would
have turned the imitation into a complimentary allu-
sion. He used another line (52) of *The Feasts* for his motto
to the Moscow canto (Seven, 1827–28, pub. 1830) and
subtly referred to ll. 129–39 in his Four : XLV (see n. to
Four : XLV : 1, 7).

Pushkin—the Pushkin of 1819—is described in Bara-
tïnski's piece (ll. 210–13) as:

> . . . the enchanting minstrel
> of love, and liberty, and pleasure—
> young P., volatile and wise,
> a confidant of fun and fame . . .

In the revised edition of *The Feasts* (1826), when it
came out together with Baratïnski's narrative poem
Eda, the allusion to Pushkin goes:

> Our P . . . . . n, you to whom 'tis given
> to sing heroes and wine,
> wild passions and an escapade,
> who with a prankish mind can blend
> a wondrous knowledge of the heart,
> and who can be (not a small thing, meseems!)
> most amiable at table.

In the final text of 1835 "wondrous" is altered to
"true," and the next two lines are condensed into one:

> and over wine is the best guest.

Baratïnski disliked *EO* and in a letter of 1832 de-
scribed it as a brilliant but juvenile imitation of Byron.

*

When forwarding, on Feb. 20, 1826, from Mihaylov-
skoe, a copy of Baratïnski's *The Feasts* and *Eda* (pub.
Feb. 1, 1826) to Praskovia Osipov, then in the province
of Tver, Pushkin loyally described this *Eda: a Finnish
Tale* as a "chef-d'œuvre de grâce, d'élégance et de senti-

ment." This singularly uncouth and banal poem, consisting of 683 iambic tetrameters freely rhymed, was begun in 1824, published in 1826, and revised in 1835. The Finnish maid Eda, who is seduced by the Russian hussar Vladimir, is (in ll. 63–69), by an unhappy coincidence, not unlike Vladimir Lenski's Olga in appearance (*EO*, Two : XXIII : 5–8):

> A tender color in her cheeks,
> an airy figure, golden hair
> in careless ringlets o'er her shoulders,
> and pale-blue eyes
> akin to Finnish skies,
> in a pure heart the readiness to feel—
> there's Eda for you!

(In the final text of 1835, this last little cry is canceled.)

Eda's and Vladimir's kiss is described as a *vlazhnïy plamen*', "humid flame" (l. 159), borrowed, I notice, from Charles Millevoye's *Le Déjeuner*:

> Un long baiser, le baiser du départ
> Vient m'embraser de son humide flamme.

1 / languorous / *tómnoy*: This characteristic favorite of Pushkin's and his school—*tomnaya glava*, "her languished head"; *tomnïe glaza*, "languishing eyes"; *tomnïy vzor*, "a dying eye"—is basically equivalent to all the varieties of "languish" typical of the French and English sentimental writers; but because of its resemblance to *tyomnïy*, "dark," and owing to its Italianate fullness of sound, the Russian epithet surpasses in somber sonority its English counterpart and lacks the slight ridicule attached to the latter. It will be noted that the state and sensation of *nega*, "sensual languor," is close to the more superficial and, as a rule, less pleasurable condition defined as *tomnost'*. That this feeling, though often saturated with lyrical sentiment, is intrinsically not a pleasant one is confirmed by another

philologism, *tomlenie*, the antiquated English noun,
"languish"—a painful void, an irksome satiety (Three :
VII : 12). The verb is *tomit'*, "to irk," "to oppress," "to
weigh upon" (which brings the intransitive *tomit'sya*
into the *toskovat'*, "to pine," series). The adjective *tom-
nïy*, "languid," shades off into the *vyalïy* series—"list-
less," "limp."

12–13 It was in Finland that Baratïnski wrote the first poem
that revealed his talent to discriminating readers. This
is *Finlyandiya*, first published, 1820, in the magazine
*The Champion of Enlightenment and Benefaction (Sorev-
novatel' prosveshcheniya i blagotvoreniya)*. This Ossianic
elegy, consisting of seventy-two free iambics, begins:

> Great everlasting rocks, deserts of granite,
> you gave the wanderer refuge and shelter

and closes:

> O golden phantoms, golden visions,
> ardent desires, come flying in a crowd!
> Let my deluded soul drink avidly the magic
> of error from the cup of youth!
> What matter past or future races?
> I strum my dull strings not for them.
> Though heeded not, I am in full rewarded
> for sounds by sounds, for dreams by dreams.

14 / worry / *górya*: The reference is not to the grief of
separation but to the grievous predicament in which
Pushkin places Pushkin in this matter of having to put
into Russian verse an imaginary French epistle.

XXXI

1 / Tatiana's letter is before me: Its presence in the hands
of Pushkin, considered as a character in the novel, may
be explained, for instance, by Onegin's transcribing it

for him in Odessa, in the course of their resuming, in
1823–24, the evocation of past loves that used to grace
their rambles on the Neva quay in 1820 (see *Onegin's
Journey*, comm. to Eight, MS st. XXX).

In the course of the novel Pushkin quotes the writings
of all three main characters: Tatiana's letter, Lenski's
last elegy, and Onegin's letter.

2 / *Egó ya svyáto beregú*: The French formula "je la con-
serve religieusement" has helped me to render this in
English.

5–6 / *Kto eý vnushál i étu nézhnost'*, | *I slóv lyubéznuyu
nebrézhnost'?*: The answer is: Parny. See, for example,
his idiom in *Le Lendemain* (*Poésies érotiques*, bk. I):

> Et ton âme plus attendrie
> S'abandonne nonchalamment
> Au délicieux sentiment
> D'une douce mélancolie

which falls automatically into romanticist Russian: *i
umilyónnaya dushá predayótsya nebrézhno sládostnomu
chúvstvu grústi nézhnoy*.

6 / *lyubéznuyu nebrézhnost'*: A Gallicism: *aimable abandon*.

7 / [tosh] / *vzdor*: Misprinted *vzor*, "gaze," in the 1837 edn.

13 / *Freischütz* / *Freyshíts*: The reference is to the overture
of *Der Freischütz* (*Le Franc Archer*, The Seventh Bul-
let, *Volshébnïy strelók*), a romantic opera by Carl Maria
von Weber (1786–1826), first produced in Berlin June
18, 1821, and first performed in Paris Dec. 7, 1824 (as
Robin des Bois).

A wood demon furnishes a marksman with magical
bullets. The villain of the play, Kaspar, has sold himself

to this demon, both being in love with Agatha, the daughter of the head ranger to the Duke of Bohemia, etc. In act II, Agatha in melancholy mood opens her window and lets the moonlight flood the room. The incantational music in the Wolf's Glen is said by George P. Upton and Felix Borowski, in their *Opera Guide* (New York, 1928), to have never been surpassed in weirdness, mystery, etc. Specters, skeletons, and grotesque animals terrify Max, Agatha's betrothed, who has gone to that glen, persuaded by Kaspar to meet the demon there, etc.

Vyazemski (Mar. 24, 1824) wrote from Moscow to A. Turgenev in St. Petersburg: "Send my wife everything there is for the piano from the opera *Der Freischütz*: waltzes, marches, overture, and so forth." On Apr. 4 Turgenev replied that he would try to get the music. On Apr. 10, Vyazemski wrote that the thing could be obtained in Moscow.

Votaries of biographical romances should imagine Princess Vyazemski and Countess Vorontsov, about June 10, 1824, in Odessa, learning to play this overture in the presence of Pushkin, who developed an *amitié amoureuse* for the former and was passionately in love with the latter. About the same time, all three defied the turbulent succession of waves on the Odessa shore, a little event that may have led our poet to recombine the *Tavrida* theme (see nn. to One : XXXIII).

VARIANT

13 The draft (2370, f. 4ᵛ) has "Mozart and Dietz" instead of *Freyshits*.

Wolfgang Amadeus Mozart (1756–91), Austrian composer, and Ferdinand Dietz (1742–98), Tsar Alexander's violin teacher and author of the music to Dmitriev's *Moans the Gray-blue Little Dove* (*Stonet sizïy golubochek*), one of the most popular songs of the time.

TATIANA'S LETTER TO ONEGIN

Seventy-nine lines in iambic tetrameter, with a free pattern of rhymes: ababacceffeggihhijojo; babaaceec; ababececiddifoofogoog; aabeebiicoco; babaceeciddi; baba. (The spacing is perfunctory; the identity of letters in these six parts does not imply a similarity of rhymes; in Russian editions the piece is usually spaced after ll. 21, 30, and 75.)

Tatiana is supposed to have written her letter in French; and it is indeed much easier to turn it into conventional French prose than into English iambics. The four French prose versions I have consulted are:

In the *Eugène Onéguine* of H. Dupont, *Œuvres choisies de A. S. Pouchkine*, vol. I (St. Petersburg and Paris, 1847).

In the *Onéguine* published by Ivan Turgenev and Louis Viardot in the Parisian *Revue nationale*, XII and XIII, 48–51 (1863); Tatiana's letter is in XIII, 49 (May 10, 1863).

The "Lettre de Tatiana à Oniéguine" in fragments of *Eugène Oniéguine* in *Œuvres choisies*, translated by André Lirondelle (Paris, 1926).

The similarly entitled piece in Jacques David's *Anthologie de la poésie russe* (Paris, 1946).

Of these four translations the best is Lirondelle's, with the heavier Turgenev-Viardot running a close second. Both are exact. Dupont's version nicely reflects here and there the French idiom of Pushkin's time, but contains a number of gross blunders (such as l. 16, "penser à un homme unique" for *dúmat' ob odnóm*, which in the original of course means "to think of one thing" and not "of one person") and besides is rather vulgar. Much vulgarer, however, is David's version, which flaunts such cheap inexactitudes as l. 16, "de faire en un seul rêve tous les rêves"; l. 34, "et le ciel m'a faite pour toi"; and ll. 68–71, "considère . . . que me taire c'est mourir."

In the literal French translation of Tatiana's letter given below, which, I repeat, slips beautifully into flat French, I have initialed the borrowed lines: Dupont [Du], Turgenev-Viardot [TV], Lirondelle [L], and David [Da]. The uninitialed lines are my contribution.

```
      Je vous écris—en faut-il plus?                      [L]
      Que pourrais-je dire encore?                   [Da+Du]
      Maintenant, je le sais, il est en votre pouvoir   [TV]
 4    de me punir par le mépris.                          [L]
      Mais si vous gardez                                [Da]
      une goutte de pitié pour mon malheureux sort      [TV]
      vous ne m'abandonnerez pas.                        [Du]
 8    Je voulais d'abord me taire.                       [Du]
      Croyez-moi: jamais vous n'auriez                   [Du]
      connu ma honte                                     [Du]
      si j'avais eu l'espoir                              [L]
12    —ne fut-ce que rarement, ne fut-ce qu'une
            fois par semaine—                            [TV]
      de vous voir dans notre campagne,                  [Du]
      rien que pour entendre vos propos,
      vous dire un mot et puis                            [L]
16    penser, penser à une seule chose
      jour et nuit, jusqu'au revoir.                      [L]
      Mais, dit-on, vous fuyez le monde                  [Du]
      dans ce coin perdu de la campagne tout
            vous ennuie                              [Da+Du]
20    et nous ne brillons par rien                       [TV]
      bien que nous soyons naïvement heureux de
            vous voir.                                   [TV]

      Pourquoi être venu chez nous?                       [L]
      Au fond d'une campagne ignorée,
24    je ne vous aurais jamais connu,                    [TV]
      je n'aurais pas connu ces amers tourments.         [TV]
      Ayant avec le temps—qui sait—calmé                  [L]
      l'émoi d'une âme novice,                        [L+Du]
28    j'aurais trouvé un ami selon mon cœur          [Du+Da]
      et j'aurais été fidèle épouse                       [L]
      ainsi que mère vertueuse.                           [L]
```

```
      Un autre! . . . Non, à nul autre au monde        [TV]
32 je n'aurais donné mon cœur!                          [TV]
      C'est ainsi qu'en a décidé le conseil d'en-haut,    [L]
      c'est la volonté du ciel: je suis à toi.       [Du, TV]
      Ma vie entière fut le gage                          [L]
36 de notre rencontre certaine;                          [L]
      Dieu t'envoie à moi, je le sais;                    [L]
      tu seras mon gardien jusqu'à la tombe . . .   [TV+L]
      Tu m'apparaissais dans mes songes                 [Du]
40 invisible, tu m'étais déjà cher;                  [TV+L]
      ton regard merveilleux me troublait;
      ta voix résonnait dans mon âme                      [L]
      depuis longtemps. . . . Non, ce n'était pas un
                               rêve;                     [Du]
44 à peine tu étais entré, aussitôt je te reconnus,    [L]
      je me pâmais, je brûlais,
      et je me dis: C'est lui!                         [Du+L]
      N'est-ce pas, je t'avais déjà entendu:            [TV]
48 tu me parlais dans le silence             [TV, L, Da]
      lorsque je secourais les pauvres             [Du, L]
      ou que j'adoucissais par la prière           [L+TV]
      l'angoisse de mon âme agitée?                [Du+L]

52 Et même à ce moment-ci
      n'est-ce pas toi, chère vision,                   [TV]
      qui vient de passer dans l'ombre transparente
      et de se pencher doucement sur mon chevet?
56 N'est-ce pas toi qui me murmures                     [TV]
      avec joie et amour des mots d'espoir?              [L]
      Qui es tu? Mon ange gardien          [TV, L, Da]
      ou un perfide tentateur?                      [TV, L]
60 Résous mes doutes.                                   [TV]
      Peut-être que tout cela est vide de sens
      et n'est que l'égarement d'une âme novice,
      et tout autre chose m'attend. . . .

64 Mais s'en est fait. Dès à présent                    [TV]
      je te confie mon sort.                            [Du]
      je verse mes larmes devant toi,
      j'implore ta défense.                             [Du]
68 Imagine-toi: je suis seule ici;                 [Du+TV]
      personne ne me comprend,              [Du, TV, L]
      ma raison succombe,                               [TV]
```

et je dois périr en silence.   [Du]
72 Je t'attends: d'un seul regard
viens ranimer les espérances de mon
    cœur . . .   [Du+TV]
ou bien interromps le songe pesant
d'un reproche, hélas, mérité.   [L, Da]

76 Je finis. Je n'ose relire.   [L+TV]
Je me meurs de honte et d'effroi.   [TV]
Mais votre honneur me sert de garantie—   [Du]
je m'y confie hardiment.   [TV]

1 /*Ya k vám pishú—chegó zhe bóle?*: Among the clumsy
pieces in Russian syllabic verse that patch up the love
scenes in an anonymous novella of the early eighteenth
century that Gukovski reprints in his anthology (Mos-
cow, 1938; see n. to One : XLVIII : 12), *The History of
Aleksandr, Russian Nobleman* (hideously adapted from
a mawkish German romance), there occur the following
lines in the love plaint of the heroine (p. 19):

    Predáy níne smérti, ne tomí menyá bóle,
    Tï mya múchish, v tvoéy ést' vóle.

    Put me now to death, let me languish no more,
    you are tormenting me, 'tis in your power.

5–7 / But you . . . keeping . . . one drop of pity, you'll not
abandon me: Cf. Mme de Krüdener, *Valérie*: "Vous ne
me refuserez pas votre pitié; vous me lirez sans colère"
(Linar to Valérie, Letter XLV).

See also in Julie's first long letter to Saint-Preux:
". . . si quelque étincelle de vertu brilla dans ton âme . . ."
(Rousseau, *Julie*, pt. I, Letter IV).

The separate edition of the chapter gives the following
variant of l. 7:

    I ne ostávite menyá.
    indeed will not abandon me.

13, 19, 23 / at our country place . . . in backwoods, in the
country . . . In the backwoods of a forgotten village / *V
derévne náshey . . . v glushí, v derévne . . . V glushí
zabítogo selén'ya*: In England, Tatiana Larin would have
been named Rosamund Gray (see under that title
Charles Lamb's unconscious parody of a sentimental
novelette, with a rake, and a rape, and rural roses) and
would have lived in a cottage; but the Larins live in a
country house of at least twenty rooms, with extensive
grounds, a park, flower and vegetable gardens, stables,
cattle sheds, grainfields, and so forth. I would reckon the
amount of their land at some 350 desyatins (1000 acres)
or more, which is a small estate for that region, and the
number of their serfs at two hundred souls, not counting
women and infants. A number of these were household
slaves, while the rest lived in the log cabins that consti-
tuted a village (or several small hamlets). The name of
the village, or of the nearest of the hamlets, would be
that of the whole estate with its fields and forest. The
Larins' neighbors, Onegin and Lenski, were consider-
ably wealthier and might each have had more than two
thousand souls.

18 / *No govoryát, vï nelyudím*: With an inner note con-
cisely echoing a passage in Constant's *Adolphe* (ch. 3):
". . . ce caractère qu'on dit bizarre et sauvage, ce cœur
. . . solitaire au milieu des hommes" (cf. Pichot's *Le
Corsaire*, quoted in my n. to Three : XII : 10).

In a letter to Vyazemski from Mihaylovskoe, Nov. 29,
1824, Pushkin writes:

How came you to have Tanya's letter? N.B. explain
this to me [it had been circulated no doubt by Lev Push-
kin]. In answer to your criticism: a *nelyudim* is not a mis-
anthrope, i.e., not a hater of people, but one who avoids
people. Onegin is a *nelyudim* [an unsociable person] in
the opinion of neighboring country squires; Tanya thinks

the reason for this [for his being unsociable] is that in the backwoods, in the country, all bores him, and that brilliancy alone might attract him. If, however, the sense is not quite precise, the more truth there is in the letter— the letter of a woman—and, on top of that, a seventeen-year-old one—and, on top of *that*, a woman in love.

A famous line in *Childe Harold* (III, LXIX, 1) goes:

To fly from, need not be to hate, mankind.

22 / *Why* did you visit us? / *Zachém vï posetíli nás?*: In laying this pathetic emphasis on *why*, I may have been influenced by a wonderful record (played for me one day in Talcottville by Edmund Wilson) of Tarasova's recitation of Tatiana's letter.

26, 62 / The tumult of an inexperienced soul . . . an inexperienced soul's delusion / *Dushí neópïtnoy volnén'ya . . . Obmán neópïtnoy dushí* [gen.]: *Neopïtnaya dusha* (nom.) is a Gallicism, *une âme novice*, so often met with in the literature of the day. Thus the beginning of the quatrain serving as master motto for *Werther* in Sevelinges' French (1804) reads:

Ainsi dans les transports d'une première ardeur
Aime et veut être aimée une âme encore novice.

The good reader will also note that "Ainsi dans les transports d'une première ardeur" bears a certain resemblance to a line from Vyazemski (*First Snow*, l. 75), which Pushkin at one time planned to borrow for the motto to One:

Po zhízni ták skol'zít goryáchnost' molodáya . . .
O'er life thus glides young ardor . . .

31 / Another!: A common rhetorical formula of European romances. Cf. Chénier, *Les Amours*, no. IX (in *Œuvres*, ed. Walter), an elegy beginning "Reste, reste avec nous . . ." (l. 75): "Un autre! Ah! je ne puis . . ."; or

Byron, *The Bride of Abydos* (1813), I, VII, 197–98: "To
bid thee with another dwell: Another! . . ."

34 Cf. Rousseau's *Julie* (Saint-Preux to Julie, pt. I, Letter
XXVI): "Non . . . un éternel arrêt du ciel nous destina
l'un pour l'autre . . ."

It is at this point that Tatiana switches from the
formal second person plural to the passionate second
person singular, a device well known in French episto-
lary novels of the time. Thus in her third short note to
Saint-Preux Julie starts to *tutoyer* him, mingling the *tu*
with *vous*. In Tatiana's letter the initial *vous* comes back
only at the very end (l. 78, *vásha chést'*, "your sense of
honor").

A misprint in the 1837 edn. turns the word *to* ("that")
into the absurd *no* ("but").

35–46 / my entire life . . . It is he: Tatiana may have seen
(among the contributions to her sister's album, perhaps)
an elegy of 1819 by Marceline Desbordes-Valmore
(1786–1859), a kind of female Musset minus the color
and the wit:

> J'étais à toi peut-être avant de t'avoir vu.
> Ma vie, en se formant, fut promise à la tienne;
> .   .   .   .
> . . . j'avais dit: Le voilà!

45 Tatiana has read the *Phèdre* (1677), I, iii, of Racine (who
had read Virgil):

> Je le vis, je rougis, je pâlis à sa vue;
> Un trouble s'éleva dans mon âme éperdue;
> Mes yeux ne voyoient plus, je ne pouvois parler;
> Je sentis tout mon corps et transir et brûler . . .

I have translated *obomléla* by "felt all faint," but the
latter lacks the melting and tremulous quality of the

Russian term, which is somewhat better, but far from perfectly, rendered by the French *se pâmer* or *défaillir*.

49 A sentimental fashion of the times. One thinks of such French prints as *La bonne Châtelaine*: young lady from castle—small basket of provisions on arm—bottle of wine sticking out—doorway of hovel—rag-bedded old villager inside vigorously raising eyes and arms to heaven—wife clasping her hands piously—child receiving a doll.

53–55 Cf. Vincent Campenon, in *Almanach des Muses* (1805):

> Loin de lui, seule avec moi-même,
> Je crois et l'entendre et le voir;
> La nuit, son fantôme que j'aime
> Près de ma couche vient s'asseoir.

Here parallel passages might be multiplied.

55 / bed head / *izgolóv'yu* (dat.): Fr. *chevet*. A very Gallic situation—this bedside phantasm, this praying girl, this angel-demon hybrid. There is but one step here from the sentimental vision to the Gothic succubus—both of them insipid products of the Age of Reason.

56 / with [joy] / *s otrádoy*: A treacherous misprint in the 1837 edn. turns this into *s otrávoy* ("with poison").

61 / 'tis nonsense all / *éto vsyó pustóe*: Cf. " 'So very fond of me!' 'tis nonsense all" (Fanny's rill of consciousness running over Miss Crawford's letter in Jane Austen's *Mansfield Park*, vol. III, ch. 13).

It is curious that Jane Austen was not popular in Tatiana's Russia, although as early as 1815 *Raison et sensibilité, ou les Deux Manières d'aimer*, "traduit librement" by Isabelle de Montolieu (Elisabeth Jeanne

Commentary

Pauline Polier de Bottens), had been published in Paris,
followed next year by Henri Villemain's *Le Parc de
Mansfield, ou les Trois Cousines* (actually, two sisters
and their cousin Fanny).

78 | *No mné porúkoy vásha chést'*: This is difficult to render
exactly. "But your honor is my security," "Your sense
of honor is my guarantee." In Three : XXXIV : 5, the
nurse uses the same expression, substituting "God" for
"honor," and in Four : XIV : 5, Onegin says that "con-
science" is his *poruka*.

Cf. Rousseau, *Julie* (Julie's first long letter to Saint-
Preux, pt. I, Letter IV): "Toutefois . . . s'il y reste [in
her correspondent's soul] encore quelque trace des senti-
ments d'honneur . . ." and ". . . mon honneur s'ose
confier au tien . . ."

VARIANTS

The draft is in Cahier 2370, beginning after the draft of
XXXI, f. 4ᵛ, going on to both sides of f. 5 and then to
ff. 6ʳ and 7ʳ.

P. Annenkov, *A. S. Pushkin. Materialï dlya ego
biografii i otsenki proizvedeniy* (2nd edn., St. Peters-
burg, 1873), pp. 132–33, was the first to observe that
our poet had started by jotting down Tatiana's letter
in Russian prose. ". . . Upon which," says Annenkov,
"Pushkin transposed this meager program into wondrous
verse." (A similar program was made later for Onegin's
sermon in Chapter Four.)

On f. 5ʳ, there is the draft of a prose paragraph, which
is reproduced photographically in Acad 1937, facing p.
314:

I know that you despise [the end of the sentence is
illegible]. For a long time I wished to be silent—I thought
I would see you. I do not want anything, I want to see you
—I have nobody to . . . Come. You must be . . . this and

that. If not, God has deceived me . . . but upon rereading my letter, I do not have the strength to sign it. Guess . . .

Under this, on the same folio, the draft of the letter, with innumerable but insignificant corrections, continues in verse till l. 21, after which there is a line in prose: "Why did I ever see you—but now it is too late." F. 5ᵛ begins with l. 26.

Draft (l. 4a):

> My end not distant I foresee . . .

Canceled readings (ll. 1, 4a, 7):

> I love you—what then would one more?
> My shame inevitable I foresee . . .
> I love you so, I am so wretched.

In the vicinity of l. 3, there is a canceled line in prose: "My shame, my guilt are now known to you."

There exist the following variants to the passage 24–30:

Final draft (2370, f. 5ᵛ):

> My humble folks,
> secluded strolls,
> and books—true friends—
> 'tis all I would have loved.

Canceled in draft (ibid.):

> Unto a country husband [*derevénskomu suprúgu*]
> perhaps I would have given my hand . . .

51 After l. 51, additional lines (a, b, c, d) read in the fair copy:

> 'Twas you inspired my prayers,
> and the graced ardency of Faith,
> and melancholy, and the tears of tender feeling
>   [*attendrissement*]
> —was it not all your secret gift?

Commentary

79 After this last line of her letter, there are in the draft
(2370, f. 7ᵛ) two unstanzaed lines, which could only be
ll. 5–6 of a succeeding stanza, since it is a feminine-
rhymed couplet:

> *Podúmala chto skázhut lyúdi?*
> *I podpisála T. L.*

> she wondered what people would say,
> and signed T. L.

In Russian this produces an identical rhyme because of
the use of special mnemonic names for letters in the old
Russian alphabet: the word for *L* is *Lyudi*. The reader
should imagine that in the English alphabet the letter
T were labeled, say, "Tough," and the letter *L*, "Little."

> And after pondering a little
> she wrote her signature: Tough, Little.

> *Podúmala chto skázhut lyúdi?*
> *I podpisála Tvérdo, Lyúdi.*

XXXII

In the left-hand margin of the draft (2370, f. 7ᵛ; repro-
duced by Efros, p. 203), alongside ll. 5–7, Pushkin drew
his concept of Tatiana. It is a charming melancholy fig-
ure, the face inclined upon the hand, the dark hair fall-
ing upon the naked shoulder, the parting of the breasts
delicately marked in the opening of the flimsy shift. (See
also n. to One : XLVIII : 2.) Below, there is a profile recog-
nizable as that of Pushkin's father, whom he saw, or was
to see, at Mihaylovskoe after a separation of more than
four years.

I think that Pushkin may have reached this stanza in
June, 1824, a month and a half before leaving Odessa for
Mihaylovskoe; but it is also clear that he resumed work
on the same stanza Three : XXXII only about Sept. 5,
1824, at Mihaylovskoe.

The autographs should be studied.

1 / sighs and ohs / *to vzdohnyót, to óhnet*: The untranslatable Russian exclamation *oh* of weariness and distress is akin to the Irish "och," but is more a groan than a moan, and ends in a very rough aspirate.

3 / *Oblátka rózovaya*: This was before the invention of envelopes; the folded letter was sealed by means of an adhesive disk of dried paste, colored pink in the present case. To this a personal seal might be added by letting a drop of gaudy wax fall upon the paper and impressing one's monogram upon it (see XXXIII : 3–4).

5 / *golóvushkoy*: "Her gentle head," "her heavy head"; a kind of compassionate diminutive (from *golova*), often used in plaintive folk songs. The usual diminutive is the nastily coy *golovka*. (See n. to Four : XVII : 8.)

6 A young lady in the 1820's would wear her day shift, a flimsy, very low-necked affair, to bed, putting a nightdress or a special jacket, or both, over it. For evening ablutions, an Anglicized belle might have a tin bathtub in her dressing room, filled with hot water (brought up in jugs or pails)—and under the circumstances, I suppose, a change of linen would also occur. A Russian provincial miss, however, would probably rely for her weekly bath on the bagnio (*banya*), bathhouse, which every squire had on his grounds. That particular night Tatiana did not go to bed at all—and apparently slipped her dress on just before the nurse entered.

14 Under the last line of the corrected draft of the established text in Cahier 2370, f. 11ᵛ, Pushkin made the following note: "5 sentyabrya 1824 u.l.d. E.W."

This is deciphered as "5 September 1824 eu lettre de Elise Worontzow." Pushkin linked the two initials monogrammatically as they are in known signatures of

Countess Elizaveta Vorontsov. He had not seen her since
the end of July. (She returned to Odessa from the Crimea
on July 25.) Countess Vorontsov's profile is sketched by
him on f. 9ᵛ of the same cahier. The drafts of XXXII begin
on f. 7ᵛ.

It would seem that between June 13, 1824, and Sept. 5
Pushkin had not worked at his novel. He left Odessa on
July 31, traveled post along a police-prescribed route via
Nikolaev, Elizavetgrad, Kremenchug, Chernigov, Mo-
gilev, and Vitebsk, and arrived in Opochka Aug. 9, hav-
ing covered 1075 miles in ten days. On Oct. 4, the Pskov
provincial governor, B. Aderkas, reported to the Baltic
governor general, F. Pauluchi (Paulucci), that the "state
councilor" Sergey Pushkin had agreed to act for the
government and keep his son under close observation at
Mihaylovskoe, their estate near Opochka. In the course
of October this led to a family row, and about Nov. 17
his parents left Mihaylovskoe.

VARIANT

The following variant, with many deletions, can be
made out in 2370, f. 7ᵛ:

⟨In agitation sitting⟩ on the bed
Tatiana scarce could breathe,
not daring verily the letter
4 ⟨either read o'er or sign⟩.
'Tis late, the moon loses its luster
and quiet morning beams
into her window through the linden's branches,
8 but to our maid 'tis all the same.
She, turned to stone, leans on one elbow. . . .
The bed ⟨. . . . .⟩ is hot.
Down from her ⟨charming⟩ shoulder
12 the light chemise has slid,
⟨over her eyes her curls have tumbled,
upon her breasts a tear has dropped.⟩

XXXIII

1 / *Oná zarí ne zamecháet*: The reader of the Russian text should mark very carefully the long-drawn intonation of this line, so simple in literal sense, so evocative in melody. This same plaintive and languorous leitmotiv will vibrate again in Five : XXII : 1 and in the last chapter, Eight : XXX : 1 and XLII : 1, each time opening the stanza.

3–4 Cf. Byron, *Don Juan*, I, CXCVII, Julia's letter:

> I have no more to say, but linger still,
> And dare not set my seal upon this sheet . . .

Pichot (1823): "Je n'ai plus rien à dire, et je ne puis quitter la plume; je n'ose poser mon cachet sur ce papier."

6 / gray Filatievna / *Filát'evna sedáya*: Daughter of Filat: an elderly and respectable person of the lower class was often referred to by his or her patronymic only. We never learn the old nurse's given name or surname. For some reason, Pushkin had trouble in deciding what to call her, and all three patronymics he used for her begin with *F*. She is "Fadeevna" (daughter of Thaddeus) in the draft and fair copy, and "Filipievna" (daughter of Philip) in the 1827 and 1833 edns., before becoming "Filatievna" (daughter of Philetus) in 1837.

13 / No trace at all of the night's fret / *Toskí nochnóy i slédu nét*: Still closer in sound would be: "Of night's annoy no trace is left."

VARIANT

4 A canceled draft (2370, f. 11ᵛ) has "carnelian seal."

XXXIV

2, 5, 11 / darling . . . My friend . . . my dear / *rodnáya*

. . . *Moy drúg* . . . *mílaya moyá*: The pet names (nine
in all) used by the old nurse are XVIII : 7, "my sweet"
(*moy svét*; literally, "my light"); XIX : 6, 12 and XXXIII: 8,
"my child" (*dityá moyó*); XX : 3 and XXXV : 2, "friend of
my heart" (*Serdéchnïy drúg*; literally, "heart friend");
XXXIII : 9, "pretty one" (*krasávitsa*); XXXIII : 10, "my
early birdie" (*ptáshka ránnyaya moyá*); XXXIV : 2,
"darling" (*rodnáya*, "own one," "kindred one");
XXXIV : 5, "My friend" (*Moy drúg*); XXXIV : 11, "my
dear" (*mílaya moyá*, "my dear one"); and XXXV : 10,
"my dear soul" (*dushá moyá*, literally, "my soul").

6 / [the nurse's] grandson: For all we know, this may be
the pedee (his name was Trishka, from Trifon, in the
first draft) who serves the cream in Three : XXXVII : 8,
or the even smaller lad with the hand sled in Five : II :
9–14.

7–8 / *k Ó* . . . *k tomú* . . . | *K sosédu*: Tatiana starts to pro-
nounce Onegin's name but does not go further than the
little gasp of the *O*, then attempts to define him (that
man, that person), and finally finds the saving formula,
"to the neighbor" (*that* neighbor for her, but one of the
many local squires for the nurse).

It is very curious that Tatiana, even if she wanted to
go on with the name, could not have done so since the
initial *O* as part of the name precedes an accented syl-
lable and *Onéginu* does not fit in that compartment of
the line. Had she named him, the verse would not scan:
s zapískoy étoy k Onéginu. The fact that the *O* falls on
an ictus suggests that Tatiana uses it as a cipher (cf. the
monogram in XXXVII : 14).

Tatiana's confusion and broken breathing is beauti-
fully rendered in l. 8:

K sosédu . . . *da velét' emú*

by means of the scud on the second foot (*du da*), after which she rapidly continues:

> *Chtob ón ne govoríl ni slóva,*
> *Chtob ón ne nazïvál menyá*

where an exceptionally rare sequence of stresses (semi-scud, scud, accent, accent) occurs twice in a row:

$$\cup \overset{-}{\cdot} \cup - \cup \overset{\prime}{\cdot} \cup \overset{\prime}{\cdot} \cup$$

$$\cup \overset{-}{\cdot} \cup - \cup \overset{\prime}{\cdot} \cup \overset{\prime}{\cdot}$$

The separate edition of the chapter drops the third *k* in l. 8, which does not impair the dative.

8 / him / *emú*: The grandson, of course.

XXXV

The first draft (in pencil) is on f. 12ʳ of Cahier 2370, under stanza XXV (the Parny paraphrase), which is not in the fair copy and is thought to have been composed in the last week of September, 1824 (after the stanzas leading to Tatiana's letter, the letter itself, and XXXII–XXXIV were ready).

6 / *Ah, nyánya, nyánya! do togó li?*: "Is it [the time, the mood] for that?"

8 / it is about a letter / *délo o pis'mé*: "Il s'agit d'une lettre." Tatiana's Gallicism in this conversation is very piquant, since it is followed immediately by the nanny's very Russian *délo, délo* (l. 9), "Now you're talking," "This makes sense."

12 / pale again: Psychologically sound: the plunge has been taken, the letter has left Tatiana's hands.

xxxva

The following stanza, replacing XXXVI, is canceled in the
fair copy:

> At present how her heart begins to throb,
> to ache as if before calamity.
> How can it be? What happened to me?
> 4 Why did I write, good God!
> She at her mother dares not glance,
> now she all burns, now she all blanches,
> all day with downcast gaze is mute,
> 8 and nearly cries, and trembles.
> The nurse's grandson came back late.
> The neighbor he had seen: to him
> in person had handed the letter.
> 12 And he, the neighbor? He was getting on his horse
> and put the letter in his pocket.
> Ah, what will be the end of the romance?

The device of reported speech, so characteristic of
European eighteenth-century writing, comes here in
three varieties: (1) Tatiana's inner monologue, (2) her
dialogue with the little messenger or the nurse, and (3)
the author's (or reader's!) anxious query.

In the same fair copy the first five lines in a variant
reading stand thus:

> Scarce had the nurse withdrawn
> when as before calamity the heart
> of the poor girl began to throb;
> she cried out: Good God, what's the matter with me!
> She rises. At her mother dares not glance . . .

XXXVI

2 / nothing yet / *vsyo nét, kak nét*: "Still none as none can
be": a denial of the particular (*vsyo net*, "still no [let-
ter]'") in terms of the general (*kak net*, "as if no [letter
existed]'").

3 / since morning dressed: Dressed for visitors, waiting for
Onegin.

8 The tone of this remark vaguely implies more than one
previous visit on Onegin's part. We know, however,
that there had been only one. There will be only two
more—before Chapter Eight.

The spacing of Onegin's three visits to the Larins' is
as follows: first visit, end of June, 1820 (the reader should
remember that Old Style is used everywhere in my
notes, unless otherwise specified); second visit—end of
July; third visit—Jan. 12 of the next year. Pushkin's
chronology is not very "realistic" here.

12 Meaning that Onegin's correspondence has held him up.
Tatiana understands it—for one dreadful instant—as
meaning that Onegin is still in the act of studying her
letter and writing a lengthy answer to it.

Of course, reticent Onegin had not told frank Lenski
about Tatiana's letter, and so Lenski's reference to the
mail was quite innocent.

XXXVII

11 / the dear soul / *moyá dushá*: Literally, "my soul." Push-
kin uses the nurse's vocabulary (see XXXV : 10).

14 / *Zavétnïy vénzel' Ó da É*: "The secret, sacred mono-
gram, an O [linked] with an E."

A very curious case of affinity is the earlier appearance
of this cherished monogram—namely in Goethe's *Die
Wahlverwandtschaften* (1809), pt. I, ch. 9, where a
drinking glass is described, on which one could see "die
Buchstaben E und O in sehr zierlicher Verschlingung
eingeschnitten: es war eins der Gläser, die für Eduarden
in seiner Jugend verfertigt worden." The earliest French

translation seems to have been the anonymous *Les Affinités électives* (Paris, 1810), actually translated by Raymond, A. Serieys, Godailh, J. L. Manget, and G. B. Depping.

8 This pedee is called "Trishka" in the draft (2370, f. 17ᵛ) and in the fair copy.

XXXVIII

2 It is extremely doubtful that a gaze, *vzor*, can be "full of tears," *pólon slyóz*.

The obsessive recurrence of terms pertaining to sight is characteristic of Russian literature. Russ. *vzorï, ochi, glaza* = Fr. *regards, prunelles, yeux*. (See also n. to Eight : xv : 4.)

3–4 Elton: ". . . a sudden pawing, | A tramp outside, a trot! . . ."

4 / Coming fast / *skáchut*: Here *skachut* does not necessarily mean "they [horsemen] are galloping." It merely means, I think, that Eugene is briskly driving up to the house in his coachman-conducted carriage, drawn by (presumably) three horses. Illustrators seem to have assumed, however, that he arrived on horseback.

4, 7 / in the yard . . . outdoors / *na dvór . . . na dvór*: This curious word *dvor* is a welcome *cheville* for the versificator but a bugbear for the translator. The word reflects a conflict between different relations to an enclosure. It may mean "the outside" in such formulas as *holodno na dvore*, "it is cold outdoors" (or "out there," "abroad," "in the open," etc.), or it may mean "the inside" in such formulas as *ehat' so dvora*, "to drive off the premises" (as in Six : XXIV : 14), in which *dvor* is either, generically, "habitation," "homestead," any group of buildings relating to one household, or, specifically, a courtyard; since a yard is not within the house, we have at this point a kind of link between the outside idea and the inside. *Dvor* may also mean the imperial court, as in Eight : XLIV : 10. (See also nn. to One : IV : 4; Two : XXXIV : 14; and Five : I : 2.)

5 / "*Áh*": The *h* is rough, as in *oh*; see n. to XXXII : 1. The verb is left out in the Russian locution. Pushkin had already used (1813) this formula in *The Monk*, can. III, a long poem written when he was fourteen ("Pankrátiy: '*Ah!*'—and sudden he awoke").

This form should be compared to those discussed in the next note.

6 / Tatiana skips / *Tat'yána príg*: From *prígnut'*, "to jump." *Príg* is the so-called "interjectional" verb (the indeclinable *príg* instead of the third-person past-perfective feminine *prígnula*), which coincides grammatically with the "verbal interjection" (i.e., an interjection used as an interjectional verb—cf. Five : XII : 8: *Tat'-yána* "*ah!*"—since *ah* can also be regarded as the interjectional abbreviation of the verb *ahnut'*), and is close to another very Russian form, the "conjugate infinitive," e.g., ibid.: *on revét'*, "he [starts] to roar." There is yet a third form in this series: when the action is so instantaneous that the verb is not even represented (e.g., Six : XIX : 14: *i na kríl'tsó*, "and out onto the porch").

14–XXXIX : 1 / on a bench has dropped: A rare case of one stanza overflowing into another. The device admirably renders Tatiana's excitement. This will be echoed by the similar rhythm of Onegin's belated rush in Chapter Eight (XXXIX : 14–XL : 1).

What struck Tatiana was not the fact of Onegin's having come (she had been expecting him in XXXVI, and Lenski had just said he would come), but the fact of his not having answered her letter before coming. In the epistolary novels that had educated her sentiments, the answer came by letter, not by word of mouth. Casual reality impinges here upon ordered romance.

Pushkin's description of Tatiana's dash from dining room to park bench gives the reader an idea of the grounds. Leaving the house from a side porch, she flitted out of doors (*na dvór*) and made for the garden (*sad*). She then negotiated (*obezhála*) the disks, lunes, and rectangles of its beds (*kurtíni*), the small bridges (*móstiki*) laid across its ditches, and a lawn (*luzhók*; a *kósheni̇̆ luzhók*, "mown lawn," is canceled in the fair copy). She entered the park by the avenue (*alléya*) leading through a bosquet (*lesók*) to the lake (*ózero*); but before reaching the latter she turned off the path, to break through one of those Russian floreta (*tsvetníki*) that were so prominent in Russian country places. I read "bushes, lilac" (*Syringa vulgaris* L., first imported from Asia, via Turkey and Austria, in the sixteenth century, an emancipated relative of the utilitarian olive). See also *siren'* in Lexicon.

Tatiana reaches a bench (*skam'yá*) on a path skirting a brook (and leading back to the avenue in Three : XLI). Beyond the brook there is the vegetable garden, or the orchard, where slave girls are gathering berries. It is along this kitchen garden that she and Onegin will return to the house in Four : XVII (after meeting in the linden avenue to which she walks back in Three : XLI— and which she will recall in Seven : LIII : 13–14 and Eight : XLII : 11).

XXXIX

8, 11 / berries . . . berry / *yágodï* [acc. pl.] . . . *yágodï*
[gen. sing.]: These are identified as "gooseberries" in
an incomplete draft (2370, f. 19ʳ) and as "raspberries"
and "scarlet barberries" in canceled readings. They are
the revived ingredients of the preserves in Three : III,
and thus link the end of the chapter to its beginning. In
XXXIX : 12, the singular (*yagoda*) is used collectively
(cf. "fruit").

THE SONG OF THE GIRLS

In *devushka* as used in the title, *Pésnya dévushek*, "The
Song of the Girls," there is the implication of "serf
girl," "servant girl" (cf. "maid"); otherwise it means
"adolescent girl" or "unmarried woman." The word
dévitsa, used in the song itself, means "girl" in a general
sense, with a folksy accent on the first syllable (the simi-
larly spelled, but differently accented, *devítsa* is a syno-
nym of *devushka*, in the sense of unmarried person of the
female sex, thus used, for instance, in Seven : XXIII : 3).

"The Song of the Girls" is the only noniambic set of
verses in *EO*. It consists of eighteen lines, each a trochaic
trimeter with a long terminal. Its ultima may be so ac-
cented in actual song as to mimic the ictus of a fourth
scudded foot. (At this point the reader should consult
App. II, "Notes on Prosody: 3. The Scud.")

Seventeen lines of the song scud either on the first
foot (ll. 3–5, 7–12, 15, 17) or on the second (1–2, 6,
13–14, 16), and the last is scudless (18: *Ígrï náshi dévi-
ch'i*, $\perp \cup \perp \cup \perp \cup \bar{\cup}$). The slight difference of accentuation
between a trisyllable making the long terminal (ictus-
depression-depression) of the trochaic line and a tri-
syllable beginning a trochaic line (scudded on II) is
exceptionally nicely expressed when the terminal word
of a line is repeated at the beginning of the next verse:

> *Zatyaníte pésenku,*
> *Pésenku zavétnuyu*
>
> $- \cup \acute{} \cup \acute{} \cup \bar{}$
> $\acute{} \cup - \cup \acute{} \cup \bar{}$

Although the themes and formulas of this song existed endemically in the Russian counterpart of the

> Little Arcady between
> Servants' hall and village green

the berries have been artificially colored and flavored, and Pushkin's elegant little product only summarizes eighteenth-century stylizations of folklore stuff couched in neat trochees. This "Song of the Girls" was reprinted in *The Northern Chanter*, "a collection of the newest and most excellent *romances* [Fr., romantic ballads] and songs dedicated to ladies and gentlemen cultivating the arts," pt. I, 1830, and in the *Songbook for a Lady's Reticule and Dressing Table*, 1832, both published by the Lazarev brothers, in Moscow, and instrumental in propagating, for the benefit of solemn ethnographers, several "folk songs" (such as *Devushki krasotochki*, c. 1850) strummed by lackeys and artisans. Thus transits a poet's glory.

The song is a charming pastiche. I find it printed everywhere in one block of lines; but the changing tone, and especially the envoylike ending, surely warrant the breaking up I have suggested.

In order to render exactly the rhythm of the thing, I have devised the following onomatopoeic imitation, the sense of which has, of course, nothing to do with the two lines (3–4) it parrots:

> You're the brightest, Davison,
> You're the lightest, Milligan.
>
> (*Razïgráytes'*, *dévitsï*,
> *Razgulyáytes'*, *mílïe!*)

3–4 The verbs *razïgrat'sya* and *razgulyat'sya* used here
come from *igrat'*, "to play," and *gulyat'*, "to have a good
time." The prefix *raz* connotes a spreading of action, its
freedom and thoroughness.

VARIANT

In Cahier 2370, f. 19ᵛ, above the established version of
the song, there is the draft of a first version consisting of
four quatrains, in alternate trochaic tetrameter and trim-
eter, with paired feminine rhymes:

> Dunya came out on the road,
> having said her prayers.
> Dunya weeps and wails
> 4 as she sees her lover off.
>
> He is gone to a strange land,
> a remote countree . . .
> Oh, that strange land is for me
> 8 bitter desolation!
>
> In that land there are young women,
> there are maidens fair;
> I remain, the young one,
> 12 a bitter-hearted widow.
>
> Oh, remember me, young me,
> or else I'll be jealous;
> oh, remember me when out of sight,
> even though not on purpose.

In ll. 13–16:

> *Vspomyaní menyá mladúyu,*
> *Ál' ya prirevnúyu;*
> *Vspomyaní menyá zaóchno,*
> *Hot' i ne naróchno*

an approximate echo of rhyme and rhythm would be:

> You don't need my heart, or do you?
> Formerly I knew you;
> You don't need my heart, but watch it
> Even while you notch it.

XL

1 / They sing . . . / *Oní poyút* . . . : A similar classical in-
tonation occurs elsewhere in Pushkin, namely after the
Tatar song of the Khan's wives in *The Fountain of
Bahchisaray*.

Pushkin, while anxious to quote the berry-picking
song he had composed, was not quite certain whether to
have Tatiana listen to it (which under the circumstances
she could hardly have been expected to do) or to ignore it
(in which case the reader should be hardly expected to
be concerned with it either). The draft of the stanza has
the song "reverberating in the fields" and Tatiana
"harkening to it involuntarily."

5–6 / *Chtobï proshló lanít pïlán'e.* | *No v pérsyah tó zhe
trepetán'e*: Mark the alliterations: *lo-la-la* for the cheeks
and *per-to-tre-pe-ta* for the breasts. The melody con-
dones a poetical platitude, which is so meaningless, for
instance, in Thomson's unmusical *Spring*, ll. 968–69:

> . . . her wishing bosom heaves
> With palpitations wild . . .

VARIANT

9–11 In the canceled fair copy the butterfly is slightly
different:

> A prankster thus, upon a rose
> will capture by its feet [*lápki*]
> a charming butterfly.

I like the *lápki*.

XLI

5–6 It will be noted that on this summer day of 1820
Tatiana sees Onegin as a demonic character in a Gothic
novel or Byronic romance—that is, in terms of Three :

XII, which lists Onegin's reading in 1820 (and that of young girls in 1824, at the time of Pushkin's composing the stanza), rather than in terms of Thrée : IX, wherein Tatiana's own favorites are listed prior to the spring of 1821, when, in Onegin's study, she will read Maturin and Byron for the first time (Chapter Seven).

8 / she stopped / *Ostanovílasya oná*: This will be repeated in her dream (Five : XI : 14). Incidentally, it is curious to mark here one of the cases when in *EO* a Russian line of eight syllables dwindles to the minimum of two in its English exact translation. Another such case is the *Blagoslovénnïe krayá*, "Blest climes" (or "Blest parts") of *Onegin's Journey*, XXIII : 14.

On the other hand, there are a few cases in *EO* when the eight-syllable line of the Russian text finds its most accurate English equivalent in a hexameter.

12–14 In Tressan's version of Ariosto's *Roland furieux* (to use the language in which it was familiar to Pushkin) can. III concludes with this device: "Vous en apprendrez le sujet [of a sudden outcry in an inn]; mais ce ne sera que dans le chant suivant, car il est temps que ma voix se repose."

The poem speaks at one point of certain "poissons souvent troublés dans leurs amours secrets" (can. VII), which have always puzzled me. And in can. X (there are forty-six of them in all) Angélique is prostrated on some sand "toute nue . . . sans un seul voile qui put couvrir les lys et les roses vermeilles placés à propos," Gallic emblemata, which the reader will find also in the very first metrical poems in Russian (Trediakovski, Lomonosov), as well as in a passage from Vyazemski's *First Snow* recalled by Pushkin in connection with Five : III (see my n. to Five : III : 6), where however they refer to the facial garden:

> Fresher the roses of your red cheeks blush,
> and fresher on your brow the lily whitens.

Cf. Thomas Campion, *Fourth Book of Airs*, VII:

> There is a garden in her face,
> Where roses and white lilies grow . . .

*

Pushkin dated the finished chapter with the month in Russian (not French as before): "2 *okt.* 1825."

Chapter Four

La morale est dans la nature des choses: *Necker*: "La morale doit être placée au-dessus du calcul. La morale est la nature des choses dans l'ordre intellectuel; et comme, dans l'ordre physique, le calcul part de la nature des choses, et ne peut y apporter aucun changement, il doit, dans l'ordre intellectuel, partir de la même donnée, c'est-à-dire, de la morale" (Mme de Staël, *De la Littérature*, pt. II, ch. 6; 1818 edn., vol. II, p. 226).

"Vous avez trop d'esprit, disoit un jour M. Necker à Mirabeau, pour ne pas reconnoître tôt ou tard que la morale est dans la nature des choses" (Mme de Staël, *Considérations sur les principaux événemens de la Révolution française* (1818), pt. II, ch. 20; *Œuvres*, XII, 404).

Pushkin completed Chapter Four on Jan. 3, 1826, a few days after he had learned of the Decembrist rising; and in this light it is curious to note that the passage from which the quotation is taken is immediately preceded by the following: "J'ai eu entre les mains une lettre de Mirabeau, écrite pour être montrée au roi; il y offroit tous les moyens pour rendre à la France une monarchie forte et digne, mais limitée . . . *Je ne voudrois pas avoir travaillé* [said Mirabeau] *seulement à une vaste destruction.*" Some forty words further comes the Necker quotation.

There are two epigraphs heading Chapter Four in the fair copy (PB 14):

> [Ma dimmi:] al tempo de' dolci sospiri
> A che e come concedette amore
> Che conosceste i dubbiosi desiri?
>   Dante inf[erno] Cant[o] v [ll. 118–20]

and

> Collection of the flaming marks
> of the rich life of youthful years.
>   Ba[ratïnski]

The first is also written on the title page of the fair copy of Three (see n. to its motto). The second motto is also on the cover of the first fair copy of One (Odessa, 1823; see n. to its mottoes): it comes from Baratïnski's *Feasts* (ll. 252–53) and is paraphrased in the last lines (15–17) of the Prefatory Piece (1837 edn.), which appeared as a dedication to Pletnyov in the separate edition of Four and Five (1828).

The first six stanzas were omitted (wisely) by Pushkin in the complete editions. By 1833 he had been married to Natalia Goncharov as long as Prince N., in 1824, had been married to Tatiana Larin: about two years. The first four stanzas, under the heading "Women: a Fragment from *Eugene Onegin*," appeared in the *Moscow Herald* (*Moskovskiy vestnik*), pt. 5, no. 20 (1827), 365–67; the fair copy is in MB 3515. Sts. v and vi are represented by drafts in Cahier 2370, ff. 31^r, 32^v, and 41^v. Here are these six rejected stanzas:

I

In the beginning of my life ruled me
the charming, sly, weak sex;
I then would set myself for law
4 nought but its arbitrary will.
My soul had just begun to kindle,
and to my heart woman appeared
as some pure deity.
8 Controlling feelings, intellect,
she was resplendent with perfection.
In front of her I melted in the stillness:
her love seemed to me
12 bliss unattainable.
To live, to die at the dear feet—
nought else could I desire.

II

Or suddenly I would detest her,
and quiver, and shed tears,
with heartache and with terror see in her
4 the product of malignant secret forces;
her penetrating gaze,
smile, voice, discourses—
all in her was envenomed,
8 infused with wicked treachery,
all in her thirsted for my tears and moans,
fed on my blood. . . .
Or suddenly I saw in her the marble
12 before Pygmalion's prayer,
still cold and mute,
but presently hot and alive.

5–7 There is a curious echo here of the intonation discussed
in my note to Olga's portrait (Two : XXIII : 5–8).

III

In the words of a vatic poet
I also am allowed to say:
"Thamyra, Daphne, and Lileta
4 I've long forgotten like a dream."
But there is one among their throng . . .

> By one I was enraptured long—
> but was I loved, and loved by whom,
> 8 and where, and did it last? . . .Why should
> you know? 'Tis not the matter!
> What *was* is past, is twaddle;
> the matter is that ever since
> 12 the heart in me became already cold,
> it closed for love,
> and all within it is empty and dark.

A facsimile of the draft (2370, f. 41ʳ) is published by Tomashevski, "Pushkin i frantsuzskaya literatura," *Lit. nasl.*, nos. 31–32 (1937), p. 23. In the right margin, alongside ll. 9–14, Pushkin drew a nightcapped profile of Voltaire, and there is a Mirabeau, and another Voltaire, capless, lower down on the same page.

3 / *Temíra, Dáfna i Liléta*: From a then MS ode, written c. 1815, by Delvig, *To Fani*, published (by Gofman) in 1922:

> Thamyra, Daphne, and Lileta
> I've long forgotten like a dream,
> and for a poet's recollection
> only a happy line preserves them.

"Thémire" and "Daphné" are frequently mentioned by French Arcadians (Gresset, Houdar de la Motte, etc.). "Lileta," or "Lila," was Batyushkov's favorite shepherdess.

IV

> I have discovered that ladies themselves,
> betraying their soul's secret,
> cannot stop marveling at us
> 4 when in all fairness they appraise themselves.
> Our wayward transports
> appear to them very amusing;
> and really, on our part,
> 8 we're inexcusably absurd.

Self-bondaged rashly,
their love we, in reward, expect,
in folly call for love,
12 as if it were possible to demand
from butterflies or lilies
deep sentiments and passions.

The following variant to IV is drafted in 2370, f. 34ʳ:

Of course, the solemn Fashionable,
the systematical Faublas,
professed attendant of the fair,
4 is funny, though right, in tormenting you.
But pitiful is he who without art,
the soul's exalted sentiments,
believing in the magic dream,
8 to a fair lady immolates,
and having rashly spent himself,
expects but love as his reward,
in folly calls for love,
12 as if it were possible to demand
from butterflies and lilies
deep sentiments and passions.

2 / Faublas: See n. to One : XII : 9–10.
    Works 1949, p. 529, adds an incomplete variant said
to follow var. IV in the draft:

Happy who shares his pleasure,
clever who was alone to feel,
who was of an involuntary inclination,
4 the egoistic master,
who would accept without intoxication
and leave without regret,
when winged love
⟨. . . .⟩ abandoning himself again.

Tomashevski (Acad 1937, p. 338) also refers to a draft
of IV in MS 22/3366 ("Sobolevski coll."), with the
(author's?) note: "Avant les voyages" (i.e., to precede
Onegin's Journey).

V

Shall I confess to you? Pleasure alone
I at the time possessed;
blindness was dear to me,
4 I afterward regretted it.
But by the luring riddle
not long was I tormented furtively . . .
⟨. . . themselves did help me greatly⟩
8 by whispering to me the *word*;
⟨for a long time⟩ known to the world of fashion,
and it had even ceased to seem
funny to anyone.
12 Thus ⟨having solved that riddle⟩
I said: So this is all, my friends?
How slow-witted I am!

8 / the *word* / *slóvo*: A Gallicism, *le mot de l'énigme*. One
wonders what was its simple solution. Perhaps: "le
fruit de l'amour mondain n'est autre chose que la
jouissance . . ." (Pierre de Bourdeilles, Seigneur de
Brantôme, *Recueil des dames*, pt. II, *Les Dames galantes*,
Discours II).

See also Seven : XXV : 2.

VI

The restless worries of the passions
have gone, will not return again!
The dormancy of a numb soul
4 by love no longer can be shaken.
Of vice the empty beauty
glitters and pleases for a term.
'Tis time the misdeeds of young days
8 were by my life effaced!
Rumor, in play, has blackened
my opening years.
Slander lent it a hand
12 and only friendships' mirth excited;
but happily the verdict of blind rumor
may sometimes be reversed!

VII

10 / sapajous: Pushkin echoes a moralistic passage in his
own letter written in French from Kishinev to his
brother in Moscow in the autumn of 1822: "moins
on aime une femme plus on est sûr de l'avoir . . .
mais cette jouissance est digne d'un vieux sapajou du
dix-huitième siècle."

12 / *Lovlásov obvetshála sláva*: A French form derived from
the name of Richardson's villain in *Clarissa Harlowe*:
un lovelace (*ove* as *ov* in "Soviet"; *ace* as in "Laplace").

VIII

7–8 One wonders if the terminal of the first of these two
lines:

> *Kotórïh né bïlo i nét*
> *U dévochki v trinádtsat' lét!*

was not influenced subliminally by the *-nette* in *L'Heure
du berger*, an eclogue by Parny (in *Poésies érotiques*,
bk. I):

> —J'ai quatorze ans,
> Répond Nicette;
> Suis trop jeunette
> Pour les amants.

IX

This stanza in the draft (2370, f. 29ᵛ) was initially in the
first person and may have been intended as part of
Onegin's speech.

1 / Exactly thus my Eugene thought / *Tak tóchno dúmal
móy Evgéniy*: We are about to go back to Eugene's
youth in Petersburg; and there is a pleasing parallel
between the intonation of this line and that of One :

II : 1, "Thus a young scapegrace thought," *Tak dúmal molodóy povésa.*

The whole instrumentation of the quatrain is magnificent. See next note.

2–4 / *On v pérvoy yúnosti svoéy | Bïl zhértvoy búrnïh zabluzhdéniy | I neobúzdannïh strastéy*: Mark the internal assonance *pérvoy-zhértvoy*; and the alliterative bubbling over (slightly reminiscent of the surf in One : XXXIII) of the *b, bu, blu, bu* series in ll. 3–4, ending in a spacious flow.

8, 9 / irked / *tomim*: The use of *tomim* makes very vague sense here. Was he oppressed by longings or did he grow sick of them? Did success wear him out or produce ennui? Should one translate "discouraged"? The epithet "slowly," *médlenno*, does not help much.

10 / harking / *Vnimáya*: *Vnimát'* in the strict sense implies more attention on the hearer's part than does "to listen" (*slushat'*). *Vnimat'*, like "hearken" and "hark," is usually, though not always, employed with the dative. Pushkin's choice between *vnimat'* and *slushat'* and their derivatives is governed solely by the requirements of scansion; *vnimat'* fits into the even-odd sections of the iambic tetrameter and rhymes with thousands of other infinitives. *Slushat'* (employed only with the accusative, as *vnimat'* is sometimes—e.g., One : XIX : 2) goes into the odd-even sections and has only two or three usable rhymes. It will be marked that auditory-sense terms are more frequently met with in Russian than in English but less so than visual-sense ones.

What is now st. IX began initially (Cahier 2370, f. 29^v) with the quatrain:

> I am the victim of long errors
> and riotry of flaming passions,
> and thirst for violent impressions,
> and my tempestuous youth.

Whatever our poet's plan was—to continue his personal confession or to have Onegin make his to Tatiana—this he dropped, and IX was revamped into an authorial transition.

X

2 / dangled / *volochílsya*: This verb, *volochit'sya* (which also has a noun form, *volokitstvo*, "philandering," and *volokita*, masc., "philanderer"), has a slightly different shade of sense from the more or less equivalent English formulas "to dangle after petticoats," "to dally with," "to court a woman," and so forth. It has in Russian more of a "dragging-oneself" sense than of a "suspending-oneself" sense, and in fact comes from *vlachit'*, *volochit'*, "to drag along the ground" (so that *volokita*, fem., means "procrastination"). Pushkin uses *volochit'sya* in two other passages of *EO*: Six : XLIII : 8 and Eight : III : 12. Cf. Fr. *se traîner*: *se mouvoir à genoux, se prosterner aux pieds d'une femme.*

XI

2 / *zhívo trónut*: A Gallicism, *vivement touché.*

7 In its usual sense the noun *son* means "sleep" or "dream"; in the latter case it is synonymous with *snovidenie*, "vision in sleep." In poetry, however, it is constantly used as a mere substitute for *mechta*, "daydream," "fancy." *Son* rhymes well in the nominative singular, still better in all plural cases (*sní*, *snov*, etc.), and in the genitive

singular (*sna*) joins the great and powerful clan of rhymes in -*na*.

XII

1 / *Minútï dvé*:. "About two minutes," "For a couple of minutes"; but all this is false literality. I do not think we can imagine the two facing each other in perfect silence for more than fifteen seconds.

13 / Hear my confession / *Primíte íspoved' moyú*: Baratïnski has the same line (873) in his narrative poem *The Concubine* (*Nalozhnitsa*). See n. to Two : XXXVII : 1.

XIV

5 / *sóvest' v tóm porúkoy*: See my n. to Three : Tatiana's Letter : 78 (after nn. to XXXI).

9–14 Cf. Senancour, *Oberman*, Letter XLV: ". . . c'est une misère à laquelle on ne peut espérer de terme, de ne pouvoir que plaindre celle . . . qui n'oppose à notre indignation que des larmes pieuses. . . ."

XVI

7 / for dreams light dreams / *Mechtámi lyógkie mechtí*: Logically, if not grammatically, the epithet refers to both.

10–11 / There is a very evocative rhyme, with a kind of didactic pause, at the suspension of l. 11: *suzhdenó* ("destined") and *nó* ("but").

VARIANTS

XII–XVI

Onegin's little sermon had been jotted down at first in the same manner as Pushkin's initial notes for Tatiana's letter. (It seems rather clear to me that Pushkin at one time planned to have Onegin answer Tatiana by letter.) The draft of these prose lines (2370, f. 71ᵛ) reads:

Had I been thinking of marriage, had a peaceful family life attracted my fancy, then I would have elected you and none other . . . I would have found in you [cf. XIII] . . . but I am not made for bliss [cf. XIV] . . . unworthy . . . How could I join my destiny to yours [cf. XV] . . . You elected me. Probably I am your first *passion* [crush], but are you certain that . . . Allow me to give you advice [cf. XVI].

Other fragments, of incomplete stanzas pertaining to Onegin's monologue, are found in Cahier 2370, f. 41ʳ:

A (l. 1)

I have revealed myself frankly to you . . .

B (ll. 1–5)

No, I am no voluptuous fiend:
ashamed I would be to deceive
the trust of a fine soul
.   .   .   .   .   .
No, you are worthy to be loved . . .

C (ll. 1–7)

Not all, of course. Without a doubt
.   .   .   .   .   .
It's possible to find exceptions
and you of this present a live example
but as a rule—I swear to you—
women themselves know not
why they . . .

D (ll. 6–10)

Lured by your beauty,
imagination, intellect
.   .   .   .   .
like a voluptuous fiend who seeks
a minute of enjoyment anywhere . . .

XVII

2 This is ludicrously paraphrased by Miss Deutsch thus:

> And blinded by the tears that glistened
> Unheeded in her great dark eyes.

6 / as it is said: "mechanically" / *Kak govorítsya, ma-shinál'no*: This was a modish Gallicism, *machinalement*, which the French Academy had admitted in 1740. It had not been quite assimilated in Russian. Vyazemski, May (or Apr.) 30, 1820, in a letter to Pushkin, writes it *mahinal'no* (Fr. *machine* being translated as *mahina*; now only jocular), and so writes Pushkin in the draft of XVII : 6 (2370, f. 51ᵛ).

In Jane Austen's *Pride and Prejudice* (1813), vol. III, ch. 1, Elizabeth Bennet (when Darcy suddenly appears while she is seeing his seat Pemberley and learning many good things about him through "the praise of an intelligent servant," Mrs. Reynolds, his housekeeper) answers her aunt "mechanically" (the same Gallicism).

8 / little head: The word used here is *golóvka* instead of the *golóvushka* of Three : XXXII : 5 (to which see n.).

9 The 1837 edn. misprints *poshlá* ("she went") for the correct *poshlí* ("they went").

XVIIa

In a moment of irritation with his neighbors, Pushkin made a false start. The following stanza is drafted in Cahier 2370, f. 51ᵛ:

> But you, province of Pskov,
> hothouse of my young days,
> what can be, stagnant country,
> 4 more trying than your misses?

They do not have—I shall observe in passing—
either the subtle courtesy of rank
or the ⟨frivolity⟩ of winsome trulls.
8 Esteeming as I do the Russian spirit,
I would forgive their tattle, uppishness,
the wit of family jokes,
sometimes uncleanliness of teeth,
12 ⟨indecency and⟩ affectation—
but how can one forgive their ⟨modish⟩ raves
and clumsy etiquette?

1 *No tí—gubérniya Pskovskáya*: It is important to note that
the canceled text of XVIIa : 1 reads: "But there is the
province of Pskov," *No ést' gubérniya Pskovskáya*, which
indicates that this was *not* the province where the Larins
lived.

11 / *Poróyu zúb nechistotú*: Some editions read *Poróki zúb*,
nechistotú, "defects of teeth, uncleanliness." A canceled
draft of 11 has: "Uncleanliness of teeth and linen." The
whole thing makes rather painful reading, especially
if we think of the ("toutes mauvaises") Osipov girls.

XVIII

4–7 There are echoes of this passage in Eight : IX. In both
cases the purpose is purely structural. Here it is a matter
of thematic transition. A digression follows (XVIII : 12–14
to XXII: from "friends" through "kinsfolk" and "tender
beauties" to one's "own self").

13 / Ah me, those friends / *Uzh éti mné druz'yá*: The in-
tonation is less hearty here than in the opening line of
Three : I : 1, where the same exclamatory formula is
used (. . . *Uzh éti mné poétï!*). The repetition of *druz'yá*
enhances the troubled, head-shaking note in the present
passage.

XIX

1–2 Cf. the intonation in Byron's *Don Juan*, XIV, VII, 2 (see also n. to *EO*, Four : XX : 1): ". . . nothing; a mere speculation" (Pichot, 1824: ". . . Rien . . . c'est une simple méditation").

4–6 /   *Chto nét prezrénnoy klevetí,*
            Na cherdaké vralyóm rozhdyónnoy
            I svétskoy chérn'yu obodryónnoy . . .

The upper floor of house No. 12 in the Srednyaya Pod'yacheskaya Street, St. Petersburg, where the playwright and theatrical director Prince Shahovskoy (see n. to One : XVIII : 4–10) regularly gave gay-dog parties with the co-operation of dancing girls, was dubbed "The Garret" (*cherdak*), and since it was there that a certain rumor insulting to Pushkin's honor was circulated in the spring of 1820, commentators see more than a coincidence in the use of the word "garret" in this tremendous stanza, with its fierce growl of alliterative *r*'s and its prophetic strain. (Ivan Turgenev says in a footnote to Viardot's French translation that Pushkin seems here "prédire les causes de sa mort.") However, it is also true (1) that the "babbler," *vral'*, spawned the calumny not in the "garret," but imparted it to the "garret's" patrons from Moscow, and (2) that a "garret," Fr. *grenier*, is a *lieu commun* in its association with gossip.

A *vral'* (which, for want of a more comprehensive term, I have translated "babbler") is a trivial liar, a leasing-monger, a twaddle, a fribbling rogue, *un drôle qui divague*, a boastful driveler, an irresponsible fool who invents or spreads false information. The verb *vrat'*, in the parlance of the time, meant not only "to fib" (as it does today), but to babble and boast, to talk nonsense, to spout braggadocian rot. Griboedov's Repetilov and Gogol's Nozdryov and Hlestakov are famous *vrali*. In the next line, *obodryonnïy* is a Gallicism, *encouragé*.

It should be noted that in the draft (2370, f. 72ᵛ) l. 5 has no garret or babbler and is a stronger lunge in the direction of the calumniator our poet had in mind:

Kartyózhnoy svóloch'yu rozhdyónnoy . . .
spawned by the gaming scum . . .

(*Svoloch'* = Fr. *canaille*, "riffraff," "pack of scoundrels.")

Pushkin had been brought to Shahovskoy's *cherdak* for the first time in early December, 1818. In a letter to Katenin (whom he had not seen since 1820), written in early September, 1825, Pushkin recalls, in connection with fragments of Katenin's tragedy *Andromache* (*Andromaha*), which had recently appeared in Bulgarin's *Russian Thalia*, "one of the best evenings in my life; remember? in the *cherdak* of Prince Shahovskoy." And in the same letter our poet informs his correspondent that "four cantos of *Onegin* are now ready, and many bits besides; but I have no time for them just now [being busy with *Boris Godunov*]."

About Apr. 15, 1820, the military governor of St. Petersburg, Count Mihail Miloradovich (1771–1825), a gallant soldier, *bon vivant*, and a somewhat bizarre administrator, invited Pushkin to come and talk things over in connection with the MS circulation of antidespotic verses attributed to Pushkin. The interview was a gentlemanly one. In the governor's presence Pushkin wrote down his great ode *Liberty*, his rather silly *Noël* ("Hurray, posthaste to Russia the royal despot hies"), and possibly other short pieces that have not reached us. Had not Miloradovich conducted the whole affair so amiably, it is doubtful that Alexander I could have been persuaded by Pushkin's influential friends (Karamzin, Zhukovski, Aleksandr Turgenev, Chaadaev) to have Pushkin attached to the chancellery of fatherly General Ivan Inzov, Chief Trustee of the Interests of Foreign Colonists in the Southern Territory of Russia, and permitted to spend

the summer in the Caucasus and the Crimea for re-
cuperation—instead of being banished in chains to some
arctic wilderness.

In the meantime a rumor had reached Moscow, and
ricocheted back to St. Petersburg, to the effect that, act-
ing upon the orders of the tsar, Count Miloradovich had
had Pushkin flogged in the secret chancellery of the
Ministry of the Interior in St. Petersburg. Pushkin be-
came aware of this rumor in the last days of April, could
not locate its source, and fought a duel (which remained
unknown to the government) with a person who had
repeated it in St. Petersburg.

On May 4, Count Karl Robert Nesselrode (1780–
1862), Minister of Foreign Affairs, ordered a thousand
rubles for traveling expenses to be given to the "col-
legiate secretary" Pushkin and to have him dispatched
as courier to Ekaterinoslav, where Inzov's headquarters
were. Pushkin left Petersburg in the course of the next
few days, and only from a letter received later (possibly
in the Caucasus) learned that the famous rake Count
Fyodor Tolstoy (1782–1846; his first cousin, Nikolay,
was Leo Tolstoy's father), from Moscow, was regaling his
Petersburg friends with lurid accounts of the "flogging."
(Internal evidence leads me to assume that Shahovskoy
and Katenin energetically refuted the rumor.)

Fyodor Tolstoy's nickname, "the American," is a good
sample of Russian humor: in 1803, while taking part in
the first lap of Admiral Krusenstern's famous voyage
around the world, Tolstoy was dumped for insubordina-
tion on Rat Island, in the Aleutians, and had to wander
back via Siberia, which took him a couple of years. He
was a hero of two wars, the Russo-Swedish (1808–09)
and the Russo-French (1812). He had killed eleven
gentlemen in duels. He was known to cheat at cards.
Pushkin during his six years of exile kept looking forward
to meeting Tolstoy in single combat and immediately

challenged him upon arrival in Moscow in September, 1826. Pushkin's friends managed to bring about a complete reconciliation between them; and, oddly enough, Tolstoy became Pushkin's spokesman in the days of Pushkin's courtship of Natalia Goncharov.

In the Epilogue (composed in July, 1820, at Pyatigorsk) of *Ruslan and Lyudmila* and in the Dedication (addressed in 1821 to Nikolay Raevski) of *The Caucasian Captive*, our poet mentions "the noisy gossiping of fools" (Epilogue, l. 8) and his being "victim of slander and revengeful fools" (Dedication, l. 39). In retaliation to the slander, he alluded twice, in short poems (1820, 1821), to Tolstoy's low morals.* On Apr. 23, 1825, our poet wrote from Mihaylovskoe to his brother in Petersburg thus: "I shall have Tolstoy appear in all his beauty in Canto Four of *Onegin*, if his scurrilous epigram is worth it." The reference is to a rather neat, albeit virulent, set of MS Alexandrines that at the end of 1821 Tolstoy had written in reply to Pushkin's diatribes. Pushkin heard *about* it in 1822.

In this epigram consisting of six Alexandrines Tolstoy reminds "Chushkin" (from *chush'*, "rubbish," and *chushka*, "piggy") that "he has cheeks." How Pushkin, vindictive Pushkin, with his acute sense of honor and *amour-propre*, could ever forgive this piece of rudeness is incomprehensible. Tolstoy must have made some really extraordinary amends in September, 1826.

I suggest that, when planning his Chapter Four, Pushkin prepared the following two incomplete stanzas (which Kaverin transcribed in Kaluga on Aug. 1, 1825,

---

*In the eighty-four Alexandrines addressed to Chaadaev in 1821 the allusion is in lines 55–58:

"Or that philosopher who in past days
Amazed four continents with his lewd ways,
But, growing civilized, effaced his shame,
Abandoned wine, and a cardsharp became."

Sobolevski wrote down from memory for Longinov about 1855, and Annenkov published as an epigram in 1857), with a view to developing the "despicable slander" theme, and, possibly, depicting Tolstoy in stanzas devoted to Moscow, whither the Larins were to travel in this canto (see XXIVa):

AA

O Muse of the flaming satire!
Come to my summoning call!
I do not need the plangent lyre,
4 hand me the scourge of Juvenal!
Not for cold imitators,
not for hungry translators,
not for defenseless rhymesters,
8 do I prepare the sting of epigram!
Peace unto you, poor poets,
peace, humble fools;
but as for you, mean villains . . .

BB

Approach, you pack of scoundrels!
I'll rack all with the punishment of shame;
but if I happen to omit a person,
4 please do remind me, gentlemen!
How many faces pale and brazen,
how many foreheads broad and dense,
are ready to receive from me
8 the brand indelible! . . .

Between the beginning of July and September, 1825, Pushkin, in Mihaylovskoe, drafted a letter to the tsar (never sent) in which the following lines occur:

Des propos inconsidérés, des vers satiriques me firent remarquer dans le public, le bruit se répandit que j'avais été traduit et fou[etté] à la Ch[ancellerie] sec[rète].
Je fus le dernier à apprendre ce bruit qui était devenu général, je me vis flétri dans l'opinion, je fus découragé—je me battais. J'avais 20 ans en 1820—je délibérais si je ne ferais pas bien de me suicider ou d'assassin[er]—

The wiggle that follows is read as a V, but it is neither the initial of a word nor its last letter, judging by the dash before and the wavy line after it. I have little doubt that it stands for "Miloradovich," with the v hypertrophied.

It is incomprehensible how commentators could have imagined that the V stands for "Votre Majesté" (especially in view of the succeeding context, wherein Pushkin defines his potential victim as "un homme auquel tenait tout"—which, if applied to the tsar, would have been an impossible understatement—and of whose "talent" he had been "l'admirateur involontaire"). It is also incomprehensible how and why the words "fus découragé" could have been read as "suis découragé" by D. Blagoy, the editor of Acad 1937, XIII, 227, in which edition a facsimile of the MS shows quite clearly the similarity between this "fus" and the "fus" at the beginning of the paragraph.

Who was the person with whom Pushkin fought a pistol duel in the spring of 1820?

In a diary kept by a young officer, Fyodor Luginin, during his stay in Kishinev (May 15–June 19, 1822),* he notes, in an entry of June 15, that Pushkin, with whom he had struck up a brief friendship, had had a duel in St. Petersburg in connection with the spreading of the rumors about his having been whipped in the secret chancellery.

In a letter of Mar. 24, 1825, from Mihaylovskoe, to Aleksandr Bestuzhev (pseud. Marlinski), in St. Petersburg, Pushkin, after good-naturedly asserting that he esteems Rïleev's poetry so highly as actually to see a rival in him, adds: "I regret very much that I did not shoot him dead [*zastrelil*] when I had the occasion to do so, but how the devil could I have known?"

---

*Pub. by Oksman, in *Lit. nasl.*, nos. 16–18 (1934), pp. 666–78.

This is not only an allusion to a duel but also to an affair of which Bestuzhev evidently knew so well that it was not necessary to explain anything.

Pushkin's acquaintance with Rïleev (1795–1826) could have taken place only in the spring of 1820, when Rïleev lived in Petersburg and on his nearby estate Batovo (belonging to his mother, Anastasia, daughter of Matvey Essen; it had been bought in 1805; situated a couple of miles W of Rozhestveno, a village in the Tsarskoe Selo district, forty-five miles S of St. Petersburg, on the highway to Luga). Pushkin memorized Rïleev's face so vividly that more than five years after seeing him he drew his profile with the ledged nose, the protruding underlip, and the lank hair. I also note that Pushkin mentions Batovo in his correspondence as a place familiar to him: on June 29, 1825, in Mihaylovskoe, he forwards two letters to Praskovia Osipov, who was in Riga, one from his mother, "the other from Batovo." We know that early in 1820 Rïleev had sent or taken his pregnant wife to her family's seat in the province of Voronezh and that a daughter was born on May 23. His own movements between the end of 1819 and the end of 1820 seem to be very little known (see Oksman's notes to his edition of Rïleev's works, Moscow, 1956).

When did Pushkin actually leave St. Petersburg?

According to V. Gaevski, Delvig's biographer, who had it from Mihail Yakovlev (see *Sovremennik*, September, 1854), Pushkin left the city on May 6. According to Aleksandr Turgenev (in a letter of May 6 to his brother Sergey), our poet was to leave next day, May 7. He set out on either of these two days with his valet, Nikita Kozlov; two friends "accompanied him as far as Tsarskoe" (14½ miles from Petersburg in the direction of Luga). These two friends were Delvig and Pavel Yakovlev (1796–1835; Pushkin's coworker at the Foreign Office and brother of Pushkin's classmate, Mihail Yakovlev).

In his Kishinev diary, in the May 9, 1821, entry, Pushkin notes that exactly a year has passed since his leaving St. Petersburg. He may have actually left town on May 6, 1820. But if he had spent the next days, till the ninth, in its direct vicinity, he was justified in saying he left Petersburg on the ninth. Pushkin was very particular about his fatidic dates.

My hypothesis thus is that about May 1, 1820, Rïleev, in his antigovernmental fervor, repeated the rumor as a fact (e.g., "The government is now flogging our best poets!"), and that Pushkin challenged him to a duel; that Pushkin's seconds were Delvig and Pavel Yakovlev; and that the duel was fought between May 6 and May 9 in the vicinity of St. Petersburg, possibly at Rïleev's maternal countryseat, Batovo. After this Pushkin immediately left for the south, via Luga, Velikie Luki, Vitebsk, Mogilev, etc., arriving in Ekaterinoslav on May 20 or 21.

The estate of Batovo later belonged to my grandparents, Dmitri Nikolaevich Nabokov, Minister of Justice under Alexander II, and Maria Ferdinandovna, née Baroness von Korff. A beautiful forest road led to it from my parents' estate, Vïra, which was separated by the curving river Oredezh both from Batovo (a mile W of Vïra) and, immediately east, from my uncle Rukavishnikov's countryseat, Rozhestveno (which had been the residence of Aleksey, son of Peter the Great, in the second decade of the eighteenth century, and was inherited by me, at my uncle Vasiliy's death, in 1916). Visits to Batovo by calash, charabanc, or automobile were regular features of every summer from as far as I can summon myself out of those tremulous green depths, say 1902, to the revolution of 1917, when, of course, all private lands were nationalized by the Soviets. I remember the mock duels I fought with a cousin in the *grande allée* of Batovo (a splendid avenue of huge lindens and birches ending in a transverse line of poplars), where, according to a vague family tradition, Rīleev had had a real duel. I also remember a certain trail through the woods beyond Batovo, a long, "grown-up" ramble to be looked forward to, which had been known to two or three generations of governess-bred little Nabokovs as Le Chemin du Pendu: it had been, a hundred years before, the favorite walk of Rīleev, *le Pendu*, the Hanged One. I am aware that an article on Batovo (V. Nechaev, "Usad'ba Rīleeva") appeared, or was to appear, c. 1950, in the Soviet publication *Zven'ya*, no. 7, but that issue, to the best of my knowledge, never reached America, though no. 8 did.

XX

1 Cf. Byron, *Don Juan*, XIV, VII, 2: "Gent. reader . . ."

12–13 Votaries of the biographic approach will see here a recollection of Countess Vorontsov's suddenly skimming away with her husband in mid-June, 1824, from Odessa to the Crimea.

14 / long life / *dólgi dní*: The idiom is "lang dags"—to transpose into another Northern tongue.

XXI

5–8 The eloquent accumulation of possibilities in this uncommonly poor stanza is introduced by the peg-up device of beginning every phrase with a "but":

> No doubt, so. But the whirl of fashion—
> but nature's waywardness—
> but the stream of the *monde*'s opinion—
> while the amiable sex is light as fluff.

XXII

9–10 / *Prizráka súetnïy iskátel'*, / *Trudóv naprásno ne gubyá*: The construction in the text is:

A futile seeker of a phantom,
efforts in vain not wasting . . .

11 / love your own self . . .: Another weak and trite stanza.
Cf. Heine—*Die Heimkehr* (1823–24), no. LXIV, ll. 9, 11–
12—who expresses it much better:

> Braver Mann! . . .
>
> . . . .
>
> Schade, dass ich ihn nicht küssen kann!
> Denn ich bin selbst dieser brave Mann.

XXIII

9–11 Again a listing, reminiscent of Two : XXII : 5–8, with
"smile," *Ulïbka*, falling into place.

13–14 Under the corrected draft of this stanza (2370, f. 52),
Pushkin, with his usual superstitious attitude to dates,
wrote:

> 1 Genv. 1825   31 dek. 1824

The symbols of "storm," "day," etc., were frequently
used by him in regard to his own fate, both in verse and
in prose. And it should be remembered that Tatiana is a
cousin of his Muse (see Eight : V : 11–14). Indeed, one
critic has seen the end of the novel as an allegory of
Pushkin's losing his Muse not to Prince N. but to General
Benckendorff of the tinkling spurs (see n. to Eight :
XLVIII : 5)!

XXIV

2 / is wasting / *gásnet*: A Gallicism, *se consume*. "She
sinks as dies the lamp," as Moore has it in *Lalla Rookh*.

14 / my dear Tatiana: Her maker will now ignore her (except for an allusion to her coming name day, in Four : XLIX) for twenty-eight stanzas—i.e., until Five : IV (where the divination-dream-name-day theme begins, to end in Six : III). In terms of fictional time, this means that Tatiana goes on wilting and sinking for at least six months—a protracted agony, checked by her visit to Onegin's abandoned castle in Seven, after which we leave for Moscow.

VARIANTS

Pushkin drafted several versions of stanza XXIV.

XXIVa

There is a canceled draft in Cahier 2370, f. 52ᵛ:

> Relations shake their heads,
> neighbors whisper among themselves:
> time, time she married!
> 8 The mother thinks so too; her friends'
> advice seeks quietly.
> The friends' advice is that in winter
> the entire family take off for Moscow;
> 12 perchance, within the throng of the *grand monde*
> a suitor for Tatiana may be found,
> more likable, or luckier, than others.

XXIVb

Another draft (2370, f. 53ᵛ), continuing the Moscow idea, reads:

> Much did the old dame like
> that commonsensible advice;
> for Moscow she decided ⟨to set out⟩
> 4 as soon as there ⟨would be⟩ the winter surface.
> The sky already breathed of autumn,
> The sun already shone more seldom . . .

The stanza continues as in XL : 7–14.

b: 6 A variant reads:

⟨the rainbow⟩ already shone more seldom . . .

Pushkin, at this point, wondered what to do further
with his novel, which, after the first explosion of plot,
was about to peter out. Creative intuition suggested that
he postpone the journey to Moscow indicated here. Ta-
tiana will be taken there only in Chapter Seven. Of the
grands mouvements of the first six chapters—Tatiana's
falling in love with Onegin, and the nightmarish name
day with its tragic consequences—the second is to be
started at the end of Four.

XXIVc

A draft in 2370, f. 53^r, reads:

'Twas not the first time that one nominated
suitors for my Tatiana,
all tended to congratulate beforehand
4 the Larin family.
. . . .
She had been sought, but until now
she had refused every proposal.
8 Her good old mother took some pride in this.
Her neighbors ⟨listed everyone⟩
and on their fingers ⟨even⟩ counted them,
got to Onegin,
12 ⟨then zestfully discussed him⟩
—and prophesied already a divorce
. . . ⟨not later than⟩ next year.

XXIVd

Another draft (ibid.) reads (ll. 1–3):

But ⟨soon⟩ the tattle ⟨stopped⟩;
the suitor did not think to make an offer;
and Tanya . . .

d: 2 A canceled draft (ibid.) reads:

> Onegin did not come again . . .

XXIVe

Another draft (2370, f. 53ᵛ) reads:

> When spring begins to waft our way
> and all at once the sky is animated,
> I like with hasty hand
> 4 the double window to take out.
> 'Tis with a kind of doleful delectation
> that I imbibe the breath
> of ⟨vivid⟩ freshness; but the spring
> 8 around here is not gladsome; she
> is rich in mud, not flowers.
> One's avid glance beckons in vain
> the captivating pattern ⟨of the meadows⟩;
> 12 the songster does not whistle o'er the waters,
> violets are absent, and instead of roses
> melted manure is in the fields.

e: 3–4 / *Dvoynóe vístavit' oknó*: Russian houses had, and possibly still have, large casement windows with two sturdy frames, one of which is removed in spring. A snug padding of cotton wool, a few inches thick, between the frames, insulation along the hinges, inner shutters of whitewashed wood, thick lateral curtains, and flouncy blinds kept out the cold. Our "storm windows" are dollhouse fixtures in comparison to those defenses.

e: 12 / the songster: "Songstress" or "chauntress" would be more traditional in English verse in regard to the nightingale that is meant here, which is masculine (*solovéy*) in Russian. A canceled draft (2370, f. 53ᵛ) pleas-

ingly has the "bulbul," a Persian species, of which Push-
kin knew from the jejune and frigid French adaptations
and imitations of Oriental tales that were so popular in
the eighteenth century.

e: 13–14 / instead of roses . . . manure / *vmésto róz . . .
navóz*: Note the "realistic" rhyme here, in contrast to
the conventional *róz-moróz* of XXIVf : 5–6 (see also n.
to Four : XLII : 1–3).

XXIVf

There is another draft in 2370, f. 54ʳ:

> What is our Northern summer?
> A caricature of Southern winters.
> It will glance by and vanish: this is known,
> 4 though to admit it we don't wish.
> Not sough of groves, not shade, not roses—
> we are allotted frosts,
> the blizzard, a sky-vault of lead,
> 8 a leafless silvery wood,
> bright-snowy wastes
> where the sledge runners whistle
> ⟨amidst the coldly⟩ clouded nights,
> 12 kibitkas, daredevil songs,
> double panes, bathhouse steam,
> the dressing gown, the stove seat, and stove
> fumes.

f: 5–6 Note the rhyme *rózï* ("roses"), *morózï* ("frosts"),
of which Pushkin makes fun in the established text of
Four : XLII : 1–3.

XXV

For some reason, the four English versions of this stanza
are particularly abominable. Spalding has Lenski rove
with Olga "Around the meadow and the grove" (l. 8) and
"dally with a dishevelled tress" (l. 13); Elton has them

(ll. 7–8) "... to the gardens fare, | Clasp hands, and
take the morning air" (evidently some Oriental ritual);
Miss Deutsch sees them as "... sitting | In her room
while the light is flitting" (ll. 5–6) or going out to "ex-
plore the garden's charm" (l. 8); and Miss Radin rewrites
Pushkin thus (ll. 9–14):

> And then what else? Perplexed and seized
> With shame and hopelessly ensnared,
> The most that he had ever dared
> (And that when Olga smiled and teased)
> Was just to smooth a loosened curl
> Or kiss the dress of his dear girl.

A pretty picture.

XXVI

13–14 I have seen somewhere—perhaps in the magazine
The Graphic Survey (*Zhivopisnoe obozrenie*—c. 1899?)
—a chess problem ("Lenski begins and is mated by Olga
in one move") humorously based by its composer upon
this irregular capture, the solution being: white's pawn
takes white's rook.

Pushkin played an average game and would probably
have been beaten by Leo Tolstoy. Incidentally, he had
in his library the very charming book on chess, *Shahmat-
naya igra* (1824), by Aleksandr Petrov, a celebrated
master, with a dedication to Pushkin in the author's
hand. He also possessed François André Danican Phili-
dor's *Analyse du jeu des échecs* (1820).

VARIANTS

3–4 Pushkin does not seem to have been quite sure of his
ground here in using Chateaubriand's great name.
The draft (2370, f. 58ʳ) reads (ll. 3–4):

> wherein the modest author ⟨knows⟩
> ⟨more⟩ about morals ⟨than Chateaubriand⟩ . . .

with a canceled reading (l. 3):

> wherein the modest German author

—a crack at August Lafontaine.

13–14 A canceled draft (ibid.) may be reconstructed, I think, as:

> *I péshkoy svoegó sloná*
> *Beryót v razséyan'i oná.*
>
> and with a pawn her bishop
> takes in abstraction she.

XXVII

1 / When he drives home, at home he also / *Poédet li domóy; i dóma:* The exact intonation is: "Does he drive home, at home he also . . ."

3 / fugitive leaves / *Letúchie listkí: Letuchiy* is, grammatically, "flying," and *listok,* "small leaf," *feuillet.* A *feuille volante* in French is a loose page or a flyleaf; but *letúchie listkí* are not flyleaves. "Flying" turns into "fleeing," or "fugitive." A curious interrelation of terms.

5 / agrestic views / *sél'ski vídï:* The use of the archaic truncation of the adjective (*sel'ski* instead of *sel'skie,* three syllables) gives an effect of stylization attaining the maudlin subject itself.

VARIANT

5–6 Fair copy:

> He draws in it a floweret,
> two hearts within a wreath, a brooklet . . .

This brooklet, these two hearts, and a harp (in draft),

combine with the gravestone of the final text to form the main Lenskian emblems.

XXIX

1–4 Cf. Swift, *Verses Wrote in a Lady's Ivory Table-book* (c. 1698):

> Here you may read (*Dear Charming Saint*)
> Beneath (*A new Receit for Paint*)
> Here in Beau-spelling (*tru tel deth*) . . .

and Prior, *Cupid and Ganymede* (c. 1690), ll. 19–20:

> Two Table-Books in Shagreen Covers;
> Fill'd with good Verse from real Lovers . . .

5 / military / *arméyskiy*: Technically: "of the regular army," "of the line"; but here merely implying the swagger of garrison vulgarity.

5–6 Spalding has:

> Some army poet therein may
> Have smuggled his flagitious lay

—which is much too sinister.

I notice that Miss Deutsch has simply omitted these lines, reducing the stanza to twelve lines.

6 / a roguish rhyme / *stishók zlodéyskiy*: Fr. "un petit vers scélérat," as Turgenev-Viardot correctly translate.

VARIANTS

2 There is a "little dog under a rose tree" half hidden in a canceled draft (2370, f. 74^r).

13 The separate edition of Four and Five gives *vérno*, "surely," for *vázhno*, "solemnly."

XXX

6 / Tolstoy's: The reference is to Count Fyodor Petrovich
Tolstoy (1783–1873), a well-known artist (not to be con-
fused with Count Fyodor Ivanovich Tolstoy, dubbed
"the American"; see n. to Four : XIX : 5). In a letter to
Lev Pushkin and Pletnyov, from Mihaylovskoe to St.
Petersburg, May 15, 1825, when sending them the MS
collection of his short poems for publication, Pushkin
clamored (in vain) for them to be headed by a vignette
("Psyche, lost in thought, over a flower") and added:
"What about having it done by Tolstoy's magic brush?
'No—too expensive, but how terrifically sweet' " (part
of ll. 50–51 of Dmitriev's tale in free iambics, *The
Fashionable Woman, Modnaya zhena*, published 1792
in the *Moscow Journal*).

10 / proffers / *podayót*: The separate edition of Four and
Five gives *podnesyót*, "will present."

Walter Scott in his *Journal* (Nov. 20, 1825) terms a
lady's album "a most troublesome shape of mendicity."

XXXI

Very pleasingly, in this part of the canto, where Pushkin
discusses poem forms, he gives to the octave in the stanza
that closes his topic the two rhymes of an Italian sonnet:

> *Ne madrigáli Lénskiy píshet*
> *V al'bóme Ól'gi molodóy;*
> *Egó peró lyubóv'yu díshet,*
> 4 *Ne hládno bléshchet ostrotóy;*
> *Chto ni zamétit, ni uslíshit*
> *Ob Ól'ge, ón pro tó i píshet:*
> *I pólni ístinï zhivóy*
> 8 *Tekút elégii rekóy.*
> *Tak tï, Yazïkov vdohnovénnïy,*
> *V porívah sérdtsa svoegó,*

> *Poyósh', Bog védaet, kogó,*
> 12 *I svód elégiy dragotsénnïy*
> *Predstávit nékogda tebé*
> *Vsyu póvest' o tvoéy sud'bé.*

The repetition of a rhyme word (*píshet*, "writes") would not be tolerated, of course, by a classical sonneteer.

An approach to the two-rhyme scheme is also found in Five : X, where, however, the consonance of the feminine rhymes *-áni* and *-áne* is technically inexact.

2 / of young Olga / *Ól'gi molodóy*: A Gallic formula, "de la jeune Olga." Cf. Seven : V : 11: *Táni molodóy*, "de la jeune Tanya."

9 / inspired Yazïkov: The reference is to Nikolay Yazïkov (1803–46), a minor poet, vastly overrated by Pushkin, whom he first saw in 1826, during a summer sojourn with Pushkin's country neighbors, the Osipovs. (Aleksey Vulf, Praskovia Osipov's son, was Yazïkov's fellow student at Dorpat.) He is also mentioned at the end of *Onegin's Journey* (see nn. to ultimate st., 6–11).

12 / code of elegies / *svód elégiy*: Chénier, in a piece inscribed to Ponce Denis Ecouchard Lebrun (*Epître*, II, 3, ll. 16–17, in *Œuvres*, ed. Walter), speaks of "l'Elégie à la voix gémissante, | Au ris mêlé de pleurs . . ." Pushkin borrowed the metaphor of the "codex" from ll. 60–61 in the same piece:

> Ainsi que mes écrits, enfants de ma jeunesse,
> Soient un code d'amour, de plaisir, de tendresse.

XXXII

1 / soft! / *tíshe!*: English equivalents, such as "hark!" "list!" "whist!" "hush!" etc., are all related to hearing or silence. The Russian *chu!* connotes the idea of *chuyat'*,

"to sense," thus invoking all the faculties. *Tishe* is the comparative of *tiho*, "quiet."

1 / a critic stern: This *kritik strógiy* is Küchelbecker, who published (June 12, 1824) an essay voluminously entitled "On the Tendency of Our Poetry, Especially Lyrical, in the Last Decade" ("O napravlenii nashey poezii, osobenno liricheskoy, v poslednee desyatiletie," in *Mnemosyne*, pt. II [1824], pp. 29–44), in which he correctly criticized the Russian elegy for its colorless vagueness, anonymous retrospection, trite vocabulary, and so on, but quirkishly praised the (frequently bombastic and opportunist) Russian ode as the height of inspired lyricism. Pushkin, who composed the stanza in January, 1825, prepared about the same time, or had prepared already, a foreword (see above, "Dropped Introductions," pp. 10–11) for the separate edition of Chapter One (1825) wherein he refers to the same essay—which disturbed him because the vocabulary of his own elegies, despite their marvelous melodiousness, was well within the range of Küchelbecker's attack (in fact, Küchelbecker did say: "When one reads any elegy by Pushkin or Baratïnski, everything is familiar . . ."). Moreover, Pushkin left a MS note (see *Works* 1949, VII, 40 and 663) in which he answers both the June essay and another by the same author, "Conversation with Mr. Bulgarin," in the October issue (*Mnemosyne*, pt. III, 1824), accuses Küchelbecker of confusing *vostorg* (the initial rapture of creative perception) with *vdohnovenie* (true inspiration, cool and continuous, "which is necessary in poetry as well as in geometry"), and wrongly maintains that an ode (Pindar, Derzhavin) excludes both planning and the "constant labor without which there is no real greatness."

Vilgelm Kyuhelbeker was of German descent: Wilhelm von Küchelbecker, according to the dedication

Goethe inscribed on a copy of *Werther* he gave him at
Weimar, Nov. 22, 1820, N.S. He survived Pushkin al-
most by a decade (1797–1846). A curious archaic poet,
an impotent playwright, one of Schiller's victims, a
brave idealist, a heroic Decembrist, a pathetic figure,
who after 1825 spent ten years of imprisonment in vari-
ous fortresses and the rest of his days in Siberian exile. He
was Pushkin's schoolmate; "les fameux écrivailleurs
[those notorious scribblers], Pouschkine et Küchel-
becker"—thus the Grand Duke Konstantin couples their
names in a private letter to Fyodor Opochinin, Feb. 16,
1826, from Warsaw, asking about a Guriev, if he is their
classmate.

Bartenev's note (1852) on a duel that Pushkin had
with Küchelbecker in 1818* has no foundation in fact,
although several anecdotes refer to it; at best it may have
been a practical joke played on Küchelbecker by his
cynical friends.

Only at the very end of a singularly sad and futile
literary career, and in the twilight of his life, first jeered
at by friend and foe alike, then forgotten by all; a sick,
blind man, broken by years of exile, Küchelbecker pro-
duced a few admirable poems, one of which is a brilliant
masterpiece, a production of first-rate genius—the
twenty-line-long *Destiny of Russian Poets* (written in
the province of Tobolsk, 1845). I quote its last lines:

> . . . thrown into a black prison,
> killed by the frost of hopeless banishment;
>
> or sickness overcasts with night and gloom
> the eyes of the inspired, the seers!
> Or else the hand of some vile lady's man
> impels a bullet at their sacred brow;

Russkiy arhiv, 1910, teste Yuriy Tïnyanov, "Pushkin i
Kyuhelbeker," *Lit. nasl.*, nos. 16–18 (1934), pp. 321–78.

Or the deaf rabble rises in revolt—
and him the rabble will to pieces tear
whose wingèd course, ablaze with thunderbolts,
might drench in radiance the motherland.

The bullet killed Pushkin, the rabble murdered Griboedov.

A tragic entry in Küchelbecker's diary reads: "If a man were ever unhappy, it is I. Around me there is not one heart against which I might press myself" (Aksha, September, 1842).

Küchelbecker, in criticizing the elegy, listed examples of its vapid vocabulary: *mechta* ("reverie"), *prizrak* ("phantom"), *mnitsya* ("appears to the mind"), *chudit'-sya* ("appears to the eye"), *kazhetsya* ("seems"), *budto bï* ("as if"), *kak bï* ("as though"), *nechto* ("a something"), *chto to* ("a something or other"):

When one reads any elegy by Zhukovski, Pushkin, or Baratïnski, everything is familiar. . . . The feeling of dejection engulfs all other feelings [this is the sentence Pushkin quotes in his foreword to One, 1825]. . . . The images are everywhere the same: the moon, which is always "mournful and pale," rocks, groves, sunsets, the evening star, long shadows and apparitions, something or other invisible, something or other uncanny, banal allegories, pallid and tasteless personifications of *Trud* ["work"], *Nega* ["voluptuousness"], *Pokoy* ["peace"], *Vesel'e* ["gaiety"], *Pechal'* ["sadness"], of the poet's *Len'* ["indolence"] and of the reader's *Skuka* ["boredom"]; and especially *tuman* ["mist"], mists over water, mists over fir woods, mists over fields, mist in the writer's head. . . .

The gist of all this, Küchelbecker had, I notice, borrowed from the second of two articles on Byron, signed "R" [by Etienne Becquet], in the *Journal des débats* (Paris, Apr. 23–24 and May 1, 1821): "Vous pouvez être sûr d'avance qu'il y a un *vague indéfinissable* dans leur figure, du vague dans leurs mouvements, du vague dans

Commentary

leur conduite, parce qu'il y a beaucoup de vague dans la tête du poète."

Cf. the description of Lenski's elegies in Two : x.

6 The separate edition of Four and Five gives "or" for "and."

14 / Write odes / *Pishíte ódï*: The first ode in Russian syllabic verse was the *Ode on the Surrender of the Town of Gdansk* (Danzig), by Vasiliy Trediakovski (1703–69), published as a separate pamphlet in 1734. It is a deliberate imitation of Boileau's *Ode sur la prise de Namur* (1693). Trediakovski also followed Boileau in distinguishing two main varieties of ode, the eulogistic and the tender, and in advocating a lyrical disorder in odes (*krasnïy besporyadok*, "a beautiful disorder"). A heroic ode was the first form Russian metrical verse took, with Lomonosov's *Ode on the Taking of Hotin* (written 1739, published 1751), which is examined in App. II, "Notes on Prosody," where I discuss the inauguration of the iambic tetrameter in Russia through the adoption of German prosody and a French strophic form. This is the beautiful *strophe de dix vers*, in the syllabic equivalent of a tetrameter, invented by Ronsard (e.g., strophe I of an ode of fifty-six lines beginning "Comme un qui prend une coupe," composed in 1547, published at the beginning of bk. I of his *Odes* in 1550; bk. I, no. II, in *Œuvres*, ed. Cohen) and popularized by Malherbe. It consists of a *quatrain à rimes croisées*, abab, and of two tercets with rhymes eeciic (the order of feminine-masculine is sometimes reversed: babaccedde), and the number of syllables, not counting the feminine ultima, may be seven or eight. A good example (which, moreover, has a curious Oneginesque intonation—the inventorial strain) is Malherbe's *Sur l'attentat commis en la personne de Henry le Grand, le 19 Décembre 1605*, of which st. XVIII goes

448

(*La Poésie de M. de Malherbe*, ed. Jacques Lavaud, Paris, 1936–37):

> Soit que l'ardeur de la priere
> Le tienne devant un autel,
> Soit que l'honneur à la barriere
> L'appelle à débattre un cartel;
> Soit que dans la chambre il médite,
> Soit qu'aux bois la chasse l'invite,
> Jamais ne t'escarte si loin,
> Qu'aux embusches qu'on luy peut tendre
> Tu ne soit prest à le deffendre,
> Sitost qu'il en aura besoin.

Both the French odic stanza and the *EO* stanza are related to the sonnet. It will be noted that the stanza of fourteen lines invented by Pushkin for *EO* is technically a French odic stanza from the waist up (the first seven lines being rhymed similarly in both). It may be said that the *EO* stanza is half ode and half sonnet. We might term it the mermaid stanza. Its tail part is rhymed ciddiff; the nether part of the odic stanza is iic.

The French odic stanza of ten lines (ababeeciic) if compared to a regular sonnet (abababeeciic) will be seen to be an incomplete sonnet, i.e., a sonnet lacking the second quatrain.

Houdar de la Motte, in his chilly *Réflexions sur la critique*, pt. IV (*Œuvres* [1754], III, 256), curiously defines it as "un air, dont le quatrain est la première partie, et dont les deux tercets sont la reprise. . . ." It does not have any clear-cut counterpart in English. Prior (1695), in his parodies of Boileau's *Ode sur la prise de Namur*, shows as little comprehension of the mechanism of the *strophe de dix vers* as Boileau has of Pindar's technique; while Cowley (1656) substitutes for Pindar's extremely accurate odic form a mere nebula of gusty lyricism.

For Pushkin the idea of "ode" was associated with heroic pieces in the manner of Trediakovski and Lo-

Commentary

monosov. He seems to dismiss the fact that the greatest
Russian poems of the eighteenth century are Derzhavin's
majestic odes to his queen and his God (and the greatest
poem of the first two decades of the nineteenth century
is Pushkin's own ode, *Liberty*). He was not an admirer
of the French official odes, and he did not know the Eng-
lish ode of his time (the Collins to Keats strain), with its
new romantic infusion of passionate poetry. It seems
clear that when he says "ode," he is thinking of an ag-
glomeration of bombastic, awkward rhetorical trends,
and is polemically aware of the ponderous use made of
the ode by Slavonizers (Archaists, Ancients). Küchel-
becker was not alone in preferring the old Lomonosov-
Derzhavin type of ode to the romantic elegy of his time.
Shevïryov, a forerunner (in certain tricks of archaic
demeanor and mythopoeic imagery) of Tyutchev (whose
genius he lacked), had similar predilections. Classifica-
tors distinguish two main groups of poets: the Archaists
(Derzhavin, Krïlov, Griboedov, Küchelbecker) and the
Romanticists (Zhukovski, Pushkin, Baratïnski, Ler-
montov). In Tyutchev the two lines merged.

XXXIII

6 The reference here is to *Chuzhoy tolk*, 1795 (*chuzhoy*,
"another's," "of others"; *tolk*, "view," "notion," "in-
terpretation," "sense," "opinion," "attitude," "belief,"
"comments," "talk"), the title of a satire of 150 lines, in
iambic hexameter couplets, by Ivan Dmitriev (1760–
1837). The title has also been understood to mean "a
foreign doctrine," in reference to French pseudoclassi-
cism—although Dmitriev was the last person who
should have deplored any French influence.

There are four characters involved in this muddled
and heavy piece. An Old Gentleman, who complains to
the author about Russian heroic odes and wonders why

they are so bad; the Author himself (Pushkin's "satirist"), whom this talk about his fellow poets embarrasses; a Critic, who joins in the discussion and explains to the first gentleman why Russian odes are bad (lack of time, mercenary intentions); and an Odist (Pushkin's "shrewd lyrist," or "pompous lyrist" in a canceled draft), whose mechanical way of composing the Critic describes. The piece ends with the Critic saying in effect, "Break your lyre, you are no poet if in Catherine's glorious age you are incapable of singing that glory"; whereupon the Author turns to his comrades and suggests that they all compose a good long satire on the Critic who has commented so insultingly on them.

The Pushkin-Küchelbecker quarrel sounds rather tedious today. The matter is largely one of terminology, since specifically an "ode" may be as perfect as any other formal poem, depending on individual genius.

14 / set . . . by the ears / *ssórit'*: The Russian verb has no simple English equivalent. It means "to make [them] quarrel with each other." It is also employed in Six : VI : 13 (*possórit'*).

The two ages that Pushkin did not wish to see at each other's throats are the eighteenth and the nineteenth centuries, or, more exactly, the era of Lomonosov and Derzhavin, which, expressed in terms of their creative years (1739–65 and 1776–1816) occupied more than half a century, and the 1800–25 period that had seen the rise of the romantic elegy (Zhukovski, Pushkin, and many others).

XXXIV–XXXV

In the drafts of these stanzas (Jan. 18, 1825; Cahier 2370, ff. 75ᵛ and 76ʳ) are intercalated jottings referring to the prophetic dream of Grigoriy in pt. I of *Boris Godunov*,

Commentary

the "romantic drama" Pushkin was composing at the time (December, 1824–Nov. 7, 1825).

XXXV

3 / nurse / *nyáni*: This is Arina daughter of Rodion: Arina (or Irina) Rodionovna (1758–1828), Pushkin's housekeeper in Mihaylovskoe, whither he removed, or rather was removed, from Odessa in 1824. She should not be confused either with the generalized nurse Pushkin gives the Larin girls (a confusion Pushkin deliberately promoted in a letter to Shvarts that I quote in a note to Three : XVI : 14) or with the nurse he had as a child.

Arina had been originally brought to Moscow from her native village of Kobrino (near Suida, province of St. Petersburg) to nurse our poet's sister Olga (1797–1868), his senior by two years. The estates Mihaylovskoe (province of Pskov) and Kobrino (or rather Runovo, as the estate itself was called) had been inherited in 1782 by Osip Gannibal from his father Abram (Pushkin's maternal great-grandfather); Kobrino was sold in 1800, but Arina was not. She is a tremendous favorite with demophile Pushkinists. The influence of her folk tales on Pushkin has been enthusiastically and ridiculously exaggerated. It is doubtful that Pushkin ever read *EO* to her, as some commentators and illustrators have believed. In the twenties she ruled the household with a firm hand, terrorized the servant maids, and was extremely fond of the bottle. Pushkin, who followed all the literary fashions of his time, romanticized her in his verse, although it is quite true that he was very fond of her and her tales. In my time all Russian children used to learn by heart the stanzas *Winter Eve* (written 1825, first published in the *Northern Flowers* for 1830), four octets in trochaic tetrameters, beginning "Storm with gloom the heavens covers." St. III begins:

452

> Let us drink,
> kindly friend of my poor youth,
> drink from grief. Where is the mug?
> Gayer to the heart 'twill be.
> Sing a song to me . . .

Pushkin also dedicated to her the touching elegy (un-
finished) written in 1826, twelve iambic tetrameters and
half a verse, beginning:

> Companion of my austere days,
> my dear decrepit friend [*golubka*]*
> alone, deep in the pinewoods
> long, long you wait for me . . .

And he remembers her as sharing his years of exile in the
country (1824–26) and telling him tales "that since
childhood" he "knew by heart but never tired of hear-
ing," in his poem *Mihaylovskoe Revisited* (as it might be
entitled; see my n. to Two : 1 : 2), composed there in
1835.

Our poet's own nurse, his *mamushka*, in the years of
his infancy was not Arina, but another woman, a widow
named Uliana, of whom unfortunately very little is
known. Her patronymic seems to have been Yakovlevna,
daughter of Yakov, Jacob. She was born about 1765.

3–4 In a fragment entitled *The Dream (Son)*, 220 freely
rhymed pentameters, written by Pushkin in 1816, he
says about Uliana (ll. 173–79, 183–86):

> Ah, can I fail to speak about my mammy
> and the enchantment of mysterious nights,
> when, in a mobcap, in old-fashioned garments,
> she, having turned off specters with a prayer,
> would cross me with a most assiduous air
> and in a whisper would begin to tell me
> about dead men, about Bova's exploits

**Golúbka drýahlaya moyá*; but to say "my decrepit doveling"
was too much, even for a literalist.

. . . .
Beneath the icon a plain earthenware
night lampad dimly brought out her deep wrinkles,
my great-grandmother's mob—a dear antique—
and that long mouth where two or three teeth knocked.

In an elegy of 1822 composed in Kishinev (beginning
"The bosom friend of magic ancientry"—*Napérsnitsa
volshébnoy starinï*), consisting of twenty-six freely
rhymed iambic pentameters, Pushkin describes the two
masks under which the Muse attended him: an old nurse
(ll. 5–12) and a young enchantress (ll. 18–26):

[*To His Muse*]

The bosom friend of magic ancientry,
the friend of fantasies playful and sad!
I knew you in my springtime's days,
4 in days of games and pristine dreams.
I waited for you; in the vesper stillness
you would appear as a merry old woman
and by me you would sit, in a warm jacket
[*v shushuné*],
8 large spectacles, and with a friskful rattle.
You, rocking the infantine cradle,
with chantings captivated my young hearing
and 'mongst the swaddling bands left a reed pipe
12 o'er which a spell yourself had cast.

This again is Uliana. It seems evident to me that only
beginning with the close of 1824 in Mihaylovskoe does
Pushkin start to identify in retrospect Arina (now his
housekeeper, formerly his sister's nurse) with a kind of
collective "my nurse." Let us, by all means, remember
Arina, but let us not forget good Uliana.

8 / I choke him in a corner with a tragedy: The tragedy is
Boris Godunov; see n. to XXXIV–XXXV.
    Cf. the penultimate line (475) in Horace's *Art of
Poetry*:

quem vero arripuit, tenet occiditque legendo . . .

"Whomever he can seize upon, he holds him and reads him to death" (or "kills him with reciting").

In the corrected draft, instead of "a tragedy" Pushkin had *poema*, "a long poem," and in the canceled draft, *kupletï* (Fr. *couplets*, a term he applied loosely to "strophes" or "stanzas"), thus a reference to *EO*.

9–14 As early as 1815, in a tetrametric poem *To My Aristarch* (his teacher of Latin at the Lyceum, N. Koshanski, 1785–1831), Pushkin had the wonderful lines:

> Whether I roam near tranquil waters,
> or in a dense and darksome park,
> pensive I grow—throw up my arms
> and start to speak in rhyme.

XXXVI

Published only in the separate edition of Four and Five:

> By now afar my gaze is seeking them;
> while stealing through the wood the shotman
> damns poetry, and whistles,
> 4 releasing carefully the cock.
> Each has his sport,
> his favorite concern:
> one aims a gun at ducks;
> 8 one is entranced by rhymes, as I;
> one with a flapper slays impudent flies;
> one rules the multitude in planful thought;
> one entertains himself with war;
> 12 one basks in woeful sentiments;
> one occupies himself with drink:
> and Good is mixed with Evil.

This is an exceptionally poor stanza. The opening quatrain is a jumble of broken images, among which we vaguely distinguish the following ideas: a poet scares ducks with his declamation; a hunter shoots them, pulling the trigger "carefully"; the duck hunter was stealing

Commentary

through the wood but now curses the poet and whistles
for his dog.

8–9 Instead of this insipid couplet, Pushkin, in order to elim-
inate the image of the flies (which Onegin's uncle had
crushed with a dull thumb on the windowpane: see Two :
III : 1–4), changed it by hand in the margin of his own
copy of the separate edition of Four and Five (published
Jan. 31–Feb. 2, 1828, and bound with One, Two, Three,
and Six):

> another with his epigrams, as I,
> shoots at the jacksnipe in reviews. *

It is here, in this bound collection of Chapters One
through Six (MB 8318), that Pushkin also wrote in the
one line of the Vyazemski motto (One), the "O Rus"
epigraph (Two), and the word "witch" instead of
"raven" (see n. to Five : XXIV : 7–8).

XXXVII

9 / Gulnare: Russ. *Gyul'nára*, from Fr. Gulnare. Edward
William Lane, in a note to ch. 23 of his genteel version
of *The Thousand and One Nights* (London, 1839–41),
says (III, 305): " 'Jullanár' (vulgarly pronounced
'Julnár') is from the Persian 'gulnár' and signifies
'pomegranate-flower.' " Dictionaries corroborate this.

In *The Corsair*, II, XII, Byron describes his heroine as:

> That form, with eye so dark, and cheek so fair,
> And auburn waves of gemmed and braided hair.

In a letter to Anna Kern, Dec. 8, 1825, Pushkin writes:
"Byron vient d'acquérir pour moi un nouveau charme
. . . c'est vous que je verrai dans Gulnare. . . ."

*G. Georgievski, "Avtografï A. S. Pushkina," *Zapiski otdela
rukopisey* (describing certain autographs in the Lenin Library,
Moscow), no. 1 (1938), publishes a facsimile of these two lines
(p. 14).

456

10 / Hellespont: The strait between the Sea of Marmara and the Aegean Sea; the Dardanelles.

Byron wrote to Henry Drury, May 3, 1810: "This morning I *swam* from *Sestos* to *Abydos*. The immediate distance is not above a mile but the current renders it hazardous. . . . [I made it] in an hour and ten minutes."

See also the delightful end lines of *Don Juan*, II, CV:

> [Juan] could, perhaps, have passed the Hellespont,
> As once (a feat on which ourselves we prided)
> Leander, Mr. Ekenhead, and I did.

Pushkin knew these lines from Pichot's version of 1820.

Leander, a legendary Greek, swam the strait nightly from Abydos to Sestos and back in order to visit his lady, a priestess of Aphrodite at Sestos, on the Hellespont. He was finally drowned. Mr. Ekenhead was a British officer, Byron's fellow swimmer.

VARIANTS

13–14 The fair copy (PB 14) has the following two lines, canceled, with a careful note in the margin reading: "en blanc."

> and dressed—only I doubt
> you ever wore such an attire:

XXXVIII

The two var. lines of XXXVII are followed by st. XXXVIII, likewise canceled. Pushkin started to give Onegin his own clothes but then thought better of it.

> he wore a Russian blouse,
> sashed with a silken kerchief;
> an open Tatar caftan,
> 4 and a hat with a curb roof, like a house
> transportable. This wondrous garb,
> "immoral and foolhardy,"
> greatly distressed
> 8 Madame Durín, of Pskov,

> and with her one Mizínchikov. Eugene
> perhaps despised the comments
> or, what's more likely, did not know them,
> 12 but, anyway, his habits
> he did not change to satisfy them—
> for which his fellows could not suffer him.

1 / he wore . . .: When rambling in the environs of his countryseat Mihaylovskoe, Pushkin dressed very fancifully, a self-assertive gesture, the last stronghold of personal freedom. The police and helpful neighbors saw through the disguise. A local tradesman by the name of Lapin wrote down in his diary (May 29, 1825),* in Svyatïe Gorï (Holy Hills):

And here I had the fortune of seeing Mr. Pushkin, who, in a manner of speaking, surprised me by the strangeness of his dress, to wit: he wore a big hat of straw, and a peasant shirt of red calico, with a sky-blue ribbon for sash. He carried an iron club. He wore his side whiskers very long; they looked more like a beard; and his fingernails were also very long: with them he kept shelling [sic] one orange after another and ate them with great appetite; I daresay he consumed half a dozen of them.

Pushkin carried an iron club to strengthen and steady his pistol hand in view of a duel he intended to have with Fyodor Tolstoy at the first opportunity (see n. to Four : XIX : 5). He had done so since a quarrel he had had with a Moldavian Feb. 4, 1822, in Kishinev, according to I. Liprandi (*Russkiy arhiv* [1866], p. 1424), who says the club weighed about eighteen pounds. Another source† gives eight pounds as the weight of the club he carried in Mihaylovskoe.

The journalist A. Izmaylov (see n. to Three : XXVII : 4) wrote to a friend, Sept. 11, 1825, from Petersburg, that

---

*L. Sofiyski, *Gorod Opochka* (Pskov, 1912), p. 203.
†K. Timofeev, in *Zhurnal Ministerstva Narodnogo Prosveshcheniya*, 1859; quoted by V. Veresaev, *Pushkin v zhizni* (5th edn., Moscow and Leningrad, 1932), p. 185.

Pushkin had been at the Svyatïe Gorï Fair on May 29, 1825, surrounded by beggars and crushing oranges with both hands. He wore a red Russian blouse with a gold-embroidered collar.

The "big hat of straw" was (according to Vulf's diary) a white hat of plaited pith, *kornevaya shlyapa*, from Odessa. It should not be confused with another headgear our poet wore, described below (see n. to var. 4).

3 / caftan / *armyak*: This variety of *kaftan* is a kind of smock frock in cut, made, typically, of camel's wool.

8 The qualification *pskovskaya* — Pskovan, or hailing from Pskov — as applied to this Madame Durin ("Dame Goose") does not necessarily mean that the locus of the novel coincides with Pushkin's country place in the Pskovan province. On the contrary, several scattered details suggest a place somewhat east of it; but it is also true that a kind of superposition of details occurs here and there throughout *EO*, with Pushkin's own impressions of rural life coloring the planned pattern of a generalized Russian *rus*.

9 / Mizínchikov: A comedy name, which, however, had its counterpart in the name of one of Pushkin's country neighbors, Palchikov, which comes from *pal'chik*, "fingerlet." Mizinchikov is derived from *mizinchik*, which is the diminutive of *mizinets*, the cuddy-finger (Yorkshire), the pinkie (Scotland), the curnie-wurnie, the minimus, the ear-finger, the auricular, Fr. *l'auriculaire*, so that the shocked gentleman here is "Mr. Earfingerlet."

VARIANTS

4 Draft (2370, f. 76ᵛ):

a cap with a white peak . . .

Commentary

Canceled draft:

>   a cap with a huge peak . . .

In a pencil sketch along the margin of sts. Five : III–
IV, draft (2370, f. 80ʳ), reproduced by Efros, p. 215,
Pushkin portrayed himself standing, with this cap on
his head and a riding crop in his hand (*not* the celebrated
iron club, as Efros conjectures).

XXXIX

1–4 One of the best examples that one can choose to illus-
trate some of the special difficulties that Pushkin's trans-
lators should be aware of is this quatrain of st. XXXIX,
which describes Onegin's life in the summer of 1820 on
his country estate:

>   *Progúlki, chtén'e, són glubókoy,*
>   *Lesnáya tén', zhurchán'e strúy,*
>   *Poróy belyánki chernoókoy*
>   *Mladóy i svézhiy potselúy . . .*

In the first line (which Turgenev-Viardot translated
correctly as "La promenade, la lecture, un sommeil pro-
fond et salutaire"), *progulki* cannot be rendered by the
obvious "walks," since the Russian term includes the
additional idea of riding for exercise or pleasure. I did
not care for "promenades" and settled for "rambles"
because one can ramble about on horseback as well as on
foot. The next word means "reading," and then comes a
teaser: *glubokoy son* means not only "deep sleep" but
also "sound sleep" (hence the double epithet in the
French translation) and of course implies "sleep by
night" (in fact, a cancellation in the draft reads: *Pro-
gúlki, nóch'yu són glubókoy*). One is tempted to use
"slumber," which would nicely echo in another key the
alliterations of the text (*progulki–glubokoy*, "rambles–
slumber"), but of these elegancies the translator should

460

beware. The most direct rendering of the line seems
to be:

> Rambles, reading, sound sleep . . .

which is comparable to Pope's "Sound sleep by night;
study and ease," in *Ode on Solitude* (1717), or Thomson's
"Retirement, rural quiet, friendship, books," in *Spring*,
l. 1162.

In the next line:

> *Lesnáya tén', zhurchán'e strúy* . . .

Lesnaya ten' is "the forest's shade," or, in better con-
cord, "the sylvan shade"; and now comes another diffi-
culty—the catch in *zhurchan'e struy*, which I finally
rendered as "the purl of streams," is that *strui* (nom.
pl.) has two meanings: its ordinary one is the old sense
of the English "streams" designating not bodies of water
but rather limbs of water, the shafts of a running river
(e.g., Charles Cotton, *The Retirement*, l. 48: "And
Loire's pure streams . . ."; see also *The Oxford English
Dictionary*), while the other meaning is an attempt on
Pushkin's part to express the French *ondes*, "waters";
for it should be clear to Pushkin's translator that the line

> the sylvan shade, the purl of streams

(or, as an old English rhymester might have put it, "the
greenwood shade, the purling rillets") deliberately re-
flects an idyllic ideal dear to the Arcadian poets. The
wood and the water, "les ruisseaux et les bois," can be
found together in countless *éloges de la campagne* prais-
ing the "green retreats" that were theoretically favored
by eighteenth-century French and English poets. An-
toine Bertin's "Le silence des bois, le murmure de
l'onde (*Les Amours*, bk. III: *Elégie* XXII) and Parny's
"dans l'épaisseur du bois, | Au doux bruit des ruisseaux"
(*Poésies érotiques*, bk. I: *Fragment d'Alcée*) are typical
commonplaces of this kind.

Commentary

With the assistance of these minor French poets, we have now translated the first two lines of the stanza. Its entire first quatrain runs:

> Rambles, reading, sound sleep,
> the sylvan shade, the purl of streams,
> sometimes a white-skinned, dark-eyed girl's
> young and fresh kiss . . .

In ll. 3–4:

> *Poróy belyánki chernoókoy*
> *Mladóy i svézhiy potselúy*

the translator is confronted with the fact that Pushkin masks an autobiographical allusion under the disguise of a literal translation from André Chénier, whom, however, he does not mention in any appended note. I am very much against stressing the human-interest angle in the discussion of literary works; and such emphasis would be especially incongruous in the case of Pushkin's novel, in which a stylized, and thus fantastic, Pushkin is one of the main characters. However, there is little doubt that, by means of a device that in 1825 was unique, our poet camouflaged in the present stanza his own experience—namely, an affair he was having that summer at Mihaylovskoe, the maternal estate of the Pushkins in the province of Pskov, with a delicate-looking slave girl, Olga Kalashnikov (b. about 1805), daughter of Mihail Kalashnikov (1775–1858), steward of the estate at the time and later steward of Boldino, the paternal estate of the Pushkins in the province of Nizhni. In late April, 1826, Pushkin dispatched her, big with child, to Moscow, asking Vyazemski to send her on to Boldino after the birth of her child and to have the child eventually tucked away at one of Vyazemski's countryseats. It is not clear what arrangement was eventually made. The child, a boy, was born July 1, 1826, at Boldino, registered as the son of the peasant Yakov Ivanov, by profession a sexton (*prichyotnik*), and christened Pavel. We know nothing of his fate. His mother, after her arrival in Boldino, was married off (in 1831) to one Pavel Klyuchnikov, petty landowner and drunkard.

If we now turn to Chénier, we find, in a fragment dated 1789, *Elégies*, III (in *Œuvres*, ed. Walter), pub. by H. de Latouche, 1819 (ll. 5–8):

> Il a, dans sa paisible et sainte solitude,
> Du loisir, du sommeil, et les bois, et l'étude,
> Le banquet des amis, et quelquefois, les soirs,
> Le baiser jeune et frais d'une blanche aux yeux noirs.

None of the translators of Pushkin—English, German, or French—have noticed what several Russian students of Pushkin discovered independently,* that the first two lines of our st. XXXIX are a paraphrase, and the next two a metaphrase, of Chénier's lines. Chénier's curious preoccupation (in this and other poems) with the whiteness of a woman's skin and Pushkin's vision of his own frail young mistress fuse to form a marvelous mask, the disguise of a personal emotion; for it will be noted that our author, who was generally rather careful about the identification of that type of source, nowhere reveals his direct borrowing here, as if by referring to the literary origin of these lines he might impinge on the mystery of his own romance. The curious part is that he actually had the opportunity to quote his source. The critic Mihail Dmitriev, adversely reviewing this canto in the *Athenaeum* (*Ateney*), pt. 1, no. 4 (1828), pp. 76–89, took our poet to task for his "obscure expressions." In the rough draft of Pushkin's answer to this review, he objects that "a young and fresh kiss" instead of "the kiss of young and fresh lips" is a very simple metaphor; but he does not appeal to Chénier's authority, as he had here the occasion to do.

---

*A discovery first published, I believe, by S. Savchenko: "Elegiya Lenskogo i frantsuzskaya elegiya," in *Pushkin v mirovoy literature* (Leningrad, 1926), p. 361–62n.

Chénier, in these lines and elsewhere (e.g., in his *Epîtres*, II, 1, l. 39 (ed. Walter), to Lebrun: "Les ruisseaux et les bois et Vénus et l'étude . . ."), is imitating Horace. See, for instance, Horace, *Satires*, II, VI, ll. 60–62 (the beginning of which is used by Pushkin for the motto of *EO*, Two; see n.):

> o rus, quando ego te aspiciam! quandoque licebit
> nunc veterum libris, nunc somno et inertibus horis,
> ducere sollicitae iucunda oblivia vitae!

English translators, who were completely unaware of all the implications and niceties I have discussed in connection with this stanza, have had a good deal of trouble with it. Spalding stresses the hygienic side of the event:

> The uncontaminated kiss
> Of a young dark-eyed country maid . . .

Miss Radin produces the dreadful:

> A kiss at times from some fair maiden,
> Dark-eyed, with bright and youthful looks . . .

Miss Deutsch, apparently not realizing that Pushkin is alluding to Onegin's carnal relations with his serf girls, comes up with the incredibly coy:

> And, if a black-eyed girl permitted,
> Sometimes a kiss as fresh as she . . .

and Professor Elton, who in such cases can always be depended upon for triteness and awkwardness, reverses the act and peroxides the concubine:

> [Onegin] At times, a fresh young kiss bestowing
> Upon some blond and dark-eyed maid . . .

Pushkin's l. 3 is, by the bye, an excellent illustration of what I mean by literalism, literality, literal interpretation. I take "literalism" to mean "absolute accuracy." If such accuracy sometimes results in the strange allegoric scene suggested by the phrase "the letter has killed the spirit," only one reason can be imagined: there must

have been something wrong either with the original let-
ter or with the original spirit, and this is not really a
translator's concern. Pushkin has literally (i.e., with ab-
solute accuracy) rendered Chénier's "une blanche" by
belyanka, and the English translator should reincarnate
here both Pushkin and Chénier. It would be false
literalism to render *belyanka* ("une blanche") as "a
white one"—or, still worse, "a white female"; and it
would be ambiguous to say "fair-faced." The accurate
meaning is "a white-skinned female," certainly
"young," hence "a white-skinned girl," with dark eyes
and, presumably, dark hair enhancing by contrast the
luminous fairness of unpigmented skin.

Pushkin had already (January, 1820) accurately trans-
lated a line from Chénier. With this line he closed a poem
of six Alexandrines, *To Dorida*:

> *I láskovïh imyón mladéncheskaya nézhnost'.*
> and of caressing names the childish tenderness.

Cf. Chénier, *L'Art d'aimer*, IV, 7, l. 5 (ed. Walter):

> Et des mots caressants la mollesse enfantine . . .

In connection with this note, see Chénier, *Epîtres*, VII
(*Epître sur ses ouvrages*, ed. Walter), ll. 97–102, 137–40:

> Un juge sourcilleux, épiant mes ouvrages,
> Tout à coup à grands cris dénonce vingt passages
> Traduits de tel auteur qu'il nomme; et, les trouvant,
> Il s'admire et se plaît de se voir si savant.
> Que ne vient-il vers moi? je lui ferai connaître
> Mille de mes larcins qu'il ignore peut-être.
> . . . .
> Le critique imprudent, qui se croit bien habile,
> Donnera sur ma joue un soufflet à Virgile.
> Et ceci (tu peux voir si j'observe ma loi),
> Montaigne, s'il t'en souvient, l'avait dit avant moi.

Chénier here refers to the following passage in Mon-
taigne, *Essais* (1580): "Des Livres," bk. II, ch. 10 (spell-

ing conforming to Bordeaux MS as published by A.
Armaingaud, Paris, 1927): "Je veus qu'ils donent une
nasarde à Plutarq sur mon nez: et qu'ils s'eschaudent à
injurier Seneque en moi."

12–14. The idea of a campestral cure after the dissipations
of the city is, of course, a classical commonplace, done to
death by the *petits poètes* of the eighteenth century. See,
for example, Claude Joseph Dorat, *Le Pot-pourri*:

> Après les frivoles tendresses
> De nos élégantes beautés,
> Ce long commerce de foiblesses,
> D'ennuis et d'infidélités . . .
> .   .   .   .
> Combien il est doux pour le sage
> De s'échapper dans les forêts;
> Et de chiffonner les attraits
> De quelque nymphe de village!

XL

6 / the sun / *sólnïshko*: "Small sol," "dear sol," "dear little
sun," "good sun," "nice sunshine." There is no way to
render in English the diminutive of *solntse*, "sun," with
the same unobtrusiveness as in Russian.

14 / at the door / *u dvorá*: "By the stead," "near the
premises," "at the gate." See n. to Five : 1 : 2.

XLI

1–4. The quatrain of this stanza provides a fine example of
perfect interconnection between theme and rhythm:

Vstayót zaryá vo mglé holódnoy;
Na nívah shúm rabót umólk;
S svoéy volchíhoyu golódnoy
Vïhódit na dorógu vólk . . .

The first two "regular lines" display two statements
—cold morning, silent countryside—made in a narrative
tone. Then a "flowing line" introduces the ominous wolf
motif; and a "slow line" puts on the dramatic brakes (*na
dorogu*)—to have the he-wolf appear in sudden strong
relief.

7 / sweeps uphill at top speed / *Nesyótsya v góru vo ves'
dúh*: In the draft of his notes for the 1833 edn. (PD
172), Pushkin says:

Those who criticized the rhythm of this line were
wrong:
$$\cup - \cup - \cup \cup -$$

is one of the variations of the iambic tetrameter, which,
anyway, is rather monotonous.

To this Pushkin adds another example (Three : v : 14:
"and thenceforth the whole way was mute") of what he
considered a plain pyrrhic based on the same words *vo ves'*
(lit. "in all," which, however, cannot be rendered by the
same English equivalent in both cases):

I pósle vo ves' pút' molchál.
$$\cup - \cup \cup \cup \quad - \cup \quad -$$

There are, of course, no true "pyrrhics" here. Bul-
garin, who quoted this line in his critique of Three
(*Northern Bee*, no. 124, 1827) as a mistake in versifica-

tion, wisely did not go into details; but Pushkin, in his
defense of it, does not see the point of a possible objection.

The lines in question actually scan thus (Four : XLI : 7
and Three : V : 14):

> *Nesyótsya v góru vo ves' dúh*
> goes téaring úphill at top spéed
> ‿ ´ ‿ ´ ‿ – ‿ ´

> *I pósle vo ves' pút' molchál*
> and thenceforth the whole way was mute
> ‿ ´ ‿ – ‿ ´ ‿ ´

The rhythm of *vo ves'* in both examples (contextually
"at top" and "the whole") is not a "pyrrhic" (‿‿), but
what I have termed in my discussion of prosody a "re-
verse tilt" (–´). The stress of the foot coincides with the
unaccented *vo* ("at," "the"), forming a scud (–), i.e.,
an unaccented stress, instead of the regular, accented
stress (´), as in the other feet of the lines under con-
sideration; this is a usual variation; but what jars the ear
is that the depression (unstressed part) of the foot co-
incides with *ves'* ("top," "whole"), a word that is defi-
nitely accented in the locution *vo ves'* ("at tóp," "the
whóle"); this is what constitutes the "reverse tilt," and
this is what is ill-sounding. For further details see App.
II, "Notes on Prosody."

9, 11 The cattle mentioned here have been driven to
Krasnogorie all the way from the calcareous plateau of
the Vexin Normand, where Chaulieu, in *Les Louanges
de la vie champêtre* (noticed elsewhere; see n. to One :
LVI : 2), sang at the top of his clerical falsetto:

> Quel plaisir de voir les troupeaux,
> Quand le midi brûle l'herbette,
> Rangés autour de la houlette [sheephook],
> Chercher le frais sous ces ormeaux!

Why the sight of cows standing around a shepherd's
crook should please anybody is a mystery solved only in
terms of literary fashions or conventions.

12 / maiden / *déva*: In his n. 23, Pushkin is referring to a
critique by Boris Fyodorov, who reviewed Chapters Four
and Five in the first and only issue of the magazine *The
St. Petersburg Spectator* (*Sanktpeterburgskiy zritel'*),
1828. Pushkin used the "noble," poetical term, *deva*, in-
stead of *devushka*, *devitsa*, or *devka*; and in Five : XXVIII :
9, he used *devchonki* instead of *devï* or *barïshni* ("young
ladies").

In a MS note (*Works* 1949, VII, 176) Pushkin has
more to say on the subject:

Mr. Fyodorov, in a magazine that he started to publish,
examined rather benevolently Chapters Four and Five;
he observed, however, that in the description of autumn
several lines [only two, really: Four : XL : 5 and 6; there
is another "already" in mid-line 14] begin with the
particle *uzh* [a contraction of *uzhe*, "already," Fr. *jà*,
déjà], and such lines he therefore termed *uzhi* [a pun:
uzh also means "natrix," the common European ringed
snake, pl. *uzhi*] . . .

The recurrence of "already" in Russian narrative
poetry is a distressing factor to the conscientious trans-
lator, who has to use a heavy trisyllable in order to render
a more or less tautological monosyllable that his author
inserted merely as a stopgap!

Commodious brevity and smoothness of sound allow
Russians to use this little word both in speech and in
writing much more frequently than its counterpart is
used in English. Its soft sibilant is constantly heard
ushering in a phrase; and to render it every time by
"already" tends to make the translation resemble the
comedy English of a Russian-born New Yorker. The
word is much in evidence in *EO* and may be considered

something of a philologism. I have endeavored to keep
it intact as "already" in passages where it is a stylistic
accessory. Here and there *uzhe* or *uzh* can be adequately
rendered by "now," "practically," etc. It is curious to
note that owing to the origin of the English word, such
a common Russian phrase as *on uzhe gotov* becomes
the amusing and impossible "he is already ready."
See Lexicon for all the meanings of the word in *EO*.

12–14 I have not looked up French translations of
Thomson's *Seasons*, but I suspect that some shadow of
ll. 134–37 of that author's *Winter* (1726) was present in
Pushkin's mind:

> Even, as the matron, at her nightly task,
> With pensive labour draws the flaxen thread,
> The wasted taper and the crackling flame
> Foretell the blast.

14 / splintlight / *luchinka*: Diminutive of *luchina*, a splinter
of resinous wood used as a candle.

14–XLII : 1 / crackles . . . crackle / *Treshchit . . . treshchát*:
This repetition is not very felicitous. The clean crack of
frost (e.g., in a hyperborean forest, where low tempera-
tures are known to have split great tree trunks and set
the very ground a-twanging) is different from the snap
and splutter of resinous matchwood used for lighting in
a peasant's log cabin.

XLII

1–3 *Morózï*, "frosts," *rózï*, "roses," is a Russian example
of what Pope calls (in his *Essay on Criticism*, ll. 349–51)
"sure returns of still-expected rhymes":

Where-e'er you find *the cooling western breeze,*
In the next line, it *whispers thro' the trees* . . .

In a poem to Zhukovski written in 1821, Vyazemski,
in discussing rhymes, uses the same device:

and right 'mid summer's heat, while searching
meads for "roses" [*rózï*],
drive thither, by sheer force, from Ural
Mountains, "frosts" [*morózï*] . . .

The rhyme (*moroza–roza*) occurs in our poet's own
lines of 1827, the second quatrain of an eight-line
madrigal beginning *Est' róza dívnaya*, addressed pre-
sumably to some Moscow belle:

Paphos and Cytherea vainly
are blasted by the breath of frost:
among one-minute roses
there glistens an unfading rose

and as a masculine rhyme (*moróz–róz*) in some other
tetrameters, written in the winter of 1828 (ll. 1–8 of a
twelve-line fragment):

How fast in open country runs,
reshoed, my steed,
how ringingly under his hoof
the frozen ground resounds!
Good for the Russian health
is our strengthening frost:
cheeks, brighter than spring roses,
sparkle with cold and blood . . .

In his *Pushkin, psihologiya tvorchestva* (Paris, 1928),
p. 208, Gofman notes that prior to the composing of
Four : XLII (written, I think, in the first week of
January, 1826) Pushkin had never used the rhyme
morozï–rozï. See, however, XXIVf : 5–6.

7 | *Mal'chíshek rádostnïy naród*: The epithet is clumsily

balanced on two semantic levels; Pushkin meant to say
vesyólïy naród ("the merry troop"), but this would not
have scanned. The use of *narod* (lit. "people," "nation,"
etc.) in this colloquial and mildly jocose sense should be
compared by the curious to the neoclassical variations
on a natural-philosophic theme in Thomson's *Seasons*
(1726–46), "the feathery people," "the plumy nation,"
"the tuneful race," and "the weak tribes," all referring
to birds.

8 The critic mentioned in Pushkin's n. 24 is Mihail Dmi-
triev, who reviewed Four and Five in the *Athenaeum*
(*Ateney*), 1828.

9 "The same critic," says Pushkin in a MS note, "under-
stands that the intention of the heavy goose is to use *red*
[i.e., not black or any other color] feet for swimming,
and correctly remarks that *red* feet will not help one
swim very far."

The word *lápki* (sing. *lapka*) here is not meant as a
diminutive (which, grammatically, it is), but as merely
signifying the feet of a fowl. Actually, however, the
full form of the word (sing. *lapa*, pl. *lapï*) would have
been better Russian as applied to this particular animal
in the live state (heavy as a goose may be, there is no
contrast between his body and his large flat feet). The
feet of unspecified birds, from wren to peacock, those of
insects (in the perfect stage), and the paws of small or
portable quadrupeds (e.g., lap dogs, rabbits, domestic
cats) are properly called *lapki*. The paws of hounds,
wolves, bears, and tigers, the feet of large waterfowl,
ostriches, eagles, vultures, and the like, as well as the
pawlike feet of tortoises and camels, are *lapï*. The feet of
caterpillars and children, and the legs of chairs, are
nozhki, which, grammatically, is the endearing diminu-
tive of *nogi* (feet or legs).

13 / first snow: This is December, 1820, and constitutes the first of three descriptions in the novel of the coming of winter. The other two are in Five : I (which refers to the same winter, but is seen through Tatiana's eyes) and Seven : XXIX–XXX (November, 1821).

The allusions to winter in the *editio optima* are:

One : XVI : powder of the frost besilvers his beaver collar (November or December, 1819)

XXII : fidgeting horses, freezing coachmen

XXVII : rainbow light on the snow

XXXII : small foot on iron of the grate

XXXV : morning snow singing underfoot

Four : XL : a travesty of Southern winters

XLI : the friend of winter nights

XLII : frost, skating, first snow glitters (December, 1820)

XLIII : winter pastimes

XLIV : bath with ice

XLV–L : fireside supper (Jan. 5, 1821)

Five : I : snow comes for good (Jan. 2–3, 1821) (note the overlapping with Four)

II : the simple pleasures of the poor

III : Vyazemski and Baratïnski

IV : sunlit hoarfrost, pink evening snows

IX : clear night, frost, creaking snow

XI : winter scene in Tatiana's dream (Jan. 5, 1821)

XII : snowdrift and bear

XIII : snow-burdened pines

XIV : crumbly snow, crisp snow

XV : desolate snow

XX : frosty darkness

XXI : crimson ray on frosty pane

XXIV : "blizzard" in dream book

XXV : sleighfuls of guests (Jan. 12, 1821)

Commentary

*

This description of the coming of winter—XL : 5–14, XLI, and XLII : 2, 5–14—is translated (with a number of inaccuracies, which I have italicized) by Edmund Wilson, in his "In Honor of Pushkin," in *The Triple Thinkers*, rev. edn. (New York, 1948), pp. 34–35. He is the first to have adopted unrhymed iambics for rendering *EO*.

Already now the sky was breathing autumn, already the dear sun more seldom gleamed, shorter grew the day, the forest's *secret shadow* was stripped away with *sighing* sound, mist *lay* upon the fields, the caravan of *loud-tongued* geese *stretched* toward the south: drew near the *duller* season; November stood already at the door.

Rises the dawn in cold murk; in the fields the sound of work is still; the wolf with his hungry mate comes out upon the road; *sniffing*, the road-horse snorts—and the traveler *who is wise* makes full speed up the hill; the herdsman now *at last* by morning light no longer drives his *cattle* from the byre; at mid-day to their huddle his horn no longer calls them; inside her hut, the *farm* girl, singing, spins, while—friend of winter nights—her little flare of kindling snaps *beside* her.

And now the *heavy* frosts are snapping and spread their silver through the fields . . . smoother than a *smart* parquet glistens the ice-bound stream. The merry *mob* of *little* boys with skates cut ringingly the ice; on *small* red feet the lumbering goose, *hoping* to float on the water's breast, steps carefully but slips and topples; gaily the first snow *flashes* and whirls about, falling in stars on the bank.

VARIANT

12–14 A canceled draft (2370, f. 77ʳ) reads much more pleasingly:

> slidders and falls. The gay
> small rabbit comes out. The first snow
> in stars falls on the bank.

XLIII

1 / What do then: Cf. Keats, *Fancy* (1820), ll. 15–18:

> . . . What do then?
> Sit thee by the ingle, when
> The sear faggot blazes bright,
> Spirit of a winter's night . . .

See also the end of Four : XLI.

5–8 Pushkin closes a letter to Vyazemski (Jan. 28, 1825, from Trigorskoe, near Mihaylovskoe, to Moscow) with the words: "I am writing you from [the Osipovs], with one arm bruised—have fallen upon the ice not *from* my horse but *with* my horse, which makes a great difference to my equestrian vanity." It is the difference between a cropper and a crumpler.

10 / Pradt: Dominique de Pradt (1759–1837), French political writer. His most obvious work in Onegin's library that winter would be *L'Europe après le congrès d'Aix-la-Chapelle, faisant suite au congrès de Vienne* (Paris, 1819), where the following amusing passage occurs (pp. 36–42):

Les accroissemens de la population en Russie suivent les mêmes degrès qu'on voit parcourir en Amérique. . . .Il est calculé qu'en 1920 [la] population [des Etats-Unis] surpassera 100,000,000 h[abitans]. . . . [Dans] cent ans la population de la Russie excédera cent millions

d'hommes. . . . Ajoutez que la Russie . . . est la seule
puissance de l'Europe qui possède encore, dans une très-
grande abondance, une des machines les plus essentielles
de la guerre, un des principes vitaux de l'état militaire
d'un pays, les chevaux . . . [et] sous ce rapport, la Russie
ressemble à . . . l'Amérique. . . .

Pradt's main point was (p. 42): "Le congrès de Vienne,
en sanctionnant l'occupation de la Pologne, a faussé la
politique de l'Europe qui exigeait d'éloigner la Russie à
tout prix."

10 / Walter Scott: For instance, *Ivanhoé, ou le Retour du
croisé*, tr. Auguste Jean Baptiste Defauconpret (Paris,
1820).

VARIANT

1–4 The fair copy reads:

> What do then in the backwoods at that time?
> Promenade? But all places are bare
> as the bald pate of Saturn
> or serfdom's destitution.

The draft (2370, f. 77ᵛ) is marked "2 *genv.* 1826."
  Brodski, of course, makes a lot of this allusion to rural
conditions before Lenin and Stalin.
  There is a wonderful alliterative play on *g* and *l*:

> *V glushí chto délat' v éto vrémya?*
> *Gulyát'? No góli vsé mestá,*
> *Kak lísoe Satúrna témya*
> *Il' krepostnáya nishchetá.*

Saturn is the ancient god of time or of seasons, and is
usually represented as a gray-bearded old man with a
bald pate and a scythe. He eats up his own children, "as
revolutions eat up the liberties they engender" (as
Vergniaud, the Girondist, said).

XLIV

1 / Childe Harold / *Chíl'd Garól'dom* (instr.): Pushkin
gave an English value to the *Ch* of the first word, but
pronounced the vowel in the French manner, producing
a vowel sound between "chilled" and "shield." He com-
menced the next word with the transliteration *G*, used
for rendering the English and German *h*; he accented
the word on a kind of open *old* (rhyming with "dolled"),
à la française, and wound up with a Russian instru-
mental-case termination (*om*).

The rhyme itself is most striking. In order to stress
still more sarcastically the triteness of the *morozï–rozï*
rhyme tossed into the reader's lap in XLII, Pushkin now
shows what he can do: *Só l'dom* ("with ice") is accented
upon the preposition, and this folksy intonation is in
prodigious contrast to the cosmopolitan *Garól'dom*. The
English reader is reminded that the *rime richissime*,
even when consisting of two words as here, does not have
in Russian the vulgar jocular tone of its English counter-
part. A curious example is at hand.

In the jocular lines devoted to the siege of Izmail in
can. VII of *Don Juan*, among bungled Russian names
that had already been misspelled in their passage
through German transliteration into French and Eng-
lish, names with ragged *w*'s and shoddy *sch*'s still hang-
ing about them or, on the contrary, losing their *h*'s in
Frenchified forms, there is, in st. XVII, a "Mouskin
Pouskin" (Musin-Pushkin) rhyming with "through
skin" and "new skin." (The Counts Musin-Pushkin are
distantly related to the plain Pushkins.)

According to E. H. Coleridge's footnote in his edition
of *Don Juan*, this is a reference to Count Aleksey Ivano-
vich Musin-Pushkin (1744–1817), statesman and arche-
ologist; there was another person of that name, who also
died in 1817, and was also known to English memoirists,

Commentary

Count (1779) Aleksey Semyonovich Musin-Pushkin, ambassador of Catherine II in London and Stockholm.

The name seems to have sorely puzzled Englishmen: "The author of the pretended tour is a Russian prince, Mouska Pouska . . . [nobody] could possibly equal his misrepresentations about English society." Thus writes George Brummell to a lady, from Caen, on Jan. 1, 1836, a year before he began losing his mind (quoted in Jesse, *Brummell*, vol. II, ch. 22). The traveler Edward Daniel Clarke (1769–1822), who visited Russia in 1800, has, however, the name almost correctly transliterated in a footnote (*Travels in Various Countries of Europe, Asia and Africa* [4th edn., London, 1817], II, 126): Alexis Mussin Pushkin.

In November, 1825, Pushkin, from Mihaylovskoe, writes Vyazemski, in Moscow, that he knows only the first five cantos of *Don Juan* (in Pichot's French prose). On July 21, 1825, he had reminded Anna Vulf, who had gone to Riga, where her cousin Anna Kern lived, to send him Pichot's prose version of the remaining cantos (this is the Paris edition of 1824), which Anna Kern had promised to obtain for him. He probably got it early in 1826. Pichot's version of the "new skin" passage goes :

. . . et Mouskin-Pouskin, tout aussi belliqueux que quiconque [a] fendu un homme en deux. . . . Ils se souciaient peu de Mahomet . . . à moins qu'ils n'eussent pensé à faire un tambour de leur peau.

In a critical MS note of 1827 (*Works* 1936, V, 23) Pushkin writes:

Byron used to say he would never undertake to describe a country he had not seen with his own eyes. Nevertheless, in *Don Juan* he describes Russia; in result, certain errors can be detected: a *kibitka* [is not] an uncomfortable carriage without springs [Byron confused it with *telega*]. And there are other, more important mistakes. . . .

The reference is to *Don Juan*, IX, xxx: "A curséd sort

of carriage without springs," which Pushkin's source (Pichot, 1824) translates "maudite sorte de voiture non suspendue."

Russians on the whole had less trouble with Byron's and his characters' names than Byron had with Russian ones (he rhymed, for instance, "Soúvaroff–lover of" and "Suwárrow–sorrow" instead of the correct "Suvórov–more of"). Byron's works, as I am not tired of repeating, came to most Russians in French versions. The French pronunciation of his name is "Birong," with the accent on the nasalized ultima; no Russian counterpart of this sound exists; there were some attempts in Russia to imitate the French form of the name by writing it "Birón" (rhyming with "here-on"). This, however, did not work, owing to confusing associations with the name of a famous favorite of Empress Anna (Bühren, Russianized as Biron). The correct pronunciation was hit upon with "Báyron," which renders perfectly the English vowel sound; but, concurrently, another linguistic school evolved the horrible "Béyron," which was persistently used by Katenin, Vyazemski, Rïleev, Yazïkov, and various writers of the Moscow-Germanophile group. This *ey*, pronounced somewhat like *ey* in "Bey" or *ay* in "bay," but with a longer, hollower, yellower sound to it, is a result of a Germanic, or rather Rigan, influence. Knowing, theoretically, that the English "by" is similar to the German *bei*, Baltic scholars pronounced "Byron" as if it were a German word (written, for instance, *bei-ronn*), but since the Baltic pronunciation of the German *ei* resembles the Russian *ey*, Byron became Beyron. (See also n. to One : XXXVIII : 9.)

13 / *Na tróyke chálïh loshadéy*: Lenski arrives in a sleigh drawn by a troika, three horses abreast. A *troyka* (with the "of horses" omitted) is also used elliptically to mean a carriage-and-three. It almost rhymes with "toy car."

I see that one of the English translators, Spalding (1881), has Lenski take the reins as would an English nobleman driving his curricle or phaeton; but we are in provincial Russia, and there is a coachman between the nobleman and the three horses.

The meaning of *chalïy*, implying as it does a more or less even mixture of a pale brownish tint with a grayish one, varies slightly in different localities. I see it here as a rather light, delicate dunnish gray coat with dark tail and mane, but I may be influenced by riding-school memories of St. Petersburg. Turgenev-Viardot translate it "fleur-de-pêcher," which is a blend of reddish and white hairs; and Ivan Turgenev was an expert in the matter.

VARIANT

6 A canceled draft (2370, f. 77ᵛ) has Onegin

sharpen a cue, rub it with chalk . . .

XLV

1–7 / Veuve Cliquot . . . Moët . . . a simile [and see XLVI : 5, 6 / *Aï*]: Voltaire, *Le Mondain*, sees in the "écume pétillante" of Ay (or Aï) wine "l'image brillante" "de nos Français."

Byron, *Don Juan*, XV, LXV, 8, speaks of the foam of champagne "As white as Cleopatra's melted pearls."

Baratïnski, in *The Feasts*, l. 139, finds in champagne "a simile of youthful life." (See below.)

The surname of Jean Remi Moët (1758–1841), founder of the famous champagne firm and genial *maire* of Epernay, rhymes in Russian with *poét*. The diaeresis over the *e* of Moët and over the *i* of Aï (pronounced "Ah-ee," with the accent on the *ee*) indicate in French the splitting of the diphthong into two syllables (naïf, Baïf) and should not be confused with the diacritical sign over *i* that, in my transliteration of Russian, has been arbitrarily chosen to render the transformation of *i* into its open-mouth variety, as in *tï*, Krïm, Yazïkov, etc. (See "Method of Transliteration," vol. 1, pp. xix, xxi–xxii.)

The name of this glorious champagne comes from Aï or Ay, a town in the Marne Department, northern France, where the original vineyard was situated in the Marne watershed, near Epernay.

Pushkin's n. 25 is part of an epistle (trochaic tetrameter, thirty-six lines) addressed to his brother Lev. It starts: "Well, and what about the wine," and is a mere sketch written in early December, 1824.

It would seem at first blush that Pushkin had realized that his Four : XLV : 7 might sound like a mocking allusion to the line in *The Feasts* of Baratïnski, whose feelings he was always morbidly anxious to spare; and that, therefore, he tactfully and laconically quoted his own lame lines as a kind of prototype in retrospect to prove he never had Baratïnski in view.

But there might be another, subtler reason for his imitation and his note.

Here is the passage referring to champagne in Baratïnski's *Feasts* (1821 edn., ll. 129–39):

> Into plain cups the god of tippling
> luxuriously to sons of glee
> pours out his fondest drink, Ay:
> courage within it is concealed;
> its liquid, twinkling starrily,
> is full of a celestial soul.
> It sparkles free.
> Like a proud mind, it cannot bear captivity;
> it bursts its cork with sportive surf
> and merrily its foam doth spurt
> —a simile of youthful life . . .

In the edition of 1826, just after the Decembrist rising, the censor objected to this simile (ll. 135–36) involving freedom and pride:

Kak górdïy úm, ne térpit pléna . . .

which was then altered (possibly by Delvig, as Gofman
suggests in his 1915 edn. of Baratïnski's works) to:

> It bubbles joyously.
> Like a proud steed, it cannot bear captivity . . .

What horse could, man could not.

(In the final, 1835, edition, this became: "It glistens,
bubbles like a daring mind," etc.)

In a letter to Baratïnski, his friend Delvig, who at-
tended to the printing of *The Feasts* and *Eda* (published
together), speaks of his fruitless attempts to have the
censor pass the original lines: "Censorship," he writes,
"has gone completely crazy after the *André Chénier*
affair."

It is quite possible that Pushkin, who at the time was
in correspondence with both Delvig and Baratïnski,
commemorated his awareness of the ridiculous alteration
demanded by the police, and affixed to his sly line, "a
simile of this and that," an innocent-looking quotation
that immediately recalled *The Feasts* to those who were
in the know.

The *André Chénier* mentioned by Delvig is an elegy
composed by Pushkin early in 1825, bemoaning Ché-
nier's death under the knife of the guillotine in 1794, at
the close of the era of popular tyranny. It consists of 185
free iambics, is inscribed to Nikolay Raevski, and was
first published, with the deletion by the censor (Oct. 8,
1825) of some forty lines (21–64 and 150), in *Poems of
Aleksandr Pushkin*, which came out Dec. 28, 1825, a
fortnight after the Decembrist revolt. Malicious or naïve
readers circulated MS copies of these lines (in which
Chénier is made to invoke "sacred liberty" and the over-
throw of kings) under the spurious title (given them by
a certain Andrey Leopoldov, Moscow University stu-
dent), *The Fourteenth of December*, in consequence of

which the puzzled police pestered Pushkin and arrested the possessors of MS copies. The elegy, including the censored passage, has really nothing to do with Russian events, except by casual association: in the course of its attack on Robespierre's regime of Terror, it eulogizes (as *Vol'nost'* had done in 1817) Liberty based on Law.

2 Cf. Vyazemski, a tetrametric piece inscribed to the poet Davïdov (1815; ll. 49–52):

> ... the magic gift
> of blest Ay
> fizzes, with surging sparks and foam:
> thus fizzes life in youthful days ...

5 / Hippocrene: A fountain on Mount Helicon, in Bœotia, sacred to the Muses. It spurted from the spot struck by the hoof of Pegasus, a winged horse, emblem of poetic inspiration.

9 / last poor lepton: Tomashevski observes (in *Works* 1957, p. 597) that this is an ironic quotation from Zhukovski's epistle in 484 Alexandrines, *To the Emperor Alexander* (1814; ll. 442–43):

> When even poverty under oblivion's roof
> its last poor lepton for your likeness gives ...

XLVI

Both this and the previous stanza, XLV, are very poor, bubbling with imported platitudes.

3 / Bordeaux: Bordeaux's "sanguine frothy juice" is also John Gay's choice (*Wine*, 1708).

Ducis, in a verse *A Mme Georgette W. C.*, praises Bordeaux in similar terms (ll. 2, 8):

> Oui, je bois [ses] coupes vermeilles;
> .   .   .   .
> Calme et vieux, c'est le vin des sages.

5, 6 / Ay: See n. to XLV : 1–7.

11–14 A good example of the sobering and braking effect
accomplished by a run of second-foot scudders after a
burst of record modulations. The following paraphrase
is meant only to render the rhythm:

> No matter at what time or place
> A comrade and a ready helper,
> In leisure, and in lonely rue:
> My gratitude, Bordeaux, to you!

XLVII

4–7 In a MS note (see *Works* 1949, VII, 171) Pushkin
writes:

For a long time the reviewers left me in peace. This did
them honor: I was far away, and in unfavorable circum-
stances. They became used to considering me still a very
young man. The first inimical reviewals began to appear
after the publication of *EO*, Four and Five [early in 1828].
A critique published in the *Athenaeum* [1828, signed
"V.," written by Mihail Dmitriev] surprised me by its
bon ton, its good style, and the oddity of its carpings. The
most usual rhetorical figures and tropes puzzled the critic,
such as "the glass fizzes" instead of "the wine fizzes in
the glass" or "the grate exhales" instead of "the vapor
issues from the grate."

9–13 The intonation of this parenthetical remark is very
like the one about Rousseau in One : XXIV : 9–14.

12 / between wolf and dog / *mezh vólka i sobáki*: A familiar
Gallicism, *entre chien et loup*, going back to the thirteenth
century (*entre chien et leu*), meaning dusk—a time of day
when it is already too dark for the shepherd to distinguish

his dog from a wolf. An evolutionist sense has also been read into the locution; namely, the reference to the blending of day with night in terms of an intermediary stage between two closely allied species of animals.

XLVIII

VARIANTS

10 The separate edition of Four and Five (1828) has the variant:

> or else, *mon cher*, judge for yourself . . .

13–14 and XLIX : 1: A canceled draft (2370, f. 78^v) has "Saturday," as in the final fair copy, but the corrected draft (ibid.) reads:

> *Da chtó?—kakóy zhe yá bolván—*
> *Chut' ne zabíl—v chetvérg tï zván—*

> But stay—what a blockhead I am—
> almost forgot—you are invited Thursday—

This "Thursday" is retained in a variant of the fair copy, where the next stanza begins:

> *Tï zván v chetvérg na imenínï . . .*
> You are invited Thursday to the name day . . .

However, in 1821, which is the only possible year here, Jan. 12 fell on a Wednesday, and it would have been quite easy for Pushkin to say *Chut' ne zabíl—tï v srédu zván* and *Tï v srédu zván na imenínï.* It fell on a Saturday in 1818 and in 1824, on a Monday in 1825, and on a Tuesday in 1826, the year this chapter was finished.

XLIX

Everybody forgets something here: Lenski forgets (but then unfortunately remembers) the invitation; Onegin

forgets the situation in which Tatiana is placed; and
Pushkin forgets his calendar. Had not Lenski suddenly
recalled what his guardian angel was trying to make him
forget, there would have been no dance, no duel, and no
death. Here begins, on Onegin's part, the series of care-
less, irresponsible acts that fatally lead to the disaster.
It would seem that the small family party promised by
Lenski in his naïve eagerness to have his friend come
should have seemed even less acceptable to Onegin—
though for a different reason—than a big one. What can
lead him to prefer the intimacy to the crowd? Cruel
curiosity? Or has Tatiana been growing upon him since
he last saw her more than five months earlier?

1–2 / Tatiana's name day is Saturday / *Tat'yáni imeníni* /
V subbótu: Jan. 12, St. Tatiana of Rome, c. 230, martyr.
   Here and elsewhere I have reduced to "name day"
the term used by the English of the time: "name's-day"
or "his (her) fête."

VARIANTS

1 See XLVIII : var. 13–14.

13 A canceled draft (2370, f. 78ᵛ) charmingly reads:

> *Nakínul sínyuyu shinél'*
> threw on his blue carrick

and (presumably) drove off into the blizzard (*myatél'*).

L

9 / enemies of Hymen / *vragí Giména*: A cacophonic clash
of consonants (*gi-gi*) unlike anything else in *EO*. Or did
Pushkin pronounce it "Hiména"?

12 / Lafontaine: Pushkin's n. 26, on this "author of numer-
ous familistic novels" (*semeystvennïh romanov*), refers

to August (also spelled Auguste) Heinrich Julius Lafontaine (1758–1831), German novelist. He was as mediocre as he was prolific, begetting more than 150 volumes, and was tremendously popular abroad in French translations. Pushkin may have had in mind specifically *Les Deux Amis* (*Die beiden Freunde*), tr. Countess de Montholon (Paris, 1817, 3 vols.); or *Les Aveux au tombeau* (*Das Bekenntniss am Grabe*), tr. Elise Voïart (Paris, 1817, 4 vols.); or, still more likely, *La Famille de Halden* (*Die Familie von Halden*, 1789), tr. H. Villemain (Paris, 1803, 4 vols.), a copy of which (according to Modzalevski's laconic note in *P. i ego sovr.*, I, 1 [1903], p. 27) was in the library of Mme Osipov, Pushkin's neighbor, at Trigorskoe.

LI

Under this, in the draft (2370, f. 79^r): "6 *genv*" (Jan. 6, 1826).

Chapter Five

MOTTO

Two lines from the epilogue of Zhukovski's ballad *Svetlana* (1812), referred to in my nn. to Three : V : 2–4 and Five : X : 6.

The two conclusive stanzas of the ballad are addressed to Aleksandra Protasov (1797–1829), Zhukovski's godchild and niece (his sister's daughter). In 1814 she married the minor poet and critic, Aleksandr Voeykov (1778–1839), who treated her cruelly. She did know "these frightful dreams" and died young in Italy. Aleksandr Turgenev was in love with her; in a letter of Oct. 19, 1832, Zhukovski sent him an inscription in ecclesiastic Russian for her tomb in Livorno (*Arhiv brat'ev Turgenevïh*, no. 6 [1921], p. 461). She was the sister of Maria Protasov (1793–1823)—the great love of Zhukovski's life—who in 1817 married the distinguished surgeon, Dr. Ivan Moyer (Johann Christian Moier, 1786–1858).

The fair copy of Five (PB 14) has a suggestion of two epigraphs: the first two words of the Petrarch lines that are used for Six—probably only a false start here; and *Svetlana*, st. II, ll. 1–8, which contain a theme that leads us back to Three : V:

The moon's light is lusterless
in the darkness of the mist;
silent is and melancholy
dear Svetlana.
Sweet companion, what ails you,
no word uttering?
Hearken to the roundelay,
and take out your ring.

I

At the top of the draft (2370, f. 79ᵛ) Pushkin wrote the date "4 *genv.*" (Jan. 4, 1826).

2 / abroad / *na dvoré*; 7 / yard / *dvor*; 11 / outside / *na dvoré*: *Dvor* in l. 7 is a specific item (the yard) among other items (flower beds, etc.). *Na dvoré* in l. 11 may mean "in the yard" or (as it is more likely to be understood here) "outside," "out of doors." In l. 2 the *na dvoré* conveys a still vaguer, more general and abstract notion of something taking place at large, in the open. Indeed, the *na dvore* in this idiomatic phrase, *osénnyaya pogóda* ("fall weather") *stoyála* ("stood") . . . *na dvoré* ("on the premises," "on the scene"), means hardly more than the adverb would in the colloquial Americanism "the man stood around" or "it's raining out." In consequence, ll. 1–2:

> *V tot gód osénnyaya pogóda*
> *Stoyála dólgo na dvoré*

merely signify that this kind of weather (autumnal) continued, or endured, that year (1820) for a long time (till January, 1821), but since the act of enduring must take place somewhere, the Russian way is to round up the phrase with *na dvore*.

3, 10, 13 / winter: "Winter" (*zimá*, adj. *zímniy*) is repeated three times in this stanza.

489

It will be noted that in a preceding chapter (Four : XL) November rather incongruously closes summer, and this clashes with the definition of a Northern summer's brevity (Four : XL : 3), since fall weather in the region where the Larins' countryseat was would have normally set in not later than the last days of August (Old Style, of course). Otherwise, the lateness of the seasons, both autumn and winter, in the year "1820" is not too clearly defined in Four, although actually Four : XL–L (from November to the beginning of January) cover the same time stretch as Five : I–II. Pushkin's "1820" differs from the historical 1820, which was marked in NW Russia by a very *early* snowfall (Sept. 28, in the St. Petersburg region, judging by a letter from Karamzin to Dmitriev).

5 All four English translators—Spalding, Deutsch, Elton, and Radin—make a mistake in the date, understanding *na trét'e* as "on the third"!

9 / patterns / *uzórï*: The reference is to frostwork.

12 / *myágko*: Fr. *moelleusement*, a blend of "yieldingly" and "thickly."

14 / *Vsyo yárko, vsyó beló krugóm*: Cf. Thomson, *Winter* (1730–38 edns.), ll. 232–34:

> Sudden the fields
> Put on their winter-robe of purest white.
> 'Tis brightness all . . .

VARIANT

1–4 Canceled draft (2370, f. 79^v):

> That year fall weather
> remained a long time. The barometer
> froze up. Poor nature
> . . . ⟨the wind⟩ . . .

"Wind," *vetr*, could be the only possible rhyme to
barométr here. It had already been used by Zhukovski
in a facetious poem of 1811, *A Kaleidoscopically
Curious Scene Between Mr. Leander, Pagliaccio, and the
Dignified Herr Doktor (Kolovratno-Kur'oznaya stsena
mezhdu gospodinom Leandrom, Pal'yasom i vazhnïm
gospodinom doktorom).*

II

This stanza often appears in Russian schoolbooks as a
separate poem entitled *Winter*; and in 1899, a certain
Plosaykevich made a "Child chorus for two voices" out
of the stanza, of which he dubbed the octave "The
Russian Winter" and the sextet "The Sportive Lad"
(*Mal'chik-Zabavnik*).

1–4 Spalding (1881):

> Winter! The peasant blithely goes
> To labour in his sledge forgot,
> His pony sniffing the fresh snows
> Just manages a feeble trot . . .

C. F. Coxwell, *Russian Poems* (London, 1929):

> Winter . . . The Peasant shows his glee
> Sleighing along the frozen road;
> Whose faithful horse, since it has snowed,
> Maintains a trot but cautiously.

Deutsch (1936):

> Here's winter! . . .The triumphant peasant
> Upon his sledge tries out the road;
> His mare scents snow upon the pleasant
> Keen air, and trots without a goad.

Elton (1937):

> Winter! the peasant's heart now dances;
> Again he journeys in his sleigh.

> The old mare sniffs the snow, advances
> With shambling trot, as best she may.

Radin (1937):

> Winter! The peasant in its honor
> Marks out the roadway with his sleigh;
> His poor horse plowing through the furrows
> Goes jogging, stumbling, on its way.

The sledge forgot, the triumphant peasant showing his glee on the frozen road, the pleasant keen air, the incredible goad, the dancing heart of the peasant, the old mare, the honor of winter, the plowing through furrows, the poor stumbling horse—all this forms a mass of nonsense that of course has nothing in common with *EO*.

10 / pooch / *zhúchka* (italics in Russ. text): Any kind of small house dog. It occurs to me that *zhuchka* may come from "Joujou" (or "Bijou"), a toy dog's common French name, which one can imagine passing from a Frenchified Russian lady's drawing room to the servants' quarters and growing there the curled mongrel tail of a Russian diminutive.

VARIANTS

1 Canceled draft (2370, f. 70ʳ):

> Winter! . . . Our muzhik not lamenting . . .

12–14 Draft (2370, f. 70ᵛ):

> standing, the merry coachman drives,
> and the brave little bell
> under the new shaft-bow resounds.

III

3 / lowly nature: Here Brodski idiotically comments: "Lords and ladies were shocked by realistic descriptions of nature." Actually, of course, Pushkin has in mind the

Frenchified common reader, whose genteel taste (*le bon goût*) might be shocked.

6 / another poet; 7–13 / first snow . . . : A MS note (PD 172), prepared for the 1833 edn., reads:

First Snow, by Vyazemski. A handsome outcomer [*krasivïy vïhodets*], etc. The end [of the poem]. Barat[ïnski] in Finl[and].

The passage in Vyazemski's *First Snow* (1819; see my n. to One : motto) goes:

A handsome outcomer from mettled herds,
rival in pace of the wing'd-footed doe,
shall sweep us o'er the field, trampling the crumbly snow.
And black and glistening are your sable furs,
the tribute of Siberian forests . . .

. . . .

Fresher the roses of your red cheeks blush,
and fresher on your brow the lily whitens.

This is a good example of Vyazemski's florid and redundant style, full of definitions, and definitions of definitions. The poem ends (ll. 104–05):

O Winter's firstling, brilliant and morose,
first snow, the virgin fabric of our fields.

Pushkin easily overtook and left behind both Vyazemski and Baratïnski (see next n.) in his short poems *Winter* (1829) and *Winter Morning* (1829), in which the colors are beautifully pure, with everything harmonious, concise, and colloquially fluent.

13–14 A reference to a fragment of Baratïnski's *Eda*, published in *Mnemosyne*, early 1825, and also in *The Polar Star* of the same year. The fragment differs slightly from the 1826 text (ll. 623–31):

The winter cold has shackled torrents,
and o'er their precipices
from granite mountains they,
mountains of ice, already hang.
From under snowdrifts
the crags loom black. The snow in mounds [*bugrami*]

lies on the centenary pines.
Around, all is deserted. Noisily
the winter blizzards have begun to wail.

Our poet apparently changed his mind and decided to
compete with Baratïnski, after all—which was not too
difficult. In Tatiana's dream, Pushkin unshackles those
torrents (Five : XI) and improves those pines (Five : XIII).
Baratïnski replaced the pines with a "hoary, undulating,
sky-covering gloam" in the 1826 edn. of *Eda*.

IV

6–7 / at late dawn, the radiance of pink snows / *zaryóyu
pózdnoy* | *Siyán'e rózovïh snegóv*: Cf. Thomas Moore,
Loves of the Angels (1823), ll. 98–99, "First Angel's
Story": ". . . snow | When rosy with a sunset glow."

"Mr. Moore's poetry," wrote *The Edinburgh Review*
in February, 1823, "is the thornless rose—its touch is
velvet, its hue vermilion. . . . Lord Byron's is a prickly
bramble, or sometimes a deadly Upas." (See n. to One :
XXXIII : 3–4.)

In this image of *rózovïh snegóv* our poet amalgamates
the frosts and the roses (*morozï–rozï*) of the "expected
rhyme" tossed into the reader's lap in Four : XLII.

14 / husbands: The accusative plural used here is *muzh'yóv*,
a vulgarism more suitable to the speech of these servant
maids than the regular *muzhéy* (which appears in the
1828 edn., and is later in the same year corrected to the
established reading in the errata appended to Six). Note
that the prediction came true: Olga married an uhlan,
and Tatiana a distinguished general.

V

9–12 The same superstition was current in Wales, according to the following observation (R. P. Hampton Roberts, in *Notes and Queries*, 5th ser., VII [Feb. 17, 1877], 136):

> When in Anglesey I used to be told that this act of pussy's [washing her face] presaged, not rain [as it is commonly held in England], but the advent of a visitor. If the face only was washed, the date of the visitor's call was not fixed; but if the paw went over the ear, he might be expected the same day.

9 / *Zhemánnïy kót*: The 1828 edn. adds *l'* after *zhemánnïy*, giving the sense of "did" or "if" or "whenever."

*

In the margin of the drafts (2370, ff. 80^v and 81^v) Pushkin, while working on sts. V–VI and IX–X, three weeks or so after the disastrous Decembrist rising in Petersburg (Dec. 14, 1825), sketched the profiles of several conspirators he personally knew. Among various Mirabeaulike and Voltairelike profiles, one can make out those of the Decembrists P. Pestel and Rïleev, which shows tremendous power of visualization on Pushkin's part, since he had seen Pestel more than four years before (spring, 1821, Kishinev) and Rïleev five and a half years before (spring, 1820, Petersburg). See vol. 3, p. 361 and n.

VI

2–7 "I have known the shooting of a Star spoil a Night's Rest. . . . There is nothing so inconsiderable that may not appear dreadful to an Imagination that is filled with Omens and Prognosticks" (Addison, *The Spectator*, No. 7, March 8, 1711, where he is very witty in regard to superstititous ladies).

Shooting stars have been portentous ever since the world was made.

VII

1 / And yet / *Chto zh?*: This interrogative formula means here "What would you think?" or "Strange to say."

Commentary

11 / *U grobovóy svoéy doskí*: Idiom for "at the door of the grave."

2 / submerged wax / *vósk potóplennïy*: Pushkin's epithet seems to have been affected by *rastopit'*, "to melt" (trans.); *topit'*, meaning both "to drown" (trans.) and "to dissolve" (trans.). Instead of hot wax, tin (*olovo*) is sometimes melted down and placed in water, wherein it assumes prophetic shapes. A ritual book, the *Potrebnik*, of 1639, mentions sorcerers of both kinds: *voskoley* and *olovoley*, wax dissolvers and tin dissolvers (or "pourers" of these substances).

5–8 The Yuletide and Twelfth-night singing of dish-divination songs (*podblyudnïe pesni*) opens with a carol beginning "Glory [*Sláva*] be to God in heaven, Glory!" Girls and women wishing to divine drop rings and other trinkets into a dish or bowl containing water. The dish (*blyudo*) is then covered with a cloth, and the carols commence. At the end of each song a trinket is drawn at random, and its owner deduces an omen from the nature of the song that has just been sung over her token.

7 / turned up / *vínulos'*: The obvious translation, "was taken out," does not convey the element of chance and lot pertaining to the Russian verb as used here.

9 / the countrymen / *muzhichki-to*: This diminutive and the folksy filler, *-to*, cannot be adequately rendered in English.

9–12 This is a well-known *svyatochnïy* song (the adjective comes from *svyatki*, the twelve days from the birth of Christ, Dec. 25, to Epiphany (*Kreshchenie*, Baptism of Christ), Jan. 6. The song goes:

In Our Saviour's parish, in Chigásï beyond the Yáuza,
Glory!
Rich peasants live;
Glory!
They dig up gold by the spadeful,
Glory!
Bright silver by the basketful,
Glory!

Yauza River is a tributary of Moskva River east of the Kremlin. The brick church of Our Saviour was built in 1483. The usual portent of this song is death for elderly people.

14 / Kit / *koshúrka*: The carol goes:

Tomcat calls Kit:
Glory!
You come, my Kit, to sleep in the stove nook,
Glory!
I, Tomcat, have a flask of rye,
Glory!
A flask of rye and the end of a pie,
Glory!
And soft is the bed of Tomcat,
Glory!

This "sweeter" song foretells marriage, as Pushkin remarks in his n. 29.

VARIANT

2 Canceled drafts (2370, f. 81ʳ) have *vósk rastóplennïy*, "melted wax," and *vósk i ólovo*, "wax and tin."

IX

5 / in low-cut frock / *V otkrítom plát'itse*: Spalding has "In a half-open dressing-gown"; Elton, "Bareheaded, in a kerchief"; Miss Deutsch, "careless of the cold"; only Miss Radin has it right.

6 / she trains a mirror on the moon; 13 / What is your
name: These are well-known outdoor methods of div-
ination. Not only this Frenchified bare-shouldered miss,
but also a Russian peasant girl, booted and kerchiefed,
would go out onto the rural crossroads and direct her
looking glass at the moon, urging her destined husband
to appear in it. The reader may recall the old English
invocation:

> Moon, good moon, all hail to thee.
> I prithee, moon, reveal to me
> Who my husband must be.

Another old charm (not mentioned by Pushkin, but
opening Zhukovski's *Svetlana*) consisted in throwing
one's slipper over the gate onto the road. As it lay on the
snow, it pointed in the direction one's husband's home
would be.

The stanza ends with a ritual that one doubts shy
Tatiana really performed: this was to go beyond the gate
and challenge the first foot passenger.

13 / He looks: The verb "to look"—*smotret'*, *glyadet'* (Six :
XXIV : 13)—is used more often in Russian than in Eng-
lish. It is sometimes a mere syntactical pointer directing
the attention of the reader to a coming action or event
(as here) or sets a certain mood (of surprise or uncer-
tainty): "The prince looks at Onegin" (Eight : XVII : 11).
Also common is a perfective verb variant, *vzglyanut'*,
"to glance": "I shall glance at the house" (Seven : XVI :
3–4). But the most enervating phenomenon of this
order is the Russian equivalents of the noun "look"—
vzglyad (specifically "glance") and *vzor* (specifically
"gaze"). They are easy to rhyme and, when bolstered
by an epithet ("languorous," "sad," "glad," "gloomy"),
become ready-made formulas conveying a state of mind
through a person's facial expression.

14 / Agafón: Agafon, pronounced something like "Ah-gah-fawn," comes as a grotesque shock. This Russian version of Agatho or Agathonicus (see Pushkin's n. 13 to Two : XXIV : 2, on euphonious Greek names) is elephantine and rustic to the Russian ear. Its counterpart may be found among the Biblical names in England. We should imagine an English young lady of 1820 slipping out of the manor gate to ask a passing laborer his name and discovering that her husband will be called not Allan but Noah.

VARIANT

14 In the draft of this stanza (2370, f. 81ᵛ, pencil; published by Efros in *Lit. nasl.*, nos. 16–18 [1934], between pp. 928 and 929), Pushkin crossed out *Agafón* and wrote above it *Haritón*—which, had he retained it in the final text, would have nicely prophesied the Hariton Lane in the Hariton (St. Chariton) Parish whither, a year later, Tatiana will be taken on a matrimonial quest.

A canceled draft has *Mirón*, and a variant in the fair copy reads *Paramón*.

X

1, 5, 8, 9, 14 / Tatiana: It will be marked that Tatiana's name is repeated as many as five times in the course of this catoptromantic stanza, and there are other repetitions in it. One wonders if this is not the echo of her incantations; and one recalls the repetition of words in the first stanza of this canto. Her mirror may be compared to Pushkin's "magic crystal" in Eight : L.

1–3 / nurse's . . . in the bathhouse / *nyáni . . . v báni*: The ultima of the locative in l. 3 accommodates itself to the rhyme. The correct form is, of course, *v bane* (or, in the old orthography, used throughout the nineteenth century, *v banye*).

In Arabia the jinn's "chief abode is the bath" (Thomas Patrick Hughes, *A Dictionary of Islam* [London, 1885], p. 136).

We shall not divine with Tatiana in the Larins' bagnio. Instead, in Seven, we shall accompany her to an abandoned castle, where, enchanted in a fashionable cell, she will raise a daemon by studying magic signs in the margins of his books. *Her* books have bred, too. The mirror under her pillow, which had reflected the dancing moon, replaced *Werther*, which had been lying there, and that romance in its turn will be replaced by *Adolphe*.

6–8 Cf. other sympathetic phrases concerning Tatiana.

6 / Svetlana: Yet another allusion to Zhukovski's beautiful ballad, which our poet mentions in Three : v : 2–4 (see n.), and which provides Five with a motto. Svetlana engages in divination and conjuration before a candlelit mirror at a table laid for two. Bright-eyed and uncanny, her lover, after a year's absence, suddenly appears and, as in Bürger's *Lenore*, carries her off—to his own grave. The whole event, however, turns out to be a dream; and on the morrow, Svetlana's lover comes home safely, and they are married. The ballad ends with a twelve-line epilogue (or envoy—to use the term for a type of complimentary poem also termed "ballad"):

> Never know these frightful dreams,
> You, O my Svetlana!

and eight lines lower, to the end of the piece:

> Let all your life be bright
> as on the bosom of a mead
> a brooklet's pleasant gleam!

A Lenskian landscape.

St. v of *Svetlana* is, not without a special reason, at the back of Pushkin's prismatic mind:

> Here is the fair one alone;
>   sits her at the mirror;
> with a secret dread regards
> 4   herself in the mirror;
> in the mirror it is dark.
>   All around, dead silence;
> scarcely with a trembling fire,
> 8   candles pour their luster.
> Terror makes her bosom heave,
> to glance back she is afraid,
>   fear her eyes is dimming . . .
> 12 With a crackling spurts the flame,
> plaintively the cricket cries,
>   messenger of midnight.

In each of the twenty stanzas, the rhymes go: babaceceddiffi.

L. 13 yielded the nickname by which Pushkin was known in 1817–18 at the goose-dinner club, Arzamas, where each convive was labeled by a title or term derived from Zhukovski's ballads (see my n. to Eight : XIV : 13). An echo of these dinners, the skeleton of the goose and the remains of its crimson coif, will be found in Tatiana's dream, Five : XVII : 3–4.

11 *Lel'*, Ukrainian Lelo, Polish Lelum (Snegiryov, *Russkie prostonarodnïe prazdniki*, I, 119, 165, 184): a pagan god (of love and grove), or supposedly one; probably derived from a mere refrain; comparable to the *leli, leli, leli* and *ay lyuli lyuli* of Russian songs. One also remembers the beginning of the old English ballad: "Down in the valley, the sun setting clearly. | Lilly o lille, lilly o lee."

An old Whitsuntide song goes:

> *I ya vídu molodá*
> *Za novïe vorotá;*
>   *Dído, kálina!*
>   *Lélyo, málina!*

> And forth shall I, young maid,
> Go beyond the new gate;

> Diddle, whitten tree!
> Lilly, raspberree!

In this and other Russian songs the *kálina* and *málina* are common rhyme words almost devoid of meaning (and fancifully accented); but since Russo-English dictionaries are hopelessly inept in dealing with botanical terms, the following information may be helpful.

Kalina, "whitten tree," one of the many names of *Viburnum opulus* L. In his *Herball* (1562), William Turner christened it "ople tre," from the French *opier*, now (*viorne*) *obier* or *aubier*. Is it the "whipultre" of Chaucer? It is also called "cranberry tree" (a silly and confusing appellation, since it has nothing to do with cranberry); gardeners know it as "snowball tree" or "guelder-rose." It is represented by allied species (various haws) in North America.

Malina is the common European raspberry, *Rubus idaeus* L.

12–13 Cf. John Brand, *Observations on the Popular Antiquities of Great Britain* (London, 1882), II, 165–66: "In the north [of England] slices of the bride-cake are thrice . . . put through the wedding-ring, which are afterwards by young persons laid under their pillows when they go to bed, for the purpose of . . . [producing] dreams . . . [showing] 'the man or woman whom Heaven designed should be his or her wedded mate.' "

In England there also is or was a form of divination by means of "St. Thomas' onion": girls peel an onion and put it under the pillow at night with a prayer to that saint to show them their true love in a dream.

XI

1–2 / And dreams a wondrous dream Tatiana. She dreams that she / *I snítsya chúdnïy són Tat'yáne;* / *Ey snítsya, búdto-bï oná*: Exactly the same intonation was used by Pushkin in *Ruslan and Lyudmila*, can. v, ll. 456–57: "And dreams a vatic dream the hero; he dreams that the princess . . . " *I snítsya véshchïy són geróyu,* | *On vídit búdto bï knyazhná* . . . (note the same ending in *na*).

10 / footbridge: This I regard as a reflected image, within the dream, of yet another instrument of divination. Snegiryov (in the work mentioned in n. to X : 11, vol. II [1838], p. 52) and anonymous compilers in various editions of *Martïn Zadek* (e.g., 1880) give the following information. A small bridge of birch withes (such as those used for a *venik*, the short besom, with which steam-bathing Russians switch their scarlet backs) is put together and placed under the maiden's pillow. At bedtime she incants: "He who is my *suzhenïy* [the one destined me] will help me over the bridge." He appears to her in a dream and leads her across by the hand.

It will be noted that the bear, Onegin's chum (Five : XV : 11), who helps Tatiana to cross over in her prophetic dream (XII : 7–13), foreshadows her future husband, the corpulent general, a relation of Onegin's. An interesting structural move in the development of Pushkin's precise composition that blends creative intuition and artistic foresight.

14 / she stopped / *Ostanovílasya oná*: The dream echoes of rhythms and terms previously attached to Tatiana's experience in the last stanzas of Three are a remarkable feature of this and the next stanzas. Her dream is both a travesty of the past and a travesty of the future. Five : XI : 14 repeats exactly Three : XLI : 8.

XII

2, 13 / brook / *ruchéy*: Although Pushkin gives an unusually wide sense to this word (cf. the "roar" of Caucasian "brooks" in *Onegin's Journey*, var. xiic : 8), I think we can admit here the characteristic transformation of dream objects: the raging torrent of romance that dins in xi dwindles to the familiar rill in Larino (Three : xxxviii : 13) without surprising the dreamer.

8 / *Tat'yána "ah!"*: This locution is another subtle reminder of Tatiana's wild dash to the brook in Three : xxxviii (see my n. to *Ah!* in l. 5).

14 / and what then? / *i chtó zh?*: A rhetorical formula meaning here "And what do you think happened next?" Cf. Five : vii : 1.

XIII

3 / from the shaggy footman / *ot kosmátogo lakéya*: Throughout the greater part of the nineteenth century it was customary for a young lady of noble birth, when going for a walk with her governess or *dame de compagnie*, to be followed by a footman in livery. As late as c. 1865, in Tolstoy's *Anna Karenin*, pt. I, ch. 6, we glimpse little Princess Kitty Shcherbatski (one of Tatiana's granddaughters) promenading on Tverskoy Boulevard, in Moscow, with her two elder sisters and Mlle Linon, all four "escorted by a footman with a gilt cockade upon his hat." Shakespeare's "rugged Russian bear" (*Macbeth*, iii, iv, 100) might provide a closer epithet for the rendering of *kosmatïy*.

12 / precipices / *stremnínï*: It is curious that even a Russian winter comes to Pushkin through French poems, or from French versions of English poems. In the present case, one thinks of Thomson's *Winter*, ll. 300–01: ". . . precipices huge | Smoothed up with snow . . ."

13 / o'er-drifted / *zanesént*: The same word ("swept over," "overblown") is repeated in XV : 8 (*zanesyón*).

XIV

6 / in the crumbly snow / *v hrúpkom snége*: The usual locative is *v snegu*. The general sense of *hrupkiy* is "brittle." Here it is derived from the verb *hrupat'*, which means "to make a crisp, crackly, crunchy sound."

Vyazemski, in *First Snow* (see quotation in n. to Five : III : 6), uses the same epithet for snow. See also Krïlov, in his admirable, poetical *The Spendthrift and the Swallow* (1818), *Fables*, bk. VII, no. IV, ll. 19–22:

> . . . again . . . come frosts;
> on crumbly snow the freight sleighs creak;
> from chimneys smoke in columns rises; frostwork
> scumbles the windowpanes . . .

In two other evocations of winter, One : XXXV : 8–11 and Five : I : 9, Pushkin repeats two of these images, the smoke and the frostwork.

XV

1–3 / deftly . . . submissive / *provórno . . . pokórna*: The rhyme seems to presage the equally inexact rhyme of XLIV : 1–3: *zadórnïy . . . provórno* (see n. to Five : XLIV : 3).

VARIANTS

9–10 When preparing the 1833 edn., Pushkin jotted down (PD 172):

> And now the bear taps on the window
> and in the hut there sounds a noise . . .

The 1828 edn. gives (l. 10):

> and in the hut there's dreadful noise . . .

XVI

4 / big funeral: Perhaps a recollection of the burial of Onegin's uncle (One : LIII), as described to Tatiana by those who had attended it. The allusion is to the noisy arval, the feast following the actual interment.

7 / *I chtó zhe! vídit . . . za stolóm*: Thus in the 1837 edn., instead of *I chtó zhe vídit? . . . za stolóm*, "and what does she see? . . . at the table."

14 / half crane and half cat: Cf. Mme de Staël on *Faust*, in *De l'Allemagne*, pt. II, ch. 23: "Mephistopheles conduit Faust chez une sorcière, qui tient à ses ordres des animaux moitié singes et moitié chats."

It is very odd that Schlegel, who assisted Mme de Staël in her labors, did not correct her strange mistake. The animal mentioned by Goethe in his *Hexenküche* scene has nothing to do with a "cat" or a "half cat"; it is simply an African long-tailed monkey (*Cercopithecus*), *eine Meerkatze*.

VARIANTS

To judge by the corrections in the drafts (2370, ff. 83^r, 83^v) and fair copy (PB 14), Pushkin had considerable trouble in choosing his animals. (See also vars. to XVII.)

9–10 Canceled drafts (2370, 83^r):

> with horns and a bear's muzzle;
> another with a mouse's head . . .

10 Fair copy:

> another with a donkey's head . . .

12 Canceled drafts (ibid.):

> . . . with a tiger's mane [sic] . . .
> rat paws . . .
> hawk nose . . .
> red eye . . .

Fair copy:

> there stirs a proud proboscis . . .

13 Canceled draft (ibid.):

> a fish with feet . . .

14 Draft (ibid.):

> . . . half crane, half mole.

XVII

1 / *Eshchyó strashnéy, eshchyó chudnée*: This line bears an amusing resemblance to the "Curiouser and curiouser" of Lewis Carroll's *Alice's Adventures in Wonderland*, (1865), ch. 2.

3–4 / goose's neck . . . red calpack: A Russian calpack or *kolpak* is a more or less conical cap of cloth, cotton, felt, fur, etc. It is tempting to see here a last memory of the Arzamas dinners of 1817–18. See n. to Five : x : 6 and Eight : XIV : 13.

5 / windmill . . . dances: Tomashevski (1936, *Vremennik pushkinskoy kommissii*, II, Moscow) published a pencil sketch by Pushkin showing the windmill of Tatiana's dream and a small dancing skeleton. Pushkin drew it in his copy of the separate edition of Four and Five. The vanes or sails of a windmill are termed "wings," *kríl'ya*, in Russian.

In a MS variant of Eight : XLVI, Tatiana recalls the local windmill (canceled reading in the PB fair copy). This is not the mill (Six : XII : 11 and XXV : 10), apparently a water mill (Six : XXVI : 1), near which Lenski falls in his duel with Onegin, but the Russian reader is reminded of it since any flour mill is *mel'nitza*.

The squat-jig is, of course, the well-known Russian masculine dance performed with bent legs.

In the *Dneprovskaya Rusalka* (see n. to Two : XII : 14), a burlesque personage is changed into a bear, a tree is transformed into a windmill, and bags of flour perform a dance. Pushkin may have seen it in his youth in St. Petersburg.

7 The separate edition of Four and Five gives "Yells" for "Barks."

7–8 See my n. to One : XXII : 5–6, where the leitmotiv represented by these lines is discussed for the whole novel.

The guests, who in Tatiana's waking life will be present at the name-day party, and later at the balls in Moscow, are benightmared and foreshadowed by the fairy-tale ghouls and hybrid monsters in her dream.

*

In Ivan Hemnitser's fable *The Two Neighbors* (*Fables*, 1779) a similar intonation occurs (ll. 24–25):

> Here's bark of dogs, and porcine squeal,
> And cry of men, and thump of blows.

In a remarkable poem, a beautiful tale about a magic castle, by the precursor of Russian romanticism, Gavrila Kamenev (1772–1803), entitled *Gromval* (pub. 1804), and consisting of unrhymed quatrains with masculine endings, the first two verses of each in dactylic tetrameter (a most unusual combination), the following two lines (105–106) express a similar theme in a similar manner:

> *Dúhi, skelétï, rukámi skhvatyás',*
> *Gárkayut, vóyut, hohóchut, svistyát . . .*

> Skeletons, spirits, with hands interlocked,
> bellow and whistle, and wail, and guffaw . . .

And, finally, in a dream that Sofia invents when speaking to her father, Pavel Famusov, in Griboedov's *Woe from Wit*, there occurs in act I, l. 173:

... *stón, ryov, hóhot, svíst chudóvishch!*
... groans, roar, laughter, whistles of monsters!

The formula is international. Tennyson has much the same intonation in *The Day Dream: The Revival* (1842), ll. 3–4:

And feet that ran, and doors that clapt,
And barking dogs, and crowing cocks ...

*

The reviewers Pushkin takes to task in his n. 31 (which see) contended that in the case of *hlop*, "clap," and *top*, "stamp," the full form (*hlópanie, tópanie*) alone was correct. Pushkin uses *hlop* and *top* in *The Bridegroom* (see below), ll. 139 and 137 respectively.

In 1826 Pushkin revised, or invented, a folk song (one of a set of three) about Stenka (Stepan) Razin, the famous Volga bandit (a rebellious Don Cossack caught and quartered in 1671), which starts:

Not the stamp of horse, not the parle of man
— 'tis the good old weather whistling,
luring me, Stenka Razin,
to roam the sea ...

A similar intonation occurs in Pushkin's great ballad *The Bridegroom: a Folk Tale*, composed in July, 1825, at Mihaylovskoe and consisting of forty-six stanzas of masculine-rhymed iambic tetrameters and feminine-rhymed iambic trimeters (babaccee), ll. 137, 153:

Then cries I heard, the stamp of horse ...
Cries, laughter, songs, and noise, and clink ...

Natasha, a merchant's daughter, disappears for three days (she gets lost in a wood, as we discover later) and returns, bewildered and silent. After a while she reverts to her usual rosy cheerfulness, until one evening the sight of a young man driving a dashing three-in-hand past her porch makes her blanch again. He asks her in ·marriage, and her father forces her to accept the offer. At the wedding feast she relates what purports to be a dream (she tells of a forest trail that led her to a log cabin full of sparkling jewels), but is really the story of a murder committed by the young man, who is then and there arrested. The ballad, which verbally is superior even to Zhukovski's *Svetlana*, is magnificently onomatopoeic; ll. 117–20, for example, render to perfection the soughing of a dense wood:

> . . . *v glushí*
> *Ne slíshno bílo ni dushí*
> *I sósnï lish da éli*
> *Vershínami shuméli.*

> . . . in the forest depth
> one did not hear a single soul;
> only the pines and firs
> made murmur with their crests.

I could not render the *s-s-s* and *sh-sh-sh-sh-sh* of the original and retain the sense.

8 / parle of man and stamp of steed: Cf. Praed, *The Red Fisherman*, l. 117:

> Neigh of steed, and clang of steel . . .

VARIANTS

1 Drafts (2370, f. 83ᵛ):

> ⟨Rats in rose-colored livery⟩ . . .
> Roosters in colored livery . . .

Canceled fair copy and separate edn. (1828) of chapter:

> ⟨A rat in light-blue livery⟩ . . .
> ⟨A raven in a light-blue livery⟩ . . .
> A fidgety hedgehog in livery . . .

Notes for 1833 edn. (PD 172):

> ⟨A horned owl on a winged snake⟩ . . .
> A goggled snake, hedgehog in livery . . .

5 / Drafts (2370, f. 83ᵛ):

> ⟨there on a chair a windmill dances⟩ . . .
> there a live windmill dances . . .

Fair copy and separate edn. of chapter:

> in uniform a windmill dances . . .

XVIII

Compare with various details and intonations of Ta-
tiana's dream the end of ch. 15 of Nodier's *Sbogar*, where
Antonia is telling Jean of her delirium:

> Tout, ici, étoit plein de fantômes.—On y voyoit des
> aspics d'un vert éclatant, comme ceux qui se cachent dans
> le tronc des saules; d'autres reptiles bien plus hideux, qui
> ont un visage humain; des géants démesurés et sans
> formes; des têtes nouvellement tombées . . . et toi, tu
> étois aussi debout au milieu d'eux, comme le magicien
> qui présidoit à tous les enchantements de la mort.

12 / his eyes sparkling: In Dmitriev's *Prichudnitsa*, the
heroine, Vetrana (*Anglice* Zephyrina), a frivolous belle
full of freaks, who has everything, including a good hus-
band, but feels sorely ennuied, is transported in a dream
by an enchantress, who wishes to teach her a lesson, into
a perilous forest where a robber, "his eyes sparkling,"
snatches her up, gallops off with her, and tosses her into a
river.

This *vzórami sverkáya* in *EO*, Five : XVIII : 12, is a
recollection of the *blistáya vzórami*, "eyes blazing," in
the last stanza of Three (XLI : 5), when Onegin suddenly
appears before her, fulfilling as it were the request
Tatiana makes in l. 74 of her letter (Three : before

XXXII): ". . . interrupt the heavy dream." Now the reveries have built up, Onegin's image continues to develop along the demoniac lines already suggested by l. 59 of her letter. The blazing gazes will, however, be transformed into the "wondrous tender" (*chúdno nézhen*) "look of his eyes" (*vzór egó ochéy*) of Five : XXXIV : 8–9 (recollected further as "the momentary softness of his eyes," *Mgnovennaya nezhnost'* [nom.] *ochey*, Six : III : 2).

13 / with a clatter / *gremyá*: Producing a loud, clangorous noise by pushing back his chair.

    Ll. 12–13 link up the past (Three : XLI : 5) and the future (Five : XXXV : 1).

XIX

9–14 In this Boschian assemblage the *usï* in the beginning of l. 11 may mean the whiskers of a felid or the feelers of an arthropod as well as an ogre's mustachio. Parts of elephants and boars, and the tail of a diabolical poodle or lion, can be vaguely made out among the conventional medievalisms.

13 / all point as one / *Vsyó ukazúet*: "All points," "the whole [crowd] points," is the same idiomatic form as in the opening phrase of One : XXI, *Vsyo hlópaet*, "All clap as one," "All claps," "The whole [house] claps."

XX

5–7 / Onegin gently . . . .: The critic alluded to in Pushkin's n. 32 is Boris Fyodorov, who, in reviewing Four and Five (1828) in his magazine, *The St. Petersburg Spectator*, accused Pushkin of immorality and flippancy.

    The verb *uvlekat'*, Fr. *entraîner*, as used in l. 5, stands somewhere between "to draw" and "to sweep away," and, despite our poet's protestations, does connote a certain degree of blandishment and enticement, as, of course, it should in this passage.

The *slagáet* ("deposits," Fr. *dépose*) in the next line is associated in Russian with related forms meaning "to fold," "to join," and so on, and conveys, in the present context, a singularly limp-jointed and yielding state on the part of the subject. It is used here in a sense close to *ukladïvat'*, which means "to have one lie down," a connotation enhancing the deliberate and purposeful quality of Onegin's action.

10–XXI : 3 / Lenski . . .: M. Gershenzon, in his article "Snï Pushkina" (Dreams in Pushkin),* argues that Tatiana subconsciously knows in her dream that (1) Lenski, despite his poetry, is nothing but a budding vulgarian and that (2) Onegin subconsciously hates him for this.

There is, however, nothing in Tatiana's dream to justify this statement. "Onegin," writes Gershenzon, in his remarkably silly paper, "is nauseated by the trite, Philistine, maudlin quality of Lenski's romance; and how human, how comprehensible it is that he gives way to his vexation, roils Lenski, and whirls away Olga, like any lad pitching a pebble at a pair of cooing doves"!

Gershenzon also mentions a little book by S. Sudienko, whom he considers a crank, *Tayna poemï A. S. Pushkina "Evgeniy Onegin"* (The Enigma of Pushkin's Poem Eugene Onegin; Tver, 1909), in which an allegoric meaning is attributed to various details of Tatiana's dream, the two sticks forming the bridge, for example, being the two meetings that she had had with Onegin, and so on.

---

*Published in *Pushkin*, a collection of essays by various authors, ed. N. Piksanov (Moscow, 1924), pp. 79–96.

Commentary

1 Canceled drafts (2370, f. 84ʳ):

> "Mine!" said Eugene in a bass voice . . .
> "Mine!" said pale Eugene . . .

9–10 In a canceled draft (ibid.), Olga comes in:

> with a pale lamp in her hand,
> followed by Lenski . . .

XXI

1–3 See n. to XX : 10.

XXII

1 / *No tá, sestrí ne zamecháya*: The long-drawn, wistful chant of this line is an echo of Three : XXXIII : 1, *Oná zarí ne zamecháet*, "She takes no notice of the sunrise," and is in its turn echoed by similar first-line intonations in Eight : XXXI, *Oná egó ne zamecháet*, "She does not notice him," and Eight : XLII, *Oná egó ne podïmáet*, "She does not bid him rise." An incantatory and recitative leitmotiv.

12 / Martin Zadeck / *Martín Zadéka*: I am inclined to regard this personage as the fabrication, in 1770, of an anonymous German-Swiss ephemerist who may have derived his sage's name from zaddik, a rabbinical title meaning the "specially righteous," or from Zadok, a priest in the time of Solomon, or from Zedechias, the *fameux cabaliste* who, in the reign of Pepin the Short (eighth century), proved to scoffers that the elements are inhabited by sylphs, whom he advised to show themselves to men, which they did, riding in splendid airships (according to the Abbé Montfaucon de Villars, in a ro-

mance directed against the Rosicrucians, *Le Comte de Gabalis, ou Entretiens sur les sciences secrètes*, Paris, 1670).

The University Library of Basel possesses a collection of eighteenth-century pamphlets entitled *Historische Schriften* on the flyleaf and *Varia historica* on the cover (indexed as *Leseges. Brosch*. No. 17). Mlle Eugénie Lange, librarian at the Swiss National Library, kindly obtained for me a photostat of the fourth pamphlet in the series. It is a four-page affair bearing the title "Wunderbare und merkwürdige Prophezeyung des berühmten Martin Zadecks, eines Schweitzers bey Solothurn der im 106ten Jahr seines Alters, vor seinem Tode den 20. Dezember, und nach seinem Tode den 22ten Dez. 1769. in Gegenwart seiner Freunde prophezeyet hat, auf gegenwärtige und zukünftige Zeiten." The brochure gives a short description of his life (he retired to the Alps in 1739, subsisted on herbs there for thirty years in holy solitude, and died in a poor hut not far from Soleure) and of the predictions he made on his deathbed (such as Turkey's disintegration, the coming opulence of Scandinavia and Russia, Danzig's dazzling grandeur, the conquest of Italy by France, the complete invasion of Africa by three Northern nations, the destruction of most of the New World by cataclysms, and the end of the world in 1969). The pamphlet was evidently widely distributed; versions of it were included in various divinatory compilations, German and Russian. The name of Martin Zadeck (spelled in Russian Martïn Zadek or Martïn Zadeka) appears with those of Tycho Brahe and Johann Kaspar Lavater on the title page of a 454-page *Oraculum* in three books published in Moscow in 1814, and there are many other editions, such as *The Ancient and New Oraculum Discovered after the Death of a Hundred-and-Six-Year-Old Recluse Martin Zadeck* (Moscow, 1821) and *The New Complete*

Oraculum and Enchanter, containing "The Interpretation of Dreams" and "The Predictions of Bruce and Zadeck" (Moscow, 1880).

XXIII

5 / *Malvina*: *Malvina*, by Mme Cottin (Paris, 1800; 1801, according to L. C. Sykes, author of an admirable study, *Madame Cottin*, Oxford, 1949). Mme Cottin was also the author of *Mathilde*; see n. to Three : IX : 8, on Malek-Adhel.

Malvina de Sorcy, after the death of her friend Milady Sheridan (niece, one supposes, of Rousseau's Lord Bomston), goes to live with a relation, Mistriss (the *iss* is a French specialty of the time) Birton, in Scotland, where M. Prior, a Catholic priest, and Sir Edmund, a rake, both fall in love with her. The malice of Mistriss Birton occasions various dreadful and complicated events in consequence of which Malvina loses what mind she has.

To judge by a canceled draft of l. 5 (in 2368, f. 49ᵛ, ". . . with a Russian Malvina"), Pushkin may have meant the Russian version that had appeared in 1816–18 (according to Brodski, p. 231), and in that case Tatiana would hardly have read it.

6 / three rubles fifty: Probably (as noted by Lozinski, 1937), in paper money ("assignations"), which would equal one ruble in silver.

8 / collection of common fables / *Sobrán'e básen ploshchadníh*: The reference is to chapbooks meant for the lower classes—merchants, artisans, more or less literate retainers, and so forth.

9 / two "Petriads": Among the half-dozen "Petriads"

516

(epics devoted to Peter I, miserable imitations of miserable French "Henriades") known to have circulated at the time, there was a grotesque *Lyric Hymn*, in eight cantos, by Prince Sergey Shihmatov, the publication of which (in 1810) provoked Batyushkov's witty epigram, *Advice to an Epic Poet*:

> Choose any name to designate
> Your half-barbaric song:
> Peter the Big, Peter the Long
> —But not Peter the Great.

Two other heroic poems dealing with Peter are those by Roman Sladkovski (1803) and Aleksandr Gruzintsev (1812); and there is a French tragedy in verse, *Pierre le Grand* (Paris, 1779), by Dorat. The best of the lot is Lomonosov's *Pyotr Velikiy, geroicheskaya poema*, in 1250 iambic hexameters (rhyming bbaaccee). It consists of an exordium (64 lines, dated Nov. 1, 1760) and two cantos (632 and 554 ll.). Ll. 171–73 of can. I are pleasantly prophetic:

> Russian Columbuses, despising gloomy fate,
> shall open a new path mid ice floes to the east,
> and to America our empire shall extend.

10 / Marmontel, tome three: In Marmontel's *Œuvres complettes* (Paris, 1787, 17 vols.), the third volume contains *Contes moraux*, which had first appeared in 1761 (in a La Haye edn., 2 vols.), followed by *Nouveaux contes moraux* (Paris, 1765). Pushkin's library contained the 1818–19 edn. of the complete works.* I notice that Brodski (1950, p. 49) writes *Contes morales* and that Chizhevski (1953, p. 212) misspells the author's name "Marmontelle."

The association in Pushkin's mind between Peter the Great and Marmontel may have been owing to a recollec-

---

*See B. Modzalevski, "Biblioteka Pushkina (bibliograficheskoe o pisanie)," *P. i ego sovr.*, III, 9–10 (1909), p. 282.

Commentary

tion of Gilbert's satire *Le Dix-huitième Siècle* (1775), wherein Antoine Léonard Thomas is mentioned, author of *La Petréide*, an epic in honor of that tsar, interrupted by the poet's death in 1785:

> Thomas est en travail d'un gros poême épique;
> Marmontel enjolive un roman poétique . . .

VARIANTS

8–9 In canceled drafts (2368, f. 49ᵛ) the book hawker takes in exchange "Lhomond" and *vokábulï da chást' Levéka*. The allusions here are obviously to *Elémens de la grammaire françoise*, by Charles François Lhomond (Paris, 1780), which went through countless editions and revisions; and to *Histoire de Russie*, by Pierre Charles Levesque (Paris, 1782, 5 vols.), or to his *Histoire des différents peuples soumis à la domination des Russes* (Paris, 1783, 2 vols.), which Pushkin had in his library.

XXIV

7–8 The "alphabetic" order of the Russian words is incorrect: the sequence of the words in *m* should be *medved'*, *metel'*, *mostok*, *mrak*.

The "raven" is a pentimento (see var. XVII : 1, canceled fair copy), and so is the "hedgehog" (see ibid., fair copy and separate edn. of Four and Five). "Raven" appears in the fair copy of XXIV : 7 (PB 14) and in all three editions. However, Acad 1937 prints *véd'ma*, "witch," instead of *vóron*, on the strength of a MS correction that Pushkin made in his copy of the five printed issues of the novel bound together (Chapters One through Six; preserved in MB 8318) sometime or soon after Six was published (March 23, 1828). The *voron* worried Pushkin. In the margin of the draft of *Winter*, dated Nov. 2, 1829 (2382, f. 15ᵛ), he jotted down *voron* as a memorandum note above another one referring to Seven : XXXI : 1–4 (see n. to Seven : XXXI : 1–4). Perhaps he meant to reinstate the "raven in a light-blue livery," canceled in XVII : 1.

In the draft (2368, f. 49ᵛ), XXIV : 8 reads:

> *Medvéd', mostók, muká, metél'* . . .
> bear, footbridge, flour, snowstorm . . .

This "flour" is an allusion to the dancing windmill in Tatiana's dream, but it also affords interesting proof of Pushkin's psychological indebtedness to the *Dneprovskaya Rusalka*, in which bags of flour dance on the stage (see nn. to Two : XII : 14 and Five : XVII : 5).

Other words looked up by Tatiana are, in the draft (2368, f. 49ᵛ), *zhenít'ba* ("marriage"), *shatyór* ("tent"), *shalásh* ("hut"), with the canceled *dom* ("house"); also *ruchéy* ("brook"), *sér'gi* ("earrings"), and a few other tentative ones that can be hardly made out in Pushkin's MS.

To judge by certain details of style, the oneirocritical index (*sonnik*) in the 1880 edn. of *Martïn Zadeka*, which I have consulted, should not differ (apart from a few obvious additions to the basic text) from early nineteenth-century versions of the dream book. True, the 1880 index does not contain all the words Tatiana looked up, but it does list "raven," "fir tree," and "bear." It says that if a raven is vocal in your dream (and all Tatiana's animals were very much so) this forebodes the death of a relative —which takes care of her sister's fiancé; a "fir tree" means marriage—and Tatiana will marry next year; a "bear" spells affluence—and her husband will be the wealthy Prince N. In other words, Zadeck should have solved at least some of her "doubts." Curiously enough, there is not much more Tatiana could have looked up in connection with her dream, except perhaps "goat," "crane," and "windmill," all of which foretell trouble, whereas hoofs and barking portend, respectively, marriage and a quarrel.

13 / *Dney néskol'ko oná potóm*: The line is accented in an interesting way, the strongest word (*dney*) coinciding with a depression and forming a false spondee with the accented first syllable of *néskol'ko*, while *oná* and *potóm* are weak words with semiscuds on their ultimas: ◡ ́− ◡ − ◡ ̆ ◡ ́.

XXV

1 / *bagryánoyu rukóyu*: The epithet *bagryanïy*, "crimson," is synonymous with *purpurnïy*, "porphyrous," and implies a rich tone of red, the French *pourpre*, not the English "purple," which is deep violet (Russ. *fioletovïy*).

The *bagryanaya ruka* strikes, or should strike, a Russian as amusing because the Homeric *rhododactylos Eos*, "rose-fingered dawn" or "dawn of the rosy arms" (see Simaetha's invocation of the moon in Theocritus' *Idyl* II), is given by the Russian epithet the scarlet hands and arms of a washerwoman (as Vyazemski quips in a short poem of 1862).

A French poet would have said "rosy hands" (e.g., Casimir Delavigne: "Déjà l'Aurore aux mains vermeilles . . .").

As far as I can make out (and frankly, I have not gone into the question beyond its shallows), there were two kinds of classical purples: the Tyrian purple, which was crimson, the color of blood and dawn; and the Tarentine dye, said by poets to rival the hue of the violet. French poets in their use of *pourpre* drove the Tyrian idea to a point where sight ceased to be of any moment; and an abstract sunburst replaced the perception of any specific hue; they were followed by the Russians, whose *purpur* is merely the conventional crimson of a heavy curtain in an allegory or apotheosis; but the once woaded English, with their Saxon cult of color, turned to the plum, and the Purple Emperor butterfly, and the heather in bloom, and remote hills—in short, to "amethyst" and "violet" for their conception of purple. "You violets . . . | By your pure purple mantles known," writes Sir Henry Wotton (1568–1639) in a poem addressed to Elizabeth of Bohemia. Shakespeare's "long purples" (*Hamlet*, IV, vii, 170) become characteristically "fleurs rougeâtres" with Letourneur, which, of course, makes nonsense of the comparison to the bluish fingers of dead men in the same passage. The bright-red variety of purple does crop up as a Europeanism in Shakespeare and other poets of his time, but its real ascendancy, of short duration happily, comes with the age of pseudoclassicism, when Pope seems to have deliberately conformed to the French use of *pourpre*; Pope's pupil, Byron, followed suit, and Pichot can hardly be accused of erring in his choice of hue when he makes of *Don Juan*, II, CL, 2–3 (". . . the lady, in whose cheek | The pale contended with the purple rose"): ". . . la jolie personne, sur les joues de laquelle le vermillon de la rose semblait le disputer à la pâleur des lis"—which (while automatically interpolating the accepted counterpart, "lily," in one of the tritest formulas in literature) identifies purple with the color of blood.

1–4. In one of his *Nonsensical Odes* (*Vzdornïe odï*), Aleksandr Sumarokov (1718–77), an influential rhymester of the time, parodies Lomonosov's imagery thus:

> The grass with a green hand
> has covered many places;
> Aurora with a crimson foot
> leads forth new years.

Pushkin's n. 34 to the quatrain of xxv quotes the opening of Lomonosov's *Ode on the Anniversary of the Ascent to the Throne of Her Majesty Empress Elizaveta Petrovna* (1748), in twenty-four stanzas rhyming ababeeciic.

Another "crimson hand" occurs in Lomonosov's ode on an earlier anniversary of the same reign (1746), in twenty-seven stanzas (ll. 11–14):

> And lo, with crimson hand already
> Aurora on the world opens the gate,
> sheds from her raiment rosy light
> on fields, on wood, on town, on seas.

But the first "crimson hand" in Lomonosov occurs even earlier, in an ode known only from a fragment, which he published in his *Manual of Rhetoric* (1744). It slips rather easily into English rhyme:

> From golden fields descends Aurora
> On us with crimson hand to strew
> Her brilliants, sparks, festoons of Flora,
> To give the fields a rosy hue;
> To hide the dark with her bright cloak
> And birds to mellow songs provoke.
> Most pure, the ray of blessings thine
> Doth ornament my zealous line;
> Grows clearer in thy purple's fire
> The tone of my most humble lyre.

Porfira, the "royal purple" in l. 9 of Lomonosov's piece, is not always seen as blood red by Russian poets. It is given a fiery-amber color (*v porfírah ógnenno-yantárnïh*) in l. 6 of Shevïryov's remarkable *A Dream* (*Son*; fifty-three iambic tetrameters, published in 1827). Franciszek Malewski (1800–70), a Polish man of letters, has left a note in his diary to the effect that this *Dream* was criticized (as "the delusion of a champagne drinker") at a party in Polevoy's house, where Pushkin, Vyazemski, and Dmitriev were present. * Shevïryov apparently knew English: his epithet seems to come from Milton's *L'Allegro* (1645), ll. 59–61:

> Right against the Eastern gate,
> Where the great Sun begins his state,
> Rob'd in flames, and Amber light . . .

VARIANTS

5–10 Drafts (2368, f. 43ᵛ), ll. 5–6:

> with children and their tutors
> whole families of neighbors . . .

Canceled draft (ibid.), l. 5:

> with governesses and with tutors . . .
> *s madámami, s uchitelyámi* . . .

Another draft (ibid.), ll. 5–10:

greetings, kind words [*láski*] await Tatiana:
the day before already two calashes [*kolyáski*],
a hooded coach [*kibítka*], three sledded coaches [*trí vozká*],
whole families of neighbors
. . . with mammies . . . servants . . .
young daughters, children.

In a canceled draft (ibid., f. 41ᵛ), referring to Five : XXIX : 1–2, the attendants are taken care of as follows:

> the tutors, governesses, nurses
> eat with the children in the drawing room . . .

XXVI

2–12 / Pustyakóv . . .: These are comedy names, also found elsewhere, and with obvious counterparts in English

---

*Incidentally, the commentary to this diary, in *Lit. nasl.*, LVIII (1952), 268, n. 30, makes the incredible mistake of assigning that criticism to the dream of Svyatoslav in *Slovo o polku Igoreve*.

literature: Pustyakov (a descendant of Fonvizin's Pro-
stakov, "Mr. Noddy") corresponds to "Mr. Trifle" (in
nice contrast to his corpulence); Gvozdín, to "Squire
Clout"; Skotínin (the maternal uncle of the Minor in
Fonvizin's *Nedorosl'*, 1782; see n. to One : XVIII : 3), to
"Mr. Brutish"; Petushkóv, to "Young Cockahoop,"
and Flyánov, to "Judge Flan"—grotesque personages
waiting for Gogol to transfer them from a rather obvious
comedy of hoggish manners and Hogarthian noses into
his own fantastic and poetical world.

9 / Buyánov ["Mr. Rowdy"], my first cousin: The hero of
The Dangerous Neighbor (*Opasnïy sosed*), a narrative
poem of 154 lines in Alexandrine couplets by Vasiliy
Pushkin, our poet's uncle (1770–1830), the elder brother
of Sergey Pushkin. Vasiliy Pushkin had already been
complimented by his young nephew in 1814 on this
rather unexpected achievement, in the latter's iambic
trimeters, *Small Town* (*Gorodok*); and Baratïnski, in an
epigram of 1826, wittily suggested that only a pact with
the devil could explain the sudden spurt of talent coming
from the dull and inept poetaster that Vasiliy Pushkin
had been before (and was to be after).

A *galant* poem in the French sense rather than an ob-
scene one, although full of rowdy national connotations,
this racy little epic was composed in April, 1811, and mer-
rily circulated in manuscript copies among littérateurs
and *bons vivants*, who learned it by heart so thoroughly
that in 1815 a Russian diplomat (Baron P. Schilling),
when trying out some Russian lithographic implementa
in Munich, casually printed it from memory—thus be-
ing responsible for its first edition! * The second edition, a

------

*Apart from a very small edition (now known from a unique
copy in PD) privately printed by the author about Jan. 1, 1812,
in St. Petersburg.

Leipzig one in 1855, was brought out from a MS gladly
supplied by the author in 1830. The first edition pub-
lished in Russia was Burtsev's, Petersburg, 1901. For
these notes I have used a Moscow edition of 1918
(Bibliofil) and a Petersburg edition of 1922 (Atheneum).

The poem begins as follows:

Och! Let me rest and muster all my strength.
What would avail me to be cagey, friends?
I'll tell you everything. Buyanov,
my neighbor, who spent in eight years his fortune
on gypsy girls, whores, taverns, and crack coachmen, *
called yesterday on me: mustache unshaven,
tousled, fluff-covered, wearing a peaked cap
—he came, and the whole place reeked of the pothouse.

This "dangerous neighbor" (dangerous because genial
rakes lead their friends into trouble) invites the narrator
to a bawdyhouse to sample a young whore, Varyushka
(little Barbara), who, however, turns out to be poxy, ac-
cording to an older female with whom the narrator even-
tually retires; he is interrupted in his undertaking by a
drunken row conducted by Buyanov. Although com-
posed in pleasingly flowing colloquial verse, the poem is
far from being the masterpiece it is generally considered
to be. The reader will note that Buyanov, the rowdy
rake, fresh from dallying with young Varyushka, is not
only invited by Vasiliy Pushkin's nephew (the "cousin"
of his uncle's brain child) to Tatiana's name-day party,
but is permitted, in Seven : XXVI : 2, to seek Tatiana's
hand and to be mentioned by the mother as a possible
candidate. In gratitude to his nephew for this kindness
to Buyanov, Vasiliy Pushkin mentioned Tatiana in a
worthless narrative poem in tetrameters, *Captain
Hrabrov* (Captain "Bold"; 1829), wherein the captain is
told by a lady visitor:

---

*In the 1918 edn., "male dancers."

> . . . I read a lot,
> romanticism enchants me:
> the other day, Miss Larin—Tatiana—
> gave me to read "Caliban" [*Kalibana*]

The reference is, I suspect, to Küchelbecker's "Dramatic Joke in two acts," *Shakespeare's Ghosts* (*Shekspirovï duhi*; St. Petersburg, 1825), which is discussed by Aleksandr Pushkin in the draft of a letter to Küchelbecker (first week of December, 1825: "On the other hand, Caliban is charming"), who, however, never got it: he was arrested for participation in the Decembrist revolt (Dec. 14, 1825).

Long before writing *EO*, our poet, in a letter to Vyazemski of Jan. 2, 1822, from Kishinev to Moscow, had formulated his opinion of his uncle's poetry: "All his works are not worth his Buyanov; and what will happen to him in posterity? I apprehend greatly [*krayne opasayus'*] that my cousin may be taken for my son . . ."

10 The detail about the "fluff" often crops up in descriptions of this or that disreputable Russian; its presence is owing to his sleeping with his clothes on in a drunkard's world of leaky feather beds and unswept floors. Elton understood *v puhú* as "With downy face," and Miss Radin has, still more ridiculously, "Unshaven"! Spalding twists the *puh* into a "wadded coat"; and Miss Deutsch puts the down into Buyanov's hair.

VARIANTS

2 In a canceled draft (2368, f. 42^r) Pustyakov is Tumakov ("Mr. Whack").

5–12 Draft (2368, f. 43^r):

> Mrs. Hlipkov, thrice young,
> with children of all ages, counting
> from two to thirty years:

> five sons and seven daughters.
> Buyanov, my first cousin,
> complete with skullcap, copper chains,
> embroidered jacket, and mustache.
> And the retired Counselor Lyánov . . .

who, in the fair copy (PB 14), is (ll. 13–14):

> a heavy gossip, lady's clown,
> a glutton, usurer, and rogue.

XXVII

1 / Panfíl Harlikóv: Panfil is the popular form of Pamphilus (a Syrian saint). Harlikov is a comedy name ("Mr. Throttle") derived from *harlo,* a dialect form of *gorlo,* "throat" (cf. Fr. *gosier*), from which the verb *gorlanit'* (or *harlit'*), which means "to speak at the top of one's voice" (*à plein gosier*), is derived:

> And with Pamphilus Throttle's family
> Also arrived the Frenchman Trick,
> A wit, come recently from Tambov,
> With spectacles and red perwick

—as I once had it in my first, and sinful, attempt (1950) at rendering *EO* in rhyme.

6 / stanza / *kuplét*: This is not a "couplet" (two rhyming verses) in the English technical sense, but a strophe of several lines, often with a refrain. Pushkin actually used the term *kuplet* for the *EO* stanza. The application is French. (See also n. to Four : XXXV : 8.)

8–13 / "Réveillez-vous, belle endormie" . . . "belle Niná": It is curious to note that, in a sense, Tatiana is the fair sleeper and that she does not really awake from her magic dream, which foreshadowed the grotesque guests.

The reference here is to one of the many imitations of *La Belle Dormeuse* (c. 1710), attributed to Charles

Rivière Dufresny (1648–1724), who (according to Philoxène Boyer) composed tunes for his plays without knowing music and sang them to the composer Nicolas Ragot de Grandval (1676–1753), who took them down in score. The first and third lines of the first quatrain went (according to Tomashevski, in *P. i ego sovr.*, VII [1917], 67) "Réveillez-vous, belle endormie" and "Dormez profondément, ma mie" respectively, in the version Pushkin might have had in mind. The text published by Boyer, in *Les Petits Poètes français* (1861), III, 129, goes:

> Réveillez-vous, belle dormeuse,
> Si ce baiser vous fait plaisir;
> Mais si vous êtes scrupuleuse,
> Dormez, ou feignez de dormir.
>
> Craignez que je ne vous réveille,
> Favorisez ma trahison;
> Vous soupirez, votre cœur veille,
> Laissez dormir votre raison.
>
> Pendant que la raison sommeille
> On aime sans y consentir,
> Pourvu qu'amour ne nous réveille
> Qu'autant qu'il faut pour le sentir.
>
> Si je vous apparais en songe
> Profitez d'une douce erreur;
> Goûtez le plaisir du mensonge,
> Si la vérité vous fait peur.

Julien Tiersot, *Chansons populaires recueillies dans les Alpes françaises (Savoie et Dauphiné)* (Grenoble and Moutiers, 1903), p. 243, traces the publication of the first stanza of the ballad given above to the collection *La Clef des Chansonniers, ou Recueil des vaudevilles depuis cent ans et plus* (Ballard, 1717) and doubts that its author was Dufresny, to whom it is assigned by *L'Anthologie française* (1765). Tiersot also quotes half a dozen stanzas,

with music, of a so-called "folk song" (i.e., the cor-
rupted anonymous echo of an individual effort) that he
believes to have provided the theme and the tune of the
Anthologie française piece. It begins (as in *EO*, Five :
XXVII : 8):

> Réveillez-vous, belle endormie,
> Réveillez-vous, car il est jour;
> Mettez la tête à la fenêtre:
> Vous entendrez parler de vous!

It was, however, the more polished product that
reached Russia. The words have the powder-puff touch
of genteel lubricity so typical of Dufresny's age, but the
air is graceful and by 1820 had long become a favorite
with editors of songs for children and young ladies. By
then the original lines (of which one hears some dim
echoes in Tatiana's letter, e.g., ll. 39 and 62) were for-
gotten and replaced by more demure ones in various
congratulatory arrangements, such as:

> Il faut vous appeler Julie,
> Ce nom nous tire d'embarras,
> Il rime trop bien à "jolie"
> Pour qu'il ne nous convienne pas.

Something of this kind, discovered in some old *Chan-
sonnier des Grâces* or *Almanach chantant*, was recited by
Triquet. Leafing through my own childhood memories,
I find—dim but still legible—the following madrigal,
seen in an old songbook or album:

> Chérissez ce que la nature
> De sa douce main vous donna,
> Portez sa brillante parure,
> Toujours, toujours, belle Nina.

The elimination of one "toujours" ("Toujours, belle
Tatiana") would have turned the octosyllabic trick in
Triquet's case. Note that Pushkin, in ll. 13 and 14, ig-

nores metrically the *e muet* (but he makes three syllables of the Italian *niente* in One : LV : 7!).

The name Triquet ("Mr. Trick") is a comedy one and had been used in a slightly different form by Krïlov, in his completely mediocre three-act farce, *The Fashion Shop* (*Modnaya lavka*; written 1805, first produced July 27, 1806), in which there is an unscrupulous Frenchman called M. Trichet ("Mr. Trickster").

"Niná" was a French idyllic name much in vogue in the eighteenth century. See, for instance, *Le Bouquet*, a dialogue between "Nina et Daphné," by Nicolas Germain Léonard (1744–93).

Tatiana's name is pronounced here (XXVII : 14) in a French manner, "Ta-tee-a-ná," four syllables, with accent on last.

It is typical of Chaykovski's slapdash opera *Eugene Onegin* that *his* Triquet sings a totally different tune.

The Dufresny-Grandval tune goes:

Ré - veil - lez vous, belle en - dor - mi - e, Si ce bai - ser vous fait plai - sir;

Dor - mez pro - fon - dé - ment, ma mi - e, Dor - mez ou fei - gnez de dor - mir.

VARIANT

1–2 In a corrected draft (2368, f. 43ʳ) the Frenchman arrives as the escort of a giddy widow of forty years, Mrs. Lazorkin ("Mrs. Azure").

XXVIII

6 / *Muzïka . . . polkováya*: A military band.

9 / The young things skip / *Devchónki prígayut*: See n. to Four : XLI : 12.

10 / *kúshat' pódali*: "Dinner they have served." The an-
nouncement was (by the butler): *Kushat' podano*, "The
meal [To eat] is served."

13 / *krestyás'*: An allusion to the preprandial rapid little
sign of the cross that a Russian makes with bunched
fingers over the breastbone at the very moment he
sinks into his chair (which the footman behind him
slips under him). The movement is mechanical, no
heads are inclined, no grace is said; it is little more than
a checked button.

XXIX

4 / of glasses / *ryúmok*: An allusion to ponies of vodka
rather than to goblets of wine. The wine comes later
(XXXII : 8).

5–8 The rhythm of these lines, especially in the original, is
very similar to Swift's; cf. *The Journal of a Modern
Lady*, ll. 174–78:

> Now Voices over Voices rise;
> While each to be the loudest vies,
> They contradict, affirm, dispute,
> No single Tongue one Moment mute;
> All mad to speak, and none to hearken . . .

At this point, no doubt, Tatiana, with an inward gasp,
recalls the loud ghouls of her dream—and next moment
the blinding eye of Onegin is upon her.

9 / door leaves / *dvéri*: The reference is to a double door,
porte à deux battants (or *vantaux*), sometimes called,
not quite correctly, a folding door; but "double door"
is also ambiguous.

10–11 / Maker . . . / *Tvoréts* . . .: Spalding has the amus-

Commentary

ing howler: " 'Ah! | At last the author [Lenski]!' cries Mamma."

12–13 / each shifts covers, chairs / *vsyák otvódit* | *Pribórï, stúl'ya*: This is a little ambiguous, since the verb may also mean "assigns," "allots"; but our poet should have added *im* ("to them," "for them") if he wished to say that the covers and chairs are being prepared for the two newcomers by the guests who *tesnyátsya*, "make room" (or, grammatically, "press themselves closer together").

13 / covers / *Pribórï*; 14 / friends / *druzéy*; XXX : 1: seat them directly facing Tanya / *Sazháyut prýamo prótiv Táni*: The alliterations *pr* and the first *dr* (to be taken up by *tr*) prepare the wonderful instrumentation of the next lines, when the sounds of moving and making room at the end of XXIX are now repeated in a new emotional key (XXX : 2–3):

> *I, útrenney luní blednéy*,
> and than the morning moon paler,
> *I trépetney goními láni* . . .
> and more tremulous than the hunted doe . . .

Note that *útrenney* ("than the morning") is perfectly paralleled by *trépetney* ("more tremulous")—same consonants, same ending, same metrical position in same slow "swooning" line. The *ey* and *ney* repetitions are carried on from the rhyme closing one stanza into the next through the *ney* of *útrenney*, *blednéy*, and *trépetney* to *temnéyushchih* and to the *ey* of *ochéy* in ll. 4–5, with an emotional *ch* alliteration beautifully rounding up the symphony:

Ona	*temnéyushchih*	*ochéy* . . .
she	darkening	eyes . . .

Incidentally, it is curious to compare this delicate "morning moon" emblematizing Tatiana to the "stupid" nocturnal moon resembling Olga's face in Three : v. See App. II for a scheme of the scuds in this stanza.

XXX

1–5 See n. to XXIX : 13.

6 The separate edition of Four and Five gives "secret" (*táynïy*) for the redundant "passionate" (*strástnïy*).

VARIANT

7–14 In a variant (2368, f. 41ʳ) abounding in agitated enjambments, Pushkin had planned at first to have Tatiana behave like a more ordinary heroine:

> the two friends' greetings she
> 8 does not hear; the tears from her eyes
> are on the point of gushing. Suddenly has fallen
> the poor thing ⟨in a faint⟩; at once
> they carry her out; fussing,
> 12 the crowd of guests ⟨begins to prattle⟩.
> At Eugene everybody looks
> as if accusing him of everything.

XXXI

13 / inwardly / *v dushé svoéy*: "In his soul."

XXXII

4 / pie: The *piróg*, a meat pie or cabbage pie, was an important part of an old-fashioned name-day feast.

7 / blancmanger (pronounced as in French): This almond-milk jelly (an old French and English sweet, not to be confused with our modern "blancmange") might be

artificially colored. Its presence (as well as the presence of the Russian champagne) at Dame Larin's festive table stresses both the old-world style of her household and a comparative meagerness of means.

In Pushkin's short story "The Young Lady Turned Peasant Girl" (1830), the servants of a wealthy squire's household get for dessert "blancmanger, blue, red, and candy-striped."

At big dinners, landscapes in colored blancmanger were the fashion in eighteenth-century England.

8 / Tsïmlyánskoe: A sparkling wine from Tsïmlyanskaya Stanitsa, a Cossack settlement on the Don.

11 / Zizí: Zizi Vulf, Tatiana's name-day mate.

Pushkin's relations with the Osipov family, his country neighbors, are not easily duplicated in the annals of literary amours. During his years of enforced rustication (August, 1824, to September, 1826) at Mihaylovskoe, province of Pskov, and later on visits to the Vulfs in their province-of-Tver lands, he courted five or six members of the clan—in Malinniki, which had belonged to Nikolay Vulf; Pavlovsk, Pavel Vulf's seat, and Bernovo, that of Ivan Vulf.

There was the chatelaine herself, Praskovia Osipov, née Vïndomski (1781–1859), owner of Trigorsk, or Trigorski, or Trigorskoe, near Pushkin's place, in the province of Pskov, and of Malinniki, in the province of Tver, some twenty-five miles from Staritsa; she had lost two husbands, Nikolay Vulf (d. 1813) and Ivan Osipov (d. 1822). Her signature, in Russian French, reads consecutively: Prascovie de Windomsky, Prascovie Woulff, and Prascovie d'Ossipoff. Whether or not Pushkin conducted an intrigue with her is not clear, but there seems to be no doubt of her being in love with him.

There was Zina, or Zizi, otherwise Euphrosine, or

Euphrasie, Frenchified forms of Evpraksia, Eupraxia, or
Eufraxia—Zizi Vulf (1809–83), youngest daughter of
Mme Osipov. Pushkin made fugitive verses for her, and
from Mihaylóvskoe wrote to her brother in St. Petersburg
in late October, 1824, that he, Aleksandr Pushkin, aged
twenty-five, and she, Zizi, aged fifteen, had the same
waist measurements. To judge by a preserved silhouette,
she was on the plump side at the time, and the compari-
son in Five : XXXII to a slim wineglass is meant as a joke. *
He was her lover briefly in 1829. She married Baron
Vrevski in 1831. St. Eufraxia is honored on St. Tatiana's
Day, and Zizi's shade appears at the Larins' name-day
dinner of the fictitious "Jan. 12, 1821," two days before
Lenski's fictitious death. The real Zina Vrevski, during
a visit to St. Petersburg, dined on Jan. 26, 1837, with
Pushkin and her sister, on the eve of *his* mortal duel.

There was Zizi's elder sister, Anna, Annette Vulf
(1799–1857), who passionately and faithfully adored our
poet, and whom our poet deliberately and cynically de-
bauched in 1825. Her mother whisked her away in the
beginning of February, 1826, at the peak of the romance.
Annette's letters to Pushkin, in 1826, from Malinniki
are heart-rending.

There was another Anna, Netty Vulf, daughter of
Ivan Vulf, and cousin of Annette and Zizi. She is the
"tender, languorous, hysterical Netty" of a later letter
from Pushkin to Annette's and Zizi's brother, Aleksey.

There was Aline, Aleksandra Osipov, Mme Osipov's
stepdaughter, daughter of her second husband from a
previous marriage (and mistress of Aleksey Vulf, 1805–
81, rake and diarist), later Bekleshov. Pushkin's passion
for her ran parallel to the above-mentioned loves but
flourished especially in the autumns of 1828 and 1829,
during visits to the Vulf country places.

_____

*See also vol. 3, p. 310.

And, finally, there was Mme Osipov's niece, Anna Kern (1800–79), daughter of Pyotr Poltoratski and Nikolay Vulf's sister. Anna's first husband, whom she married as a very young girl, was Major General Ermolay Kern (Cairn, 1765–1841). Pushkin courted her in vain during her visits to Trigorskoe in the summer of 1825. Soon after this she had an intrigue with her cousin Aleksey Vulf, and only in February, 1828, in Petersburg, did she become, technically, Pushkin's mistress.

11 / *kristál*: Meaning here "flute glass of crystal."

VARIANT

11–12 The draft (2370, f. 40ᵛ) alludes not to Zina Vulf, but presumably to Eliza Vorontsov:

> Liza, friend of my soul,
> the rival of French fashion plates.

XXXIII, XXXIV

Observe the agitated enjambments in these two stanzas.

XXXV

3 / luscious hive / *lákomogo úl'ya* [gen.]: *Lakomïy kusok* is a "relishing morsel." The adjective means "dainty," "delicious," "attractive to the taste," "sapid," "saporous." I have been influenced in my choice by the "luscious cells" in Thomas Hood's *Ode: Autumn* (1823), l. 34.

6 / neighbor in front of neighbor / *Soséd . . . pered sosédom*: *Sosed* is used here and elsewhere in the sense of "country neighbor," owner of land in the same area.

7 / have settled / *Podséli*: The verb *podsest'*, as used here,

conveys both the idea of drawing up to a certain point
and sitting down there. See Seven : XLIX : 11, *Knéy* . . .
podsél, "[moved over to her and] sat down beside her."

11 / omber: A card game of Spanish origin, popular in
Europe in the seventeenth and eighteenth centuries. It
is often mentioned in satirical verse. See Vasiliy May-
kov's *The Omber Player* (*Igrok Lombera*), a poem in
three cantos. (See my n. to Eight : Ia : 3.)

VARIANT

11–12 In the draft (2370, f. 39ᵛ) "boston and *kvíntich*" lure
the elderly guests, and "the rapid écarté" succeeds the
older games.

For the game of boston, see n. to One : XXXVIII : 11.
Ecarté does not need elucidation, and *kvintich* is pre-
sumably an ancestor of *vint,* the common Russian card
game of later decades. Cf. "quint," a sequence of five
cards of the same suit, in piquet.

XXXVI

1 / rubbers / *róbertov* [gen. pl. of *robert*]: The origin of the
English word is obscure; as used in relation to other
games and sports, it goes back to the sixteenth century.
In Pushkin's time the French said *robre,* and the Ger-
mans *Robber.* The mysterious *t*—which suggests a false
derivation for the Russian eighteenth-century *robert*—
is, I think, really owing to the Dutch corruption of
"rubber": *een robbertje whisten.*

8 / Bréguet: See n. to One : XV : 13.

13 "Homer" is *Omír* in old-fashioned poetic Russian. Else-
where our poet uses the correct Russian *Gomér.* Earlier

(1818–20) he had completely Gallicized the name by writing it *Omér*. See *Ruslan and Lyudmila*, can. IV, ll. 147–53:

> I'm not Omér; in lofty verses
> he may alone sing the repasts
> of Grecian troops,
> the clink and foam of wine cups deep.
> Parny I much prefer to follow
> and have my casual lyre extol
> a naked shape in the night's darkness.

The "divine" is also a Gallicism, and the reference to Homer's feasts is a literary commonplace. Cf. Byron, *Don Juan*, XV, LXII, 3–6:

> . . . but what Muse since Homer's able
>   (His feasts are not the worst part of his works)
> To draw up in array a single day-bill
>   Of modern dinners? . . .

And Voltaire, *La Pucelle*, can. X:

> . . . tous ces auteurs divins,
>   . . . ce bavard Homère
>
> .   .   .   .
>
> Ne manquent point . . .
> L'occasion de parler d'un repas.

If, as it is generally assumed, the mysterious Greek poet Homer flourished about the ninth century B.C., Pushkin erred by four centuries, as did most scholars of his day. Unhomerically, but not unwisely, he did not describe the supper in the beginning of Six.

XXXVII, XXXVIII

The following charming two stanzas appeared only in the separate Four and Five edition of 1828. Because of the tender (and really unwarranted) allusion to Istomina (see n. to One : XX : 5–14) Pushkin, a married man by 1833, dropped this stanza and its continuation in the complete editions.

XXXVII

In feasts I'm ready disobediently
with your divinity to grapple;
but magnanimously I do concede
4 that elsewhere you have vanquished me:
your savage heroes,
your irregular battles,
your Cypris, your Zeus,
8 have a great prevalence
over chilly Onegin;
over the drowsy dreariness of fields;
over my I[stomina];
12 o'er our fashionable education.
But Tanya, 'pon my word, is more endearing
than your nasty Helen.

In the corrected draft (2370, ff. 39ʳ, 38ᵛ) there is the following variant of ll. 10–12:

over my *brigadírsha*,
over the dreariness of ⟨northern⟩ fields,
o'er our fashionable education.

Brigadírsha: Mrs. Larin, widow of a *brigadír* (see Two : XXXVI : 13). The term has a slight shade of opprobrium (good-natured here) since the day of Fonvízin's comedy *The Brigadier General* (written 1766, pub. 1786), in which the Brigadier's wife, Akulína, is a tightfisted, ridiculously ignorant woman, heartless toward the serfs, and ready to "endure the spotted fever" (as her son puts it) for money's sake.

XXXVIII

No one will even argue here,
though Menelaus because of Helen

for yet a hundred years cease not
4 to chastise the poor Phrygian region;
though round the worthy Priam,
the assembly of Pergamum's elders,
on sighting her, decide again
8 that Menelaus is right, and Paris right.
As for the battles, just a little
I shall ask you to wait:
kindly read on;
12 do not judge sternly the beginning;
a battle there shall be, I do not lie,
my word of honor I can give.

XXXIX

3, 13 / hall: I do not know if anybody has ever pointed out
the curious difficulty attending the finding of equiva-
lent terms for the parts of a house in different languages.
The Russian word here comes from the German *Saal*
and French *salle*, and has the unique distinction in Rus-
sian of possessing all three genders (*zal*, *zala*, *zalo*). It
means a "reception hall" or "assembly room," differing
from a drawing room (*salon*, *gostinaya*) in being more
spacious, or in the present case "longer," with the furni-
ture (gilt chairs, a grandfather clock, consoles, and so
forth) relegated to wallflower positions and with a
sufficient area of parquet for dancing. It is intermediate
between a music room and a regular ballroom. The
word *zal* is also employed in the sense of theater or
concert hall.

7 / the Paris of surrounding townlets: Instead of this
"Paris" (son of Priam, Aphrodite's champion, Helen's
lover), canceled fair copy reads *Dyupór*, the reference
being to Louis Duport (1781–1853), a first-rate French
dancer, who (says *La Grande Encyclopédie*, vol. XV,
with disgust), "abandonnant l'Opéra, quitta furtive-
ment Paris en 1808, au mépris de ses engagements, pour

se rendre à Saint-Pétersbourg," where he danced successfully till 1812. Pushkin changed *Dyupor* to *Lovlás* before finding *París*—which sounds ambiguous (not so in Russian, the capital of France being *Parizh*).

12 / *Pustyakóvu*: Russian usage with its absence of title does not disclose whether the name refers to a Miss or to a Mrs. Logically, it should be "Miss"; but in XXVI : 1–2, where the Pustyakov pair appears, no daughter is mentioned; and it would satisfy the demands of comedy humor to have disreputable Buyanov whirl away Mr. Trifle's corpulent wife.

*

The draft of this stanza and those of XL–XLV are lost.

XL

3 / *Al'bána*: Albane, the Frenchified form of Albano or Albani. This Francesco Albani, a second-rate Italian painter (1578–1660), was extremely popular in the eighteenth century. Cloying and coy, he specialized in flat mythological scenes with a pseudoclassical slant dear to the Age of Reason, and since he never painted a ball or any other contemporaneous assembly, the explanation of this allusion is either that Pushkin recalled in a retrospective flash some *Vénus procédant à sa toilette*, which may have prompted the simile in One : XXV : 12 (see n.), or else that he selected at random the name of what was then a famous painter. For rococo reasons, French writers of the eighteenth century placed l'Albane beside Raphael (the darling of the nineteenth century) and even called him "l'Anacréon de la peinture." *Phoebus conduisant son char* is still represented by crude prints in the parlors of central-European boardinghouses.

Albano's sad case is one of the most striking examples of fading fame; he is practically never mentioned today; but the references to him in European literature of the eighteenth and early nineteenth centuries are numberless. I can mention only a few:

Gentil-Bernard (1710–75), *L'Art d'aimer*, can. I, ll. 57–58:

> Dans mes tableaux, Albane plus fidèle,
> Peignons l'Amour comme on peint une belle . . .

and ll. 199–202, 205–06, 244:

> Ce sont les jeux des Amours triomphants;
> Albane eût peint ces folâtres enfants:
> L'un, pour servir une flamme secrète,
> Contre un jaloux dirige une lunette;
> .   .   .   .
>
> Tel à sa voix joint un clavier sonore;
> Tel autre esquisse un objet qu'il adore.
> .   .   .   .   .   .
>
> Et dans nos bals, vrais temples de l'Amour . . .

La Harpe (1799), *Lycée, ou Cours de littérature* (the manual Pushkin knew so well), VIII, 189 (1825 edn.), quotes from Voltaire's *Henriade* (1728), can. IX:

> Les folâtres Plaisirs, dans le sein du repos,
> Les Amours enfantins désarmaient ce héros:
> L'un tenait sa cuirasse encor de sang trempée;
> L'autre avait détaché sa redoutable épée,
> Et riait en tenant dans ses débiles mains
> Ce fer, l'appui du trône, et l'effroi des humains . . .

and adds: "Cette touche est de l'Albane . . ."

The same La Harpe, ibid. (1825 edn.), XIII, 560, speaking of Beaumarchais' *Noces de Figaro*, says: "Ce charmant page [Chérubin] entre ces deux charmantes femmes occupées à le déshabiller et à le rhabiller est un tableau de l'Albane" (cf. *EO*, One : XXIII : 4, "is dressed, undressed, and dressed again").

Lebrun, *Odes*, bk. v, no. xii, has:

> D'azur il peint une cabane,
> Et son art, au pinceau d'Albane,
> Prête d'infidèles vernis.

Antoine Lemierre (1723–93), *La Peinture* (1769), can. iii, has:

> La foule des Amours de tous côtés assiège
> L'atelier de l'Albane et celui de Corrège . . .

Hazlitt, "On *Gusto*," in his *Round Table* essays (1817), remarks: "There is a gusto in the colouring of Titian. . . . Rubens makes his flesh-colour like flowers; Albano's is like ivory . . ."

Byron in 1823, speaking of one of the pictures at Norman Abbey, *Don Juan*, XIII, lxxi, 5, has: "Here danced Albano's boys [cupids] . . ."

Casimir Delavigne, *Messéniennes*, ii (*Messéniennes et poésies diverses*, 1823), exclaims:

> Adieu, Corrége, Albane, immortel Phidias;
> Adieu, les arts et le génie!

J. A. Amar, in an "Avertissement" to the 1820 edn. of the *Œuvres* of Jean Baptiste Rousseau, author of tedious odes and bewigged cantatas, describes the latter as "exécutés avec le pinceau de l'Albane ou du Corrège."

Pushkin himself, in his Frenchified youth, alluded several times to "l'Albane." In *The Monk* (1813), can. iii, there is the passage:

> With a firm hand I would have seized a brush
> and having downed a bumper of champagne,
> I would have set my ardent head to work
> like Titian or the passionate Alban
> to represent Natalia's charms. . . .

In the third quatrain of the tetrametric *To a Painter* (to his schoolmate Illichevski; 1815), young Pushkin had:

> Around the slender waist of Hebe
> the zone of Venus bind;
> with Alban's secret charm
> surround my queen [another schoolmate's sister,
>   Katerina Bakunin].

In *The Dream* (1816), one of his very first poems of real worth (see n. to Four : XXXV : 3–4), Pushkin clamors for "Alban's tender brush to depict love and youth" (l. 200).

XLI

1–3 / *bezúmnïy . . . vál'sa víhor'*: In *Justification* (*Opravdanie*, 1824), a tetrametric poem of forty lines, Baratïnski had depicted, in his usual awkward but eloquent manner, the "mad waltz" wherein he would whirl various nymphs:

> Brushing their perfumed curls
> with my face, clasping with an avid hand
>   [*zhádnoy dlán'yu*]
> their graceful waists . . .

See also the dreadful Sainte-Beuve performance, in *Vie, poésies et pensées de Joseph Delorme* (1829), in n. to One : XXXVIII : 3–4.

11–12 / *Spustyá minútï dvé, potóm | Vnov' s néyu vál's on prodolzháet*: I have attempted to reproduce the tautological elements of this poor passage. "A couple of minutes later he goes on waltzing with her" was what our poet *intended* to say.

14 / *sóbstvennïm glazám*: A common Gallicism (*ses propres yeux*) instead of the correct *svoim glazam*, "his own eyes."

XLII

8 / in . . . towns / *v gorodáh*: I suggest that this is a misprint for *v gorodkáh*, "in small towns."

XLIII

Ll. 1–4 are in the fair copy. Ll. 5–14 were published in
the 1828 edn. The whole stanza was omitted in the 1833
and 1837 edns.

> As the whip drives in manège sand
> the frisky fillies on the longe,
> the men, in a tumultuous ring,
> 4 have driven, jerked the maidens:
> the hobs, the spurs of Petushkóv
> (retired chancery clerk)
> resound. Buyanov's heel
> 8 breaks verily the floor around.
> Crash, stamping, rumble come in turn,
> the deeper in the woods, the more the logs.
> Crack hoofers now take over;
> 12 they all but plunge into a squat-jig.
> Ah, easy, easy! Heels
> will crush the ladies' toes!

6 / *kantselyarísta*: Instead of the expected *kavalerísta*,
"cavalryman."

10 / woods . . . logs: "The deeper you go into a wood, the
more logs there are," says a Russian proverb, inept as
all proverbs are, but hitting the line here with just the
right crack. Pushkin is stressing the barbarous vulgarity
of a provincial ball.

XLIV

1 See XXVI : 9–11 and note to it.

3 / Deft: It will be noticed how nicely the "deftly" at the
end of XV : 1 is echoed by the "deft" here.

9–10 In a short poem written in Kishinev, *To a Greek Lady*
(Calypso Polychroni, who was said to have been Byron's

mistress), Pushkin had, in 1822, used a similar intonation:

> 23 Unconsciously a tremor started
> in your conceited breast,
> and you, leaning upon his shoulder . . .
> no, no, my dear, the jealous dream's
> 27 flame I don't wish to nourish . . . .

XLV

It is amusing to examine what live Byron was doing while Pushkin's creature danced, dreamed, died:

On Jan. 12, 1821, O.S. (Jan. 24, N.S.), while Lenski in northwestern Russia went to his last ball, Byron in Ravenna, Italy, noted in his diary: ". . . met some masques in the Corso . . . they dance and sing and make merry, 'for tomorrow they may die.' "

Next evening, Jan. 13 (Jan. 25, N.S.), while Lenski was writing his last elegy, Byron noted: "One day more is over . . . but 'which is best, life or death, the gods only know,' as Socrates said to his judges . . ."

And Jan. 14 (Jan. 26, N.S.), the day Lenski and Onegin were having their duel, Byron jotted down: "Rode—fired pistols—good shooting."

This will probably remain the classical case of life's playing up to art.

11 / *trébuet konyá*: I would have understood this as "calls for his horse," "orders his horse to be brought out," if it were not more likely that Lenski and Onegin had come to the party in the latter's sleigh, and now the former has to borrow a mount from the Larins' stable.

14 The separate 1828 edn. of Four and Five gives:

> *Kak ráz reshát sud'bú egó.*
> shall adequately solve his fate.

But in order to avoid the fusion of *kak raz* ("just in the right way" or "time") with the next word (*reshat*), Pushkin, in the errata appended two months later to Six, altered the line to:

> *Vdrug razreshát sud'bú egó.*
> shall in a trice resolve his fate.

COMMENTARY TO *EUGENE ONEGIN*

PART 2

Chapter Six

This is a fragmentary quotation (ll. 49 and 51) from Petrarch's *In vita di Laura*, Canzone XXVIII, beginning "O aspettata in ciel beata e bella." With l. 50, which Pushkin omitted, the passage reads:

> Là sotto i giorni nubilosi e brevi,
> Nemica naturalmente di pace,
> Nasce una gente, a cui 'l morir non dole.

> There, beneath days misty and brief,
> inimical to peace by nature,
> a race is born t'whom dying is not painful.

I

| 1 *Zamétiv, chto Vladímir skrílsya*: "Having noticed that Vladimir had withdrawn." But this does not retain the "disappearance" in *skrílsya*.

10–12 Cf. Robert Lyall, *The Character of the Russians, and a Detailed History of Moscow* (London, 1823), pp. liii–liv, lvii:

A *fête* was to be given by Madame [Poltoratski], the mother of the gentleman whom I accompanied . . . on

the Sunday subsequent to our arrival at that estate [Gru-
zino, near Torzhok]. Throughout the Saturday, carriages
filled with nobles continued to arrive from time to time.
. . . Although the house of Madame [Poltoratski] was of
considerable size, it was matter of astonishment to me,
where the whole party, amounting to nearly fifty indi-
viduals, were to find rooms for their accommodation in
the night. . . . Conversation and cards were the evening
amusements, and at 11 o'clock an elegant supper was
served up, and at its conclusion, a scene of bustle and con-
fusion followed which riveted my attention. The dining-
room, the drawing-room, the hall, the whole suit of
apartments, in which we had passed the evening, were
converted into bed-rooms. . . . The number of bed-steads
. . . [being] insufficient . . . a number of beds were im-
mediately arranged on the floor, some upon chairs. . . .

I made a *morning visit about eleven o'clock* on the follow-
ing day, to one of the houses, in which were lodged some
of my male acquaintances. . . . The hall and the drawing-
room were literally a barracks;—sofas, divans, and chairs
put together, covered with beds, and their fatigued or
lazy tenants . . . half a dozen noblemen . . . [in one such
den] wrapped up in splendid silk night-gowns, some lying
down, some sitting up in bed, some drinking coffee and
tea, and smoking tobacco, amidst mephitic air, and sur-
rounded by chamber utensils, and other disagreeable
trumpery, formed a curious motley association.

II

1–3 The inimitable Elton has:

> All quiet! In the parlour snorting
> Was heard the ponderous Pustyakov,
> With ponderous better-half consorting . . .

3 / better half / *polovínoy* [instr.]: A Gallicism, *moitié*.
French poets of the *sublime*, or *cheville*, school have used
the term *moitié* in perfectly serious verse. Voltaire has
somewhere in the *Henriade*: "Et leurs tristes moitiés,
compagnes de leurs pas" ("and their sad halves, com-
panions of their steps").

8 / underwaistcoat: The term used by Pushkin is *fufáyka*, which comes, I suppose, from the German *Futterhemd*. It corresponds to the French *camisole de laine* or *gilet de flanelle*. The eighteenth-century English word I have chosen is the *gilet de dessous* of c. 1800. In my time, *fufáyka* was used mainly in the sense of "jersey" or "sweater," but with the epithet *natel'naya* ("next the skin") it might stand for "undershirt" or "T shirt." I see Triquet as remaining in his flannel vest for the night.

11 / *Odná pechál'no*: I suspect that this should be *Odna, pechal'na*, "alone, sad."

14 "Field," *póle*, is used in the sense of "open country." The same intonation occurs in Pushkin's earlier long poem *The Gypsies* (*Tsïganï*), ll. 26–29:

> In one tent an old man sleeps not:
> before the coals he sits
>
> .   .   .   .
>
> and into the far field he looks . . .

III

8–9 In a Russian version of can. XXIII, octaves C–CXII, of Ariosto's *Orlando furioso* (or, rather, of the French version, *Roland furieux*), composed by Pushkin in 1826 (see my n. to One : LIV : 4), our poet rendered a passage from the French ("son cœur se glace: il lui semble qu'une main froide le lui presse") by the tetrametric lines:

> it is as if a chilly hand
> compressed his heart in awful fashion . . .

Strange migrations and transmigrations!

The Italian text reads (can. XXIII, octave CXI, 6):

> Stringersi il cor sentia con fredda mano . . .

Lodovico Ariosto (1474–1533) began this story of knightly amours in 1505 and worked on it for eleven years. The first edition (1516) contains forty and the 1532 edn. forty-six cantos (4842 octaves). A French gentleman of parts, Louis Elisabeth de La Vergne, Comte de Tressan (1705–83), took three months to paraphrase in easy French prose the elaborate melodies of the divine Lodovico. Although it was preceded by several much more faithful versions, it was Tressan's *Roland furieux*, "poème héroïque de l'Arioste" (1780), that went through a multitude of more or less revised editions (e.g., Pannelier, 1823) throughout the nineteenth century.

IV

3 / Five versts from Krasnogórie: *Anglice*, "Three miles from Fairhill." In Slavic place names the idea of *krasnïy*, "beautiful," "festive," is sometimes allied to the idea of *krasnïy* as expressing anciently the live magic of fire, springtime, and so on; and from *krasnïy*, "flamelike," there always has been an easy step to *krasnïy*, "red," its usual meaning today. Whether Pushkin desired it or not, the not-uncommon name of Lenski's countryseat has more links with myths and enchantments than matter-of-fact "Fairhill" would have. Such combinations as Krasnaya Gorka ("Bright Hillock") are associated not only with the idea of vivid natural beauty (or, specifically, with the color of red stone, red sand, red pine bark), but also with some of those enthusiastic but repetitious May-Day pagan rites and Floralian games that are so dull to read about in anthropological works.

6 / *V filosofícheskoy pustíne*: *Pustïnya* is the *désert* of French pseudoclassicism. It is also *retraite*. Cf. Marmontel, "La Leçon du Malheur," in *Contes moraux*: "Tout le monde connaît la retraite philosophique qu'il s'était faite au bord de la Seine."

7 / Zarétski: Some amateurs of prototype wrongly see in this character a skit on Fyodor Tolstoy (see nn. to Four : XIX : 5 and Six : VI : 5–8).

10 / Cf. Two : XXXVI : 9.

13 A note in Lerner* sent me to a sentence of Voltaire's *Candide* (1759), ch. 30: "Il n'y eut pas jusqu'à frère Giro-flée qui ne rendît service; il fut un très bon menuisier, et même devint honnête homme . . ."

(Incidentally, another good example of what I mean by sloppy "translation" is John Butt's rendering of this passage in the Penguin Books execrable English para-phrase (1947) of *Candide*: "No one refused to work, not even Brother Giroflée, who was [instead of "who turned out to be"] a good carpenter [instead of "worker in wood"], and thus [instead of "even"] became an honest [instead of "honorable"] man.")

Chizhevski (p. 267) draws here a completely erroneous analogy with Gogol's use of "even" (*dazhe*) in "The Carrick" (*Shinel'*).

14 / *Tak ispravlyáetsya nash vék*: I take *vek* to mean here "epoch" rather than "life span" (as, for instance, in Eight : X : 13); neither, however, makes more than trivial sense. The line, in fact, is a clumsy Gallicism. Cf. Voltaire, footnote of 1768 to *La Guerre civile de Genève*, begin-ning of can. IV: "Observez, cher lecteur, combien le siècle se perfectionne."

V

4 / *V pyatí sazhényah*: "At five sagenes." A sagene is seven feet, 2.134 meters, 2.33 yards. A yard in measuring dis-tances is one pace, and twelve paces was a popular range

*Zven'ya, no. 5 (1935), p. 77.

7

in pistol duels. Byron (according to his *Life* by Moore, p. 319) could snuff out a candle with a pistol-shot at the distance of twenty paces.

9 / swine drunk / *Kak zyúzya p'yánïy*: "Soused as a swine." In Russian, *zyuzya* has several meanings besides "pig," one of which is exactly a "soused" or "drunk" person, and another a "blubbery" person. The English noun "souse" also means a pickled pig and may have come from L. *sal*, "salt," while the verb may have been influenced by the Fr. *saoûl*, which comes from L. *satietas*. *Zyuzya* sounds as if it came directly from *sus*, Latin for "pig," but is probably a product of suctorial onomatopoeia (cf. *susurrus*). Cf. "as drunk as David's sow" (Ray's *Proverbs*, 1670).

Denis Davïdov uses a similar locution (*kak zyuzya natyanusya*, "I shall suck up my fill," "I shall get as tight as a sow") in his brilliant poem *The Decisive Evening* (three Alexandrine quatrains, c. 1818).

11 The allusion is to the Roman general Marcus Atilius Regulus (d. c. 250 B.C.), hero of the first Punic War. After his defeat by the Carthaginians he was dispatched by his captors to Rome with harsh terms of peace. There he insisted instead that the war be continued. Although he knew that he would pay for this with his life, he returned into captivity as he had promised to do.

13 / Véry's: Café Véry, an old café-restaurant in Paris, originally (1805–17) on the Terrasse des Feuillants, in the Jardin des Tuileries, and famous, especially among military men, for its exceptionally fine cuisine. I cannot understand why Captain Jesse, in his *Brummell*, writes "Vérey," and why Spalding (followed by Elton) writes "Verrey." Anthelme Brillat-Savarin's *Physiologie du goût* (1825) mentions the wonderful *entrées truffées*

served by the brothers Véry. In her journal (1818), *Passages from my Autobiography* (London, 1859), Sydney, Lady Morgan, who flaunts some fluent but also atrocious French (full of mistakes and of idioms completely out of idiomatic focus), mentions (p. 52) being taken "to dine at Vérey's, aux jardins des Tuileries."

VI

5–8 These lines may well be a faint echo of what our poet had intended to say, but did not, about Fyodor Tolstoy, against whom he had fumed for six years on account of the rumors he accused that commonplace babbler and rake of spreading about him (see nn. to Four : XIX : 5).

VII

4 / with babble / *vran'yóm*: For a discussion of the word *vrat'* in the rakish cant of the time, see my n. to Four : XIX : 5.

5 "Autres temps, autres mœurs"—French proverb.

9 Among some fifty college students whom I once happened to ask (in planned illustration of the incredible ignorance concerning natural objects that characterizes young Americans of today) the name of the tree, an American elm, that they could see through the classroom windows, none was able to identify it: some hesitantly suggested it might be an oak, others were silent; one, a girl, said she guessed it was just a shade tree. The translator, when tackling botanical names in his author, should try to be more precise.

In *EO*, Six : VII, Pushkin describes his reformed rake, Zaretski, as having retired to the country and found refuge or shelter (*ukrívshis'*) under certain plants. The line to be analyzed goes thus:

> *Pod sén' cheryómuh i akátsiy . . .*

The translation of *pod* ("beneath," "under") *sen'* (the overhead shelter provided by anything in the way of covert, roof, pend, arch, eaves, "leafy ceil," "sylvan shed," screen, canopy, scug, metaphorical wing, and so forth) presents only a minor difficulty; true, it is an irritating one, because *pod sen'* (acc. sing.), *pod sen'yu* (instr. sing.), and other formulas founded on *sen'* (fem. sing.) and *seni* (pl.; not to be confused with the well-known word for "hall" or "vestibule") are metrically very tractable and therefore too much favored by Russian poets for their translator's comfort. *Sen'* cannot always be rendered in English by any one word. The specious "shade" does not lure the incorruptible literalist, for the important reason that its exact Russian equivalent, *ten'*, in phrases similar to those given above is not quite synonymous with *sen'*, and in fact may occur with it in the same passage as a sheepish rhyme. However, the sensuous meaning of *sen'* is so evanescent that in many instances—of which this is one—none should deem it a crime if "beneath" or "under" be used instead of "beneath the shed" (see Collins, *Ode to Evening*, l. 49, in Dodsley's *Collection* of 1748) or "in the shelter." But let us return to the passage under consideration:

Pod sén' cheryómuh i akátsiy . . .

The bower alluded to in the line under discussion is formed by two kinds of shrubs or trees. Do their mere names suggest anything to the Russian reader? We all know that the popular name of a plant may strike the imagination differently in different languages; its stress may be on color in one country and on structure in another; it may have beautiful classical connotations; it may be redolent of unbelievable Floridas; it may contain a honeydrop as a residue of the cumulative romantic sense bestowed upon it by generations of elegiasts; it may be, in floral disguise, a plaque commemorating (like the dahlia) the name of an old botanist or (like the camellia) that of a roving Jesuit back from Luzon. The words *cheryomuh* and *akatsiy* (both fem. gen. pl.) convey to the Russian mind two flowery masses and what may be termed a stylized blend of aromas, one part of which, as will presently be shown, is artificial. I do not think that it is the translator's duty to trouble much about the rendering of associations in his text, but he should explain them in his notes. It is certainly a pity that the euphonious French name of some plant, say, *l'alidore* (to invent one), with its evocations of love philters and auroral mists, should become in England hog's wart (because of the singular form of its flowers), or cotton bud (because of the texture of its young leaves), or parson's button (allusion untraceable). But unless a name of that kind might puzzle or mislead the reader by referring to a dozen different plants (and then the Latin specific name should be given), the translator is entitled to use any available term as long as it is exact.

Dictionaries usually translate *cheryomuha* as "bird cherry," which is so vague as to be practically meaningless. Specifically, *cheryomuha* is the "racemose old-world bird cherry," Fr. *putier racémeux, Padus racemosa* Schneider. The Russian word, with its fluffy and dreamy syllables, admirably suits this beautiful tree, distinguished by its long racemes of flowers, giving the whole of it, when in bloom, a gentle pendulous appearance. A common and popular woodland plant in Russia, it is equally at home among the riverside alders and on the pine barren; its creamy-white, musky, Maytime bloom is associated in Russian hearts with the poetical emotions of youth. This racemose bird cherry lacks such a specific English designation (it has a few generic ones, all of them either uncouth or homonymous, or both) as would be neither as pedantic nor as irresponsible as the nonsense names that harmful drudges carefully transport from one Russian-English dictionary to another. At one time I followed the usually reliable Dahl's *Dictionary* in calling the tree "mahaleb," which proves to be, however, another plant altogether. Later I coined the term "musk cherry," which renders rather well the sound of *cheryomuha* and the fragrance of its bloom, but unfortunately evokes a taste that is not characteristic of its small, grainy, black fruit. I now formally introduce the simple and euphonious "racemosa" used as a noun and rhyming with "mimosa."

We now turn to its companion, *akatsiya*, and the question is: should the translator take the name of a plant at its face value (sticking to his dictionary, which says that *akatsiya* is "acacia") or should he find out what the word really means, in its contextual habitat, within the terms of a certain imagined place and in the light of a certain literary device? I advocate following the second course.

While racemosas grow wild throughout the habitat of our novel (northwestern and central Russia), the true acacia does not. The latter is a beautiful and useful genus of tropical mimosaceous tree, of which one, the Australian *A. dealbata* F.v.M., the silver wattle of nurserymen, is acclimatized in coastal Caucasia: it used to be sold—after Pushkin's time—as a *mimoza* by St. Petersburg florists. Neither is the *akatsiya* of our text the "locust" of one translator, although it is true that to southern Russians *belaya akatsiya* ("white acacia") means only one thing, the sweetly perfumed American *Robinia pseudoacacia* Linn., cultivated in the Ukraine and sung by hundreds of Odessa rhymesters. It is neither the mimosa nor the false acacia. What, then, is the *akatsiya* of our text? It is quite certainly a yellow-flowering *Caragana* species, namely *C. arborescens* Lam., imported from Asia and cultivated in gentlemen's bowers and along garden alleys in northern Russia. French tutors called it "l'acacia de Sibérie"; little boys would slit open its dark beanlet in a certain way and produce a nasty blare by blowing into it between their cupped hands. But what really settles the identity of the plant with absolute certainty is the following consideration. Pushkin's line is a parody of two passages in a poem entitled *Bower of Muses* (*Besedka Muz*, 1817), by Batyushkov, minor poet and literary pioneer, to whose idiom Pushkin owed at least as much as he did to the style of Karamzin and Zhukovski. The poem, which is written in free, or fable, iambics—i.e., iambics of varied length —begins:

> In the shade of milky racemosas
> and golden-glistening pea trees [*akátsiy*] . . .

and closes with:

> carefree as is the child of ever carefree Graces,
> someday he'll come to sigh in the dense shelter
>   of his racemosas and pea trees.

The epithet in the second line of the poem suits the bright flower of *Caragana* well and does not suit the white blossoms of the false acacia at all. Consequently, the correct way to translate *EO*, Six : VII : 9, is:

> beneath the racemosas and the pea trees

—leaving other trees to those noble paraphrasts whom Sir John Denham praised three centuries ago, in his address to another worthy, Sir Richard Fanshawe (see Dryden's Preface to *Ovid's Epistles*, 1680):

> That servile path thou nobly do'st decline,
> Of tracing word by word and Line by Line . . .

*

The first edition of Batyushkov's works, in two consecutive volumes, came out in St. Petersburg, 1817, under the title *Essays* [*Opïtï*] *in Verse and Prose*. Konstantin

Commentary

Batyushkov was born in 1787. His first published poem,
Mechta, was composed in 1802, his last, a little master-
piece, in 1821 (or early in 1824, during a lucid interval,
after reading the latest edition of Zhukovski's poems—
according to Aleksandr Turgenev):

> Do you recall the cry
> Of gray Melchizedek when he prepared to die?
> Man, he exclaimed, is born a slave; a slave
> He must descend into the grave,
> And Death will hardly tell him why
> He haunts the magic vale of tears,
> Suffers and weeps, endures and disappears.

In 1822, Batyushkov attempted to take his own life.
He died in 1855, after thirty-three years of insanity.

In his brief heyday of creative endeavor, Batyushkov
had translated Gresset, Parny, Boileau, and Tasso and
written in the style of his favorite poets. He and Zhukov-
ski were the predecessors of Pushkin, and in our poet's
youth, Batyushkov was his best-loved Russian master.
Harmony and precision—these were the literary virtues
Pushkin learned from both, although even his boyish
verses were more vivid and vigorous than those of his
teachers. Later he was critical of Batyushkov, and left
some interesting notes in the margin of the *Essays*; but
in *Eugene Onegin* there still echoes something of Ba-
tyushkov's new-found fluency, certain predilections of
idiom and various improved characteristics of his style.

I notice that his name was given four syllables (Bá-ty-
úsh-kov) by the only English poet (a very minor one)
who mentions him, namely Bernard Barton, in some
stanzas (1824) addressed to John Bowring, who trans-
lated Batyushkov for his Russian anthology (st. III):

> Derzhavin's noble numbers, soaring high,
>   Replete with inspiration's genuine force,
> And Batiushkov's milder melody,
>   Warm from domestic pleasure's sweetest source.

12 / plants cabbages like Horace: Chizhevski at this point
wonders why Horace is made to plant cabbages. Actually,
this is a common Gallicism: *planter des (ses) choux,*
"to grow cabbages," meaning "to rusticate." But quite
apart from this, Horace did have a green thumb. The
generalized plain garden vegetable *olus* or *holus,* which
may include *brassica,* cabbage, is mentioned in *Satires,*
bk. II, no. I, 74, and bk. II, no. VI, 64 (see n. to motto of
EO, Two); and *Epistles,* bk. I, no. XVII, 13. And there is
a specific reference to *caule* in *Satires,* bk. II, no. IV, 15,
cabbages or cabbage stalks (or "coleworts," as David
Watson has it) "growing sweeter on parched soil than
in suburban gardens."

A similar, and possibly prototypical, locution in
French, *planter* (or *cultiver*) *ses laitues (à Salone),* al-
ludes to a letter that the retired Roman emperor
Diocletian wrote from Salona (in Dalmatia) to his col-
league, Maximian, wherein he rates the pleasure of
raising vegetables with his own hands higher than any
delights of political power.

VIII

2 / heart in him / *sérdtsa* [gen.] *v nyóm*: "Heart" is taken
here as meaning the seat of moral virtues such as gen-
erosity, sensibility, and integrity, all of which Zaretski
lacked. Cf. "man of heart," *homme de cœur.* A little
further, "heart" (*serdtse*) is employed in the Russian
sense of "ire" (Lenski's *mladóe sérdtse,* XI : 4). The posi-
tion of the chess pieces now arrived at by Pushkin is in-
consistent with the plan behind the first moves of the
game. We could make ourselves believe that the moody
beau might strike up a friendship with poetical Lenski
(replacing, as it were, the narrator in Onegin's af-
fections), but Zaretski, who after all is but another edi-
tion of Buyanov, while displaying all the traits of the

rural "scum" criticized by Onegin, seems hardly suitable for him as a crony. On the other hand, Onegin's intimate knowledge and exaggerated fears of the man's libelous wit are absolutely necessary to the plot.

11 / with gaze atwinkle / *osklábya vzór*: The verb *osklabit'sya*, seldom used today, would be more suggestive of a fleering, or smirking, or grinning, or *goguenard* look than of the kind of smile Pushkin has, I think, in view here.

IX

4 / *Zval . . . na duél'*: Challenged his friend to a duel, called upon his friend for a hostile meeting. The *zval* is a Gallicism, *appeler en duel, appeler en combat singulier*.

In modern Russia, where little remains of the idea of honor—pure personal honor (I am not speaking of Stahanovets competition, political touchiness, or nationalistic *gonor*)—readers, if not accepting passively the Lenski-Onegin duel in terms of some curious "feodal" legend or operatic libretto, are puzzled by its cause and baffled by its details. Actually, not only was a gentleman of 1820, anywhere in the civilized world, perfectly justified in challenging to a duel another gentleman who had behaved in regard to him and his fiancée as Onegin had in regard to Lenski at the Larin ball, but it is indeed a wonder that young Lenski had had enough self-control not to send Onegin a cartel of defiance (*lettre d'appel*) immediately after the latter's vulgar remarks about mediocre Madonnas and round moons half a year earlier. Lenski's course of action, far from being a temperamental extravaganza, is the only logical course an honorable man could have taken in that set in those times; it is Onegin who behaves oddly (i.e., out of tune with the mentality given him by his maker in previous chapters),

16

when he not only accepts the challenge but fires first and shoots to kill. It should be remembered that a gentleman's honor was purified not so much by his own fire as by his coolly enduring that of his adversary (see nn. to XXVIII : 7 and 14).

X

8 / At eighteen: See Two : X : 14, "not quite eighteen." How old was Lenski? Surely, not seventeen to eighteen, as suggested in Six, when his fiery recklessness in calling out Onegin is pronounced excusable in the case of an eighteen-year-old dreamer; but the age datum sounds as theoretical as the reference in Four to a thirteen-year-old girl, in the generalities leading to Onegin's attitude toward Tatiana (who is seventeen). Although it was not uncommon for gifted boys to be sent to foreign universities at fourteen or fifteen (on the other hand, we have Adolphe, in Constant's novel, opening it with the words: "Je venais de finir à vingt-deux ans mes études à l'université de Göttingue"), it sounds highly unlikely that Lenski at eighteen would have been on the point of marrying Olga (who was sixteen); our wealthy young landowner seems definitely to have reached or to be about to reach his majority; I do not think he could be more than five or six years younger than Onegin (who would be twenty-six in the spring of 1821).

XI

12 / *I vót—obshchéstvennoe mnén'e*: The first of three references in *EO* (see Seven : third motto and Eight : XIII : 14) to *Woe from Wit* (*Gore ot uma*), a four-act comedy in fable iambics—i.e., freely rhymed iambic lines of varying length (from one syllable to thirteen)— by Aleksandr Griboedov (1795–1829). The quoted line is Chatski's speech (IV, x, 286):

17

> Fools have believed it, they tell others,
> old dames at once sound the alarm,
> and here it is—public opinion!

This was unpublished at the time of Pushkin's inserting it in this stanza (end of 1826). Only scenes vii–x of Act I and the whole of Act III had come out—in Bulgarin's collection *The Russian Thalia* ("a present for the amatores and amatrices of the patrial theater"), mid-December, 1824 (and were reviewed at the same time as *EO*, Chapter One). The publication of the complete play was for a long time deferred by whimsical censorship. Planned by its author as early as 1818, actually begun in 1822, and finished in 1824, this work of genius, strikingly superior to the author's first theatrical pieces, was familiar to Pushkin from one of the many manuscript copies in circulation, owing to the clerical activities of Griboedov's friend, the playwright Zhandr (Gendre), and the latter's copyists. One of the few friends who visited the Mihaylovskoe exile was his former schoolmate, Ivan Pushchin. He arrived on Jan. 11, 1825, on the eve of Tatiana's (and Euphraxia's) day, bringing Pushkin one of these transcripts of Griboedov's comedy, and left after midnight. By that date our poet had reached at least *EO*, Four : XXVII. A year later, in Six : XI : 12, he quoted the line from *Gore ot uma*.

The first edition of the whole play, with cuts, came out in Moscow posthumously in 1833; but parts of Act I had been staged in Petersburg in 1829, and there had been other fragmentary performances before the first more or less complete one given Jan. 26, 1831. The fate of Russian letters seems to have timed things in such a way as to have the two greatest verse masterpieces in Russian appear in print simultaneously.

13 / Honor's mainspring, our idol: And see XXVIII : 14, "false shame" (*fausse honte*). A literary commonplace of the time. Cf. Steele, *The Spectator*, no. 84 (June 6, 1711):

. . . by the Force of a Tyrant Custom, which is mis-named a Point of Honour, the Duellist kills his Friend whom he loves. . . . Shame is the greatest of all Evils . . .

and Cowper, *Conversation* (in *Poems*, 1782), ll. 181–82:

> The fear of tyrant custom, and the fear
> Lest fops should censure us, and fools should sneer.

(*Conversation* is a didactic piece 908 ll. long, with a section, ll. 163–202, devoted to dueling, in which Cowper suggests that matters of honor be settled by fist fights.) We have had "fashion, our tyrant" at a less serious occasion in Five : XLII : 13.

XII

3 / grandiloquent neighbor / *soséd velerechívïy*: I notice that Zaretski was linked up in Pushkin's mind with the hero of Vasiliy Pushkin's *The Dangerous Neighbor* (see n. to Five : XXVI : 9), Buyanov making a speech at the bordello (l. 58):

> *Ni s mésta—prodolzhál soséd velerechívïy . . .*
> "Stir not," went on the grandiloquent neighbor . . .

10 A curious echo of Tatiana's Letter (l. 60) and her consultation of the dream book (Five : XXIV : 9–10).

13 / *Vzvestí drug ná druga kurók*: Note the shift of accent onto the *na* ("on," "at").

XIII

5 / gave up / *Mahnúl rukóyu*: There is one obvious case in which literalism has to yield (and settle for an exhaustive gloss): when the phrase concerns national gestures or facial movements, which become meaningless in accurate English; the Russian gesture of relinquishment that *mahnul rukoy* (or *rukoyu*) conveys is a

one-hand downward flip of weary or hasty dismissal and renouncement. If analyzed in slow motion by the performer, he will see that his right hand, with fingers held rather loose, sketches a half turn from left to right, while at the same time his head makes a slight half turn from right to left. In other words, the gesture really consists of two simultaneous little movements: the hand abandons what it held, or hoped to hold, and the head turns away from the scene of defeat or condemnation.

Now, there is no way to translate *mahnul rukoy* by means of a verb and of the word "hand" or "with hand" so as to render both the loose shake itself and the associations of relinquishment that it has. Of my predecessors, only Miss Radin caught at least the spirit of the thing.

Spalding (1881):

> His watch, the sun in turn he views—
> Finally tost his arms in air
> And lo! he is already there!

Miss Deutsch (1936):

> He marked the time, and presently
> He waved his hand, as one who'd rue it
> And was at Olga's ere he knew it!

Elton (1937):

> Scanned watch, observed the sun; and yet
> Waved hand at last, and soon was quitting,
> And there, amidst his neighbours, sitting!

Miss Radin (1937):

> Takes out his watch, surveys the sun,
> Is tempted, and capitulates—
> And here he's at his neighbors' gates.

8 / by his coming / *Svoím priézdom*: "By his driving over." As is usual in Russian, the not-on-foot character of coming is specified.

10 / to meet / *Na vstréchu*: Fr. *à la rencontre.*

12 / *Podóbna vétrenoy nadézhde*: Cf. One : XXV : 12, *Podób-
nïy vétrenoy Venére,* and the attributes of "hope" in
Five : VII : 6–14.

XIV

9 / *On smótrit v sládkom umilén'e*: "Il regarde avec un
doux attendrissement." See n. to Seven : II : 5.

XV–XVI

These two stanzas (and XXXVIII) are known only from
their publication by Ya. Grot in *Pushkin i ego litseyskie
tovarishchi i nastavniki* (Pushkin and His Lyceum
Schoolmates and Teachers; St. Petersburg, 1887), pp.
211–13 (see Tomashevski, Acad 1937), from a transcript
(now lost) made by Prince V. Odoevski.

XV

    Yes, yes, because the fits of jealousy
    are just as much a sickness as the plague,
    as black spleen, as the agues,
4 as the derangement of the mind.
    It flames like a pyrexia,
    it has its fever, its delirium,
    evil dreams, phantoms of its own.
8 The Lord be merciful, my friends!
    There is no penalty on earth more painful
    than its dire lacerations.
    Believe me: he who has endured them
12 quite certainly without fear will
    ascend the flaming stake
    or bend his neck under the ax.

3 / black spleen: See nn. to One : XXXVII : 6–10 and XXXVIII :
  3–4.

XVI

With an empty reproach I do not wish
to trouble the tomb's peace;
you are no more, O you to whom
4 in tempests of young life
I owed awesome experience
and a voluptuous glimpse of paradise.
As one who teaches a weak child
8 tainting the tender soul,
deep sorrow you taught it.
With sensuousness you roused the blood,
in it you kindled love
12 and the flame of cruel jealousy.
But it is gone, that grievous day.
Sleep ye, tormenting shade!

XVIII

1–2 In 1819 Marceline Desbordes-Valmore (see Comm. to
Three, between XXXI and XXXII, n. to Tatiana's Letter, ll.
35–46) published a *Romance* beginning "S'il avait su
quelle âme il a blessée . . ."

7–8 / her love might have conjoined the friends again:
She would have recalled, moreover, that Rousseau's
Julie d'Etange (whose father, the grim Baron, had killed
a friend in the field and was forever haunted by that
recollection) manages to prevent a duel between her
lover and his best friend in Part I of the novel.

XIX

4 / with knitted brow / *nahmúrya bróv'*: The literal sense
is "having knitted the eyebrow," a curious solecism: the
plural (*brovi*, "eyebrows," "brows") would be the cor-
rect form. "To frown" is *nahmuritsya*.

14 / Nothing / *Tak*: A kind of vocal shrug.

XX

12–14 Baron Anton Delvig (Aug. 6, 1798–Jan. 14, 1831),
one of Pushkin's dearest friends, a minor poet, author of
pleasant idyls, folk songs, well-made sonnets, and some
excellent dactylic hexameters, curiously combined the
classical strain and the folksy one, the amphora and the
samovar. A very expressive drawing (c. 1820) represent-
ing him, full of mirth and wine, bespectacled and di-
sheveled, is reproduced from a contemporaneous album,
in I. Medvedev's paper, "Pavel Yakovlev i ego al'bom"
(Pavel Yakovlev and His Album).*

By a marvelous coincidence, Delvig died on the anni-
versary of the death of the fictional Lenski (who is com-
pared to him here on the eve of a fatal duel); and the
wake commemorating Delvig's death was held by his
friends (Pushkin, Vyazemski, Baratïnski, and Yazïkov)
in a Moscow restaurant, on Jan. 27, 1831, exactly six
years before Pushkin's fatal duel.

It was Delvig who quipped that the nearer to heaven,
the colder one's verses get (as reported by Pushkin in a
MS note), and it was Delvig who intended to kiss Der-
zhavin's hand when the latter visited the Lyceum (see n.
to Eight : II : 3).

Delvig's best poem is the one he dedicated to Pushkin,
his schoolmate, in January, 1815 (published the same
year in *Russian Museum, Rossiyskiy muzeum,* no. 9). A
boy of sixteen, prophesying in exact detail literary im-
mortality to a boy of fifteen, and doing it in a poem that
is itself immortal—this is a combination of intuitive
genius and actual destiny to which I can find no parallel
in the history of world poetry:

> He—a swan born in blooming Ausonia—
> who is crowned with the myrtle and laurel;

---

*In *Zven'ya*, no. 6 (1936), p. 127.

23

who one May night, 'mid hovering choruses,
in sweet dreams from his mother was weaned,

does not quibble in councils; he does not
on his walls hang the flags of the fallen,
or in front of the temple of Ares
deck with enemy rostrums a column.

Fleets with treasures untold from America,
weighty gold that with blood has been purchased
—not for him do those ships in their wanderings
twice disturb the equator;

but since infancy he has been learning
how to sing subcelestial beauty,
and his cheeks are aflame from the greetings
of the wondering crowd.

And the nebulous cloud from his vision
is by Pallas dispelled, and already
as a youth sacred truth he distinguishes,
and the lowering glances of vice.

Pushkin! Even the woods cannot hide him!
With loud singing his lyre will expose him,
and from mortals Apollo will carry
the immortal to cheering Olympus.

XXI

1 / chanced / *na slúchay* [= *sluchayno*]: "The verses are
by chance preserved." Pushkin did not preserve them as
"religiously" (*svyato*) as he did Tatiana's letter (see
Three : XXXI : 1–4).

3 / Whither, ah! whither, are ye fled / *Kudá, kudá vï
udalílis'*: Quite literally, "Whither, whither have you
receded," but I have preferred to echo the cry so often
heard in English seventeenth- and eighteenth-century
poetry:

John Collop, *Spirit, Flesh* (1656):

>Whither? ah, whither flies my soul . . .

Thomas Fletcher (1692):

>Whither fond soul, ah, whither wouldst thou fly?

Pope, adaptation of the emperor Hadrian's *Animula vagula blandula*, l. 5:

>Whither, ah whither art thou flying!

(In 1713, Pope sent John Caryll two versions of Hadrian's piece; it is in the second of these, beginning "Ah, fleeting spirit!," entitled "The same by another hand"—Pope's other hand, presumably—that the "whithers" occur.)

James Beattie, *Ode to Hope* (c. 1760), l. 78:

>Whither, ah whither are ye fled?

Anna Laetitia Barbauld, *Life* (c. 1811):

>O whither, whither dost thou fly . . .

Barry Cornwall, *Song* (c. 1820):

>Whither, ah! whither is my lost love straying . . .

Keats, *Endymion* (1818), bk. I, ll. 970–71:

>. . . Ah! where
>Are those swift moments? Whither are they fled?

4 / my springtime's . . . days / *Vesní moéy . . . dní*: A well-worn Gallicism. I can mention only a few examples, jotted down in the course of casual reading:

Clément Marot, *De soy mesme* (1537):

>Plus ne suis ce que j'ay esté,
>Et ne le sçaurois jamais estre;
>Mon beau printemps et mon esté
>Ont fait le saut par la fenestre.

Guillaume de Chaulieu, *Sur la première attaque de goutte* (1695), ll. 12–13:

>Et déjà de mon printemps
>Toutes les fleurs sont fanées.

Voltaire, *Epître* XV (1719), ll. 8–10:

> Tu vis la calomnie . . .
> Des plus beaux jours de mon printemps
> Obscurcir la naissante aurore.

André Chénier, *Elégies*, I (*Œuvres*, ed. Walter; no. XVI in *Œuvres posthumes*, 1826), ll. 1–2:

> O jours de mon printemps, jours couronnés de rose,
> A votre fuite en vain un long regret s'oppose.

*

Cf. Mihail Milonov (1792–1821), *The Unfortunate Poet*, a very liberal translation of *Le Poète malheureux*, by Laurent Gilbert. The second hemistich of Gilbert's l. 23 reads: "ô printemps de mes jours!" The rest is rendered by Milonov in limp paraphrase (ll. 1, 12–14):

> O springtime of my days! Whither have vanished you?
> . . . .
>   . . . your radiance,
> still charmed, imagination tries to capture [*lóvit*].
> Who knows what fate for me in future holds [*gotóvit*] . . .

See also Charles Hubert Millevoye (1782–1816), *Elégies*, bk. I, *La Chute des feuilles* (*première version*):

> Et je meurs! de leur froide haleine
> M'ont touché les sombres autans;
> Et j'ai vu, comme une ombre vaine,
> S'évanouir mon beau printemps.

And his *Priez pour moi*, "composé . . . huit jours avant sa mort":

> Je meurs au printemps de mon âge,
> Mais du sort je subis la loi . . .

Russian commentators (referred to by Brodski, in his commentary to *EO*, p. 241) have drawn attention to prototypes of Lenski's verses in various Russian elegies of the time, among which we find Vasiliy Tumanski's

Werther and Charlotte (1819), in iambic pentameters
("... when with tremulous beams the moon will gilt my
simple monument, O come to dream of me and with
your bitter tears asperge that urn where your friend's
dust is hidden"); Küchelbecker's *Awakening* (1820), in
trochaic tetrameters ("What will bring the coming day?
Withered are my flowers . . ."); and especially an
anonymous *Morning* (attributed by V. Gippius to V.
Perevoshchikov), in an anthology of 1808 ("First days of
love! . . . Whither, ah, whither are ye fled . . .").

Young Pushkin himself had foreshadowed young
Lenski: *Again I'm yours* . . . (1817): "Days of my glad-
ness, ye have fled" (*umchalis'*); *To M. Shcherbinin*
(1819): ". . . but young days shall fly by"; (1820): "I've
no regret for you, years of my spring"; *Extinguished is
the orb of day* . . . (1820): ". . . the secret sweethearts of
my golden [*zlatïya*, arch., gen. sing. fem.] spring."

In English poetry an obvious example of the locution
is Peacock's "The bright and happy springtime of our
days" (*The Visions of Love*, in *Palmyra and Other
Poems*, 1806).

*

In commenting on similar terms used by Catullus in *Ad
Manlium*, an amusing Frenchman, François Noël, who
is under the impression that he has translated that poet,
Poésies de Catulle (Paris, 1803), II, 439—a book Push-
kin possessed—has this to say of l. 16:

Ver . . . florida. Ces expressions riantes: "la fleur de
l'âge, le printemps de la vie," supposent beaucoup
d'imagination dans les premiers écrivains qui s'en sont
servis. Dans Pétrarque, par exemple, qui a dit fort
heureusement:
  Ch'era dell' anno, e di mia etate aprile;
mais fort peu dans ceux qui les imitent. C'est ce qui rend
la langue poétique si difficile. Commun ou bizarre, ces
deux écueils ne sont séparés que par un sentier étroit et
glissant.

27

These were the times when *traduction* meant an elegant paraphrase, when *la langue poétique* was synonymous with *le bon goût*, when people of *goût* were shocked by "les bizarreries de Sakhespear" (sic; Noël, II, 453), and when Jean Baptiste Rousseau was deemed a poet.

The curious paradox is that, though eighteenth-century translations into French from modern and ancient poets are the worst in existence, the French translations of a later era are the best in the world, one reason being that the French use their marvelously precise and omnipotent prose for the rendering of foreign verse instead of shackling themselves with trivial and treacherous rhyme.

Théophile Gautier, as early as 1836,* wrote:

Une traduction, pour être bonne, doit être en quelque sorte un lexique interlinéaire. . . . Un traducteur doit être une contre-épreuve de son auteur; il doit en reproduire jusqu'au moindre petit signe particulier.

4 / golden days: If the "springtime" comes from France, the "golden days" come from Germany.

Zhukovski, in 1812, made a Russian version of Schiller's *Die Ideale* (see n. to XXIII : 8), calling it *Mechtï* (*Fantasies*, a word that occurs in l. 2 of the original).

O! meines Lebens goldne Zeit?

is rendered as:

O dnéy moíh vesná zlatáya . . .
O golden springtime of my days . . .

Cf. Milonov, *The Fall of the Leaves: an Elegy* (1819; an imitation of Millevoye's *La Chute des feuilles*; see previous note), ll. 21–24:

_____
*In a review of a translation of E. T. A. Hoffmann's *Erzählungen*; reprinted in *Souvenirs de théâtre, d'art et de critique* (Paris, 1883), p. 49.

> *Osénni vétrï vozshuméli*
> *I dïshut hládom sred' poléy,*
> *Kak prízrak lyógkiy uletéli*
> *Zlatïe dní vesní moéy!*

> Autumnal winds have started wailing
> and breathe their chill amid the fields;
> away have flown like a light phantom
> the golden days of my springtime.

Millevoye's *Chute des feuilles* was also imitated by Baratïnski (1823–7), ll. 21–22:

> You've flown away, O golden dreams
> of my brief youth . . .

8 / *Net núzhdï; práv sud'bï zakón*: I was tempted to render the intonation of *Net nuzhdï* by "let be," but it did not seem literal enough.

It should be noted that Pushkin repeated the end of Lenski's melancholy line ten years later—in l. 22 of his (not completed) poem dedicated to the twenty-fifth anniversary of the Lyceum and recited by him at the reunion of Oct. 19, 1836, which was to be his last. The poem consists of eight stanzas of eight iambic pentameters each. The last line of st. VIII is not finished. The strophic rhyme scheme is baabecec (ll. 19–22):

> The years have fled . . .
> . . . how they have changed us!
> .   .   .   .
> Do not complain. Such is the law of fate.
> [*takóv sud'bï zakón*]

The combination *sud'bï zakon*, "of fate the law," is not only in sense but also in sound close to a line in Millevoye's *Priez pour moi*:

> . . . du sort je subis la loi . . .

11 I have been influenced in my choice of rendering *Vsyo blágo* (*blago* meaning "the good," "the beneficial," all

that contributes to human felicity) by Pope's Leibnitzian
"all is right," known to Pushkin through Voltaire's
ironical refrain "tout est bon, tout est bien" in his
pamphlet-novel *Candide, ou l'Optimisme* (Geneva,
1759); see, for instance, chs. 10, 19, 23. Pope's line (*An
Essay on Man*, ep. I, l. 294) goes:

> One truth is clear, "Whatever IS, is RIGHT."

(See also *Essay*, ep. IV, the first hemistich of 145 and the
second of 394.) The tone of Lenski's elegy seems defi-
nitely to contain this current echo of Optimism, the
original name of the doctrine propounded by Gottfried
Wilhelm von Leibnitz or Leibniz, German philosopher
and mathematician of genius (1646–1716). Voltaire as a
thinker was infinitely inferior to him, whereas Pope's
thematic imitativeness is at least saved from ridicule
(which Voltaire's criticism is not) by that poet's ex-
ceptional talent for placing the best words possible in the
best possible order.

In a poem, *L'Homme*, addressed to Byron and pub-
lished in *Méditations poétiques* (Paris, 1820), Lamartine
explains in l. 56:

> Tout est bien, tout est bon, tout est grand à sa place . . .

XXII

8 / maid of beauty / *déva krasotí*: *Fille de la beauté*, a
pseudoclassic Gallicism; e.g., in the beginning of "an
imitation of Horace," *Odes*, bk. I, no. XVI, by Etienne
Augustin de Wailly (1770–1821), in *Almanach des
Muses* (1808), p. 117, and separate edition, *Odes de
Horace* (1817).

14 / spouse / *suprúg*: Another Gallicism on Lenski's part,
a literal translation of *époux*, which, in the French senti-
mental literature of the time, meant not only "spouse"

in the modern sense, but also "fiancé," "betrothed mate," "bridegroom." There is a similar obsolete sense of "spouse" in English literature. The *Pridí, pridí* ("viens, viens") is presumably an invitation to visit his urn. See the quotation in my n. to XL : 14.

XXIII

1–2 / "obscurely" and "limply" / *temnó i vyálo*: For years I had sought in vain an illustration of this obvious Gallicism, when I hit upon the following in Chateaubriand's "Remarques" to his *Le Paradis perdu* (1836), a marvelous prose translation of Milton's poem:

> Souvent, en relisant mes pages, j'ai cru les trouver obscures ou traînantes, j'ai essayé de faire mieux: lorsque la période a été debout *élégante* ou *claire*, au lieu de *Milton*, je n'ai recontré que *Bitaubé*; ma prose lucide n'étoit plus qu'une prose commune ou artificielle, telle qu'on en trouve dans tous les écrits communs du genre classique. Je suis revenu à ma première traduction.

Some idea of what Pushkin meant by *temno* and *vyalo* may be gathered from a marginal note in his copy of Batyushkov's *Essays in Verse and Prose*, II, 166, *Epistle to I. Muravyov-Apostol* (1815). Ll. 77–80 refer to the author of *To the Volga* and *Ermak*:

How often Dmitriev, disclaiming worldly dues,
Would lead us in the wake of his fortunate Muse
As pure as are the streams of the bright waters' queen
Whereon for the first time the sunrise he had seen . . .

Our poet marked ll. 79–80 *vyalo*; he marked the last two lines of the same poem (99–100) *temno*. Ll. 98–100:

Feels strongly everything, with eye, with ear all captures,
Delights in everything, and, in fine, everywhere
Tribute his coming priest for Phoebus doth prepare.

Pushkin italicized "obscurely and limply," perhaps

quoting some reviewer's definition of the romantic style. The two epithets to a certain degree do describe Lenski's poem. The "coming day" lurking "in deep gloom"; the formidable inversion in the original: "I of the tomb shall descend into the mysterious shelter"; the Ossianic "maiden of beauty," and the dedication to her of the doleful dawn, all this is no doubt both obscure and flabby, *vers traînants et obscurs, style languissant et flasque*, nebulous and feeble.

2 / romanticism: As happens in zoological nomenclature when a string of obsolete, synonymous, or misapplied names keeps following the correct designation of a creature throughout the years, and not only cannot be shaken off, or ignored, or obliterated within brackets, but actually grows on with time, so in literary history the vague terms "classicism," "sentimentalism" "romanticism," "realism," and the like straggle on and on, from textbook to textbook. There are teachers and students with square minds who are by nature meant to undergo the fascination of categories. For them, "schools" and "movements" are everything; by painting a group symbol on the brow of mediocrity, they condone their own incomprehension of true genius.

I cannot think of any masterpiece the appreciation of which would be enhanced in any degree or manner by the knowledge that it belonged to this or that school; and, conversely, I could name any number of third-rate works that are kept artificially alive for centuries through their being assigned by the schoolman to this or that "movement" in the past.

These concepts are harmful chiefly because they distract the student from direct contact with, and direct delight in, the quiddity of individual artistic achievement (which, after all, alone matters and alone survives); but, moreover, each of them is subject to such a variety of interpretation as to become meaningless in its own field, that of the classification of knowledge. Since, however, these terms exist and keep banging against every cobble over which their tagged victims keep trying to escape the gross identification, we are forced to reckon with them. For the needs of the present comments, I am prepared to accept the following practical definitions:

"Classical" in regard to a literary work of our era suggests the imitation of ancient models, in traditional matter and manner. Russians use the term "pseudoclassical" for anachronistic imitations in which the Roman or Greek wears a powdered wig.

"Sentimental" implies little beyond the shedding of conventional tears over the misadventure of conventional virtue in verse or prose.

A "realistic" work of fiction is one wherein the author is ready to name or describe without fear of traditional restriction any physical or moral detail pertaining to the world he perceives. (In this sense *EO* is neither sentimental nor realistic, while containing elements of both; it parodies the classical and leans toward the romantic.)

The fourth term in this series, "romanticism," requires a closer discussion of its main varieties as known in Pushkin's time. We can distinguish at least eleven forms or phases of the thing:

(1) The primitive, popular sense: Johnson's *Dictionary* defines a "romance" as "a military fable of the middle ages." But the "military fable" has an Arcadian sequel, and in the seventeenth century, in England, "romantic" is definitely suggestive of the delightful lives of shepherds and retired knights living on honey and cheese. Both the "military" and "pastoral" parts fall under our first definition of "romantic" as characterizing the flights of fancy in popular literature during a period of time between the fall of Rome and the revival of letters.

(2) "The addition of strangeness to beauty" (Walter

Commentary

Pater, *Appreciations*: "Postscript"). An intensive pre-occupation with the passionate and the fantastic. The retired knight is a necromancer; the moon rises over Arcadia in a new part of the ruined sky. As early as 1665–66, Pepys describes a site (Windsor Castle) as "the most romantique castle that is in the world." In 1799, Campbell notes that " 'Tis distance lends enchantment to the view."

(3) The Highland subspecies and the eerie note. To paraphrase Beattie, *The Minstrel* (1772), "The grotesque and ghostly appearance of a landscape, especially by the light of the moon, diffuses an habitual gloom over the fancy and gives it that romantic cast that disposes to invention and that melancholy which inclines one to the fear of unseen things."

(4) The romanesque: a "romanesque" person feels as "romantic" such landscapes, lakescapes, and seascapes as recall either direct emotion (love, friendship, old ambitions and longings) or the description of similar places in popular novels and poems of the sentimental or fantastic kind. "Il [Fonsalbe] a rendu à mes déserts quelque chose de leur beauté heureuse, et du *romantisme* de leur sites *alpestres*" (Senancour, *Oberman*, Letter LXXXVII).

(5) The German subspecies (a hybrid, with a strong strain of sentimentalism). Reveries, visions, apparitions, tombstones, moonshine. The pictorial grading into the metaphysical. Lofty sentiments couched in a flaccid and nebulous idiom. The expression in poetry of the soul's endless approach to a dimly perceived perfection.

(6) The textbook synthetic conception of c. 1810: a combination of "melancholy" as the essence of Northern (Germanic, "Ossianic") poetry and of Renaissance vividness and vigor (e.g., Shakespeare). Romantic as implying "modern and picturesque" and as opposed to "classical" (the latter standing for "antique and sculpturesque"): this seems to be the end product of cogita-

34

tions on the matter by the well-meaning but hardly readable cofounder (with his brother, Friedrich, the philosopher, 1772–1829) of the romantic school of German literature, August Wilhelm von Schlegel (1767–1845), tutor of Mme de Staël's children (c. 1805–15); he assisted her in her work *De l'Allemagne*; was ennobled and invested with many decorations, and delivered his lectures on dramatic art and literature in Vienna, 1808. *

(7) A romantic epic is one in which the tragic and the comic, the lofty and the lowly, the sacred and the profane, the metaphysical generalization and the physical detail, and so forth are pleasingly mingled (cf. the program of *EO* as set down in the Prefatory Piece).

(8) "Romantic" as applied to a style abounding in vivid specific details (local color, exotic landscapes, national peculiarities, realistic popular traits, new shades of perception, emotion, and meaning, etc.) as opposed, in such writings as those by Chateaubriand or Victor Hugo, to the generalized mist of sentimentalism; e.g., the waters of Lamartine (it will be noticed that, on the other hand, the mist plus the melancholy is somehow also "romantic," although directly opposed to the specific brightness and this is why the same Lamartine figures among the romantics).

(9) A new style in poetry, free of classic rigidity and conventionalism, permitting enjambments, mobile caesuras, and other liberties.

(10) Literary genres not known to the ancients.

(11) "Modern" as opposed to "ancient" in any literary form.

There is a good deal of overlapping in these concepts,

---

*His *Über dramatische Kunst und Literatur* (1809–11) was translated into French (*Cours de littérature dramatique*, Paris, 1814, 3 vols.) by Albertine Adrienne Necker de Saussure, Mme de Staël's cousin; and this translation Pushkin had carefully read.

Commentary

and no wonder some muddle existed in Pushkin's mind as to what should be termed "romantic" in the strict sense, a question that interested him and his fellow writers more acutely than it does us.

In a note entitled "On Poetry Classical and Romantic" (1825), our poet accuses French critics of confusing the issue by referring to romanticism all such poetry as is characterized either by "the stamp of dreaminess and Germanic ideology" or is founded upon "the prejudices and traditions of the common people." He maintains that the distinction between classicism and romanticism can be drawn only in terms of form and not of subject matter. His definition of romantic poetry reads: "All such genres of poetical composition as were not known to the ancients or have since changed in form." According to our poet, western European poetry in the Dark Ages was at best an elegant bauble, a troubadour's triolet. Two circumstances, however, had a vigorous influence on its eventual course: the invasion of the Moors, "who inspired it with frenzy and tenderness, a leaning toward the marvelous and rich Oriental eloquence," and the Crusades, which imbued it "with piety and naïveté, a new code of heroism, and the loose morals of camp life." This was, according to Pushkin, the origin of romanticism.

In the same note, and elsewhere, Pushkin is hard on French "pseudoclassicism" as personified by Boileau: "It originated belowstairs and never went further than the salon. . . . It dressed the maudlin conceits of medieval romanticism in the severe garb of classicism." In a postscriptum, however, to this 1825 note he praises La Fontaine's *Contes* and Voltaire's *Pucelle* as masterpieces of pure romantic poetry. We should not forget that "pure French classicists," such as Corneille, Racine, and Molière, were among Pushkin's favorite writers.

In another MS note (1830), Pushkin continues:

The French critics have their own notions of romanticism. They either assign to it all works bearing the stamp of melancholy and reverie or apply the term to neologisms and bad grammar. Thus André Chénier, a poet permeated with the spirit of antiquity, a poet whose very defects are owing to his desire to give the French language the forms of Greek versification [this is a singular error on Pushkin's part], becomes a romanticist for them.

7 / "ideal": Schiller's *Die Ideale* (Ideals; from the *Musen-almanach* for 1796), an elegy of eighty-eight iambic tetrameters in eleven strophes, begins:

> So willst du treulos von mir scheiden,
> Mit deinen holden Phantasien,
> Mit deinen Schmerzen, deinen Freuden,
> Mit allen unerbittlich fliehn?
> Kann nichts dich, Fliehende! verweilen,
> O! meines Lebens goldne Zeit?
> . . . .
> Erloschen sind die heitern Sonnen,
> Die meiner Jugend Pfad erhellt,
> Die Ideale sind zerronnen . . .

Mme de Staël, *De l'Allemagne*, pt. II, ch. 13, observes:

Il seroit intéressant de comparer les stances de Schiller sur la perte de la jeunesse, intitulées *l'Idéal*, avec celles de Voltaire:
> Si vous voulez que j'aime encore,
> Rendez-moi l'âge des amours, etc.

I have acted upon her suggestion, but it is not *intéressant* at all; in fact, her observation is completely irrelevant.

Lamartine (on the night he wrote the piece mentioned in the n. to XXI : 10), in the autumn of 1818, read *Childe Harold*, in the incomplete French version of the Bibliothèque Universelle de Genève, all night and finally "[s'endormit] de lassitude, la tête sur le volume comme sur le sein d'un ami" (Lamartine, *Vie de Byron*, 1865).

10–14 / *uzh soséd* ("already the neighbor") . . . *sed'móy uzh chás* ("seventh already hour") . . . *zhdyót uzh nás* ("is awaiting already us"). I have kept these "adders" (see n. to Eight : LI : 3–4).

XXIV

4 / *Vésper*: By a strange oversight, Pushkin calls the morning star "Vesper" or Hesperus (which is the evening star), instead of the correct Lucifer or Phosphor. All these names were given by the ancients to the planet Venus. In certain districts of Russia the word *zornitsa* or *zarnitsa* (which otherwise means "summer lightning," "sheet lightning") is used for the morning star and evening star. (See *vechérniya zarnítsï*, "of the evening star," in Milonov's elegy quoted in n. to XLI : 1–4, and *utrennyuyu zarnitzu*, "the morning star," in Tolstoy's *Anna Karenin*, pt. VI, ch. 12.)

7 / shifting flurries / *perelyótnaya myatél'*: The epithet means "flying from one place to another," and *myatel'* or *metel'* is not "snowstorm" or "blizzard" (as it would be in a general sense of "driving snow"), but what is more specifically termed in Russian *zamet'*, namely, spinners of powdery surface snow caused by gusts of wind on a morning of bright sun and keen frost.

12 / *póli závesa*: The two parts, or "skirts," of a bed curtain.

XXV

2 / Guillot: This is, technically, a French comedy name. It is mentioned as a typically humble name, among other lowly ones ("Pierre, Guillot et Michel"), in Montaigne's essay "Des Noms," written c. 1573 (*Essais*, bk. I, ch. 46). As that of a shepherd, the same first name occurs twice in La Fontaine's *Fables* (1668–79), bk. III, no. III, "Le

Loup devenu Berger," and bk. IX, no. XIX, "Le Berger et
son Troupeau." Pushkin, I think, uses the name as a
surname (cf. "Picard," in *Count Nulin*, 1825). Griboe-
dov, in *Woe from Wit* (known since 1825), has Chatski
mention a volatile French dance master in Moscow
whom he calls "Guillaumet" (Act I, ll. 405–11). The
French translator of Shakespeare (in 20 vols., 1776–83),
Pierre Letourneur (1736–88), was baptized by Bernar-
din Félix Guillot, vicar of Valognes (Basse Normandie);
and there are other Guillots in the margin of history.

11–14 The text is clumsy: Onegin "bids his valet to carry"
the pistol case and (bids) "the horses" (including sleigh
and coachman) "to drive off" into a field.

12 / Lepage's / *Lepázha*: The reference is to Jean Le Page
or Lepage (1779–1822), Parisian gunsmith.

I happen to notice that in the Rudolph J. Nunne-
macher Collection of projectile arms* there is only one
Lepage pistol, and that its make has been misread by the
author of the description of the collection as "Lgiage"
(the looptail of the *p* in "Lepage" having been assigned
by the transcriber to the preceding *e*, to form a *g*).

12 / fell tubes / *stvóli rokovíe*: I find in a spirited paragraph
of Leigh Hunt's *Table-Talk* (London, 1851), "Sport-
ing," pp. 158–63, the application of "death-tubes" to
the weapon of sportsmen who "crack the legs of par-
tridges" and "strew the brakes with agonies of feathered
wounds."

XXVI

9 / *iz chúvstva*: I am not sure that "out of feeling" renders

*See John Metschl's paper in *Bulletin of the Public Museum of
Milwaukee*, IX (1928), 446.

as well as the Russian equivalent does Zaretski's professional fondness for order and thoroughness in the conduct of these affairs.

XXVII

9 / if you are willing / *pozhály*: A fading word that from an initial sense of "please," "if you please," Fr. *s'il vous plaît*, shaded subsequently into an expression of bland deference to another's desire (as here) and soon dwindled to a casual locution expressing merely the acceptance of a suggestion or possibility ("I think one might . . ." and so forth).

Hodasevich, *O Pushkine* (Berlin, 1937), p. 79, sagaciously observes that the long-drawn and dejected tone of the musical phrase *Nachnyom pozhaluy* ("Yes, if you like, let's start"), given to the tenor in Chaykovski's opera *Eugene Onegin*, makes a whining weakling of Pushkin's virile Lenski.

XXVIII

7 To the oneirologist, Onegin's behavior throughout that morning has an uncanny dreamlike quality, as if he had been infected by Tatiana's recent nightmare. We all know that dream sensation of "lateness," those casual "substitutions" (as here—the valet turned second), those "omissions," that odd discomfort followed by its carefree dismissal. Onegin behaves as he never would have behaved in a normal state of moral awareness. He deals Lenski a gratuitous insult by grossly oversleeping, in result of which the fuming youth has to wait a couple of hours or more in an icy wind. He omits somehow to secure a witness, and while knowing as well as Zaretski does that in an encounter between gentlemen the seconds must be of equal rank in society with the principals

they attend, he turns up with a servant, thus dealing
Lenski yet another silly insult. He fires first and shoots
to kill, which is quite out of character. Lenski, no doubt,
has murderous intentions, but Onegin, a fearless and
scornful marksman, would, if in his right mind, have
certainly reserved his fire, and not even returned it but,
if still alive, thrown it away, i.e., discharged his pistol
into the air. When Lenski falls, one almost expects
Onegin to wake (as Tatiana does) and realize that it has
all been a dream.

10–11 / laughing while their hand is not encrimsoned /
poká | Ne obagrílas' ih ruká [their hand]: Cf. dawn's
"crimson hand," n. to Five : XXV : 1–4.
   One wonders if Lomonosov's shade is not laughing,
too.

13–14 "Le faux point d'honneur, leur [aux gens du monde]
inspire une crainte farouche, et les arrête" (Turgenev-
Viardot translation).

14 / false shame: *Lózhnïy stíd*; *fausse honte, mauvaise
honte*. It seems clear to me that this very trite couplet
reflects a reminiscence of Boileau's *Epistres*, III (1674),
ll. 28, 37–38:

   Des jugemens d'autrui nous tremblons follement,
   .   .   .   .
   Quelle fausse pudeur à feindre vous oblige?
   "Qu'avez-vous?"—"Je n'ai rien."...

(Cf. Lenski's exit.)
   See also n. to Six : IX : 4.

XXIX

3 / *uhódyat púli*: Each of the two balls goes into its

respective pistol barrel, which is polyhedral (hence "cut," *granyonïy*) in cross section.

4 Cf. Byron, *Don Juan*, IV, XLI, 1–2:

> It has a strange quick jar upon the ear,
> That cocking of a pistol . . .

Pichot (1823): "C'est une étrange sensation que produit sur l'oreille le bruit qu'on fait en armant un pistolet . . ."

5–6 / The powder . . . is poured / *póroh . . . sípletsya*: "The early arms of Lepage of Paris," says Major H. B. C. Pollard in *A History of Firearms* (London, 1926), p. 113, "show attempts to use loose powder evolved by Pulat of Paris, 1818."

9 / Behind a near stump . . . Guillot: In Ilya Repin's most famous and most execrable picture of the Lenski-Onegin duel, in which everything, including the attitudes and positions of the combatants, is ludicrously wrong, Guillot, whom a puny sliver does not screen, is in the line of Onegin's fire and in danger of sharing the fate of a second who was shot in a bungled duel, on a Wednesday morning in November, on Bagshot Heath (as recorded by the *Morning Chronicle*, Nov. 26, 1821). It is doubtful that the "great" Russian painter had read Pushkin's novel (although he certainly had seen the opera by the "great" composer) when he painted his *Duel of Onegin and Lenski* (1899). As in the opera, everything in the picture insults Pushkin's masterpiece. The two duelists, two stolid dummies, stand stockstill, one foot thrust forward, *la taille cambrée*, pointing their dummy pistols at each other. Lenski is in the same pose as young Pushkin reading his verses to Derzhavin, in another ridiculous picture (1911) by the same painter. These ignoble daubs are lovingly reproduced in all illustrated editions of Pushkin's works.

The society (Obshchestvo Imeni A. I. Kuindzhi) that accorded Repin a prize of three thousand rubles and a golden medal for the "Lyceum examination" picture declared that it was rewarding him not so much for the picture itself as because of his being abused by the *dekadentï* (*avant-garde* painters).

13 / his friends / *Druzéy*: Russian construction allows an ambiguity here: the meaning may be "the two friends" just as well as "his friends"; but the opening ejaculation of XXVIII seems to preclude the former interpretation.

XXIX–XXX

The hostile meeting described here is the classical duel *à volonté* of the French code, partly derived from the Irish and English pistol duel, for which the basic code duello was adopted in Tipperary about 1775. According to this Clonmel Code and to an additional rule adopted in Galway, firing was regulated by signal, or word of command, or at pleasure, and in the last case, either party might advance "even to touch muzzle." In the favorite Continental variation, however, a stretch of ground at mid-distance could not be trespassed upon, and this was called the *barrière* (a term stemming from the oldest form of any pistol duel, the French one, which was fought on horseback, with the combatants divided by posts placed some ten yards asunder to represent the nearest range from which they were permitted to fire). The affair was conducted as follows.

The adjustment of the preliminary ceremonies would comprise not only the actual "calling out" or, in English parlance of the time, "calling upon," with the dispatch of a written challenge or "message," technically termed "cartel of defiance" (Six : IX), but also a conference between the seconds; we shall note that the latter formality is omitted in the present case, nor are the conditions of combat set down in writing by the witnesses, as formal usage would demand. It is not necessary to assume that suicide notes, at least, have been deposited, with a view to exempt the survivor from prosecution; officially, duels were forbidden, which did not affect, however, their frequency; the participants remained unpunished when no death followed, but even in case of a fatal result influence in high places helped to mitigate, or eliminate altogether, such penalties as imprisonment or banishment.

The parties repair to the selected spot. The seconds mark the ground at a certain number of paces (yards); for instance, in the present case, thirty-two yards are measured off, and the combatants, after a given signal, are allowed to reduce the distance by walking toward each other (otherwise, twelve paces or less would do). The limits of this progression are fixed by a number of paces being told off between the extreme marks, leaving a space of, say, twelve paces in the center of the ground: this is *la barrière*, the boundary, a kind of no man's land beyond the inner limits of which neither man can advance; its boundaries would be generally marked by the coats, carricks, or pelisses doffed by the combatants.

The pistols are loaded or "charged" by the seconds, and the duel begins. The principals take their positions at the extreme points of the ground, facing each other and keeping the muzzles of their pistols pointing down. At a given signal (*Marchez! Skhodites'!*, meaning "March toward each other"), they advance upon each other and may fire whenever they think proper. Onegin starts gently leveling his pistol when both have advanced four paces; they walk another five, and Lenski is killed on the first fire. If Onegin, while taking aim, had discharged his pistol without effect, or if it had snapped, or even if a severe hit had not utterly disabled Lenski,

the latter might have made him come up to the *barrière*
limit and at twelve paces taken a long cool aim at him.
This was one of the reasons why serious duelists pre-
ferred to have the other fellow fire first. If after the ex-
change the adversaries still felt bloodthirsty, they might
have the pistols reloaded (or use a fresh brace) and begin
all over again. This type of duel, with variations (for ex-
ample, the *barrière* idea seems to have been less clearly
defined in the Irish and English duels), was popular in
France, Russia, Great Britain, and the Southern states of
America from the end of the eighteenth century to about
1840 and was still fought in Latin and Slav countries in
our time. The reader should not imagine, when reading
this chapter, anything resembling the "back-to-back-
march-face-about-fire" affair popularized in modern
times by movies and cartoons. This was a variant in-
vented in France in the 1830's and popular with Parisian
journalists later on.

The description of the Lenski-Onegin duel is, on our
poet's part, a personal recollection in regard to various
details, and, in regard to its issue, a personal prediction.

Pushkin had been out at least three times before his
fatal meeting with d'Anthès. His first, with Rïleev, oc-
curred presumably between May 6 and 9, 1820, in the
district of Tsarskoe Selo (see my n. to Four : XIX : 5).
In his next affair (1822, first week of January, 9 A.M., at
a mile and a half from Kishinev), with Colonel Starov,
commander of the Chasseur Regiment, for adversary,
accurate aim was impaired by a raging snowstorm; the
boundary was set at sixteen paces for the first exchange
and narrowed to twelve for the second. In the spring of
the same year, in a vineyard near Kishinev, he fought
with another military man named Zubov. In these three
duels no blood was shed; very few details are known
about them, but it would seem that in the first and third
Pushkin discharged his pistol into the air.

In his fourth and last encounter, with Baron Georges
Charles d'Anthès, also known as Baron Georges de
Heeckeren, on January 27, at 4:30 P.M., near St. Peters-
burg (on the north side of the Neva, some 1500 feet
north of the Black River, in a pine grove a little way off
the Kolomyaki road), the parties took their ground at a
distance of twenty paces, and Pushkin was mortally
wounded at the first fire. Here are the conditions of the
duel.

1. Les deux adversaires seront placés à vingt pas de
distance, à cinq pas chacun des deux barrières qui seront
distantes de dix pas entre elles.
2. Armés chacun d'un pistolet, à un signal donné, ils
pourront en s'avançant l'un sur l'autre, sans cependant
dans aucun cas dépasser la barrière, faire usage de leurs
armes.
3. Il reste convenu en outre qu'un coup de feu parti,
il ne sera plus permis à chacun des deux adversaires de
changer de place pour que celui des deux qui aura tiré le
premier essuie dans tous les cas le feu de son adversaire à
la même distance.
4. Les deux parties ayant tiré, s'il n'y a point de résul-
tat on recommencerait l'affaire . . . en remettant les adver-
saires à la même distance de vingt pas. . . .

The six clauses, of which I quote four, were signed on
Jan. 27, 1837, at 2:30 P.M., in St. Petersburg. Two hours
later Pushkin received a wound in the lower abdomen
and died of traumatic peritonitis at 2:45 P.M., January 29.

The circumstances that led to Pushkin's tragic death
can be briefly summarized as follows.

In 1833 the Dutch minister, Baron Jacob Theodore
van Heeckeren (Jacques Thierry Borchard Anne van
Heeckeren-Beverwaert, 1791–1884), who after a leave
of absence was returning to his post in St. Petersburg,
at an inn befriended a young Alsatian gentleman going
the same way. This was Georges Charles d'Anthès (1812–
95), a native of Colmar and onetime student at Saint-

Cyr. According to Louis Metman, the official (and not always reliable) biographer of the family, the d'Anthès had originated on Gottland Island and had been established since the seventeenth century in Alsace, where a Jean Henri Anthès, *manufacteur d'armes blanches*, was ennobled in 1731. The father of Georges d'Anthès had been baronized by Napoleon I. Our hero's military studies in France had been interrupted by the July Revolution, which ended the reign of Charles X (1824–30) and hoisted Louis Philippe upon the throne. D'Anthès remained faithful to Charles and went to seek his fortune at the court of Tsar Nicholas I, who liked legitimists.

Georges d'Anthès and his protector arrived by steamer on Oct. 8, 1833. Pushkin, who happened to be keeping a journal at the time, jotted down on Jan. 26, 1834, almost exactly three years before his fatal duel, that a foreigner, Baron d'Anthès, had been received into the Chevalier Guards. He met d'Anthès in St. Petersburg at the end of July, 1834. Natalia Pushkin and the two children, Maria and Aleksandr, were spending the summer on her mother's estate in the province of Kaluga, after a miscarriage she had suffered in March of that year. She returned to St. Petersburg in the autumn and bore a third child (Grigoriy) in May, 1835, and a fourth (Natalia) a year later. There is no proof that her relations with d'Anthès, who fell in love with her at the close of 1834, ever went further than flirtatious conversations and snatched kisses; this was bad enough, but it is also true that her husband had affairs with other women, among whom was her sister Alexandra. Her other (elder) sister, Ekaterina, was madly enamored of d'Anthès.

In the summer of 1836, the Pushkins rented a villa in the suburbs, near the Black River (I have read somewhere that the name Black River, known as early as 1710, came from its peculiar dusky tint, owing to the fact that the dense alder shrubs growing along its banks and dipping their roots in the water produced a dark, tawny suffusion of alnein in it), and both Natalia and Ekaterina saw a good deal of d'Anthès. July passed in an atmosphere full of billets-doux, *petits jeux*, rides, and picnics, and somehow, in the course of that month, Ekaterina Goncharov became pregnant (a circumstance carefully camouflaged in the annals of the Heeckeren-d'Anthès family, but conclusively proved by Grossman in *Krasnaya niva*, XXIV, 1929). It is certain that by the early fall of 1836 rumors were circulating about a possible marriage between her and d'Anthès (by now Baron de Heeckeren—his father having officially ceded him in April of that year to the Dutch minister). It is also certain that d'Anthès' courtship of Natalia Pushkin, a source of passionate interest to the *grand monde*, went on just as before.

Vienna society a few years earlier had found great fun in conferring on people various absurd certificates. A coterie of effeminate young men decided to renew the fad in St. Petersburg. A member of this giggling clique, Prince Pyotr Dolgoruki (nicknamed in society *le bancal*, "bowlegs"), cooked up an anonymous letter that Pushkin and his friends received by the (recently inaugurated) city mail on Nov. 4, 1836:

Les Grands-Croix, Commandeurs et Chevaliers du Séré-nissime Ordre des *Cocus*, réunis en grand Chapitre sous la présidence du vénérable grand-Maître de l'Ordre, S. E. D. L. Narychkine, *ont nommé à l'unanimité Mr. Alexandre Pouchkine coadjuteur du grand Maître de l'Ordre des Cocus et historiographe de l'Ordre.*

Le secrétaire pérpétuel: Cte J. Borch

I have preserved the orthography. The secretary is Count Joseph Borch: him and his wife, Lyubov, the *monde* dubbed a model couple because "she lived with the coachman, and he with the postilion." The vener-

able Grand Master is His Excellency Dmitri Lvovich
Narïshkin, whose wife, Maria, had been the mistress of
Tsar Alexander I for many years. It is surmised that this
"certificate" should be construed in the sense that Push-
kin had been cocufied by the tsar. This was not so. Al-
though the potentate had had his eye on Natalia Pushkin
even before she married, she is thought to have become
his mistress for a brief spell only after our poet's death.

That the hand is a Russian's is clear from the very at-
tempts to disguise it (for example, by forming the French
u as a Russian *i*, which in block-letter script is the mirror
image of *N*); but Pushkin, for some reason never ex-
plained, decided it had been written by Heeckeren.
Soviet graphologists proved (in 1927) that it was Dol-
goruki's work; his subsequent forgeries lend strong
psychological support to his authorship. He belonged to
the Heeckeren set, but it was Heeckeren and d'Anthès
whom Pushkin immediately saw as the main villains.
On November 7 he called out Lieutenant d'Anthès; a
hectic period of *pourparlers* ensued, with Pushkin's
friend Zhukovski doing his best to patch up matters. On
November 17 Pushkin took back his challenge on the
grounds that d'Anthès had proposed to Ekaterina Gon-
charov—which it was high time he did, since she was
now five months with child. He married her on Jan. 10,
1837. On January 24 Pushkin had a mysterious inter-
view with the tsar. During the fortnight following his
wedding d'Anthès continued to pay court to Natalia
Pushkin on every possible occasion.

On January 26 Pushkin sent an insulting letter to the
Dutch minister, accusing him of being "the pimp of
his bastard." This last epithet was a perfectly gratuitous
insult since Heeckeren was a confirmed homosexual, a
fact well known to our poet. For reasons of protocol,
Heeckeren abstained from challenging Pushkin, and it
was d'Anthès who immediately called him out.

Pushkin's second was his old schoolmate, Lieutenant Colonel Konstantin Danzas, and that of d'Anthès was Viscount Laurent d'Archiac, a secretary of the French embassy. The duel took place on Wednesday, January 27. Both sleighs arrived in the vicinity of the so-called Commandant's Villa about 4 P.M., with dusk already dulling the frosty air. While the two seconds and d'Anthès were engaged in trampling out a twenty-yard-long path in the snow, Pushkin, enveloped in a bearskin pelisse, sat waiting on a snowdrift. The seconds marked the ten-yard boundary with their shed carricks, and the duel began. Pushkin at once walked up his five paces to the boundary. D'Anthès made four paces and fired. Pushkin fell on Danzas' military carrick, but after a pause of a few seconds raised himself on one arm and declared he had enough strength to fire. His pistol had stuck barrel down in the snow; another was given him, and Pushkin took slow careful aim at his adversary, whom he had ordered to come up to the boundary. The shock of the ball, which hit d'Anthès in the forearm, bowled him over, and Pushkin, thinking he had killed him, exclaimed, "Bravo!" and threw his pistol up into the air. He was carried to the livery coupe that had conveyed the passionately anxious Dutch minister to the vicinity of the ground (Heeckeren then quietly transferred himself to one of the hack sleighs).

D'Anthès later had a distinguished career in France. In *Les Châtiments*, bk. IV, no. VI, a fine diatribe of thirty resounding Alexandrines "Ecrit le 17 Juillet 1851, en descendant de la tribune," Victor Hugo qualified the members of Napoleon III's senate, including d'Anthès, as follows (ll. 1–2, 7):

Ces hommes qui mourront, foule abjecte et grossière,
Sont de la boue avant d'être de la poussière.
.   .   .   .
Ils mordent les talons de qui marche en avant.

It is extremely curious to discover—as I have from a work by Baron Ludovic de Vaux, *Les Tireurs de pistolet* (Paris, 1883), pp. 149–50—that the son of Georges and Catherine Heeckeren d'Anthès, Louis Joseph Maurice Charles Georges (1843–1902), was one of the most celebrated duelists of his day. "Baron Georges de Heeckeren . . . grand, gros et fort, yeux clairs et barbe blonde," while heading in the sixties a counterguerrilla action in Mexico, "se prit de querelle," at a hotel in Monterey, "avec un Américain qui mettait les pieds sur la table avant le dessert" and fought a duel with him "à l'américaine au revolver et lui brisa le bras. . . . Rentré en France il eut un duel à l'épée avec Albert Roge. . . . Tout le monde se rappelle son duel avec le Prince Dolgorouki dans lequel il fracassa l'épaule de son adversaire après avoir subi son feu à dix pas. . . . C'est un charmant viveur . . . qui compte beaucoup d'amis à Paris et qui le mérite bien."

XXX

3 / *Pohódkoy tvyórdoy, tího, róvno*: The rhythm of the duelist's grim advance, stressed by these thudding epithets, is curiously anticipated at the end of pt. I of Pushkin's earlier poem, *The Caucasian Captive* (1820–27), in which the protagonist recalls his former encounters (ll. 349–52):

> A thrall of honor, merciless [honor],
> he at close range had seen his end
> when in a duel he, firm, cold [*tvyórdïy, hládnïy*],
> would face the fateful lead.

The "thrall of honor," *nevól'nik chésti*, was to be borrowed in 1837 by Lermontov for a famous poem on Pushkin's death.

13 / hours / *Chasť*: The appointed hours of his life come to an end as the last one strikes.

XXXI

6 / lump of snow / *glíba snegováya*: A *glíba* conveys the idea of larger bulk than "lump," midway between it and "mass."

When, in Pushkin's *EO*, Six : XXXI : 4–6, Lenski's falling in the fatal duel is illustrated by the comparison "Thus, slowly, down the slope of hills, shining with sparkles in the sun, a lump of snow descends," we visualize, with the Russian author, a Russian bright winter day, but cannot help recalling that when in Macpherson's *Fingal*, bk. III, Agandecca is slain by Starno, she falls "like a wreath of snow, which slides from the rocks of Ronan." When Lermontov, in *A Hero of Our Time* (pt. II, "Princess Mary"), compares Mt. Mashuk in the northern Caucasus (elev. 3258 ft.) to a shaggy (*mohnataya*) Persian fur cap, or defines other, low, timbered mountains as *kudryavïe gorï*, we remember the many "shaggy mountains" in *The Poems of Ossian* (e.g., in the beginning of *Darthula*). And when Tolstoy begins and ends his marvelous story "Haji-Murad" (1896–98; 1901–04) with an elaborate comparison involving the crushing of a vigorous thistle and the death of a Caucasian chieftain, we note the faint but indubitable prompting of "they fell like the thistle's head," a recurrent phrase in *Ossian* (e.g., in *Sul-malla of Lumon*).

10–14; XXXII : 9–14 The torrent of unrelated images with which XXXI closes—young bard, untimely end, the storm has blown, the bloom has withered, the flame upon the altar has gone out—is a deliberate accumulation of conventional poetical formulas by means of which Pushkin mimics poor Lenski's own style (cf. XXI–XXII, Lenski's

52

last elegy); but the rich and original metaphor of the deserted house, closed inner shutters, whitened window-panes, departed female owner (the soul being feminine in Russian), with which XXXII ends, is Pushkin's own contribution, a sample as it were of what *he* can do.

In the 1820's neither Shelley nor Keats was yet famous enough to be widely read in French versions as were the more grossly grained and more easily paraphrased Macpherson, Byron, and Moore. When Pushkin was writing Chapter Six of *EO*, he certainly did not know *Adonais*, Shelley's poem on the death of Keats, written in June, 1821, and published the same year. As with so many other parallelisms mentioned in my notes, the similarity between the metaphors accumulated around Lenski's death and the images in *Adonais*, VI, 7–9—

> The bloom, whose petals, nipped before they blew,
> Died . . .
> The broken lily lies—the storm is overpast

—is readily explained by the logic of literary evolution working on the same fund of immemorial formulas. Pushkin's image of the abandoned house is, however, more original in specific detail than the metaphor of the "angel soul" who was the "earthly guest" of the "innocent breast" in *Adonais*, XVII.

XXXII

1–2 Cf. Browning's *After* (1855), the soliloquy of a duelist who has killed his adversary:

> How he lies in his rights of a man!
> Death has done all death can.
> And, absorbed in the new life he leads,
> He recks not, he heeds
> Nor his wrong nor my vengeance; both strike
> On his senses alike,
> And are lost in the solemn and strange
> Surprise of the change.

8 | *Igrála zhízn'*, *kipéla króv'*: Even a professed literalist is stopped by "played life, boiled blood."

9–14 See n. to Six : XXXI : 10–14.

12–14 By Jan. 6, 1827, Vyazemski had read Six (brought by Pushkin to Moscow) and, for the nonce, was enthusiastic. He admired, with great acumen, the metaphor of the abandoned house (see letter of that date to Aleksandr Turgenev and Zhukovski, who were abroad).

The "window boards," *stávni*, are folding shutters on the inside of the casement panes.

14 | *Propál i sléd*: "Has disappeared even the trace."

XXXIII

12 | at a gentlemanly distance | *Na blagoródnom rasstoyán'i*: Cf. Byron, *Don Juan*, IV, XLI, 4–6:

> . . . twelve yards off, or so;
> A gentlemanly distance, not too near,
> If you have got a former friend for foe.

Twelve yards is twelve paces (thirty-six feet), three eighths of the distance in the Onegin-Lenski duel. Actually, they were at a distance of fourteen yards from each other when Onegin fired. In duels where family honor was involved the distance might be considerably less. Thus Rïleev and Prince Konstantin Shahovskoy fought at *three* paces (Feb. 22, 1824)—with their bullets colliding in mid-air.

Pichot (1823): "C'est une distance honorable . . ."

The formula was not Byron's invention, either. See Sheridan's silly *The Rivals*, V, iii, where Sir Lucius O'Trigger, the second of the comedy coward Acres, measures paces and remarks: "There now, that is a very pretty distance—a pretty gentleman's distance." (Acres thinks "forty, or eight and thirty yards" is "a good dis-

tance," with the duelists *not* walking toward each other
as the Franco-Russian code allowed.)

XXXIV

VARIANTS

Drafted continuations, in the Maykov collection (PD
155):

XXXIVa

It is praiseworthy to be ⟨brave⟩ in battle,
but who's not brave in our courageous age?
One and all boldly fight, lie brazenly.
4 Hero, be first a human being!
At one time sensibility was current
even in our Northern nature.
When burning grapeshot
8 tears off the head from a friend's shoulders,
weep, warrior, do not be ashamed, weep freely!
Caesar, too, shed tears
⟨when he learned⟩ of a friend's ⟨death⟩
12 and was himself most badly wounded
(I don't remember where, I don't remember how);
he was, of course, ⟨no⟩ fool.

10–14 Here, Pushkin vaguely recollects a passage from
Plutarch's *Lives* (read in Jacques Amyot's French), in
which Caesar in Alexandria, on being presented with
Pompey's head, "ne put retenir ses larmes" (*Vies des
hommes illustres*: "César," LIII). It was near the statue
of Pompey that, at the meeting of the Senate, Caesar
received a first gash in the neck (dealt by Casca) before
being killed (ibid. LXXI)—hence the mention here of his
being wounded.

Works 1949, p. 612, adds a draft where Cassius and
Brutus replace Caesar and his friend (ll. 10–11):

> *I Kássiy slyózï prolivál,*
> *Kogdá on Brúta smért' uznál . . .*

> And Cassius also tears did shed
> When he found out that Brut was dead . . .

It was the other way round. This vagueness of classical knowledge is curious.

xxxivb

> But one can also weep without a wound
> over a friend if he was dear,
> did not tease us imprudently,
> 4 and served our whims.
> But if the fatal Reaper,
> ensanguined, blind,
> in fire and smoke, before a father's eyes,
> 8 smites his stray youngling—
> O dread! O bitter moment!
> O St[roganov]—when your son
> fell, smitten, and you were alone,
> 12 ⟨glory⟩ and battle ⟨you forgot⟩
> and you abandoned to another's glory
> success encouraged by yourself.

10 / St[roganov]; 13 / another's: Count Pavel Stroganov, who commanded a division in the battle of Craonne, near Laon, France, Mar. 7, 1814, N.S., left the field upon learning that his son Aleksandr, aged nineteen, had been decapitated by a cannon ball.

The "another" is (according to Tïnyanov, *Lit. nasl.*, nos. 16–18 [1934], pp. 369–70) Pushkin's bête noire, Count Vorontsov, to whom contemporaries assigned the final success of the battle at Laon on March 9.

xxxivc

1 Like a lugubrious groan, like the grave's cold . . .

xxxv

4 / neighbor / *soséd*: This seems incongruous here—unless we realize that, besides connoting fellow landowner and

country neighbor, the term echoes here XII : 4 (to which see note).

10 / lading / *klad*: Apparently a mistake for *klad'*. *Klad* means "treasure," especially "hidden treasure."

12 / jib / *b'yútsya*: It will be noticed by the bilingual reader that Pushkin employs the same verb he did for the "fidgeting" horses in One : XXII : 9 (*b'yútsya kóni*). Here a stronger English verb is needed to convey the dramatic restiveness of these flinging and plunging steeds.

XXXVI

13 / [token]: Gofman, in a special Pushkin issue (1937) of the Russian-language periodical *Illyustrirovannaya Rossiya* (Paris), publishes with facsimiles (pp. 30 and 31) one of the few autographs extant of Chapter Six—a MS page in the possession of a Russian lady, Olga Kuprovich, in Viipuri, Finland, which is the final draft or corrected fair copy of Six : XXXVI and XXXVII. The variants are insignificant except for XXXVI : 13, where the word *priznak* ("sign," "index," "token," "evidence," etc.) is clearly written and thus should replace the word "phantom" (*prizrak*, "ghost," "shade," "apparition," etc.), which is, as Gofman correctly points out, a misprint in the published texts (1828, 1833, 1837). Cf. *Conversation of Bookseller with Poet*, l. 111: ". . . God's token, Inspiration,". . . *priznak bóga, vdohnovén'e* (see Comm., "Dropped Introductions").

XXXVII

13 / rush up / *domchítsya*: This verb combines the idea of "rushing" and "reaching."

13 / to it / *K néy*: "To her" (*ten'*, "shade," is feminine).

XXXVIII

This stanza is known only from Grot's publication (see
n. to XV–XVI).

> Having imbued his life with venom,
> not having done much good,
> alas, he might have with undying fame
> 4 the issues of newspapers filled.
> Teaching men, gulling brethren,
> to the thunder of plaudits or of curses,
> a grim course he might have achieved,
> 8 so as to breathe his last
> in sight of solemn trophies
> like our Kutuzov, or like Nelson,
> or like Napoleon, in exile,
> 12 or on the gallows, like Rïleev . . .

The two last lines, whatever they were, may have been
left out by Grot for reasons of censorship.

1–7 This image is on Pushkin's part a case of second sight,
since these traits refer to a type of beloved and hated
publicist of the fifties, sixties, and seventies, such as the
radicals Chernïshevski, Pisarev, and other civic, politico-
literary critics, a harsh type that did not yet exist in
1826, when this admirable stanza was composed.

12 Kondratiy Rïleev (1795–1826), a leading Decembrist,
who joined the Decembrist movement in the beginning
of 1823 and was executed by hanging. He is the com-
pletely mediocre author of *Meditations* (*Dumï*, 1821–
23), twenty-one patriotic poems on historical subjects
(one of them, a monologue by Boris Godunov, is curi-
ously echoed in so far as certain intonations go, two years
later, in a passage of Pushkin's tragedy of the same
name). He also wrote a long poem, *Voynarovskiy*, on a
Ukrainian theme (Mazepa, etc.), the separate edition of
which appeared in mid-March, 1825.

See also n. to Four : XIX : 5.

XL

5–14 The brook and the branches are tenacious of life, even
after their chanter's death. In his first published poem
(1814) to a rhyming friend, Pushkin advised him to for-
go "brooks, woods, and gloomy tombs." But the mood is
catching.

It will be noted that the Lenskian rill winds its way
into the domain of Onegin. And Onegin's *Idol mio*, the
last sound we hear him emit (Eight : xxxviii : 13), is
somehow congeneric to Lenski's "ideal" (Six : xxiii : 8),
the last word he writes in our presence. Thus also the
"ideal" in the last stanza of the novel recalls the ad-
jectival "ideal" of the Prefatory Piece. There is a con-
spiracy of words signaling to one another, throughout
the novel, from one part to another.

The "streamlets of the . . . brook" (ll. 8–9), *strúyki*
(a diminutive of the *strúi* in Four : xxxix : 2) . . . |
Ruch'ya, which suddenly develop "waves" (l. 12),
vólnï, remind us of certain aqueous transformations in
Tatiana's dream (Five : xi : 5–14; xii : 1–2, 13); but
then, on the other hand, *volnï* in both passages may be
hardly more than an attempt to render the French
ondes, which has no exact equivalent in Russian, while,
generally speaking, *ruchey* is used in a very large sense
by Pushkin, often being a mere synonym of the *potok*
("torrent").

Note also that "There is a spot," *Est' mesto* (l. 5), has
the very classical intonation of *est locus* (e.g., "est locus
Italiae medio sub montibus altis," *Aeneid*, vii, 563).

5–14 [and see xli; Seven : vi–vii] Professor Chizhevski says
(p. 270): ". . . this theme [the grave of a youth] was used
by K. Delavigne (Messenie)." There is no such poet as
"K. Delavigne," and if this is meant for Casimir De-
lavigne (as the index belatedly suggests), then neither

he nor anybody else wrote anything called "Messenie";
and if this is meant for Delavigne's collection of patriotic
elegies, *Les Messéniennes*, then there is no grave of any
youth sung therein.

14 [and see XLI : 13; Seven : VII : 9, 12] The simplicity of
the monument is yet another thematic convention in
the "bloom–doom" or "doom–tomb" series. Cf. the *ro-
mance*, in four elegiac quatrains, entitled *Werther à
Charlotte, une heure avant de mourir*, by André François
de Coupigny (1766–1835), st. III (in *Almanach des Muses*
[1801], p. 106):

> Vers le soir, près de l'urne où ma cendre paisible
> Dormira sous l'abri d'un simple monument,
> Viens rêver quelquefois; que ton âme sensible
> Plaigne l'infortuné qui mourut en t'aimant . . .

This is the model of Tumanski's elegy that I quote in my
n. to Six : XXI : 4.

See also Byron's allusion to General Marceau's tomb,
in *Childe Harold*, III, LVI, 1–2:

> By Coblentz, on a rise of gentle ground,
>   There is a small and simple Pyramid . . .

There is also a "simple monument" in Pushkin's ode
of 1814, *Recollections at Tsarskoe Selo* (see n. to Eight :
IC : 12).

XLI

1–4 Cf. Millevoye, *La Chute des feuilles* (*première version*):

> Mais son amante ne vint pas
> Visiter la pierre isolée;
> Et le pâtre de la vallée
> Troubla seul du bruit de ses pas
> Le silence du mausolée.

Batyushkov, *The Last Spring* (1815), rendered the end of Millevoye's elegy thus:

> And Delia did not visit
> his lonesome monument;
> only the shepherd in the quiet hour
> of sunrise, as he drove his flock
> into the field, with mournful song
> disturbed the sepulcher's dead silence.

The clumsy (in Russian) locution *kak . . . stado vïgon-yal* ("as he drove the flock" or "herd") instead of *kogda* ("when") is oddly echoed by Pushkin in Six : XLI : 1–2, "as [*kak*] begins to drip spring rain."

Mihail Milonov, *The Fall of the Leaves* (1819; see n. to Six : XXI : 4), winds up his bizarre version thus:

> Close to the oak is the youth's grave;
> but with woe in her soul
> his love here did not come;
> only the shepherd, guest of the bare fields,
> when at the hour of the evening star
> he off the meadow drives his flocks,
> disturbs the sepulcher's
> deep silence with the rustle of his steps.

Chizhevski (p. 274) makes at least five mistakes in quoting the five lines of the French original.

Baratïnski, in *his* rendering (1823), used the *deuxième version* of Millevoye's elegy, in which the author replaced the shepherd with the dead youth's mother (they *both* appear in a *troisième version*).

The theme is taken up again in the next chapter. Thus, after death has proved to exist in Arcadia, Lenski remains surrounded by the intertwined emblemata of minor poetry. He is buried by the side of a path, in pastoral solitude, not only out of elegiac considerations, but also because the consecrated ground of a churchyard was denied the suicide a dead duelist was assumed to be by the Church.

5 This young townswoman, the herdsman, and the women reapers are very pleasant stylizations. The herdsman will still be plaiting his shoe in Seven, and the young Amazon will, in a sense, become the Muse of Eight.

8 / *Nesyótsya po polyám*: Fr. *parcourt la plaine, les champs, la campagne.*

13 Its text will be given in Seven : VI.

14 / *nézhnïe glazá*: Alas, "tender eyes" is spoiled nowadays and hereabouts by consonance ("tenderize").

XLII

1 / in open champaign / *v chistom póle*: Fr. *dans la campagne*, "in open country." Karamzin (in 1793) artificially employed *v chistom pole* in the sense of *à la campagne, aux champs* (locution of the seventeenth century). Pushkin himself, in his French translations of (eleven) Russian songs (he used N. Novikov's *New and Complete Collection of Russian Songs*, pt. I, Moscow, 1780), rendered *chistoe pole* "la plaine déserte"!

XLIII

1–2 There is something pleasantly grotesque about this declaration of love for one's hero when one has just dispatched poor Lenski. See other declarations in Four : XXIV : 13, 14 and Two : XV : 1–2.

4 / *No mné tepér' ne do negó*: An intimate phrase combining the ideas of not being in the mood, not having the time for somebody or something, and not being up to the matter. See also n. to Three : XXXV : 6.

5–6 "And, to confess a truth ... [the author] | Grows weary of his long-lov'd mistress, Rhyme," says Dryden in his excellent Prologue (ll. 7–8) to his ridiculous tragedy *Aureng-Zebe* (performed spring, 1675).

XLIV

5–6 Should obsolete or otherwise unusual forms of Russian be rendered by unusual forms of English?

The noun *mólodost'* ("youth," as a state or a period) has an archaic form, *mládost'*, no longer in use even in poetry. In *EO* and elsewhere Pushkin employs both forms and their adjectives (*molodóy* and *mladóy*) indiscriminately, merely choosing that form which slips more easily into the right metrical compartment. Sometimes *molodóy* (masc. nom. sing. and fem. gen. sing.) or *molodáya* (fem. nom. sing.) dwindles to a shadow epithet with the Gallic intonation of, say, *la jeune Olga*, regardless of our already knowing that she is young. "Youthful," which of course is not archaic in the sense *mladóy* is, is hardly worth using when "young" can do just as well; but in the course of *EO* there are passages where *mládost'* should be rendered by "youthhood" or by an even more obsolete word. Thus, when in Six : XLIV Pushkin laments the passing of youth and mentions a twinning of rhyme words that in our times would not come about, one twin being dead—

> *Mechtí, mechtí! gde vásha sládost'?*
> *Gde, véchnaya k ney rífma, "mládost' "?*

—this translator has not been able to resist the temptation of:

> Dreams, dreams! Where is your dulcitude?
> Where is (its stock rhyme) juventude?

It may be argued that in no age has dulcitude– juventude cropped up commonly in English poetry as *sládost'–mládost'* did in Pushkin's day and that therefore the analogy is strained. It might have been wiser to render the terminals as "sweetness" and "youth" and explain the situation in a note.

Commentary

The flirtation with "pranksome rhyme" (see XLIII : 6), *shalún'ya rífma* (Fr. *la rime espiègle* or *polissonne*), can be traced back to the gratuitous "rose" of Four : XLII : 3.

7–8 / *i vprávdu nakonéts | Uvyál, uvyál eyó* [*mladosti*] *venéts*; 11: Thus Pushkin identifies in retrospect the Lenskian theme of withered bloom (Two : X : 13–14, Six : XXI : 3–4, and Six : XXXI : 12–13) with the effusions of his own youth. At twenty-one, in an elegy beginning "I have outlived my aspirations," he wrote (ll. 5–8):

> Under the storms of cruel fate
> My bloomy wreath has withered fast;
> Alone, forlorn, I live, and wait
> When will the end arrive at last.

(Three quatrains composed Feb. 22, 1821, at Kamenka, province of Kiev, and at first intended for insertion after l. 55 of the long poem *The Caucasian Captive*, which our poet was finishing at the time; it was completed the following day, and an epilogue was added May 15 of the same year, during a brief visit to Odessa.)

14 / thirty soon: This stanza (as well as XLIII and XLV) was written Aug. 10, 1827, at Mihaylovskoe. Our poet was twenty-eight years old.

Cf. Bertin, *Les Amours*, bk. III, *Elégie* XXII (1785):

> La douce illusion ne sied qu'à la jeunesse;
> Et déjà l'austère Sagesse
> Vient tout bas m'avertir que j'ai vu trente hivers.

The drafts of XLIII (2368, f. 24ʳ), XLIV (ibid.), and XLV (f. 24ᵛ) are one of the three autographs of Six that have reached us (the others are: the drafts of XXXIVa, b, and c, PD 155, and a final draft or first fair copy of XXXVI–XXXVII, coll. Kuprovich) and bear the date "10 *avg* [1826]" (the year, according to Tomashevski, Acad 1937, p. 661). See also n. to Six : XLVI : 1–4.

XLV

1 / My noontide: Cf. Jean Baptiste Rousseau, *Odes*, bk. I,
no. x (c. 1695), "tirée du cantique d'Ezéchias, Isaïe, chap.
38, verset 9 et suiv. (*Ego dixi: in dimidio dierum
meorum . . .*)":

> Au midi de mes années
> Je touchois à mon couchant . . .

("In the noontide of my days," Psalm of Hezekiah, king
of Judah, in Isa. 38 : 10)
The romanticists improved on this: Cf. Byron, *Don
Juan*, X, XXVII, 4–5:

> That horrid equinox, that hateful section
> Of human years—that half-way house . . .

XLVI

1–4 Pushkin wrote down this quatrain (already published in
the 1828 and 1833 edns.), together with a quotation from
Coleridge, Oct. 2, 1835, at Trigorskoe, in the gold-tooled
red morocco album belonging to his inamorata of ten
years before, Annette Vulf. The quotation is the begin-
ning of a five-line epigram written by Coleridge in 1802:

> How seldom, friend! a good great man inherits
> Honour or wealth with all his worth and pains!

1 / coverts / *séni*: The reference here (as in Two : I : 12) is
to the shelter of trees. See my nn. to Six : VII : 9.

8 / nook / *úgol*: "Corner" or "hole" would seem to be less
exact here. Elsewhere I have used "nook" for *ugolok*,
the diminutive of *ugol*. See my nn. to Two : I : 2.

VARIANT

13–14 In the first edition of *EO*, Chapter Six ended in the
following (see Pushkin's n. 40):

Commentary

amidst the soulless proudlings,
amidst the brilliant fools,

XLVII

amidst the crafty, the fainthearted,
crazy, spoiled children,
villains both ludicrous and dull,
4 obtuse and captious judges;
amidst devout coquettes;
amidst the voluntary lackeys;
amidst the daily modish scenes
8 of courteous, affectionate betrayals;
amidst cold verdicts
of cruel-hearted vanity;
amidst the vexing emptiness
12 of schemes, of thoughts and conversations;
in that slough where with you
I bathe, dear friends!

XLVII : 11–12 / amidst the vexing emptiness of schemes, of thoughts and conversations / *Sredi dosádnoy pustotí* / *Raschyótov, dúm i razgovórov*: In a copy of the separate edition of Chapter Six (bound with the previous chapters), Pushkin, sometime in 1828, altered by hand *dum*, "of thoughts," to *dush*, "of souls." This hardly affects the meaning of the whole rather colorless passage (a very ordinary tabulation); in fact, both *dush* and *dum* might be rendered in English by "of mentalities." Pushkin obviously did not bother much about this correction, for the stanza, when relegated to the notes in the complete 1833 and 1837 edns., retains the reading *dum*.

Raschyotï means "schemes," "calculations," "computations," "estimates." *Dushi*, as already mentioned, means "souls." Brodski (*EO* commentary, pp. 250–51), in his sociological fervor, abolishes the comma between *raschyotov* and *dush*, gives "souls" the sense of "souls of peasants" (serfs being reckoned by "souls," as cattle are by "heads"), and makes the two lines read:

> amidst the vexing emptiness
> of estimates of serfs and conversations . . .

implying that Pushkin is here satirizing barons who in
high society engaged in shop talk, in calculating the
number of slaves each possesses and haggling about their
prices! This is sheer nonsense, of course: no such talk was
typical of the beau-monde prattle. Besides, the construc-
tion *raschyotov dush* is impossibly clumsy and themati-
cally throws out of balance both the "vexing emptiness"
and the unspecified "conversations."

XLIII–XLVI

In the last four stanzas of this chapter Pushkin passes in
review, among other things, some of the favorite words
of his vocabulary.

Chapter Seven

The first motto is Dmitriev's poem *The Liberation of Moscow* (1795), ll. 11–12.

In the opening lines of the greatest ode in Russian, Pushkin's *Liberty* (composed 1817):

> Be gone, be hidden from my eyes,
> weak queen of Cythera!

our poet slightly imitates Dmitriev's worthless *Liberation of Moscow* (liberation from Troubled Times, Poland, and Pretenders in 1613, when Prince Dmitri Pozharski vanquished the Lithuanians and the first Romanov was elected to the throne), ll. 3–4:

> I wish to sing not noisy pleasures,
> not sweets of Cytherean bonds.

Dmitriev's poem (162 iambic tetrameters, irregularly rhymed) is marked, incidentally, by the most formidable clash of consonants known in Russian poetry (l. 14):

> a diamond scepter in your hands . . .
> *Almáznïy skíptr v tvoíh rukáh . . .*

ptrvtv!

The second motto to Seven is Baratïnski's *Feasts* (1821), l. 52 (see n. to Three : XXX : 1).

The third is Griboedov's *Woe from Wit* (finished 1824), I, vii, Sofia's taunt, Chatski's retort (see n. to Six : XI : 12).

For reasons that will transpire in the course of the notes to this chapter, one would like to suggest that Pushkin might have also used a fourth motto—from Kozlov's *Princess Natalia Dolgoruki*, can. II, st. IV:

> . . . Moscow appears . . .
> The eye now sees Ivan Velikiy;
> its crown glows ember-bright . . .

The name "Big John" is applied to the tallest steeple of the city: ". . . the great campanile of Ivan Veliky, erected in the Lombardo-Byzantine style by Boris Godunov, in 1600, rises to the height of 271 ft. (318 ft. including the cross), and contains many bells, one of which weighs 64⅓ tons" (Prince Peter Kropotkin and John Thomas Bealby, in *The Encyclopaedia Britannica*, 11th edn., New York, 1911).

I

1–3 / vernal beams . . . turbid streams: A literary, not a local spring. In many western European poems fashionable at the time, we find similar "rills | Let loose in spring-time from the snowy hills," from Moore's *Lalla Rookh* (1817): "The Veiled Prophet of Khorassan" (5th edn., London, 1817, p. 30), and the earlier "Dissolving snows in livid torrents lost," from Thomson's *Spring*, l. 16. Their real source is Virgil; cf. *Georgics*, I, 43–44:

> Vere novo gelidus canis montibus humor
> liquitur . . .

or imitations of Virgil:

Au retour du printemps, quand du sommet des montagnes qu'elle blanchissait, la neige fondue commence à s'écouler . . .

Commentary

4 / onto the inundated fields / *Na potoplyónnïe lugá*; II : 2 /
spring, spring, season of love / *Vesná, vesná! porá lyubví*:
A curious rewording of Baratïnski's *Spring* (six tetra-
metric staves rhymed abbab, first published December,
1822, in *The Polar Star*), ll. 5–10, 28–30:

> The earth has risen from her sleep
> .   .   .   .   .   .
> The snows in torrents flow;
> in hills again the horns resound;
> again the zephyrs fly
> onto the renovated fields [*Na obnovlyónnïe lugá*].
> .   .   .   .   .   .
> Ah, if the generous gods allowed
> that to a mortal would return
> the season of love with the season of flowers [*Porá
>   lyubví s poróy tsvetóv*]!

10 / after the tribute of the field / *za dán'yu polevóy*: To
fetch the mead's meed, duty, due; to tax the meadow.
Cf. Jean Antoine de Baïf (1532–89), *Passetemps*, bk.
I: *Du printemps*, st. IX:

> Les ménagères avettes
> .   .   .   .
> Voletant par les fleurettes
> Pour cueillir ce qui leur duit.

This also stems from Virgil and not from direct ob-
servation.

11 / waxen cell: A commonplace in both English and French
poetry. See, for instance, Gay, *Rural Sports, a Georgic
. . . to Mr. Pope* (1713), can. I, l. 88: "[bees] with sweets
the waxen cells distend," or André Chénier, *Elégies*, I
(ed. Walter; XVI, *Œuvres posthumes*, 1826), l. 33: "Sa
cellule de cire"; there are many other examples.
In his commentary to *EO*, Brodski (p. 253) drags in a
bit of Russian "folklore," wherein is mentioned a little
cell of honey, which is obviously the work of some minor

Russian poet of the beginning of the nineteenth century who had read French poets or their Russian imitators.

13 / *Stadá shumyát*: The herds and flocks bellow and bleat.

II

There are a number of analogies (probably coincidental or going back to Chateaubriand) between sts. II and III and Letters XXII–XXIV of Senancour's *Oberman* (for instance, end of XXII: ". . . tout existe en vain devant lui, il vit seul, il est absent dans le monde vivant"; and XXIV: ". . . cette volupté de la mélancolie . . . printemps. . . . Saison du bonheur! je vous redoute trop dans mon ardente inquiétude").

See also a passage of Chateaubriand's *Mémoires d'outre-tombe*, the chapter on his sojourn of 1793 on Jersey, written 1822 (ed. Levaillant, pt. I, bk. x, ch. 3):

Ce qui enchante dans l'âge des liaisons devient dans l'âge délaissé un objet de souffrance et de regret. On ne souhaite plus le retour des mois . . . une belle soirée de la fin d'avril . . . ces choses qui donnent le besoin et le désir du bonheur, vous tuent.

2 See n. to Seven : I : 4.

3 / dark / *tyómnoe*: Other editions have *Kakóe tómnoe volnén'e*, "What a languorous agitation."

5 / tender feeling / *umilén'em* (instr.): The word can be accurately rendered only by the French *attendrissement*, for which the horrible "inteneration" has been suggested in English. It can be paraphrased by "melting mood," "softheartedness," "tender emotion," and the like. It is related to compassion as charm is to beauty or a dewy eye to one brimming with tears. See n. to Six : XIV : 9.

12–13 In a draft of II (Leonid Maykov coll., PD 108) a variant (possibly of 12–13) reads:

> Give back to me snowstorms and blizzards
> and the long shade of winter nights . . .

III

See my n. at beginning of II.

IV

1 / Now is the time / *Vot vrémya*: Cf. Thomson, *Winter* (1726), ll. 33–35, 39:

> . . . Then is the time [fair autumn],
> For those, whom wisdom, and whom nature charm,
> To steal themselves from the degenerate crowd,
> .   .   .   .
> And woo lone quiet, in her silent walks.

1 / good lazybones / *dóbrïe lenívtsï*: Fr. *bons paresseux. Len'*, in the idiom of the time, meant "the enjoyment of outward inactivity in contrast to the simultaneous animation of the inner senses" (Hodasevich, c. 1930, quoted from his *Literaturnïe stat'i i vospominaniya*, New York, 1954). It has, moreover, a Gallic turn of meaning. Cf. the delightful note of indolence in Gresset's *Epître* V, to Father Bougeant, in which he speaks of the "smiling ease" of his verses, which have earned him

> . . . l'indulgence
> Des voluptueux délicats,
> Des meilleurs paresseux de France,
> Les seuls juges dont je fais cas.

4 / you, fledglings [*ptentsï*] of the Lyóvshin school: Students of Lyovshin's works (not "peasants," as some Russian commentators have thought!).

Vasiliy Lyovshin (1746–1826), a Tula landowner, prolific compiler, author of over eighty works in 190 volumes, including various tragedies and novels, and whatnots, mostly translated from the German, such as *The Enchanted Labyrinth* (*Ocharovannïy labirint*), an Oriental tale in three parts (1779–80), and a *Life of Nelson* (1807). I have seen a work of his on windmills, steam mills, and water mills. He was known in the 1820's for his voluminous compilations dealing with *Flower Gardens* and *Vegetable Gardens*, and for a *Manual of Agriculture* (1802–04). At present he is remembered only for his rather remarkable *Russian Tales* (*Russkie skazki*), "containing the most ancient accounts of famous bogatïrs [peasant knights, strong men], folk tales, and other adventures remaining in the memory through their retelling" (Moscow, 1780–83). Of all his works only this is mentioned by D. Blagoy, *Istoriya russkoy literaturï XVIII veka* (Moscow, 1945), pp. 271–72, who is also my authority on the pronunciation of the name.

5 / Priams: Priam, last king of Troy, a gentle old man with more than fifty children. His life ended in despair and ruin. *Un Priam* is generally used in the sense of *type d'extrême malheur* rather than in that of a venerable rusticator or rural paterfamilias, as apparently Pushkin has it here, through some twist of literary memory.

14 / start to trek / *Tyanites'*: Inf. *tyanut'sya*. A term difficult to translate wholly. It blends the idea of "tending," "stretching," and "progressing in a long, slow line." The same verb is used for the caravan of geese in Four : XL : 12.

VARIANT

4 The draft reads (2371, f. 3ʳ):

you, carefree songsters . . .

V

2 / calash / *kolyáske*: A four-wheeled open carriage with a folding hood. Also spelled, in eighteenth-century England, with a *g* (after its passage through Germany). It is the true French *calèche*—which, incidentally, the American reader should be careful not to confuse with the similarly named Canadian vehicle, a rude two-wheeled contraption (depicted, for example, in *Webster's New International Dictionary*, 1957). A later variety of *kolyaska* is the victoria.

6; VI : 5–6: The Batyushkov and Millevoye *décor* is again described as we revisit Lenski's tomb with the Amazon, an ally of Pushkin's Muse. The following observation may be of interest to the Pushkinian scholar.

In one of his greatest short poems, *The Lord Forbid My Going Mad* (1832), Pushkin, in his special code, signals an awareness of Batyushkov's madness: Batyushkov, in his elegy *The Last Spring* (1815), an imitation of Millevoye's *La Chute des feuilles* (discussed in my n. to Six : XLI : 1–4), had used an epithet for the nightingale that was unusual in Russian poetry (ll. 3–4):

> The brilliant [*yárkiy*] voice of Philomela
> has charmed the gloomy pinewood . . .

Pushkin, in his 1833 piece of five six-line stanzas, with masculine lines bbcddc, in iambic tetrameter (b, d) and trimeter (c), echoes Batyushkov's lines in the last stanza:

> And I shall hear at night neither the brilliant
> voice of the nightingale,
> nor the dense forest's murmur,
> but my companions' cries,
> the oaths of the night wardens,
> shrill sounds, the clink of chains.

Batyushkov's and Pushkin's epithet is, really, a simple

Gallicism. See, for example, Dudoyer (Gérard, marquis du Doyer de Gastels, 1732–98), in a madrigal to Mlle Doligny (a charming actress, whom he eventually married), May 1, 1769 (*Almanach des Muses* [1809], p. 35):

   . . . des oiseaux la voix brillante . . .

VI

2–3 Cf. Addison, *The Spectator*, no. 37 (Apr. 12, 1711): ". . . a little Rivulet which runs through a Green Meadow . . ."

5–6 See n. to Seven : V : 6.

6 / cinnamon rose / *shipóvnik*: European brier with fragrant pink flowers and soft red fruit, *Rosa cinnamomea* L., the modest country cousin of some six thousand cultivated varieties of roses. It blooms in June. L. H. Bailey, *Manual of Cultivated Plants* (New York, 1949), p. 536, pleasingly says: "an old garden rose, running wild and persisting about old premises, along fences, in cemeteries, and by roadsides." Russian sources, on the contrary, consider it to be the ancestor of garden roses (M. Neyshtadt, *Opredelitel' rasteniy* [Moscow, 1947–48], p. 263).

10 / to the stranger / *Prishél'tsu*: *Prishelets* means grammatically "he who comes from another place," and possibly Pushkin used this loosely for *prohozhiy*, "passenger," "wayfarer," Lat. *viator*.

VII

2–4 A poet's tomb, with a wreath and lyre suspended from the branches over it, had been sung by Zhukovski in a

famous elegy of 1811 entitled *The Bard* (*Pevets*). It con-
sists of six stanzas of eight verses each, with rhymes
abbaceec. Its meter is curious and was a great novelty in
Russian prosody: four iambic pentameters are followed
in every stanza by three iambic tetrameters, and the
closing verse is a dactylic dimeter (ll. 41–48):

> Gone is the bard, and from these haunts his traces
> Have disappeared, the voice we heard is still,
> And all is melancholy, dale and hill,
> And all is mute. Only the quiet zephyrs
>   Shaking the withered wreath, when they
>   Over the tomb sometimes suspire,
>   Are sadly echoed by the lyre:
>   Piteous bard [*Bédnïy pevéts*]!

It will be noted that the term *bednïy pevets*, "poor
songster," "luckless poet," is applied to Lenski in Six :
XIII : 10, *Na vstréchu bédnogo pevtsá*, "à la rencontre
du pauvre chantre."

9–10, 12 See n. to Six : XL : 14.

9–11 In describing Lenski's neglected tomb by the road-
side in Russian Arcadia, Pushkin expresses the work of
weeds and oblivion by means of two remarkable en-
jambments:

> *No nïne . . . pámyatnik untlïy*
> *Zabït. K nemú privïchnïy sléd*
> *Zaglóh. Venká na vétvi nét . . .*

The translator would dearly wish to preserve the exact
cut and the alliterations (the long-drawn *nï*, the recur-
rent rhythm of the two disyllables in *z*), but must content
himself with the following:

> but now . . . the drear memorial is
> forgot. The wonted trail to it,
> weed-choked. No wreath is on the bough.

The opening word in l. 11 is most accurately translated by "weed-choked," but, strictly speaking, no Russian equivalent of "weed" actually appears within *zagloh*. This would not matter much, had not the presence of "weed" in English improved upon a situation that is quite extraordinary enough. I doubt very much that at the time this was written (between autumn, 1827, and Feb. 19, 1828) Pushkin had acquired enough English not only to read through an English poem of almost two thousand lines but to catch niceties of English rhythm. Howbeit, the fact remains that *EO*, Seven : VII : 9–11 bears a striking resemblance, both in mood and modulation, to a passage of Wordsworth's *The White Doe of Rylstone* (composed 1807–08, pub. 1815), can. VII, ll. 1570–71, 1575–76:

> Pools, terraces, and walks are sown
> With weeds; the bowers are overthrown,
>
> .   .   .   .
>
> The lordly Mansion of its pride
> Is stripped; the ravage hath spread wide . . .

12 / beneath / *pod*: Misprinted *nad*, "above," in the 1837 edn.

VARIANT

1–10 In a draft of this stanza (2368, ff. 36ʳ, 37ʳ):

> Around it blooms the cinnamon rose,
> brief herald of warm days,
> and ivy twines, lover of tombs;
> the nightingale resounds and trills
> in the hush of the muted wilderness,
> and over the white urn, 'tis said,
> the fresh breeze in the morning
> sometimes will sway a wreath
> upon the boughs of two old pines,
> and on the urn a scripture says . . .

According to Tsyavlovski (*Works* 1936, I, 757), the following quatrain is twice repeated on the same page

(2368, f. 36ʳ, according to Tomashevski, Acad 1937, p. 417):

> Around it blooms the cinnamon rose,
> brief herald of warm days;
> the ivy twines, lover of tombs,
> anight there trills the nightingale.

Then the following seven lines in dactylic and anapaestic hexameter with feminine endings, unrhymed, are jotted down (1827):

In the groves of Caryae, dear to the hunters, a cavern is
    hidden:
Lithe pines bend their branches around, and its entrance
Is screened by the freely twining and rambling
Ivy, lover of crags and crevices. Flowing from stone
To stone, in a sonant arc, a boisterous brook
Floods the cave's bottom and, cleaving a deep bed,
    meanders
Afar through a dense grove, which with its purl it
    gladdens.

VIII

In draft (2371, f. 4):

> ⟨But⟩ once, at eventide,
> one of the maidens hither came.
> It seemed, with grievous heartache,
> 4 she was disturbed.
> As by fear agitated,
> in tears, in front of the dear dust
> she stood, with downcast head
> 8 and with her hands in tremor joined.
> But then, with hurried strides,
> a young uhlan overtook her,
> tight-laced, well built and rosy-cheeked,
> 12 flaunting a black mustache,
> inclining his broad shoulders,
> and proudly making his spurs sound.

IX

In draft (2371, f. 4):

> She at the warrior glanced.
> His gaze burned with vexation,
> and she grew pale ⟨and⟩ sighed,
> 4 but said nothing.
> And Lenski's bride in silence
> leaving the orphaned spot
> with him retreated and henceforth
> 8 came no more from beyond the hills.
> 'Tis so! Indifferent oblivion
> beyond the sepulcher awaits us.
> The voice of foes, of friends, of loves
> 12 falls silent suddenly. Alone over the estate
> the angry chorus of the heirs
> starts an indecent squabble.

9–14 It will be noted that when Pushkin dropped VIII and IX he transferred these lines to XI : 9–14.

X

1–2 / Pining away, she did not weep: A common construction with Pushkin instead of "she neither pined nor wept."

5–8 / [*ulán*] *uvlyók . . . uspél . . . umél . . .*: All three Russian verbs in this alliterative sequence are difficult to render exactly: *uvlyok* is "carried away" when the object is a person; *uspel* can be understood here either as "succeeded" or "had time to"; and *umel* (a Gallicism) connotes "had the ability" and "found a way" (Fr. *sut*).

13–14 A shocking picture. We have gone far since our first impression of naïve little Olga, the sinless charmer gamboling with the lad Vladimir in the ancestral park

Commentary

(Two : XXI). There is now something of a cunning young demon about Olga, strangely changed ever since that nightmare ball. What does that slight smile imply? Why this glow in a virgin? Should we not suppose—and I think we should—that the uhlan will have a difficult time with this bride—a sly nymph, a dangerous flirt, as Pushkin's own wife is to be a few years later (1831–37)?

This is the human-interest type of commentary.

XI

2 / deaf / *gluhóy*: The epithet is ambiguous. In reference to a region, *gluhoy* (*gluhoy kray, gluhaya storona*) means "dense," "dull," "gloomy," "muffled," "remote," "stagnant," etc.

9–14 See n. to IX : 9–14.

VARIANT

9–14 A draft (2371, f. 4ᵛ) reads:

> At least, out of the grave
> there did not rise on that sad day
> his jealous shade,
> and at the late hour dear to Hymen,
> no traces of sepulchral visitations
> frightened the newlywed.

XII

A very poor stanza—after a series of magnificent ones. As often happens with Pushkin, when he is obliged to attend to the plot and to outline a series of actions that do not interest him, his attempts at hurried conciseness result in dismembered platitudes and naïve awkwardness. Neither he nor any novelist of his time had mastered the art of transition that Flaubert was to discover three decades later.

XIII

St. XIII (2371, ff. 5ʳ–5ᵛ) is dated Feb. 19 [1828], at the top of the draft (f. 5ʳ; the year according to Tomashevski, Acad 1937, p. 661).

6 / own dear / *rodnáya*: There is a subtle ambiguity here since, basically, *rodnaya* means "kindred," and Olga *was* Tatiana's "kindred" darling.

Incidentally, this passionate fondness for her younger sister is new to the reader, who will be wondering, when he reaches Eight, why Tatiana does not remember Olga any more.

XV

1–2 Pushkin writes in a note (Boldino, 1830; draft in MB 2387A—a cahier sewed up from loose leaves by the police after our poet's death—f. 22; first published 1841):

I glanced through the review of Chapter Seven in the *Northern Bee** at a house where I was a guest and at a minute when I was not concerned with *Onegin*. I noticed some very well-written verse and a rather amusing joke about a beetle. I have:

'Twas evening. The sky darkened. Waters streamed quietly. The beetle churred.

The reviewer [Faddey Bulgarin] welcomed the appearance of a new personage and expected him to prove a better sustained [*vïderzhannïy*] character than the others.

2 / The beetle churred / *zhúk zhuzhzhál*: The reference is to a cockchafer, a scarabaeoid beetle, the European maybug, either of the two species of *Melolontha*, which flies at dusk, with a bumbling, blind perseverance, along country lanes in May and June. Some poets have con-

---

*No. 35, Mar. 22, 1830; see my n. to Eight: XXXV: 9.

fused its drone, or whir, with the hum of hawkmoths bombinating at nightfall over flowers; and a dung beetle (*Geotrupes* sp.) has been suggested in Shakespeare's case (quoted below); but why Miss Deutsch should think fit to transform a coleopterous insect into an orthopterous one ("One heard the crickets' slender choir") is incomprehensible—especially since the chafer is a common component of descriptions of dusk in English poetry. When Bulgarin ironically welcomed Pushkin's beetle as a new character, he was wrong: it was a very old character indeed.

Shakespeare, *Macbeth* (1623), III, ii, 42–43:

> The shard-born beetle with his drowsy hums
> Hath rung night's yawning peal . . .

William Collins, *Ode to Evening* (1746), ll. 11–14:

> Or where the Beetle winds
> His small but sullen Horn,
> As oft he rises 'midst the twilight Path,
> Against the Pilgrim born in heedless Hum.

Thomas Gray, *An Elegy Wrote in a Country Church Yard* (1751), l. 7:

> . . . the beetle wheels his droning flight . . .

James Macpherson, *The Songs of Selma* (the "royal residence" of Fingal; 1765):

The flies of evening are on their feeble wings; the hum of their course is on the field.

Robert Southey, *To Contemplation* (written in Bristol, 1792; pub. 1797), ll. 26–28, 31:

> Or lead me where amid the tranquil vale
> The broken streamlet flows in silver light;
> And I will linger . . .
> .   .   .   .
> And hearken the dull beetle's drowsy flight . . .

Crabbe incorrectly transfers "the beetle's hum" to the "light and shade" of an autumnal evening (*The Cathedral-Walk*, in *Tales of the Hall*, 1819).

Young Zhukovski, in his famous, admirably modulated first version, the iambic one (1802), of Gray's elegy, loyally did his best (l. 7):

Lish' izredka, zhuzhzhá, vechérniy zhúk mel'káet . . .
only at times, with drone, the evening beetle passes . . .

In his second translation (1839) Zhukovski used dactylic hexameter, unrhymed:

. . . Only at intervals passes
Swiftly the beetle, with heavy somniferous hum.

(Zhukovski is influenced here by Southey.)

But in Chateaubriand's version of the elegy, *Les Tombeaux champêtres* (London, 1796), *Melolontha grayi* undergoes the following change:

On n'entend que le bruit de l'insecte incertain

—a very uncertain insect, indeed; but then the Age of Good Taste prohibited one's using the "specific and low" word *hanneton*. Forty years later the great French writer redeemed this surrender by his excellent translation of *Paradise Lost*.

8–14; XVI : 1–7 All this is embarrassingly close to a passage in Kozlov, *Princess Natalia Dolgoruki* (known in 1827, pub. 1828), can. I, ll. 11–32, and is only a slight improvement on the blind poet's description of Natalia's approaching her former home (ll. 11–13, 24–26, 28–32):

she walks, her heart beats;
there is a meadow with a grove before her;
yonder a path winds to a village
. . . .
but suddenly transfixed by something,
she stops, woeful and pale;

perplexity is in her eyes,

.   .   .   .

she does not go on [villageward], does not go back,
she casts around a timid glance:
"Oh, if down there . . . And I whom fate
bids to lie hidden . . . May be . . . No!
Who'd know me? . . ."

Kozlov's long poem, in two cantos, consists of irregu-
larly rhymed iambic tetrameters with staves of varying
length; it recalls the misfortunes, Gothic rather than
Slavic in nature, of the daughter of Count Boris Shere-
metev, a field marshal of Peter I. At one point, the ghost
of her husband appears before her and, in order to show
that he has been decapitated, takes off his head like a cap.

See also nn. to Seven : XXIX : 5–7 and XXXII : 13–14.

As said in my "Notes on Prosody" (see App. II),
Pushkin's text in XVI : 2–6 illustrates the longest se-
quence of scudless lines (in one stanza) in the entire
work; the influence, perhaps, of a bad conscience.

13 / the heart in her: Since *sérdtse* ("heart") is accented
fore and *egó* ("his") or *eyó* ("her") aft, it follows that
"his [her] heart" cannot be used within a Russian iambic
or trochaic line. Hence the awkward *serdtse v nyóm* ("in
him") or *v néy* ("in her"), of which there are several
examples in *EO*.

XVI

14 / lady / *bárïnyu*: I suspect that *barïnya* may be a mis-
print for *barïshnya*, "miss," Fr. *la demoiselle*.

XVIII

The way Anisia (a close relative of Tatiana's nurse), as
she rambles on, imperceptibly switches from Eugene to
his uncle is a great artistic achievement on our poet's

part. The real master for the old housekeeper was not
the young blade from St. Petersburg, but the old gentle-
man who had grumbled at her since 1780.

2 / late Lenski / *Pokóynïy Lénskiy*: This is, of course, an
impossible form of reference on the old serf woman's
part. She would have referred to poor Lenski by his first
name and patronymic or said *Krasnogorskiy barin*. Be-
sides, she must have known that the host had killed the
guest.

11 / tomfools / *durachkí*: A simple card game, played in
Russia now mainly by children.

13 / to his dear bones / *kóstochkam egó*: This affectionate
diminutive cannot be rendered by "bonelets" or "os-
sicles."

XIX

11–14 At this point the reader should be reminded of the
fascination that Byron exercised on Continental minds
in the 1820's. His image was the romantic counterpart
of that of Napoleon, "the man of fate," whom a myste-
rious force kept driving on, toward an ever-receding
horizon of world domination. Byron's image was seen
as that of a tortured soul wandering in constant quest of
a haven beyond the haze, as in Pierre Lebrun's *En
apprenant la mort de Lord Byron* (1824), II, 17–20:

> Ainsi, loin des cités, sur les monts, sur les mers,
> Cherchant un idéal qui le fuyait sans cesse,
> Martyr des maux rêvés plus que des maux soufferts,
> Au gré d'une inconstante et sauvage tristesse . . .

12 / puppet: The old word for statue (now *statuya*) is
kumir ("idol"), and the old word for statuette (now

statuetka) is *kúkla* ("puppet"), which is the word
Pushkin uses here. He had used it before in a short
poem, *Epistle to Pavel Yudin*, a schoolmate of his,
written in the summer of 1815 (ll. 22–26):

> contented with a humble lot,
> I asked myself why should bards have
> brilliants, and topazes, and sapphires,
> and empty porphyritic vases,
> and in the niches precious puppets?

VARIANT

13–14 The draft (2371, f. 6ᵛ) leads us back to One : XXIV:

> crystal, and bronze, and china,
> ⟨and⟩ an array of ⟨modish⟩ little brushes.

XXI–XXII

VARIANTS

In a canceled variant of XXI : 10–14 and in XXII alternate,
we are introduced to an album Tatiana finds in Onegin's
study.

10–14 This alternate ending of XXI, in the fair copy (PB 43),
reads:

> At first she was not in a mood for books,
> ⟨when suddenly among them was revealed⟩
> ⟨an album⟩, and fell to reading
> Tatiana with an avid soul;
> and a different world revealed itself to her.

XXII alt. This variant, in the fair copy (PB 43), reads:

> Along the edges neatly banded
> with gilded silver,
> with writings, drawings it was covered
> 4 all over in Onegin's hand.
> 'Mongst unintelligible scribbling
> there flickered thoughts, remarks,
> portraits, dates, names,

8 also initials, cryptographs,
   fragments, rough drafts of letters—
   it was, in brief, a candid journal
   where had poured out his soul
12 Onegin in his youthful days:
   a diary of dreamings and of pranks.
   Some passages I'll copy out for you.

Similarly, Antonia, in Nodier's novel *Sbogar* (1818;
see n. to Three : XII : 11), after Sbogar's disappearance,
comes across his jottings, some of which are in ink; others,
in pencil; a few, in blood.

"Onegin's Album" begins immediately after XXI in
the draft (cahier 2371), with XXI on f. 7^r and XXII alt.
(followed by the "Album") on f. 7^v.

An album was a fashionable thing in those times.
Compare Captain Jesse's description of Beau Brummell's
album, *Brummell*, vol. I, ch. 11:

The corners and clasps are of massive embossed silver gilt,
like those on old missals, and the binding is dark-blue
velvet. . . . It contains no fewer than two hundred twenty-
six pieces of poetry [by eminent contemporaries] . . . in-
serted with his own hand.

Onegin's album, the binding of which is also fortified
with silver at the edges, seems to be, however, more on
the lines of a diary than of a scrapbook.

After having had Tatiana learn—or think she learned
—something of Onegin's nature from his album, or from
the marginalia in his books (XXIII—XXIV), our poet planned
at first to leave her brooding there in the desolate castle
and to take up its former occupant again (see further,
XXV alt.).

ONEGIN'S ALBUM

Twelve entries in fair copy. Numbered by Pushkin (no
doubt, provisionally). MS in the Saltïkov-Shchedrin
Public Library, Leningrad (PB 43).

I

I am disliked and vilified;
in a male circle I'm unbearable;
before me young things quiver;
4 dames look at me askance.
Why is it? Because conversations
we're glad to take for deeds;
because to trifling men trifles are grave;
8 because stupidity is volatile and wicked;
because of fiery souls the rashness
to smug nonentity
is either insulting or absurd;
12 because, by liking room, wit cramps.

It will be noted that ll. 6–12 (except for one word in 7) are identical to Eight : IX : 9–10, 12, 11, 5–8 (in that order), but have a more positive, less interrogative, tone.

II

"You are afraid of Countess -ov,"
said to them Eliza K.
"Yes," retorted austere N. N.;
4 "we are afraid of Countess -ov,
as you are of a spider."

VARIANTS

1 / Draft (2371, f. 8ʳ):

. . . maiden Princess R—ov

Canceled variants:

. . . Eliza R—ov
. . . old [Mrs.] K—ov
. . . Countess K—ov

Fair copy, canceled (PB 43):

. . . old [Mrs.] Z. K.
. . . old [Mrs.] V. K.

3 "N. N." is "[Mr.] E. K." in the draft (ibid.). "N. N." is not Tatiana's husband-to-be, whom Pushkin had not yet

evolved. Russians use the Latin *N* for the names of people or places as others use *X*.

III

> In the Koran sound thoughts are many:
> This, for instance: "Before every sleep
> pray, beware of devious ways,
> 4 revere God and don't argue with a fool."

2–4 This "quotation," a very vague paraphrase of a passage in the Koran, which Pushkin knew from French versions, seems to be based on part of sura (section) LXXIII, referring to night prayer, where 8 and 10 read, in Richard Bell's translation, *The Qur'an* (Edinburgh, 1937–39), p. 614: "But remember the name of thy Lord and devote thyself entirely to Him . . . And have patience under what they [the unbelievers] say, and withdraw from them gracefully." The last is rendered by Edouard Montet, in his translation, *Le Coran* (Paris, 1925), p. 236: ". . . et éloigne-toi d'eux dans une retraite digne."

4 See end of *Pamyatnik* (or *Exegi monumentum*), quoted in my n. to Two : XL : var. 5–8.

IV

> The bloom of fields, the leaf of groves
> in a Caucasian brook are petrified:
> thus, in life's turmoil deaden
> 4 a giddy nature and a tender one.

1–2 This petrifactive phenomenon is also referred to in the closing lines, 27–28, of a posthumously published poem of twelve quatrains (beginning "You're right, my friend"—a most melodious piece, with a Byronian slant, which Pushkin addressed to Vladimir Raevski in 1822):

Commentary

> . . . thus the light leaf of groves
> in the Caucasian springs is turned to stone.

Vladimir Raevski (1795–1872) was a (very minor) poet and Decembrist (not a member of General Nikolay Raevski's family).

Additional lines: Draft (2371, f. 8ᵛ):

> If the burden oppressing me
> were passion, I would throw it off.
> Thus, by a straining of strong will,
> a frantic passion we subdue,
> endure disaster with proud soul,
> and sweeten woe with hope;
> ⟨but how . . . to comfort⟩
> ⟨heartache, the frantic heartache [*toskú*]⟩.

V

> The sixth, went to a ball at V.'s.
> The *salle* was rather empty.
> R. C. as pretty as an angel:
> 4 Something so free about her manner,
> her smile, the languorous movement of her eyes.
> What sensuousness and what a soul!
> (She mentioned—*nota bene!*—
> 8 that she would go to Célimène's tomorrow.)

VI

> R. C. said yesternight to me:
> "I have long wished to meet you."
> "Why?" "Everybody has been telling me
> 4 that I would hate you."
> "What for?" "For your sharp talk,
> your flippant views
> on everything; your caustic scorn
> 8 of everyone. But that's all nonsense.
> You may well laugh at me—
> but you are not so dangerous at all,
> and did you know before this time
> 12 that simply—you are very kind?"

1 "R. C." is "L. C." in the draft (2371, f. 9ʳ), with the can-
cellation: "S. M."

VII

    The treasures of our native letters,
    grave minds will note,
    for foreign lisping
4 we in our folly have neglected.
    We love the toys of foreign Muses,
    rattles of foreign idioms,
    and read not our own books.
8 But where are they? Let's have 'em.
    And where, then, did we our first knowledge
    and first ideas find?
    Where do we verify our trials?
12 Where do we learn earth's fate?
    Not in barbarous translations,
    not in belated works,
    wherein the Russian mind and Russian spirit
    rehash old stuff and lie for two.

Except for two changed words (in 9 and 11), this is an
amalgam of Three: XXVIa: 1–8 and XXVIb: 1–8.

VIII

    Frost and sunshine! a splendid day;
    but seemingly our ladies are too lazy
    to step down porches, and above the Neva
4 gleam with cold beauty.
    They stay at home. In vain lures them,
    sprinkled with sand, the granite.
    Wise is the Oriental system,
8 and right the custom of the old:
    they were born for the harem,
10 or for the thralldom of the *terems.*

10 The *terem* was a kind of lady's bower, a special apartment
to which Russian women were relegated in ancient
Russia.

IX

⟨Last night, at V.'s⟩, leaving the feast,
R. C. flew zephyrlike,
not hearkening to plaints and lamentations,
4 while we down polished stairs
flew, in a noisy crowd,
after the youthful odalisque.
The last sound of her last discourse
8 I was in time to catch;
I with black sable clothed
her blazing shoulders;
on the curls of her dear head
12 I flung a green shawl;
before the Venus of the Neva, I
parted the amorous throng.

X

1 I love you . . .

"I love you etc." is all there is under this heading.
Gofman, in *P. i ego sovr.*, IX (1922), 181n, suggests that
Pushkin may have planned to insert here some version
of the discarded Three : XXIIIa ("But you, avowed co-
quettes, I love you . . .").

XI

Today I was to her presented.
Quite half an hour gazed at her husband.
⟨He is important.⟩ Dyes his hair.
4 From having brains his rank exempts him.

[XII–XIII]

Two more entries are found in the draft, between II and
III (2371, f. 8ʳ):

[XII]

I do not like maiden Princess S. L.:
⟨of her involuntary coquetry⟩
she makes a ⟨means⟩.
4 Shorter would be to take it for a goal.

[XIII]

A rather ⟨dull time⟩ yesterday.
⟨Had in the morning visitors⟩.
What was it she desired so much?
4 The first three letters shall I tell?
C, R, A—cra . . . What? Cranberries?

5 Cf. the second motto to a fragment (c. 1827) that seems to be the beginning of a long poem with scene laid in Italy. The fragment opens with the quasi-Goethian query, "Who knows the land," *Kto znáet kráy*, and the first of the two mottoes refers to the first line of Mignon's song heading Goethe's *Wilhelm Meisters Lehrjahre* (1795–96), bk. III, ch. 1.

The second motto reads: *Po klyúkvu, po klyúkvu | Po yágodu, po klyúkvu* (a folk ditty, or pseudo-folk ditty, referring to the picking of cranberries, *Oxycoccus palustris*). It is an allusion to the whim of a Russian tourist, the young Countess Maria Musin-Pushkin, who said that what she had missed most in Italy was cranberries.

I. Shlyapkin, *Iz neizdannïh bumag A. S. Pushkina* (St. Petersburg, 1903), p. 3, attributes the following draft to the "Album":

Of course, it is not hard to scorn
separatedly every fool;
'tis likewise senseless to be cross
with a separate knave [*stramtsá*],
but in a heap 'tis somehow complicated

⟨to scorn⟩ . . .
their common epigrams
borrowed from *Bievriana.*

For the collection of puns to which *Bievriana* applies, see
n. to Two : Motto.

*

These thirteen or fourteen "entries" represent all we
have of "Onegin's Album." We now return to the main
road: Seven : XXII.

XXII

5 / *Pevtsá* [Fr. *le chantre*] *Gyaúra i Zhuána*: Byron's poem
The Giaour (1813) was known to Pushkin and Onegin
in the Chastopalli translation (1820). Onegin might have
marked such a passage as:

Les plus cruelles angoisses de la douleur seraient des
plaisirs en comparaison de ce vide effrayant, de ce désert
aride d'un cœur dont tous les sentiments sont devenus sans
objet

(after shedding de Salle, Pichot replaced "ce désert" by
"cette solitude" in the 1822 edn.). This is a dreadful
paraphrase of Byron's ll. 957–60:

> The keenest pangs the wretched find
> Are rapture to the dreary void,
> The leafless desert of the mind,
> The waste of feelings unemployed.

In the 1820 Chastopalli translation (Pichot's contri-
bution) of the first two cantos of Byron's *Don Juan*
(1819), Tatiana (in June, 1821) might have found the
following passage marked by Onegin:

C'en est fait! jamais mon cœur ne sentira plus descendre
sur lui cette fraîche rosée qui retire de tout ce que nous
voyons d'aimable, des émotions nobles et nouvelles; tré-
sor semblable à celui que l'abeille porte dans son sein
[sic]!

94

This is supposed to render I : CCXIV : 1–5:

No more—no more—Oh! never more on me
 The freshness of the heart can fall like dew,
Which out of all the lovely things we see
 Extracts emotions beautiful and new,
Hived in our bosoms like the bag o' the bee.

Tatiana might also have found:

Les jours de l'amour sont finis pour moi: adieu les
charmes des jeunes beautés, de l'hymen. . . . J'ai perdu
l'espoir d'une tendresse mutuelle!

This is apparently I, CCXVI : 1–5:

My days of love are over; me no more
 The charms of maid, wife . . .
Can make the fool . . .

. . . .
The credulous hope of mutual minds is o'er . . .

Don Juan was composed between autumn, 1818, and
spring, 1823, and the cantos were published at intervals:
I and II, July 15, 1819 (this and the following dates are
given N.S.); III, IV, V, Aug. 8, 1821; the rest, from
July 15, 1823, to Mar. 26, 1824. The reference in *EO* is,
of course, to the French version of *Don Juan* (1820,
1823–24), in Pichot's *Œuvres de Lord Byron*.

In the separate edition of Chapter Seven, l. 5 reads:

Pevtsá Manfréda i Zhuána . . .

The reference is to *Manfred*, Byron's drama in blank
verse (written 1816–17, pub. 1817), translated by Pichot
and de Salle in 1819.

6 / two or three novels / *dva-trí romána*: At this point one
 of the English "translations" (Miss Deutsch's) reads:
 ". . . two or three bright-backed imported | Romances."

Commentary

3–12 The draft contains two variants. The first (2371, f. 17ʳ) reads:

> However, several works
> he took with him on trips.
> Among these chosen . . . volumes
> . . . to you familiar
> not much you would have found:
> Hume, Robertson, Rousseau, Mably,
> Baron d'Holbach, Voltaire, Helvétius,
> Locke, Fontenelle . . . Diderot,
> . . . Lamotte,
> and Horace, Cicero, Lucretius . . .

The second variant (2371, f. 68ʳ) reads (ll. 3–5):

> Several favorite works
> he took with him merely from habit:
> *Melmoth, René,* Constant's *Adolphe* . . .

Canceled drafts (ibid.) also contain: "The whole of Scott" and "*Corinne* by Staël." The latter, of course, would have hardly surprised Tatiana, who had read *Delphine.*

These tabulations of names of authors and titles of works were well known in French and English literature (see n. to Eight : XXXV : 2–6). What amused Pushkin was to iambize and rhyme them.

In the first list are David Hume (1711–76), Scottish philosopher and historian, and William Robertson (1721–93), Scottish historian. There were several translations of their works; e.g., Hume's *Histoire d'Angleterre,* tr. J. B. D. Desprès (Paris, 1819–22), and Robertson's *Histoire d'Ecosse,* tr. V. Campenon (Paris, 1821).

John Locke, English philosopher (1632–1704), was also much translated; e.g., his *Essay Concerning Human Understanding* came out in a French version by P. Coste (Amsterdam, 1700), etc.

The rest are: Gabriel Bonnot, Abbé de Mably, French

political writer (1709–85); Bernard le Bovier de Fonte-
nelle, French writer (1657–1757); and three French
philosophers, Paul Henri Thiry, Baron d'Holbach
(1723–89), Denis Diderot (1713–84), Claude Adrien
Helvétius (1715–71).

Which Lamotte? Hardly François de La Mothe le
Vayer. The least implausible candidates among the
many La Mottes, all of them mediocre, who survive in
bibliographic works are Antoine Houdar de la Motte
(1672–1731), literary critic and playwright, and Fried-
rich Heinrich Karl, Baron de La Motte Fouqué (1777–
1843), German poet and novelist, read by Russians in
French. Houdar de la Motte and Fontenelle belonged to
a literary school that sought in and demanded of poetry
des pensées raisonnables. In La Motte's *Œuvres* (1754),
Onegin might have found various essays on literary mat-
ters that students of literature were still supposed to be
acquainted with in 1824, such as the correct forms of
elegies and odes.

La Motte Fouqué is the author of the romance *Undine*
(1811), in French *Ondine*, "traduit librement" by the
indefatigable Mme de Montolieu (Paris, 1822), and imi-
tated by Zhukovski (*Undina. Starinnaya povest'*, 1833–
36). His *Pique-Dame*, "Berichte aus dem Irrenhause in
Briefen. Nach dem Schwedischen" (Berlin, 1826), was,
I suggest, known to Pushkin (in a French or Russian
version) when he wrote his "Queen of Spades" (*Pikovaya
Dama*). I intend to publish a note on the matter else-
where.

The three Romans are the poets Quintus Horatius
Flaccus (65–8 B.C.) and Titus Lucretius Carus (d. 55 B.C.)
and the statesman and orator, Marcus Tullius Cicero
(106–43 B.C.). *Kikeron*, instead of the usual Russian form,
Tsitseron, looks suspicious to me. The MS should be re-
examined.

In the second list, *Melmoth the Wanderer* (1820) is

the novel by Maturin, in Cohen's French version (see n. to Three : XII : 9).

René, a work of genius by the greatest French writer of his time, François (Auguste) René, Vicomte de Chateaubriand (1768–1848; see n. to One : XXXVIII : 3–4), was, he says, thought up under the very elm at Harrow, in Middlesex, England, where Byron "s'abandonnait aux caprices de son âge" (*Mémoires d'outre-tombe*, ed. Levaillant, pt. I, bk. XII, ch. 4). This admirable short novel, whose art and *charme velouté* only Senancour's *Oberman* (1804) can approach, appeared in the second volume of Chateaubriand's *Le Génie du Christianisme* (1802) and through four editions (1802–04) remained attached to its mother volume. The sonorous sequence of titles and subtitles reads:

> *Génie du Christianisme; ou Beautés poétiques et morales de la religion chrétienne*. Seconde partie. Poétique du christianisme. Livre IV. Suite de la poésie dans ses rapports avec les hommes. Suite des Passions. René, par François-Auguste de Chateaubriand.

In a pirated edition (Paris, 1802), the little novel came out under the title *René, ou les Effets des passions*.

In the next authorized edition (Paris, 1805), *René* accompanied *Atala* (another portion of the *Génie*, first pub. 1801).

In the wilds of Louisiana, under a sassafras tree, René, a French expatriate, "un jeune homme entêté de chimères, à qui tout déplaît, et qui s'est soustrait aux charges de la société pour se livrer à d'inutiles rêveries," tells the story of his romantic past to Father Souël: *

> Mon humeur étoit impétueuse, mon caractère inégal.
> . . . Chaque automne je revenois au château paternel, situé au milieu des forêts, près d'un lac, dans une province reculée.

---

* *René*, ed. Weil (1935), pp. 77, 16–17, 17–18, 23, 24, 25, 37, 40, 51, 59, 67.

The rhythm and richness of phrasing are admirable; Flaubert could not have done better.

Tantôt nous [René and his sister Amélie] marchions en silence, prêtant l'oreille au sourd mugissement de l'automne, ou au bruit des feuilles séchées, que nous traînions tristement sous nos pas; tantôt, dans nos jeux innocens, nous poursuivions l'hirondelle dans la prairie, l'arc-en-ciel sur les collines pluvieuses . . .

These rain-blurred hills slope toward a new world of artistic prose.

The melancholic and tender narrator, after the death of his father, wanders in the resounding and solitary cloisters of a monastery where he half thinks of retiring (". . . la lune éclairoit à demi les piliers des arcades, et dessinoit leur ombre sur le mur opposé"). Then he decides to travel:

. . . Je m'en allai m'asseyant sur les débris de Rome et de la Grèce [where the next traveler, Childe Harold, will never recall his predecessor]. . . . La lune, se levant dans un ciel pur, entre deux urnes cinéraires à moitié brisées, me montrait les pâles tombeaux.

We find him next before the statue of Charles II in London. Up in the Highlands, he muses on the heroes of Morven. After a visit to Sicily, he returns to his country, which he finds corrupted and debased by the Revolution: "Traité partout d'esprit romanesque, honteux du rôle que je jouois, dégoûté de plus en plus des choses et des hommes, je pris le parti de me retirer dans un faubourg . . ." These intonations are echoed in the stanzas of *EO*, Chapter Eight, dealing with Onegin's return to St. Petersburg and his state of mind, which has affinities with René's ennui in Paris:

Je me fatiguai de la répétition des mêmes scènes et des mêmes idées. Je me mis à sonder mon cœur, à me demander ce que je désirois. Je ne le savois pas; mais je crus

tout-à-coup que les bois me seroient délicieux. Me voilà
soudain résolu d'achever, dans un exil champêtre, une
carrière à peine commencée, et dans laquelle j'avois déjà
dévoré des siècles.

He contemplates suicide, but Amélie comes and saves
him: ". . . elle tenoit de la femme la timidité et l'amour,
et de l'ange la pureté et la mélodie." A subtle perfume of
incest permeates their relationship: "cher et trop cher
René . . ."

She leaves him for a convent. In her passionate letter
to him there is "je ne sais quoi de si triste et de si tendre,
que tout mon cœur se fondoit." After a wonderful visit
to the country estate where they had lived, and a descrip-
tion of her consecration (at which she admits her "crimi-
nelle passion"), René sets out for America.

Constant's remarkable novel (written 1807, pub.
1816) *Adolphe*, "anecdote trouvée dans les papiers d'un
inconnu, et publiée par M. Benjamin Constant" (Henri
Benjamin Constant de Rebecque, 1767–1830), was
represented in Pushkin's library by an 1824 edition; but
he had read it earlier. *Adolphe* is a contrived, dry,
evenly gray, but very attractive work. The hero courts,
adores, and torments a more or less Polish lady, Ellénore
(a niece of Rousseau's Wolmar), first in a vague German
setting, then in a still vaguer Polish one, between 1789
and 1793, when (unmentioned) events and conditions
in France prevented the author from localizing a purely
psychological romance (where a bright specific backdrop
would be a needless distraction) within such familiar
surroundings as might be taken for granted; that pale
Poland is at least pale, and the artist has managed to
outwit history.

In an epistolary afterword to his novel, Constant
describes Adolphe as blending egotism and sensibility,
and as foreseeing evil but retreating in despair when
the advance of evil is imminent. His is a checkered na-

ture, now knight, now cad. From sobs of devotion he
passes to fits of infantile cruelty, and then again dis-
solves in saltless tears. Whatever gifts he is supposed to
possess, these are betrayed and abolished in the course
of his pursuing this or that whim and of letting himself
be driven by forces that are but vibrations of his own
irritable temper. "On change de situation, mais . . .
comme on ne se corrige pas en se déplaçant, l'on se trouve
seulement avoir ajouté des remords aux regrets et des
fautes aux souffrances."

The analogies with Onegin are several, all of them
obvious; it would be a great bore to go into further de-
tails. One thing should be marked, however: physically,
Adolphe hardly exists. He glides and sidles, a faceless
figure in an impalpable world. But as a character, as a
case history, as a field of emotional tensions on display,
he is vigorously alive, and his romance is a masterpiece
of artistic saturation. In contrast to him, Onegin (if,
for the nonce, we consider him a "real" person) is seen
to grow fluid and flaccid as soon as he starts to feel, as
soon as he departs from the existence he has acquired
from his maker in terms of colorful parody and as a
catchall for many irrelevant and immortal matters. On
the other hand, as a physical being, Onegin, in com-
parison to the gray engraving of Adolphe, is superbly
stereoscopic, a man with a wardrobe, a man with a set
of recognizable gestures, a man existing forever in a
local world colored and crowded with Pushkin's people,
Pushkin's emotions, memories, melodies, and fancies.
In this sense, Pushkin transcends French neoclassicism;
Constant does not.

On Jan. 1, 1830, in the first issue of the *Literary Ga-
zette* (*Literaturnaya gazeta*), published by Delvig, Orest
Somov, Vyazemski, Pushkin, and Zhukovski (in that
order of management), our poet published the following
unsigned note:

Commentary

Prince Vyazemski has translated and is soon to publish Benj. Constant's celebrated novel. *Adolphe* belongs to the number of "two or three novels

> in which the epoch is reflected
> and modern man
> rather correctly represented
> with his immoral soul,
> selfish and dry,
> to dreaming measurelessly given,
> with his embittered mind
> boiling in empty action."

Constant was the first to bring out this character, which later the genius of Lord Byron popularized. We await the appearance of this book with impatience. It will be curious to see if the experienced and live pen of Prince Vyazemski is able to overcome the difficulties of Constant's metaphysical language, always harmonious, elegant, and often inspired. In this respect the translation should be an original creation and an important event in the history of our literature.

(It was not. Polevoy, an influential reviewer who had translated the same book some ten years before, but with even less success, was right in accusing Vyazemski's version, which came out in spring, 1830, with a dedication to Pushkin, of being clumsy and inexact.)

Neither Chateaubriand nor Constant seems to have been highly appreciated by English critics. Of Chateaubriand's *Atala*, *The Edinburgh Review*, an influential Philistine sheet of the period, wrote, no. LXIX (March, 1821), p. 178: "The subject, conduct, and language of it, are, to our apprehension, quite ludicrous and insane." And Constant is referred to (same page) as "the author of a poor novel called 'Adolphe.' "

XXIII

1–2 One recalls that in Sheridan's famous but singularly inept comedy, *The Rivals*, Lydia Languish says of Lady

Slattern that she "cherishes her nails for the convenience of making marginal notes" (I, ii). The art is a lost one today.

XXV

This stanza and the next three are wanting in Cahier 2371. None is numbered in the draft. The next stanza drafted (2371, f. 71ᵛ) is the XXIX of the established text.

2 / the word: A Gallicism, *le mot de l'énigme.* The key word, the solution.

8 / with a groan / *krehtyá*: A participle from *krehtet'* or *kryahtet'* that cannot be rendered by one verb in English. It is to emit a deep diaphragmatic sound between a grunt and a groan in sign or result of a feeling of oppression or indecision.

13 / I'll not marry [him, you] / *Neydú* [*za negó, za vás*]: A contraction of *ne idu*, "I do not go," "I do not accept." Cf. XXVI : 7, *poydyót*, "she will accept."

ALTERNATE

Draft in 2371, f. 69ʳ. In Tomashevski's recension of 1937 (p. 442, XXIVa) the cancellations are shown; they are not shown in the text published in his commentary of 1949 (p. 543) and 1957 (p. 546), where, moreover, one line reads differently (Acad 1937: "the driver lashed out, whistled"). I have been obliged, as in other cases, to follow 1937 for the deletions and 1949 (or 1957) for the actual wording.

> On her discovery we shall congratulate
> my dear Tatiana,
> and turn our course aside,
> 4 lest I forget of whom I sing.

> After he'd killed his inexperienced friend,
> the irk of ⟨rural⟩ leisure
> Onegin was unable ⟨to bear⟩;
> 8 ⟨to seat himself in a kibitka he decided⟩.
> The full-toned yoke bell ⟨sounded⟩,
> the dashing driver whistled,
> and our Onegin sped away
> 12 ⟨to seek a gladdening⟩ of dull ⟨life⟩
> in distant parts,
> himself not knowing where exactly.

In the course of composing Chapter Seven, Pushkin was twice faced with alternate routes: one branches off after XXI : 9 and the next (upon his returning to the main road) after XXIV.

At the bifurcation of XXI, he toyed, as we have seen, with the idea of having Tatiana discover Onegin's St. Petersburg diary (kept by the melancholy rake *before* his retiring to the country in May, 1820). This first alternate route is followed through XXII alt. (description of the album) to a kind of plateau with the ruins of the album's contents (accumulated in the moonlight), of which some fourteen, unstanzaed, entries, making about a hundred lines, are tentatively quoted. The idea fizzled out.

By omitting Tatiana's discovery and perusal of Onegin's St. Petersburg diary, Pushkin no doubt showed good taste and saved Tatiana from a brazen inquisitiveness hardly in keeping with her character. There is a world of difference between, on one hand, reading a private letter placed in a borrowed book and, on the other, deducing its owner's character from the scholia in its margins. However, one cannot help thinking that Pushkin might still not have deprived us of finding those picturesque fragments inset in his story at that particular place, if he had let Tatiana turn away in all modesty from the discovered album while allowing the reader to dip into it behind her back.

Upon returning to the main road Pushkin continued (XXI : 10, etc.) as we know from the established text: Tatiana reads Onegin's books (XXI : 10–14, XXII), and from the marks in their margins (XXIII) deduces more or less clearly their owner's character (XXIV).

After XXIV comes the next bifurcation. Our poet follows an alternate route for the stretch of one stanza (XXV alt.), in which he plans to leave Tatiana to her thoughts in the deserted château and to describe Onegin's sudden departure (say, in February or March, 1821) from his countryseat, whereupon, presumably, the rest of Seven would have been devoted to his arrival in St. Petersburg and the surge of patriotic sentiments that send him on the Journey, of which we have at least two thirds. But after composing XXV alt. Pushkin again changed his mind and returned to the highway. He remained with Tatiana (XXV) and launched, in the same stanza, upon the matrimonial theme that leads to Moscow.

XXVI

6 | *mélkim bésom rassïpálsya*: The idiom is: "[he], a regular petty devil, dispersed himself [in crafty compliments]." Cf. Fr. *se répandit en compliments.*

XXVIII

Tatiana's soliloquy should be compared to Lenski's elegy in Six : XXI–XXII.

5–9; XXXII : 11–12: The intonation is a familiar one. See, for example, Pope's *Winter: The Fourth* (and last) *Pastoral* (1709), l. 89 (with three to go):

Adieu, ye vales, ye mountains, streams and groves . . .

XXIX

5–7 Cf. Kozlov, *Princess Natalia Dolgoruki* (1828), can. I,
XIV, 16, 18–19:

> . . . pond, trees, flowers—
>
> .   .   .   .   .
>
> these unforgotten friends
> she meets again . . .

See nn. to Seven : XV : 8–14; XVI : 1–7.

VARIANT

5–6 Draft (2371, f. 71^v):

> with oak grove, meadows,
> as with dear friends . . .

XXXI

1–3 / overdue . . . made solid / *prosróchen . . . upróchen*: To
judge by a note (Cahier 2382, f. 15^v; first published in
Rukoyu Pushkina, p. 321) in the margin of the draft of
the short poem *Winter*—" 'Tis winter: what can one do
in the country?" (dated Nov. 2, 1829)—Pushkin in-
tended at the time to change the order of the lines in
the quatrain to 3, 4, 1, 2, and replace the rhyme *upró-
chen–prosróchen* by *isprávlen–ob'yávlen* ("is mended"
–"has been announced"). Above this is the word *voron*
("raven"), a memento referring to a contemplated
change (never made) in the already published Five :
XXIV : 7 (to which see note).

5 / *kibitki*: In common with the traveling coach, these are
also on runners in winter.

14 / eighteen nags: In a canceled draft (2371, f. 72^r), Push-
kin had "six troikas" (6 x 3 = 18).

XXXII

11–12 / Farewell . . .: Before his arrival in Mihaylovskoe
from Odessa, in August, 1824, for a two-year stay, Push-
kin had visited it twice: in the summer of 1817, soon
after graduating from the Lyceum, and in the summer
of 1819. During his first visit, he made the acquaintance
of the Osipov family in nearby Trigorskoe, and on Aug.
17, 1817, before returning to Petersburg, dedicated to
them a little elegy of sixteen iambic tetrameters that
starts (ll. 1–2, 5, 11–12):

> Farewell, ye faithful coppices,
> farewell, ye carefree peace of fields . . .
>
> .   .   .   .   .   .
>
> Farewell, Trigorskoe! . . .
>
> .   .   .   .   .
>
> Perhaps (delicious reverie!)
> I shall come back . . .

and it is, indeed, to Trigorskoe rather than to his own
Mihaylovskoe that our poet returns in the last retrospec-
tive digression of *Onegin's Journey* (1830).

    Cf. also Lenski's elegy in Six : XXI–XXII. And see n. to
Seven : XXVIII : 5–9.

13 / *Uvízhu l' vás?* / Shall I see you?: The implied "again"
is drowned in a sob.

13–14 Cf. Kozlov, *Princess Natalia Dolgoruki*, can. II, end
of V:

> . . . and sudden from her eyes
> [flow] streams of tears . . .

which has the same rhyme, *ochey–ruchey*.

See nn. to Seven : XV : 8–14; XVI : 1–7; and XXIX : 5–7.

    Cf. a similar ending of a verse paragraph in Baratïn-
ski's *Eda* (1826), ll. 262–65:

> Ah, where are you, peace of my soul?
> To find you, whither shall I go?

And infantine involuntary tears
flow from her eyes.

XXXIII

4 / *Filosofícheskih tablíts*: This final reading is jotted down
in the copybook (2382, f. 107ʳ) that contains drafts of
Onegin's travels, with the note "Canto VII."

Pushkin apparently wrote (the autographs, fide
Tomashevski, are not very legible) in his draft (2371,
f. 72ᵛ) *polistatícheskih* after canceling "Dupin's com-
parative tables" and *geostatícheskih tablíts*. The reference
is to Charles Dupin ("le Baron Pierre Charles François
Dupin, Membre de l'Institut," as he was styled; 1784–
1873) and to his statistical tables (*statistícheskih tablíts*,
gen. pl., was what Pushkin wished to say, but was one
syllable short).

In the glorious afterglow of her victories over Na-
poleon, political Russia, a young and acutely self-con-
scious world power, was greatly interested in anything
the wary West wrote about her. Hence the vogue of
Dupin's *Observations sur la puissance de l'Angleterre
et sur celle de la Russie au sujet du parallèle établi par
M. de Pradt entre ces puissances* (Paris, 1824; for the
parallèle established by that prophet in regard to Amer-
ica and Russia, see my n. to Four : XLIII : 10). In a later
work, *Forces productives et commerciales de la France*
(Paris, 1827, 2 vols.), Dupin discusses (II, 284–85n) the
routes transversales and the *routes radicales* in France;
"Espérons," he says, "que le gouvernement . . . com-
plétera notre système de communications transversales:
c'est un des moyens les plus efficaces de favoriser le
commerce, l'agriculture et l'industrie" (see, below,
Vyazemski's fireside crack). In his tables Dupin com-
pares the populations of the ·principal European states
including Russia and predicts (II, 332) that by 1850 the

population of Paris will rise to 1,460,000. In 1827–28, Dupin also produced *Le Petit Producteur français*, in six handy volumes, with a "petit tableau des forces productives de la France" in vol. I.

5–14 Alexander I was almost pathologically interested in roads; many of them were built in his reign, and liberal critics had a great time poking fun at their defects (see Comm., Ten : VI : 5).

Cf. a passage (quatrain IV, ll. 1–2) in Vyazemski's ponderous but picturesque and witty *Winter Caricatures* (1828), with the subtitle "Ruts, Caravans" (*Uhabï, Obozï*), published in Maksimovich's literary almanac, *Sunrise* (*Dennitsa*), for 1831 (and highly praised by Pushkin in a letter to its author, Jan. 2, 1831):

> In armchair, by the hearth, I'm no less than Dupin
> cheered by the overplus of earthly force in motion . . .

but (to paraphrase the next lines) "I curse agriculture and commerce when I have to travel on roads that have been ruined by the heavy train of Moscow-bound wagons loaded with the produce of the land."

XXXIV

1 The passage in Pushkin's n. 42 is from *The Station* (*Stantsiya*)—meaning the stopping place, the roadside inn or the like, in a stage route—a poem by Vyazemski, pub. Apr. 4, 1829, in the literary almanac *Snowdrop* (*Podsnezhnik*).

The line "for passers-by!," *dlya prohodyashchih*, which Vyazemski quotes in his poem (meaning occasional strollers who can admire the roadside trees, but are not obliged to endure the ruts), is the last in *The Passer-by*, in Dmitriev's *Fables*, pt. III, bk. II, no. VII (5th edn., Moscow, 1818):

109

A passer-by (*un passant*, a passenger) visits a monastery and is enchanted with the view from the steeple. "Is it not beautiful!" he cries;

> And with a sigh
> "Yes," answered a laborious brother—
> "for passers-by!"

Dmitriev's little fable is based on an old French anecdote, cropping up in eighteenth-century collections of bons mots and ascribed to various persons. A version of it appears in the first edition (1834–36, edited by L. J. N. de Monmerqué, J. A. Taschereau, and H. de Châteaugiron, who had the MS since 1803) of the posthumous *Historiettes* written in 1657–59 by the gifted and witty Gédéon Tallemant des Réaux (1619–92; he died on the eve of his seventy-third birthday), whose name, incidentally, Chizhevski (p. 278) not only mutilates in three ways, but also transforms into the designation of a vacuum: "the anonymous [sic] *Les Historiettes de Tallement* [sic] *de* [sic] *Reaux* [sic]" (I defy, moreover, anyone to understand the same compiler's reference, in the same sentence, to Henri IV). The edition of the *Historiettes* that I have consulted is the third (1854–60), brought out in Paris by Monmerqué and Paulin. The anecdote is found under No. 108 in ch. 477, vol. VII (1858), p. 463. It goes:

Henry IVᵉ, estant à Cisteaux, disoit: "Ah! que voicy qui est beau! mon Dieu, le bel endroit!" Un gros moine, à toutes louanges que le Roy donnoit à leur maison, disoit tousjours: *Transeuntibus*. Le Roy y prit garde, et luy demanda ce qu'il vouloit dire: "Je veux dire, Sire, que cela est beau pour les passans, et non pas pour ceux qui y demeurent tousjours."

In discussing the location of the MS, Monmerqué says that there have been earlier leakages (see VIII, 2). I suggest that Dmitriev saw the anecdote in Marmontel's *Essai sur le bonheur* (1787):

Aussi triste que le chartreux, à qui l'on vantait la beauté du désert qui environnait sa cellule, tu diras: "Oui, cela est beau pour les passans," *transeuntibus.*

McAdam, McEve (in Pushkin's n. 42): "Macadamization" (a fashionable topic; see, for example, *The London Magazine*, X [Oct., 1824], 350–52) was the paving of roads with small stones and shingles. The inventor was John L. McAdam (1756–1836), a Scottish engineer. Vyazemski's painful pun turns on the gender of the word for "winter" in Russian, *zima*, which is feminine (see, for example, Seven : XXIX : 13–14).

XXXV

5 / Automedon: The charioteer of Achilles (hero of Homer's *Iliad*).

7–8 In reference to Pushkin's n. 43, Spalding (1881, p. 271) calls this a "somewhat musty joke" and darkly adds: "Most Englishmen, if we were to replace verst-posts with milestones and substitute a graveyard for a palisade, would instantly recognize its Yankee extraction."

14 General evidence weighed, and particular circumstances considered, the most the Larins could have made that winter (January or February, 1822), with their four heavy sleighs and eighteen hoary jades, in a week, would have been two hundred miles (a distance that could be covered in as little as two days by traveling post in a light sleigh and changing horses every few miles). This and other considerations suggest locating their estate two hundred miles west of Moscow, about halfway between it and Opochka (province of Pskov), near which Pushkin's estate was situated. This would place the Larins' seat in the present Kalininskiy Region (consisting of the northern part of the former province of Smolensk and

the western part of the former province of Tver). This district is about four hundred miles south of St. Petersburg and is bounded on the west by the source of the Western Dvina and on the east by the sources of the Volga. It will be noticed a little further (XXXVII, Petrovskiy Castle; XXXVIII, Tverskaya Street) that the Larin procession penetrates Moscow from the northwest, where Pushkin himself entered it upon his arrival there from his Mihaylovskoe exile, in the midst of writing the preceding canto (on Sept. 7, 1826).

Caesar, who is said by Gibbon to have posted one hundred miles a day with hired carriages, could not have competed with his Russian colleagues. The Empress Elizabeth, daughter of Peter the Great, in the 1750's, had a special sleigh-coach, containing among other things a stove and a card table; by hitching twelve horses (which were changed every few miles) to this vehicle, she used to equal her father's record of making the journey on snow from St. Petersburg to Moscow (486 miles) in forty-eight hours. Alexander I, about 1810, beat the record by covering that distance in forty-two hours, and Nicholas I, in December, 1833, made it (according to a note in Pushkin's journal) in the phenomenal time of thirty-eight hours.

On the other hand, winter might pile up so much snow that traveling "on the snow track" was no better than in the seasons of slosh and mud. Thus, Vulf remarks in his diary that owing to a particularly abundant snowfall it took him, with his uncle's troika, a whole day, from early morning to eight in the evening, to cover the forty miles between Torzhok and Malinniki, in the province of Tver. The heavy Larin caravan must have crawled not much faster.

In his draft (2371, f. 73^r) Pushkin at first wrote "a week," then struck it out and altered it to "about ten days."

Brodski (*EO* commentary, p. 399) gives the wrong date for the arrival of the Larins in Moscow. They arrived there at the very beginning (not at the very end) of 1822, soon after Christmas, 1821 (see XLI : 13). By August, 1824, Tatiana has been married to Prince N. for about two years (see Eight : XVIII : 2).

VARIANT

1–6 A false start to the stanza is represented by the following lines in the draft (2371, f. 71ᵛ):

> The nurse, ⟨regarding still⟩
> Tatiana as a child,
> promises her a merry time, exhausting
> the rhetoric of her eulogy.
> ⟨In vain⟩ grandiloquently [she]
> describes vividly Moscow . . .

XXXVI

8 / *chertógov*: Luxurious ceremonial halls, splendid buildings, palazzos.

12 / Moscow! . . .: Cf. the first line of a poem in Pierce Egan's *Life in London*, bk. I, ch. 2:

> London! thou comprehensive word . . .

VARIANT

9–14 The draft (2368, f. 22ᵛ) reads:

> Moscow! . . . . How much within that sound
> is blended for a Russian heart,
> how strongly it is echoed there!
> ⟨In exile, sorrow, separation,
> Moscow, how I loved you,
> my sacred native town!⟩

XXXVII

2 / Petrovskiy Castle: John Lloyd Stephens, *Incidents of*

Commentary

Travel in Greece, Turkey, Russia, and Poland (2 vols., New York, 1838), II, 72–73:

Pedroski [sic] is a place dear to the heart of every Russian. . . . The chateau is an old and singular, but interesting building of red brick, with a green dome and white cornices. . . . The principal promenade is . . . through a forest of majestic old trees.

The Petrovskiy Park is thus described in 1845 by Mihail Dmitriev, a minor poet, *Moskovskie elegii* (Moscow, 1858), pp. 40–41:

Merrily looks at the crowd our Petrovskiy Gothic old castle:
Circular towers, spirals of chimneys, ogives of windows;
Cut of white stone are its columns, its walls are dark red.
There, in the dark dense and wide greenery of ancient pine trees,
Merry and stately, it stands, a grandsire 'mid merry young grandsons.

This Mihail Dmitriev (1796–1866) was Ivan's nephew and Pushkin's Zoilus.

4–14 Fires had already started here and there on Sept. 3/15, 1812, at the time of Napoleon's entrance into Moscow. He removed from his quarters in the burning Kremlin, in the center of Moscow, to Petrovskiy Castle, in the western suburbs, on Sept. 4. The following day was overcast. A downpour at night and rain on the sixth extinguished the conflagration.

XXXVIII

6–14 There is a slight echo of Tatiana's dream in this accumulation of impressions.

9 / Bokharans / *Buhártsï*: Inhabitants of Bokhara (Bohara, Buhara), Russian Asia, north of Afghanistan. In Moscow they were hawkers of Oriental wares, such as Samarkand rugs and robes.

13 / lions on the gates: Lions of iron or alabaster, painted a
reptile green and put up, generally in pairs, on or before
house gates, as heraldic intimations. In their jaws they
often held imposing iron rings, which, however, were
only symbolic since they in no way controlled the open-
ing of the gates.

In Pisemski's *A Thousand Souls*, a kind of Russian
Le Rouge et le Noir, and on the same level of paltry
literary style, there is an amusing passage concerning
leonine ornaments (pt. IV, ch. 5):

On almost every holiday [the scene is laid in a pro-
vincial town], this rake and his valet would perch on the
gateposts, tuck up their legs, put great rings in their
mouths, and, forming certain grimaces with their noses,
would represent, rather accurately, lions.

VARIANTS

6–14 In canceled drafts (2368, f. 23ʳ) the list includes
"dummies in wigs," "bright-colored shop signs," "col-
umns," "popes," "wenches," and "Germans."

XXXIX

Perhaps a feigned omission to suggest the blurry repeti-
tion of trivial impressions.

XL

3 / by St. Chariton's / *u Haritón'ya*: A Moscovite identified
his habitation by its proximity to this or that church.
The saint figuring here was a martyr in the Orient,
under Diocletian, about 303.

Pushkin lodged the Larins in the same "upper-class
residential" quarter where he had spent several years
as a child. St. Chariton's parish was in East Moscow, so
that is why the Larins, who entered by the western gate,
had to traverse the entire city.

Commentary

Our poet was born (May 26, 1799) in a rented house, long gone, in Nemetskaya Street (now renamed Bauman Street in honor of a young revolutionist killed in 1905 in an affray with the police). The autumn and winter of 1799 were spent at the maternal estate of Mihaylovskoe, province of Pskov. After a brief stay in St. Petersburg, the Pushkin family lived again in Moscow, from 1800 to 1811, with summer sojourns at Zaharino (or Zaharovo), an estate acquired in 1804 (and sold in 1811) by our poet's maternal grandmother, Maria Gannibal, in the Zvenigorod district, some twenty-five miles from Moscow. The Pushkins resided (from 1802 to 1807), at No. 8 Greater Haritonievski Lane. Our poet's uncle, Vasiliy Pushkin, lived in Lesser Haritonievski Lane. For some of the information in this note I am indebted to Messrs. Levinson, Miller, and Chulkov, joint authors of *Pushkinskaya Moskva* (Moscow, 1937), and to N. Ashukin's *Moskva v zhizni i tvorchestve A. S. Pushkina* (Moscow, 1949).

XLI

12 / by St. Simeon's / *u Simeona*: Simeonovskiy Lane in that parish (see n. to XL : 3). St. Simeon Stylites the Elder (390?–459) was a Syrian hermit who spent thirty-seven dull years on a pillar about sixty-six feet high and about three feet in width.

13 The "Christmas Eve" establishes the date of the arrival of Tatiana and her mother in Moscow (January or February, 1822).

VARIANTS

9–10 Draft (2371, f. 74ʳ):

> Coz, you remember Grandison,
> and at our house that ball? . . .

13–14 Canceled draft (ibid.):

> He is a Senator, he's got a married son,
> he visited me recently.

XLII

1 / As to the other / *A tót*: *Tot* here may also mean "the latter." In fact, it is not too clear whether Aunt Aline is still speaking of the son of her cousin's former beau or is referring to that "other Grandison" who formerly courted *her*, Aline.

XLIII

11 / The darkness thins / *Redéet súmrak*: An English poet would have said: "Night wanes" (e.g., Byron, *Lara*, beginning of can. II).

XLIV

8–14 It is not at all clear where and when these Moscow relatives could have seen Tatiana as a child. We may suppose that some of them had visited the Larins in the country.

11 / And since I pulled you by the ears: Cf. Griboedov, *Woe from Wit*, act III, ll. 391–92 (Beldam Hlyostov's speech):

> You, I recall, danced with him as a child,
> I used to pull him by the ears—too seldom!

XLV

3–10 Aunt Aline (Frenchified diminutive of Aleksandra), Pauline Larin's cousin, whom we have already met, and this Aunt Elena are both spinsters and presumably sisters; both come from a titled family (they might be the Princesses Shcherbatski). Lukeria Lvovna (i.e., daughter of Lev) is presumably another grandaunt of Tatiana's.

Lyubov, Ivan, and Semyon are evidently siblings, their father being Pyotr, possibly the father of Dmitri Larin. Palageya or Pelageya, daughter of Nikolay, may be a cousin of either Dame Larin or her late husband; and M. Finemouche may have been a former tutor of Pelageya's children.

12 / sedulous clubman / *klúba chlén isprávnïy*: Presumably a member of Moscow's so-called English Club (which was neither "English," nor, strictly speaking, a "club"), famed for its good food and gambling tables. It had at the time about six hundred members. This Moscow English Club should not be confused with the considerably more fashionable St. Petersburg English Club, with three hundred members, founded Mar. 1, 1770, by one Cornelius Gardiner (appearing as *Garner* in Russian sources), an English banker.

VARIANT

14 The separate edition (1830) has:

> and just as gravely catches flies.

XLVI

2 / Moscow's young graces / *Mladíe grátsii Moskví*: A most melodious line. The first syllable lingers voluptuously on the *m* before resolving itself in the liquid Oriental *la* of the vowel; then another foot touches off the ardent roll of *grátzii* (which has the full sound of the Italian *grazie*), flowing on to a dying scud in the third foot.

12 Moscow and Petersburg fashions closely followed Paris and London, so that this passage—C. Willett Cunnington, *English Women's Clothing in the Nineteenth Century* (London, 1937), p. 95—is relevant:

All through the decade [1820–30] there was a steady increase in the apparent size of the [female] head, and especially in the breadth. The hair, instead of hanging in vertical ringlets by the side of the face [as was still fashionable in 1822], was now [c. 1824] puffed out in curls on the temples, causing the face to assume a round shape.

XLVII

5 / Pushkin is at his best in evolving the erotic euphony of this line, with its petaled *p*'s and lapping *l*'s; and indeed the entire passage portraying those soft Muscovite *demi-vierges*, whom he knew so well, is lovely. The madrigal to the majestic lady in Seven : LII is considerably more formal and trite.

XLIX

1 / "archival youths" / *Arhívnï yúnoshi*: A nickname coined by Pushkin's friend Sobolevski (according to Pushkin, in the draft—MB 2387A, f. 22^r—of some critical notes, autumn, 1830) for denoting his, Sobolevski's, colleagues, young men of gentle stock enjoying soft jobs at the Moscow Archives (Office of Records) of the Ministry of Foreign Affairs (Moskovskiy arhiv kollegii inostrannïh del; see also n. to Two : XXX : 13–14). Pushkinists have made halfhearted attempts to explain the attitude our poet supposes that these youths would take toward Tatiana by the fact that the office harbored certain Muscovite littérateurs (such as Prince Odoevski, Shevïryov, and Venevitinov) who were immersed in Germanic mists of idealistic philosophic thought (Muscovized Schelling, especially) that were foreign to Pushkin's mind. In the draft (1–4), however, Pushkin had the archival youths enthusiastically admire "the dear girl."

It may be recalled that the prig and toady Molchalin,

in Griboedov's *Woe from Wit*, is also attached to the Archives (act III, l. 165), or, as an English commentator has it, "[is] on the rolls of the Records Office" (*Gore ot uma*, ed. D. F. Costello [Oxford, 1951], p. 177).

Pushkin's Zoilus, the minor poet Mihail Dmitriev (see n. to XXXVII : 2), was also employed there.

The employment was nominal; and the choice of that branch of civil service among young men who did not care to go into the army was owing to the fact that of all nonmilitary institutions only the Foreign Office (to which, in Moscow, only the Archives belonged at the time) was considered, in the 1820's, a fit place for a nobleman to serve.

5 The "sad coxcomb" (*shút pechál'nïy*) is replaced in the draft (2368, f. 31ᵛ) by "of Moscow dames the sad poet," and there are canceled readings: *poét pechál'nïy i zhurnál'nïy* ("topical") and *poét bul'várnïy* ("cheap," "popular," "meretricious"). Cf. vol. 2, p. 16n.

Shut has a variety of meanings, the main semantic subspecies being: court jester, clown, punchinello, and a jocose euphemism for "devil" and "house goblin," whence branches the (familiar and good-natured) equivalent of "rascal" in the parlance of Pushkin's time (a Gallicism, *le drôle*; see n. to XLIX : 10).

10 / V[yazemski]: The name is completed in the draft (2368, f. 31ᵛ).

There is something very pleasing in Pushkin's device of having his best friends entertain his favorite characters. In One : XVI : 5–6, Kaverin is there to meet Onegin at a fashionable Petersburg restaurant, and now Vyazemski in Moscow, by alleviating Tanya's boredom with his charming talk, provides her with the first moment of pleasure she has experienced since she left her dear woods. The bewigged old party who is fascinated by

Vyazemski's new acquaintance is of course not Prince N., Onegin's former fellow rake, now a fat general, whom Tatiana will presently meet, but a kind of forerunner.

Vyazemski, in a letter to his wife, from Petersburg, Jan. 23, 1828, writes in reference to the fragment of the chapter that had come out in the *Moscow Herald*:

> Pushkin's description of Moscow does not quite live up to his talent. It is limp and frigid, although, of course, containing many nice things. The rascal [*shut*] put me in, too.

The critic N. Nadezhdin, reviewing the chapter in the *Messenger of Europe* (*Vestnik Evropï*), 1830, found that the description was made in a manner "truly Hogarthian" (*istinno Gogartovskiy*).

L

VARIANTS

11–14 Contrary to the final text, Pushkin in his draft (2368, f. 32ʳ) had Tatiana create quite a stir in the theater: lorgnettes and spyglasses did turn toward her; and the stanza is followed by the false start of La (f. 32ᵛ), ll. 1–3:

> Questions were bruited in the pit:
> who is that on the right-hand side,
> in the fourth box? . . .

LI

1 / Sobránie / *Sobrán'e*: Vigel thus describes its appearance in the beginning of the nineteenth century; *Zapiski* (Moscow, 1928), I, 116:

> A three-story palace, all white, all full of columns, so brightly lit that it seemed on fire . . . and at the end of a ballroom, on a pedestal, the marble effigy of Catherine smiling upon the general gaiety.

The full name of the club (founded in 1783) was, since 1810, the Russian Assembly of Nobility (*Russkoe blagorodnoe sobranie*). It was also known as Dvoryanskiy Klub or Club de la Noblesse.

13–14 / haste to arrive . . . flash . . . and wing away: A well-known intonation in Western poetry. Cf. Moore, *Lalla Rookh*: "The Fire-worshippers" (5th edn., London, 1817, p. 184):

> To show his plumage for a day
> To wondering eyes, and wing away!

VARIANTS

10–11 A draft (A. Onegin coll., PD 156) reads:

> an empty head, a corset,
> starched neckcloth, quizzing glass . . .

with the cancellation (l. 11):

> here a starched pedant . . .

LIa

1–4 A draft (Maykov coll., PD 108), continuing LI, reads:

> How ⟨vividly⟩ did caustic Griboedov
> in a satire describe the grandsons
> as had F[on]v[izin] the grandsires described!
> ⟨All⟩ Moscow ⟨he invited⟩ to a ball . . .

LII

1 / charming stars / *zvyózd preléstnïh*: Some understand this as "wanton stars" (*prelestnitsa* being a "fallen woman," and a "falling star" being a *prelestnaya zvezda*), but this is farfetched.

1–4 / stars . . . moon: Commentators have seen a parody of the *Elegy to the Unforgettable One* here:

... and among young and charming maidens,
as among stars the moon, she shone ...

—a dreadful little poem by Mihail Yakovlev, in Voey-
kov's magazine *Literary News* (*Novosti literaturï*), no.
15 (St. Petersburg, 1826), p. 149.

And going further back, there is Semyon Bobrov's
Tavrida (1798), quoted by Brodski, *EO* commentary
(1950), p. 274:

> O thou of winsome mien, Zarena!
> All stars are brilliant in the North,
> all daughters of the North are fair,
> but thou alone art moon among them ...

1–14 Scholars have diligently tried to identify the faceless
recipient of this madrigal.

2 / in Moscow / *na Moskvé*: "On Moscow," in the sense of
"on the Moscow scene." The expression is ambiguous,
since it may also be understood as "on the river Moskva."

LIII

14 / used to appear / *yavlyálsya*: She had seen him actually
only once in the shade of those old limes, but, as we know
from the end of Three : xv and the beginning of Three :
xvi, he had "appeared" there to her more than once in
her adolescent hallucinations.

VARIANTS

12–13 Canceled draft (2368, f. 35^r), l. 12:

> back to the country, to roses and tulips ...

Draft (ibid.), l. 13:

> to avenues of apple trees ...

These last would have been more suggestive (unpleas-
antly so) of an orchard than of the private park to which
the lindens of the canceled draft and final text belong.

LIV

12 / There where . . . those two / *Tam, gde eshchyó . . .
dvóe*: *Eshchyo* means "more," and from a formal point
of view it would seem that besides the fat general there
were two more military men standing there; but it
seems to me that the *eshchyo* has merely the idiomatic
emphasis of a pointer demanding *more* attention to a
more specific point within a *more* limited space.

VARIANT

14 Draft (2371, f. 74ᵛ):

What, that old general?

In the light of Eight : XVIII : 7 and XXIII : 3–4, Onegin's
chum could have been at the most ten years his senior
(thus about thirty-seven in 1822).

LV

11 / aslant and askew / *vkós' i vkriv'*: There is a family re-
semblance here to Cowper's definition of digression as
"continual zigzags in a book" (*Conversation*, l. 861).

VARIANTS

5–6 In the draft (2371, f. 75ʳ), the epithet to "hero" is
"half-Russian" (cf. Lenski, Two : XII : 5).

9 Canceled draft (ibid.):

O Muse of Pulci and Parini . . .

Italian poets, Luigi Pulci (1432–84), author of *Morgante
Maggiore* (1481, 1483), known to Pushkin from an
anonymous French version, *L'Histoire de Morgant le
géant* (Paris, 1625); and Giuseppe Parini (1729–99),
author of *Il Mattino* (1763), being a set of ironical in-
structions to a Milanese scapegrace on how to spend his

day, followed by *Il Mezzogiorno* (1765), etc., known to Pushkin from a "traduction libre" (by the Abbé Joseph Grillet-Desprades) entitled *L'Art de s'amuser à la ville, ou les Quatre parties du jour* (Paris, 1778).

*

On Nov. 28, 1830, at Boldino, Pushkin wrote the following note (Cahier MB 2387B, ff. 36 and 62), with which at the time he planned to preface a separate edition of two chapters, "Eight" (now *Onegin's Journey*) and "Nine" (now Eight)—a plan not realized:

With us, it is rather difficult for the author himself to find out the impression that his work produces upon the public. All he learns from literary magazines is their editors' opinion, upon which, for a number of reasons, it is impossible to depend. The opinion of his friends is, needless to say, partial, whereas strangers will certainly not berate his work to his face, even though it may deserve this.

When Canto Seven of *Onegin* came out, in general the reviewers reported on it very unfavorably. I would have readily believed them, had not their verdict clashed so inordinately with what they had said about the earlier chapters of my novel. After the excessive and undeserved praises that they lavished on the six parts of the same work, I found it odd to read, for example, the following critique.

Bulgarin's review in the *Northern Bee* (*Severnaya pchela*), Mar. 22, 1830, is meant, according to two footnotes in the same MS; the text was not copied out by Pushkin, but is given here as implied (see in footnote to Introd.: "The Publication of *EO*," no. 13, Bulgarin's fawning note to the lines on Moscow—Seven : XXXV–LIII—which he reprinted two years before):

Can one demand the public's attention to such compositions as, for example, Chapter Seven of *Eugene Onegin*? We thought at first that this was some mystification, merely a joke or a parody, and would not believe this Chapter Seven to be the work of the author of *Ruslan and*

Lyudmila until the booksellers convinced us of this being indeed so. This Chapter Seven—two small printed sheets —is variegated with such verses and such clowning that even *Eugene Velski** appears in comparison to be something having a semblance of common sense.

The following lines, coming after "critique," were intended by Pushkin as a footnote:

I beg the pardon of a poet unknown to me if I am forced to repeat this piece of rudeness. Judging by the fragments of his poem, I see no injury whatever to myself in the rating of *Onegin* lower than *Velski*.

Bulgarin continues:

Not one idea in this watery Chapter Seven, not one sentiment, not one picture worthy of contemplation! A complete comedown, *chute complète*. . . . Our readers may ask: What is the subject matter of this Chapter Seven consisting of 57 small pages? The verses in *Onegin* carry us away and force us to answer this question in rhyme:

> How then to chase her grief away?
> Here's how: place Tanya on a sleigh.
> From her dear countryside she rides
> "to Moscow, to the mart of brides!"
> Daughter is bored, mother laments.
> Full stop. Here Chapter Seven ends.

Exactly, dear readers, the whole subject of the chapter is that Tanya is to be removed from the country to Moscow!

Pushkin intended to append a second footnote:

These verses are very good, but the criticism they contain is baseless. The most insignificant subject may be selected by the author for his poem. Critics need not discuss *what* the author describes. They should discuss *how* he describes it.

In one of our reviews it was said that Chapter Seven could not have any success because the age and Russia go forward whereas the author of the poem remains on the

---

*An anonymous novel, in Onegin stanzas, in three chapters (Moscow, 1828–29).

same spot. This verdict is unjust (i.e., in its conclusion). If the age may be said to progress, if sciences, philosophy, and civilization may perfect themselves and change, poetry remains stationary and neither ages nor changes. Her goal, her means remain the same, and while the conception, the works, the discoveries of the great representatives of ancient astronomy, physics, medicine, and philosophy have grown obsolete and are daily replaced by something else, the works of true poets remain ever fresh and young.

A work of poetry may be weak; it may be a fallacy or a failure; but then it is the author's talent that is at fault and not the age that has moved forward away from him.

Probably the critic wished to say that Eugene Onegin and his entire cortege are no longer a novelty to the public and that it is as much bored by him as are the reviewers.

Anyway, I venture to try the patience of the public again. Here are two more chapters of *Eugene Onegin*— the last ones, at least for publication. Those who would seek entertaining events in them may rest assured that there is less action in these chapters than in all the preceding ones. Chapter Eight [*Onegin's Journey*] I had all but resolved to abolish altogether and to replace it with a Roman numeral; the fear of criticism, however, stopped me. Moreover, many excerpts from it had already been published. The thought that a humorous parody might be taken for disrespect in regard to a great and sacred memory also restrained me. But *Childe Harold* stands so high that whatever the tone in which it is spoken about, the thought of a possible offense to it could not have arisen in me.*

During the same autumn Pushkin jotted down another note of the same kind (draft in MB 2387A, f. 64ʳ; first published 1841):

The omitted stanzas have repeatedly provided a pretext for blame.† The fact that *Eugene Onegin* contained

---

*See my introductory remarks to *Onegin's Journey*.

†Bulgarin, in his critique of Seven, wrote: "On p. 13 we find with a sense of the greatest enjoyment two stanzas omitted by the author himself and replaced by two beautiful Roman numbers, VIII and IX."

stanzas that I could not or did not wish to publish should not be deemed surprising. But since their exclusion interrupts the coherence of the story, it is necessary to indicate the place where they ought to have been. It might have been better to replace those stanzas by others, or to rework and recombine those I kept. But pardon me, I am much too lazy. Moreover, I humbly submit that two stanzas are left out of *Don Juan.*

There are more omissions than two stanzas in the text from which Pichot translated, but Pushkin may have been thinking of the first canto only. In the first editions of the original (1819–24), the following stanzas or parts of stanzas were excluded and replaced with dots:

I, xv, allusion to the suicide of Sir Samuel Romilly; cxxix, 7–8, cxxx, 7–8, and cxxxi, play on the "smallpox" and the "great."

V, lxi, friendship of Queen Semiramis with a horse.

XI, lvii, 5–8, literary occupations of the Rev. George Croly; lviii, Henry Hart Milman.

"Nous ignorons," says Pichot in his n. 2 to *Don Juan,* can. I, vol. VI (1823), p. 477, "si ces lacunes doivent être attribuées à l'éditeur anglais, ou à l'auteur lui-même." And in his n. 39 to can. XI, vol. VII (1824), p. 383, he observes further: "Les points existent dans le texte, ce qu'il est bon de dire depuis que les points sont devenus une spéculation de librairie."

Incidentally, in *Don Juan,* can. I, the numeration after cix differs from the original in Pichot (1820 and 1823), who does not have Byron's cx, a stanza ending in a reference to the author's mother. In other words, Pichot has 221 stanzas in I, and Byron has 222. I have not been able to discover how and why this happened.

Chapter Eight

The beginning of Byron's famous and mediocre stanzas, *Fare Thee Well*, on his domestic circumstances, first published in the London *Champion*, Apr. 14, 1816.

I

1 / In those days / *V te dní*: It is curious to note that this first stanza (as well as the dropped stanzas following it; see Ia, b, and e), written at the close of 1829, begins with the same formula and intonation as Pushkin's short poem *The Demon* (1823), which I discuss in a note to Eight : XII : 7, where it is mentioned.

1 / in the Lyceum's gardens / *v sadáh Litséya*: The reference is to the Aleksandrovskiy Litsey, Lycée de l'Empereur Alexandre I, founded by that tsar Aug. 12, 1810, at Tsarskoe Selo (now Pushkin), twenty-two versts from St. Petersburg. Pushkin passed the entrance examinations in August, 1811. The Lyceum opened Oct. 19, 1811, with thirty pupils. The anniversary of this date was to

be piously celebrated by Pushkin, in company or in solitude, twenty times (1817–36). In modern terms, the Lyceum might be defined as a boarding school for young gentlemen, which offered three years of preparatory school and three years of junior college. Each of the thirty boys had his own room. The infliction of corporal punishment of any kind was absolutely forbidden, a great advance in comparison to the flogging and other brutal practices characteristic of the best English and Continental schools of the time.

It was in the Lyceum that Pushkin composed his first poems. Of these, the first to be published was *To a Friend Who Makes Verses* (*K drugu stihotvortsu*), in the *Messenger of Europe* (*Vestnik Evropï*), edited by Vladimir Izmaylov, pt. 76, no. 13 (July 4, 1814), pp. 9–12, signed "Aleksandr N.k.sh.p." To judge by final marks, Pushkin did "excellently" in literature (French and Russian) and in fencing; "extremely well" in Latin, state economy, and finances; "well" in sacred studies, logic, moral philosophy, and Russian civil and criminal law; and "also studied" history, geography, statistics, mathematics, and German. On June 9, 1817, he was graduated with the rank of collegiate secretary (the tenth rung in the civil-service ladder), was nominally attached to the Ministry of Foreign Affairs, and spent most of the next three years in St. Petersburg, leading the life of a rake, a poet, and a *frondeur*.

To the end of his life he remained deeply attached to what he considered his real home, the Lyceum, and to his former fellow students. He has commemorated these recollections, and the annual reunions on Oct. 19, in several poems. There is something symbolic in the fact that the one he composed for the last anniversary feast he attended was not completed. On the occasion of the Oct. 19 reunion of 1838, his schoolmate Küchelbecker, an exile in Aksha, Siberia, wrote in a wonderful piece:

At present with our Delvig he is feasting,
At present he is with my Griboedov . . .

On nĭne s náshim Dél'vigom pirúet,
On nĭne s Griboédovĭm moĭm . . .

The term *litsey* comes from the Parisian *lycée.* In 1781
Jean François Pilâtre de Rozier (b. 1756) established an
institute in Paris called the Musée, where natural sci-
ences were taught. Then, in 1785, after his death in a
balloon accident, his Musée was reorganized under the
name Lycée, and Jean François de La Harpe was invited
to lecture there on world literature. He taught this
course for several years, and began publishing his fa-
mous manual (1799–1805), *Lycée, ou Cours de littéra-*
ture ancienne et moderne, which was used at the Litsey
eight years after his death.

In his letters of 1831 from Tsarskoe Selo, where he
spent the first months (end of May to October) of his
marriage and put the last touches to *EO,* Pushkin takes
pleasure in referring to the place by its old Westernized
name, "Sarskoe Selo" or "Sarsko-Selo."

3 / Apuleius: Lucius Apuleius, Latin writer of the second
century, author of the *Metamorphoses* (also known as
the *Asinus aureus,* the *Aureate Ass,* imitated from the
Greek), by Russians read mainly in tawdry French ver-
sions, such as, for instance, *Les Métamorphoses, ou l' Ane*
d'or d'Apulée, tr. Abbé Compain de Saint-Martin (2
vols., Paris, 1707, and later editions), upon which a
clumsy Russian adaptation, by Ermil Kostrov (Moscow,
1780–81), was based. This once-famous romance, deal-
ing with the narrator's adventures when he is trans-
formed into a donkey, contains some brilliant erotic
images, but, on the whole, strikes the reader of today
as even more boring than Cicero seemed to Pushkin in
1815—or to Montaigne in 1580.

See also my n. to One : XXXIII : 3–4.

1a–f

Pushkin scrapped a longer account of his youth at the
Lyceum. We possess four stanzas in a fair copy (PB 21–
26), which I have marked 1a, 1d, 1e, and 1f; and two in
drafts (MB 2382, f. 25ᵛ), of which the second is incom-
plete. These two I have marked 1b (it is headed "Dec. 24,
1829," and was apparently the first one in this chapter
to be written) and 1c. It will be noted that 1a : 1–4 is
only a variant of 1b : 1–4 and that both have been used
for 1 : 1–4. The batch 1a, 1d, 1e, 1f, 11, and 111 is marked
from "1" to "v1" in the fair copy.

1a

In those days when in the Lyceum's gardens
I bloomed serenely;
would eagerly read *Eliséy*,
4 while cursing Cicero;
in those days when it would be a rare poem
to which I'd not prefer a well-aimed ball;
when things scholastic I deemed nonsense,
8 and jumped into the garden o'er the fence;
when I would be now diligent,
now lazy, now stubborn,
now sly, now frank,
12 now subdued, now unruly,
now sad, silent,
now cordially talkative;

1b

In those days when in the Lyceum's gardens
I bloomed serenely;
would furtively read Apuleius,
4 while yawning over Virgil;
when I was lazy, full of pranks,
o'er the roof and into the window climbed,
and would forget the Latin class
8 for red lips and black eyes;
when was beginning to disturb
my heart vague sadness;

when the mysterious distance
12 enticed my dreamings,
and in the summer [. . .] for the day
would wake me gaily;

IC

when I was dubbed "the Frenchman"
by cocky friends;
when pedagogues prognosticated
4 I'd be a scapegrace all my life;
when on the field of roses
we to our heart's content frisked and went wild;
when in the shade of alleys dense
8 I listened to the calls of swans
as I surveyed the luminous waters;
or when among the plains

.   .   .   .   .   .

12 while visiting the Kagul marble

Id

When, in a trance, before the class
I now and then lost sight and hearing;
and tried to speak in a bass voice,
4 and trimmed the first down o'er my lip;
in those days . . . in those days when first
I noticed the live features
of a charming maiden, and love
8 roused my young blood;
and yearning hopelessly,
oppressed by the deceit of fiery dreams,
I sought her traces everywhere,
12 lapsed into tender thoughts of her,
awaited all day long a minute's meeting,
and learned the bliss of secret pangs;

Ie

in those days—in the gloom of grovy arches,
near waters flowing in the stillness
in corners of Lyceum corridors,
4 the Muse started to appear to me.
My student cell,

> hitherto strange to gaiety,
> was suddenly alight! In it the Muse
> 8 opened a feast of her devices;
> farewell, cold knowledges!
> Farewell, games of first years!
> I've changed: I am a poet;
> 12 within my soul nothing but sounds
> are modulating, are alive,
> are running into measures sweet.

                    If

> And with first tenderness obsessed,
> to me the Muse sang, sang again
> (*amorem canat aetas prima*)
> 4 of love incessantly, and yet of love,
> I echoed her. Young friends
> during enfranchised leisures
> were fond of listening to my voice.
> 8 They, with partisan souls
> devoted to our brotherhood,
> presented me with my first wreath,
> so that their songster might adorn with it
> 12 his bashful Muse.
> O triumph in the days of innocence!
> Sweet is your dream unto my soul!

                    Ia

3 / *Eliséy*: *Elisey, or Irate Bacchus* (1771), by Vasiliy Maykov (1728–78), a Scarronic poem of 2234 Alexandrine lines, in five cantos. A second edition came out in 1778, and it was reprinted in Maykov's *Works* (1809). The poem is known to have influenced *The Dangerous Neighbor*, by Pushkin's uncle, Vasiliy Pushkin, alluded to in *EO*, Five : XXVI : 9. Its hero is a Petersburg crack driver of hackney troikas. He is introduced (I, 94) as

        Cardplayer, drunkard, rowdy, pugilist.

Bacchus chooses Elisey as his ally in his fight with the liquor contractors who charge forbidding prices. Elisey's favorite *vino* is pimpinella, otherwise anisated vodka, which he drinks by the tankard (I, 152–55). Although of not very high literary quality, *Elisey* contains some excellent passages, such as I, 559 (describing the black mustache that Hermes, in order to impersonate a policeman, makes of his two wings, by gluing them to his upperlip); the incidental merchant of Old Believers faith who, as he says his evening prayer, "makes the schismatic cross upon his lardy forehead" (IV, 361); and the fine denunciation of bear-baiting (V, 239–40): "with a bored yawn to watch | dogs tearing innocent beasts"). The fun is coarse, albeit picturesque; for example, in I, 274, crimson-booted Bacchus speeds on winged tigers to the throne of drunken and drowsy Jove, whom he finds in the act of releasing "doves" (*golubey*, acc. pl., slang for "silent flatuses").

5–6 Canceled fair copy (PB 21–26) reads:

> in those days when to the black copybook
> I would prefer a nimble ball . . .

The reference is to exercise books used at Pushkin's school; they were bound in black cloth (oilcloth?).

6 / a well-aimed ball: The reference is presumably to *lapta*, a rudimentary form of baseball, in which a stick replaces the bat, and a serve-throw, pitching. Tagging is a conspicuous feature, the small, hard, hurtful ball being deftly hurled at the runner.

Ib

The stanza is headed "Dec. 24, 1829," which date also refers, presumably, to Ic (both in 2382, f. 25ᵛ).

Ic

1 / dubbed "the Frenchman": Pushkin's French, acquired in infancy from home tutors, was as idiomatic and

fluent, but also as ready-made, as that of any Russian nobleman in the nineteenth century. Not special proficiency in the language, but young Pushkin's agility and fierce temper earned him that nickname at school. A clue to its real meaning is given in the following explanation, added by Pushkin on Oct. 19, 1828, in St. Petersburg, to his signature, "the Frenchman" (*Frantsuz*), in the minutes of the annual reunion of the Lyceum alumni:* "A cross between a monkey and a tiger" (*smes' obyezianï* [sic] *s tigrom*). I find that Voltaire, *Candide*, ch. 22, defines France as "ce pays où des singes agacent [tease] des tigres," and in a letter to Mme du Deffand (Nov. 21, 1766) uses the same metaphor to divide the French into mocking monkeys and truculent tigers.

In the proclamation, written by Admiral Shishkov (who, despite his Gallophobia, knew French literature very well; see n. to Eight : XIV : 13), telling the nation of Napoleon's departure from Moscow (beginning of October, 1812), its author remarked that even the writers of France "described the nature of that people as a merging of the tiger with the monkey" (*sliyanie tigra s obez'yanoy*).

It is amusing to note that Pushkin's teacher of French literature and history at the Lyceum was one of the three brothers of Jean Paul Mara, alias Marat (1743–93), celebrated headman of the French regime of Terror. Dr. Augustin Cabanès (*Marat inconnu*, Paris, 1891; rev. edn., 1911) is positive that this brother, known in Russia, whither he emigrated in the 1780's, as "de Boudry" (from the place name in Switzerland), was Henri Mara (b. 1745). The two other brothers were David (b. 1756), referred to in his youth as *le borgne* (he had apparently lost one eye), and Jean Pierre (b. 1767). According to the

---

*Published by Yakov Grot, in *Russkiy arhiv*, XIII, 1 (1875), 490.

Lyceum professor's obituary (d. Sept. 23, 1821, O.S.),
however, he was David Mara ("David Ivanovich de
Budri"), born in Neustadt in 1756. A Russian gentleman
traveling abroad, Vasiliy Saltïkov, engaged him as tutor
for his children in 1784.* In a cartoon by Illichevski
(1816) depicting Lyceum teachers, many times pub-
lished, Boudry has both his eyes (a glass one would not
have escaped a schoolboy's notice), but does not look to
be seventy, as Henri Mara would have been at the time.
The whole question seems to invite some additional
research.

1–2 There is a beautiful buzzing alliteration in these lines:

> Kogdá frantsúzom nazïváli
> Menyá zadórnïe druz'yá . . .

5 / *Po rózovomu pólyu:* The so-called Champ des Roses in
the Tsarskoe Selo park, which had been a floretum in the
days of Catherine II.

12 / the Kagul marble / *kagúl'skiy mrámor:* Fr. *le marbre
de Cagoul*, a Gallic-toned reference to the marble obe-
lisk erected in the park of Tsarskoe Selo by Catherine II,
in 1771, to commemorate a Russian victory, gained on
July 12 of the previous year, over the Turks on the
Kagul, a river in Moldavia. It is also mentioned in Push-
kin's pseudoclassical *Recollections at Tsarskoe Selo* (see
n. to II : 3), written in 1814, ll. 49–52:

> In the dense shade of gloomy pine trees
> A simple monument doth stand.
> How baneful 'tis to thee, O Kagul's brink! How glorious
> To our belovéd native land!

The poetical abbreviation of trisyllabic adjectives in
Russian (*dragoy* instead of *dorogoy*, "beloved") finds a

---

*See Grot, in *Russkiy arhiv*, XIV (1876), 482.

curious counterpart in the poetical lengthening of English epithets (be-lov-ed).

1d

5–14 This young lady has been satisfactorily identified by Pushkinists as Ekaterina Bakunin (1795–1869), the sister of one of Pushkin's schoolmates. In an entry of Nov. 29, 1815, in his Lyceum diary young Pushkin dedicated an indifferent elegy to her (followed, in 1816, by some much better ones) and added a little effusion in prose:

I was happy! No, yesterday I was not happy: in the morning, racked by the ordeal of waiting, in a state of indescribable excitement I stood at the window and looked at the snowy road—she was not to be seen! Finally, I lost hope. All at once, I happened to meet her on the stairs. Delicious minute! . . . How charming she was! How becoming was [*pristalo*] that black dress to charming Miss Bakunin!

1f

1 / *I pervoy nezhnost'u tomima.* Thus in *Works* 1960.

3 / *amorem canat aetas prima*: Adapted from Sextus Propertius (c. 50–10 B.C.), *Elegies*, bk. II, no. X, l. 7:

aetas prima canat veneres, extrema tumultus . . .
Young age sings lust; mature age, tumult . . .

With this line Pushkin epigraphed his first collection of short poems, 1826 (Dec. 28, 1825). *Veneres* was bowdlerized to *amorem*. When Pletnyov brought this volume to Karamzin, the latter understood *tumultus* as an allusion to the December insurrection and was horrified; but Pletnyov explained to him that Pushkin meant "strong emotions," "the tumult of the soul." Propertius meant "the tumult of war."

3 / Derzhavin: Gavrila Derzhavin (1743–1816) is Russia's first outstanding poet. His celebrated *God: an Ode* (1784), with its curious borrowings from Friedrich Gottlieb Klopstock (German poet, 1724–1803, author of *Messias*, 1748–73) and Edward Young (English poet, 1683–1765, author of *Night Thoughts*, 1742–45), his odes of the same period to *Felitsa* (Catherine II), and such poems of the 1790's as *The Grandee* and *The Waterfall* contain many great passages, colorful images, rough touches of genius. He made interesting experiments in broken meter and assonance, techniques that did not interest the next generation, the iambophile poets of Pushkin's time. Derzhavin influenced Tyutchev much more than he did our poet, whose diction came early under the spell of Karamzin, Bogdanovich, Dmitriev, and especially Batyushkov and Zhukovski.

In his memoirs (1852), Sergey Aksakov (1791–1859), a very minor writer, tremendously puffed up by Slavophile groups, recalls that in December, 1815, Derzhavin told him that the schoolboy Pushkin would grow to be another Derzhavin. Aksakov's recollection was at the time almost half a century old.

Pushkin himself modestly implies a certain act of succession:

> The aged Derzhavin noticed us—
> and blessed us . . .

Not to young Pushkin, however, but to Zhukovski did old Derzhavin address the lines:

> To you in legacy, Zhukovski,
> My antiquated lyre I hand,
> While o'er the slippery grave abysmal
> Already with bent brow I stand.

And not Derzhavin, but Zhukovski did young Pushkin apostrophize in the final stanza of his ode *Recollections at Tsarskoe Selo* (an enthusiastic survey of historical associations, in 176 iambic lines of varying length with alternate rhymes, composed in 1814), which jolted Derzhavin out of his senile somnolence. But let us turn to Pushkin's own notes of 1830 (*Works* 1936, V, 461):

I saw Derzhavin only once in my life but shall never forget that occasion. It was in 1815 [Jan. 8] at a public examination in the Lyceum. When we boys learned that Derzhavin was coming, all of us grew excited. Delvig went out on the stairs to wait for him and kiss his hand, the hand that had written *The Waterfall*. Derzhavin arrived. He entered the vestibule, and Delvig heard him ask the janitor: "Where is the privy here, my good fellow?" This prosaic question disenchanted Delvig, who canceled his intent and returned to the reception hall. Delvig told me the story with wonderful bonhomie and good humor. Derzhavin was very old. He was in uniform and wore velveteen boots. Our examination was very wearisome to him. He sat with his head propped on one hand. His expression was inane, his eyes were dull, his lip hung; the portrait that shows him in housecap and dressing gown is very like him. He dozed until the beginning of the examination in Russian literature. *Then* he came to life, his eyes sparkled; he was transfigured. It was, of course, *his* poems that were read, *his* poems that were analyzed, *his* poems that were praised every minute. He listened with extraordinary animation [*s zhivost'yu neobïknovennoy*]. At last I was called. I recited my *Recollections at Tsarskoe Selo* while standing within two yards of Derzhavin. I cannot describe the state of my soul; when I reached the verse where Derzhavin's name is mentioned [l. 63], my adolescent voice vibrated and my heart throbbed with intoxicating rapture. . . . I do not remember how I finished my recitation [he turned to Derzhavin as he launched upon the last sixteen lines, which were really addressed to Zhukovski, but might be taken to mean Derzhavin]. I do not remember whither I fled. Derzhavin was delighted; he demanded I come, he desired to embrace me. . . . There was a search for me, but I was not discovered.

The passage referring to Derzhavin (ll. 63–64) goes:

Derzhavin and Petrov twanged paeans to the heroes
  On strings of thunder-sounding lyres.

Vasiliy Petrov (1736–99) was a third-rate Bellonian odist.

In November or December, 1815, Pushkin composed a
satirical poem, *Fonvizin's Shade* (first pub. 1936, in
Vremennik, vol. I), in which he parodies Derzhavin's
*Lyrico-Epic Hymn on the Occasion of the Expulsion of
the French from the Fatherland* (in ll. 231–40) and pro-
ceeds to exclaim (ll. 265–66):

> Denis! he will be always famous,
> But, O why should one live so long!

"Denis" is the satirist Fonvizin (see One : XVIII : 3
and n.), and "he" is old Derzhavin, who had "blessed"
our young poet less than a year before.

5–14 The fair copy gives the ten lines omitted in the estab-
lished text:

> And Dmítrev [sic] was not our detractor;
> and the custodian of Russian lore,
> leaving his scrolls, would heed us
> 8 and stroke [our] timid Muse.
> And you, deeply inspired
> bard of all that is beautiful,
> you, idol of virginal hearts:
> 12 was it not you, by partisanship driven,
> was it not you who stretched a hand to me
> and summoned to pure fame?

5 / Dmitrev: a poetical elision of Dmitriev.

Ivan Dmitriev (1760–1837), a very minor poet,
shackled in his art by his indebtedness to French *petits
poètes*. He is mainly remembered for a song (*Moans the
Gray-blue Little Dove*), a satire (*As Others See It*; see
Four : XXXIII : 6 and n.), and a few fables (see n. to
Seven : XXXIV : 1). His only distinction really is that of
having perfected and purified Russian poetical style

when the national Muse was still a clumsy infant. He had even less to say than Zhukovski and unfortunate Batyushkov, and what he did say was worded with considerably less talent. He has left an autobiography in good, limpid prose.

Venevitinov, in a letter to Shevïryov, Jan. 28, 1827, accuses Dmitriev of being an envious person, ever ready to lower Pushkin's reputation if given a chance. However, in 1818 (and this is the recollection in II : 5), in a letter to A. Turgenev, dated Sept. 19, Dmitriev termed young Pushkin "a beautiful flower of poetry that will not fade soon." He was critical, however, of *Ruslan and Lyudmila*: "I find in it a great deal of brilliant poetry and narrative ease; but it is a pity that he often slips into *le burlesque*, and more pity still that he did not take for motto a famous verse [Piron's], slightly altered: 'La mère en défendra la lecture à sa fille' " (letter to Vyazemski, Oct. 20, 1820). (See also vol. 2, p. 240.)

An interesting situation arises when, in referring to an author, Pushkin uses a phrase that constitutes a parody of that author's diction. Yet even more interesting are such passages as those in which the aped phrase is found in the Russian version of the French translation of an English author, so that in result Pushkin's pastiche (which *we* have to render in English) is three times removed from its model! What should the translator do in the following case? The line about Dmitriev reads:

> *I Dmítrev né bïl násh hulítel'* . . .
> And Dmitriev was not our detractor . . .

Now, if we turn to Dmitriev's colorless version (1789), in Alexandrine couplets, of Pope's *Epistle to Dr. Arbuthnot* (1734–35), we discover in the second hemistich of Dmitriev's l. 176 the model of Pushkin's phrase:

> *Kongrév* applauded me, *Svift* was not my detractor . . .

Dmitriev, who had no English, used a French translation of Pope (probably La Porte's), and this explains the Gallic garb of Congreve (which Dmitriev mentally rhymes with *grève*). If we look up Pope's text, we find that Dmitriev's line is a paraphrase of Pope's l. 138:

And Congreve lov'd, and Swift endur'd, my Lays . . .

But Pushkin, in *EO*, Eight : II : 5, is thinking not of Pope or La Porte, but of Dmitriev, and I submit that, in an accurate English translation, we should keep the "detractor" and resist the formidable temptation to render Pushkin's line:

And Dmitriev, too, endured my lays . . .

6–8 / custodian of Russian lore: The reference is to Nikolay Karamzin (1766–1826). Pushkin had been well acquainted with him in 1818–20, and appreciated him chiefly as a reformer of language and as the historian of Russia. Karamzin's *Letters of a Russian Traveler* (1792), an account of a trip he took through western Europe, had had a tremendous impact on the preceding generation. As a novelist, he is negligible. He has been called the Russian Sterne; but Karamzin's prim and pallid fiction is the very opposite of the great English prose poet's rich, lewd, and fantastic style: Sterne came to Russia in French versions and imitations and was classified as a sentimentalist; Karamzin was a deliberate one. Sharing with other Russian and French writers of his time a blissful lack of originality, Karamzin had nothing to say in his stories that was not imitative. His novella *Poor Liza* (1792) proved, however, most popular. Liza, a young country girl who lives with her aged mother in a hut (how these infirm and utterly decrepit old women in European lachrymose tales managed to bear children is a separate problem), is seduced near a moonlit pond by a frivolous nobleman graced with the comedy name of Erast, although the scene is laid in a suburb of Moscow.

There is nothing much more to say about this tale except that it reveals certain new niceties of prose diction.

Karamzin's charming, graceful, but now seldom remembered verses (*My Trifles*, 1794), which his friend Dmitriev followed up next year with his *And My Trifles*, are artistically above his prose fiction.

In his truly marvelous reform of the Russian literary language, Karamzin neatly weeded out rank Church Slavonic and archaic Germanic constructions (comparable, in their florid, involved, and uncouth character, to bombastic Latinisms of an earlier period in western Europe); he banned inversions, ponderous compounds, and monstrous conjunctions, and introduced a lighter syntax, a Gallic precision of diction, and the simplicity of natural-sounding neologisms exactly suited to the semantic needs, both romantic and realistic, of his tremendously style-conscious time. Not only his close followers, Zhukovski and Batyushkov, but eclectic Pushkin and reluctant Tyutchev remained eternally in Karamzin's debt. Whilst, no doubt, in the idiom Karamzin promoted, the windows of a gentleman's well-waxed drawing room open wide onto a Le Nôtre garden with its tame fountains and trim turf, it is also true that, through those same French windows, the healthy air of rural Russia came flowing in from beyond the topiary. But it was Krïlov (followed by Griboedov), not Karamzin, who first made of colloquial, earthy Russian a truly literary language by completely integrating it in the poetic patterns that had come into existence after Karamzin's reform.

This is not the place to discuss the value of Karamzin's historical conceptions. His *History of the Russian State* was a revelation to an eager audience. The first edition, consisting of the first eight volumes, was published Feb. 1, 1818, and the total printing of three thousand copies was exhausted in the course of one month. A French translation made by two French professors in Russia (St. Thomas and A. Jauffret) began to appear in Paris as early as 1819.

Karamzin is also the author of one of the best Russian epigrams (Dec. 31, 1797):

Life? A romance. By whom? Anonymous.
We spell it out; it makes us laugh and weep,
And then puts us
To sleep.

And in a *bouts-rimés* exchange (using rhymes supplied by Dmitriev), Karamzin made the following New Year prophecy for 1799 (which was to be the year of Pushkin's birth):

To sing all things, Pindar will be reborn.

9–14 / And you, deeply inspired . . .: The reference is to Vasiliy Zhukovski (1783–1852), Pushkin's lifelong friend, a prudent mediator in our poet's clashes with the government, and his amiable teacher in matters of prosody and poetical idiom. Zhukovski owned a strong and delicate instrument that he had strung himself, but the trouble was he had very little to say. Hence his continuous quest for subject matter in the works of German and English poets. His versions of foreign poetry are not really translations but talented adaptations remarkably melodious and engaging; and they seem especially so when the original is not known to the reader. Zhukovski at his best communicates to his reader much of the enjoyment he obviously experiences himself in molding and modulating a young language while having his verses go through this or that impersonation act. His main defects are constant tendencies to simplify and delocalize his text (a method consistent with French translatory practice of the time) and to replace with a pious generalization every rough and rare peculiarity. The student who knows Russian will find it profitable to compare, for instance, Zhukovski's *Smaylhome Castle*

Commentary

(*Zamok Smal'gol'm*, 1822) with its model, *The Eve of St. John*, by Walter Scott. It will be seen that Scott's specific details are consistently neutralized. The "plate-jack" and "vaunt-brace" of quatrain III become with Zhukovski merely "armor of iron"; the charming under-the-breath line about the page (VII, "His name was English Will") is ignored; the "bittern" is changed into an "owl"; the colorful description of Sir Richard's plume, shield, and crest is replaced by a very primitive and conventional blazon, and so on; but, on the other hand, there is in the Russian text a somewhat finer breath of mystery; everything about Scott's rather matter-of-fact adulteress acquires a more romantic and pathetic air with Zhukovski, and what is especially noteworthy, he evolves throughout the piece a set of wonderful, exotic sonorities by employing the least number of words to fill his muscular line and by making his musically transliterated names—*Broterstón* (Brotherstone), *Duglás* (Douglas), *Kol'dingám* (Coldinghame), *El'dón* (Eildon)—resonantly participate in his Russian rhymes and rhythms. There is a wonderful orchestration of letters in such lines as *S Ankrammórskih krovávïh poléy* (last line of XXXV, meaning "From the Ankrammor gory fields," and corresponding in sense to the first line of XXXV in Scott, "The Ancram moor is red with gore"), and this kind of thing counterbalances the loss of lilt. The cadential swing of Scott's piece, in which, technically speaking, broken anapaestic lines commingle with iambic ones, is rendered in Zhukovski's Russian by regular anapaestic tetrameters alternating with regular anapaestic trimeters, whereas in Scott's typically balladic lilt the more or less anapaestic (sometimes frankly iambic) lines of four beats alternate with iambic (or sometimes semi-anapaestic) lines of three beats. Zhukovski retains the masculine endings of the alternate rhymes and reproduces some of the internal consonances.

Zhukovski met Pushkin a few months after that cele-
brated Lyceum examination which Derzhavin attended.
In a letter to Vyazemski dated Sept. 19, 1815, Zhukovski
writes:

I have made another agreeable acquaintance—this
time with our young wonder-worker Pushkin. I visited
him for a minute at Tsarskoe Selo. What a charming,
lively creature! . . . He is the hope of our literature.

Zhukovski's portrait of 1820, a lithograph by E.
Oesterreich, shows within its oval the poet's charm-
ing young features with a melancholy and penetrative
expression about the lips and eyes. Under the oval,
Zhukovski wrote, when presenting Pushkin with a copy
of the portrait:

To the victorious pupil from the defeated teacher on
that most solemn day when he finished his poem *Ruslan
and Lyudmila,* Mar. 26, 1820, Good Friday.

In a five-line inscription, *To Zhukovski's Portrait* (an
earlier portrait, by Pyotr Sokolov, published in the *Mes-
senger of Europe,* 1817), paying deserved tribute to the
evocative melody of his friend's poetry, Pushkin said
late in 1817 or early in 1818 (ll. 1–2):

Egó stihóv plenítel'naya sládost'
Proydyót vekóv zavístlivuyu dal' . . .

The captivating sweetness of his verses
shall cross the envious distance of the ages . . .

(*Plenitel'naya sladost'*, incidentally, occurs in Mrs.
Radcliffe's *The Romance of the Forest* [1791], ch. 1:
"[Adeline's] features . . . had gained from distress an
expression of captivating sweetness." But Pushkin was
thinking of *douceur captivante,* a common formula of
the time.)

*

As early as 1816, in a poem of 122 iambic hexameters
dedicated to Zhukovski (starting *Blagoslovi, poét,* "Bless

me, poet," which sounds comically like the "bless me,
Reverend Father," *blagoslovi, vladïko*, of the Russian
church ritual), Pushkin mentioned the three poets of
EO, Eight : II, in a somewhat similar combination:
"Dmitriev praised with a smile my feeble talent,"
"Derzhavin in tears embraced me with a faltering arm"
(or would have, had not our poet fled), and "Zhukovski
gave me his hand in token of sacred friendship."

VARIANT

13–14 Canceled in fair copy:

> called me to take the glorious road
> and told me: Be my brother.

III

4, 9 / frisky, frisked / *rézvuyu, rezvílas'*; **5, 12** / riotous,
riotously / *búynïh, búyno*: These awkward repetitions
are difficult to explain, given the tremendous trouble
Pushkin took over the beginning of this canto.

13–14 / and I was proud 'mong friends of my volatile
mistress / *Podrúgoy vétrenoy moéy*: The same intona-
tion and rhymes occur in Baratïnski's *The Concubine*
(*Nalozhnitsa*; composed 1829–30), ll. 779–80:

> To his volatile mistress
> he daily was more dear . . .
>
> *Podrúge vétrenoy svoéy*
> *On ezhednévno bïl miléy* . . .

IV

1–11 The instrumentation of the first eleven lines in the
final text of this stanza (of which a lexical translation is

given below) is truly remarkable. The alliterations are built around the vowel *a* (which is also the sound of the unaccented *o*) and the consonants *l, s, z, k.*

> *No yá otstál ot íh soyúza*
> But I dropped out of their alliance
> *I vdál' bezhál . . . oná za mnóy.*
> and afar fled. She after me.
> *Kak chásto láskovaya Múza*
> How often the gentle Muse
> 4 *Mne uslazhdála pút' nemóy*
> to me made sweet the way [which was] mute
> *Volshébstvom táynogo rasskáza!*
> with the bewitchment of a secret tale!
> *Kak chásto, po skalám Kavkáza,*
> How often on the crags of the Caucasus
> *Oná Lenóroy, pri luné,*
> she Lenorelike, by the light of the moon,
> 8 *So mnóy skakála na koné!*
> with me galloped on a steed!
> *Kak chásto po bregám Tavrídï*
> How often on the shores of Tauris
> *Oná menyá vo mglé nochnóy*
> she me in murk of night
> *Vodíla slúshat' shúm morskóy . . .*
> led to listen the sound of the sea . . .

```
. . . . . . . .al. . . . . . . .za
. . . . . . . . .al. .aza. . . .
ka. . .as. .lask. . . . . . .za
4 . . . .sla. . . .la. . . . . . . .
.al. . . . . . . . . . . . . . . .as kaza
ka. . .as. . .askala.ka.kaza
. .al. . . . . . . . . .l. . .
8 . . . . . .skakala. .ka. .
ka. . .as. . . . . . . . . . . . . . .
. . . . . . . . . . . . .l. . . . . . . .
. . . .lasl. . . . . . . . . . . .sk. .
```

The play of inner assonances that is so striking in *EO* and other poems by Pushkin occurs, not infrequently, in English verse. One remembers Dryden's beautifully counterpointed lines (in his imitation, 1692, of Juvenal, *Satires*, VI) in which the confusion of intoxication is rendered by words echoing and mimicking each other (ll. 422–23; my italics):

> When *vapours* to their swimming brains ad*v*ance,
> And *double tapers* on the *table dance*.

"Table" combines the first syllable of "tapers" and the second of "double"; "vapours" rhymes with "tapers"; and the initial consonants of these two words are repeated in the terminal rhyme, "advance–dance." One also recalls the technique by means of which Wordsworth, in *Poems on the Naming of Places*, VI (composed 1800–02; pub. 1815), renders the surf of an imaginary sea, heard through the murmur of a fir grove (ll. 106–08; my italics):

> . . . and, with a store
> Of indist*inguish*able sympathies,
> Mi*ng*ling most earnest *wishe*s for the day . . .

1–2 / But I dropped out of their alliance—and fled afar . . . she followed me / *No yá otstál ot íh soyúza | I vdál' bezhál . . . oná za mnóy*: I note here a curious reminiscence, the faint echo of a passage in Batyushkov's *Bacchante* (twenty-eight lines in trochaic tetrameter, 1816, imitating Parny's *Déguisements de Vénus*, IX, 1808 edn.):

> The young nymph dropped back.
> I then followed her—she fled . . .
>
> *Nímfa yúnaya otstála.*
> *Yá za néy . . . oná bezhála . . .*

2 I am reminded by the intonation of Pushkin's line, and by the sense of Batyushkov's trochaic one, of a line in *The Fall*, a poem by Sir Charles Sedley (c. 1639–1701), of whom neither could have known anything:

I follow'd close, the Fair still flew . . .

2 / fled afar; 6 / Caucasia's crags; 9 / shores of Tauris;
v : 3 / Moldavia; 11 / in my garden: Pushkin's pere-
grinations have been alluded to several times in this
commentary. After he fled (or rather was expelled) from
Petersburg in the beginning of May, 1820, Pushkin
spent most of the summer in the Caucasus and then
stayed for three weeks in southern Crimea. These two
stages are commemorated by the first draft of *The
Caucasian Captive* (begun August, 1820) and *The Foun-
tain of Bahchisaray*, which he wrote at his next official
domicile, Kishinev, in the general region of Moldavia or
Bessarabia (the scene of his *Gypsies*, 1823–24), where he
had his headquarters from autumn, 1820, to summer,
1823, thence moving to Odessa. "My garden" refers to
his countryseat Mihaylovskoe, in the province of Pskov,
to which he was confined by governmental order from
August, 1824, to September, 1826.

It has become a commonplace with commentators to
deplore Pushkin's "exile." Actually, it may be argued
that during those six years he wrote more and better than
he would, had he remained in St. Petersburg. He was
not permitted to return to the capital; this no doubt
greatly irritated our poet during his years of provincial
office and rural seclusion (1820–24, 1824–26). The
biographer should not, however, exaggerate the hard-
ships of his banishment. His chief, General Inzov, was a
cultured and sympathetic person. Pushkin's vegetation
in Kishinev was an easier life than that of many a mili-
tary man gambling and drinking in the provincial hole
where his duty took him and his regiment. His life of
fashionable dissipation and romantic adventure in gay,
sophisticated Odessa was a very pleasant form of exile in-
deed, despite his feud with Count Vorontsov. And the
quiet of Mihaylovskoe, with the friendly Osipov family

at the end of the pinewood ride, was in fact sought out by
our poet again very soon after he was permitted to reside
where he wished.

6 / on . . . crags / *po skalám*; 9 / on the shores / *po bregám*:
The preposition *po* cannot be rendered by one word in
English. It combines the idea of "on" (*na*) and that of
"along" (*vdol'*).

7–8 / *Oná Lenóroy, pri luné,* | *So mnóy skakála na koné*:
Lenore is the celebrated ballad written at Gelliehausen,
near Göttingen, in the summer of 1773, by Gottfried
August Bürger (1747–94). He had been assiduously
reading the *Reliques of Ancient English Poetry* (3 vols.,
London, 1765), collected by Thomas Percy (1729–1811),
later Bishop of Dromore. *Lenore* consists of 256 lines, or
thirty-two stanzas of eight iambic lines, with a rhyme
scheme going babaccee and with the masculine-ending
lines in tetrameter and the feminine-ending ones in
trimeter—a most ingenious arrangement. This pattern
is exactly imitated by Zhukovski in his mediocre trans-
lation of 1831 (*Lenora*), and is exactly the stanza of
Pushkin's *The Bridegroom* (*Zhenih*, 1825), a poem far
surpassing in artistic genius anything that Bürger wrote.
His *Lenore* owes a great deal to old English ballads; his
achievement is to have consolidated and concentrated
in a technically perfect piece the moon-tomb-ghost
theme that was, in a sense, the logical result of Death's
presence in Arcadia, and the cornerstone of Goethe's
Romanticism.

Scott's version of the ballad—*William and Helen*
(1796)—is well known (ll. 113–16):

> We saddle late—from Hungary
> I rode since darkness fell;
> And to its bourne we both return
> Before the matin-bell.

Incidentally, the idea of magically rapid transit occurs, with a curious echoing ring about it, in *The Song of Igor's Campaign*, where in one famous passage or interpolation, concerning a necromancing prince (Vseslav, Prince of Polotsk, 1044–1101), the latter is said to have been able to travel ("enveloped in a blue mist") so fast across Russia that while the matin bells were ringing at his departure from Polotsk he would be in time to hear them still chiming in Kiev; and from Kiev he would reach the Black Sea before cockcrowing. This Vseslav is a kind of Slavic Michael Scot (c. 1175–c. 1234).

Zhukovski imitated Bürger's *Lenore* twice: in 1808 (*Lyudmila*, an approximate version, in 126 tetrametric couplets, among which we find one of the sources of Pushkin's information on *Lenore* in such a passage as: "the moon glistens, the dale silvers, the dead man with the maid gallops") and in his wonderful ballad of 1812, *Svetlana*, which I discuss in my n. to Three : V : 2–4.

Zhukovski had German, but most Russian men of letters knew Bürger's ballad only from Mme de Staël's *De l'Allemagne*, which contains an analysis of it, and from French versions. The title of the first French version beautifully brings out the method: *Léonora*, "traduction de l'anglais" (i.e., based upon W. R. Spencer's English version) by S. Ad. de La Madelaine (Paris, 1811). Another ridiculous French imitation came from the dainty pen of Pauline de Bradi (Paris, 1814), who at least knew the German text. I think that this is the model of Pavel Katenin's *Olga* (1815), a clumsy thing in trochaic tetrameter. A much finer French version is Paul Lehr's *Lénore* (Strasbourg, 1834):

> Ses bras de lis étreignent son amant,
> Au grand galop ils volent hors d'haleine . . .

This is excellent music, though only a paraphrase of Bürger's ll. 148–49.

After Lenore, grieving over her William's absence, has thoroughly upbraided Providence (this passage was considerably toned down by Zhukovski), her lover, a dead man by now, comes to fetch her (ll. 97–105):

> Und aussen, horch! ging's trap trap trap,
> Als wie von Rosseshufen,
> Und klirrend stieg ein Reiter ab,
> An des Geländers Stufen;
> Und horch! und horch! den Pfortenring
> Ganz lose, leise klinglingling!
> Dann kamen durch die Pforte
> Vernehmlich diese Worte:

> "Holla, Holla! Thu auf, mein Kind! . . ."

The horseman warns Lenore that it is a hundred-mile ride to their nuptial bed in Bohemia, and, as transpires after a few more stanzas, this bed is his grave. Off they go in the famous lines (149):

> Und hurre hurre, hop hop hop! . . .

and (157–58):

> . . . Der Mond scheint hell!
> Hurra! die Todten reiten schnell!

At one point (st. xxv) they pass by a gibbet in the stark moonlight.

I have often wondered why Pushkin chose to identify his Muse with that frightened girl, and although no doubt his choice may be understood as an acknowledgment of the romanticism that used to tinge his early inspirations, one is tempted to decipher the figures of five spectral Decembrists dangling from those gallows by the autobiographical road over which he swiftly passes in his retrospective fancy of 1829.

12 / Nereid's / *Nereïdï*: A sea nymph, daughter of the sea-god Nereus.

VARIANT

1–4 The fair copy reads:

> But fate at me cast looks of wrath
> and bore me far. . . . She followed me.
> How oft the gentle maid
> would sweeten the nocturnal hour . . .

V

3 / Moldavia: Moldova in Romanian; part of the province
of Bessarabia, extreme SW Russia. It has already been
mentioned with the same intonation of melancholy re-
moteness in One : VIII : 13.

4–9 Pushkin has in mind his impressions of 1820–23, when
he resided in Kishinev, capital of Bessarabia, and on two
or three occasions toured the surrounding country. Thus,
in December, 1821, he took a ten-day trip to Izmail. He
revisited Moldavia briefly in January, 1824, going to
Tiraspol and Kaushani (Kaushany), where he sought in
vain the traces of Mazepa's grave. The main artistic re-
sult of all this was *The Gypsies* (*Tsïganï*), a romantic
poem of 549 iambic tetrameters, begun in winter, 1823,
in Odessa and finished in a fair copy Oct. 10, 1824, at
Mihaylovskoe.

"The scant, strange tongues and songs of the steppe"
refers to two pieces: (1) some indifferent couplets in
amphibrachic tetrameter composed by Pushkin Nov. 14,
1820, and called *Moldavian Song* (known as *The Black
Shawl*), which became a popular ballad (and is said to
have enjoyed, in a Romanian version, a new lease of
life as a "folk song"), and (2) the excellent little song of
twenty anapaestic dimeters given Zemfira to sing in *The
Gypsies*:

Commentary

> Husband old, husband fierce,
> cut me [*rezh' menyá*], burn me [*zhgi menyá*];
> I stay firm, unafraid
> of the knife or the fire.

There is said to be a genuine Moldavian gypsy song that goes "arde-ma, fride-ma" (fide Pushkin). In Romanian, *arde* is "to burn" and *fride*, "to fry" (Leonid Grossman, *Pushkin* [Moscow, 1939], transliterates *ardï ma, frïdzhe ma*).

George Henry Borrow (1803–81), *Targum; or, Metrical Translations from Thirty Languages and Dialects* (St. Petersburg, 1835), p. 19, renders the song of Pushkin's Zemfira as:

> Hoary man, hateful man!
> Gash my frame, burn my frame;
> Bold I am, scoff I can
> At the sword, at the flame.

Prosper Mérimée, in his inexact and limp prose version of Pushkin's poem, *Les Bohémiens* (1852), renders Zemfira's song as "Vieux jaloux, méchant jaloux, coupe-moi, brûle-moi," etc.; and thence it is in part transferred by Henri Meilhac and Ludovic Halévy, in their libretto of Georges Bizet's opera *Carmen* (1875), based on Mérimée's novella of that name (1847), to Carmen, who derisively sings it in I, IX.

Finally, Ivan Turgenev translated this nomadic song from *The Gypsies* for Edmond de Goncourt, who gives it as a "chanson du pays" to the gypsy woman Stepanida Roudak (also supplied by his Russian friend) in his mediocre *Les Frères Zemganno* (1879), ch. 8:

> Vieux époux, barbare époux,
> Egorge-moi! brûle-moi!

and the last quatrain:

> Je te hais!
> Je te méprise!
> C'est un autre que j'aime
> Et je me meurs en l'aimant!

11 See n. to Eight : IV : 2, 6, 9.

13–14 | *S pechál'noy dúmoyu v ocháh,* | *S Frantsúzskoy knízhkoyu v rukáh*: Perhaps this is better rendered by:

> sad brooding in her eyes,
> a French book in her hands.

This sounds like a neat little summary of the closing lines of *La Mélancolie*, by Gabriel Marie Jean Baptiste Legouvé (1764–1812):

> . . . tendre Mélancolie!
>
> .   .   .   .
> Ah! si l'art à nos yeux veut tracer ton image,
> Il doit peindre une vierge, assise sous l'ombrage,
> Qui, rêveuse et livrée à de vagues regrets,
> Nourrit au bruit des flots un chagrin plein d'attraits,
> Laisse voir, en ouvrant ses paupières timides,
> Des pleurs voluptueux dans ses regards humides,
> Et se plaît aux soupirs qui soulèvent son sein,
> Un cyprès devant elle, et Werther à la main.

(*Werther*, pronounced "Verter," rhyming with *vert*— abbreviated title of Goethe's novel in a French version.)

VARIANT

10 A fair-copy variant of this line reads:

> but the wind blew, the thunder crashed . . .

The allusion is to the events of July, 1824—Pushkin's expulsion from the civil service, and from Odessa, to rustication at Mihaylovskoe.

VI

2 / high-life rout / *svétskiy ráut*: The term *raut* was still used in St. Petersburg society as late as 1916. Vyazemski, in a letter to his wife (Aug. 1, 1833), has the jocular barbarism, *fash'onabel'nïy raut*. The French called it *raout*.

3 / steppe / *stepníe*: In a larger sense than the "steppe" of V : 9; "agrestic."

6 / *Voénnïh frántov, diplomátov*: It has been suggested (I do not remember by whom) that perhaps a misprint in all three editions (1832, 1833, and 1837) caused a comma to disappear after *voennïh*, a word that may mean either "military" or "military men." The comma would, of course, give the line a much more Pushkinian cut (besides disposing of the rather too-ostentatious image of "military fops"):

of military men, of fops, of diplomats.

14 / around . . . about / *Vkrug . . . ókolo*: The comparison is trivial, and the expression, clumsy. The whole stanza, in fact, is poor.

VARIANTS

5 The separate edition of Eight (1832) has:

Through an array of pompous magnates . . .

The draft of this stanza is on the cover of the fair copy of the canto.

10–11 Draft (2387A, f. 17^r):

the slow turmoil of guests,
apparel, feathers, speech . . .

VII

6 / nebulous / *tumánnïy*: "Misty," "bemisted," "with clouded brow"(a synonym of *pasmurnïy*, "overcast," and *sumráchnïy*, "somber," *ténébreux*, as used to characterize Onegin).

VARIANTS

1–7 Fair copy:

> Who there among them in the distance
> as a superfluous something stands?
> With none, it seems, is he in contact,
> he speaks to hardly any man
>
> .   .   .   .   .   .
>
> he seems a stranger everywhere.

And these canceled lines in the fair copy (4–6):

> lost, and forgotten, and alone,
> among the young aristocrats,
> among the transient diplomats . . .

VIII

1 / grown more peaceful / *usmirílsya*: The connotation is "tamed by life," "quieted down" in relation to "passions," etc.

2 / *kórchit . . . chudaká*: The verb *korchit'* combines two ideas: "to pose" and "to grimace." Impersonation rather than imitation is implied, and this precludes the use here of "to ape" or "to mimic."

5–7 Maturin's *Melmoth the Wanderer*, *l'Homme errant*, with the stamp of Fate and Eternity on his livid brow (see n. to Three : XII : 9).

"Cosmopolitan," a person at home in any country, but especially in Italy if an Englishman, and in France if a Russian. Onegin, however, had never been abroad.

"Patriot," a nationalist, a Slavophile. We know from *Onegin's Journey*, on which he started early in 1821, that he had gone through that phase and had come back disillusioned to Petersburg in August, 1824.

Byron's *Childe Harold*, friend of the mountains, companion of the caverns, familiar of the ocean, but in man's dwelling a restless stranger who looks at the painted world with a smile of despair and crushes his enemies with the curse of forgiveness.

"Quaker," a member of the Society of Friends, the religious sect founded by George Fox in England in the middle of the seventeenth century.

"Bigot," a blind worshiper of his own intolerance.

The bizarre beau of the time, while sitting in a state of torpor with his feet on the bars of the grate, might balance "between becoming a misanthrope and a democrat" (Maria Edgeworth, *Ennui*, ch. 5).

VIII–IX

Brodski's well-developed sociological ear distinguishes in the reported speech of these stanzas (and in XII : 1–7) a volley of abuse hurled at Onegin by conservative aristocrats. This is, of course, nonsense. Brodski forgets that Tatiana, too, questioned Eugene's genuineness. Actually, the hubbub of queries and answers here is a kind of artistic double talk on our poet's part. The reader must be made to forget for the time being that Onegin is Lenski's murderer. The "sensible people" (XII : 4) are merely the imagined reviewers of the canto. The statements that we are busybodies, that we dislike wit and cling to traditional values, had been the stock in trade of literary eloquence since the birth of satire and should not be taken seriously here. If they are, the whole passage becomes meaningless since such a phrase as "the rashness of fiery souls" is the last thing we could think of applying to Onegin, and such phrases are really smuggled in here only to create the right atmosphere for and prepare the transition to Onegin's passionately falling in love with Tatiana.

IX

8 / *Chto úm, lyubýa prostór, tesnít*: The meaning is: intelligence, needing elbowroom, squeezes fools out. *Prostor* has several meanings, all depending on the idea of spaciousness, such as "scope," "range," "open expanse," etc. The word for "space" itself is *prostranstvo*.

12 / grave are trifles / *vázhnï vzdórï*: Cf. André Chénier, *La République des lettres*, frag. VIII (ed. Walter): "S'il fuit les graves riens, noble ennui du beau monde . . ."

X, XI, XII

These three stanzas, composed in Moscow, are dated by Pushkin Oct. 2, 1829. They were at the time visualized by him as the beginning of the canto (note the proemial ring of X), which was to contain Onegin's Journey and which was to come after Chapter Seven. The established text to Eight (then Nine) was begun Dec. 24, 1829, in St. Petersburg, at Demut's Hotel. A fortnight later in a letter to Benkendorf, he asked permission (which was refused) to go abroad as a private citizen—or to accompany a Russian mission to China.

X

1 The not-very-new advice to be "young in one's youth" had
already been extended by Pushkin in a short poem of
1819 to the poetaster Yakov Tolstoy (1791–1867), whom
he had met at dinners of the Green Lamp, another of
those champagne clubs to which commentators are prone
to ascribe too much revolutionary and literary significance.

3 Miss Deutsch serenely rhymes (with "merry"):

> Who ripened, like good port or sherry . . .

XII

1–7 See n. to Eight : VIII–IX.

7 A reference to Pushkin's poem *The Demon* (October or
November, 1823). It will be noticed that the first lines
of this poem, given below, prelude Eight : I : 1:

> In those days when to me were new
> all the impressions of existence—
> and eyes of maids, and sough of grove,
> and in the night the singing of the nightingale;
> when elevated feelings,
> freedom, glory, and love,
> and inspired arts,
> so strongly roused my blood;
> the hours of hopes and of delights
> with sudden heartache having shaded,
> then did a certain wicked genius
> begin to visit me in secret.
> Sad were our meetings:

his smile, his wondrous glance,
his galling speech,
cold venom poured into my soul.
With inexhaustible detraction
he tempted Providence;
he called the beautiful a dream,
held inspiration in contempt,
did not believe in love, in freedom,
looked mockingly on life,
and nothing in all nature
did he desire to bless.

This "demon" is connected with the "Byronic" personality of Aleksandr Raevski (1795–1868), whom Pushkin first met in Pyatigorsk in the summer of 1820 and of whom he saw a good deal in Odessa, in the summer of 1823, and at intervals later, till the summer of 1824. In the draft of a letter to him, October, 1823, Pushkin calls Raevski his "constant teacher in moral affairs" and remarks upon his "Melmothlike character." When, in pt. III of the literary almanac *Mnemosyne* (c. Oct. 20, 1824), this piece appeared under the title *My Demon* (changed to *The Demon* when republished in the *Northern Flowers* for 1825 and in Pushkin's *Poems*, 1826, from which text I translate it), some readers thought they recognized Raevski, and Pushkin wrote, but did not publish, a refutation. In this MS note (1827) our poet, writing of himself in the third person, advises readers that his *Demon* is to be regarded not as the portrait of any particular individual but as the spirit influencing the morality of the age, a spirit of negation and doubt (*Works* 1936, V, 273).

Pushkin left a tentative continuation of *The Demon* in rough draft, of which the last lines read:

I started looking with his eyes

.   .   .   .   .

with his dim words
my soul would sound in unison . . .

Very similar lines Pushkin planned to use at one time in continuation of One : XLVI (see n. to ll. 5–7 of that stanza).

An interesting sequel to all this comes in the form of Pushkin's poem *The Angel*, which is a kind of amendment to *The Demon*. It is a not-uncolorful but on the whole mediocre little poem, a cross between the Byronic elegy and the Gallic madrigal, marked by very routine rhymes and a telltale poverty of scud modulation* (o, III, III, III, I, III, III, III, o, o, III, III, in contrast to the rhythm of *The Demon*: o, I–III, o, III, III, III, I–III, II, III, III, o, II, o, o, III, o, I–III, I–III, III, I–III, o, II, I, I–III). It was first published in the 1828 issue of the *Northern Flowers* and then appeared, in the form in which it is here translated, in Pushkin's *Poems* (1829), where it is dated 1827. Here it is:

The Angel

> At Eden's door a tender Angel
> let sink his radiant head,
> while, gloomy and restless, a Demon
> flew over hell's abyss.
>
> The spirit of negation, the spirit of doubt
> gazed at the stainless spirit
> and an involuntary glow of tender feeling
> for the first time he dimly knew.
>
> Quoth he: "Forgive me, I have seen you,
> and your radiance has not been lost on me:
> not everything in heaven I hated,
> not everything on earth I scorned."

It is surmised that the thing refers to Countess Vorontsov and Aleksandr Raevski, thus consolidating the presumed link between the fictional Onegin and the stylized Raevski (see n. to One : XLVI : 5–7).

A decade later, from these two poems the main strain of Lermontov's romantic epic *Demon* was evolved.

---

*See App. II, "Notes on Prosody."

9–14 The intonation here, especially in l. 13, is very like that in a passage of Chateaubriand's *René* (ed. Weil, pp. 41–42): "Sans parens, sans amis, pour ainsi dire seul sur la terre, n'ayant point encore aimé, j'étois accablé d'une surabondance de vie."

13 / *Bez slúzhbï, bez zhení, bez dél*: Without any military or civil position in the government service; without a wife; and without any affairs, private or professional.

XIII

1 / A restlessness took hold of him . . . / *Im ovladélo bespokóystvo*: A Gallicism; e.g., Chateaubriand, *Mémoires d'outre-tombe*, entry of 1838, on the death of the Duke of Enghien (ed. Levaillant, pt. II, bk. IV, ch. 2): ". . . Il me prend . . . une inquiétude qui m'obligerait à changer de climat."

See also Maria Edgeworth, *Ennui*, ch. 1: ". . . an aversion to the place I was in . . . a childish love of locomotion."

2 / toward a change of places / *k pereméne mést*: The same Gallicism (*changement de lieu*) occurs in Griboedov's *Woe from Wit*, act IV, ll. 477–79:

> Those feelings . . .
> which were not cooled in me either by distance,
> or by amusement, or by change of places.

This is also curiously close to the description of Lenski's constancy in Two : XX : 8–14:

> Neither the cooling [quality of] distance,
> nor the long years of separation . . .

10 / *Dostúpnïy chúvstvu odnomú*: An ambiguous line. "Accessible to one sensation only" (say, ennui or remorse) or

"moved only by feeling" (not "reason")? Neither makes good sense.

14 / from boat to ball / *s korablyá na bál*: An allusion to Chatski's arrival, in I, vii, of Griboedov's *Woe from Wit*. He suddenly makes his entry on a winter morning, in 1819, at Famusov's house in Moscow, whither he returns after three years spent in foreign climes (act I, l. 449). He has driven more than seven hundred versts (above four hundred miles) in forty-five hours (l. 303), without stopping, i.e., traveling post. This obviously refers to the St. Petersburg-Moscow stretch. He has come via Petersburg from abroad, apparently from a watering resort (in Germany? Liza's remark, l. 277, may also be construed as his having visited the Caucasus for his health at the start of his journey). He has, it would seem, been to France (obliquely mentioned in III, viii). The *korabl'* ("ship," "boat") in Pushkin's reference is a telescoped reminiscence of Chatski's having arrived in Russia from abroad, evidently by water (i.e., the Baltic), and of Sofia's (act I, l. 331) observing that she had been inquiring even of sailors if they had seen him passing in a mail coach. The "ball" refers to the party given at the close of the same day at Famusov's house in act III.

*

At first blush, it would seem that Onegin has arrived in St. Petersburg by sea from a foreign country beyond the Baltic. But various complications arise:

How far—if at all—should one be influenced in one's understanding of the established text by details of plot and characterization explicitly mentioned by the author only in such MS passages as he had preserved but not published? And if some degree of influence be admitted, should it depend on the category of the MS (draft, fair copy, struck-out readings, etc.), as well as on special reasons for its not being published by the author (e.g., pressure of censorship, fear of offending the living, etc.)? I am inclined to rely on the established text only.

In the established text of *EO* we find nothing of a positive nature to exclude the possibility of Onegin's having returned to Russia from a trip to western Europe (after the visit to the shores of the Black Sea, described in the passages of *Onegin's Journey* published by Pushkin). When using *all* the material we have, we find that, starting from St. Petersburg (where he had arrived soon after his duel) in summer, 1821, Onegin traveled to Moscow, Nizhni, Astrahan (Astrakhan), and the Caucasus, was in the Crimea in autumn, 1823, then visited Pushkin in Odessa, and in August, 1824, returned to St. Petersburg, thus closing the complete circle of his Russian tour, with no possibility of any trip abroad.

When in Eight : XIX Tatiana casually asks Onegin whether he had come to St. Petersburg from his country place, his reply is not given, but we can easily hear Onegin answering: "No, I came straight from Odessa"; but only by a great effort of the imagination can we have him say: "As a matter of fact, I was abroad: traversed western Europe from Marseilles to Lübeck—enfin, je viens de débarquer." I would suggest, without probing the problem any further, that the transition from deck to dance has no geographic reality and is a mere literary formula derived from a situation in *Woe from Wit*, where the "ship" is also more or less of a metaphor.

See my nn. to *Onegin's Journey*, where I give all variants and rejections.

There is another little problem here: logically, the events and moods described in the twenty-one lines from XII : 8 to the end of XIII seem to represent a consecutive series, and then Onegin should be twenty-nine now, in 1824; but stylistically one might be tempted to regard the whole of XIII as merely an illustration and develop-

Commentary

ment of the comments closing the preceding stanza
(XII : 10–14), and then Onegin would be twenty-six
now, in 1824, in which case a pluperfect turn (which
Russian does not possess) should be given to XIII ("A
restlessness had taken hold of him," etc.).

XIV–XV

In these two stanzas Tatiana's entrance with Prince N.,
her husband (the "imposing general" of XIV : 4), is ob-
served by Pushkin's wide-awake Muse, not by sluggish
and sulky Onegin. *He* will notice her only in XVI (begin-
ning with l. 8), by which time she has joined another
fashionable lady. Meanwhile Prince N. has walked up
to his kinsman—whom he has not seen for several years
—and the Spanish ambassador is paying his respects to
Tatiana.

XIV

9 / without those little mannerisms / *Bez étih málen'kih
uzhímok*: Fr. *sans ces petites mignardises*.

". . . Whatever is evidently borrowed becomes vulgar.
Original affectation is sometimes good *ton*; imitated af-
fectation always bad," writes Lady Frances to her son
Henry Pelham in Edward Bulwer-Lytton's tedious
Pelham; or, Adventures of a Gentleman (3 vols., London,
1828), vol. I, ch. 26, a work that Pushkin knew well from
a French version (which I have not seen): *Pelham, ou les
Aventures d'un gentilhomme anglais*, tr. ("librement")
Jean Cohen (4 vols., Paris, 1828).

9–10 / mannerisms . . . devices: Although the following
beautiful passage refers not to Russian wives of the
1820's but to English misses of a century before, it does
convey some idea of what these airs and mannerisms

might be; letter signed Matilda Mohair, written by
Steele, *The Spectator*, no. 492 (Sept. 24, 1712):

> *Glycera* has a dancing Walk, and keeps Time in her
> ordinary Gate. *Chloe*, her Sister . . . comes into the Room
> . . . with a familiar Run. *Dulcissa* takes Advantage of the
> Approach of the Winter, and has introduc'd a very pretty
> Shiver, closing up her Shoulders, and shrinking as she
> moves. . . . Here's a little Country Girl that's very cun-
> ning. . . . The Air that she takes is to come into Company
> after a Walk, and is very successfully out of Breath upon
> occasion. Her Mother . . . calls her Romp . . .

13 / *comme il faut*; XV : 14, "vulgar": In a letter to his wife
from Boldino to Petersburg, Pushkin wrote, Oct. 30,
1833:

> I am not jealous . . . but you know how I loathe every-
> thing that smacks of your Moscow missy, everything that
> is not *comme il faut*, everything that is "vulgar."

13 / [Shishkov]: The reference is to the leader of the
Archaic group of writers, Admiral Aleksandr Shishkov
(1754–1841), publicist, statesman, president of the
Academy of Sciences, and a cousin of my great-grand-
mother.

Shishkov's name is left out in all three editions (1832,
1833, 1837), but the presence of its first letter (*Sh*) in the
fair copy, and a marginal gloss by Vyazemski in his copy
of the novel, settle a problem, to the solution of which all
logic points. Poor Küchelbecker was pathetically wrong
when in his prison diary (entry of Feb. 21, 1832, Svea-
borg Fortress) he bitterly hinted that the dots stood for
his Christian name (Wilhelm) and that Pushkin was
poking fun at his addiction to mixing Russian and
French in his letters. Actually, he was closer in many
ways to the Archaists than to the Moderns.

Facetious references to the champion of Slavisms were
frequent in the first third of the century. Thus Karam-

zin, Shishkov's amiable opponent, writes in a letter to Dmitriev, June 30, 1814:

You are angry with me—or am I mistaken? . . . I know your "tenderness" [*nezhnost'*]—I would have said "delicacy" [*delikatnost'*, Fr. *délicatesse*], but I fear Shishkov.

Shishkov had the following to say in 1808, in commenting on his own translation of two French essays by La Harpe (I quote from Pekarski's excellent notes to his and Grot's edition of Karamzin's letters to Dmitriev, St. Petersburg, 1866):

The monstrous French Revolution, having trampled upon all that was based on the principles of Faith, Honor, and Reason, engendered in France a new language, far different from that of Fénelon and Racine.

This is presumably a reference to Chateaubriand, whose genius and originality owed nothing, of course, to any "revolution"; actually, the literature produced by the French Revolution was even more conventional, colorless, and banal than the style of Fénelon and Racine; this is a phenomenon comparable to the literary results of the Russian Revolution, with its "proletarian novels," which are, really, hopelessly bourgeois.

"Simultaneously," continues Shishkov, "our letters, too, following the model set by the new French and Frenchified-German literatures, started to lose all resemblance to Russian."

This is an attack on Karamzin's prose of the 1790's. It was in order to stop this dangerous trend that Shishkov wrote, in 1803, his *Dissertation on the Old and New Styles in the Russian Language*, followed by an addendum in 1804. (Pushkin possessed an 1818 edition of that work.) What he attacked was liberal thought rather than Gallicisms and neologisms; but he is mainly remembered for the uncouth and artificial Russisms with which he attempted to replace the current terms that had been automatically adopted in Russia from western European sources for the designation of a German abstraction or a French trinket. The struggle between him and the followers of Karamzin is of historical interest, * but it had no effect whatsoever upon the evolution of the language.

On Mar. 25, 1811, Shishkov founded the group *Beseda lyubiteley rossiyskogo slova* (Concourse of Lovers of the Russian Verb). If we discount the nominal membership of two major poets, Derzhavin and Krïlov, we can concur with Russian critics in defining the activities of the group as the naïve recreations of elderly grandees. Its doomed purpose was to support "classical" (really, neoclassical or pseudoclassical) forms of Russian against Gallicisms and other infections. Another, younger, group of literary men took up the cudgels, and there ensued a rather insipid "literary war" on the lines of those *querelles* of the *anciens* with the *modernes* which are so tedious to read about in histories of French literature.

It has been quite a tradition with Russian historians of literature, ever since the middle of the last century, to assign exaggerated importance to the Arzamas group, which arose under the following circumstances.

Prince Shahovskoy, a Besedist, wrote and produced, Sept. 23, 1815, a weak play that contained a skit on Zhukovski (*The Lipetsk Waters*; see my n. to One : XVIII : 4–10). The future well-known statesman Count Dmitri Bludov (1785–1869) countered the attack on his friend with an (even more wretched) squib modeled on French polemical badinage and entitled *A Vision in an Arzamas Tavern, Published by the Society of Learned People*. Arzamas, a town in the province of Nizhni, was deemed as provincial as Lipetsk. It was famed for its poultry and was often mentioned in the gazettes because

---

*Foreshadowing as it did the mid-century antagonism between the politico-philosophical Slavophiles (*Slavyanofïlï*) and Westerners (*Zapadniki*).

an artist of plebeian origin, with more energy than genius, Aleksandr Stupin (1775–1861), had founded there, about 1810, the first art school in Russia. The paradox (enlightenment coming from stagnation) tickled the Russian sense of humor. Moreover, Arzamas was a kind of incomplete anagram of Karamzin, the leader of the Moderns.

Zhukovski and Bludov founded the Arzamas Society (*Arzamasskoe obshchestvo bezvestnïh lyudey*, Arzamasan Society of Obscure People) Oct. 14, 1815, and the first meeting was held soon after. It was meant to stand up against the Ancients for colloquial simplicity of idiom and for modern forms of Russian (many of which had been more or less artificially derived from the French).

The meetings of Arzamas consisted of roast-goose dinners followed by the reading of painfully facetious minutes and trivial verse. The carousers, of whom there were seldom more than half a dozen (out of the final number of twenty), donned red calpacks: these *bonnets rouges* are gloated upon by leftist commentators, who forget, however, that some of the heads that these caps covered belonged (e.g., in the case of the leaders of the group, Zhukovski and Karamzin) to ardent champions of monarchy, religion, and genteel literature, and that the thread of travesty that ran through the proceedings of the club precluded the presence of any serious political (or artistic) purpose. The club's juvenile symbols had a deadening effect on the few poems of Pushkin in which the Arzamas facetiae were reflected. It should also be remembered that Zhukovski's humor was at best that of a fabulist (e.g., monkeys and cats are a priori comic) and a child (the belly is comic). The nicknames by which the members of the group went were taken from his ballads: Zhukovski was Svetlana; Bludov, Cassandra; Vyazemski, Asmodeus; Aleksandr Turgenev, Eol's Harp; Vasiliy Pushkin, Vot (Fr. *voici*, *voilà*, "here," "there," "lo!"), and so on. When Pushkin joined this merry organization in the autumn of 1817, he was dubbed Sverchok (Cricket), the source being *Svetlana*, v, 13 (see my nn. to Five : x : 6 and xvii : 3–4). The whole affair, as so frequently happens with such things, soon became a bore and waned, despite Zhukovski's efforts to inject life into it. It disintegrated in 1818.

If Shishkov's group was notable for its insufferable black-letter pedantry and reactionary attitudes, Arzamas, on the other hand, was characterized by an archness of humor that sets one's teeth on edge. Its liberalism (in contrast to the obscurantism of the Ancients) had no political significance: Zhukovski, for example, was as stanch a supporter of monarchy and religion as was Shishkov. Russian historians of literature have vastly overrated the importance of these two societies. Neither had any marked influence on the course of Russian literature, which, as all great literatures, is the product of individuals, not groups.

From tactical considerations, Pushkin, in the months preceding the printing of the first canto of *EO*, voiced patriotic respect toward the leader of the Ancients. In his *Second Epistle to the Censor* (at that time, Aleksandr Biryukov, 1772–1844, who occupied the post from 1821 to 1826), consisting of seventy-two Alexandrines and composed late in 1824, Pushkin welcomed Shishkov as the new Minister of Public Education (ll. 31–35):

> An honest minister our good tsar has elected:
> Shishkov already has the sciences directed.
> We cherish this old man. To honor, to the people,
> he is a friend. His fame is that of the year twelve;
> alone among grandees he loves the Russian Muses.

For similar reasons Pushkin, in 1824, changed his attitude toward the Besedist Prince Shahovskoy (who had been the main scapegoat of the Arzamasists) and inserted a couple of flattering verses about him in Chapter One.

XV

4 / *vzór eyó ochéy*: Fr. *Le regard de ses yeux.*

7 Cf. Vyazemski, 1815, a tetrametric poem inscribed to
Denis Davïdov (ll. 20–23):

> . . . a general's epaulets
>
> . . . .
>
> which often cause unconsciously the shoulders
> ╵ of some to rise . . .

12 The fair copy contains a much better epithet than "auto-
cratic," namely "gentle-voiced" (*tihoglásnoy*).

14 / "vulgar": The Russian adjective *vul'garnïy* was soon
to come into general use. In its more general sense of
"common" and "coarse" the term is equivalent to
ploshchadnoy (from *ploshchad*, "town square," "market
place"), which appears elsewhere in *EO* (Four : XIX : 8
and Five : XXIII : 8).

Cf. Mme de Staël, *De la Littérature* (see n. to Three :
XX : 14), pt. I, ch. 19 (1818 edn.), vol. II, p. 50n: ". . . ce
mot *la vulgarité* n'avoit pas encore été employé [au
siècle de Louis XIV]; mais je le crois bon et nécessaire."

See also n. to Eight : XIV : 13.

14–XVI : 6 The parenthetic passage from the *Ne mogu* ("I
can't—") that closes XV : 14 to the end of XVI : 6, where
it is suggested we return to the lady in question, is a rare
variety of interstrophic enjambment. In this specific in-
stance, it also plays the amusing part of a kind of door
that opens for the reader but is closed for Onegin, who
only notices the lady (whose quality the reader has al-
ready appreciated) when she settles down next to Nina
Voronskoy.

XVI

5 I have little doubt that the epigram stirring in the poet's
mind has to do with a play on "vulgar" in connection
with Bulgarin, the loathsome critic. Pushkin might have
transformed him into "Vulgárin" or he might have
given "vulgar" a Russian predicative turn and rhymed
Bulgárin–vulgáren, "Bulgarin–is vulgar."

The stanza was written, presumably, in October, 1830,
at Boldino. In the *Northern Bee*, no. 30 (Mar. 12, 1830),
Bulgarin's insulting "Anekdot" had appeared (see n. to
Eight : XXXV : 9) and, a week later, his adverse critique
of Chapter Seven* (see above, pp. 125–26).

In a Pushkin MS, among various autobiographical
odds and ends, there is the following note (*Works* 1936,
V, 461), dated Mar. 23, 1830:

I met [the critic] Nadezhdin at the house of Pogodin
[another literary man]. Nadezhdin struck me as most
plebeian, vulgar [in English], tedious, bumptious, and
devoid of manners. For instance, he picked up the hand-
kerchief I had dropped.

9–10 / Nina Voronskóy, that Cleopatra of the Neva: In
Chapter Five, the tricky magician M. Triquet substi-
tuted "Tatiana" for "Nina" in his madrigal. Like most
of the portents in that chapter (such as the "military
husbands" predicted to both Larin girls), this comes
true: Tatiana has now eclipsed "belle Nina."

Some prototypists have (incorrectly) identified this
generalized belle with a historical person, Countess Agra-
fena Zakrevski (1799–1879). Baratïnski, who fell in
love with her in the winter of 1824 in Helsingfors (her
husband was governor general of Finland), and appar-
ently became her lover in the summer of 1825, confesses

---

*See P. Stolpyanski, "Pushkin i 'Severnaya pchela,' " in *P. i
ego sovr.*, V, 19–20 (1914), 117–90.

in a letter to a friend that he imagined her when making the heroine of his tasteless *The Ball* (February, 1825–September, 1828) lose her lover, Arseniy, to an Olenka and commit suicide; but "Nina" was a fashionable literary cognomen, and the fact that Baratïnski's heroine is called Princess Nina does not prove that her glorified model is the same as that of Pushkin's "Nina Voronskoy" ("Volhovskoy" and "Taranskoy" in fair-copy cancellations).

Our only reason for thinking that Pushkin may have had a brief affair with Agrafena Zakrevski in August, 1828 (after shedding Anna Kern and while trying to shed Elizaveta Hitrovo, 1783–1839), is that her first name figures in his famous catalogue of platonically and sensually loved, successfully and unsuccessfully courted ladies (a list he wrote down in 1829 in the album of Elizaveta Ushakov, in Moscow). Of Agrafena Zakrevski he writes to Vyazemski (in a letter of Sept. 1, 1828, from St. Petersburg to Penza) thus:

I have plunged into the *monde* because I am shelterless [*bespriyuten*]. Were it not for your bronze Venus, I would have pined to death. She is consolingly amusing and charming. I write verse for her; and she has promoted me to the rank of her pimp.

Vyazemski, in his answer, punned on *bespriyuten*, inquiring if Pushkin was no longer being admitted to Priyutino, the Olenins' estate near St. Petersburg; actually, Pushkin was to visit Priyutino at least once again, on Sept. 5, when (as Annette Olenin, to whom he had not yet proposed, noted in her diary) he darkly hinted he had not the force to tear himself away from her.

The literary critic should note that "bronze" is not "marble" (XVI : 12), and that the charming woman of Pushkin's letter to Vyazemski is as different from "that Cleopatra of the Neva" (XVI : 10) as a comet is from the moon. Incidentally, I take "cette Cléopâtre de la Néva" to mean hardly more than "cette reine de la Néva," with connotations of glamour and power but with no specific reference to the legend of the three immolated lovers that Pushkin made use of in his unfinished *The Egyptian Nights.* (Cf. also "Onegin's Album": IX : 13, above, p. 92.)

Less reckless prototypists point out that another lady, Countess Elena Zavadovski (1807–74, sister-in-law of the duelist mentioned in my n. to Istomina in One : XX : 5–14), has a better claim to be Nina Voronskoy's model. Her cold, queenly beauty was the talk of society, and, as P. Shchyogolev points out,* Vyazemski, in a (still unpublished?) letter to his wife, explicitly identifies Nina Voronskoy with Countess Zavadovski.

We note, finally, that the wonderful, palpitating, pink Nina of Eight : XXVIIa is obviously a different person from the Nina of Eight : XVI.

I have gone at some length into this dreary and fundamentally inept question of the "model" of a stylized literary character in order to stress once again the difference between the reality of art and the unreality of history. The whole trouble is that memoirists and historians (no matter how honest they are) are either artists who fantastically re-create observed life or mediocrities (the more frequent case) who unconsciously distort the factual by bringing it into contact with their commonplace and simple minds. At best we can form our own judgment of a historical person if we possess what that person wrote himself—especially in the way of letters, a journal, an autobiography, and so forth. At worst we have the kind of sequence on which the prototypical school so blithely relies: poet X, an admirer of woman Z, writes a fictitious piece in which he romanticizes her (as Y) on the lines of the literary generalities of his time;

Lit. nasl., nos. 16–18 (1934), p. 558.

the news is spread that Y is Z; the real Z is seen as a complete edition of Y; Z is referred to as Y; diarists and memoirists, in describing Z, attribute to her not merely the traits of Y but the later, popularized concepts of Y (since fictitious characters grow and change, too); comes the historian, and, from the descriptions of Z (really Z plus Y plus Y^1 plus Y^2, etc.), deduces that she was the model of Y.

In the present case, the Nina of the established text (XVI) is too obviously a casual stylization to warrant the investigations undertaken to find her "prototype." But we shall presently come to the singular Olenin case, in which our materials will be the revealing writings of the people involved, and from which something will be added to our understanding of Pushkin's mind by the examination of an incidental character.

VARIANT

7–9 Fair copy:

> She sat upon a sofa [*na sofé*]
> between dread Lady Barifé
> and . . .

One wonders if this has been correctly deciphered (by Gofman). "Barife" looks Italian to me (cf. *baruffa*, "altercation"); there was an Italian traveler called Giuseppe Filippi Baruffi who left a *Voyage en Russie* at the beginning of the nineteenth century (according to Camille Koechlin in *La Grande Encyclopédie*). Or is it a real English name, e.g., Barry-Fey?

XVII

3 / [of] steppe villages / *stepníh seléniy*: In VI : 3, Pushkin had used the same epithet in speaking of his Muse, *prélesti eyó stepníe*, "her country charms," or "her agrestic charms." Basically, *stepníe* means "of the

steppe," "of the prairie," but I notice that Krïlov, for instance, in his farce *The Fashion Shop* (*Modnaya lavka*; pub. 1807), uses it both in the sense of "provincial" or "rural" and in the direct sense of "hailing from the steppe region [beyond Kursk]." Neither the rather heavily wooded country whence Pushkin's Muse came (province of Pskov) nor Tatiana's home (two hundred miles W of Moscow) can be described as steppeland.

Steppes are grasslands with, in the past, a predominance of feather grass (*Stipa pennata* L.). They extend from the Carpathians to the Altay (Altai), in the black-soil belt of Russia, south of Oryol (Orel), Tula, and Simbirsk (Ulyanovsk). The steppe proper, which has timber (cottonwoods, etc.) only in river valleys, does not reach north beyond the latitude of Harkov (Kharkov; approximately 50°), between which and the latitude of Tula to the north there is a band of *lugovaya step'* (meadow steppe), characterized by scrub oak, *Prunus*, etc. This grades insensibly northward into birch woods, where the shade is limpid. Tambov lies within this region. Several passages in our novel certainly suggest that the region where the Larin, Lenski, and Onegin seats were situated was well forested and thus must have been still farther north. I place it midway between Opochka and Moscow. (See nn. to One : I : 1–5 and Seven : XXXV : 14.)

Elsewhere Pushkin uses steppe as a mere synonym of champaign, open country, plain; but I suspect that (just as the countryside in Four is a stylized Pskovan one, encroaching here and there upon Arcadia) the kind of country implied by the epithet "steppe" in Eight : VI and XVII is such as he saw at Boldino, where, from the first week of September, 1830, to the end of November, he spent the most fertile autumn in his entire life, owing partly to the consciousness of his impending marriage— a vague vista of financial obligations and humdrum obstacles to creative life.

The estate of Boldino (province of Nizhni, district of Lukoyanov, on the river Sazanka) comprised about nineteen thousand acres and a thousand male slaves. It belonged to Pushkin's father (Sergey Pushkin, 1770–1848), who, however, had never visited it and was happy to have his elder son take charge of it. The old master house turned out to have no garden or park, but the environs were not devoid of the kind of bleak, gray grandeur that has inspired many a Russian poet. The region belongs to the prairie belt of the steppe, with scrub oak and small aspen groves. It is here that Pushkin, during those three magic months, worked on Eight and finished *EO* in its first form (nine cantos); added to this at least two fifths of a tenth canto; composed some thirty short poems, an admirable mock epic in octaves (iambic pentameter), *The Cottage in Kolomna*, the five prose *Tales of Belkin* (experimental short stories—the first stories of permanent artistic value in the Russian language), his four small tragedies—*Mozart and Salieri*, which was probably already drafted; the draft of *The Stone Guest*, completed, it is supposed, on the morning before his duel (Jan. 27, 1837); *The Feast During the Plague*, which is a translation from a French literal translation of a scene from John Wilson's *The City of the Plague*; and *The Covetous Knight*, attributed (perhaps by a French translator) to Shenstone, whose name Pushkin wrote, in Russian transliteration, with a *Ch*, owing to his thinking that *Sh* was the same kind of Gallic mispronunciation as "Shild-Arold"—and a batch of wonderful, albeit not always truthful, letters to his eighteen-year-old fiancée in Moscow.

8 / Tell me, Prince: Both Onegin and Prince N. are noblemen. Onegin, in talking to his old friend and kinsman (possibly a first cousin), uses the intimate "thou," *tï* (Fr. *tu*), and addresses him by his title, *knyaz'*, which, in this

context and under these circumstances, is on the same level of colloquial familiarity as would be *mon cher* or a surname (cf. the Onegin-Lenski dialogues in Three and Four). A brief title in this respect was merely a convenient handle. A social inferior would, and a jocose equal might, use "Your Serenity" (cf. Prince Oblonski addressing Count Vronski, in *Anna Karenin*, pt. I, ch. 17).

The American reader should be reminded that a Russian, German, or French nobleman with the title of "Prince" (which roughly corresponds to the English "Duke") is not necessarily related to the reigning family. The introduction of theeings and thouings leads in English to ridiculous associations.

9 / in the *framboise* beret / *v malínovom beréte*: A soft, brimless headgear; of crimson velvet, in this case. I have used *framboise* because "raspberry" as a color, both in Russian and in French, seems to convey a richer, more vivid sense of red than does English "raspberry." I see the latter tint as associated rather with the purplish bloom of the fresh fruit than with the bright crimson of the Russian jam, or the French jelly, made of it.

An elegant lady of 1824 would use a flat beret of claret-colored or violet velvet for day wear (the rout to which Onegin came is presumably a late-afternoon affair). The beret might be adorned with drooping feathers. According to Cunnington, *English Women's Clothing*, p. 97, English ladies in the 1820's wore "The beret-turban," made of crepe or satin and adorned with plumes; it was probably this variety that Tatiana wore. Other fashionable colors were *ponceau* (poppy red) and *rouge grenat* (garnet red). In the September, 1828, issue of the review *Moscow Telegraph*, p. 140, there is the following description, in French and in Russian, of Parisian fashions:

Dans les premiers magasins de modes on pose des fleurs en clinquant sur des bérets de crêpe bleu, rose ou ponceau.

Ces bérets admettent en outre des plumes de la couleur de l'étoffe ou blanches.

According to B. Markevich,* a toque of ponceau velvet was worn by the brilliant Caroline Sobanski (born Countess Rzhevuski, elder sister of Eva, Mme Hanski, whom Balzac was to marry in 1850) at social functions in Kiev, where Pushkin first saw her during a brief visit to that town in February, 1821. Three years later, in Odessa, he courted her, and they read *Adolphe* together. Still later, he frequented her Moscow salon and wrote her passionate letters and poems (*I Loved You*, 1829, and *What Is There in My Name for You*, 1830). She was a government spy.

The beret, plumed and plain, of the 1820's became extinct by 1835 but has been revived in many other forms in modern times.

In a fair-copy variant (Gofman, 1922), Pushkin first had a "red shawl" instead of a "yellow shawl" in Three : XXVIII : 3, and a "ponceau shawl" instead of a "green shawl" in the draft (2371, f. 9ᵛ) of "Onegin's Album," IX : 12. Finally, he limited the red to Tatiana's beret.

According to V. Glinka,† the Hermitage, the Leningrad picture gallery in Million Street (from which that clip-clap of a droshky came in One : XLVIII), possesses a nationalized portrait by (Sir George) Hayter, 1832, of Countess Elizaveta Vorontsov showing her wearing a beret *rouge-framboise*.

I suggest that, when composing Eight, Pushkin visualized not the fashions of 1824 but those of 1829–30 and, possibly, the very beret of eminence color (a pur-

---

* *Works* (St. Petersburg, 1912), XI, 425; quoted by Tsyavlovski, in *Rukoyu Pushkina*, p. 186.

† *Pushkin i Voennaya galereya Zimnego Dvortsa* (Leningrad, 1949), p. 133.

plish red) which is prominently illustrated in vol. LXII (no. 2, Pl. 2, fig. 1; Jan. 11, 1829) of the *Journal des dames et des modes*, imported into Russia from Frankfort on the Main. This issue, incidentally, carries the second and last installment of Bulgarin's *Le Partage de la succession*, a translation of his Oriental tale *Razdel nasledstva* (*Polar Star* for 1823).

10 In autumn, 1822, at the Congress of Verona, Austria, Russia, and Prussia agreed upon armed intervention in liberal Spain. A French army entered Spain in spring, 1823, and took Madrid. Despotism, with Ferdinand VII, was restored in 1823. By the winter of 1824–25, diplomatic relations between Russia and Spain (where the French remained till 1827) were, I presume, re-established, but a Spanish ambassador does not seem to have been appointed before 1825.

Lerner, in *Rukoyu Pushkina*, determines that in 1825–35 J. M. Páez de la Cadena was Spanish ambassador to Russia; and Pushkin knew him personally (Aug. 9, 1832, he discussed French politics with him at a dinner); but the incident in Eight : XVII refers to August, 1824, before Páez de la Cadena's time.

XVII–XVIII

In the course of these casual notes I have refrained from paying too much attention to the disastrous versions of *EO* in English doggerel. Here and there, however, a glance at their faults may be of some assistance in convincing readers of translations and publishers of translations that the use of rhyme, while mathematically precluding exactitude, merely helps its user to conceal what plain prose would reveal, namely his inability to render accurately the difficulties of the original. The passage I have selected for display here—end of st. XVII

(8–14) and beginning of st. XVIII (1–7)—is an especially hard one, and reveals with especial clarity the unintentional insults and injuries that the rhyming paraphrast inflicts on an innocent and unprotected text. Let me first present the text with an interlinear literal translation, then unfold four rhyming versions and comment on their particular features.

XVII

8   *"Skazhí mne, Knyáz', ne znáesh' tĭ,*
    "Tell me, prince, you don't know
    Kto tám v malínovom beréte
    who there in the *framboise* beret
    S poslóm Ispánskim govorít?"
    with the Spanish envoy is talking?"
    Knyáz' na Onégina glyadít.
    The prince at Onegin looks:
12   —*"Agá! davnó zh tĭ né bĭl v svéte.*
    "Aha! long indeed you've not been in the *monde*.
    Postóy, tebyá predstávlyu yá."
    Wait, I'll present you."
    —*"Da któ zh oná?"*—*"Zhená moyá."*
    "But who is she?" "My wife."

XVIII

    —*"Tak tĭ zhenát! ne znál ya ráne!*
    "So you're married! I did not know before!
    Davnó li?"—*"Ókolo dvuh lét."*
    How long?" "About two years."
    —*"Na kóm?"*—*"Na Lárinoy."*—*"Tat'yáne!"*
    "To whom?" "The Larin girl." "Tatiana!"
4   —*"Tĭ éy znakóm?"*—*"Ya ím soséd."*
    "You to her are known?" "I'm their neighbor."
    —*"O, tak poydyóm zhe."*—*Knyáz' podhódit*
    "Oh, then come on." The prince goes up
    K svoéy zhené, i éy podvódit
    to his wife and to her leads up
    Rodnyú i drúga svoegó.
    his kin and friend.

A "literal translation," as I understand it, is a some-
what tautological term, since only a literal rendering of
the text is, in the true sense, a translation. However,
there are certain shades to the epithet that may be worth
while preserving. First of all, "literal translation" im-
plies adherence not only to the direct sense of a word or
sentence, but to its implied sense; it is a semantically ex-
act interpretation, and not necessarily a lexical one (per-
taining to the meaning of a word out of context) or a
constructional one (conforming to the grammatical
order of words in the text). In other words, a translation
may be, and often, is, both lexical and constructional, but
it is only then literal when it is contextually correct, and
when the precise nuance and intonation of the text are
rendered.* A lexical and constructional translation of
ne znaesh' ti (XVII : 8) would be, of course, "not knowest
thou," but this does not render the idiomatic simplicity
of the Russian construction (in which the pronoun may
be placed without change of meaning either before *ne
znaesh'* or after it), while the archaic, sectarian, and
poetical implications of the second person singular in
English are absent from its plain, colloquial counterpart.

"The Larin girl" is the best I can do for *Na Larinoy*
(XVIII : 3), the noun here being the locative of *Larina*,
the feminine form of *Larin*. The difficulty of rendering
this exactly and rapidly is augmented by the absence of
the articles "a" and "the" in the Russian language, so
that to say "a Larin" (or "a Larina") would be much too
offhand, and to say "the Larin" (or, even worse, "the
Larina") would convey an impossible ring of notoriety.
This does not mean that I am absolutely satisfied with
"the Larin girl" (which is a jot more familiar than the
text); I toyed with "Mlle Larin" and "Miss Larin," and
rejected them. The Larins were a good family, and al-

---

*See also Foreword.

though Onegin had not circulated in society for some time, the prince might automatically assume that the fact of there having been a marriageable girl in that family was known to him.

Lexically *Tï ey znakom?* (XVIII : 4) is "Thou [art] to her known?" which is, or rather was, more courteous (to the lady involved) than *Tï s ney znakom?*, "Thou art with her acquainted?" This is a case in which the lexical grades into the literal.

Lexically *Ya im sosed* (XVIII : 4) is "I [am] to them neighbor," but again this would not be a literal translation, especially as the word "neighbor" itself is not as simple as it looks. The phrase means "our estates adjoin."

Let us now turn to the four versions.

Spalding (1881):

8 "Inform me, prince, pray dost thou know
    The lady in the crimson cap
    Who with the Spanish envoy speaks?"—
    The prince's eye Onéguine seeks:
12 "Ah! long the world hath missed thy shape!
    But stop! I will present thee, if
    You choose."—"But who is she?"—"My wife."

    "So thou art wed! I did not know.
    Long ago?"—" 'Tis the second year."
    "To——?"—"Làrina."—"Tattiana?"—"So.
4 And dost thou know her?"—"We live near."
    "Then come with me." The prince proceeds,
    His wife approaches, with him leads
    His relative and friend as well.

The attempts to remain faithful to the text while dallying with the rhyme are truly heroic, seeing that Spalding could not write poetry. The passage is a good example of his manner throughout the poem. It should be noted that the rhyme scheme is reduced to masculine terminals and that some of them are very weak (the lame "shape" in XVII : 12, for example, makes the reader

wonder if the cap Tatiana is made to wear should not be a
"cape"). The dialogue is that of two Quakers. The "so"
closing XVIII : 3 is dreadful. "We live near" is meaning-
less. The last two lines are ludicrous. The phrase "His
wife approaches" is supposed to mean "the prince pro-
ceeds to approach his wife."

Elton (1938):

```
 8  "—Prince, wilt thou tell me—dost thou know
        Who, in the raspberry beret yonder
        Talks with the Spanish Envoy there?"
        And the Prince answers, with a stare,
12  "So long a stranger? ha! no wonder . . .
        But see, I will present thee; stay!"
        "But who, but who?"—"My wife, I say!"

        "So, married? till to-day, I knew not!
        Married . . . some while?"—"Two years or so."
        —"To whom?"—"A Larina."—"You do not
 4  Mean, to Tatyana?"—"Her you know?"
        —"Their neighbour, I!"—"Then, come!" Preceding,
        The prince unto his wife is leading
        His friend and kinsman. . . .
```

The two Quakers are still with us. Again, the passage is
characteristic of the translator. The alternations of the
rhyme scheme are scrupulously and miserably repro-
duced. The "stare," the "ha!," and the idiotic ejacu-
lation "stay!" are impossibly vulgar. The "But who, but
who?" is a preposterous reiteration. The end of XVII ("I
say!") sounds as if the prince actually stamps his foot. A
characteristic feature of Elton's notion of versification
and syntax is the little exchange: "Her you know?"
"Their neighbour, I!" No less horrible are the "Preced-
ing" (whom?) and "is leading" of ll. 5 and 6.

Radin (1937):

```
 8  "Who is the lady yonder, Prince,
        The one in crimson over there
        With the Ambassador from Spain?"
```

The prince looked at Eugene again—
12 "You must be introduced to her,
    You've lived too long outside our life."—
    "But tell me who she is?"—"My wife."—

    "You're married, then! I didn't know it.
    And how long since?"—"Two years."—"To
        whom?"—
    "Her name was Larin."—"Not Tatyana?"—
4 "You know her?"—"I lived near their home."—
    "Then come!" In such an unforeseen
    Encounter Tanya met Eugene,
    Her husband's relative and friend.
8 She saw him come and slowly bend
    Before her. . . .

Despite their impossible English, Spalding and Elton
are, after a fashion, faithful to their text, or at least to
their notion of the text. With Miss Radin and Miss
Deutsch, the wild paraphrase triumphs. Miss Radin
clothes the entire Tatiana in crimson. The "outside our
life" (XVII : 13) is a very clumsy euphemism. The phrases
"in such an unforeseen | Encounter Tanya met Eugene"
(XVIII : 5–6) and "She saw him come and slowly bend |
Before her" are not in the original. It should be noticed
that the first quatrains of the stanza are not rhymed in
the odd lines (feminine terminals), and that all the
rhymes are masculine.
  Deutsch (1936):

8 "Forgive me, Prince, but can you not
    Say who it is that now the Spanish
    Ambassador is speaking to?
    She's wearing raspberry." "Yes, you
12 Have been away! Before you vanish
    Again, you'll meet her, 'pon my life!"
    "But tell me who she is." "My wife."

    "Well, that is news—couldn't be better!
    You're married long?" "Two years." "To whom?"
    "A Larina." "Tanya?" "You've met her?"

188

4 "I am their neighbor." "Come, resume
   Your friendship." At this invitation
   The prince's comrade and relation
   Now met his spouse. . . .

The rhyme scheme is reproduced, but the subject matter
has little to do with *EO.* Why must the prince "Forgive"
Onegin (XVII : 8)? What is the "raspberry" (11) the lady
is wearing: gown? slippers and purse? Why does the
prince think Onegin will "vanish" (12)? Why does he
swear (13)? Why does Onegin think that nothing could
be "better" (XVIII : 1) than the news of his "comrade's"
(6) marriage? Why does the prince assume that there
had been a "friendship" between Onegin and Tatiana
(5)? Is it because Onegin calls her "Tanya" (3)? None of
these questions are answered in Pushkin's text. In the
college library copy of this "translation" that I consulted,
a poor, misguided, foolish, endearing, anonymous col-
lege student has dutifully written in pencil the word
"Irony" against the "better" of XVIII : 1. Irony, indeed.

XVIII

13 / *ton*: Pushkin was fond of this French word, which the
English sometimes did not italicize in those days. It was
used in the sense of social style in Russian drawing rooms
as well as in the English ones. A Russian of today would
be apt to confuse with *ton* its homonym meaning "tone,"
individual manner of speaking, assumed attitude, and
so on. *Ton,* in the early nineteenth-century sense, was
the "bon ton." This reminds me incidentally of perhaps
the most cacophonic line ever penned by a French
rhymester, Casimir Delavigne's "Ce *bon ton dont Mon-*
cade emporta le modèle" (my italics), *Discours d'ouver-
ture du Second Théâtre Français* (1819), l. 154.

   Cf. Rousseau's *Julie* (Saint-Preux to Lord Bomston,
pt. IV, letter VI); Julie's former lover sees her, married to

another, after he had traveled for some four years:
"Elle conserva le même maintien et . . . continua de me
parler sur le même ton."

XIX

11 / *I ne iz íh li uzh storón*: A string of six monosyllabics,
oddly revealing (through the very rarity of such a
rhythm in Russian verse) a certain constraint, the mere
ghost of a stutter, distinguished by Pushkin's reader,
but not by his hero, in Tatiana's speech.

Ll. 10, 11, 13, and 14 turn on the same rhyme (*ón,
storón, vón, ón*)—an unusual monotone in the novel.

XX

7–8 / he keeps a letter: Pushkin also preserved that letter
("religiously," according to Three : XXXI : 2). We must
assume that when Onegin got together with his pal in
Odessa in the winter of 1823, he not only showed Push-
kin Tatiana's letter, but allowed him to transcribe it. It
is that copy which Pushkin has before him when trans-
lating it from the French into Russian verse in 1824.

XXII

7–14:   . . . *néskol'ko minút*
                     8 *Oní sidyát. Slová neydút
                       Iz úst Onégina. Ugryúmoy,
                       Nelóvkiy, ón edvá, edvá
                       Ey otvecháet. Golová*
                     12 *Egó polná upryámoy dúmoy.
                       Upryámo smótrit ón: oná
                       Sidít pokóyna i vol'ná.*

My purpose was to render the deliberately stumbling en-
jambments of the Russian text (echoed further on by the
staccato intonations of Tatiana's speech in XLIII and

XLVII); hence the somewhat rugged meter, which had to be made to follow both sense and scansion. The run-ons of the text are all reproduced here, but are more tuneful in Russian, filling up as they do with perfect saturation of rhythm the *en-escalier* sections of these tetrameters. The end of l. 10, *edvá, edvá,* is an idiomatic repetition, which "hardly, barely" renders rather clumsily. In the next run-on (11–12) the order of noun and pronoun (*Golová | Egó,* "head his") and their remarkable separation could not be preserved by English syntax, and I was not tempted by the artifice of "That head | of his . . ."

XXIII

3–4 Initially (fair-copy variants and cancellations) Pushkin had Tatiana's husband and Onegin recall "the stunts [*zatéi*], opinions . . . friends, belles of former years," which confirms the fact that Prince N. could not have been more than half a dozen years older than his kinsman Onegin, thus in his middle thirties.

In the published text of a famous but essentially clap-trap politico-patriotic speech, pronounced on June 8, 1880, at a public meeting of the Society of Amateurs of Russian Letters before a hysterically enthusiastic audience, Fyodor Dostoevski, a much overrated, sentimental, and Gothic novelist of the time, while ranting at length on Pushkin's Tatiana as a type of the "positive Russian woman," labors under the singular delusion that her husband is a "venerable old man." He also thinks that Onegin had "wandered in foreign countries" (repeating Prosper Mérimée's error in *Portraits historiques et lit-téraires* [Paris, 1874], ch. 14: "Oniéghine doit quitter la Russie pour plusieurs années") and that he is "in-finitely inferior socially to Prince N.'s brilliant set," all of which goes to show that Dostoevski had not really read *EO*.

Commentary

Dostoevski the publicist is one of those megaphones of elephantine platitudes (still heard today), the roar of which so ridiculously demotes Shakespeare and Pushkin to the vague level of all the plaster idols of academic tradition, from Cervantes to George Eliot (not to speak of the crumbling Manns and Faulkners of our times).

12 / [without] pedantry / *bez pedántstva*: See n. to One : v : 7.

VARIANT

15–14 The fair copy reads:

> nor did the talk contain one word
> about the rain or bonnets.

XXIIIa, b

The fair copy gives the following rejected stanzas:

XXIIIa

> In the salon authentically noble
> one shunned the elegance of speech
> and bourgeois prudishness
> 4 of priggish judges in the journals.
> ⟨By the hostess, high-life and free,
> a plain-folk language was accepted
> and did not shock her ears
> 8 with its lively bizarreness,
> at which assuredly will wonder,
> preparing his critical sheet,
> some deep reviewer;
> 12 but after all much happens in the *monde*
> of which no inkling has among us
> perhaps a single journal!⟩

XXIIIb

> ⟨None with a cold sneer
> thought of greeting an old man
> on noting the unfashionable collar

4 under the bow of his neckcloth;⟩
   nor did the hostess ⟨with her *morgue*⟩ embarrass
   the tyro from the provinces;
   alike with everybody she was
8 unconstrained and charming;
   only a far-flung traveler,
   a brilliant London jackanapes,
   provoked half-smiles
12 by his studied deportment,
   and a gaze silently exchanged
   gave him the general verdict.

a: 2–4 I have contrived to replace with a makeshift alliteration Pushkin's marvelous play on the sounds *shch* and *ch* in ll. 2–4:

> *Chuzhdális' shchegol'stvá rechéy*
> *I shchekotlívosti meshchánskoy*
> *Zhurnál'nïh chópornïh sudéy.*

b: 9–10 / a far-flung traveler, a brilliant London jacka-napes; and XXVI : 9–10 / a far-flung traveler, an over-starched jackanapes: Apart from the possible connection *
that this image has with the figure of an actual English-man, Tom Raikes, whom Pushkin met in St. Petersburg society (see my nn. to Two : XVIIa–d), I suggest that our poet's mind had reverted here to his Odessa impressions and to the arrogant Anglomania of the governor gen-eral, Count Mihail Vorontsov. This name, according to a Russian eighteenth-century official fashion of German spelling, was transliterated as Woronzoff, and Pushkin mockingly transliterated this back into Russian, giving an English value to the *W*, as Uorontsov. This General Vorontsov (1782–1856), son of Count Semyon Voront-sov, Russian ambassador in London, received an English education there. Since May 7, 1823, Vorontsov was the

---

*As first conjectured by S. Glinka, in *P. i ego sovr.*, VIII, 31–32 (1927), 105–10.

governor general of New Russia (Novorossiya, as the southern provinces of the empire were called) and viceroy of the Bessarabian region. In the 1840's, he was named viceroy of the Caucasus and given the title of prince. In a letter to Aleksandr Kaznacheev, director of Vorontsov's chancery, written beginning of June, 1824, in Odessa, Pushkin said:

Je suis fatigué de dépendre de la digestion bonne ou mauvaise de tel et tel chef, je suis ennuyé d'être traité dans ma patrie avec moins d'égard que le premier galopin anglais qui vient y promener parmi nous sa platitude et son baragouin.

(Draft, 2370, ff. 8ᵛ, 9ʳ; not to be confused with the earlier, Russian, letter to same, May 22, 1824, draft, 2370, ff. 1ʳ, 2ʳ.) A couple of months earlier, Vorontsov, in a letter to Nesselrode, characterized Pushkin as ". . . un faible imitateur d'un original très peu recommandable: Lord Byron."

In 1808, Vorontsov's only sister, Catherine, married George Augustus Herbert, Earl of Pembroke and Montgomery (1759–1827), and English relatives visited the Novorossiyan viceroy in Odessa.

XXIV

According to Tomashevski (*Works* 1957, V, 627), sts. XXIV–XXVI, including the variants, were worked over and the established ones sorted out, in June, 1831, at Tsarskoe Selo, after the canto, except for Onegin's letter, had been completed (at Boldino, late 1830). See also n. to XXVa : var. 1–9.

1 / here was / *Tut bíl*: The recurrent intonations in the listing of the participants of this noble rout, sts. XXIV–XXVI, are too close to those in Byron's *Don Juan*, XIII, LXXXIV–LXXXVIII ("There was Parolles, too, the legal

bully," "There was the Duke of Dash," "There was Dick Dubious," and so forth), to be a coincidence.

xxiva

A stanza written on the same separate leaf as XXIV (fair copy) bears the numeral 25, corrected from 26 (the numeral of the established XXIV is corrected from 25):

> And she upon whom smiled
> the grace of life in bloom;
> and she who was about
> 4 already to rule general opinion;
> and she who represented the beau monde;
> and she whose modest planet
> someday was bound
> 8 to gleam with humble happiness;
> and she whose heart, in secret
> bearing the penalty of a mad passion,
> nursed jealousy and fear;
> 12 by chance united,
> in spirit strange to one another,
> sat here together.

xxva

The following stanza appears on a separate page in the fair copy:

> Here was, to epigrams addicted,
> with everything cross, Prince Brodín,
> with the too-sweet tea of the hostess,
> 4 the women's crassness and the *ton* of men,
> the badge two orphans had been granted,
> the talk about a foggy novel,
> ⟨his wife's vacuity,
> 8 and his daughters' gaucherie⟩.
> Here was a certain ball dictator,
> a hopper, rigorous, official.
> Against the wall stood a young fopling,
> 12 as if he were a fashion plate,
> as rosy as a Palm Week cherub,
> tight-coated, mute, and motionless.

5 / badge / *vénzel'*: From the Polish *wezel*, "knot." The two orphaned (*sirotkam*, dat. pl.) young ladies had been made ladies in waiting of the empress and as such received a *venzel'* or *shifr* (Fr. *chiffre*), a court decoration with the royal initials. In another, more usual, sense, *venzel'* means simply "monogram," and is so employed in Three : XXXVII : 14.

12–14 See XXVI : 6–8 and nn. to XXVI : 6 and 7.

VARIANTS

1–9 Lerner, in *P. i ego sovr.*, I, 2 (1904), 81, published the following rough draft (a separate page, numbered 53, in the Imperial Public Library, St. Petersburg), a variant of XXVa:

> Here was, displeased with the whole world,
> angry with all things, Count Turín,
> with the house of his hostess, much too free,
>
> .   .   .   .
> .   .   .   .
> the talk about a mannered novel,
> .   .   .   .
> 8 ⟨the snow [. . . . .] the war⟩,
> the waists of his ripe daughters . . .

On the same scrap of paper there is a note (conjectured by Lerner to be written prior to the verses), in Zhukovski's hand: "Come at half-past one; we shall go to the Lyceum, where they have the examination in history." This establishes the fact that the fragment was written in June, 1831, at Tsarskoe Selo, where our poet was spending his honeymoon, in the vicinity of his old school.

6 A canceled line reads:

> ⟨the prose style of the press, the foggy day⟩ . . .

Tomashevski (Acad 1937, p. 311) publishes a draft of
xxva (PD 164) in a different form (ll. 1–2, 6–9):

> Entered, pleased only with himself,
> always cross, Prince Brodín
>
> .   .   .   .   .
>
> Poland, the foggy climate,
> the muteness of his wife,
> the waists of his ripe daughters.
> Entered Prostóv, ballroom dictator . . .

The autograph described by Lerner is designated by
Tomashevski (Acad 1937, p. 629) as a fair copy, with
canceled readings corresponding to Lerner's recension.

XXVI

1 / [. . .]: The name Prolazov, or Prolasov, is derived from
prolaz, prolaza (both masc.), something like "climber,"
"vile sycophant." Prolazov is a ridiculous personage of
eighteenth-century Russian comedies and popular pic-
tures.

The editorial tradition of filling in the blank after
"was" with the surname of Andrey Saburov (1797–
1866), later the inept director of the imperial theaters,
whom Pushkin hardly knew, is founded on a series of
wild guesses that I don't think worth while discussing.
It would be much more interesting to check if caricatures
of Olenin frequently occur among Saint-Priest's draw-
ings (preserved where?).

4 / Saint-P[riest]: The reference is to Count Emmanuil
Sen-Pri (1806–28), said to have been a gifted cartoonist.
None of his drawings seem to have been published. He
was the son of a French *émigré*, Armand Charles Em-
manuel de Guignard, Comte de Saint-Priest, who mar-
ried a Russian lady, Princess Sofia Golitsïn.

This young artist shot himself, according to some, on

Commentary

Easter Day in Italy, in church, or, according to others, in the presence of an eccentric Englishman who had promised to pay his gambling debts if granted the spectacle of self-murder.

Pushkin also alludes to Saint-Priest's caricatures in a short poem of 1829 addressed to N. N. ("You are fortunate in foolish charmers" [. . . *v preléstnïh dúrah*]).

6 / like a fashion plate / *kartínkoyu zhurnál'noy*: "Like a [fashion] magazine picture."

7 / *vérbnïy heruvím*: *Verbnïy* from *verba*, various species of sallow. The allusion is to paper figures of cherubs (glued to gingerbread, etc.), sold at the annual fair on what is translated as Palm Week, Willow Week, and (more appropriately) Catkin Week—the week preceding Easter.

9–10 See also n. to Eight : xxiiib : 9–10.

10 / overstarched: The reference is to the neckcloth. Beau Brummell, in the first decade and a half of the century, had set the fashion of having it slightly starched. His followers, in the late 1820's, shocked French and Russian taste by overdoing it. Brummell himself, in the last period of his life, when dwelling at Caen (he began losing his mind about 1837, and became hopelessly imbecile by summer, 1838), seems to have starched his cambric cravats more heavily than before.

XXVIa

This stanza appears on a separate page in the fair copy:

> Here was Prolasov, who had gained
> distinction by the baseness of his soul
> who had blunted in all albums,
> 4 Saint-Priest, your pencils;

here was ⟨Prince [?] M.⟩, a Frenchman, married
to a wasted and hunchbacked doll
and seven thousand serfs;
8 here was, with all his decorations,
⟨a member of the censorship board⟩ inflexible
(this awesome Cato recently
had been removed for taking bribes).
12 Here also was a sleepy senator
who had at cards spent his life span:
for government a needed man.

Ll. 12–14 have been cut off. The reconstruction is based
on the text published in the *Messenger of Europe*, vol. I
(1883), by A. Ott-Onegin, who then possessed the auto-
graph.

5–6 A cancellation in the fair copy reads:

here was a great patrician married
to a yellow and hunchbacked doll . . .

5–11 The "wasted and hunchbacked," *cháhloy i gorbátoy*
(fem. loc.), of the fair copy of XXVIa, recalls the "so
diminutive," the epithet in some drafts to be mentioned
further, which certainly refer to Olenin's daughter,
Anna (1808–88). The *gorbatoy* is a vicious allusion to her
somewhat prominent shoulder blades. It is curious to
note that eventually (about 1840) she did marry a person
of French extraction (Fyodor Andro, Fr. Andrault, a
military man and later a senator). I do not know if the
letters *K. M.*, referring to the husband of the debile doll,
have been correctly deciphered in the draft, but if they
have, I suspect that *K.* is the usual initial for "Prince"
(*knyaz'*).

If XXVIa : 5–7 represents a coarse travesty, with added
details for camouflage, of Annette Olenin, the same may
be said of ll. 8–11 in regard to her father. He did not take
bribes, but he did like wearing his decorations. The
words beginning l. 9, *Pravlén'ya Tsénsor*, are a sole-

cistical ellipsis for *chlen Glavnogo Upravleniya Tsenzuri*,
"member of the Chief Board [or Administration] of
Censorship."

By a decree of 1828, censorship in Russia was sub-
ordinated to the Ministry of Public Education, and
among the members of its higher council were presi-
dents of learned institutions. Aleksey Olenin became an
ex officio member of the Chief Board of Censorship on
Sept. 6, 1828, and remained one till 1834; he was no
doubt acquainted with the work of the special institu-
tion (a Provisional Supreme Commission, consisting of
Prince Viktor Kochubey, Count Pyotr A. Tolstoy, and
Prince Aleksandr Golitsïn), which, from Apr. 28, 1828,
to Dec. 31, 1828, examined the *Gavriliada* case (see be-
low). I cannot find, however, if Olenin was ever "dis-
missed" from the board, and I suppose this dismissal and
its cause are meant as a makeshift camouflage just as is
the marital state of the "hunchbacked doll."

In the draft of XXVIa (2382, f. 32^v), ll. 11–14, Liza
Losin (from *los'*, "moose," in allusion to *olen'*, "stag")
is described with bitter fury as being:

> so mannered, so diminutive,
> so slatternly, so shrill,
> that every guest unconsciously
> conjectured wit and spite in her.

(Natalia Pushkin, on the other hand, was almost five feet
six inches tall, very elegant, and so stately-looking that
people seeing her at balls thought her to be cold and
brainless.) I assume that these lines were penned by our
poet during his honeymoon, in Tsarskoe Selo, 1831. Is
all this merely a little present of his past that a hypo-
critical and passionate young husband makes to his young
wife, or is it, as I think much more plausible, a rejected
suitor's unquenchable exasperation with an unforget-
table girl and her Philistine parents?

She produces a "shudder" in Onegin (canceled draft of XXVIa : 7, in 2382, f. 32ᵛ). In these cancellations she is "hunchbacked," with a "hunchbacked little zero" for father, and on the same f. 32ᵛ Tomashevski deciphers (ll. 7–10):

Annette ⟨Lisette⟩ Olénine [Fr.] here was [*tút bïlá*], so very [*uzh ták*] mannered, so diminutive [*ták malá*], so scatterbrained, so shrill, that she seemed quite the picture of her parents [*Chto vsyá bïlá v otsá i mát'*] . . .

Had I had access to Pushkin's MSS, I would have managed probably to give a fuller and clearer picture of the reflection in them of Pushkin, the rejected suitor, and Pushkin, the artist. The artist (and the gentleman) triumphed, and no trace of Annette Olenin or her father subsists in the established text. There is no doubt of one thing, however: that the heart of our poet was more deeply involved in his courtship of Annette Olenin than in his sensual enchantment with his bride.

Pushkin had probably first seen Annette when she was a pale child of eleven, at her father's house, and, for all we know, she may have taken part in the charades at that very party in 1819 where he flirted with her cousin Anna Kern (his *maîtresse en titre* in 1828), and where Krïlov recited the fable about the honorable donkey (one line from which was to become the starting point of *EO* in 1823; see n. to One : 1 : 1). As so often happens with well-studied lives, an artistically satisfying pattern appears at this point of our inquiry, linking up the beginning of *EO* with its end.

In her journal, written partly in Russian and partly in French (*Dnevnik Annï Alekseevnï Oleninoy, 1828–1829*, edited by Olga Oom, who appears to have lavishly corrected her grandmother's Russian, Paris, 1936), Anna Olenin describes Pushkin as avidly watching her very small feet "glissant sur le parquet" at a ball in St. Petersburg, in winter, 1827–28. "Parmi les singularités du poète était celle d'avoir une passion pour les petits pieds, que dans un de ses poèmes il avouait préférer à la beauté même" (entry of July 18, 1828). In the same entry she writes (in Russian):

God, having endowed him with unique genius, did not grant him an attractive exterior. His face was, of course, expressive, but a certain malevolence and sarcasm eclipsed the intelligence that one could see in his blue, or better say vitreous, eye. A Negro profile acquired from his maternal generation did not embellish his face. Add to this: dreadful side whiskers, disheveled hair, fingernails like claws, a small stature, affected manners, an arrogant way of looking at the women he chose to love, the oddities of his natural character and of his assumed one, and a boundless *amour-propre*. . . .

She dubbed Pushkin "Red Rover" after the hero of James Fenimore Cooper's novel *The Red Rover* (written in the summer of 1827 in a village near Paris). This is the name of a pirate ship flying a blood-red ensign and it is also the nickname of her captain, William Heidegger. He is a man of vacillating moods who "indulges in glimmerings of wayward and sarcastic humor" and relapses into "brooding reveries." His extravagant gesticulation, while "smiles and dark thoughts" pass over his face, makes one fancy that he is the victim of "some unholy and licentious passion." "His body is not large but it contains the spirit of a giant."

Annette Olenin was at twenty a small graceful blonde, "as cute and as quick as a mouse," says Vyazemski (in a letter of May 3, 1828, to his wife). In a poem (seventeen iambic tetrameters, beginning abaab, with the rest alternate) entitled *Her Eyes*, Pushkin wrote in the spring of 1828 in Petersburg or at Priyutino, the Olenins' estate, seventeen versts out of town, beyond the Okhta suburb (ll. 9–17):

the eyes of my Olenin!*
What pensive genius dwells in them,
what infantine simplicity,
what languorous expression,
and how much tenderness and fancy!
When with Lel's smile she casts them down,
the triumph of shy graces they reflect,
and when she raises them—Raphael's angel
thus contemplates divinity.

In a transcript made in an unknown hand in Anna
Olenin's album, it is signed (in that hand) *Arap Pushkin,*
"Pushkin the Blackamoor."

Among the poems addressed by Pushkin to Annette
Olenin there is one that is exceptionally interesting. Its
draft is in 2371, f. 13^r—that is, in the midst of Chapter
Seven (the draft of Seven : XIII, dated "Feb. 19," 1828,
is in 2371, f. 5^r; "Onegin's Album" ends in 2371, f. 10^r;
and Seven : XXII, *Hotya mï znaem chto Evgeniy* . . . , is
in 2371, f. 17^r):

⟨Alas! the tongue of love loquacious,
an incomplete [?] and simple tongue,
with its negligent prose
4 bores you, my angel⟩.
But sweet is to the ear of a dear girl
vainglorious Apollo,
⟨dear to her⟩ are the measured songs,
8 ⟨sweet to her⟩ is the rhyme's proud ringing.
You are afraid of love's confession,
and a love letter you will tear,
but an epistle writ in verse
12 you will read with a tender smile.
Ah, blesséd be henceforth the gift
on me by destiny conferred!
Up to now in the wilderness of life
16 it brought me only persecution
⟨or slander, or⟩ imprisonment
and, seldom, frigid praise.

---

*Replaced by "Elodia" in the *Northern Flowers* for 1829.

Commentary

Under the draft of this poem (⟨*Uví!*⟩ *yazík lyubví boltlívoy*) there is the following date: "May 9, 1828." After this comes the word: "Sea" (*Móre*). This is immediately followed by two words that can be read as "on day" (Eng.)—perhaps, a reference to the poem having been composed on the (fatidic) day, May 9, the anniversary, by Pushkin's calendar, of his expulsion from St. Petersburg in 1820.

Anna Andro, née Olenin, in a letter to Vyazemski written (in bad Russian) on Apr. 18, 1857, recollects a trip to Kronstadt made on May 25, 1828:*

> Do you remember that happy time when we were young and merry, and in good health? When Pushkin, Griboedov, and you accompanied us [the Olenin family] to Kronstadt on the Neva steamship [steamships started to run regularly between St. Petersburg and Kronstadt in 1815]. Ah, how beautiful everything was then, with life flowing like a rapid noisy stream!

Tsyavlovski, who reads the words after "Sea" as "on day," comes, however, to a strange conclusion:† "This has no sense. If Pushkin wanted to say *dnyom* [in the afternoon], it should have been 'by day' [Eng.]." Other commentators have suggested a slip for "one day" (which is meaningless).

On the other hand, *Works* 1949, vol. III, pt. 2, p. 651, deciphers this as *Ol*[*enins*,] *Dau* (this tome was edited by Tsyavlovski, who died before its completion, and Tatiana Tsyavlovski-Zenger took over); *Dau* is an incorrect Russian transcription (delta, alpha, upsilon) of Dawe, the name of an English painter, which Pushkin transliterated elsewhere (*Journey to Erzerum*, 1829, in

---

*Quoted by Olga Popov, in an article on Griboedov, in *Lit. nasl.*, nos. 47–48 (1946), p. 237.
†"Pushkin i angliyskiy yazík," in *P. i ego sovr.*, V, 17–18 (1913), 66n.

description of General Ermolov) as *Dov*, the way French-speaking Russians did.

A poem entitled by Pushkin *To Dawe, Esqr.* reads:

> Why draw with your pencil sublime
> My Negro profile? Though transmitted
> By you it be to future time,
> It will be by Mephisto twitted.
>
> Draw fair Olenin's features, in the glow
> Of heart-engendered inspiration:
> Only on youth and beauty should bestow
> A genius its adoration.

The epithet to "pencil" in the first line is *dívnïy*, a word that resembles in sound the French *divin*, "divine." Cf. Voltaire, *Poésies mêlées*, CXX: *A Madame de Pompadour, dessinant une tête*:

> Pompadour, ton crayon divin . . .

George Dawe (1781–1829), English portrait painter and mezzotint engraver, had been invited to Russia by Tsar Alexander to depict the heroes of the 1812–14 campaigns in a special "military" gallery of the Winter Palace, St. Petersburg. Dawe arrived in 1819 and by 1825 had personally completed 150 portraits. He left Russia in May, 1828, having depicted in all 332 generals at a settled price of a thousand rubles each. The unknown drawing he made of Pushkin may be in Dawe's papers if these are preserved anywhere. Dawe visited Russia again the following winter and left for Warsaw, in the retinue of Tsar Nicholas, in spring, 1829, hopelessly ill.

In the autumn of 1828 Pushkin was in trouble: MS copies of his poem *Gavriliada* (1821), pleasantly depicting in the irreligious and elegantly lewd style of his French models an intrigue between the Archangel and the old carpenter's young wife, had come to the notice of the government. On Oct. 2 Pushkin wrote the tsar a frank letter (which has not reached us) and was pardoned. The poem (in iambic pentameters, rhymed) contains some marvelous passages but is spoiled by a juvenile look-how-naughty-I-am strain running through it.

Anagrams in French of "Annette Olénine" blossom here and there in the margins of our poet's manuscripts. One finds it written backward in the drafts of *Poltava* (2371, f. 11ᵛ; first half of October, 1828): *ettenna eninelo*; and the earnestness of his hopes is reflected in "Annette Pouchkine" jotted among the drafts of the first canto of *Poltava*, apparently on the very day that the repentant letter about the Gabriel poem was written to the tsar.

Some time in the winter of 1828–29 Pushkin proposed to Annette Olenin and was refused. Her parents (much as they admired Pushkin's genius) were a conservative, career-minded couple and no doubt did not relish his immoral verses, his amours, his addiction to stuss. But it is also quite clear that Annette Olenin did not love him and hoped for a much more brilliant marriage.

VARIANTS

In various drafts, corrected or canceled, referring to XXVI and XXVIa (2382, ff. 32, 33ʳ, 34ʳ), the first quatrain describes a person ("Count D.," "Prígov," "Stásov," "Tásov," "Prolásov") who is "a good fellow" and is known for his "baseness" and his "passion for opening balls."

A canceled draft of l. 1 (f. 32ʳ) has also:

> a hussar, handsome, with blond hair . . .

and another canceled draft of ll. 1–3 reads:

> Here was a ball dictator, gloomy [*hmúroy*]
> . . . .
> here was with his charming goose [*preléstnoy dúroy*] . . .

The "other" ballroom dictator appears in a draft (f.

32ᵛ) as "⟨Hrushchóv⟩ . . . author of a French elegy" (ll. 5–6) and as the father of "Liza Losin."

A draft of l. 7 (f. 33ʳ) reads:

> here was Liza Losin . . .

Her father is depicted in a first variant of ll. 10–11 (f. 32ᵛ) as:

> a little zero with two little feet . . .

and a canceled draft identifies him quite certainly:

> here was her father Ꝗ . . .

This is the monogram of Aleksey Olenin (1763–1843), director of the Public Library since 1811, president of the Academy of Arts since 1817, and an artist in his own right.

Several years earlier, in a letter to Gnedich, Mar. 24, 1821, Pushkin, thanking the latter for sending him a copy of the first edition of *Ruslan and Lyudmila* (which Gnedich had seen through the press), expresses his delight with the title-page vignette executed by Olenin: "My cordial thanks to the esteemed Ꝗ." This frontispiece (actually drawn by another hand from Olenin's sketch) represents four scenes from the poem, among which one distinguishes the wizard Chernomor, with Ruslan clinging to his beard, flying over the notched tower of an extremely Western-looking castle.

It should not be forgotten that Olenin, together with Karamzin, Zhukovski, Gnedich, Chaadaev, and, last but not least, Aleksandr Turgenev, had done his best to intercede with the court and with the cabinet ministers on behalf of Pushkin when (April, 1820) the tsar threatened to dispatch him to a monastery in the polar region —namely, to the Solovetskiy Monastïr, where, a hundred years later, the Soviets were to have one of their most infamous and inhuman concentration camps.

XXVII

This strophe, with its trivial generalizations, is considerably inferior to the superb variants given below.

XXVIIa

The draft (2371, f. 88ᵛ) contains the following alternate stanza:

> ⟨Look:⟩ Nina comes into the ballroom,
> stops at the door,
> and lets her abstract gaze
> 4 roam over the attentive guests:
> her bosom palpitates, her shoulders glisten;
> her head with diamonds burns,
> around her figure twines and quivers
> 8 in a transparent network lace
> and silk, in patterned gossamer,
> shines through on her pink legs.
> ⟨Alone Onegin⟩ [. . . . .]
> 12 ⟨before this magic picture⟩
> struck only by Tatiana,
> only Tatiana does he see.

This and the second alternate stanza, XXVIIb, abound in unusually rich imagery. Nina certainly would have eclipsed Tatiana, had our poet kept these voluptuous verses.

Her head, which "burns with diamonds," *Gorít v almázah golová*, is doubtlessly a reminiscence of Baratínski's *The Ball* (pub. 1828), in which the hairdress of the ballroom belles is described (1951 edn., ll. 16–17) as "burning with precious stones," *Dragími kámnyami u níh | Goryát ubórï golovnïe*, and the "diamonds" of Princess Nina's flickering earrings (ll. 481–82) "burn behind her black curls," *Almáz mel'káyushchih seryóg | Gorít za chyórnïmi kudryámi*. It will be remembered that the description of carriages at the door of the festively lit mansion in *EO*, One : XXVII, affected the beginning of Baratïnski's *The Ball*; and now we have a reverse process: the end of *EO* (see XXVIIb, XLIV : 14, and n. to XLIV : 6–14) echoes *The Ball*. A curious pattern of give-and-take.

11 *Works* 1960 gives the very Gallic "and all is in transport, in heavens" for 11 and leaves out 13–14.

XXVIIb

This stanza, in fair copy, is thought by Tomashevski (*Works* 1957, p. 556) to have replaced XXVIIa, draft:

> And in a ballroom bright and rich,
> when into the hushed close circle,
> akin to a winged lily,
> 4 balancing, enters Lalla Rookh,
> and above the bending crowd
> is radiant with her regal head,
> and gently weaves and glides—
> 8 a starlike Charis among Charites,
> and the gaze of commingled generations
> streams, glowing with devotion,
> now toward her, now toward the tsar—
> 12 for them no eyes has only Eugene;
> struck only by Tatiana,
> only Tatiana does he see.

1–4 This splendid quatrain, with its unusually bright imagery, is magnificently orchestrated. There is a subtle alliterative play on the letters *l*, *k*, and *r*. Note how the six last syllables of the third line of the Russian text are echoed by the closing three syllables in the last line of the quatrain:

> *I v zále yárkoy i bogátoy,*
> *Kogdá v umólkshiy, tésnïy krúg,*
> *Podóbna lílii krïlátoy*
> *Koléblyas' vhódit Lálla-Rúk . . .*

What a pity that Pushkin had to discard this exceptionally beautiful stanza, one of the best he ever composed! It is, of course, impossibly anachronistic. Yielding to personal recollections of 1827–29, Pushkin describes a ball in the first years of the reign of Nicholas I (1825–55) and momentarily dismisses the fact that the balls and routs at which Onegin saw Tatiana are supposed to take place in the autumn of 1824, in the reign of Alexander I (1801–25). Naturally, the stanza would never have been allowed to appear in print so long as Onegin preferred Tatiana N. to the imperial couple.

4 / Lalla Rookh: The young Empress Alexandra of Russia (1798–1860), who had been Princess Charlotte of Prussia (daughter of King Frederick William III and Queen Louise) when Nicholas married her in 1817, had received this *nom de société* ever since she appeared in a piece of fashionable pageantry, disguised as the heroine of Thomas Moore's very long poem, *Lalla Rookh; an Oriental Romance* (1817). She was sung under that name by her teacher of Russian, Zhukovski, who devoted three poems to the fashionable theme of Lalla Rookh when staying in Berlin, where, in January, 1821, various court festivals (described, with illustrations, in a special album: *Lallah Roukh, divertissement mêlé de chants et de danses*, Berlin, 1822) took place with Princess Alexandra in the part of the Oriental princess and the Grand Duke Nicholas in the part of Aliris. Of these three poems, the sixty-four trochaic lines addressed to Alexandra, beginning "Winsome dream, the soul's enchanter," are singularly close in imagery to Pushkin's overrated madrigal to Anna Kern beginning "I recollect a wondrous moment" (July, 1825), twenty-four iambic tetrameters, which he gave her, with *EO*, One, in exchange for a heliotrope sprig from her bosom. Pushkin repeats twice (ll. 4 and 20), with the addition of an initial monosyllable (*kak*,

"like"), needed to iambize it, Zhukovski's trochee (l. 42), which reads:

Spirit of pure loveliness

—a phrase that Zhukovski also uses elsewhere.

The young empress' innocent-looking beauty is said (by Bartenev, who had it from Nashchokin) to have had, like that of Anna Kern, a strong sensuous attraction for Pushkin.

The habitat of Moore's princess is in the India of eighteenth-century jejune fantasies. She is entertained by a minstrel in a wilderness of monotonous couplets and Gallic *chevilles*. Pushkin, as other Russians of his time, knew the poem from Amédée Pichot's prose version, *Lalla Roukh, ou la Princesse mogole, histoire orientale* (2 vols., Paris, 1820).

8 It is curious to note that the Charites come from Baratïnski's *The Ball*, l. 23, "around the captivating Charites," *Vokrúg plenítel'nïh harít.*

XXX

10 / fluffy boa / *Boá pushístïy*: The fair copy contains a modish image: *zmeyú soból'yu*, "the snake of sable."

13 / the motley host / *pyóstrïy pólk*: Influenced probably by the French descriptive term for lackeys, *le peuple bariolé*, a common formula of the seventeenth century.

XXXa

In a false start, Pushkin continued XXX (in fair copy):

> Days pass, weeks fly,
> Onegin thinks of but one thing,

> finds for himself no other aim
> 4 than only, openly or secretly,
> no matter where to meet the princess
> in order to observe upon her face
> at least anxiety or wrath.
> 8 His *sauvage* nature having daunted,
> at a soiree, ball, everywhere,
> at the theater, at the artistes of modes,
> on the embankment of the frozen waters,*
> 12 in street, in vestibule, in ballroom—
> he chases like a shadow after her.
> Whither is gone his indolence?

XXXI

8 Pushkin knew better, but pathetically used this pious didacticism to influence his bride, who, had she read Pushkin, might have been led to cast aside her "Moscow miss" affectations.

XXXII

7 There is no punctuation mark at the end of this line in the text, but surely that is a clerical or typographical oversight.

14 / word for word / *toch' v tóch'*: Should we understand that the *toch' v toch'* ("as exact as exact can be") refers not to a literal translation but to a faithful copy (it may mean either), and that Onegin, in concession to Princess N.'s genuine unaffectedness and in contrast to Tatiana's derivative romanticism of Chapter Three, couches his

---

*The Neva was *not* frozen in October, 1824, which is the latest possible date here.

otherwise very Gallic epistle in neo-Karamzinian Russian and not in the conventional French of its literary models? One wonders. Anyway, the method of bringing this letter into the novel is direct and matter-of-fact. The reader will recall the trouble Pushkin said he had (Three : XXVI–XXXI) in "translating" Tatiana's letter.

VARIANT

14 Before Pushkin added Onegin's letter between XXXII and XXXIII, the last line of XXXII read:

He waits for the answer day and night.

It is then followed by the "no answer" beginning XXXIII.

ONEGIN'S LETTER TO TATIANA

Sixty lines in iambic tetrameter, freely rhymed: baabecec, aabeebicicoddo, babacece, babacceded, ababececididobbo, baab; the spacing is the one generally adopted in Russian editions; coincidence in literation, owing to a paucity of available vowels, does not imply a similarity of rhymes, except in the case of the first lines of the second and third sections (where b denotes the same rhyme, in *-as*) and in the penultimate section (where b denotes a rhyme in *-or*); the feminine rhyme in the last section echoes the identical one, *ból̈e*, "more," and *vól̈e*, "will," of ll. 1 and 3 in Tatiana's letter, which is nineteen lines longer.

1 Cf. Rousseau, *Julie* (Saint-Preux to Julie), pt. 1, letter II: "Je sens d'avance le poids de votre indignation . . ."

10 / a spark of tenderness: Cf. the "drop of pity" in Tatiana's letter, l. 6, and the "étincelle de vertu" in Julie's first long letter to Saint-Preux.

12 / sweet habit / *Privíchke míloy* [fem. dat.]: A Gallicism, *douce habitude*, *doux penchant*. Onegin's literary model seems to have been a passage in Laclos' *Les Liaisons dangereuses* (1782), letter XXVIII: "Quoi! je perdrois la douce habitude de vous voir chaque jour!" The term crops up commonly, from Chaulieu to Constant.

16 / a hapless victim Lenski fell / *Neschástnoy zhértvoy Lénskiy pál*: This is very oddly phrased by Onegin. *Bon goût* and a bad conscience combine to blur his style here. Victim of what? Jealousy? Honor? Fate? Onegin's marksmanship? Onegin's ennui?

A profound commentator might suggest that while a hyppish Englishman shoots himself, a Russian chondriac shoots a friend—committing suicide by proxy, so to speak.

17–18 This rhetorical turn was a great favorite with poets of the time. Cf. Baratïnski, *The Ball*, ll. 223–24:

> and clasping Nina to his heart,
> his heart from Nina he concealed . . .

20–21 / I thought: liberty and peace [*vól'nost' i pokóy*] are a substitute for happiness: Cf. the last line of Pushkin's *Liberty: an Ode* (1817), and his short poem beginning " 'Tis time, my dear, 'tis time" (eight iambic hexameters, composed about 1835), l. 5:

> *Na svéte schást'ya nét, no ést' pokóy i vólya.*
> On earth there is no happiness, but there is
> peace and freedom.

Pokoy combines the meanings of "peace," "rest," "repose," and "mental ease." (See also *Onegin's Journey*: [XVIII] : 13.) Elsewhere (Two : XXX : 14) the substitute is "habit."

29 / to melt in agonies before you; 38–40 / that my life may

be prolonged I must be certain . . . of seeing you; 49–
52 / to embrace your knees . . . ; 53 / and in the mean-
time . . . : As pointed out by Russian commentators,*
Onegin's letter is full of echoes of Constant's *Adolphe*
(see my n. to Seven : XXII : 6–7). It is the same hard,
petulant tone: "Mais je dois vous voir s'il faut que je
vive" (ch. 3), with paraphrases of "Mais alors même,
lorsque tout mon être s'élance vers vous, lorsque j'aurais
un tel besoin de me reposer de tant d'angoisses, de poser
ma tête sur vos genoux, de donner un libre cours à mes
larmes, il faut que je me contraigne avec violence . . .
(ibid.)."

30 / grow pale and waste away / *Blednét' i gásnut'*: This is
an almost exact echo of Four : XXIV : 2: [*Tat'yana*]
Blednéet, gásnet.

49 / to embrace your knees. An amphoral enfoldment of
supplication and devotion constantly met with in Euro-
pean fiction of the day. See, for example, Mme de
Krüdener, *Valérie*, letter XLII: "Je [Linar] m'élançai à
ses [Valérie's] genoux, que je serrai convulsivement."

In Richardson's epistolary novel *The History of Sir
Charles Grandison*, vol. I, letter XXIX to Miss Selby,
Monday, Feb. 20, Miss Byron is taken in a chair by
treacherous chairmen to a house where Sir Hargrave
Pollexfen "threw himself at my feet"; "[she] sunk down
on [her] knees wrapping [her] arms about [one of the
women who were withdrawing]." Then she kneels be-
fore the wretch. Then she throws herself upon the win-
dow seat. Then he throws himself at her feet. Then he

*N. Dashkevich, in the collection *Pamyati Pushkina* (Kiev,
1899); Lerner, in the Petersburg daily, *Rech'*, Jan. 12, 1915;
and especially Anna Ahmatov, " 'Adol'f Benzhamena Kon-
stana v tvorchestve Pushkina," in *Vremennik*, I (1936), 91–
114.

embraces her knees with his odious arms (see a similar scene in Mme de Staël, my n. to Three : x : 3).

49–51 Gentil-Bernard's recommendations to the would-be lover in *L'Art d'aimer* (1761), can. II, ll. 218–19:

> Meurs à ses pieds, embrasse ses genoux,
> Baigne de pleurs cette main qu'elle oublie . . .

are followed by Onegin in Eight : XLI–XLII.

53–54 Cf. Rousseau, *Julie* (Saint-Preux complaining to Lord Bomston), pt. IV, letter VI: "Quel supplice de traiter en étrangère celle qu'on porte au fond de son cœur!" The Saint-Preux tone of Onegin's letter was already noted in 1832 (Feb. 21) by Küchelbecker in his prison diary.

VARIANTS

9–53 The draft (PD 165) gives the following alternate lines:

> 9 But let it be: against myself
> I cannot struggle any more.
> I've been the victim more than once
> 12 of insane passions and of fate . . .
>
> . . . .
>
> 23 I had forgotten your dear image,
> the tender sound of your shy speech,
> and with a sullen soul I bore
> 26 life as a purifying pain.
>
> . . . .
>
> 50 Granted—I am insane; but is it
> so very much that I am asking?
> O could you comprehend only the shadow
> 53 of what I carry in my heart!

55–61 Tomashevski and Modzalevski, in *Rukopisi* (1937), facing p. 72, publish the facsimile of a fair copy from the Maykov collection:

> look at you with a cheerful look,
> maintain a trivial conversation.

With this inferno you are not acquainted.
What then? Now this is what I want:
walk for a little at your side,
imbibe sweet poison drop by drop,
and gratefully lapse into silence.

Here the letter ends.

Under the last line of the draft (PD 165) Pushkin wrote: "Oct. 5, 1831, S[arskoe] S[elo]." This is the last date we have pertaining to Pushkin's work on the novel. The canto was published three months later.

XXXIII

6 / *Egó ne vídyat, s ním ni slóva*: Her apparent indifference is idiomatically rendered by the omission of the subject and by the vague plural in which the verb stands: "him [they] not see, with him no word." Something of this slightly jocular, or at least familiar, intonation might be rendered in English by "My lady sees him not . . ." It is really a Gallicism: "On ne le voit pas, on ne lui parle pas."

XXXV

2–6 The listing-of-authors device, although characteristic of Pushkin (who has a particular fondness for the tabulations of objects, names, emotions, actions, etc.), is not his invention. Indeed, the list in this stanza is nothing beside the fabulous catalogue of books read by Faublas (in Louvet de Couvray's *Une Année de la vie du Chevalier de Faublas*; see n. to One : XII : 9–10) during a spell of enforced solitude. In his list of forty authors, against Onegin's ten, the reader will recognize old friends, such as Colardeau, Dorat, Beaumarchais, Marmontel, de Bièvre, Gresset, Mably, Jean Baptiste Rousseau, Jean Jacques Rousseau, Delille, Voltaire, and others.

We shall also note that Pushkin omitted to give his

hero to read, in the winter of 1824–25, the two foreign
books that were most avidly read that season, the con-
troversial *Mémoires de Joseph Fouché, duc d'Otrante*—
Fouché had been Napoleon's chief of police (2 vols.,
Paris, September and November, 1824); and *Les Con-
versations de Lord Byron* (Pichot's version of Medwin's
Journal of the Conversations . . . ; see n. to Three : XII :
10).

*

The tabulation device was a great favorite also with
Pushkin's uncle, Vasiliy Pushkin, and was parodied by
Dmitriev, who published (Moscow, 1808; fifty copies for
private distribution) a charming poem in iambic tetram-
eter dealing with Vasiliy Pushkin's trip abroad (in 1803;
see the latter's own reports in the June and October issues
of the *Messenger of Europe* for that year). It is entitled
The Journey of N. N. to Paris and London. The follow-
ing lines (21–27) occur in pt. III:

> What dress coats! pantaloons!
> All in the newest fashion!
> What a fine choice of books!
> Count them—I'll tell you in a second:
> *Byuffón, Russó, Mablí, Korníliy,*
> *Gomér, Plutárh, Tatsít, Virgíliy,*
> all *Shakespír,* all *Póp* and *Gyúm.*

Korníliy, facetious form of Corneille; *Shakespír,* three
syllables, French pronunciation; *Póp,* French pronuncia-
tion of Pope; *Gyúm,* Russianized French pronunciation
of Hume; the rest, in Russian form and transcript.

For the unfinished novella now known as *The Blacka-
moor of Peter the Great,* begun July 31, 1827, Pushkin,
to judge by a MS medley of mottoes, planned to head the
first chapter with a quotation from the *Journey of a
Traveler* (sic):

> . . . I'm in Paris.
> I have begun to live—not breathe.

218

2 / Gibbon: Edward Gibbon (1737–94), English historian. Onegin might have read the French translation (Paris, 1793) of Gibbon's memoirs, an edition Pushkin had in his own library. The eighteen volumes of the *Histoire de la décadence et de la chute de l'empire romain* (Paris, 1788–95), Leclerc de Sept-Chênes' translation of Gibbon's *Decline and Fall*, should have kept Onegin busy for at least a month.

2 / Rousseau: After taking his fill of Gibbon, I suppose Onegin turned to Jean Jacques' *Julie* (see n. to Three : IX : 7) or *Confessions* rather than to the didactic works. Two weeks of Rousseau would probably satisfy him.

3 / Manzoni: Alessandro Francesco Tommaso Antonio Manzoni (1785–1873), the laborious, pious, and naïve author of such mediocre works as the "romantic" tragedy *Il Conte de Carmagnola* (Milan, 1820), which Onegin could have read in Claude Fauriel's French version, *Le Comte de Carmagnola* (Paris, 1823). It had also been translated by Auguste Trognon (Paris, 1822). I suspect Pushkin wished to lend Onegin *Les Fiancés, histoire milanaise*, etc., the French version, by Rey Dussueil (Paris, 1828), of Manzoni's romance *I Promessi sposi* (1827), an echo of Mrs. Radcliffe's divagations, but this came out too late for his purpose.

There is a canceled reading, "Lalande" (Joseph Jérôme Le Français de Lalande, 1732–1807, French astronomer), instead of "Manzoni," in the fair copy.

3 / Herder: Johann Gottfried von Herder (1744–1803), German philosopher.

Unless our hero knew German, which we know was not the case, or had obtained an advance copy of the French version by Edgar Quinet, who at twenty-two, in 1825, translated the first volume of Herder's *Ideen zur*

Philosophie der Geschichte der Menschheit (1784–91; *Idées sur la philosophie de l'histoire de l'humanité*, of which I have reluctantly seen an 1827–28 edn.), it is not clear how exactly the Rigan thinker, who "rappelait l'humeur souffrante de Rousseau fugitif et vieilli," could have in 1824 communicated with *Onéguine fugitif et vieilli*.

3 / Chamfort: The reference is no doubt to the *Maximes et pensées* in the *Œuvres de* [Sébastien Roch Nicolas] *Chamfort*, "recueillies et publiées par un de ses amis" (vol. IV, Paris, 1796; Pushkin had the 1812 edn.).

Onegin may have thumbnailed the following items (pp. 384, 344, 366, and 552):

Je demandais à M. N. pourquoi il n'allait plus dans le monde? Il me répondit: "C'est que je n'aime plus les femmes, et que je connais les hommes."

Le Médecin Bouvard avait sur le visage une balafre, en forme de C, qui le défigurait beaucoup. Diderot disait que c'était un coup qu'il s'était donné, en tenant maladroitement la faulx de la mort.

Pendant la guerre d'Amérique, un Ecossais disait à un Français en lui montrant quelques prisonniers américains: "Vous vous êtes battu pour votre maître, moi, pour le mien; mais ces gens-ci, pour qui se battent-ils?"

Je ne sais quel homme disait: "Je voudrais voir le dernier des Rois étranglé avec le boyau du dernier des Prêtres."

The last reference is to the lines (which La Harpe, *Lycée*, attributes to Diderot):

> Et des boyaux du dernier prêtre
> Serrons le cou du dernier roi.

According to O. Guerlac, *Les Citations françaises* (Paris, 1931), p. 218n:

On a longtemps attribué ces vers à Diderot qui a, en effet, dans les *Eleuthéromanes ou abdication d'un Roi de la Fève* (1772), écrit deux vers similaires. Mais ceux-ci, dont on ignore le véritable auteur, ne sont que la paraphrase d'un vœu du curé d'Etrépigny en Champagne, Jean Meslier, dont Voltaire publia un extrait de testament, d'ailleurs considéré comme apocryphe, où se lisent ces mots: "Je voudrais, et ce sera le dernier et le plus ardent de mes souhaits, je voudrais que le dernier des rois fût étranglé avec les boyaux du dernier prêtre."

The lines were paraphrased in a Russian quatrain of c. 1820, attributed by some to Pushkin, but probably written by Baratïnski. It circulated in a variant with "Russian" instead of "last" in reference to "a priest" and "the tsar":

> Good citizens we shall amuse,
> and at the pillory
> with the last priest's intestine
> we'll strangle the last tsar.

4 / Mme de Staël: Onegin, according to a canceled passage in One, had read this popular lady's work on German literature in his youth. He may now have turned to *Delphine*, which, with *Julie*, had been among young Tatiana's favorite novels.

4 / Bichat: The great physician, anatomist, and physiologist, Marie François Xavier Bichat (1771–1802), author of *Recherches physiologiques sur la vie et la mort* (Paris, 1799; 3rd edn. seen, 1805). He distinguished two lives in a creature: "organic life," depending on the body's asymmetrical internal structure, and "animal life," depending on the body's symmetrical external structure. Onegin may have been especially interested in Article Six, on the physiology of passions, in which the author proves that all passions affect the functions of the organism. Bichat has left wonderful pages on the death of the

heart, the death of the lung, the death of the brain; he died at an even earlier age than Pushkin.

4 / Tissot: Simon André, according to some, Samuel Auguste André, according to others, Tissot (1728–97), a famous Swiss doctor, author of *De la santé des gens de lettres* (Lausanne and Lyon, 1768).

Onegin may have also noted (pp. 31, 91):

Il y a eu des tyrans qui ont condamné à la mort des philosophes qu'ils haïssaient, mais ils n'ont pu la leur faire craindre. Combien auraient-ils été plus cruels, si en leur accordant la vie, ils eussent pu leur inspirer les craintes qui sont le tourment des hypocondriques?

Rien au monde ne contribue plus à la santé que la gayeté que la société anime et que la retraite tue. . . . Elle produit cette misantropie, cet esprit chagrin . . . ce dégoût de tout. . . .

In reading Tissot, Onegin followed the advice of Beaumarchais:

. . . Si votre dîner fut mauvais . . . ah! laissez mon *Barbier* . . . parcourez les chefs-d'œuvres de Tissot sur la tempérance, et faites des réflexions politiques, économiques, diététiques, philosophiques ou morales.

("Lettre modérée sur la chute et la critique du *Barbier de Séville*," which is an introduction to *Le Barbier de Seville, ou la Précaution inutile*, "comédie en quatre actes, représentée et tombée sur le Théâtre de la Comédie Française, aux Tuileries, le 23 de Février 1775," in *Œuvres complètes de Pierre Augustin Caron de Beaumarchais*, Paris, 1809, vol. I.)

It is curious to note that in his diminutive drama *Mozart and Salieri* (composed 1830), Pushkin has Beaumarchais give Salieri, according to Salieri, a very different piece of advice (sc. ii, ll. 31–35):

. . . Beaumarchais
was wont to say to me: Look, friend Salieri,

whenever by black thoughts you are beset,
uncork a bottle of champagne or else
reread *Figaro's Marriage.*

Some commentators have dragged in another, completely irrelevant, Tissot: Pierre François (1768–1854), author of a *Précis des guerres de la Révolution jusqu'a 1815* (Paris, 1820) and *De la poésie latine* (Paris, 1821).

5 / the skeptic Bayle: Pierre Bayle (1647–1706), French philosopher.

What was it exactly? Perhaps his marvelously cynical and misleading account of Abélard (d. 1142) and Héloïse (d. 1163), with lewd footnotes, in his *Dictionnaire historique et critique* (Rotterdam, 1697; Pushkin possessed A. J. Q. Beuchot's 1820–24 edn., in 16 vols.).

6 / works of Fontenelle: Bernard le Bovier de Fontenelle (1657–1757), in a new edition of his complete works (3 vols., Paris, 1818), might have tempted Onegin with his *Entretiens sur la pluralité des mondes* (1686), or, more practically, *Discours de la patience* (1687).

A still better choice, prompted by Lenski's shade and by a recollection of that careless talk on Arcadian topics (Three : I–II), may have been *Poésies pastorales, avec un Traité sur la nature de l'églogue* (1688). His best work, however, is *Dialogues des morts* (1683), in which, through the airy wit and rigid rationalization of his time, one distinguishes an individual flow of strong, lucid thought.

7–8 Among Russian poetical works that appeared at the end of 1824 and at the beginning of 1825, the following are especially mentioned by contemporaneous critics: a collection of Zhúkovski's poems; Pushkin's *Fountain of Bahchisaray*; fragments of Griboedov's *Woe from Wit* (in *The Russian Thalia*; see n. to One : XXI : 5–14).

Commentary

Furthermore, Rïleev's *Meditations* (*Dumï*), and various magazine pieces by Pushkin, Baratïnski, Küchelbecker, Delvig, Yazïkov, and Kozlov received good reviews.

In Delvig's literary "almanac" for 1825, *Northern Flowers*, which came out about Christmas, 1824, Onegin might have found a fragment, four stanzas (Chapter Two : VII–X) describing the pure soul of the young idealist he had dispatched four years before (Jan. 14, 1821).

In the last week of February, 1825, having acquired Chapter One, he might have read with a smile, half amused and half nostalgic, about himself, Kaverin, Chaadaev, Katenin, and Istomina in his old pal's sympathetic survey of a young rake's life in 1819–20.

About the same time (beginning of 1825) he could have seen in the first three issues of *The Son of the Fatherland* for that year Bulgarin's venomous criticism of Karamzin's *History of the Russian Empire*, vols. X and XI (Bulgarin considered Karamzin wrong in making a villain of Tsar Boris Godunov).

9 / *al'manáhi, i zhurnáli*: The main literary magazines, or collections, termed "almanacs" (which differed from *zhurnalï*—literary reviews—mainly in appearing at erratic intervals, sometimes as "annual miscellanies," and in leaning toward the anthological in pocket form), were, in 1824–25, *Mnemosyne* (ed. Odoevski and Küchelbecker), *Northern Flowers* (ed. Delvig), Bulgarin's theatrical review, *The Russian Thalia*, and others. The *al'manah* I am holding at the moment is *The Polar Star* (*Polyarnaya zvezda*), 1824, "a pocket book for female and male lovers of Russian letters, edited by A. Bestuzhev and K. Rïleev, St. Petersburg, 322 pages, illustrated."

The term "almanac," as used in Russia in the sense of a more or less periodical collection of new literary pieces, stems from Karamzin's venture of 1796, *Almanac of the Aonids*, in imitation of the famous French *Almanach des Muses*, a *recueil* of fugitive poems (with a sprinkling of enduring ones), published at intervals from 1764 to 1833.

Among the *zhurnalï* (literary reviews, weeklies, monthlies, and quarterlies) of 1824–25, we may mention *The Messenger of Europe*, *The Literary News*, and *The Son of the Fatherland*. The most successful were Bulgarin's *Northern Bee* and Polevoy's fortnightly *Moscow Telegraph*. In the latter Pushkin was attacked in 1830 (see, for example, Polevoy's harsh critique of Chapter Seven in no. 5). In the former, Bulgarin, in 1824–25, had eulogized Pushkin in various brief references to his poems. An abrupt change occurs only in 1830; that year, in no. 5, in reference to Pushkin's short poem entitled *May 26, 1828*, Bulgarin still speaks of our poet's "inspiration of genius," but then in no. 30 (Mar. 12, 1830) Bulgarin publishes a piece called "Anekdot," grossly insulting to Pushkin, followed by a violent critique of Seven in no. 35 (Mar. 22, 1830) and no. 39 (Apr. 1, 1830).

Pushkin wrote to the chief of the Gendarmes Corps, General Benkendorf (Count Alexander Benckendorff, 1783–1844), Mar. 24, 1830, Moscow:

. . . M. Boulgarine, qui dit avoir de l'influence auprès de vous [Bulgarin was a police agent], est devenu un de mes ennemis les plus acharnés à propos d'une critique qu'il m'a attribuée . . .

It is true that Delvig's journal, *The Literary Gazette*, of which Pushkin was the leading spirit, had harshly criticized Bulgarin's two very mediocre and popular novels, published March, 1829, and March, 1830, respectively (*Ivan Vïzhigin*, a moral satire, 1086 pp., and *The False Demetrius*, a historical romance, 1551 pp.);

especially blasting was Delvig's unsigned review (*Literary Gazette*, no. 14, 1830), which Bulgarin attributed to Pushkin; but the specific cause that prompted Bulgarin's attack was a MS epigram by Pushkin (written February, 1829, and circulated in MS). It goes:

> The harm is not that you're a Pole:
> so are Kosciusko and Mickiewicz;
> a Tatar be, for all I care:
> likewise no shame can I see there;
> or be a Jew, no harm there either;
> the harm is you're Vidocq Figlyarin.

The allusion is to François Eugène Vidocq (1775–1857), chief of the secret police in France, whose spurious *Memoirs* were such a hit in 1828–29. "Figlyarin," drawn from *figlyar* ("zany") and rhyming with the subject's real name.

Bulgarin boldly published this epigram, unsigned, in the review *Son of the Fatherland*, XI, 17 (Apr. 26, 1830), 303, with a note saying: "This curious epigram by a well-known poet circulates in Moscow and has come here [St. Petersburg] to be distributed." Bulgarin changed the last two words of the epigram to "Faddey Bulgarin," thus making it look like a direct libel.

The "Anekdot" (subtitled "From an English Journal") reads, in part:

Travelers are cross with our Old England because the rabble here behaves discourteously toward foreigners and employs the name of a foreign nation as an invective [possibly an allusion to the derivation of "bugger" from "Bulgar"]. . . . In civilized France [where] foreign-born writers enjoy the particular esteem of the natives . . . there appeared a French rhymester who, after deceiving the public for a long time by aping Byron and Schiller (whom he did not understand in the original), fell at last into disesteem and switched from poetry to criticism.

The "Anekdot" goes on to relate how this shameless person vilified a distinguished German-born writer, and rounds up the attack on Pushkin by describing this "Frenchman" as a trivial versificator "with the cold and mute heart of an oyster," a tippler, a sycophant, and a cardsharper. *

12 / *such* madrigals: Although on the whole Pushkin's first long poems, *Ruslan and Lyudmila*, *The Caucasian Captive*, and *The Fountain of Bahchisaray*, were met with ecstatic applause by the reviewers, there were a few ferocious dissenters, such as the viciously conservative Mihail Dmitriev, who, in *The Messenger of Europe*, no. 3 (Feb. 13, 1825), denied Pushkin the status of true poet and affirmed that the "lauded music of his verse can mean nothing to posterity, nor does it mean much to contemporaries."

XXXVI

In a work in which, on the whole, the poet is at pains to keep his imagery within the limits of the accepted, the rational, the not-too-bizarre, the *déjà dit* (with melodious novelty supplied by its Russian garb), sts. XXXVI and XXXVII stand out as something very special. The wording may fool one at first, for it seems a routine display of formulas to which *EO* has accustomed us—"dreams," and "desires," and "legends," and the usual epithets "secret," "forgotten," and so forth. Yet very soon the inner eye and the inner ear begin to distinguish other colors and sounds. The elements are the old ones but their combination results in a marvelous transmutation of meaning.

The passage is not easy to render accurately. The *I chtó zh?*, opening it, is not the plain "Eh, bien, quoi?

---

*For quotations from Bulgarin's article I rely upon P. Stolpyanski's "Pushkin i 'Severnaya pchela,' " in *P. i ego sovr.*, VI, 23–24 (1916), 127–94 and VIII, 31–32 (1927), 129–46.

Tué" (*Nu, chtó zh? ubít*) of Zaretski (Six : XXXV : 4) or the storyteller's oratory in Tatiana's dream (. . . *i chtó zh? medvéd' za néy*, Five : XII : 14). I have translated it "And lo—" because nothing short of it would render the mysterious tone of warning in the particular "And what?"

There is a kind of irrational suggestiveness, a hypnotic and quaint quality, about those *táynïe predán'ya*, "secret legends [or traditions] of the heart's dark [or obscure] past," *tyómnoy starinï*, where two great romantic themes, folklore and heartlore, merge as Onegin is lulled into one of those predormant states in which levels of meaning shift slightly and a mirage shimmer alters the outline of random thoughts. Especially remarkable in enigmatic tone are the *ugrózï, tólki, predskazán'ya*—"threats" (what threats? evil omens? fatidic menaces?), "rumors" (or, perhaps, "interpretations," strange glosses in the margin of life?), "presages" (are these omens related to those which so beautifully linked up Tatiana's dream with her name-day party?). The gay patter of l. 13 resembles those little voices which start to narrate vivacious nonsense in one's ear as one is about to doze off; and Tatiana's only letter to Onegin is miraculously multiplied in the last prismatic line. The next stanza contains one of the most original images of the novel.

In connection with these considerations, one is tempted to quote a passage from Baron E. Rozen's fine "Reference to the Dead" (in *The Son of the Fatherland*, 1847), which I slightly condense:

Pushkin was addicted to deep, somber brooding; and in order to relieve his natural taciturnity he sought every pretext for mirth. There was something forced about that bright laughter of his. Frequently what provoked it was the unexpected, the unusual, the fantastically monstrous, the contrived. And when nothing could satisfy this need, he, that prodigy of harmonious thought, would depart

from his stately norm to compose strange verses, delib-
erate nonsense, but the nonsense of genius. And *those*
verses he never committed to paper.

13 / of a long tale / *dlínnoy skázki*: It is difficult to decide
whether *skazka* here means "fairy tale" or merely a
conte in the French sense.

XXXVII

4 The magnificent image of the faro game has us recall the
stanzas on gambling in Canto Two that our poet rejected.
The dead youth is forever encamped in Onegin's mind,
forever Zaretski's casual croak reverberates there, and
forever the snow of that frosty morning melts under
shed blood and scalding tears of remorse.

VARIANT

5–6 A rough draft published by Shlyapkin (1903), p. 24,
and mentioned in *Rukopisi* (from Shlyapkin's collec-
tion), dated September, 1830, has:

> Quick visions slyly
> glide left and right . . .

and Onegin has "lost all the stakes of life" (last line?).
In the left-hand corner, Pushkin wrote in pencil the
following aphorism in prose: "Translators are the post
horses of enlightenment."

XXXVIII

5 / magnetism: A year later, namely in December, 1825, a
committee in Paris was appointed by the French Acad-
emy of Science to examine the claims of magnetism,
otherwise hypnotism. After five and a half years of cogi-
tation, the committee announced that the effects of
magnetism were sometimes produced by lassitude, en-

nui, and imagination. Pushkin has apparently in view here self-hypnotism leading in some cases to automatic rhyming, graphomania.

Cf. Pierre Lebrun, *L'Inspiration poétique* (written in 1823):

> Le poëte! . . .
>
> .   .   .   .
>
> Dans l'inspiration, pareil
> A l'enfant que l'art mesmérique
> Fait parler durant son sommeil . . .

12 / "Benedetta": Pushkin, in July, 1825, wrote to Pletnyov:

> Tell [Ivan] Kozlov from me that our part of the world [Trigorskoe] is visited by one charmer [Anna Kern] who divinely sings his *Venetian Night* [*Venetsianskaya noch'*, *fantaziya*, composed 1824] to the tune of a gondolier's recitative ["Benedetta sia la madre"]. I promised to communicate this to the dear inspired blindman. Pity he cannot see her; but let him imagine, at least, the beauty and the soulfulness. God grant that he may hear her.

The end of this stanza is a curious echo of the themes in One : XLVIII–XLIX (see nn. to these stanzas).

12–13 / "Benedetta" . . . "Idol mio": "Benedetta sia la madre," "Let the mother be blessed," a Venetian barcarolle. To this tune were adapted the Russian trochaic tetrameters of Kozlov's *Venetian Night*, inscribed to Pletnyov, published in the review *The Polar Star* (1825):

> 'Twas a night in springtime, breathing,
> Full of Southern beauty bright,
> With the Brenta gently streaming
> Silvery in Luna's light . . .

"Idol mio, piu pace non ho," "My idol, I have no peace any longer": the refrain in a duettino ("Se, o cara, sorridi," "If only, my dear, you would smile") by Vincenzo Gabussi (1800–46).

13–14 Elton has the hilarious:

> . . . *The News*
> Drops in the fire—or else his shoes.

XXXIX

5–9 I am inclined to select the morning of Apr. 7, 1825, as the date of Onegin's awakening from hibernation, this being the first anniversary (O.S.) of Byron's death at Missolonghi. On that day Pushkin and Anna Vulf, in the province of Pskov, had Greek-Orthodox rites performed in commemoration of "the Lord's slave Georgiy" at the local churches on their lands of "Mihaylovsky" and "Trigorsky" (as Pushkin Frenchified these names). Writing that May from Trigorskoe to his brother in St. Petersburg, our poet compares these prayers to "la messe de Frédéric II pour le repos de Monsieur de Voltaire."

7 / *zimovál on kak surók*: A locution adapted from the French (*hiverner comme une marmotte*). *Surok* corresponds to the generic marmot, but the rodent known to the French as *la marmotte* (*Marmota marmota* L.) is restricted to the mountains of western Europe. It is replaced in southern and eastern Russia by *Marmota bobac* Schreber, Fr. *boubak*, Russ. *baybak*, Eng. bobac, also known in England as the "Polish marmot" and in America as the "Russian woodchuck"; and apparently, i.e., as far as a nonmammological taxonomist can make out, it is congeneric with the three American marmots (the Eastern "ground hog," the Western "yellow-bellied marmot," and the "gray marmot" or "whistler"). The "prairie dog" belongs to another genus.

It is curious to note incidentally that the bobac is

described, with fabulous details, in La Fontaine's *Fables*, bk. IX: "Discours à madame de la Sablière."

Onegin went into hibernation just before the calamitous inundation of Nov. 7, 1824 (after which, expensive social festivities such as those at which he could see Tatiana were temporarily forbidden by government decree). In other words, Pushkin very conveniently, for the structure of the novel, has Eugene sleep through the disaster. Another Eugene, however, is in the meantime losing his betrothed to the raging waters and being driven mad by the fancied gallop of an equestrian statue in the poem Pushkin devoted to that flood, *The Bronze Horseman* (composed 1833). The way Eugene Onegin, while hibernating, lends his first name to this unfortunate man is very amusing (pt. I, ll. 1–15, rhymed arbitrarily aabebeccibbicco):

> O'er the ensombered Town of Peter
> November breathed with autumn chill.
> Plashing with noisy wave against
> the margins of her trim embankment,
> 5 the Neva tossed about
> like a sick man upon his restless bed.
> 'Twas late and dark. The rain
> beat crossly on the windowpane,
> and the wind blew with a sad howl.
> 10 At this time from a visit
> came home young Eugene.
> We'll call our hero
> by this name. It
> sounds pleasingly. With it, moreover,
> 15 my pen somehow has long been friends.

The Bronze Horseman is also linked up with *EO* by a remarkable series of stanzas in *EO* rhyme sequence, *The Pedigree of My Hero* (*Rodoslovnaya moego geroya*, 1832); Pushkin hesitated to which of the two Eugenes to apply it, and then chose another hero altogether (Ivan Ezerski). See my Epilogue, following nn. to Ten.

11 The ice of the Neva starts breaking up and moving be-
tween mid-March and mid-April (end of March and end
of April, N.S.). Generally, two or three weeks later the
river is quite free of ice, but sometimes ice keeps floating
as late as the second week of May. In XXXIX, the snow in
the streets has given place to mud. Some readers under-
stand the *issechyónnïe l'dï* of the text as "scarred ice,"
floating remnants of ice cut up by the action of water,
friction, and thaw, rather than those splendid aqua-
marine blocks that are hacked out of the frozen Neva and
stand on its sparkling snows, ready to be conveyed wher-
ever needed. On Turgenev's suggestion, Viardot writes:
"le soleil se joue sur les blocs bleuâtres de la glace qu'on
en a tirée."

Cf. ll. 81–83 in the exordium of *The Bronze Horseman*
(composed October, 1833), ll. 75–83:

> O military capital, I love
> the smoke and thunder of your fortress [gun]*
> when of the Midnight Realm the empress
> gives the imperial house a son
> or victory over the foe
> Russia again is celebrating,
> or having shattered her blue ice,
> the Neva bears it to the seas
> and, sensing vernal days, rejoices.

On the same Palace Quay, it will be recalled, Onegin and
Pushkin strolled in May, 1820.

14.–XL : 1 A type of enjambment from one stanza to another
of which only a few examples occur in the novel (see In-
troduction). There is beautiful logic in the fact that a
similar run-on occurs in Chapter Three (XXXVIII : 14–
XXXIX : 1: "panting, on a bench she drops"), where
Tatiana flees into the park, only to be discovered there

---

*Whose puff is seen from the opposite Palace Quay an instant
before the detonation is heard.

and sermonized by Onegin. Now the roles are reversed, and it is Onegin who is breathlessly heading for the place where *he* will be lectured on love.

XL

My predecessors vie here, as elsewhere, in grotesque achievement. Spalding has: "Pallid and with dishevelled hair, | Gazing upon a note below"; Elton: ". . . sitting full in sight, | Still in her *négligé*, and white"; Miss Deutsch: "Looking too corpselike to be nobby, | He walks into the empty lobby"; and Miss Radin: ". . . and his passion swelled | To bursting as he saw she held | the letter he had sent . . ."

5–8 There is a dreamlike atmosphere about all this. As in a fairy tale, silent doors open before him. He penetrates into the enchanted castle. And, as in a dream, he finds Tatiana rereading one of his three letters.

12 / *kakóe-to*: Ordinarily, the meaning of this word is less close to "some . . . or another" than to a plain "a," but the way it sprawls all over the line reflects on the sense here.

XLI

10 Cf. Saint-Preux's appearance, in Rousseau's *Julie* (Julie to Mme d'Orbe), pt. III, letter XIII: "pâle, défait, mal en ordre," bidding adieu to sick Julie. And Linar's moan, in Mme de Krüdener's *Valérie*, letter XLII: ". . . voyez ces yeux éteints, cette pâleur sinistre, cette poitrine oppressée . . ."

XLII

In one of Tatiana's favorite novels, Goethe's *Werther*, in the French of Sevelinges (1804), the theme of confession and separation takes a more violent turn: "[Werther] couvrit ses lèvres tremblantes de baisers de flamme. [Charlotte] le repoussait mollement. . . . 'Werther,' s'écria-t-elle enfin du ton le plus imposant et le plus noble. [Werther] la laissa échapper de ses bras," and fainted. She ran out of the room. He scrambled up and cried through the door: "Adieu!"

1 / *Oná egó ne podïmáet*: "Elle ne le relève pas." (See n. to Three : XXXIII : 1.)

2–6 / *ochéy . . . Beschúvstvennoy . . . O chyóm . . . mechtán'e . . . molchán'e*: There is a charming alliteration on *ch* here—and an echo of the "insensibly submissive" qualifying her condition in Five : XV : 3.

5 / *O chyóm tepér' eyó mechtán'e*: I have tried to retain the queer turn of the original.

XLIII

2 / I was . . . better-looking / *Ya lúchshe . . . bïlá*: Basically and grammatically *luchshe* means "better"; it is the comparative of *horosh*, fem. *horosha*, "is good." But this predicative *horosh*, *horosha*, has a secondary meaning (of Gallic origin), namely "is good-looking" (cf. *il, elle est bien de sa personne*, "he, she is a good-looking person"). In other words, when rendering the second line of this stanza, the translator has to choose between "I was a better person" and "I was a better-looking person." I chose the "looks," as also did Turgenev-Viardot (". . . plus jolie, peut-être").

Tatiana, if anything, is now a much better person than the romanesque adolescent who (in Three) drinks the philter of erotic longings and, in secret, sends a love letter to a young man whom she has seen only once. Although she may be said to have sacrificed certain impassioned ideals of youth when yielding to the sobs of her mother, it is also obvious that her newly acquired exquisite simplicity, her mature calm, and her uncompromising constancy are ample compensations, morally speaking, for whatever naïveté she has lost with the rather morbid and definitely sensuous reveries that romances had formerly developed in her. On the other hand, the ravages of age (she is now at least twenty-one) have, in her own mind, impaired her former looks, her pristine delicacy of complexion and feature. What, however, seems to me the decisive factor in settling the meaning of *luchshe* is the intonation of "I think" or "I daresay" (*kazhetsya*), which, while not interfering with the straightforwardness of a statement referring to physical beauty ("I was younger and, I think, prettier"), would be arch and artificial in reference to one's soul. One does not "think" that one used to be "a better person"; one knows it, and keeps it to one's self. And, moreover, from Tatiana's point of view, Onegin neither then nor now could or can care much for moral qualities.

Three English paraphrasts have "better."
Spalding:

> Onéguine, I was younger then,
> And better, if I judge aright . . .

Deutsch:

> Then I was younger, maybe better,
> Onegin . . .

Elton:

> I then, Onegin, they may tell me,
> Was better:—younger, too, was I!

And only one version gives the correct sense of *luchshe* in l. 2; Radin:

> Onegin, I was then much younger,—
> And better-looking, possibly . . .

See also the rhymed version of a fragment of *EO* by Prince Vladimir Baryatinski, in *Pushkinskiy sbornik* (St. Petersburg, 1899):

> Onéguine, autrefois plus belle
> Et, certes, plus jeune j'étais.

See also Pushkin's *The Gypsies*, ll. 170–71:

> *A dévï . . . Kak tï lúchshe íh*
> *I bez naryádov dorogíh . . .*

> And maidens . . . How fairer than they are you
> even without adornments dear . . .

13 / *Vï bíli právï predo mnóy*: "You acted correctly in regard to me," "your attitude toward me was the right one." The idiom is "you were right before me."

XLIV

1 / *Then—is it not so?* / *Togdá—ne právda li?*: There is the usual trouble here in translating Gallic intonations: "Jadis—n'est-ce pas?"

1 / in the wilderness / *v pustíne*: I have already discussed this Gallicism. It has a romantic tang here, in Tatiana's speech.

The most beautiful use of the word that I know of occurs in Senancour's marvelous description of the birch tree (*Oberman*, letter XI): "J'aime le bouleau . . . la mobilité des feuilles; et tout cet abandon, simplicité de la nature, attitude des déserts."

6–14 We recall that Tatiana had read Mme de Staël's *Delphine* (Delphine to the man Léonce, suggesting they separate), pt. IV, letter XX: "Demandez-vous si cette espèce de prestige dont la faveur du monde . . . [m'entourait] ne séduisoit pas votre imagination . . ."

However, *soblaznítel'nuyu* (fem. acc.) is also "scandalous," and Pushkin certainly recalls here Baratïnski's *The Ball*, ll. 82–84:

> Is not the ear of people tired
> by rumors of her shameless conquests
> and scandalous passions?

Cf. Goethe, *Werther* (tr. Sevelinges, p. 234; Charlotte, Albert's wife, saying to Werther, who has become to her "infiniment cher"):

Pourquoi faut-il que ce soit moi, Werther, moi, précisément, la propriété d'un autre? Je crains, je crains bien que ce ne soit que l'impossibilité de me posséder qui rend vos désirs si ardents!

9 / maimed / *izuvéchen*: This is a strong term on a romantic heroine's lips. We never find out what scars Prince N. bore. We know he was fat; the tinkling of his spurs and his proud port suggest his legs were intact. Had he lost an arm?

10 / *Chto nás za tó laskáet Dvór*: Lexically and constructionally "because us for that caresses the Court." The separate edition (1832) of the canto gives: *Chto mílostiv za tó k nam Dvór*, "because is graciously disposed for that to us the Court." The change was prompted, I suggest, by Pushkin's noticing the cacophonic intrusion of *óknam* (dat. of "windows"!).

VARIANT

13–14 The fair copy reads:

> *Podíte . . . pólno—Yá molchú—*
> *Ya vás i vídet' ne hochú!*
>
> Go, 'tis sufficient, I am silent,
> I do not want even to *see* you!

Note the hysterical little yelp *Ya vas i videt'* . . . *!* "even
to *see* you!" How this telltale note would have encour-
aged Onegin!

XLV

1–2 Odd talk. When had she been *his* Tanya? It would seem
that Princess N. has again fallen under the spell of the
novels she read as a girl, in which an epistolary custom
made young ladies speak of themselves to their corre-
spondents as "your Julie," "your Corinne," and so forth,
not only in the signature. The author may have relied
on the reader's recollecting Four : XI and on its providing
an illusion of logic for accepting the diminutive here.

8–10 / *K moím mladéncheskim mechtám* | *Togdá iméli ví
hot' zhálost',* | *Hot' uvazhénie* . . .: Here is a very pretty
play on the maudlin repetition of *m* with an emotional
transition to the strong swelling *zh*, as if, after the mur-
mur and the moan, the lady's nostrils were dilating in a
spasm of wholesome but somewhat exaggerated scorn.

14 / *chúvstva mélkogo:* "D'un sentiment mesquin."

XLVI

VARIANT

8–9 Fair copy:

> for our small house, for the wild garden,
> and for the mill, and for the ruins . . .

Gorodíshche: the ruins of some former habitation; an
abandoned fortress or the like (but also a place in or near
a village where peasant girls would gather for choral
dances and games, while their masters looked on).

There is a *gorodíshche* named Voronich, the remnants

Commentary

of a huge earthen rampart of the seventeenth century,
at Trigorskoe, near Mihaylovskoe.* As to the mill, it
would have been unseemly to remind Onegin of *that*.

XLVII

5–6 Cf. in Rousseau's novel (the scene occurs in pt. III,
letter XVIII, Julie to Saint-Preux) Julie's father, the
Baron d'Etange, sobbing, kneeling before his daughter,
imploring her to marry the opulent Pole. (Technically,
all this is needed in novels for the sole purpose of keeping
the noblehearted heroines beyond any suspicion of their
being swayed by mercenary motives in marrying wealth
or position while remaining true to their first love, the
haggard rover.)

12 / I love you (why dissimulate?) / *Ya vás lyublyú (k
chemú lukávit'?)*: Cf. Julie de Wolmar, in her last letter
to Saint-Preux, in the last part of Rousseau's novel, con-
fessing she loves him (pt. VI, letter XII): "Eh! Pourquoi
craindrois-je d'exprimer tout ce que je sens?"

13–14 / but to another I've been given away: to him I shall
be faithful all my life / *No yá drugómu otdaná;* | *Ya
búdu vék emú verná*: Cf. *Julie*, pt. III, letter XVIII (Julie
to Saint-Preux): "Liée au sort d'un époux . . . j'entre
dans une nouvelle carrière qui ne doit finir qu'à la
mort." And ibid.: ". . . ma bouche et mon cœur . . .
promirent [obéissance et fidélité parfaite à celui que
j'acceptois pour époux]. Je . . . tiendrai [ce serment]
jusqu'à la mort."

There can be no doubt that Pushkin intended Princess
N.'s decision to be a final one; but has he achieved his
purpose?

*See photograph, 1936, in *Pushkin v portretah i illyustratsiyah*,
collected by Matvey Kalaushin (2nd edn., Leningrad, 1954),
p. 145.

Ninety-nine per cent of the amorphous mass of comments produced with monstrous fluency by the *ideynaya kritika* (ideological critique) that has been worrying Pushkin's novel for more than a hundred years is devoted to passionately patriotic eulogies of Tatiana's virtue. This, cry the enthusiastic journalists of the Belinski-Dostoevski-Sidorov type, is your pure, frank, responsible, altruistic, heroic Russian woman. Actually, the French, English, and German women of Tatiana's favorite novels were quite as fervid and virtuous as she; even more so, perhaps, for at the risk of breaking the hearts of the admirers of "Princess Gremin" (as the two bright minds that concocted Chaykovski's libretto dubbed Princess N.), I deem it necessary to point out that her answer to Onegin does not at all ring with such dignified finality as commentators have supposed it to do. Mark the intonations in XLVII, the heaving breast, the broken speech, the anguished, poignant, palpitating, enchanting, almost voluptuous, almost alluring enjambments (ll. 1–2, 2–3, 3–4, 5–6, 6–7, 8–9, 10–11), a veritable orgy of run-ons, culminating in a confession of love that must have made Eugene's experienced heart leap with joy. And after those sobbing twelve lines— what clinches them? The hollow perfunctory sound of the pat couplet "wife–life": shrill virtue repeating its cue!

In June, 1836, while on a diplomatic mission to Russia, a Parisian littérateur of German extraction, Loewe de Weimars or Loève-Veimars, baronized by Thiers, persuaded Pushkin to translate several Russian folk ditties into French. In 1885 (*Russkiy arhiv*, pt. I) Bartenev published our poet's very pallid French versions of eleven pieces, the originals of which are all found in N. Novikov's *New and Complete Collection of Russian Songs*, pt. I (Moscow, 1780). One of these contains the following pertinent passage:

Le jeune seigneur tentait de faire entendre raison à la
   jeune fille.
"Ne pleure pas, ma belle jeune fille! Ne pleure pas, ma
   belle amie!
Je te marierai à mon fidèle esclave,
   Tu seras l'épouse de l'esclave, et la douce amie du maître;
   Tu feras son lit et tu coucheras avec moi."
La jeune fille répond au jeune homme:
"Je serai la douce amie de celui dont je serai la femme;
   Je coucherai avec celui dont je ferai le lit."

Komu budu ladushka, tomu milen'kiy druzhok,
Pod slugu budu postelyu slat', s slugoy vmeste spat':
I shall be sweetheart of him, whose bonnie wife I shall be,
   If I make the bed for your servant to lie in [meaning: if
   I marry him]—with your servant I shall sleep.

In MS subscribed "Chansons Russes" in Pushkin's hand.
Under this, on the cover, the Baron has written: "Tra-
duites par Alex. de Pouschkine pour son ami L. de
Veimars, aux îles de Neva, Datcha Brovolcki, Juin,
1836." (The correct address: Kamennïy Ostrov, Villa
[rented from] F. Dolivo-Dobrovolski.)

*

My predecessors had a horrible time with this couplet:
   Spalding:

> But I am now another's bride—
> For ever faithful will abide.

Miss Deutsch:

> But I became another's wife;
> I shall be true to him through life.

Elton:

> But am another's, pledged; and I
> To him stay constant, till I die.

Miss Radin:

> But I am someone else's wife
> And shall be faithful all my life.

13 / *otdaná* (= am given): Küchelbecker, in his remarkable journal, in an entry made Feb. 17, 1832, Sveaborg Fortress, notes that Pushkin is very like the Tatiana of Chapter Eight: he is full of feelings (liberal ideas) that he does not want the world to know, but is given to another (Tsar Nicholas).

XLVIII

5 / clink of spurs / *shpór . . . zvón*: As we part with Onegin, a curious type of poetical vengeance swoops down upon the rhymesters who have betrayed him in English. The Deutsch version commits a kind of rhetorical hara-kiri by inquiring (XLVIII : 5): "But are those stirrups he is hearing?" They are not. They are spurs. Yet an even more comic predicament fell to the lot of the Elton jingle at the time it was serially appearing in *The Slavonic Review* and had reached Chapter Two. In an essay published in English in *The Slavonic Review* (London), XV (Jan., 1937), 305–09, under the misleading title "On New Translations of Pushkin" and the equally misleading subtitle "How Should Pushkin Be Translated?" (there is nothing about actual translations in it—except an accidental and shocking sample to be discussed presently), V. Burtsev suggests that in future original and foreign editions of *EO* should be published in nine cantos "as Pushkin . . . would have liked to publish it" (which, of course, is a meaningless phrase). In the course of this essay, Burtsev (in his Russian original, of which the *Review* article is a translation) quotes Eight : XLVIII, and metaphorically remarks that the *shpór nezápnïy zvón* might have heralded the appearance of the Chief of Police, Count Benkendorf (Benckendorff), whose shadow caused Pushkin to interrupt his novel. Prof. Elton was asked to supply the translation of Eight : XLVIII, and this he did; but he did not understand the

passage in question, and betrayed not only Pushkin, but poor Burtsev, by putting:

> *Like sudden spur*, a bell his hearing
> Strikes—it is Tanya's lord, appearing!

This bell should be considered the toll announcing the death of all doggerels posing as translations.*

13 / land: Cf. *Roland furieux*, by "L'Arioste" (de Tressan), can. XLVI (the last):

> . . . J'espère découvrir bientôt le port . . . je craignois de m'être égaré de ma route! . . . Mais déjà . . . c'est bien la terre que je découvre. . . . Oui, ce sont ceux qui m'aiment . . . je les vois accourir sur le rivage . . .

XLVIIIa

1–5 See above, vol. 1, p. 333, and below, vol. 3, p. 253.

XLIX

1 / Whoever you be / *Kto b ni bïl tï*: "Qui que tu sois"— Gallic rhetoric.

6–12 This tabulation is an echo of the closing lines of the Prefatory Piece.

L

8 / many days: Three thousand seventy-one days (May 9, 1823–Oct. 5, 1831).

13 / magic crystal / *magícheskiy kristál*: I find it curious that "crystal" had been applied in an analogous sense by

---

*Elton later corrected his translation to "A sudden, tinkling spur his hearing | Strikes . . ."

our poet to his inkstand in a trimetric poem of 1821, ll. 29–30:

> Your cherished [*zavetnïy*] crystal
> contains celestial fire.

Lerner, *Zven'ya*, no. 5 (1935), 105–08, has a rather naïve little essay on crystal gazing (which, incidentally, was not, in its typical sense, a Russian form of divination).

LI

3–4 / "Some are no more, others are distant" / *Inïh uzh nét, a té daléche* / as erstwhiles Sadi [Muslih-ud-Din Sadi, Persian poet of the thirteenth century] said: *Uzh*, the Russian "already," redundant in English; *a té*, grammatically "whereas those"; *daléche*, the rarer word for "far"; *daleko* or *dalyoko* would be the usual, less evocative, form today.

There exist four expressions of the same idea in Russian prior to 1830:

(1) An Alexandrine line reading "Some friends already are no more; others [are] in the distance" (*Druzéy inïh uzh nét; drugie v otdalén'e*, "in removal"), in a poem of 1814 by the minor poet Vladimir Filimonov (1787–1858).* There is also Byron's: "But some are dead and some are gone . . . And some are in a far countrie" (*Siege of Corinth*, lines 24 and 30).

(2) The prose motto, probably translated from the French, that Pushkin prefixed to his Oriental romance, *The Fountain of Bahchisaray*, which he considered "better than the whole poem." This motto reads: "Many, similarly to me, visited [*poseshchali*] this Fountain; but some are no more, others are journeying far" (*inïh uzhe net, drugie stranstvuyut daleche*). The wording of the second sentence seems to have been suggested by Filimonov's line.

---

*As first noted by Yuriy Ivask, in the review *Opïtï* (Essays; New York), no. 8 (1957).

(3) The last two lines of the sixth quatrain of Bara-
tïnski's poem *Mara* (the name of the poet's estate in the
province of Tambov)—ten quatrains in iambic tetram-
eter, rhymed abab, composed in 1827, but published in
full only in 1835 (it had appeared, *without* quatrain VI,
as *Stanzas*, in January, 1828, in the review *The Moscow
Telegraph*. This quatrain, which Pushkin may or may
not have been acquainted with in 1830, reads (ll. 21–24):

> Brethren I knew; but youthful dreams
> brought us together for one moment:
> far, in necessity, are some,
> and others are no more already on the earth.
>
> *Daléche bédstvuyut inîe
> I v mîre nét uzhé drugíh.*

(4) In the draft of an elegy (presumably addressed to
Natalia Goncharov), which in its final form begins,
"Upon the hills of Georgia night's gloom lies" (*Na hól-
mah Grúzii . . .*), composed in 1829, during his visit to
Transcaucasia, Pushkin struck out a stanza containing a
similar phrase (ll. 9–12):

> Days after days went by. Vanished have many years.
> Where are you, dearest of dear beings [*bestsénnïe
>   sozdán'ya*]?
> Some are far, some on earth already are no more [*Inîe
> dalekó, inîh uzh v mîre nét*],
> With me are only recollections.*

It will be seen that Baratïnski transposed the two
clauses of the second sentence of Pushkin's motto, sub-
stituted for *stranstvuyut* the very similarly sounding
bédstvuyut ("live in necessity"), added "on the earth,"
changed the order of the words *inïh uzhe net* (*inïe* and
drugie are similar in meaning). It will be also seen that
Pushkin's verse, Eight : LI : 3, although in the same

---

*See M. Sultan-Shah's discussion of this piece in the collection
Pushkin (Moscow, 1956), pp. 262–66.

meter as Baratïnski's quatrain, is less close to it than to his own seven-year-old motto: he now uses the abbreviated form of *uzhe*; *drugie* has been turned into the more elegant and remote-sounding *a te*; the verb has been dropped; but otherwise the words are the same in the same order.

Baratïnski's quatrain alludes to the friends he had among the unfortunate conspirators of December, 1825, some (five) of whom had been executed, while others lived in dingy exile on the Siberian confines of northern China. Evidently the wording of his lines written in 1827 was suggested by the fact that Pushkin's motto, which in 1824 was a quite innocent bit of nostalgic literature in the pseudo-Oriental style of the day, had now received a specific political slant through the following chain of events. * In the beginning of 1827, *The Moscow Telegraph* had published an article by the critic Polevoy, "A Glance at Russian Literature for 1825 and 1826," subtitled "A Letter to S. P. [Sergey Poltoratski] in New York." A government agent (probably Bulgarin) reported that the article contained a clear allusion to the Decembrists, and indeed the allusion *is* clear in Polevoy's sentence, "I look at the circle of our friends, formerly so lively and gay, and often repeat sadly the words of Sadi, or of Pushkin, who rendered them, 'some are no more, others are far.' " Henceforth, the epigraph to Pushkin's *Fountain* (kept in the next editions, 1827 and 1830, but dropped in the edition of 1835) received a retrospective meaning. When in 1832 Pushkin published Chapter Eight of *EO* separately, readers had no difficulty in deciphering the enriched allusion.

Pushkin's main contact with the men variously involved in the revolutionary activities that after the events of December, 1825, were to be known as "De-

---

*First noted by Lerner, *Zven'ya*, no. 5 (1935), pp. 108–11.

cembrism" (see my n. to Ten : XIII : 3) goes back to
1818–20, before his expulsion from Petersburg, and to a
sojourn he made in the winter of 1820–21 at Kamenka,
province of Kiev, the countryseat of the retired General
Aleksandr Davïdov, where Pushkin saw several De-
cembrists, such as Davïdov's brother Vasiliy, Orlov,
Yakushkin, and others. Between his starting to compose
EO (May 9, 1823) and the Decembrist rising (Dec. 14,
1825), Pushkin had not actually read the first cantos "at
friendly meetings" to any of the five conspirators who
were to die on the gallows July 13, 1826 (see my n. to
Five : V–VI, IX–X, on Pushkin's sketches); he had seen
Rïleev (at a gentlemanly distance) before he left Peters-
burg, and his brief acquaintance with Pestel in Kishinev
was prior to the writing of Canto One. Among those De-
cembrists who were at the moment "far," i.e., in Si-
berian exile, Pushkin's intimate friend Ivan Pushchin
had presumably heard our poet recite three and a half
cantos when he visited Pushkin in Mihaylovskoe, Jan.
11, 1825. But otherwise we must accept as a piece of
lyrical exaggeration the vision of Pushkin reading *EO* at
gatherings of Decembrists before he had started to write
it; neither is there any proof that Pushkin read the first
two cantos of *EO* in Odessa to people he was very little
acquainted with, such as the Decembrists Nikolay
Basargin, Prince Aleksandr Baryatinski, and Matvey
Muravyov-Apostol, who visited Odessa in 1823–24. It is
not worth while discussing other suggestions that have
been made. We know for certain of only one Decembrist
in Odessa who heard Pushkin recite at least the first
chapter of *EO*, and this is Prince Sergey Volkonski
(among the wives of Decembrists, we may conjecture
that Ekaterina Orlov and Maria Raevski, later Volkonski,
were more or less acquainted with the beginning of
EO). According to a, not-altogether convincing, tradi-
tion stemming from the Volkonski family, Sergey Vol-

konski had been asked by the Southern Society to enroll
Pushkin, but in the course of their meeting in Odessa
(presumably, in June, 1824) he decided that for this the
poet's tongue was too careless, his nature too frivolous,
and his life too precious. That Volkonski knew Canto
One in 1824 is proved by a phrase in his letter of Oct.
18, 1824, to Pushkin, who by that time had already been in
Mihaylovskoe two months:

> Dear Aleksandr Sergeevich, When I left Odessa I did
> not think that upon my return from the Caucasus I would
> not see you. . . . I am forwarding you a letter from Mel-
> moth [Aleksandr Raevski]. . . . You will be glad to hear
> of my engagement to Maria Raevski. . . . P.S. . . . I have
> helped enroll in the Lyceum the son of the majestical
> cornuto [Aleksandr Davïdov, whose mother owned Ka-
> menka; brother of Vasiliy Davïdov, the Decembrist].

This definition is a quotation from One : XII : 12.

Other Decembrists said to have visited Odessa in
1823–24 are V. Davïdov and perhaps Pestel, but whether
Pushkin read *EO* to them is unknown.

*

I have not been able to discover the exact source of Push-
kin's motto, which is at the back of LI : 3–4. *Goulistan,
ou l'Empire des roses*, by Sadi, had appeared in a loose
French version by André du Ryer (Paris, 1634), and an
anonymous collection of selections and adaptations de-
rived from it came out in Paris in 1765. I have found
nothing suitable in versions of this work, of which a
literal French translation, not seen by me, by N. Seme-
let, *Gulistan, ou le Parterre-de-fleurs du Cheikh Moslih-
eddin Sâdi de Chiraz* (Paris, 1834), was in Pushkin's
library.

The nearest I can get to the quotation is a passage in a
long poem in ten "portals," the *Bustan*, or *Bostan*, or
Bashtan (*The Aromatarium*, as one would like to trans-

late it instead of *The Orchard*), by Sadi, 1257:

> On dit que le bienheureux Djemschîd fit graver ces mots sur une pierre au dessus d'une fontaine. "Beaucoup d'autres avant nous se sont reposés au bord de cette source, qui ont disparu en un clin d'œil. Ils avaient conquis le monde par leur vaillance, mais ils ne l'ont pas emporté avec eux dans la tombe; ils sont partis . . . ne laissant après eux qu'un souvenir d'estime ou de réprobation.

I do not know how the words "fontaine," "d'autres," "ont disparu," and "ils sont partis" may have been combined in the French version Pushkin saw. Could it have been the fragments of the *Bustan* reproduced in French by Silvestre de Sacy in 1819 in his notes on the *Pandnamah* (Scroll of Wisdom)? The translation I have consulted is *Le Boustan ou Verger*, tr. A. C. Barbier de Meynard (Paris, 1880), p. 34.

In The Wisdom of the East series, there is a worthless adaptation of *The Bustān of Sadi*, "translated" into "polite English" by A. Hart Edwards (London, 1911). In "Chapter IX," p. 115, of this product I find the following vague connection with Pushkin's lines: "Our friends have departed, and we are on the road."

Finally, Tomashevski observes in his *Pushkin* (1956, vol. I, p. 506n) that in Moore's *Lalla Rookh* (in the prose passage preceding the poem "Paradise and the Peri") there occur the words: ". . . a fountain on which some hand had rudely traced those well-known words from the Garden of Sadi, 'Many like me have viewed this fountain, but they are gone and their eyes are closed for ever!' "—translated by Pichot as "Plusieurs ont vu, comme moi, cette fontaine: mais ils sont loin et leurs yeux sont fermés à jamais."

6 / And she from whom . . . / *A tá, s kotóroy* . . .: With a delightful alliterative play on *ta* (*ta . . . Tat'yanï*).

Cf. the echo in *Onegin's Journey*, XVI : 10, *A tam . . . tatar.*

Gofman, *Pushkin, psihologiya tvorchestva,* p. 22n, says that in the fair copy the line reads:

> and those from whom . . .
> *A té s kotórïh . . .*

and correctly argues that whatever Pushkin's reasons (euphonic ones, I think) for using the singular in the published text, it would be a waste of time to look for a historic "prototype" of Tatiana.

9–11 / life's banquet . . . goblet full of wine: One recalls André Chénier's beautiful lines in the poem known as *La jeune Captive* (ll. 25–30):

> Mon beau voyage encore est si loin de sa fin!
> Je pars, et des ormeaux qui bordent le chemin
> J'ai passé les premiers à peine,
> Au banquet de la vie à peine commencé,
> Un instant seulement mes lèvres ont pressé
> La coupe en mes mains encor pleine.

(Ode addressed to Aimée Franquetot de Coigny, Duchesse de Fleury; composed in prison in 1794; first published in *La Décade philosophique,* 20 Nivôse, An III, i.e., Jan. 10, 1795—if I have calculated this correctly— and then in the *Almanach des Muses* for 1796.)

11 The fair copy has instead of *Bokála pólnogo viná* the much better *Bokálov yárkogo viná,* "goblets of gaudy wine." Beneath this last stanza is the date: *Boldino sent.* [Sept., 1830] *25 3¼* [P.M.?]. At the end of the separate edition (1832) a note reads: "The end of the eighth, and last, chapter."

Notes to *Eugene Onegin*

Notes to *Eugene Onegin* / *Primechaniya k Evgeniyu Oneginu*: Pushkin's forty-four notes come immediately after Chapter Eight in the final editions of the novel (1833, 1837). They have no compositional value. Their choice is haphazard, their matter rather inept. But they are Pushkin's and belong to the work as published by him.

Fragments of *Onegin's Journey*

Fragments of *Onegin's Journey* / *Otrïvki iz Puteshestviya Onegina*: Immediately after the forty-four notes, Pushkin added in the final editions of 1833 and 1837 a commentary entitled "Fragments of *Onegin's Journey*," in which he embedded the first five lines of a dropped stanza pertaining to the established Eight, as well as stanzas, and fragments of stanzas, describing Onegin's tour of Russia, which is mentioned in Eight : XIII.

Eight : XLVIIIa : 1 / 'Tis time: the pen for peace is asking / *Porá: peró pokóya prósit*: One wonders if this stanza was really completed or if Pushkin got to l. 5 and stopped there because of the difficulty of finding a rhyme to *Kaménam*, dat. pl. of *Kamena* (Camena, one of the Roman water nymphs identified with the Greek Muses). *Izménam* ("to the betrayals")? *Pereménam* ("to the changes")? *Kolénam* ("to the knees")?

The intonation of the first line is an obvious confirmation of the *pora* ending XLVIII : 14. *Porá . . . pokóya prósit* is curiously echoed in the poem to his wife (*Porá, moy drúg, porá, pokóya sérdtse prósit*, " 'Tis time, my dear, 'tis time, for peace the heart is asking") written some five years later (see also, after nn. to XXXII, n. to Eight : Onegin's Letter : 20–21). *Pokoy* includes the ideas of "peace," "ease," "repose," "rest," "calm," "serenity," and "quiet."

Katenin: Katenin, in his *Vospominaniya o Pushkine* (Recollections of Pushkin),* describes an interview he had with the poet July 18, 1852, in a villa on the Peterhof Road, near St. Petersburg, concerning *EO*, the last chapter of which had recently appeared:

> I remarked upon the omission [of *Onegin's Journey*] and guessed that [these stanzas] had contained an imitation of *Childe Harold* canceled by Pushkin presumably because the inferior quality of places and things had not allowed him to compete with the Byronian model. Without saying a word, Pushkin inserted what I had said among his notes [to the complete editions].

Katenin makes a curious mistake here. It is not this ridiculous remark about the "inferior quality of places and things," but another, somewhat less trivial, observation of his that Pushkin mentions. Our poet's respect for Katenin remains inexplicable.

THE FRAGMENTS (INCLUDING EXPUNGED STANZAS)

Initially, in 1827, when only the stanzas describing Odessa had been composed (they were written in 1825), our poet planned to deal with Onegin's travels in Chapter Seven, on which he was working at the time. In the stanza (which is our Seven : XXV alt.) that was to follow XXIV, he intended to leave Tatiana brooding over Onegin's books and to turn his course in another direction:

> After he'd killed his inexperienced friend,
> the irk of ⟨rural⟩ leisure

---

*Written Apr. 9, 1852; published, with Y. Oksman's notes, in *Lit. nasl.*, nos. 16–18 (1934), pp. 617–56.

Onegin was unable ⟨to bear⟩;
8 ⟨to seat himself in a kibitka he decided⟩.
 The full-toned yoke bell ⟨sounded⟩,
 the dashing driver whistled,
 and our Onegin sped away
12 ⟨to seek a gladdening⟩ of dull ⟨life⟩
 in distant parts,
 himself not knowing where exactly.

Here Onegin, in a hooded sleigh, sets out in January or February, 1821, from his countryseat, presumably for Petersburg (which he will leave for his tour of Russia on June 3, 1822, in the later text, *Journey*, VI), and a description of his travels was to follow.

After canceling the idea of thus devoting the second part of Chapter Seven to Onegin's travels, and after replacing them with Tatiana's journey to Moscow, Pushkin decided to assign a whole chapter, the next one, to the pilgrimage. By the fall of 1830, the plan had been realized, and (as more exactly described in "The Genesis of *EO*"; see my Introduction) Pushkin jotted down (Sept. 26, 1830) the complete pattern of the poem he had begun May 9, 1823:

Part First

Cantos
    One: Hypochondria
    Two: The Poet
    Three: The Damsel

Part Second

Cantos
    Four: The Countryside
    Five: The Name Day
    Six: The Duel

Part Three

Cantos
    Seven: Moscow
    Eight: The Wandering
    Nine: High Life

To this in the course of the next three weeks he added at least eighteen stanzas of a Canto Ten, "The Decembrists."

In the course of 1831 he changed his plan. "The Wandering" was expelled from its place in the arrangement of chapters, the parts were abolished, and "chapters" replaced "cantos." Had our poet set down the new order of *Onegin* as it was to be published in 1833, the program would have looked as follows:

Chapters
   One: Hypochondria
   Two: The Poet
   Three: The Damsel
   Four: The Countryside
   Five: The Name Day
   Six: The Duel
   Seven: Moscow
   Eight: The Grand Monde
Notes to *Eugene Onegin* (44 items)
Fragments of *Onegin's Journey* (including comments)

The complete text of *Onegin's Journey* does not exist in its initial form, i.e., as "Canto Eight." It has been, however, restored in its major part, quantitatively speaking. The first stanza was probably the one that later became st. x of Chapter Eight. Then, after II, came, presumably, sts. XI and XII of the present Chapter Eight. It is clear that a number of stanzas—anything from ten to twenty—are missing. We may suppose that at first, in September, 1830, the Decembrism themes were dealt with in certain stanzas of "Canto Eight: The Wandering." It is also likely that there were allusions to political circumstances that Pushkin thought wise to leave out. In 1853, Katenin wrote to Annenkov, the first intelligent editor of Pushkin's works:

Concerning the eighth chapter of *Onegin*, I heard from the late poet in 1832 that besides the Nizhni market and the Odessa port, Eugene saw the military settlements organized by Count Arakcheev,* and here occurred remarks, judgments, expressions that were too violent for publication and that he decided were best assigned to eternal oblivion. Therefore he discarded the whole chapter from his tale—a chapter that after that cancellation had become too short and, so to speak, impoverished.

For *Onegin's Journey* Pushkin used a combination of impressions stemming from his Southern tour of 1820 and from his second visit to the Caucasus in the summer of 1829. The stanzas referring to the description of life in Odessa (a fragment including XX to the first line of XXIX) were composed at the end of 1825 and were published anonymously on Mar. 19, 1827, under the title "Odessa (From the seventh chapter of *Eugene Onegin*)," in the *Moscow Herald*, pt. II, no. 6, pp. 113–18. The rest of the *Journey* was composed, after Pushkin's return from the Caucasus, in Moscow (Oct. 2, 1829); at Pavlovskoe, Pavel Vulf's countryseat (second part of October, 1829); and at Boldino (autumn of 1830).

In the rough draft of an Introduction that our poet planned to prefix to the *Journey* when, as Chapter Eight, it preceded the *grand-monde* chapter, Pushkin wrote:

I deliberated with myself if I should not destroy this chapter, being tempted to do so by the fear that a playful parody might be regarded as an expression of disrespect toward a great and sacred memory. *Childe Harold*, however, stands on such a height that, whatever the tone adopted in speaking of it, I could not have harbored the thought of any possibility of insult existing there.

Since the *Journey* has nothing "playful" about it (except, perhaps, the bits about the plump oysters and the traffic conditions in Odessa) and, moreover, bears no resemblance whatsoever to the Childe's pilgrimage, we

---

*Camps of militarized peasants in Novgorod and Staraya Russa, a faint adumbration of Soviet slave-labor camps. See n. to One : XVII : 6–7.

may assume that the reference to lighthearted parody was meant to divert the censor's attention from a too-close probing of the complete text.

I hesitated whether I should not call the thing *Onegin's Pilgrimage*, but concluded that it would be crudely emphasizing a resemblance that Pushkin himself tried to avoid. The *Pilgrimage* of Byron's title was translated by Pichot as *Pèlerinage*. When attempting, in some jottings of 1836 (MS 2386B, f. 2^r), to turn the dedication ("To Ianthe") of *Childe Harold's Pilgrimage* into Russian, with the help of an English-French dictionary, Pushkin rendered that title as *Palomnichestvo Chayl'd Garol'da* (see *Rukoyu Pushkina*, p. 97). But in Russian *palomnichestvo* (from *palomnik*, "palmer," "pilgrim") happens to connote a holy goal somehow more strongly than "pilgrimage," and this was felt by Russian translators of Byron, who rendered "pilgrimage" as *stranstvovanie*, a synonym of *palomnichestvo*, but with the stress rather on the "wandering" than on the purpose of pious peregrination. Initially, Pushkin planned to entitle the account of Onegin's tour *Stranstvie*, "Wandering," which is very close to *stranstvovanie*, but later settled for the matter-of-fact and un-Byronic *Puteshestvie*, "Journey."

In the case of Griboedov's Chatski, despite the total absence of mentioned place names, we have the definite impression—based on three or four distinct references—that in the course of his three-year-long travels Chatski has been abroad. Onegin's journey from the time of his leaving Petersburg to his returning to it in August, 1824, also lasts three years; but has he been abroad *between* his departure from his countryseat and his departure from Petersburg for his Russian tour?

Writers of the ideological school such as Dostoevski were sure that Onegin went abroad, not because they had closely studied the text, but because they knew it only vaguely and, besides, confused Onegin with Chatski. That Pushkin *might* have thought of sending his man abroad is suggested to us by two considerations: (1) in a canceled stanza (Seven : XXV alt. : 13) Onegin sets out from his countryseat (which was 400 miles E of the German border) to seek relief from *tedium vitae* "in distant parts," *po otdalyónnïm storonám*, which sounds more like an allusion to foreign countries than to Russian provinces; and (2) in a canceled stanza of the *Journey* (V) the first quatrain might be understood as Onegin's returning to Petersburg from western Europe and being sick of western Europe, after wandering about like a Melmoth. In that case, of course, we would have to take the date of his departure from Petersburg for Moscow in VI : 2 as June 3, 1822, instead of 1821—and this would get his calendar and whereabouts hopelessly entangled with those of Tatiana, since it is impossible to conceive that either in Petersburg or in Moscow, where she too lived in 1822, Onegin would not have (at least) heard about her from mutual friends, such as his cousin Prince N. or Prince Vyazemski. As things stand, however—i.e., basing ourselves only on such stanzas as Pushkin has allowed to remain—we have to limit Onegin's travels to Russia. (See also my n. to Eight : XIII : 14.)

*

I have collected below the expunged stanzas and parts of stanzas that fill the gaps between the fragments of *Onegin's Journey* (printed in vol. 1, pp. 335–45).

[I]
Blest who was youthful in his youth;
blest who matured at the right time;
who gradually the chill of life
4   with years was able to withstand;
who never was addicted to strange dreams;
who did not shun the fashionable rabble;
who was at twenty fop or blade,

8 and then at thirty, profitably married;
  who rid himself at fifty
  of private and of other debts;
  who good repute and rank
12 in due course calmly gained;
  about whom lifelong one kept saying:
  N. N. is an excellent man.

[II]
Blest he who understood the stern voice
of earthly necessity;
who walked in life on the great route,
4 the great route with its mileposts;
  who had a goal and strove to it,
  who knew wherefore into the world he came
  and who gave up the ghost to God
8 as farmer-general or general.
  "We are born," said Seneca,
  "for our fellows' good and our own"
  (one could not be plainer or clearer)—
12 but it is painful after living half a century
  to see in the past but the trace
  of lost, unprofitable years.

[III]
It is unbearable to think that to no purpose
youth was given us,
that we betrayed it every hour,
4 that it duped us;
  that our best wishes,
  that our fresh dreamings,
  in quick succession have decayed
8 like leaves in putrid autumn.
  It is unbearable to see before one
  only of dinners a long series,
  to look on life as on a rite,
12 and in the wake of the decorous crowd
  to go, not sharing with it
  either general views or passions.

[IV]
When one becomes the subject of noisy comments
it is unbearable (you will agree with that)

among sensible people
4 to pass for a sham eccentric,
   a Quaker of some kind, a Mason,
   or a home-bred Byron,
   or even for my Demon.
8 Onegin (let me take him up again),
   having in single combat killed his friend,
   having lived without a goal, without exertions,
   to the age of twenty-six,
12 oppressed in the embrace of leisure,
   without employment, wife, or business,
   could think of nothing to take up.

[v]
Grown bored of either passing for a Melmoth
or sporting any other mask,
he once awoke a patriot
4 during a rainy tedious spell.
   For Russia, gentlemen, he instantly
   felt a tremendous liking,
   and it is settled. He is now in love,
8 he raves of nothing now but Rus',
   he now hates Europe
   with its dry politics,
   with its lewd bustle.
12 Onegin is to go: he will
   see holy Rus': her fields,
   wilds, towns, and seas.

[VI]
Ready to start he got, and God be thanked.
On June the third
a light calash upon his travels
4 with posters carried him away.
   Amidst a half-wild plain
   he sees Great Novgorod.
   Quelled are its squares: midst them
8 bestilled is the rebellious bell,
   [but] roam the shades of giants—
   the Scandinavian subjugator,
   the legislator Yaroslav,
12 with the pair of redoubtable Ivans;

Commentary

and round the bowed-down churches
there seethes the people of past days.

[VII]
Ennui, ennui! Eugene makes haste
further to speed. At present,
like shadows, flicker-flick
4 Valdáy, Torzhók, and Tver before him.
Here, from the clinging peasant girls
he purchases three strings of bangle buns,
there, buys pantofles; further on,
8 along the proud banks of the Volga,
he drives asleep. The horses tear
now over hills, now by the river.
The versts flick by. Post coachmen
12 sing, whistle, squabble.
Dust swirls. . . . Now my Eugene
wakes up in Moscow, on Tverskaya Street.

[VIII]
Moscow welcomes Onegin
with her presumptuous bustle,
entices with her maidens,
4 treats to her sterlet soup.
At the assemblage of the English Club
(a tryout of parliament sessions),
wordlessly plunged in thought,
8 he hears debates on gruels.
He is remarked. He's talked about
by Rumor, varivoiced;
Moscow is occupied with him,
12 dubs him a spy,
makes verses in his honor,
and promotes him an eligible bachelor.

[IX]
1 Ennui, ennui! He makes for Nizhni,
Mínin's birthplace; before him . . .

[For ll. 3–14, see vol. 1, p. 335.]

[x]
Ennui! Eugene awaits fair weather.
Now, "paragon of rivers, lakes," the Volga
calls him onto its sumptuous waters,
4 under the canvas sails.
To win the willing is not hard.
Renting a merchant vessel,
he swiftly sails downstream.
8 The Volga swells. The haulers
leaning against boat hooks of steel,
in plangorous voices sing
about that robbers' den,
12 about those daredevil incursions
when in the old times Stenka Razin
begored the Volga wave.

[xi]
They sing of those unbidden guests
who burned and butchered. But behold—
amidst its sandy steppes
4 upon the shore of salty waters
the trading town of Astrahan unfolds.
Scarce has Onegin plunged
in memories of former days
8 when the heat of meridian rays
and clouds of malapert mosquitoes,
from all sides shrilling, humming,
meet him; and in a rage
12 the crumbly shores of Caspian waters
he forthwith leaves.
Ennui! He fares on to the Caucasus.

[For sts. XII–XIV, see vol. 1, pp. 336–37.]

[xiia]
5 Afar are the Caucasian masses.
The way to them is opened. Through their barriers,
beyond their natural ⟨divide⟩,
8 to Georgia war has rushed.
Perchance, by their wild beauty
he might be touched—

263

and so, surrounded by an escort,
12 preceded by a field gun,
⟨Onegin enters⟩ suddenly
the mountains' forecourt, their lugubrious circle.

[XIIb]
He sees: the ranging Térek
shakes and erodes its banks.
Above, from the brow of a beetling crag,
4 a deer hangs, with bent antlers.
Snowslides sweep down and flash;
along sheer cliffs the torrents swish.
'Tween mountains, 'tween two ⟨lofty⟩ walls,
8 a gorge goes; cramped
is the perilous path closer and closer;
the skies above are barely seen;
nature's lugubrious beauty everywhere
12 discloses the same savageness.
Praise, hoary Caucasus, to you:
Onegin's moved for the first time.

[XIIc]
In times of yore, agone,
⟨. . . you knew me⟩ Caucasus!
to your dense sanctuary
4 you ⟨called⟩ me more than once.
Madly I was in love with you,
and noisily ⟨you welcomed me⟩
⟨with your storms' mighty voice⟩.
8 ⟨I heard⟩ your brooks' roar
⟨and rumble⟩ of snowslides,
⟨the cry of eagles⟩, songs of maids,
the fierce roar of the Terek
12 and the far-sounding laughter of the echo;
and I saw, your weak songster,
the kingly crown of Mt. Kazbék.

[XV]
Blest who is old! blest who is ill;
over whom lies Fate's hand.
But I am hale, I am young, free.
4 What have I to expect? Ennui, ennui! . . .

Farewell, summits of snowy mountains,
and you, plains of the Kuban;
he fares to other shores,
8 he from Tamán arrives in the Crimea

[For XV : 9–14–XXIX, see vol. 1, pp. 337–39.]

[XXX]
As said, I lived then in Odessa,
among new-chosen friends,
having forgot the somber scapegrace,
4 the hero of my tale.
With me Onegin never
boasted of a postal friendship,
and I, fortunate man,
8 had never corresponded in a lifetime
with anyone. With what amazement
you may judge I was struck
when he appeared in front of me—
12 like a ghost uninvited,
how loud the friends exclaimed,
and how gladdened I was!

[XXXI]
O sacred Friendship! voice of nature!
⟨Glancing⟩ at one another, presently,
like Cicero's two augurs
4 we softly broke out laughing.

[XXXII]
Not long did we together wander
upon the shores of Euxine waters.
We by the Fates again were parted
4 and were assigned a march.
Onegin, very much cooled down
and glutted with what he had seen,
set out for Neva's banks;
8 while I, from winsome Southern ladies,
from the Black Sea's ⟨plump⟩ oysters,
from the opera, from the dark loges,
and, thank God, from grandees,

12 departed for the shade of Trigorsk woods,
   in a far Northern district,
   and sad was my arrival.

[PENULTIMATE STANZA]
Ah, wheresoever Fate assign
to me a nameless nook;
wherever I may be; withersoever she
4 impel my humble skiff;
wherever a late peace for me she destine;
wherever wait the grave for me;
everywhere, everywhere, within my soul
8 I'll bless my friends.
No, no, nowhere shall I forget
their dear affectionate discourse.
Afar, alone among men,
12 I shall imagine everlastingly
you, shadows of riverside willows,
you, peace and sleep of Trigorsk fields.

[ULTIMATE STANZA]
And Sorot's sloping bank,
and the striped hills,
and in the grove the hidden paths,
4 and the house where we feasted—
retreat, clad in the radiance of the Muses,
by young Yazïkov sung
when from the shrine of learning
8 into our rural circle he arrived
and glorified the nymph of Sorot,
and made the fields around reverberate
with his enchanting verse;
12 but there I too have left my trace,
there, as an offering to the wind, on a dark fir
I've hung my vibrant pipe.

*

Here follows the Comm. on "Fragments of *Onegin's Journey*," consecutively by stanzas, including the fragments printed in vol. 1 and those given above.

[I]

In fair copy (2382, f. 120^r). Except for a slight change in l. 11, this stanza = Eight : x. Pushkin also noted the first line in PB 18, f. 4^r.

VARIANT

13–14 Draft (PD 161):

> and who gave up the ghost
> as senator or general.

In the canceled draft (ibid.), the "senator" is replaced by *kamergér*, "gentleman of the chamber," and in the first variant of the fair copy or final corrected draft (2382, f. 120^r) by "contractor" (*otkupshchik*, "farmer-general"). See also [II] : 7–8.

[II]

In fair copy (2382, f. 119^v).

9–10 / "We are," said Seneca, "born for our fellows' good and for our own": A passage in the treatise *De otio* (On Leisure, Inactivity), by Lucius Annaeus Seneca (d. A.D. 65), addressed to his friend, Annaeus Serenus, reads (III, 3):

Hoc nempe ab homine exigitur, ut prosit hominibus, si fieri potest, multis, si minus, paucis, si minus, proximis, si minus, sibi.

What is, indeed, demanded of a man is to be useful to men: to the many if he can; if not, to the few; if not, to the near; if not, to himself.

And in an epistle (LX) to his friend Caius Lucilius, Seneca writes:

Vivit is, qui multis usui est, vivit is, qui se utitur.

He lives who is useful to many. He lives who is useful to himself.

[III]

In fair copy (2382, f. 119ᵛ). Except for the beginning of l. 1, this stanza = Eight : XI.

[IV]

In fair copy (2382, f, 100ʳ). This stanza = Eight : XII, except for IV : 5–6 and 12 as supplied by *Works* 1960.

[V]

Canceled in the fair copy. This stanza is placed by Acad 1937 and other editions in *Onegin's Journey*. But Pushkin crossed it out in the fair copy and (in a marginal note) assigned it, or part of it, in this or in another form, to Chapter Ten. See Addendum to Notes on "Chapter Ten."

VARIANT

4 By sheer luck we have a photograph of the corrected fair copy (PB 18, f. 4ʳ) of this fifth stanza (and of the first four lines of the next). It is buried in nos. 16–18 (1179 large pages) of *Lit. nasl.* (Moscow, 1934), and the number of the page (nowhere mentioned) is 409. It has been published by Tomashevski, in the course of an essay on Chapter Ten of *EO*, for the purpose of showing in the margin the note "in Canto X," meaning that this fifth stanza (or at least the lines referring to the Slavophilism in Onegin), crossed out by the same pen that scrawled the marginal note, should be transferred to Chapter Ten. The stanza was composed Oct. 2, 1829, and was copied out on or not long before Sept. 18, 1830.

What is especially lucky is that in this photograph we can study Pushkin's work on V : 4. The line of the initial text (in 2382 ff. 119ʳ, 118ᵛ) is carefully deleted here:

⟨*V* Hôtél de Lóndres *chtó v Morskóy*⟩.
in the Hôtel de Londres in Morskaya Street.

Through the erasure one can make out the first word of
the known draft, and perhaps a Latin *t* in the next.
Above this abolished verse, a new line is written:

> *Dozhdlívoy véshneyu poróy.*
> during a rainy vernal spell.

The "vernal" is struck out and the (abbreviated) word
"tedious" (*skúchnoyu*) scrawled above.

With the same heavy pen he used to write the margin-
al note, Pushkin struck out "vernal" and wrote above it
a word that is a mere thick wiggle, but which looks to
Gofman like the abbreviation of the word *skúchnoyu.**

The oldest hotel in St. Petersburg was the Hotel De-
mut, on the Moyka Canal, near Nevski Avenue. It had
been established in the 1760's by the merchant Philip
Jacob Demuth or Demouth (d. 1802). Moreover, De-
muth acquired a large house at the corner of Nevski and
Admiralty Square, where he established another hotel,
London, also known as the Hôtel de Londres. It is not far
from Morskaya Street (which crosses Nevski at a slightly
more southern point), but Pushkin erred in situating it
specifically there.

In his memoirs, Andrey Delvig (1813–87), a cousin of
the poet, mentions stopping at this hotel in his youth
(October, 1826).

William Rae Wilson, an English traveler, has this to

---

*M. Gofman, "Propuschhennïe strofï 'Evgeniya Onegina'"
(Omitted Stanzas of *EO*), in *P. i ego sovr.*, IX, 33–35
(1923), 1–328. Gofman's transcriptions, often elaborate
and sometimes doubtful, are not documented by any photo-
graphic reproductions; but then, in those years of terror
and misery, it was a great feat to produce any transcription at
all.

say in his *Travels in Russia* (London, 1828), I, 218:

> We, at length, found our way to the Hôtel de Londres, and
> . . . agreed to pay for dining-room, bed-room, and serv-
> ant's apartment, seventy-five rubles [sixty-two shillings]
> weekly.

An English physician, Dr. Augustus Bozzi Granville,
who set out for St. Petersburg in July, 1827, having been
engaged by Count Mihail Vorontsov to accompany him
and his Countess on their way back from London via Ger-
many to Russia (the Countess suffered from *mal de mer*),
says, in his chatty *St. Petersburgh. A Journal of Travels
to and from That Capital* (2 vols., London, 1828), I,
466–67:

> The *Hôtel de Londres*, placed at the corner of the [Nevski
> Avenue], and opposite the Admiralty, in a cheerful but
> noisy situation . . . [offers] a sitting-room, and a bed-
> chamber, with breakfast and dinner at the *table d'hôte* . . .
> [for] twelve rubles a day (from eight to ten shillings).

[VI]

In fair copy (PB 18, f. 4ʳ).

2 / June the third: The day after Pushkin's name day. I
note a curious coincidence—in Pope's imitation (1738),
"in the manner of Dr. Swift," of Horace, *Epistles*, bk. I,
no. VII:

> 'Tis true, my Lord, I gave my word,
> I would be with you, June the third . . .

and in Byron, *Don Juan*, I, CIII:

> 'Twas on a summer's day—the sixth of June:
> I like to be particular in dates,
>
> .   .   .   .
>
> They are a sort of post-house, where the Fates
> Change horses, making History change its tune . . .

This is the "fatal day" (I, CXXI, 2) on which Juan's ro-
mance with Julia began, to last till a vaguer date in

November, whereupon the youth was sent on a four-year-long journey, in the course of which he reached the court and bed of Catherine II of Russia in 1784–85. The curious part is that the sixth of June was (N.S., end of the eighteenth century) Pushkin's birthday. "History" did "change its tune" June 6, 1799, N.S.

Don Juan was commenced in Venice, Sept. 6, 1818, and the last complete canto was finished on May 6, 1823. Before leaving Italy for Greece, Byron had composed (May 8, 1823; all these dates are N.S.) fourteen stanzas of an additional, seventeenth, canto. At the time Pushkin was about to begin *EO* in Kishinev (May 9, O.S.; May 21, N.S.).

I do not know why, after establishing the "June the third" reading in Acad 1937, Tomashevski gives "July the third" in *Works* 1949 and 1957.

6–14 Novgorod, ancient Holmgard, was founded by the Vikings at the gray dawn of our era. The "Scandinavian conqueror" is the Norman Rurik, whom legend has invade, in the 860's, the east bank of the Volhov River, which flows through Novgorod. Rurik's descendants transferred their throne to Kiev. Yaroslav the Wise (r. 1015–54), author of the first Russian Code, granted Novgorod important privileges, and by the thirteenth century the town had gained a kind of republican independence, with a public assembly, the *veche*, governing the region through an elected chief, the *posadnik*. But with the lugubrious rise of Moscow and its ruthless despots the "Volhov Republic" fell amid horrific massacres. Ivan III in 1471 imposed his law upon it. The bell (*vechevoy kolokol*) convoking the people to the *veche* is termed "rebellious" in allusion to the efforts of the stouthearted Novgorodans to resist Moscow; but nothing availed, and Ivan IV the Terrible destroyed the last vestiges of Novgorodan liberty in 1570.

Commentary

In this stanza our poet limits himself to a singularly poor description of Novgorod: "half-wild" (*poludíkoy*) has no pictorial sense, a bell is not "amidst" public squares, "rebellious" (*myatézhnïy*) is ambiguous, though not new, the four "giants" are of very unequal stature, and the "bowed-down" or "drooping" (*poníknuvshie*) churches, around which a ghostly people swarms, resemble snowmen in a thaw.

In his letter to Pushkin of Oct. 18, 1824 (see my n. to Eight : LI : 3–4), the Decembrist Prince Sergey Volkonski, writing from St. Petersburg to Mihaylovskoe, suggested that "the vicinity of Great Novgorod, the memory of its *vechevoy kolokol*," would inspire Pushkin.

VARIANT

3 Draft (2382, f. 118ᵛ) and canceled fair copy (PB 18, f. 4ʳ):

a Viennese calash . . .

Cf. the "imported calash" of Seven : V : 2.

[VII]

In fair copy (PB 18, ff. 4ᵛ, 5ʳ).

3 / like shadows, flicker-flick / *Mel'káyut mél'kom búdto téni*: A curious prefiguration of cinematography.

4 / Valdáy, Torzhók, and Tver: This is the order of these towns in a southeastern direction, between Novgorod (which is a hundred miles S of Petersburg) and Moscow, a distance of about three hundred miles. Valday is a burg situated in a hilly region on the south shore of beautiful Valday Lake. Torzhok, a larger town, was at the time famous for its leathern and velvet goods. Onegin reaches the Volga and the large city of Tver (now Ka-

linin). He has still a hundred miles to go before reaching
Moscow.

It is curious to compare the stylized account of
Onegin's route in the stanza to Pushkin's ribald descrip-
tion of his journey along the same highway—but in an
opposite direction—in a letter of Nov. 9, 1826, from
Mihaylovskoe, to Sergey Sobolevski (a disreputable but
talented and cultured friend with whom he stayed in
Moscow on his crucial visit there from Mihaylovskoe,
September–October, 1826). He left Moscow for Opochka
on the morning of Nov. 2, broke two wheels, continued
by stage, and, via Tver, arrived next evening in Torzhok
(130 miles). At Novgorod he turned west toward Pskov.
The whole journey from Moscow to Opochka (450 miles)
took him eight days.

In this epistle there are six quatrains in trochaic
tetrameters, which he suggests be read to the tune of
Once upon a Time a Turkey (a facetious ballad of twenty
trochaic tetrameters by Baratïnski and Sobolevski),*
and which contain various viatic suggestions. At Gali-
ani's tavern (with an obscene pun, showing some knowl-
edge of Italian, on the name in the rhyme) in Tver, he
recommends macaroni with Parmesan, and at Pozhar-
ski's, in Torzhok, that restaurant's famous *côtelette*s. In
the last stanza he advises the traveler to buy bangle buns
for tea from Valday's *podátlivïh* ("yielding") peasant
girls. It will be noted that the epithet in the *Journey*
(VII : 5) is less colorful (*privyázchivïh*, "clinging," "ob-
trusive," "pertinacious," "overaffectionate").

Pushkin's letter to Sobolevski drolly adumbrates
Onegin's journey and, with its mixture of prose and
verse, its light tone, its attention to good cheer, reflects

---

*Published later, 1831, in Voeykov's *Russkiy invalid*, no. 6,
lit. suppl., under the title *A True Story* (*Bïl'*) and over the
signature "Stalinski," according to *Pushkin* (1936), pp. 522–24
(Letopisi gosudarstvennogo literaturnogo muzeya I).

in miniature the seventeenth-century joint composition known as *Le Voyage de Chapelle et de Bachaumont* (*Voyage de Languedoc*, 1656, by Claude Emmanuel Lhuillier, known as Chapelle, 1626–86, and his friend, François le Coigneux de Bachaumont, 1624–1702).

Aleksey Vulf, who traveled with Pushkin along the same route in mid-January, 1829 (from Staritsa, in the province of Tver, to St. Petersburg), calls the *baranki*-vending girls at Valday "cheap belles" (*P. i ego sovr.*, VI, 21–22 [1915–16], 52).

Aleksandr Radishchev (1749–1802), the liberal-minded author of *A Journey from St. Petersburg to Moscow*, printed on his private press, a work for which he was banished to Siberia by Catherine the Great for the rest of her reign, but which Alexander I allowed to be published in 1810. The *Journey* is a clumsily worded but fiery piece of eighteenth-century prose directed against oppression and slavery. Pushkin, who condemned its style (see his posthumously published essay, "Aleksandr Radishchev," written August, 1836), knew it well. In it there occurs the following passage (a fact suggestive of a sly attempt on Pushkin's part to smuggle Radishchev's shade into *Onegin's Journey*):

Who has not visited the Valday Hills, who does not know the Valday *baranki* and the rouged Valday wenches? Every time a traveler passes by, these brazen Valday wenches, shedding all shame, stop him and meretriciously attempt to fan the passenger's lust.

Baranki, "bangle buns," are known commercially in the U. S. as "bagels" (through the Yiddish).

11 The "versts" mean the wooden posts (painted white with black stripes) indicating the stretches. A verst is 0.6 of a mile. The coachmen, *yamshchiki*, driving the post troikas were called "post-boors" by English travelers of the time.

274

[VIII]

In fair copy (PB 18, f. 5ʳ).

5 / [Moscow] English Club: Should not be confused with the incomparably more fashionable St. Petersburg English Club (colloquially, *Angliyskiy klub* or *klob*; officially, Sankt-Peterburgskoe Angliyskoe Sobranie; it was founded in 1770, and Pushkin was a member from 1832 to his death). Cf. Blagorodnoe Sobranie (Assembly of Nobility); n. to Seven : LI : 1.

6 / of parliament sessions / *naródnïh zasedániy*: "Of the people's sessions"—meaning *parlamentskih zasedaniy*.

8 / gruels: Boiled groats, hot cereals (buckwheat, barley, millet, etc.), fancy varieties of which, boiled, served with meat, enfolded in pies, or porridged and buttered, are favorite features of a Russian's fare.

12 / spy / *shpión*: A government spy, a secret agent working for the political police, is meant here as well as in Two : XIVb : 5. Pushkin himself, even in his Odessa days, had been accused by contemptible gossips of "working for the government,"* as did one of his most glamorous lady friends (Countess Caroline Sobanski; see n. to Eight : XVII : 9). The word "promotes" (*proizvódit*), which in another connection, at the end of this stanza, echoes the "promote" of Two : XIVb : 5, tends to prove that the latter passage was in Pushkin's mind when this stanza was written (seven years later, in the autumn of 1830).

---

*See also the draft of a letter to Vyazemski (Sept. 1, 1828, St. Petersburg): "Aleksey Poltoratski, twaddling in Tver, mentioned that I am a spy, that I get 2500 rubles a month (which, thanks to craps, would have come in very handy), and distant cousins are already coming to me for situations and the tsar's favors."

14 / an eligible bachelor / *v zhenihí*: One wonders if a mysterious undated stanza, with an *EO* rhyme scheme and an *EO* family air, written on a scrap of gray paper, and first published, with the verses in a wrong sequence (1–6, 10–14, 7–9) and containing other errors, as a separate poem by I. Shlyapkin in 1903 (*Iz neizdan-nïh bumag A. S. Pushkina*, p. 22), may not have been planned by our poet to come somewhere here, where rumors of Onegin's being an eligible bachelor are circulated:

> Marry? Whom? Vera Chátski?
> Too old. Miss Rádin?* Too naïve.
> The Hálski girl? She has a silly laugh.
> 4 The Shípov girl? Too poor, too fat.
> Miss Mínski? Breathes with too much languor.
> Miss Tórbin? She composes ballads,
> her mother kisses you, father's a fool.
> 8 Well, then, Miss [N-ski?] Catch me doing that—
> and getting flunkydom for kin!
> Miss Lípski? What a *ton*!
> A million airs, grimaces.
> 12 Miss Lídin? What a family!
> You're offered walnuts at their house,
> they at the theater drink beer.

The various editions I have consulted print this as a dialogue (between Onegin and a friend suggesting he marry). I take it to be a soliloquy akin to One : I, but have not seen the MS.

Works 1949, V, 562, corrects the sequence of lines, writes "Miss Lidin" and "Grusha Lipski," and (following Shlyapkin) omits the editorial question mark after "Miss Lenski." I cannot believe Pushkin could have

---

*Shlyapkin has "Solin" for "Radin," "Masha Lanski" for "Lipski," and "Sitski" for "Lidin." *Works* 1936, I, 596, misplaces the lines (following Shlyapkin), has "Lida" (*na Líde*) instead of "Miss Lidin" (*na Lídinoy*), has "Masha Lipski" instead of Shlyapkin's "Masha Lanski," and instead of my "Miss N-ski" has "Miss Lenski."

used that name within this context—unless the passage was written not in 1829–30 (when the *Journey* was written) but between May and October, 1823 (before Canto Two, in which Lenski appears, was begun). Let us have the MS reproduced.

The name "Chatski" is probably taken from Griboedov's *Woe from Wit.* If so, this stanza must have been written not before 1825. "Radin," "Minski," and so on are invented names of the kind given to gentlefolk in novels and plays of the time. *Tsalúet mát'*, "mother kisses [you]," alludes to a provincial way a matronly hostess might have of kissing a visitor on the brow while he kisses her hand. However, in the 1957 edition, Tomashevski reads *Shalún'ya mat'*, "the mother is a romp," a not-very-convincing recension.

According to Shlyapkin, the following canceled readings can be made out (ll. 2 and 3): "Miss Sédin," "Miss Rzhévski."

I notice that Zenger, in her excellent article on certain draftings, in *Pushkin, rodonachal'nik novoy russkoy literaturï* (1941), pp. 31–47, also concludes that the stanza may refer to the Moscow section of *Onegin's Journey.*

VARIANTS

2 Draft (2382, f. 118ʳ):

. . . Oriental bustle . . .

8 Canceled draft (ibid.):

Chatámov prén'ya slíshit ón.
of Chathams the debates hears he.

William Pitt the Elder, Earl of Chatham (1708–78), English statesman.

[IX]

1 -2 From the fair copy (PB 18).

1–3 From Moscow, in July, 1821, Onegin drives directly east three hundred miles to Nizhni Novgorod (now Gorki), an old town on an old hill at the confluence of the Volga and the Oka. Nizhni's famous citizen, a butcher by trade and a politician by inclination, Kuzma Minin-Suhorukiy, was instrumental in promoting a victorious rising against the Polish invaders of the Moscow state in 1611–12.

Makariev is a reference to the famous Makariev Market in Nizhni, whither it had been transferred, in 1817, from Makariev, a town some sixty miles east of it. The fair was held in midsummer. The "bustle" is rather automatically repeated in [v] : 11 and [viii] : 2.

According to the "list of goods and capital announced at the Director's Office, at the fair of [Nizhni Novgorod], in the year 1821" (i.e., at the time of Onegin's visit), there were, among forty items of merchandise, "Small silver plate and pearls" for 1,500,000 rubles, "Wine and brandy" for 6,580,000 rubles, and "horses" for 1,160,000 rubles (as quoted by Lyall, *Travels*, II, 349–51).

[x]

From the fair copy (PB 18).

2 / "paragon of rivers, lakes," the Volga: Dmitriev's rococo ode *To the Volga*, l. 4. It consists of nine ten-line stanzas in iambic tetrameter rhymed according to the sequence in French and Russian odes: ababeeciic. Karamzin received the MS of this ode from Dmitriev Sept. 6, 1794. The passage reads (ll. 2–7):

> completed is the happy voyage,
> and you that brought us to the shore,
> O Volga, paragon of rivers, lakes,
> their chief, their queen, their honor and their glory,

O sumptuous, stately Volga,
adieu! . . .

8 / The Volga swells: In result of midsummer rains at its
upper reaches—as has been known to occur in certain
years.

13–14 / Stenka Razin . . .: The famous robber chief, hero
of several songs, a riparian Robin Hood of sorts, but con-
siderably more sanguinary than the good yeoman. L. 14
runs "begored the Volga wave." The Soviet policy being
to present Robin Razin as an early promoter of the
People's Revolution, Comrade Brodski suggests that this
l. 14 is merely a romantic reference to a song in which
Razin casts a sweetheart of his—a Persian princess—into
the Volga wave (so that cosmopolitan love may not inter-
fere with patriotic communistic activities). But Persian
princesses do not necessarily bleed when drowning—and
what about the beginning of the next stanza?

The epithet "canvas" (l. 4) also occurs in a song
about Stenka Razin (the one referred to in my n. to
Five : XVII : 7–8), derived by Pushkin from folk poetry
(l. 10):

> *Raspustí parusá polotnyánïe . . .*
> spread your canvas sails . . .

[XI]

From Nizhni Onegin sails down the Volga toward Astra-
han, a leisurely voyage of about two thousand miles,
with stops at Kazan, Sïzran, Saratov, and so on. I should
date Onegin's brief stay on the Caspian shores late
autumn, 1821.

7 I cannot understand the failure of Soviet commentators,

who are usually thankful for any scrap of revolutionary offal they can obtain from *EO*, to notice that the naïve phrase "memories [*vospominán'ya*] of former days" relates not to private but to historical memories, and refers, doubtlessly, to the civil and military rebellion in Astrahan in the reign of Peter the Great; the insurrection, starting as a protest against harsh taxes, lasted from July 30, 1705, to March 12, 1706, and more than two thousand people were executed after it had been quenched.

9 The mosquitoes of Astrahan are berated by several travelers. See, for example, Voeykov's "Logbook" in his magazine *Literary News* (*Novosti literaturï*), no. 9 (Aug., 1824). The classic account, however, of the "affecting visitation" of Tatary mosquitoes is that by E. D. Clarke (*Travels in Various Countries*, II, 59–61), whom they almost killed one July night in 1800 on the banks of the Kuban.

The draft of XI (2382, f. 117ᵛ) is dated Oct. 3 [1829, Pavlovskoe, province of Tver].

[XII]

1 / Térek: A Caucasian river that has its source in a small glacier in the Central Chain on Mt. Kazbek (see n. to XIII : 2–4). The Terek skirts the Kazbek group and flows turbulently in a general NE direction through a series of gorges (such as the Daryal Canyon) along which runs the Military Georgian Road (see n. to l. 13). Below Vladikavkaz the Terek collects the waters of various mountain streams, flows N toward the steppe country, then turns resolutely E and continues its course to the Caspian Sea.

10–12 See n. to XIIa : 8.

13 / Arágva and Kurá: Rivers S of the Central Chain. The Aragva, a mountain stream, rises NW of the Pass of the Cross (7957 ft.), flows sixty miles S, and falls into the Kura's livid waters.

The Kura, the most important river in Transcaucasia, rises NW of Kars, Turkey, and flows E across Georgia to the Caspian Sea.

The Pass of the Cross, where the highway traverses the main range of mountains, which runs roughly from NW to SE across the breadth of the Caucasus, is famous in literature for being described in the beginning of Lermontov's *A Hero of Our Time* (pub. 1839–40). (An English translation of it by Dmitri Nabokov was published New York, 1958.)

The so-called Military Georgian Road (the construction of which was begun in 1811), running from Vladikavkaz, some fifty miles N of the pass, winds through the Aragva Valley S to Tiflis, the capital of Georgia, a journey of about 135 miles.

[XIIa]

In draft (PD 168).

8 / to Georgia / *do Grúzii:* In earlier Soviet editions the reading here has always been *do glubiní,* "to the bottom," but *Works* 1957, without explications (as is the rule in this ridiculously laconic edition), prints *do Grúzii;* Georgia is the region in southern Caucasia (Transcaucasia) bounded by the Black Sea in the W and the Dagestan region in the E.

The gradual annexation of the Caucasus by Russia went on intermittently from the capture of Derbent in 1722 by Peter I to the capture of the leader of the Lezgians, Shamyl, in 1859. The advance of the Russian Empire in the Orient (narrowly watched by England

Commentary

and stubbornly opposed by Turkey) was realized by
various means, from semivoluntary integration (e.g.,
Georgia in 1801) to a series of fierce wars with the moun-
taineers, of whom various Moslemized Circassian tribes
offered the toughest resistance.

12 / by a field gun / *púshkoyu stepnóy*: A fieldpiece for use
in the steppes.

[xiib]

In draft (PD 168).

[xiic]

In draft (2382, f. 39ᵛ).

On Sept. 24, 1820, from Kishinev, Pushkin wrote to his
brother Lev, in Petersburg:

. . . Upon my arrival in Ekaterinoslav [about May 20,
1820], feeling bored, I went for a boat trip on the Dnepr,
took a dip, and, as usual with me, caught a fever. General
Raevski, who was traveling to the Caucasus with his son
[Nikolay] and his two daughters [Maria and Sofia], found
me in a Jew's shack, doctorless, with a mug of iced lemon-
ade. Young Raevski (you know our close friendship and
the important, unforgettable services he rendered me) [an
allusion to the fact that the trip to the Caucasus had been
planned at least a month earlier] suggested my traveling
also to the Caucasian spas, and the physician [a Dr.
Rudïkovski] they had with them promised not to do me
to death.

Further he describes the wild beauty of the Caucasus:

The curative springs are all situated at a short distance
from one another, in the extreme spurs of the Caucasus
Mountains. I regret, my friend, that you did not see with
me that magnificent range, those ice-covered summits,
which, from afar, at a clear sunrise, look like bizarre

clouds, varicolored and motionless; I regret you did not climb the peaks of Beshtu's five hills. . . .

(See n. to XIII : 2–4.)

4 / more than once: Pushkin visited the Caucasus twice—in the summers of 1820 and 1829. Artistically, the account in the *Journey* is much inferior to his beautiful "A Journey to Erzerum," a prose description of his 1829 trip, published 1836 in his literary review *The Contemporary* (*Sovremennik*).

Pushkin took part in the Caucasian campaign of 1829 as a poet, informal war correspondent, would-be lancer, *bon vivant*, and semiprofessional gamester. He traveled in the first week of May from Moscow to Tiflis via Kaluga and Oryol, after which he drove through the green Voronezh steppes and then by the Military Georgian Road from Ekaterinoslav to Vladikavkaz (May 21) and Tiflis, where he stayed from May 27 to June 10. Count Paskevich, the commander in chief, permitted Pushkin to ride to Erzerum (with the Nizhegorodski dragoons, in which Nikolay Raevski, Jr., and Lev Pushkin served). On June 11, near the fort Gergeti, Pushkin met the coffin of Griboedov, who had been murdered in Teheran. On June 14, he attempted to take part in a skirmish with the Turkish cavalry. His civilian coat and round hat (*chapeau rond*) puzzled the Russian troops, who mistook him for a German doctor or Lutheran clergyman. On June 27, he witnessed the taking of Erzerum and stayed there for almost a month. About July 20 he left for Tiflis and Pyatigorsk, left Pyatigorsk in the second week of September, and was back in Moscow before Sept. 21.

[XIII]

3–4 / Beshtú . . . Mashúk: The reference is to the conic peaks of Besh Tau, a five-coned eminence timbered with oak and beech N and E of Pyatigorsk, a mineral-spring resort in the northern Caucasus. These peaks are Mt. Besh (4590 ft.); Mt. Iron (Zheleznaya, 2795 ft.); Mt. Snake (Zmeinaya, 3261 ft.); Mt. Mashuk (3258 ft.); and Mt. Bald (Lïsaya, 2427 ft.). Some fifty miles to the S, in the western part of the Central Chain (running from parallel 44° in NW Caucasus to parallel 41° in SE Caucasus), loom Mt. Elbruz, the highest mountain in Europe (about 18,500 ft.), and Mt. Kazbek (about 16,500 ft.).

Onegin spends more than a year (1822) in the Caucasus. The next celebrated literary character to stay at its spas and cross its passes is Lermontov's Pechorin (1830–38).

6 / its magic brooks / *ruch'yóv egó volshébnïh*: I suspect that my translation is too nice and that Pushkin meant merely "founts" or "streams."

Cf. Fontanes' description of a similar resort (Bagnères), in his *Les Pyrénées* (c. 1805):

> Le vieillard de maux escorté,
> Le héros encor tourmenté
> De cicatrices douloureuses,
> La mélancolique beauté
> . . . .
> Viennent chercher ici les jeux ou la santé . . .
> . . . .
> L'ennui, les sombres maladies
> Et la goutte aux mains engourdies
> Tout cède au breuvage enchanté . . .

9 / Cypris: A euphemism for *Lues venerea*. Pushkin is known to have suffered from a venereal disease—gonorrhea and/or some form of syphilis—at least three times in his life (January, 1818, in St. Petersburg; spring, 1819, same place; and mid-July, 1826, after a visit to a Pskov brothel).

[XIV]

4 / [smoking] / *dïmnïe*: Misprinted *zimnïe*; "wintery." A curious repetition of the slip mentioned in Pushkin's n. 17.

VARIANT

13–14 PB 18, f. 7ᵛ:

> I also, like those gentlemen,
> with hope might be acquainted then.

[XV]

1–8 In fair copy (PB 18).

6 / Kubán: A river that rises in a glacier at the foot of Mt. Elbruz and flows N and W to the Sea of Azov.

6–8 / plains of the Kuban . . . Crimea: From central Caucasus Onegin travels some four hundred miles in a NW direction to the tip of the Taman peninsula, where he boards a ship for the Crimea. This is Pushkin's route of early August, 1820. In a letter to his brother (Sept. 24, 1820) from Kishinev to Petersburg, he writes:

> I saw [on Aug. 8, 1820] the banks of the Kuban and outposts—admired our Cossacks: always in the saddle, always ready to fight, always on the lookout. I rode in sight of inimical plains belonging to free mountain tribes. We were escorted by sixty Cossacks, and behind them there dragged a loaded cannon. . . .

Our poet saw the Crimea for the first time not from board ship but from Taman, in mid-August, 1820, across the Kerch Strait (same letter to Lev). It will be recalled that Pechorin, in Lermontov's story "Taman" (1840), sees from the town of that name, on an azure morning, "the distant shoreline of the Crimea, which stretches in a lilac band and ends in a cliff with the white of a lighthouse perceivable on its summit" (note "lilac," a color that is absent from Pushkin's classical palette).

Pushkin sailed from Taman to Kerch, his first stop on the Crimean peninsula. At Kerch (Aug. 15, at sunset) he visited the ruins of a tower called the Sepulcher of Mithridates: "There I picked a flower as a memento, and next day lost it without regret"—quoted from the "Extract from a Letter to D[elvig]" (first pub. in *Northern Flowers* for 1826), a deliberately supercilious narrative, which our poet prefixed to the third edition, 1830, of his *Fountain of Bahchisaray*.

From Kerch Pushkin traveled by land south to Feodosiya (ancient Kaffa), on the SE coast of the Crimean peninsula, sixty-three miles—a day's journey. There he spent the night (now No. 5 Olginskaya Street), and next day (Aug. 18), at dawn, with the Raevskis boarded a navy brig, which took them along the shore in a general SW direction. During the voyage he wrote a Byronic elegy ("Extinguished is the orb of day"), published at the end of the year in the review *Son of the Fatherland*, and incorrectly dated "September" by Lev Pushkin, who received it with his brother's September letter.

At dawn, Aug. 19, they landed at Gurzuf (for a discussion of the emotional mystery in the last lines of XVI, see my n. to One : XXXIII : 1). There he spent three blissful weeks with the—now reunited—Raevski family at the villa placed at their disposal by Armand Emmanuel du Plessis, Duc de Richelieu.

About Sept. 5 he left Gurzuf with the general and his son. They visited "the fabulous ruins of Diana's temple" near the Georgievskiy monastery and taking the Balaklava Road reached Bahchisaray, the very center of the Crimea, some sixty miles from the seacoast. Bahchi Saray means "garden palace," and the place lives up to its name. It was the residence of the Tatar khans from the beginning of the sixteenth century to the end of the eighteenth. A little fountain trickles from a rusty pipe into dimples of marble in a cool hall, where swallows dart in and out. I saw the place in July, 1918, during a lepidopterological excursion.

From Bahchisaray our travelers rode (on the eighth) to Simferopol, whence, via Odessa (mid-September), Pushkin reached Kishinev Sept. 21.

8 / Tamán: A Black Sea port in the extreme NW corner of the Caucasus, on Taman Gulf (an eastern inlet of Kerch Strait), about 250 miles NW of Suhum, a western Caucasian maritime town. Here, too, Lermontov's Pechorin has an adventure, in the least successful section ("Taman") of *A Hero of Our Time.*

10 / with Orestes argued Pylades: As retold in old French *mythologies*, from which Pushkin and his readers gained familiar information about these things, the legendary young man Orestes and his faithful friend Pylades, being desirous to obtain purification from a complicated vendetta that they had brought to a successful close, were directed by the oracle at Delphi, in Greece, to bring thither a statue of Artemis (Diana) from Tauric Chersonese (Korsun, near Sebastopol). So to the land of the Tauri the two sailed. King Thoas, high priest of the goddess' temple, ordered the young strangers to be sacrificed, as was the rule. Orestes and Pylades heroically argued with one another, each desiring to die in the other's place. Both escaped, with Iphigenia (a local priestess, who turned out to be the sister of Orestes) and the statue.

Pushkin calls Orestes *Atrid*, meaning "one of the Atridae."

11 / Mithridates: Mithridates the Great, King of Pontus, who in 63 B.C. ordered an obedient Gallic mercenary to

kill him. His alleged tomb and throne are shown on Mt. Mitridat, a knoll near Kerch, a port on the Sea of Azov (see above, n. to 6–8).

12–14 Adam Bernard Mickiewicz (1798–1855), Polish poet and patriot, spent four and a half years in Russia (from October, 1824, to March, 1829). During that time he visited the Crimea—five years after Pushkin; i.e., in the autumn of 1825—and composed his eighteen admirable *Crimean Sonnets* (*Sonety Krymskie*) upon his return to Odessa, completing his work on them in 1826 in Moscow. The Polish text was published there in December, 1826, and the first, very mediocre, Russian versions came out in 1827 (by Vasiliy Shchastnïy) and 1829 (by Ivan Kozlov). Mickiewicz evokes Pushkin's *Fountain of Bahchisaray* in Sonnet VIII, *Grob Potocki* (the mausoleum of a Tatar Kahn's wife believed to have been a Polish maiden of the Potocki family). In that sonnet, as well as in others, especially in Sonnet XIV, *The Pilgrim* (*Pielgrzym*), Mickiewicz nostalgically recalls his native Lithuania.

Pushkin made his acquaintance in October, 1826, in Moscow, but the cordiality of this relationship did not survive later political events. The Polish insurrection broke out Nov. 17/29, 1830, and continued for about nine months. The news of the uprising in Warsaw was communicated by Nicholas I to the officers of the guard at a trooping of colors on Nov. 26, 1830. He said that he was sure they would help to quell it. Generals and officers broke into huzzas and started to kiss the hands of Nicholas and the rump of his horse as if the man were a centaur. Pushkin, much to the distress of Vyazemski and A. Turgenev, gave the quelling of the revolt overenthusiastic support. In his iambs *To the Slanderers of Russia* (August, 1831) and in the odic *Anniversary of Borodino* (September, 1831), our poet indulges in a torrent of lurid nationalism and speaks in cold mocking tones of the defeat of rebellious Poland. In a blank-verse fragment dated Aug. 10, 1834, Petersburg, he recalls Mickiewicz's visit and happy sojourn among an "alien race" and contrasts the guest's serene discourses with the "baneful verses" ("dog's barks," in a canceled draft, a phrase that ties up with the end of Mickiewicz's poem addressed "to Russian friends," in which the voice of any Russian who might resent the Polish poet's attack on despotism is compared to the bark of a dog biting the liberating hand) that the angry poet now directs at Russia from the west: Mickiewicz in 1832–34, living in exile in Dresden and Paris, in satirical verse (copied out by Pushkin in Cahier 2373, ff. 35ᵛ, 34ᵛ) accuses his former Russian friends of being bribed by their government, of glorifying the triumph of their tyrant, and of exulting in the sufferings of the Poles. It is owing rather to Mickiewicz's fine personality than to historical reality that the idea of "liberalism" became associated at the time with the idea of "Poland," a country that in some of its periods of sovereignty was as autocratic as Russia.

Pushkin greatly admired Mickiewicz's works. In October, 1833, at Boldino, he composed one of his very few anapaestic pieces, a fine-toned but hopelessly inexact version of Mickiewicz's ballad *The Three Sons of Budrys.*

VARIANTS

12 In the fair copy (PB 18) "the inspired exile" replaces "inspired Mickiewicz."

12–14 Canceled drafts (2382, f. 115ᵛ):

> There my inspired Mickiéwicz
> .   .   .   .
> composed immortal verses.

and (l. 14):

> composed his sonnets.

[XVII–XIX]

Literary fashions are delightfully epitomized in these stanzas. They illustrate two subspecies of romanticism.

As I have noted elsewhere (see n. to Six : XXIII : 2), the generalized form of romanticism can be traced back to the contrived Arcadia of Italian and Spanish romance. From its lowland meadows distraught lovers—wretched knights and young scholars—would repair to its montane zone and run amuck there in amorous madness. Clouds masked the moon and brooks murmured in pastoral poesy as allegorically as rack and rill were to do above and below Lenski's tomb some three centuries later. In the eighteenth century, Swiss and Scottish guides pointed out to the panting poet the waterfall and its lugubrious conifers. From there it was an easy mule's ride to the desolate Byronic scene—up to the boulders above timber-line or down to the sea cliffs where the surf boomed. This generalized subspecies of romanticism is closely associated with the pathological dislike that the Age of Reason had for the specific "unpoetical" detail and with its passion for the generic term. In this sense the "romanticism" of Byron logically continues "classicism." The vague term merely became vaguer, and the moonlit ruins remained as noble and blurry as the "passions" inspired by incest in ancient plays. As I have also noted before, only in a few snowscape stylizations did Pushkin switch (in the established text) from the generalized Arcadian vista to the specific description. In the depiction of nature his leanings were always on the side of the eighteenth century. St. XVIII illustrates critically the second, specific, phase of romanticism, its interest in "ordinary" details and in "realistic" trivialities, having none of that natural poetical residue that the words "ocean" or "nightingale" had. It is in connection with this new fashion that the Flemish masters—and the Elizabethan playwrights—were rediscovered by the romanticists.

Finally, it should be noted that in these stanzas Pushkin uses an allusion to recent literary trends, the transition from the "poetical" Oriental fountain to the "unpoetical" duck pond, as an allegory of personal life. One can also find some analogy between the evolution he outlines here and that which he suggests in relation to Lenski in sts. XXXVI and XXXIX of Chapter Six.

[XVII]

VARIANT

In a draft (2382, f. 111ʳ), probably referring to l. 8, Pushkin pleasingly alludes to the shade of olive and mulberry trees—which at once reconstructs in one's mind the stony trails leading up the mountainside from the southern Crimean shore. The mulberry (and the rather unexpected pineapple) had been already mentioned by Mickiewicz in 1826, in his Sonnet XIV, *The Pilgrim*, as a component of the Crimean landscape.

[XVIII]

2 / hillside slope / *kosogór*: The Russian word implies a twofold incline: the sloping of the hillside and the slanting of a road (or some other definite stretch of ground) coming down it diagonally.

6 The word *gumno* means "barn" or "granary," including the threshing floor and the resulting store of grain.

13 / peace / *pokóy*: See n. to l. 20 of Onegin's Letter in Eight and n. to Eight : XLVIIIa : 1, above, p. 253.

14 / *shchey* [gen.; *shchi*, nom.]: Cabbage soup. In this line

Commentary

Pushkin uses a Russian proverb meaning "my fare is plain but I am my own master."

5–6 The draft (PB 18, ff. 1ʳ, 2ᵛ) reads:

> and through a sunny meadow
> afar a peasant maiden running . . .

with a variant for l. 6:

> and shapely washerwomen near the dam . . .

13 Draft (ibid.):

> a simple, quiet wife . . .

[XIX]

5–11 See *The Fountain of Bahchisaray* (a poem of 578 lines in iambic tetrameter, freely rhymed, composed, 1822, at Kishinev, and published, 1824, Moscow, with an essay by Vyazemski), especially ll. 505–59, describing Pushkin's visit to the former "Garden Palace" of the khans, where the answer to *Journey*, XIX : 7–10, is given in ll. 533–38, with the same rhyme *shum* ("noise," "purl") and *um* ("mind").

A deliberately "prosaic" description of the fountain is added by Pushkin in a note to the poem; and this may be compared to the "dross" of the *Journey*, XIX : 1–4.

[XX]

1 We are not shown Onegin actually participating in the gay Italianate life of Odessa (XX–XXIX). Not he, but our other hero, Pushkin, is seen enjoying it in these ten stanzas, which echo in a Southern strain the theatrical,

erotical, and gastronomical delights of the Petersburg life depicted in Chapter One.

In that Chapter One, Pushkin intermingled his Petersburg recollections with the circumstances of his life in Odessa at the time of his writing about them (autumn, 1823). We had a glimpse there (One : L) of his roaming along the shore line and yearning for a sail that would carry him from Russia to Africa, reversing his ancestor's route. The present stanzas of the *Journey* are being written in the enforced seclusion of Mihaylovskoe, early in 1825. The Odessa of 1823–24, a mere harbor of nostalgia at the time, is evoked now, in 1825, with as much delectation as the pleasures of Petersburg then were. And the "golden Italy" of One : XLIX has now dwindled to a recollection of melodious Italian voices in the streets of Odessa.

2 / There for a long time skies are clear: A tetrametric condensation of Tumanski's Alexandrine—the second line of his poem *Odessa* (quoted in my n. to XXI : 1–9).

VARIANTS

5–14 Gofman (1936) quotes the following rough-draft fragments (2370, f. 66ʳ; see also p. 464 in Acad 1937)—A, ll. 8–9:

> There the bland merchant's
> sportive companion [*rézvaya podrúga*, Fr.
> *compagne folâtre*] shines.

and B, ll. 5–6:

> . . . I lived there as a poet,
> logless in winter, droshkyless in summer . . .

(For A, ll. 8–9, see n. to XXVIII : 5–14.)

Apparently the gap between this and the following lines was to be filled with some reference to future improvements of Odessa's canalization. A draft reads (ll. 12–14):

> and instead of Count Vorontsov
> there will be some fresh water there—
> and thither we shall then repair.

Which reminds one of the Lord Chancellor, equated, through "M'lud," with London's "mud," in the first chapter (written November, 1851) of Dickens' *Bleak House*.

13 Canceled draft (2370, f. 66^r):

> and a black guest from my own land . . .

meaning—an African.

[XXI]

1–9 / Odessa in sonorous verses our friend Tumanski has described . . .: Tumanski, a minor poet, Pushkin's fellow clerk in Count Vorontsov's bureau, in 1824 dedicated the following ponderous iambic hexameters to Odessa:

> This region, glorified by fame of martial days,
> Where for a long time skies do gratify the gaze,
> Where murmur cottonwoods, where waves are blue and
>   bold,
> Where nature's radiance dumfounds the son of cold.
> Beneath the canopy of evening clouds so light,
> Here you may drink the breath of gardens with delight . . .

and so forth—ten limp lines more.

6–7 / roam . . . above the sea: The image of Tumanski, who "went off to roam" (*poshyól bródit'*) "above the sea," i.e., along the sea front, *nad mórem*, repeats in a lighter key the anxious "I roam above the sea" (*Brozhú nad mórem*) of One : L : 3. A curious dovetailing, at the

Odessa port, of the beginning and of the end of our novel. The harassed gray Muse of translation has granted me a natural rhyme here ("then–pen," *potóm–peróm*) in recompense for having noticed the way a theme tapers to a sparkling point of blue sea.

11 / *stép' nagáya*: Lyall, *Travels*, I, 190; passage referring to May, 1822:

> The environs of Odéssa present a pleasing sight. The former arid *step* is now covered by villages, and farms, and cultivated fields, which near the town, are intermixed with villas, nurseries, and public and private gardens.

[XXII]

3 / muddy Odessa: Lyall, *Travels*, I, 171: "The streets of Odéssa . . . are still unpaved . . . [and] indescribably dirty in autumn and spring after heavy rain . . ."

*

From Odessa, Pushkin wrote Vyazemski, Oct. 14, 1823 (by that time Onegin had already turned up): " 'Tis dull and cold, I shiver under the Southern sky." And to Aleksandr Turgenev, Dec. 1, 1823: "Two cantos are ready" (by then Onegin had supplied his biographer with the data for Chapter Two).

10 / on stilts / *na hodúlyah*: I seem to have read somewhere the remark that Odessans (who speak the worst Russian in Russia) call the clogs they wear on days of slush *hoduli* ("walkies"!); I doubt, however, that Pushkin would have used such vulgar slang in so pointless an instance. The hyperbole on which the whole stanza rests would collapse.

[XXIII]

1–3 / hammer . . . city / *mólot* . . . *górod*: An incorrect rhyme, one of the few bad ones in *EO*. The others are the terminals of Two : VI : 10–11 and Three : XIV : 10–11 (the worst).

6–8 Lyall, who visited Odessa in May, 1822, writes (*Travels*, I, 168–70):

Two powerful obstacles . . . to the commerce and increase of this town . . . always will operate,—the want of a navigable river and of a supply of water for the purposes of life. . . . The chief fountain of supply of water for Odéssa lies at the distance of [about two miles] south of the town . . . on the sea-shore. . . . The ascent of the hill is a serious draft for loaded horses, and increases the expence of the water, each small barrel of which costs from a rouble to a rouble and a half, according to the distance.

It seems a pity that Pushkin sometimes sets going the marvelous machinery of his verse in order to express merely a hackneyed idea. Jokes concerning the lack of water in Odessa had been cracked and recracked ever since the foundation of the town in the last decade of the eighteenth century. Its very name, in those days of dreadful French puns, was attributed to the frequency with which its governor (1803–15), Armand Emmanuel, Duc de Richelieu, made the optimistic retort to critics: "Assez d'eau, eau d'assez." (Later jesters derived "Odessa" from "au-dessus de la mer.")

[XXIV]

9–14 The club Casino de Commerce was an annex of the Reynaud House, where Pushkin lived, Rishelievskaya Street, corner of Deribasovskaya (the names come from those of two former governors, Richelieu and de Ribas).

Lyall writes (*Travels*, I, 183):

Assembly-rooms were many years ago erected by Monsieur Rainaud [or Reynaud], and, we understood, are well attended [May, 1822]. The great oval hall, which is surrounded by a gallery, supported on numerous columns, is used for the double purpose of ballroom, and an *Exchange*, where the merchants sometimes transact their affairs. . . .

[XXV]

1 / *Glyadísh' i plóshchad' zapestréla*: A constructional translation would read:

You look—and the square has grown motley.

Glyadish', however, means in this type of phrase "while you look," or "the next time you look," or "presently." It is a weak "behold." The verb *pestret'*, an old enemy of the translator (Two : I : 8; Seven : LI : 6), implies here *narodom*:

And lo—the square is gay with people.

12 / conflagrations / *pozhárï*: In the draft (2370, f. 67ʳ) the line reads:

I chtó Kortésï il' pozhárï . . .
and what of Cortes or of conflagrations . . .

—which makes it pretty clear that *pozharï* in the final text means "revolutions," a point that Sovpushkinists have missed.

[XXVI]

5–6 / glee . . . juventy / *rádost'* . . . *mládost'*: I have tried —not quite successfully, I am afraid—to imitate this rhyme (nowadays fallen into desuetude with the archaic *mladost'*), which was as common in Pushkin's time as the analogous one he was to criticize not quite two years later, at the close of 1826 (in Six : XLIV : 5–6, *sládost'– mládost'*). Cf. the French rhyme *allégresse–jeunesse*.

The stanza is thematically close to One : XVI, with the restaurateur Automne replacing Talon (see n. to l. 12).

8 Cf. Dorat's fable of the not-too-astute oyster: "Huître dodue: fraiche et bien nourrie | . . . animal tenace [qui] s'emprisonne | [mais] l'écaille va s'ouvrir en deux, | Et Mon Seigneur mangera la personne. . . ."

Five decades later Tolstoy was to describe in much more original language the "scabrous" (*shershavïe*) outsides and "mother-of-pearl" (*perlamutrovïe*) insides of shells, from which Oblonski detaches with a little silver fork the "plopping" (*shlyupayushchiesya*) oysters. " 'Not bad,' he kept repeating as he glanced up with humid and glistening eyes now at Lyovin and now at the Tatar waiter" (*Anna Karenin*, pt. I, ch. 10, Oblonski and Lyovin dine at a Moscow restaurant).

12 / *Otónom* [instr. sing.]: César Automne, or Autonne, restaurateur on Deribasovskaya Street, opposite the Casino. Pushkin transliterates the name in Russian *Oton*.

[XXVII]

3 / Rossini: "Rossini" rhymes with *siniy*, "blue." The only pre-Pushkinian case I can remember of *siniy* being rhymed at all is a line in an ode (1775) by Vasiliy Petrov (1736–99), in which *siniy* rhymes with *iney*, "hoarfrost."

8–14 This "sustained" comparison between music and champagne, with its disparaging closule, does not really differ much from the "suspended" one between champagne and "this and that," in Four : XLV, or "a vivacious mistress," in Four : XLVI. A more provincial brand of brisk wine is also compared to "Zizi" at the end of Five : XXXII. The harping on this theme of wine and its analogies is a little painful.

[XXVIII]

5 Alongside this line the name "Monari" (a first-rate Italian tenor of the Odessa opera) is written in the margin of the draft (2370, f. 68ʳ).

5–14 The reference seems to be to Amalia Riznich, or Risnich, née Ripp, daughter of an Austrian-Jewish banker, one of Pushkin's three or four Odessa loves. She died in Genoa in May, 1825, about the time Pushkin (who learned of her death more than a year later) was working on these stanzas (c. March). Her mother was Italian. Her husband, Ivan Riznich (or, as he wrote his name in French, Jean Risnich), was an opulent and civilized Dalmatian merchant in the grain trade.

   She is also mentioned, presumably, in a first draft of XX:

> There, the bland merchant's
> Sportive companion shines.
>
> *Tam hladnokróvnogo ⟨kuptsá⟩*
> *Blistáet rézvaya podrúga.*

See also n. to Ten : XIII : 3.

   Pushkin courted Amalia Riznich in the summer and fall of 1823 in Odessa. His passionate elegy beginning "My voice for you, caressive, languorous," is presumably addressed to her. She bore her husband a son in the beginning of 1824, and in May of that year, very ill with consumption, left Odessa for Austria and Italy, where she died.* Her husband remained in Odessa and learned of his wife's death on June 8, 1825. Tumanski, in Amfiteatrov's and Oznobishin's almanac *Northern Lyre* (*Severnaya lira*) for 1827 (pub. November, 1826), inscribed a pentametric sonnet to Pushkin dated Odessa,

---

*See A. Sivers, "Sem'ya Riznich (novïe materialï)," in *P. i ego sovr.*, VIII, 31–32 (1927), 85–104.

July, 1825, *On the Death of R.** It is odd that Pushkin
learned of Amalia Riznich's death (from Tumanski?)
only in July, 1826.

Early in 1827 Riznich married Countess Pauline
Rzhevuski, sister of Caroline Sobanski and Eveline
Hanski.

[XXIX]

It is curious to compare this pseudo-Italian night, with its
golden Rossini music (XXVII : 11) and its Odessite Auso-
nians, with the imaginary, longed-for nights of golden
Italy, invoked so romantically in One : XLIX. It will also
be noted that One : L, by means of its allusion to the
Odessa sea front, links up One with the last lines of *EO*
in its established form. Indeed, the very last line ("As
said I lived then in Odessa," which begins *Journey*, XXX,
in the MS) coincides practically with Pushkin's note to
the word "sea" on One : L : 3 ("Written in Odessa")—
the Black Sea, which sounds in the penultimate line of
EO (*Journey* : XXIX : 14) and unites, with the curve of
its horizon, the beginning and end of the established text
in one of those inner structural circles of which I have
given other examples in the course of this commentary.

[XXX]

In fair copy (PB 18, f. 1ᵛ).

1 / in Odessa / *v Odésse*: This is the last word of the estab-
lished text. It rhymes with *povese* (loc.; see next note),

---

* It begins:

"Upon this earth you were Love's fair companion,
and sweeter than the roses breathed your lips.
In your live eyes, which were not made for tears,
burned Passion, and the Southern heavens shone."

which, in the nominative, *povesa*, rhymes in the second stanza of *EO* with *Zevesa* ("of Zeus"), which in turn rhymes with "Odessa" in *Journey* : [XXII], a most pleasing exchange of echoes under the arc of our poem.

3 / having forgot the somber scapegrace / *Zabív o súmrachnom povése*: The epithet *sumrachnïy* is close here to the French *ténébreux*. The type of *le beau ténébreux* (the handsome and somber knight, from "Beltenebros," as Amadis de Gaul called himself) was a fashionable model for young men in the late 1820's.

7–9 / and I, fortunate man, had never corresponded in a lifetime with anyone: Mark in the original the jolt and the jibe of the enjambment:

> *A yá, schastlívïy chelovék,*
> *Ne perepísïvalsya vvék*
> *Ni s kém . . .*

It was, among other matters, the interception of a chatty letter to one of his numerous correspondents (possibly, Küchelbecker; see vol. 1, p. 70, and vol. 3, p. 306) that caused our poet's expulsion from Odessa in July, 1824.

13 / the friends: The place is Odessa, the time is autumn, 1823. The two friends (for this is how I understand *druz'yá*, which can also mean "our friends") have not seen each other since May, 1820, when Pushkin left the capital for Ekaterinoslav and the Caucasus, while Onegin set out for his uncle's manor, situated midway between Opochka and Moscow. The story since Chapter One has completed a full circle. The reader should suppose that now in Odessa Onegin tells Pushkin of the intervening events. The rest will be reported to Pushkin by his Muse, whom we meet in Seven : V : 5 and Eight : I–VII.

It may be worth while to summarize at this point the main journeys of our two heroes, using all available data. From his countryseat Onegin travels to Petersburg early in 1821. On June 3 (or July 3?) he starts on his Russian tour. Its Moscow and Volga part (summer of 1821, by which time Pushkin is in Kishinev) lies far to the east of Pushkin's route (May–June, 1821, Petersburg-Kiev-Ekaterinoslav-Rostov) but merges with it in the northern Caucasus.

In May, 1820, Pushkin had been attached as a super-numerary functionary (*sverhshtatnïy chinovnik*) to the bureau of General Inzov, who presided over a committee that took care of the interests of foreign-born colonists in the Southern region of Russia. Inzov's headquarters were in Ekaterinoslav (now Dnepropetrovsk), where Pushkin arrived from Petersburg about May 20, not only as a new employee, but as a courier bringing Colonial Superintendent Inzov the news that he had been made Acting Governor of Bessarabia. Between Pushkin's leaving Ekaterinoslav (May 28, with the Raevskis) on sick leave for the curative waters of Pyatigorsk, in the Caucasus, and his blissful sojourn in the Crimea (third week of August to Sept. 5), Inzov and the bureau moved to Kishinev, where Pushkin joined his chief on Sept. 21, 1820, four months after seeing Inzov in Ekaterinoslav.

Onegin's itinerary, after merging with Pushkin's at the spas of the northern Caucasus, coincides next with the journey to Georgia that, during the war with Turkey, Pushkin made in the summer of 1829. Onegin remains in the Caucasus from late 1821 to the summer of 1823, when he follows Pushkin's route of summer, 1820, via Taman to the Crimea and visits Bahchisaray in the autumn of 1823, three years after Pushkin.

In the meantime, since July, 1823, Pushkin has been transferred from Kishinev to Odessa, where he is now attached to the chancellery of a higher dignitary, the

Governor General of New Russia (including Bessarabia), Count Vorontsov, who proved to be a much more exacting and much less sympathetic chief than good old Inzov had been. In Odessa, Pushkin is reunited in late 1823 with Onegin, after a separation of more than three years, and the two pals are separated again by the end of July, 1824, when Pushkin is expelled to his Pskovan countryseat for two years of rustication, while Onegin arrives in mid-August, 1824, in Petersburg, where he again meets Tatiana, whom he had not seen since Jan. 12, 1821.

It is to be noted that another, smaller, loop, concentric to the one discussed, takes place in relation to Pushkin's Muse. In May, 1812, when the Muse first began visiting thirteen-year-old Pushkin in his student cell at the Lyceum (Eight : I), seventeen-year-old Onegin had already started his eight-year-long period of riotous life in Petersburg (One : IV). By Jan. 8, 1815 (Eight : II), she had evolved a pair of wings. In 1817–18, she is courted by the young rakes of St. Petersburg (Eight : III), and sometime in 1819–20 she and Pushkin vainly try to teach their new friend Onegin the mysteries of prosody (One : VII). In the beginning of May, 1820, Onegin leaves Petersburg for the countryside (One : I, II, LI, LII), while the Muse follows Pushkin to the Caucasus, the Crimea, and Moldavia (Eight : IV–V). She appears in Mihaylovskoe (to deal with the events after Onegin's departure) in August, 1824, by life's calendar (Eight : V); and in August, 1824, by the novel's calendar, she meets Onegin at a Petersburg rout (Eight : VI).

VARIANT

7–14 The draft (2368, f. 30^r) reads:

> and I, ⟨a lazy] man,
> could not keep up in all my life
> a constant correspondence,

in certain cases being even glad
to face a rupture only to be spared
this ceaseless torture for a while.
Really, the cause of this is laziness;
the letter-writing day is my black day.

[XXXI]

In fair copy (PB 18, f. 1ᵛ).

1 / sacred Friendship: The same mildly ironic formula was
used by Pushkin in the letter to Sobolevski summarized
in my nn. to VII: ". . . in proof of friendship (that sacred
sentiment) I am sending you my *Itinéraire* from Moscow
to Novgorod . . ."

3 / augurs: Cicero, *De divinatione*, II, 24: "Vetus autem
illud Catonis admodum scitum est, qui mirari se aiebat
quod non rideret haruspex haruspicem cum vidisset."
The haruspex was a soothsayer who foretold the future
from an examination of the entrails of animals. Although
Cicero maintains here that one knows sufficiently well
Cato's remark that he "wondered how one diviner could
see another without laughing," no such "old saying"
of Cato's has come down to us. Actually, Pushkin's
source here is not Cicero. "Les augurs de Rome qui ne
peuvent se regarder sans rire" was an old cliché of
French journalism. It was even translated back into
Latin as: "si augur augurem."

We find Lermontov using the same trite phrase ten
years later in "Princess Mary" (Pechorin's entry of
"May 13": "Then, after looking meaningly into each
other's eyes, we began to laugh as Roman augurs did,
according to Cicero".)

4 The stanza remained unfinished. Burtsev has somewhere
conjectured that the two were quietly chuckling over the

fact that they both belonged to the same revolutionary movement. I think that what made them smile was not so much the conjectures of commentators as the unholy and artificial quality of friendship that can allow two friends to forget each other completely for three years.

Cf. the last line of Pushkin's poem written in the summer of 1819 at Mihaylovskoe, addressed to Mihail Shcherbinin, a dashing friend of his in Petersburg (ll. 27–32):

> pleasure we'll find, dear friend,
> in the blurred dream of recollection,
> for then, shaking my head,
> I'll say to you at the grave's door,
> "Remember Fanny, my dear fellow?"—
> And softly both we'll smile.

It is curious that Küchelbecker, who certainly could not have known Pushkin's line "we softly broke out laughing" (*Mĭ rassmeyálisya tishkóm*), *Onegin's Journey*, XXXI : 4, uses a similar adverb (*tihomólkom*) when introducing the same not-uncommon Gallic formula of Cicero's laughing augurs in can. III of his remarkable poem *Agasfer*, *The Wandering Jew* (*Vechnïy zhid*), written in exile, mainly in 1840–42, and published long after his death (1878). Despite its odd archaism, awkward locutions, crankish ideas, and a number of structural flaws, this poem is a major piece of work, with a harshness of intonation and gaunt originality of phrasing that should deserve a special study.

[XXXII]

In draft (2382, f. 17ᵛ).

14 / sad was my arrival: During the entire spring of 1824, from the last week of March to the first week of May, Count Vorontsov, Governor General of New Russia, had been clamoring from Odessa to St. Petersburg, in letters

to Count Nesselrode, Minister of Foreign Affairs, to rid
him of the unpleasant and difficult Mr. Pushkin ("Dé-
livrez-moi de Pouchkine!"), "a weak imitator of Byron"
—but also the author of original epigrams and an ad-
mirer of the countess. The Vorontsovs' private physician,
Dr. William Hutchinson, had proved to be, despite his
taciturnity, deafness, and bad French, an interesting
interlocutor: of his "lessons of pure atheism" Pushkin
wrote to a friend, this letter was seized by the police, and
its immoral contents prompted the tsar to do something
about Vorontsov's request.* Pushkin, on his part, had
long been exasperated by Vorontsov's morgue, Anglo-
mania, and coarseness of discrimination. On May 22
Pushkin was ordered to investigate an invasion of grass-
hoppers in the Herson, Elizavetgrad, and Aleksandria
districts. Next day he was given four hundred rubles for
traveling expenses (a ruble per mile for post horses), but
whether he ever drove farther than the first 120 miles
(to Herson) is not known, and the interesting image of a
disgusted poet directing, from his traveling cart, the
beating down of the swarms with poplar branches and
the treatment of the soil with quicklime is unfortunately
not available to the historian. On June 7, the wife of one
of his greatest friends, Princess Vera Vyazemski, arrived
in Odessa with her sick children (six-year-old Nikolay
and two-year-old Nadezhda) and became the confidante
of his romance with Countess Vorontsov. The latter
sailed with her husband for the Crimea on June 14; they
came back on July 25, and two or three days later Push-
kin was informed that he was discharged (as of July 8)
from the civil service for "bad behavior" and ordered to
the maternal manor, Mihaylovskoe. On the night of
July 30 he was for the last time at the Italian opera in

---

*Or perhaps the "deaf philosopher" mentioned in Pushkin's
letter was a certain Wolsey, teacher of English at the Risheliev-
skiy Litsey in Odessa (*Works* 1962, IX, 432).

Odessa, where he saw Rossini's *Il Turco in Italia* (1814).
Next day he set off for the province of Pskov, with the
same valet (Nikita, son of Timofey Kozlov) whom he had
taken with him when leaving St. Petersburg more than
four years before. Traveling via Nikolaev, Kremenchug,
Priluki, Chernigov, Mogilev, Vitebsk, and Opochka, he
arrived in Mihaylovskoe on Aug. 9. Here he found his
parents, his brother, his sister, and twenty-nine servants.
His relations with his parents, especially with his father,
had always been cool, and their reunion was now marked
by recriminations of all sorts. On Oct. 4 the Civil Gover-
nor of the province of Pskov, Boris Aderkas, reported to
the Governor General of that province and of the Baltic
Region, General Filipp Pauluchi (Marquis Paulucci),
that Sergey Pushkin had agreed to act for the govern-
ment and keep his son under close observation. This
spying led to a dreadful row between Pushkin and his
father. His parents left for St. Petersburg about Nov. 18;
his sister Olga had left a week earlier, and Lev Pushkin
had taken a fair copy of *EO* to St. Petersburg in the first
week of November.

[PENULTIMATE STANZA]

In fair copy (PB 18, f. 8^r).

There is an obvious gap of at least one stanza between
"XXXII" and this. The friendship mentioned in Penulti-
mate : 8–10 (in contrast to the kind of casual comrade-
ship implied by the tone of XXXI) is the genuine affection
and understanding shown to Pushkin by his brother and
sister at Mihaylovskoe and by the Osipov-Vulf family in
the neighboring Trigorskoe.

[ULTIMATE STANZA]

In fair copy (PD 169). It is dated "18 *sent.* Boldino 1830."

Commentary

6–11 / young Yazïkov . . . enchanting verse: The poet Niko-
lay Yazïkov was twenty-three in the early summer of
1826 when he, a student of philosophy at the University
of Derpt, or Dorpat ("the Livonian Athens," as it was
complacently termed), was brought by his fellow stu-
dent, Aleksey Vulf, to Trigorskoe (known locally as Voro-
nich), the seat of the latter's mother, Praskovia Osipov,
Pushkin's country neighbor (see my n. to Five : XXXII :
11). In this final stanza, Yazïkov takes a curtain call as
Lenski's understudy (see Four : XXXI).

Yazïkov's poetry is marked by a sonorous, ambitious
ebullience (his iambic tetrameter is a veritable orgy of
scuds), blended, however, with a vapid vulgarity of emo-
tion and thought. Our poet, in his letters and verses,
professed enthusiastic admiration for Yazïkov; but one
wonders if Yazïkov (who in his correspondence reveals
envious disapprobation of *EO*) was pleased to have his
elegies identified by his celebrated friend with those of
the obviously mediocre Lenski (Four : XXXI : 8–14).

The only interest Yazïkov's poems present to us here
is the picture they provide of Pushkin's rural existence.
Yazïkov dedicated a number of poems to Pushkin,
Trigorskoe, and even Pushkin's housekeeper. *To Push-
kin*, 1826 (ll. 1–4):

> O you, whose friendship is to me
> dearer than fame's caressive welcome,
> sweeter than any bonny maid,
> more sacred than an emperor's life . . .

Yazïkov further recalls the golden summer just gone by
when Pushkin and he (l. 10)—

> two first-born sons of the hyperborean Muses

—concluded a poetic pact, while hot punch (prepared by
young Zizi—Eupraxia Vulf) consisting of (ll. 17–21)

> . . . mighty Rum
> with sweet Messina's fruit

> a little sugar and some wine,
> all this, fire-changed,
> streamed into giant glasses.

There are forty lines of this, ending:

> now, while good-natured Moscow,
> full of a sacred hope,
> prepares the bright day of the coronation,
> I stand with lifted brow
> before the scrolls of inspirations
> and sing the freedom of our delectations,
> and Sorot's bank I sing.

In a longer piece of the same year, *Trigorskoe* (dedicated to Praskovia Osipov), Yazïkov sings again

> . . . the blue Sorot,
> companion of mirrory lakes

and the pleasures of bathing:

> O how voluptuous, how tender
> the naiad that embraces me!

And finally, in another poem to Mrs. Osipov, 1827 (ll. 17–19, 24–30):

> and often in a dream I see
> the three hills and the handsome house,
> and the meanders of the shining Sorot.
> .   .   .   .
> . . . and those slopes,
> those grain fields, from beyond which in the distance,
> used to appear
> mounted on a black *argamak*
> and wearing an exotic hat,
> Voltaire, Racine, and Goethe, all in one,
> our famous Pushkin, making for Trigorsk . . .

(An *argamak* is a large, lean, long-legged horse of Asiatic stock.)

At the end of his last visit to Mihaylovskoe, after burying his mother, Pushkin, before returning to St. Petersburg, wrote to Yazïkov on Apr. 14, 1836, from Golubovo (the Vrevskis' seat, near Trigorskoe and Mihaylovskoe):

Guess where I am writing you from, my dear Nikolay Mihaylovich? From that part of the world . . . where exactly ten years ago the three of us [the third was Aleksey Vulf] banqueted; where sounded your verses and goblets of punch [*yonka*, a jocose Dorpatan—i.e., Germanic— corruption of *zhzhyonka**]; where we now recall you— and old times. A salute to you from the hills of Mihaylovskoe, from the coverts of Trigorskoe, from the waves of the blue Sorot', from Eupraxia Nikolaevna [Baroness Vrevski, née Vulf], formerly a half-ethereal maiden [Pushkin parodies his own *EO*, One : xx : 5], now a well-fed wife, for the fifth time big with child. . . .

Pushkin had only nine months and a half to live.

13–14 Virgil also speaks of hanging his "clear-sounding reed-pipe" on "this sacred pine"; *Bucolica*, Ecloga vii:

hic arguta sacra pendebit fistula pinu.

*

The batch of the last five stanzas was completed Sept. 18, 1830, at Boldino.

---

*The Russian *zh* or *zhzh* (identically sounded) would be transliterated *j* in French, which a German would pronounce as our *y*; hence *zhzhyonka = yonka*.

"Chapter Ten"

When we wonder about the destiny of an author's crea-
ture beyond the horizon of a discontinued romance, two
feelings prompt our fancy and direct our conjectures.
The character in the book has become so familiar to us
that we cannot bear to have him depart without leaving
us some address; and the author of the book has ac-
quainted us with so many devices that we cannot help
trying to imagine what we should do if called upon to
continue the book in his name.

Hamlet is finished not only because the Danish prince
dies, but also because those whom his ghost might haunt
have died, too. *Madame Bovary* is finished not only be-
cause Emma has killed herself, but because Homais has
at last got his decoration. *Ulysses* is finished because
everybody in it has fallen asleep (although the good
reader wonders where Stephen is going to spend the rest
of the night). *Anna Karenin* is finished not only because
Anna has been crushed by a backing freight train but be-
cause Lyovin has found his God. But *Onegin* is not
finished.

To Captain Medwin, Byron said one day
(October, eighteen twenty-one, at Pisa):
"Poor Juan will be guillotined—*has been*—

In the French Revolution . . ."
                                . . . but Eugene?

To Captain Yuzefovich, Pushkin said one day, June, 1829, in the Caucasus: "Onegin will either perish in the Caucasus or join the Decembrist movement."

Commentators suggest that in the memoirs written by Mihail Yuzefovich, a minor poet, formerly the adjutant of General Raevski, in July, 1880 (and published the same year in the *Russian Archives* [*Russkiy arhiv*], vol. XVIII, no. 3), there is some confusion after all these years: Pushkin probably meant to say that after having been connected with the Decembrist movement Onegin was to be banished to the Caucasus and killed there in a skirmish with the Circassians.

Before sailing for Greece, Byron had begun (May 8, N.S., 1823) a seventeenth canto of *Don Juan* in Italy, and after his death in 1824 fourteen complete stanzas of it were found in his room at Missolonghi (they were published for the first time by Ernest Hartley Coleridge, in 1903, in his edition of Byron's *Works*, vol. VI). But the eighteen stanzas of Pushkin's tenth canto have reached us only in a fragmentary form.

The existence of a "Chapter Ten" is referred to in the following texts:

(1) A note in the margin of a page in Cahier 2379, now in the Pushkinskiy Dom, Leningrad.

On Oct. 20, 1830, at Boldino, province of Nizhni, Pushkin finished writing his story "The Blizzard" (*Metel'*; see Comm., Ten : III : end note). On the last page of this MS, in the left-hand corner, next to the last lines of the story (" 'Goodness me, goodness me,' said M[aria] G[avrilovna], grasping his hand: 'So it was you! You, my husband. And you do not recognize me?' B[urmin] paled, and threw himself at her feet . . .") there is the note in Pushkin's hand: "Oct. 19 was burned X Canto." (The "9" is not too clear and may be read as

"1" or "8"; but of these three possible readings, the first is the best.)

(2) A note in the right-hand margin of a MS (PB 18, f. 4ʳ) of *Onegin's Journey*, now in the Pushkinskiy Dom, Leningrad.

On this page st. v is crossed out; a marginal note places it "In X Canto." I discuss its possible location in my Comm. to Ten : xviii : end note.

(3) An entry in Vyazemski's diary (Dec. 19, 1830). Pushkin visited Vyazemski at his countryseat Ostafievo (five miles from Podolsk, province of Moscow) Dec. 17, 1830 (thus two months after burning "X Canto"), and read to him, presumably from memory, a set of stanzas dealing, according to Vyazemski, with "the events of 1812 and later ones. A splendid chronicle." Onward in the same entry, Vyazemski quotes two lines from this Chapter Ten (xv : 3–4):

> At inspired Nikita's,
> at circumspect Ilya's,

thus supplying l. 4, which our poet did not reach in his cryptogram (which I discuss further), and either misquoting l. 3 or else (more probably) quoting it in the form Pushkin recited it, which is different from the text he ciphered.

(4) A letter from Aleksandr Turgenev written Aug. 11 (presumably, N.S.), 1832, from Munich, to his brother Nikolay, in Paris. This letter is published by V. Istrin in the *Journal of the Ministry of Public Education* (*Zhurnal Ministerstva Narodnogo Prosveshcheniya*), n.s. pt. XLIV (St. Petersburg, March, 1913), pp. 16–17. It contains the following passage:

. . . Here are some immortal lines about you. Aleksandr Pushkin could not publish a certain part of his *Onegin* in which he describes the latter's travels across Russia and the insurrection of 1825; he mentions you among others:

> seeing but Russia in the world,
> pursuing his ideal,
> to them did lame Turgenev hearken—

[i.e., to the conspirators]; I told him that you neither hearkened to them nor frequented [*znaval*] them.

> And whips of slavery hating,
> in this crowd of nobles foresaw
> the liberators of the peasants.

(This is Ten : XVI : 9–14; the readings "pursuing" and "whips of slavery" are represented in Pushkin's draft by "in her caressing" and "the word slavery," respectively; unless no other source exists, we cannot consider a quotation to be anything more than a variant, and have to rely on Pushkin's rough draft for our basic text.)

Let us now turn to the mysterious canto itself.

The MS fragments that we have of Chapter Ten, composed in the autumn of 1830 at Boldino, are represented by sets of lines belonging to eighteen consecutive stanzas. Our poet did not number these stanzas. I number them for easy reference, as I did in the case of *Onegin's Journey* and of various canceled verses.

The following fragments of Chapter Ten are preserved in autographs (these I describe at the end of my commentary to the chapter; see Addendum to Notes on "Chapter Ten"):

A cryptogram (PD 170) containing: the first and second lines of I–X and XII–XVII; the third lines of I–IX and XI–XVII; the fourth lines of I–IV, VI–IX, and XI–XIII; and the fifth lines of IV, VI, VIII, and XI.

Rough drafts (PD 171) of sts. XVI (which is practically complete), XVII (with the end, from l. 9 on, difficult to decipher and incomplete), and XVIII (the end of which, also from l. 9 on, is still sketchier).

Here is a reconstitution of these fragments (I have enclosed the cancellations in pointed brackets, and have square-bracketed my own suggestions or queries; I have not square-bracketed here, as I have in the cryptogram and its translation, pp. 367–73, the words or parts of words Pushkin deliberately left out, the sense of which is unquestionable; I have also added xv : 4, quoted by Vyazemski):

I
A ruler weak and wily,
a baldish fop, a foe of toil,
fortuitously by Fame befriended,
4 over us reigned then.

II
We knew him to be very tame
when not *our* cooks
plucked the two-headed eagle
4 near Bonaparte's tent.

III
The tempest of year 12
took place. Who helped us here?
The infuriation of the nation?
4 Barclay? The winter? Or the Russian God?

IV
But [God?] helped—lower grew the murmur
and, by the force of circumstances, soon
we found ourselves in Paris,
4 and the Russian tsar was the head of kings.
The seas to Albion were apportioned . . .
   .   .   .   .
14 ·   ·   ·   ·   ·   [the tsar grew fatter—]

V
—and the fatter the heavier.
O our Russian stupid nation!
Say, why indeed
4 [endure the tsars from race to race?]
   .   .   .   .
14 [Mayhap,] . . .

VI
"Mayhap"—O national shibboleth!

I'd dedicate an ode to you,
had not a highborn poetaster
4 anticipated me already.
Mayhap, the roads for us they will repair . . .

VII
Mayhap, forgetting leases,
the bigot will shut himself up in a monastery.
Mayhap, by the command of Nicholas
4 Siberia to [their] families will give back
[their sons] . . .
. . . .
14 . . . [Napoleon].

VIII
That man of destiny, that martial wanderer,
before whom groveled kings;
that horseman crowned by the Pope,
4 gone like a shadow of the dawn!
Exhausted by the torture of repose,
[mocked by the sobriquet of hero] . . .

IX
The Pyrenees shook ominously;
Naples' volcano was aflame.
The one-armed prince to the friends of Morea
4 from Kishinev already winked.

X
1 I, with my people, will curb everybody!
our tsar in congress said . . .

XI
. . . .
. . . .
and does not care a straw about you,
4 you are the slave of Alexander.
The dagger of L[ouvel], the shadow of B[erton]
⟨do not⟩ . . .

XII
Play regiment of Titan Peter,
a bodyguard of old mustaches,

who formerly betrayed a tyrant
4 to a ferocious gang of deathsmen—

XIII
Russia again grew tame,
and with more zest the tsar went reveling;
but the sparks of another flame
4 already a long time perhaps—

XIV
1 They ⟨had their own⟩ forgatherings:
they, over a goblet of wine,
they, over a glass of Russian vodka . . .

XV
For trenchant oratory famed,
the members of this group assembled
at unquiet Nikita's,
4 at circumspect Ilya's . . .

XVI
A friend of Mars, Bacchus, and Venus,
here Lúnin daringly suggested
his decisive measures
4 and muttered in a trance of inspiration;
Pushkin read his noels;
melancholy Yakushkin,
it seemed, silently bared
8 a regicidal dagger;
seeing but Russia in the world,
in her caressing his ideal,
to them did lame Turgenev hearken
12 and the word slavery hating,
in this crowd of nobles foresaw
the liberators of the peasants.

XVII
Thus was it on the icy Neva;
but there where earlier the spring
gleams over shady Kámenka
4 and over the hills of Tulchín;
where Wittgenstein's detachments
the plains washed by the Dnepr

and the steppes of the Bug enlocked,
8 there matters took another turn.
There P[estel] [an indecipherable word] of the dagger
and troops . . . mustered
the cool general,
12 and [three indecipherable words]
and full of daring and of strength
. . . hastened.

XVIII
At first these conspirations
between Laffitte and Clicquot
⟨were merely⟩ conversations
4 and did not ⟨enter⟩ deeply
the science of rebellion into hearts;
⟨all this was only⟩ boredom,
the idleness of youthful minds,
8 pastimes of grown-up scamps . . .

*

Here follows the Comm. on the foregoing fragments
of Chapter Ten.

I

1 / ruler: The abbreviation (*Vl—*) used by Pushkin for this
word of Chapter Ten suggests two, and only two, possi-
bilities: *Vlastitel'* or *Vladïka*—both meaning "sover-
eign" or "ruler." I prefer the second to the first for
reasons of euphony (since it avoids the clash of con-
sonants between the end of *vlastitel'* and the beginning
of the next word, *slabïy*, "weak") and also because Push-
kin had used *vladïka* in the same sense on previous
occasions—in the *Ode to Liberty* (1817), ll. 37–38:

> *Vladïki! vám venéts i trón*
> *Dayót Zakón, a ne priróda . . .*
>
> Rulers! to you the crown and throne
> the Law gives, and not Nature . . .

in ll. 2, 7, 33, and 53 of a poem of sixty iambics, written in December, 1823, beginning "The stirless sentinel" (*Nedvizhnïy strazh*) and consisting of ten staves, of which l. 5 is a trimeter and the rest are hexameters, with a rhyme scheme aabeeb (this poem contains several other themes related to Ten—see nn. to VIII and IX—and *vladïka* in it denotes Alexander I); and in *Anchar* (Antiaris, the Upas Tree), composed Nov. 9, 1828, ll. 31–32:

> *I úmer bédnïy ráb u nóg*
> *Nepobedímogo vladïki.*

> and died the poor slave at the feet
> of the unconquerable ruler.

2 / a baldish fop: Alexander I, officially surnamed the Blessed, in the second decade of his reign (1801–25) developed a bald spot (besides gaining weight, as noted further).

Cf. Byron, *Don Juan*, can. XIV (finished Mar. 4, 1823), st. LXXXIII, in which that witty poet addresses the English antislavery leader William Wilberforce with the following very pertinent plea:

> Shut up the bald-coot bully Alexander!
>   Ship off the Holy Three to Senegal;
> Teach them that "sauce for goose is sauce for gander,"
>   And ask them how *they* like to be in thrall?

(Pichot, 1824: "Enferme cet empereur fanfaron à la tête chauve . . .")

In the same author's *The Age of Bronze* (1823), st. X, there is another reference to Alexander:

> How well the imperial dandy prates of peace!

Had I not wished to be absolutely faithful to my text, I might have translated, perhaps, Pushkin's *Pleshívïy shchyógol'* as the "bald-coot dandy." But that would have been a literary translation and not a literal one.

II

2 / not *our* cooks: The Russian bicephalous eagle lost a con-
siderably greater amount of feathers to the French at
Austerlitz, in 1805, and at Eylau, in 1807, than he did
later to his own Russians, to those who tried to cook up
internal strife in 1825, or to those who aimed political
epigrams at the regime.

The rest of the stanza presumably dealt with the
battles unlucky to Russian arms. It is amusing to note
that Brodski says "army of the tsar" when the Russians
are beaten by Napoleon and "army of the people" when
Napoleon is beaten by the Russians.

III

1 / The tempest of year 12: Napoleon crossed the Neman
into Russia with an army of 600,000 troops on June 12,
1812 (O.S.).

In his last Lyceum-anniversary poem, recited at the
reunion of Oct. 19, 1836 (see also my n. to Six : XXI : 8),
Pushkin in an autobiographical and epic strain, without
any of the cold mocking notes characteristic of Ten,
chronicles the same general order of political events
from the rise of Napoleon to Tsar Nicholas' succession to
the throne, when "new clouds" and a "new hurri-
cane . . ." (the poem stops in the middle of its sixty-
fourth line). In l. 37 there is an interesting aftersound of
Ten : III : 1—Pushkin is recalling the beginning of the
Lyceum in 1811 (ll. 37–40):

> . . . the tempest of year 12 [*góda*]
> was still asleep. Napoleon had yet
> not tested [with invasion] a great people [*naróda*],
> he still preferred to waver and to threat.

4 General Barclay (Prince Mihail Barclay de Tolly, 1761–

1818) retreated toward Moscow, luring the French and exhausting them. Napoleon's failure in 1812 to provide against the harsh Russian winter that proved Russia's best ally, when after lingering near Moscow the puzzled conqueror began his "Great Retreat," is too well known to need any elucidation.

The Russian God. This local deity is often mentioned in Russian topical poems of the era. It is sufficient here to quote Vyazemski's poem of 1828, *The Russian God* (*Russkiy Bog*; couplets in Béranger's trivial style), which is the obvious reminiscence here. In his nine quatrains (trochaic tetrameters) Vyazemski describes the Russian God as the God of blizzards, bumps, excruciating roads, cold and hungry beggars, unproductive estates, pendant breasts and flabby buttocks, bast shoes and swollen feet, wry faces and soured cream, fruit liqueurs and marinades, mortgaged serfs, money-minded nitwits of both sexes, pectoral ribands and crosses, barefooted household slaves, and barons in sleigh-coaches with a brace of liverymen clinging behind. The Russian God is further described (we have reached quatrain VII) as full of benevolence toward fools but mercilessly severe toward intelligent people. He is the God of everything that is malapropos, outlandish, ill-fitting, ill-assorted, mustard-after-dinnerish. The God of itinerant aliens, and, especially, of Germans; "here he is, the Russian God"—a Bérangeresque refrain with which each quatrain ends. (See also n. to IV : 4, Dmitri's monologue.)

To judge by the beginning of Pushkin's next stanza, the rest of Ten : III dealt with the trials that beset the nation in 1812, such as the conflagration of Moscow.

*

As late as the end of 1830 Pushkin was still able to work up a good deal of traditional enthusiasm for Alexander I.

Russian commentators do not seem to have noticed that the story "The Blizzard" (*Metel'*, October, 1830), in the margin of which the burning of Canto Ten is commemorated, contains an all-important paragraph (I would even suggest that the entire inept tale is there merely as a framework for that paragraph) in which Pushkin, both in matter and in manner, directly rebuts with a series of almost grotesque ejaculations the contemptuous attitude toward Alexander I, the Russian eagle, and the events closing the Napoleonic wars in Chapter Ten; in consequence of which the fact of its destruction being mentioned in the margin of *that* story acquires a certain symbolic significance. The passage goes:

Meanwhile the war had ended in glory. Our troops were returning from abroad. The people ran out to meet them. The bands played the captured songs: *Vive Henri IV*, Tyrolese waltzes, and arias from *Joconde.* * . . . Time unforgettable! Time of glory and enthusiasm! How violently beat the Russian heart at the word Fatherland! How sweet were the tears of reunion! How unanimously did we blend the feeling of national pride with that of love for our Sovereign! And for Him—what a moment!

"The Blizzard" is the second of the *Tales of the Late Ivan Petrovich Belkin* series, and is supposed to have been told to the fictional Belkin by a fictional Miss K. I. T. Through this double disguise comes Pushkin's modified but quite recognizable voice.

IV

2 / by the force of circumstances / *síloyu veshchéy*: A Gallicism, *par la force des choses*. Cf. Fouché, *Mémoires* (a passage related to the events in France of December,

---

*This comic opera, *Joconde* (a young rake) *ou les Coureurs d'aventures* (Paris, 1814; St. Petersburg, 1815), is by Niccolò Isouard; in it occurs the celebrated couplet "Et l'on revient toujours | A ses premiers amours."

1813): " . . . On avait pressenti que, par la seule force des choses, tous les intérêts de la révolution que je représentais à moi seul, auraient prévalu et paré à la catastrophe."

3 / we found ourselves in Paris: In his justly celebrated letter from Paris, Apr. 25, 1814 (N.S.), addressed to D. Dashkov, Batyushkov gives a wonderful account of the Russian entrance into Paris. The description starts with the words: "I shall simply say: I am in Paris" (a formula with which Karamzin's letter from Paris, April, 1790, also starts). Alexander Turgenev, Pushkin's lifelong friend, possessed a copy of this letter, and there is little doubt that Pushkin had read it.

4 / head of kings: Cf. "O tsar of tsars," an ejaculation used in l. 10 of a mediocre hymn (six odic staves) to Alexander I, on the day of his coronation in 1801, by Dmitriev.

See also Ozerov's *Dmitri Donskoy*, a patriotic tragedy in Alexandrine couplets, first produced Jan. 14, 1807, before a wildly enthusiastic audience. Dmitri's last monologue in act v (delivered kneeling) begins:

To you the heart's first tribute, king of kings . . .

and ends:

Ye nations know: great is the Russian God.

D. Sokolov, in a paper on Pushkin's cryptogram,* quoting, if I correctly understand him, I. Zhirkevich, *Russkaya starina*, XI (December, 1874), 649, says that the expression "Vive Alexandre, vive ce roi des rois" occurred in some couplets sung by François Lays on the stage of the Opéra in Paris Mar. 10, 1814 (N.S.), to the tune of *Vive Henri IV*. The term goes back to ecclesiastic sources. "Roi des rois" is applied to Jesus in French carols.

P. i ego sovr., IV, 16 (1913), 7n.

Negus nagast, the title of Abyssinian emperors, means
"king of kings." The hyperbole is as old as the hills.

5 Beginning with the position of this verse my recension dis-
agrees thoroughly with that of Tomashevski and other
commentators.

v

4 / endure the tsars from race to race: The line accidentally
omitted by Pushkin in coding the quatrain (see Adden-
dum to Notes on "Chapter Ten") might have been (I give
this very diffidently, merely to fill up the melodic gap):

Terpét' tsaréy iz róda v ród

—the meaning being: why on earth did you suffer the
rule of tsars from generation to generation ("genera-
tion" or "race," in the sense of "lineage," rhymes with
"nation," *naród*, of the second line)?

The stanza almost certainly must have ended in a line
beginning "mayhap" (*avos'*), an adverb implying a
flaccid, fatalistic, good-natured, and vague appeal to
probability.

VI

1 / national shibboleth / *Shibolét naródnïy*: Cf. Byron, *Don
Juan*, XI, XII, 1–2:

Juan, who did not understand a word
Of English, save their shibboleth, "God damn!"

3 / highborn poetaster: Prince Ivan Dolgoruki (1764–
1823), the talentless author of the volumes of verse *The
Being of My Heart* (*Bïtiyo serdtsa moego*, Moscow,
1802) and *The Dusk of My Life* (*Sumerki moey zhizni*,
Moscow, 1808). In his facetious ode, the word *avos'*
("mayhap") is described as:

> O amiable, simple word!
> thee I shall sing in measures mine.
> Thou art indeed a Russian word,
> and thee I love with all my heart.

5 / the roads for us they will repair / *dorógi nám isprávyat*:
"We shall see our roads repaired" might hug the sense
closer.

What was the rhyme here (6)? *Zastávyat*, "will com-
pel"? *Pozabávyat*, "will amuse"? *Postávyat*, "will set
up"? *Proslávyat*, "will glorify"? *Rasstávyat*, "will place
at intervals"? *Razdávyat*, "will crush"? *Ubávyat*, "will
make less"? *Udávyat*, "will strangle"? And there are
several other less obvious candidates.

VII

1–2 / forgetting leases, the bigot / *aréndï zabïváya* | *Han-
zhá*: The meaning of the word *arendï* (which is today
"rents and leases") varied in the eighteenth and nine-
teenth centuries. Its old sense was the income paid one
by the government in lieu of the temporary enjoyment
of granted lands.

"Bigot" is an allusion to a person in power, a pious
rogue, addicted alike to some current brand of mysticism
and to the more material satisfactions of revenues; it has
not been convincingly explained at the time of my writ-
ing this note (1958). Commentators have suggested
Prince Aleksandr Golitsïn, who had been Minister of
Public Education and Ecclesiastic Affairs (1816–24) and
a member of the Investigating Committee that in 1826
handled the case of the Decembrists' insurrection. He
had also investigated our poet's morals in the *Gavriliada*
affair (see n. to Eight : XXVIa : 5–11).

4 / Siberia to [their] families will give back: There is an en-
jambment here. The first words of l. 5 must have sup-

plied the direct object of the unfinished sentence (ll. 4–5):

> *Seméystvam vozvratít Sibír'*
> [*Ih sïnovéy*] . . .

The stanza must have ended with a reference to Napoleon, perhaps with the name of Napoleon actually closing l. 14. Siberia may still return the Decembrists to their families, but it is too late now for St. Helena to release her prisoner. Thus, perhaps, might have ended the very Pushkinian inventory of trivial and momentous probabilities prompted by the *avós'*.

VIII

1 / That man of destiny: At Boldino, on the day of good resolutions, Lyceum anniversary, Oct. 19, 1830, Pushkin decided to destroy the stanzas of Chapter Ten and to transfer certain lines to another poem.

In his poem *The Hero*, composed about that time (it was ready by the beginning of November and was published in 1831), we thus find, preserved in an entirely different context (invoking a despot's courage rather than inveighing against that inherent ridiculousness of strong potentates which not even Napoleon could transcend), the following lines (14–17):

> He, always he—that martial comer
> before whom humbled themselves kings,
> that warrior crowned by liberty,
> gone like a shadow of the dawn.

A historical generality is substituted for the hand of Pius VII, and there are other minor changes. "The martial wanderer" becomes "the martial comer" (*prishléts,* "intruder," "invader," "stranger"). The "always he" is an echo of a passage in Casimir Delavigne's *Messéni-*

ennes, bk. II, no. VI, *A Napoléon* (1823): "Seul et sur un rocher . . . | Du fond de son exil encor présent partout . . ."

Further on, ll. 37–45 of *The Hero* continue what we have of Ten : VIII to an illusory end, supplying, as they do, the rhyme *pokóya*, "of repose," to *geróya*, "of hero," and completing the Onegin rhyme sequence (37–45 = ecciddiff).

35 Not there, not on his rock, whereon
   settled, racked by the torture of repose [*pokóya*],
   mocked by the sobriquet of hero [*geróya*],
   he evanesces, motionless [*nedvizhím*],
   enfolded in his cloak of battle [*boevím*],
40 no, not that picture is before me [*mnóyu*]!
   Of beds I see a long array [*stróy*],
   there lies on each a corpse alive [*zhivóy*]
   branded by the almighty plague [*chumóyu*]
   —the empress of diseases; he [*ón*]
45 not with the dead of war surrounded [*okruzhyón*]
   with knitted brows passes between the beds [*odrámi*]
   and coolly shakes hands with the plague [*chumé*].

The Hero is a dialogue between Poet and Friend. It consists of sixty-six lines and one third of a line. Excepting ll. 36–45, the arbitrary rhyme scheme bears no resemblance to *EO*. The Friend asks the Poet what moment in Napoleon's life fascinates him most, and the passage given above is the Poet's answer. The Friend then says that stern history denies that this glamorous event ever happened. The Poet, inflating his voice, retorts (ll. 63–66):

> More than a myriad of low truths
> I value the Delusion that exalts us.
> Leave the hero his heart! Without it
> what would he be? A tyrant!

And the Friend replies with quiet emphasis (l. 67):

> *Utésh'sya* [Console yourself] . . .

The allusion is to the courage officially shown by Tsar Nicholas on Sept. 29, 1830, during his visit to cholera-stricken Moscow at the peak of the epidemic, when ignorance abetted by some antigovernmental propaganda was accusing the authorities of poisoning the people.

In the famous poem of his youth that Pushkin recited in the presence of Derzhavin, *Recollections at Tsarskoe Selo*, a set of 176 iambics, composed in the three last months of 1814, in twenty-two staves, tetrametric in ll. 1, 2, 4, and 8 and hexametric in the rest, with rhymes ababecec, some of the elements of *The Hero* (1830) and of Ten : VIII (1830) are foreshadowed with a curious sharpness of detail.

In l. 138 of the *Recollections*, we find the same epithet *prishlets* ("comer," "intruder," "invader," "stranger") that replaces in *The Hero* (l. 14) the *strannik* ("rover," "wanderer," "l'homme errant") of Ten : VIII : 1; cf. ll. 137–38:

> Console yourself [*Utésh'sya*], mother of Russian cities,
> the comer's downfall contemplate!

The theme of vanishment that in Ten : VIII : 4 and in l. 17 of *The Hero* is given in terms of the disappearance of a "shadow of the dawn," *ten' zari*, is distinctly indicated in l. 152 of the *Recollections*, likewise in connection with Napoleon (ll. 149, 152):

> . . . the favorite son of Fortune and Bellona
> .   .   .   .
> gone like at morn a frightful dream.

The same theme is taken up in a poem of 1823, beginning "The stirless sentinel" (which I have already mentioned in my n. to Ten : I : 1), ll. 39–42:

> This horseman before whom kings bowed,
> rebellious Liberty's the heir and murderer
> .   .   .   .
> that king gone like a dream, like a shadow of dawn.

Ten : VIII : 5 and *The Hero*, l. 36, are adumbrated in
"The stirless sentinel . . ." by ll. 46–48 (with the same
rhyme *geróya–pokóya*):

Nothing in him betrayed the exiled hero,
when to the torture of repose
amidst the seas condemned by the command of kings . . .

3 / crowned by a Pope: The formula is a borrowed one. See,
for example, the beginning of the last strophe in Bé-
ranger's celebrated effusion (c. 1825), *Les Souvenirs du
peuple*:

> Lui, qu'un pape a couronné,
> Est mort dans une île déserte.

Another instance of Pushkin's paradoxical indebted-
ness to poetasters whom he held in contempt.

4 / a shadow of the dawn / *ten' zari*: If Pushkin had wished
to say that Napoleon vanished like "a shadow at dawn,"
he would have had to express it by *ten' na zare*. I wonder
if his strangely evocative "shadow of dawn"—an
auroral phantom, an illusion of sunrise—has not been
influenced by an image in Victor Hugo's *Buonaparte*,
written in March, 1822. The end of the last (fifth) part
of this Ode Onzième, in *Odes et Ballades*, bk. I, reads:

> Ce ne sont point là les héros!
> Ces faux dieux . . .
> Vous trompent dans votre sommeil;
> Telles ces nocturnes aurores
> Où passent de grands météores,
> Mais que ne suit pas le soleil.

Pushkin had Hugo's *Odes* (3rd edn., Paris, 1827), in
his library.

IX

1–2 / The Pyrenees shook ominously; Naples' volcano

blazed: Two easy metaphors alluding to the revolts in
Spain and in Lower Italy.

The king of Spain, Ferdinand VII, in the course of a
ruthless reign, had persecuted all liberal thought and had
outraged national pride by selling Florida to the United
States. In the beginning of 1820, a revolution broke out,
led by Riego and Quiroga at Cádiz. At the Congress of
Verona (October, 1822) the so-called Holy Alliance,
France, Austria, Russia, and Prussia, resolved to main-
tain despotism in Spain, and in May, 1823, a French army
entered Madrid. Ferdinand and despotism returned.

The volcano is Vesuvius, and its eruption is a journal-
istic one. In Naples, tyranny was met by conspiracy (the
Carbonari societies). "The discontent of the Italians" (as
an old edition of *The Encyclopaedia Britannica* puts it)
"smouldered for five years, but in 1820 broke into open
flame." Austria, ably assisted by England and France,
crushed the Italian revolution in the spring of 1821.

Cf. in "The stirless sentinel . . ." (see n. to Ten : 1 : 1)
the somewhat similar lines (21–23):

> . . . Naples rebelled,
> beyond the Pyrenees . . . a people's fate
> already was by freedom ruled.

3–4 / one-armed prince . . . Morea . . .: The Greek war for
independence (which the Russian government at first
supported, then ignored) broke out in 1821. The insur-
rection against Turkish domination was begun by
Prince Alexander Ypsilanti (Hypselantes, 1792–1828), a
Phanariot in the service of Russia. He served in the
Russian army and had lost one arm in the battle of
Dresden. Ypsilanti, who had been elected head of the
Hetaeria (a secret political organization that opposed
Turkish rule), crossed the Prut on Mar. 6, 1821, N.S.
His expedition was badly managed. In June he fled to
Austria, and Russia disowned him. The war continued

without him. Russia wavered between the urge to help anyone against her old enemy, Turkey, and the fear of backing revolutionary activities in Greece. Russian secret organizations on the other hand, while sympathizing with the Greeks and working against the despotism of Alexander I, were not at all eager to have an arrant autocrat cripple liberalism at home by assuming the role of liberator abroad.

Ypsilanti is also mentioned by Pushkin in a fugitive poem of 1821 (c. Apr. 5, Kishinev), addressed to Vasiliy Davïdov (1792–1855), active member of the Southern Society, brother of General Aleksandr Davïdov, with whose pretty wife (Aglaë, born Duchesse de Grammont) Pushkin, as many others, had had a brief affair. The poem consists of sixty iambic tetrameters freely rhymed; it begins:

> While General Orlov,
> Hymen's recruit with shaven head,
> aflame with sacred passion,
> prepares to join the ranks;
> while you, wise wag,
> spend nights in noisy converse;
> while over bottles of Ay
> sit my Raevskis;
> while everywhere young Spring,
> smiling, sets loose the mud,
> and on the Danube's bank to drown his grief
> our one-armed prince stirs strife—
> I who love you, Orlov and both Raevskis,
> and memories of Kamenka,
> desire to say a word or two
> about myself and Kishinev . . .

General Orlov—he was general at twenty-six—is Mihail Orlov (1788–1842), member of the Union of Welfare (see n. to XIII : 3); he married, May 15, 1821, Ekaterina Raevski and dropped politics. Pushkin had briefly courted Ekaterina in August, 1820, in the Crimea. He

saw the couple in Kishinev, where they dwelled in 1821.
The Raevskis are the brothers Aleksandr and Nikolay,
sons of General Nikolay Raevski. Kamenka is the estate,
in the province of Kiev, belonging to the mother of
Aleksandr and Vasiliy Davïdov; she was the niece of
Potyomkin; before marrying Lev Davïdov, she had been
married to Colonel Nikolay Raevski (d. 1771); General
Nikolay Raevski was their son.

Morea (southern part of the mainland of Greece) was
the headquarters of the Hetaeria. In the spring of 1821
Ypsilanti had started to direct operations from Kishinev,
and the rather odd "winking" is an allusion to his com-
municating with Morea, where his brother had already
landed.

In his Kishinev diary, Pushkin made the following
entry, Apr. 2, 1821:

Spent the evening at N. G.'s [not identified], a charm-
ing Greek lady. The talk was about Alexander Ypsilanti.
Among five Greeks I alone spoke as a Greek: they all
despair of success of the Hetaeria's enterprise. I am firmly
convinced that Greece will triumph and that twenty-five
million Turks will leave the flowering land of Hellas to
the rightful heirs of Homer and Themistocles.

In the same entry, and in a letter (early March, cor-
respondent not identified), our poet is enthusiastic about
Ypsilanti and his courage. The tone in Ten : IX is very
different. Already by 1823–24, Pushkin had emphat-
ically voiced his disillusion. Thus in the draft of a letter
to an unidentified correspondent from Kishinev or
Odessa, basing himself on very limited, and somewhat
provincial, observations, Pushkin calls the Greeks

. . . un tas de gueux timides, voleurs et vagabonds qui
n'ont pu même soutenir le premier feux de la mauvaise
mousqueterie turque. Quant à ce qui regarde les officiers
[Greek officers whom he met in Kishinev and Odessa], ils

sont pires que les soldats . . . nul point d'honneur. . . . Je
ne suis ni un barbare, ni un apôtre de l'Alcoran, la cause
de la Grèce m'intéresse vivement, c'est pour cela même
que je m'indigne en voyant ces misérables revêtus du
ministère sacré de défenseurs de la liberté.

The term *barbare* should be noted. It is the term used
by Nikolay Turgenev in 1831 in speaking of Pushkin
(see n. to XVI : 9–14).

X

The allusion here is probably to the Congress of Verona,
1822, at which, according to Charles Cavendish Fulke
Greville's *Diary* (entry of Jan. 25, 1823), "the Emperor
of Russia once talked to [the Duke of Wellington] of
the practicability of marching an army into Spain; and
seemed to think he might do so."

XI

Using the historical present, Pushkin apostrophizes, I
think, in this stanza the same *Zakon*, "Law," that he
made his main character in his *Liberty: an Ode* of 1817.
I have constructed (with apologies to our poet's shade)
the following dummy, merely in order to clarify my
concept of the beginning of st. XI:

> *Molchí, Zakón! Nash Tsár' tantsúet*
> *Kadríl', mazúrku i galóp,*
> *A pro tebyá i v ús ne dúet,*
> 4 *Tï—Aleksándrovskiy holóp.*
> *Kinzhál Luvélya, tén' Bertóna*
> *V vidén'yah ne trevózhat tróna . . .*

> Be silent, Law! Our Tsar is dancing
> quadrille, mazurka, and galope,
> and does not care a straw about you,
> 4 you are the slave of Alexander.
> The dagger of Louvel, the shadow of Berton
> do not in dreams disturb the throne . . .

Commentary

5 This is an enigmatic line. The word *Kinzhal*, "dagger," is
clear enough in the MS, and so are the capital letters *L*
and *B*. It is the third word of the line that is difficult to
decipher, though written in a bold hand. With most
commentators, I take it to be *ten'*, "shadow." The first
two letters of this *ten'* are formed differently from those
in the *ten'* of VIII : 4 ("shadow of the dawn"); these are,
however, duals commonly found within the limits of
one person's handwriting. What is significant is the
close similarity in the first two letters in the *ten'* of XI : 5
with the first two letters of *tem* ("the more") of V : 1;
and since the third letter in *ten'* of XI : 5 is identical with
the third letter in the *ten'* of VIII : 4, I feel certain that
no other reading then *ten'*, "shadow," is possible in XI : 5.

L is generally accepted by commentators as such. It is
the *B* that is puzzling, and some pretty silly suggestions
have been made. At one time I fancied that the not-too-
clearly written *ten'* might be read as *mech*, "sword,"
and then the sense "the sword of Bellona" seemed an ob-
vious deduction; but lately I have arrived at a different
conclusion (1952).

In an unsigned historical note published by Pushkin
in the *Literary Gazette* (*Literaturnaya gazeta*), no. 5
(1830), "On the Memoirs of Samson [Sanson], the
French Executioner," I find that Pushkin mentions
Louvel side by side with Berton. Pushkin's note reads:

What will he tell us, the man who in the course of forty
bloodstained years witnessed the last convulsions of so
many victims, some famous, some unknown, some of
sacred, others of hateful memory? All, all of them—his
acquaintances of one moment—will ascend in turn the
steps of the guillotine where he, the ferocious zany, plays
his monotonous role. Martyrs, malefactors, heroes, the
royal sufferer [Louis XVI] and his murderer [Danton],
Charlotte Corday, and the courtesan du Barry, the mad-
man Louvel and the insurgent Berton, the physician
Castaing [Dr. Edmé Samuel Castaing, 1797–1823], who

poisoned his fellow men [the two Ballet brothers, Auguste and Hippolyte, in a complicated inheritance case], and Papavoine [Louis Auguste Papavoine, 1783–1825], who killed children [a little boy and a little girl whom he stabbed in a fit of insanity as they were walking with their mother in a public park]—we shall see all of them again at their last terrible minute.

Louvel is Louis Pierre Louvel (1783–1820), the sullen saddler, who had resolved in his lunes to exterminate all the Bourbons and had commenced his imbecile task by stabbing to death the Duc de Berry, heir to the throne, in Paris on Feb. 13, 1820, N.S., a crime for which he was beheaded.

I now suggest that *B* in Ten : XI : 5 stands for Berton. This is General Jean Baptiste Berton (1769–1822), a kind of French Decembrist, who dramatically conspired against the Bourbons in 1822, and died on the block, crying in a voice of thunder, "Vive la France, vive la Liberté!"

The spurious memoirs of Charles Henri Sanson (1740–93), "exécuteur des hautes-œuvres" during the Reign of Terror in France, appeared in several editions. The earliest and best known seems to have been *Mémoires pour servir à l'histoire de la Révolution française,* "par Sanson, exécuteur des arrêts criminels pendant la Révolution" (2 vols., Paris, 1829), a mediocre concoction by two littérateurs, Honoré de Balzac, later a popular novelist (1799–1850), and Louis François l'Héritier de l'Ain (1789–1852), who was also the "editor" of that other best-selling fabrication, *Mémoires de Vidocq, chef de la police de sûreté* (4 vols., Paris, 1828–29).

XII

1 / Play regiment / *Potéshnïy pólk:* The Semyonovskiy regiment is meant. It was established for Peter I, together

with the Preobrazhenskiy regiment. This tsar was one of the most bestial, but also by far the most intelligent, of Russian potentates of the Romanov dynasty. Pushkin had an epic respect for him and used him as a colorful character in two narrative poems (*Poltava* and *The Bronze Horseman*) and in his unfinished historical novel known as *The Blackamoor of Peter the Great*. The epithet *poteshnïy*, from *poteha*, "fun," was the term applied to companies of boy soldiers, animated toy troops, which Peter in his youth played with.

2 / old mustaches / *stárïh usachéy* [acc. pl.]: A Gallicism we have already met with in Chapter Two (XVIII : 13).

3 / The word *prédali* means both "betrayed" and "delivered."

3 / tyrant: This is the lunatic Paul I (father of Alexander I and Nicholas I) who was murdered in his bedroom by a gang of courtiers on the night of Mar. 11, 1801, without the Semyonovskiy watch interfering. The event will be especially remembered as having inspired, in 1817, a magnificent passage (ll. 57–88) in Pushkin's first great work, his *Ode to Liberty*.

Two of the hanged Decembrists had served in the Semyonovskiy regiment in the 1820's, namely, Sergey Muravyov-Apostol and Mihail Bestuzhev-Ryumin. Presumably, the rest of Ten : XII continued the history of this regiment. Tsar Alexander used to say that if there was anything in the world more beautiful (*plus beau*) than the sight of a thousand identical men all performing exactly the same movement, it was the sight of a hundred thousand men performing it. Grand Duke Nicholas, later Nicholas I, had huge embarrassed grenadiers go through their steps on the parquetry of his ballroom, and, just for the fun of it, his young German wife, an *Ur*-Majorette, would strut at their side. General Shvarts, an especially brutal and pedantic commander of the Semyonovskiy regiment, had soldiers come to his house in the evening for private lessons of pointing the toe. Shvarts had a bad temper and would often slap those impassive poor faces and spit into them. Finally, on Oct. 17, 1820 (not 1821, as some compilations have it), the regiment solemnly and decorously rebelled, demanding that Shvarts be dismissed, which he was; but some eight hundred soldiers were court-martialed.

Since completely erroneous, politically inspired notions are attached by some Soviet commentators to Pushkin's above-mentioned ode, in an attempt to make naïve and misinformed modern readers see a revolutionist's message in it, it cannot be too often reiterated that *Liberty* is the work of a conservative young liberal to whom Law, *Zakon*, *les lois* (in the humanitarian and philosophic sense attached to the term by such French thinkers as Fénelon and Montesquieu), represented the primary factor in the distribution of liberties and who fully subscribed to Byron's lines (*Don Juan*, IX, xxv, 7–8):

> . . . I wish men to be free
> As much from mobs as kings . . .

Pushkin's *Vol'nost'*, in purely verbal intonation, is closer to the ode on slavery, *Na rabstvo* (1783), by Vasiliy Kapnist (1757–1824) than it is to the ode *Vol'-nost'* (c. 1783), by Aleksandr Radishchev. It should also be noted that in his *Vol'nost'* Pushkin used not the usual odic stanza of ten lines (with rhymes ababeeciic or babaccedde) but the stanza of eight lines (with rhymes babaceec, in the present case), which Derzhavin had borrowed from France for his famous *The Grandee* (*Vel'mozha*, begun 1774, final text published 1798). It is the *strophe de huit vers* or *huitain*.

Here is a translation (from Gofman's edition of Push-

kin's works in one volume, Berlin, 1937) with the iambic
tetrameter preserved, but with the rhymes sacrificed to
literal sense:

Liberty: an Ode

Begone, be hidden from my eyes,
delicate Queen of Cythera!
Where are you, where, terror of Kings,
4 the proud chantress of Freedom?
Arrive; pluck off my garland;
break the effeminated lyre!
Freedom I wish to sing unto the world,
8 to smite iniquity on thrones.

Reveal to me the noble track
of that exalted Gaul, to whom
you, 'midst awesome calamities,
12 yourself courageous hymns inspired.
Nurslings of fickle Destiny,
you, tyrants of the world, shudder!
and you take heart and hearken,
16 resuscitate, you fallen slaves!

Alas! where'er my gaze I cast
—everywhere whips, everywhere irons;
the perilous disgrace of laws,
20 the helpless tears of servitude.
Unrighteous Power everywhere
in condensed fog of prejudices
is throned—Slavery's awesome Genius
24 and Glory's fatal passion.

There only on the kingly head
suffering of nations has not fallen
where firm with Sacred Liberty
28 is the accord of mighty laws;
where spread to all is their strong shield;
where, grasped by trusty hands,
above the equal heads of citizens
32 their sword without preferment glides,

and from that elevation crime
it strikes down with a righteous sweep;
where their arm is unbribable
36 by ravenous avarice or fear.
Rulers! to you the crown and throne
the Law gives and not Nature.
Higher than the People you stand,
40 but higher than you is the eternal Law.

And grief, grief to the nations
where rashly it is drowsing,
where either the People or Kings
44 to dominate the Law are able!
As witness, you I call,
O martyr of glorious mistakes,
who for your forebears, in the noise of recent
48 laid down a kingly head.   [storms,

Louis ascends to death,
viewed by wordless posterity.
His head, now crownless, he has sunk
52 upon the bloody block of Broken Faith.
The Law is silent; silent is the People.
The criminal blade falls . . .
and lo! a villainous purple
56 has clothed the shackled Gauls.

Autocratoric Villain!
You, your throne, I abhor;
your downfall, the death of your children,
60 I see with cruel jubilation.
Upon your forehead read
Nations the stamp of malediction.
You're the world's horror, nature's shame,
64 upon earth a reproach to God.

When down upon the gloomy Neva
the star Polaris sparkles
and on the head devoid of cares
68 reposeful slumber weighs,
the pensive poet contemplates
the grimly sleeping midst the fog

339

> desolate monument of a tyrant,
> 72 a palace to oblivion cast,
>
> and hears the dreadful voice of Clio
> above yon gloom-pervaded walls,
> Caligula's last hour
> 76 vivid he sees before his eyes.
> He sees: beribanded, bestarred,
> with Wine and Rancor drunk,
> they come, the furtive assassins,
> 80 their faces brazen, hearts afraid.
>
> Silent is the untrusty watchman,
> the drawbridge silently is lowered,
> the gate is opened in the dark of night
> 84 by hired betrayal's hand.
> O shame! O horror of our days!
> Like beasts, the Janizaries have burst in!
> The infamous blows fall,
> 88 and perished has the crownéd villain!
>
> And these days learn, O Kings!
> Not punishment, not recompenses,
> not prison vaults, not altars
> 92 provide you with secure defenses.
> Be you the first to bow your heads
> beneath the Law's trustworthy shelter,
> and guard eternally the throne
> 96 shall liberty and peace of Peoples.

Here follows, by line numbers, a comm. on *Liberty*.

2 | *Tsitéri slábaya tsarítsa*: Cythera, one of the Ionian islands where stood a temple of Aphrodite, or Venus, the frail (*slabaya*, "weak," "delicate") goddess of Love.

4 | of Freedom | *Svobódï*: Sergey Turgenev (a brother of Pushkin's friends Aleksandr and Nikolay Turgenev, and a cousin of the father of Ivan Turgenev, the novelist) notes in the diary he kept in France, entry of Dec. 1, N.S.

(Nov. 19, O.S.), 1817: "[My brothers] again write to me
of Pushkin as of an unfolding talent. Ah, let them hurry
to infuse liberalism in him, and, instead of self-lamenta-
tions, let his first song be: Freedom [*Svoboda*]." To this
plea, ll. 4 and 7 of *Vol'nost'* present an obvious response,
and if we assume that Sergey Turgenev simultaneously
with his journal note voiced the same wish in his corre-
spondence, this would place the writing of the ode not
earlier than the beginning of November, O.S., since
otherwise Sergey Turgenev would have probably re-
ceived it by the time he made that entry. In his MS
"Imaginary Conversation with Alexander I" (1825)
Pushkin implies that *Vol'nost'* was written in 1817,
before his eighteenth birthday (May 26).

10 A likely candidate for the post of *vozvïshennïy Gall* is
the minor poet, Ponce Denis Ecouchard Lebrun, or Le
Brun (1729–1807). Tomashevski, in his *Pushkin* (Lenin-
grad, 1956), has discussed the question thoroughly and
has correctly stressed the tremendous, though brief,
popularity of Ecouchard's vigorous odes.

Another candidate is André Chénier, who died, aged
not quite thirty-two, on the guillotine 7 Thermidor,
Year Two (July 25, 1794). Before his arrest in 1794, he
had published only two "courageous hymns" (one of
which is *Le Jeu de paume, à David, peintre,* 1791). His
most famous piece, the elegy known as *La Jeune Captive,*
appeared in the *Décade philosophique* in 1795 and later
in several magazines (as did *La Jeune Tarentine*). Cha-
teaubriand quoted a Chénier fragment from memory in
the *Génie* (1802), in eulogizing the poet. Fayolle, more-
over, published various fragments of Chénier's work in
Mélanges littéraires, 1816. I mention this because mod-
ern Russian commentators are under the singular im-
pression that Pushkin could not have known anything
about André Chénier before August, 1819, when his

poems were first collected and published by Latouche.

11 / awesome / *groznïh*: Other editions give *slavnïh*, "glorious."

16 / resuscitate / *vosstán'te*: Grammatically, this is "rise!" or "arise!" but, as noted by Tomashevski, *Pushkin*, pp. 170–72, it is not a command to rise politically, to rebel, to start an insurrection, but means in the context (as elsewhere in Pushkin's rhetorical pieces) "wake up!" "stand up!" "revive!" and so forth.

22–24 The "prejudices" refer to the power of the Church, to her political use of superstition and directed thought. The "Genius" is an eloquent synonym of "spirit." The definition of "fame" as a "fatal passion" applies to Napoleon—who is waiting in the wings of the poem.

25 / head: There is a curious obsession with "heads" throughout the ninety-six lines of the ode. This proximal part of the body is implied in ll. 5 and 61 and named in 25, 31, 47, 50, 68, and 93.

31–32 Tomashevski, p. 162, quotes from a speech pronounced by Aleksandr Kunitsïn (1783–1840), the Lyceum professor of moral and political sciences, at the opening of the Lyceum in 1811, a citation from Guillaume Thomas François Raynal (1713–96), author of *Histoire philosophique et politique des établissemens et du commerce des Européens dans les deux Indes* (1770): "Law is nought unless it be a sword moving indiscriminately above all heads and smiting all that rise above the horizontal plane in which it moves."

32–33 Note the beautiful enjambment. Another, less striking one, links up ll. 69–72 with 73–76.

35 / their: This pronoun, as well as the "their" in ll. 29 and 32, refers to the "mighty laws" of l. 28. There is a

clumsy clash of forelimbs between ll. 30 (*rukámi*) and 35 (*ruká*).

39–40 Fénelon expresses the same thought in *Les Aventures de Télémaque, fils d'Ulysse* (1699), bk. v (1810 edn., p. 78): "Il [le roi] peut tout sur les peuples; mais les lois peuvent tout sur lui." This writer was well known to Russians of the time. Incidentally, it is a copy of the *Fables* of Fénelon (Paris, 1809) that contains the earliest sample of our poet's hand (probably 1811).

41–44 Cf. Ecouchard Lebrun's windy and cold *Ode aux français* (composed 1762), which sings martial glory rather than liberty and law (ll. 79–80):

> Malheur à qui s'élève en foulant les ruines
> Des lois et de l'état . . .

45–56 The reference is to Louis XVI, beheaded in 1793 during the French regime of Terror. Carlyle, in that admirable work *The French Revolution: a History* (1837), speaks of regicide in much the same tones (ch. 8):

> O hapless Louis! The son of sixty Kings is to die on the scaffold by form of law. O haughty, tyrannous man! Injustice breeds injustice. . . . Innocent Louis bears the sins of many generations. . . .

54 / falls: Here (*padyót*), as well as in l. 87 (*padút*) and elsewhere in our poet's works, this form (from *past'*, "to fall"), which is ordinarily employed in a future sense, is used in the present for strong brevity (instead of *padaet*, *padayut*).

55–56 / purple has clothed / *porfíra . . . lezhít*: Grammatically: "is lying."

57–64 This stanza refers to "Napoleon's purple" (as Pushkin himself remarked in a marginal note of the autograph he gave Nikolay Turgenev in 1817). In later years his attitude toward Napoleon changed considerably, acquiring the fashionable romanticist tinge characteristic of the times. Who were those "children"? I can think only of Napoleon's nephews: little Napoleon Charles Bonaparte, son of his brother Louis (1802–07), and tiny Dermide Leclerc, son of his sister Marie Pauline (1802–04).

66 / the star Polaris / *Zvezdá polúnochi*: *Polunochi* is not only "of midnight" but also (poetical) "of the North."

69 / the pensive poet / *zadúmchivïy pevéts*: According to Vigel's *Memoirs* (1864) and a letter from Nikolay Turgenev to Pyotr Bartenev (in 1867), Pushkin wrote (no doubt from memory—poets do not compose in public) the ode, or part of it, in the rooms of Nikolay Turgenev, who at the time lived in St. Petersburg on the Fontanka Quay, opposite the Mihaylovskiy Palace (also known as the Inzhenernïy Castle), whither, flushed after a champagne supper and wearing their resplendent decorations, the assassins made their way to Tsar Paul's bedroom on the night of Mar. 11, 1801.

73 / Clio: The hysterical Muse of history.

74 / above / *nad*: Other editions have *za*, "behind."

86 / Janizaries / *yanïcharï*: In general, Turkish soldiers; specifically, slave soldiers of the Sultan; here, by extension, killers.

89–96 Tomashevski, p. 170, says that this stanza was added "later." It was first published by Herzen in *The Polar Star*, bk. II (London, 1856). In the last line, *volnost'* is coupled with *pokoy*, an association that was to remain Pushkin's ideal for the rest of his life (see nn. to ll. 20–21

of Onegin's Letter in Eight, and to Eight : XLVIIIa, given
at beginning of "Fragments of *Onegin's Journey*").

XIII

3 / the sparks of a different flame: Beginning with this line
of the stanza, Pushkin starts to give his version of the
Decembrist movement. Despite his (incorrectly) mak-
ing himself a conspirator too, the manner of his account
is curiously detached, and most of the facts he lists seem
derived from documentary evidence rather than from
personal observation.

A secret union of cultured young noblemen opposed
to tyranny and slavery, the Union of Welfare (*Soyuz
Blagodenstviya*) was formed in 1818 and lasted till 1820.
This union was a tree of good, growing in a temperate,
somewhat masonic climate. Its trunk was the welfare of
the fatherland; its roots were virtue and unity; its
branches, philanthropy, education, justice, and social
economy. It was strongly nationalistic. Its disposition
toward literature, as a means of enlightenment, was
that of eighteenth-century common sense, recommend-
ing among other things in its statute "the decency [Fr.
la décence] of expressions and especially the sincere ren-
dering of lofty sentiments, urging man toward good." Its
attitude toward the government was marked by a
muffled rumble of dignified disapproval. Its seal was a
hive, with bees circumvolant. Various clubs, such as the
Green Lamp, were diffuse reflections of it.

The Union of Welfare preceded the formation of two
conspiratorial societies. These were the Northern and
Southern Societies, whose activities resulted in the
abortive coup of Dec. 14 (hence the term "Decembrist"
for the movement), 1825, on the Senate Square in St.
Petersburg. The news of Tsar Alexander's death in
Taganrog, Nov. 19, 1825, reached the capital on Nov.

27, and for the next two weeks nobody knew exactly who was going to succeed him. Finally, his brother Constantine, the rightful heir to the throne, declined to reign, and another brother, Nicholas, was proclaimed tsar. The Decembrists took advantage of the interregnum. Their plan was to overthrow the regime and to introduce a constitution. The publication of a manifesto was to be followed by a *Velikiy Sobor* (Legislative Assembly). The actual uprising fell to the lot of the Northern Society, which was less well organized and more moderate in its views than the Southern group, with its republican tendencies and military pattern of organization.

The ostensible aim of the insurgents was to stand up for Grand Duke Constantine's claims (against those of his brother Nicholas), but their real purpose was to set up a liberal form of government. On Dec. 14, 1825, the sun rose at four minutes past nine and was to set five hours and fifty-four minutes later. That morning the insurgents collected in the square with some troops; there were 671 men in all. It was very cold, and they had not much to do except form a compact *carré*. The leaders intended to compel the Senate to issue their proclamation to the people, but the people were not supposed to take any active part in the events and were merely to provide a sympathetic background, a classical *décor*. A pathetic touch was added by the confusion in the minds of the soldiers between "Constitution" and "Constantine." Everything went wrong from the start. Prince Sergey Trubetskoy had been elected dictator—but he never turned up. The bravest men among the leaders developed a strange apathy and unwonted lack of nerve. One of them, however, Lieutenant Kahovski, shot and killed Count Miloradovich, who was attempting to harangue the troops. The guns of the government, about five P.M., easily put an end to the insurrection. Of the 121 who were tried immediately after the rebellion, five were condemned to be quartered, but the sentence was commuted to hanging. Thirty-one were condemned to decapitation, and this was commuted to hard labor in Siberia. The rest received varying periods of imprisonment and exile. The five hanged were condemned on the following grounds: Colonel Pavel Pestel (b. 1794), for planning to destroy all the members of the imperial family (see n. to XVII : 9); Lieutenant Pyotr Kahovski (b. 1797), for that and for the assassination of Count Miloradovich and Colonel Stürler; Second Lieutenant Kondratiy Rïleev (b. 1795), Second Lieutenant Mihail Bestuzhev-Ryumin (b. 1803), and Lieutenant Colonel Sergey Muravyov-Apostol (b. 1791), for planning regicide. They were executed July 13, 1826, on the Crownwork Bastion of the Peter-and-Paul Fortress (north bank of the Neva, St. Petersburg).

Pushkin, in Mihaylovskoe, heard of the execution on July 24. Next day, a letter (presumably from Tumanski) informed him of the death in Italy, more than a year before, of Amalia Riznich, the young woman he had courted in Odessa. Of this coincidence he made a cryptic note at the bottom of the first fair copy (MB 3266) of the poem that on July 29 he dedicated to Mme Riznich's memory—sixteen iambics, alternate Alexandrines and tetrameters, with the rhyme scheme baba, beginning:

> Beneath the blue sky of her native scene
> She languished, she decayed;
> Decayed at last, and over me, I ween,
> Already hovered her young shade.

A famous ink drawing in Cahier 2368, f. 38^r, was made by Pushkin probably about the same time. It was first published in 1906 by Vengerov in the Brockhaus edition of Pushkin's works and has been republished and rediscussed several times since.* This f. 38^r is covered

---

*E.g., by A. Efros, *Lit. nasl.*, nos. 16–18 (1934), pp. 944–46.

with a dozen profiles, among which commentators recognize our poet's father and uncle. In the upper margin of the page Pushkin sketched a bastion and five little men dangling from a gibbet. The same drawing is repeated, with additional details, at the bottom of the same page. Above the upper gibbet, at the very top of the page, one can decipher the unfinished line

> *I yá bï móg, kak shút na . . .*
> and I might, like a clown upon . . .

Pushkin struck out the words *shut na* and repeated farther down the page, under the drawing, the first four words.

I render *shut* by the generalized "clown," but a more specific translation is possible. One may assume, I suggest, that the image in Pushkin's mind was *shut na nitke* ("string"), a pantine (Fr. *pantin*), jumping jack, manikin on a string. The association between a hanged man and a jerking clown is a common one. An obvious example (cited by Tsyavlovski in *Rukoyu Pushkina*, pp. 159–60) is found in Maykov's *Elisey*, ll. 419–20 (see n. to Eight : Ia : 3), where Zeus threatens with dire retribution that vassal who will not heed his summons:

> In plain words, I shall hang him upside down,
> And 'mid the gods he'll dangle like a clown.

On July 10, 1826, from Mihaylovskoe, Pushkin wrote to Vyazemski in Moscow: "Rebellion and revolution never pleased me, it is true; but I was connected with almost all [the Decembrists]."

From Yakushkin's memoirs (see n. to XVI : 1–8) and from those of another prominent Decembrist, Ivan Pushchin (1798–1859), one of Pushkin's schoolmates and closest friends, it is quite clear that our poet was not a member of any Decembrist organization, and the attempts of certain Soviet commentators to force him into it retrospectively are, to say the least, ridiculous. It might happen that at some dinner or casual meeting of friends, six out of seven men were Decembrists; but the seventh was Pushkin, and the mere presence of an outsider automatically divested the meeting of any conspiratorial sense. According to evidence supplied by one minor Decembrist (Gorstkin) during the inquest in January, 1826, Pushkin used to recite (*chitïval*) verses in the winter of 1819–20 at the Petersburg house of Prince Ilya Dolgoruki, one of the leaders of the Union of Welfare.* But according to Yakushkin, when he met Pushkin at Kamenka, near Kiev, in the autumn of 1820, Pushkin was very much surprised when he, Yakushkin, recited his revolutionary verses, such as *Noel'*, to the poet. It appears from Yakushkin's memoirs that at the time—winter, 1820–21—Pushkin did not know of the existence of any organized secret society and never was a member of the Southern Society (which was founded in Tulchin in March, 1821), although Pushkin was acquainted with its leader, Pestel.

In his poems directly related to the fate of the Decembrist movement, Pushkin, while expressing a solemn sympathy for the exiled men, their families, and their cause, stressed his own artistic immunity, and this blend of participation and aloofness seems to have struck some of the Decembrists as slightly tasteless. In the beginning of January, 1827, Pushkin sent the following tetrametric stanzas (rhyme scheme baba ceec diid boob) to Chita with the wife of the exiled Nikita Muravyov:

> Deep in Siberian mines
> preserve proud patience:
> not lost shall be your woeful toil,
> and the high surging of your meditations.

*See M. Nechkin, "Novoe o Pushkine i dekabristah" (New Findings Concerning Pushkin and the Decembrists), *Lit. nasl.*, LXVIII (1952), 155–66.

> Misfortune's faithful sister, Hope,
> within the gloomy underearth
> shall waken energy and gladness;
> the longed-for time shall come.
>
> Love and Friendship shall reach
> you through the gloomy bolts,
> as now into your penal burrows
> my free voice reaches.
>
> The heavy chains shall fall,
> prisons shall crumble down, and Freedom
> shall welcome you, rejoicing, at the entrance,
> and brothers shall return your sword to you.

One of the exiled Decembrists, Prince Aleksandr Odoevski, replied in four mediocre stanzas, wherein he said in effect: Do not worry, bard, we are proud of our chains and will forge swords out of them.

Later, on July 16, 1827, in fifteen iambic tetrameters (with rhymes baabeccceddiffi), entitled *Arion*, in allusion to the admirable Greek minstrel whom an appreciative dolphin saved from drowning, Pushkin evoked a boat with oarsmen (representing the Decembrists) and a poet (representing Pushkin) singing to them as they rowed. A storm wrecks the boat; all perish save the poet, who in the last lines, in a classical metaphor, is seen drying his raiments on a rock while singing his former hymns.

XIV

2 | *Oní za chásheyu viná*: What rhymed with this? There is nothing more futile, and more tempting, than filling such gaps as left here, in XIV, where l. 4 is automatically supplied by the ear: *osvobozhdáli plemená*, "freed the nations." But whether Pushkin intended this reading is another question.

XV

This stanza refers presumably to sessions of the Union of Welfare in St. Petersburg, c. 1819.

The house where the Decembrists met, belonging to Nikita Muravyov (1796–1843), is now No. 26 on the Fontanka Quay, Leningrad.* Muravyov was a member of the Union of Welfare and when, in 1820, the Northern Society was formed he became a member of its supreme council. He authored the project of a constitution that would give Russia a federal form of government, dividing Russia into states after the American pattern.

Ilya Dolgoruki (1797–1848). According to Yakushkin, the conspirators met at his house, too. He was a prominent member of the Union of Welfare but did not join the Northern Society that succeeded it. In 1820 he withdrew from secret political activities and was not arrested in December, 1825.

The two-line quotation in Vyazemski's diary, already mentioned in my introductory notes to Ten, supplies us with a variant (xv : 3: "inspired" instead of "unquiet") and with l. 4, which Pushkin did not reach in the course of enciphering this stanza.

XVI

1–8 Mihail Lunin (1787–1845) and Ivan Yakushkin (1793–1857) were active members of the Northern Society. Pushkin was personally acquainted with both.

Yakushkin's memoirs (1853–55), written in exile, can be found in vol. I of *Izbrannïe sotsial'no-politicheskie i filosofskie proizvedeniya dekabristov* (Selections from the Socio-Political and Philosophical Works of the Decem-

---

*A. Yatsevich, *Pushkinskiy Peterburg* (Leningrad, 1931).

brists; 3 vols., Leningrad, 1951; I have seen only two),
ed. I. Shchipanov, with notes by S. Shtrayh.

5 / Pushkin read his noels: In a literal sense, noels are
French Christmas carols of some historical interest but
of no poetical value. The form goes back to the eleventh
century. Parodies of such carols, with political implica-
tions, are meant here.

Young Pushkin in Petersburg certainly recited anti-
governmental poems to his friends of the Green Lamp
group and at other gay suppers, where future Decem-
brists were present. But these meetings were not con-
spiratorial sessions. In those he did not participate. As
elsewhere, our poet here stylizes his connection with the
Decembrist movement.

What exactly were these "noels"? Only one has
reached us, a rather mild piece composed probably in
1818, four iambic octaves, each consisting of five trim-
eters (1–4, 8), one Alexandrine (5), and two tetrameters
(6–7), with rhyme scheme ababecce (ll. 1–4):

> Hurrah! Posthaste to Russia
> The roving despot hies.
> Our Saviour bursts out crying,
> And all the nation cries.

Mary quietens her child, the tsar arrives "hale and stout"
and promises to fire the Director of Police, to lock up the
Secretary of Censorship in the madhouse, and "to give
people all the rights of people"—a reference to Alex-
ander's liberal speech in Warsaw to the Diet, Mar. 15,
1818. The jingle ends with the following lines (25–32):

> Then the delighted infant
> Begins to jump in bed:
> "He *really* is not joking?
> The truth he *really* said?"
> And Mary on her Child with lullabies prevails
> To close its little eyes: " 'Tis late,

> You've heard our father Tsar relate
> His bedtime fairy tales.''

All this is in Béranger's journalistic style and has little literary value—in striking contrast to the *Ode to Liberty*.

Bernard de la Monnoye (1641–1728) worked on the *Noei borguignon* in the 1670's and published them, with his translations into French, over the pen name of Gui Barôzai in 1720. Pushkin may have seen La Monnoye's *Noëls bourguignons* (which in the Burgundian original are more impious than in their French form). The edition I have consulted is found in the Leyden reprint (1865) of the rare anthology *Recueil de pièces choisies rassemblées par les soins du cosmopolite* (Armand Louis de Vignerot Duplessis Richelieu, duc d'Aiguillon, 1683–1750; Véretz in Touraine, 1735), pp. 427–500. These are flippant, sometimes impious, sometimes tender and quaint, little songs telling of Christ's birth, and so on. Noel V, st. II, goes, for example:

> A la Nativité
> Chantons, je vous supplie.
> Une Vierge a porté
> Neuf mois le fruit de vie;
> Le Saint-Esprit futé
> Fit cette œuvre jolie ["bé sutie"
>   in the Burgundian text].

I happen to notice that Ten : XVI : 5 is translated by Babette Deutsch (1943, a somewhat enlarged edition of her 1937 version of *EO*, which is remarkable only for Fritz Eichenberg's hideous and absurd illustrations):

Here Pushkin read his verses with a swagger . . .

6–8 / melancholy Yakushkin . . . regicidal dagger: Yakushkin's portraits convey an impression of dejection. He is said to have been unhappy in love. In his memoirs, he recalls that the thought of killing Alexander I overwhelmed him one day in 1817, in Moscow, when the bizarre rumor spread that the tsar was transferring his residence to Warsaw and annexing a part of Russia to Poland. Yakushkin's plan was to arm himself with a brace of pistols, one with which to shoot the tsar and the other to shoot himself, in a kind of one-man duel. He gave up this plan when the rumor proved to have no foundation in fact.

9–14 / seeing . . . lame Turgenev . . .: Nikolay Turgenev (1789–1871) was a prominent member of the moderate wing of the Secret Society and was the author of an important section of the statute in the Union of Welfare. This part dealt with the limitation of the tsar's powers.

On Apr. 9, 1824, he left for western Europe and remained there till 1856, when the Decembrists were granted amnesty. I have not been able to discover any details about his limp.

His brother, Aleksandr Turgenev (1784–1845), director of the Department of Foreign Creeds, was one of Pushkin's stanchest supporters and truest friends. It was he who helped to enroll young Pushkin in the Lyceum in 1811. It was he and Karamzin who in the last week of April, 1820, persuaded the Minister of Foreign Affairs to have Pushkin attached to General Inzov's chancellery in southern Russia—an uncommonly benign arrangement in contrast to other possibilities of exile. It was he who in the beginning of June, 1823, again spoke to Count Nesselrode and arranged Pushkin's transfer to Odessa ("A Maecenas [Vorontsov], a fine climate, the sea, historical memories—Odessa has everything," so wrote Turgenev to Vyazemski, June 15, 1823, about his protégé's new assignment). And, finally, it was he who, at midnight, on Feb. 1, 1837, after the funeral service at the Konyushennaya Church in St. Petersburg accompanied (with the gendarme Rakeev, who a quarter of a century later was to arrest the radical publicist Nikolay Chernïshevski) Pushkin's coffin to the Svyatïe Gorï monastery, province of Pskov, district of Opochka, where the poet was buried on Feb. 6, 1837, on the next day after the last rapid journey that his poor body took.

In his letters to his brother (*Arhiv brat'ev Turgene-vïh*, Petrograd, 1921), Nikolay Turgenev plays the part of a person much surprised and deeply hurt at being called a state criminal by the Russian government. "I was never interested in insurrection," "My conscience is clear."

In a letter of Apr. 26/May 6, 1826, from Edinburgh, to Aleksandr Turgenev in Petersburg, Nikolay Turgenev writes: "I always considered the Secret Society to be a thing one occupied oneself with rather in jest than in earnest." And a fortnight later:

One may ask me: but why all those secret societies, if you saw they were nonsense? What can I answer? To amuse themselves some people gamble, others dance or play blind man's buff, others again forgather to spend the time in conversations. I belong to the latter kind of person. Could I foresee that one would make a crime out of those conversations?

Another letter of June 25/July 7, 1826:

I have stated already [in a letter to the government] what I saw in secret societies. The liberation of the peasants has always been for me a most sacred cause. It was my only purpose in life. . . . But not seeing any material results, i.e., not seeing any freeing of slaves [on the part of slaveowners], which I demanded, I left at last that barren land and in recent time did not give the Secret Society a thought.

It seems to me perfectly clear that Pushkin saw these letters.

In a letter to his brother of Aug. 11, 1832, Aleksandr Turgenev quotes Ten : XVI : 9–14 and continues:

Commentary

In this part of *Eugene Onegin,* Pushkin had some delight-
ful characterizations of Russians and Russia [no doubt, the
"Mayhap" stanzas, VI and VII], but it will have to be with-
held for a long time. All he read to me in Moscow [early
December, 1831] were fragments [obviously the same
stanzas he read to Vyazemski].

To this Nikolay Turgenev replied from Paris in great
rage (the real cause of which is not clear) nine days later:

Pushkin's verses about me, communicated by you,
made me shrug my shoulders. The judges who condemned
me and condemned the others were performing their job:
the job of barbarians devoid of any civic or civilized lights.
That is in the nature of things. But here come new judges.
A person can have talent for poetry, a lot of intelligence,
and still be a barbarian. And Pushkin and all Russians are
certainly barbarians. . . . If those who were less lucky
than I and perished had no better claims to civilization
than has Pushkin, they acquired at least other rights
through self-sacrifice and sufferings that placed them
above the judgment of their compatriots.

Aleksandr Turgenev did not understand his brother's
wrath, and in a letter of Sept. 2 wrote:

Your conclusion regarding Pushkin is correct insofar
as there remains indeed some barbarism in him, and
Vyazemski in Moscow took him to task severely for his at-
titude toward Poland; but in his verses about you I do not
perceive it [the barbarism], and generally there is much
that is correct in the opinion he expressed about you. It is
only in regard to Poland that he is a barbarian.

Tomashevski, "Desyataya glava 'Evgeniya Onegina.'
Istoriya razgadki" (The Tenth Chapter of *Eugene One-
gin.* The Story of Its Solution), *Lit. nasl.,* nos. 16–18
(1934), p. 388, gives Nikolay Turgenev's answer to this
in a Russian translation (that particular letter was writ-
ten in French):

One could argue a good deal concerning the poetical
importance you assign to Pushkin and he assigns to him-

self. That would lead us too far. Byron was indubitably a poet, but it was neither his principle nor his custom to wallow in mud.

Displeasure with the crude nationalism Pushkin expressed in eloquently supporting the Russian government in the Polish question is not sufficient to explain the acute personal irritation one discerns in Nikolay Turgenev's letters. At Decembrist meetings in 1819–20, Turgenev may not have promoted his views on emancipation with the cranky perseverance described by Pushkin. It would seem that he was shocked mainly by the tone of the thing and might have mistaken Pushkin's stylization for a jeer at his most cherished idea. From our point of view, over and across the softening remoteness of time, we distinguish in Pushkin's account of the Decembrist conspiracy little more than a detached, slightly flippant note. But a reformer of Turgenev's type might have felt that any attitude save one of pious and fervid sympathy was insulting. Lerner (1915, quoted by Tomashevski, "Desyataya glava," p. 389) has suggested that Pushkin, who in 1819 had already expressed the hope of seeing slavery abolished by the tsar, must have found it ridiculous for Nikolay Turgenev to expect that a group of noblemen should perform that act. (This, of course, is exactly what happened thirty years later, when groups of altruistic noblemen prevailed on the government to liberate the serfs.)

It has also been suggested (1) that Nikolay Turgenev was displeased by Pushkin's evidently knowing of a MS essay, a *pièce de justification*, in which great stress was laid on the liberation of peasants, which Nikolay's brother had given Zhukovski in Leipzig in 1827 to show to the tsar, and in which Nikolay Turgenev harshly criticized the Decembrist movement; and (2) that he was enraged by Pushkin's making a conspirator of him, Turgenev, who emphatically denied having any connections with the Decembrists (Volkonski and others called Turgenev a liar for this).

Pushkin's esteem for Nikolay Turgenev—and for all freedom-loving, independent people as such—is evident from a marvelous epigram on Neptune (iambic tetrameters, rhymed abba cece) that heads a letter to Vyazemski, Aug. 14, 1826, from Mihaylovskoe to Petersburg:

> So 'tis the sea, the ancient assassin
> that kindles into flame your genius?
> You glorify with golden lyre
> Neptune's dread trident?
> No, praise him not! In our vile age
> gray Neptune is the Earth's ally.
> Upon all elements man is a tyrant,
> a traitor, or a prisoner.

This is an answer to a poem entitled *The Sea* that Vyazemski sent him in a letter of July 31, 1826, from Revel. Pushkin's epigram was prompted by rumors (which later proved false) to the effect that Great Britain had surrendered the political émigré, Decembrist Nikolay Turgenev, to the Russian government. In his letter following the epigram, Pushkin says: "My warmest thanks for your poem. I shall criticize it another time. Is it true that Nikolay T. has been brought by ship to Petersburg? . . ."

Vyazemski's poem is a set of twelve tetrametric staves of eight verses each (baabcece, which is a rare and harsh sequence), eulogizing the purity and beauty of the sea.

Aleksandr Turgenev's letter (see introduction to these nn. to Ten, p. 314) supplies us with the variants of two lines: 10, "pursuing [*presleduya*] his ideal"; and 12, "whips [*pleti*] of slavery."

Tomashevski's photograph ("Desyataya glava," p. 391) of Pushkin's rough draft of the stanza shows that he canceled, l. 3, "destructive," *gubitel'nïe* (replaced by "decisive," *reshitel'nïe*); l. 5, "poems," *stihi* (replaced

first by *satirï* and finally by *noeli*); l. 7, "as one who's
doomed," *kak obrechyonnïy* (replaced by "it seemed,
silently," *kazalos' molcha*); l. 12, "chains," *tsepi* (re-
placed by "whips," *pleti*); and ll. 13–14, "in this crowd
. . . foresaw the liberators" (replaced by "in this crowd
. . . saw the deliverers").

XVII

2 / earlier the spring: Pushkin now turns his attention to
the activities of the Southern Society. It consisted of
three groups, the central one, at the headquarters of the
Second Army, in Tulchin (Bratslav District, province of
Podolsk), directed by Pestel and Aleksey Yushnevski;
the group at Kamenka (Chigirin District, province of
Kiev), directed by Vasiliy Davïdov and Prince Sergey
Volkonski; and the group at Vasilkov (Vasilkov District,
province of Kiev), directed by Sergey Muravyov-Apostol
and Bestuzhev-Ryumin. The society was in touch with
Polish groups working toward the independence of
Poland.

5 Count Peter Wittgenstein (1768–1842) commanded the
Second Army, with headquarters at Tulchin. A good and
brave man, he was greatly loved by his subordinates.

9 / P[estel]: Colonel Pavel Pestel (1794–1826), adjutant of
Count Wittgenstein from 1813 to 1821 and then com-
mander of the Vyatskiy regiment. Author of a constitu-
tion (*Russkaya pravda*, Russian Justice) and the main
leader of the Southern Society, which he organized in
March, 1821, in the provinces of Podolsk and Kiev. Pestel
was by far the most intelligent, gifted, and energetic
man among the conspirators, but unfortunately was not
in St. Petersburg on Dec. 14, 1825. He said in a written
statement after his arrest:

Commentary

The events in Naples, Spain, and Portugal had a great in-
fluence upon me. I perceived there . . . the proof of the
instability of monarchic constitutions and found ample
reason to doubt that monarchs genuinely accept any such
constitutions. . . . This affirmed me very strongly in a
republican and revolutionary mentality.

Pushkin met Pestel Apr. 9, 1821, in Kishinev (and
may have first seen him at Tulchin in February). Under
this date there is the following entry in the poet's diary:

Spent the morning with Pestel [who, rather paradoxically,
had been sent by the government to Kishinev to report on
the activities of the Free Greece group there]; an intelli-
gent man in every sense of the word. Mon cœur est ma-
térialiste, mais ma raison s'y refuse [said Pestel]. Our
conversation was metaphysical, political, ethical, etc. He
is one of the most original minds that I know.

In the same entry Pushkin reports that the Greek
leader's brother, Prince Demetrius Ypsilanti, tells him
that the Greeks crossed the Danube and smashed a Turk-
ish army corps; in the next entry, May 4, he says he has
been made a mason, and in the one after that, May 9, he
notes: "Today is exactly one year since I left Peters-
burg." Pushkin saw Pestel again in Kishinev in the last
week of May, after which the latter returned to Tulchin.
(There is no evidence that they saw each other in Odessa,
which Pestel seems to have visited in the winter of 1823.)

Pushkin, in Mihaylovskoe, heard of the uprising in
Petersburg a week after the event, about Dec. 20, 1825.
In the course of the next fortnight the news of the par-
ticipation of Rïleev, Küchelbecker, and Pushchin, and
the information regarding Pestel's arrest at Lintsï, must
surely have reached our poet by means of "occasions"
(letters sent not by post but by reliable travelers). On Jan.
4 or 5, 1826, in the left margin of the draft of Five : v–vi,
which is the exact middle of the novel ("Tatiana . . .
[believed in] dreams, cartomancy, prognostications by

the moon . . .''; expected misfortune if "a swift hare . . .
would run across her path"), and farther, in the left
margin of the draft of Five : IX–X ("The night is frosty.
. . . 'What is your name?' . . . Hariton"; a mirror lies
under Tatiana's pillow for the registration of dreams'
portents), Pushkin commenced a column of profiles: in
both cases the top profile is that of Pestel. In these two
pencil sketches, Pestel has the head of an ancient Greek
with the heavy jaw of a medallic Napoleon. In the margin
of the Five : V–VI draft, the other profiles under Pestel's
represent, in the following order: a stylized combination
of Robespierre and Pushkin; under this, a large, Punch-
like Mirabeau; under this, the old-*gavroche* features of
Voltaire; and to the left from Voltaire, the duck-nosed
profile of homely Rïleev. Pushkin had last seen Pestel
more than four and a half years earlier, and Rïleev more
than five and a half years earlier; the artist's visual mem-
ory must have been exceptionally retentive. * In the draft
of Five : IX–X, the sequence of profiles under that of
Pestel represents: the very Russian features of Ivan
Pushchin (twice) and bespectacled Vyazemski (not a
Decembrist), while in the lower corner of the opposite
margin a second sketch of Rïleev's head is accompanied
by the long-nosed, chinless, and pathetic profile of Kü-
chelbecker.

Pushkin had last seen Vyazemski and Küchelbecker
some six years before. He had last seen his old friend and
schoolmate Pushchin when the latter visited him Jan. 11,
1825. According to Pushchin's memoirs, our poet knew
of his belonging to a secret society and said to him: "I do

---

*Quite apart from this fact it should be remembered that, before
photography had introduced its more flexible and more fluid
(and thus less stylized) portrayal of facial expressions, the fre-
quent occurrence of one's friend's silhouette or caricature in a
common friend's album helped to fix its typical feature in
one's mind as firmly as the endlessly recopied pictures of long
dead poets and kings.

not force you, dear Pushchin, to talk. Perhaps you are right in distrusting me. No doubt I am unworthy of your trust because of so many foolish things on my part.'' Pushkin's relations with Rïleev are tantalizingly brought out by a not-too-trustworthy account that a later friend of Pushkin's, Sobolevski, left us. It would appear that about Dec. 10, 1825, Pushkin, upon learning of Alexander I's death, decided to disobey orders and travel to St. Petersburg, where he planned to put up at Rïleev's apartment, although he had many other, closer, friends. He would have arrived just in time to participate as a sympathizer in the events of Dec. 14; but a hare crossed his path, and he turned back. If the story is true (which is not certain), the portent of the ''swift hare'' provides a nice link between Pushkin's description of Tatiana's superstitious shivers and his meditative sketches in the same Cahier 2370 of the rebels he might have joined.

11 The ''cool general'' may be a reference to the stolid, not very intelligent, but courageous and liberal Aleksey Yushnevski (1786–1844), a general in the Second Army, a friend of Pestel.

VARIANTS

A possible variant of l. 12 begins with the crossed-out words:

There R—

R may stand either for the adjective ''Russian'' or for the name Ryumin, in reference to Second Lieutenant Mihail Bestuzhev-Ryumin, a recklessly brave young man, one of the five Decembrists hanged.

Another deleted line reads:

Recruited for the Union of the Slavs . . .

and may be a variant of 10 or 11.

XVIII

2 / between Laffitte and Clicquot: This is a Gallicism, *entre deux vins*, meaning "casually," "between sips."

8 / pastimes of grown-up scamps / *Zabávï vzróslïh shalunóv*: Brodski's commentaries to this stanza are shamelessly grotesque. That Soviet toady, in his servile eagerness to prove that Pushkin was a solemn admirer of revolution, decides to apply not an "esthetic" or "textological" method but a "historical" and "ideological" one; whereupon he easily comes to the conclusion that the stanza in question should be placed before XIV, so as to represent the rudiments of the Decembrist movement in a historical sequence (the late Tomashevski in 1934 dared make some crushing remarks on Brodski's maneuvers). Brodski insinuates that *zabavï* ("pastimes," "amusements") meant "love" and "inspiration" in Pushkin's idiom, and that in the same idiom *shalun* ("scamp," "frolicker," "gay dog," "naughty boy," Fr. *polisson*) meant "a revolutionary" and "philosopher"; in result of which, the line would idiotically read: "the love and inspiration of adult philosophers" instead of Pushkin's "pastimes of grown-up scamps."

Sometime in 1824, probably in May, from Moscow Vyazemski wrote to Pushkin in Odessa:

... You have teased the government sufficiently; this will do now. The fact is that all our opposition can be marked by nothing que par des espiègleries. It is not given unto us to oppose it like men [*muzhestvovat' protiv nego*]. We can only behave like children. And persistent childish behavior is apt to become a bore.

VARIANTS

The stanza is obviously unfinished, and this leads one to think that not more than eighteen stanzas ever existed.

Commentary

Its position after XVII is also obvious, though perhaps the actions in it should be rendered by "had been" rather than by "was."

Pushkin apparently intended to start the stanza with the formula "all this was . . ." and then to enumerate the various items, conversations over wine and (canceled variant of l. 3) "couplets, friendly disputes." He then altered the "conversations" (*razgovóri*) in l. 1 to "conspirations" (*zagovóri*) and altered l. 3 to "were merely conversations"; but then he crossed out the first two words.

Another canceled variant occurs in l. 5: *myatézhnoe mechtán'e*, "rebellion's dream," instead of *myatézhnaya naúka*, "rebellion's science"; and this variant rhymed with a canceled variant of l. 6: *Vsyo éto bílo podrazhán'e*, "all this was imitation," instead of the final "all this was only boredom," *Vsyo éto bílo tól'ko skúka*.

The rest of the stanza consists of disjointed words. One can make out: "everywhere the talk of grumblers . . . knots . . . and gradually with a secret web. . . . Our tsar was dozing . . ."

*

To this batch of stanzas may be added another stanza or part of a stanza (in the fair copy of *Onegin's Journey*, V, where alongside its middle verses Pushkin drew a vertical line and wrote alongside l. 10: *v X pesn'*, "in Canto X"). It may be assumed that the chronicle of events leading to the formation of secret societies ended with Ten : XVIII and that Pushkin then took up Onegin again (he is in Petersburg, after the scene with Tatiana, in the fictional April of 1825). After a preliminary stanza (say, "Ten : XIX"), the canto may have continued (say, "XX"):

> Grown bored of either passing for a Melmoth,
> or sporting any other mask,

he once awoke a patriot
4 during a rainy tedious spell.
For Russia, gentlemen, he instantly
felt a tremendous liking,
and it is settled. He is now in love,
8 he raves of nothing now but Rus',
he now hates Europe,
with its dry politics,
with its lewd bustle

. . . .

After which Onegin may have entered into contact with the Decembrists and witnessed the uprising of Dec. 14, 1825.

ADDENDUM TO NOTES ON "CHAPTER TEN"

According to Tomashevski ("Desyataya glava," pp. 378–420), the material related to Chapter Ten, as preserved in 1934 at the Institute of Russian Literature (Pushkinskiy Dom), Leningrad, consists of two MSS (referred to further as "cryptogram" and "draft"), donated in 1904 to the autographic section of the Academy of Sciences in Petersburg, item 57 (cryptogram) and item 37 (draft), by Aleksandra Maykov, widow of Leonid Maykov, a scholar who had commenced a new edition of Pushkin's works. The two items are:

Cryptogram. A half sheet, classified (as of 1934) as IRLI 555 and (as of 1937) PD 170, folded in two, with columns of lines decipherable as sixty-three discrete verses, on the inner side of both quarters, the right-hand page containing thirty-two verses, and the left-hand page, thirty-one verses. The paper has an 1829 watermark, and the pages have been numbered in red ink by the police (in 1837) as 66 and 67. (In Tomashevski's photograph of the right-hand page, the latter figure is visible just beneath the eleventh line.)

Draft. A quarter sheet of grayish paper, watermarked 1827, classified (as of 1934) as IRLI 536 and (as of 1937)

PD 171, with the rough draft of three *Onegin* stanzas: two (the second incomplete) on one side (further termed "upper"), with the police number 55 in the middle of the left-hand margin, and a third (incomplete) stanza on the other side (further termed "lower"). These three stanzas are numbered XVI, XVII, and XVIII in my recension.

P. Morozov in 1910* easily broke the clumsy code of the cryptogram; further work on the text was accomplished by Lerner, in his notes to vol. VI of the Vengerov edition of Pushkin's works (1915), by Gofman, in his "Propushchennïe strofï 'Evgeniya Onegina' " (Omitted Strophes of *Eugene Onegin*), *P. i ego sovr.*, IX, 33–35 (1922), 311–17, and by Tomashevski, in his excellent paper in *Lit. nasl.*, nos. 16–18 (1934). My conclusions differ from those of Tomashevski and other commentators, especially Brodski. As I shall explain presently, I take the cryptogram to contain sets of lines representing not sixteen (as previously assumed) but seventeen stanzas. The study of Tomashevski's photographs of the cryptogram reveals the following:

Right-hand page

A column of sixteen lines in strong thick pen (further termed "pen 1"), representing the first lines of sts. I–X and XII–XVII.

Under this, separated by a horizontal dash, another column in smaller hand and thinner pen (further termed "pen 2"), representing the second lines of sts. I–IX.

Two sets of lines in the same pen 2, in the left-hand margin, the lines parallel to the margin; the lower marginal set represents the second lines of sts. X, XII–XIV, and the upper marginal set represents the second lines of sts. XV–XVII.

---

*"Shifrovannoe stihotvorenie Pushkina" (Pushkin's Coded Poem), *P. i ego sovr.*, IV, 13 (1910), 1–12.

Left-hand page

A column of twenty-seven lines in pen 2 down the left-hand side of the page, representing the third lines of sts. I–IX and XI–XVII, followed (without any gap or dash) by the fourth lines of sts. I–IV, VI–IX, and XI–XIII.

A column of four lines in larger hand, weak thickish pen ("pen 3"), at the top of the right-hand side of the paper, representing what I take to be the fifth lines of sts. IV, VI, VIII, XI.

Let us now follow Pushkin in his coding.

Some words he did not complete; others he omitted altogether, or used symbolic abbreviations, such as the capital Z for "tsar." All such omissions, as well as their English counterparts and my explanations, are square-bracketed in my reproduction and translation of the coded MS, with question marks denoting doubtful readings. Cancellations are as usual enclosed in pointed brackets. To avoid puzzling too much the non-Russian reader, for whom these notes are meant, I have departed from good scholarship in two respects: Pushkin's misspellings and mergings of words are not reproduced, and transcription follows, as throughout this work, the new orthography, not that of Pushkin's time. The presumable place of the line within the text of the chapter is given in roman characters for the stanza, in arabic for the line, and both are enclosed in brackets. For the sake of perfect structural correspondence I have, in certain cases, followed the Russian order of words.

Right-hand page, pen 1

[I : 1]   *Vl*[*adīka*] *slábīy i lukávīy*
         A [ruler] weak and wily
[II : 1]   *Egó mī óchen' smírn*[* īm*] *ználi*
         Him we very tame used to know
[III : 1]   *Grozá* 12[=*dvenádtsatogo*] *góda*
         The tempest of year 12

[IV : 1] *No [Bóg?] pomóg—stal rópot nízhe*
            But [God?] helped—grew the murmur lower

The questioned word is very scribbly; and if we accept this reading, the intonation seems to clash with that of III : 4. Other monosyllables, however, such as *bes*, "the devil," or *rok*, "fate," do not look any fitter scriptorially.

[V : 1]   *I chém zhirnée tém tyazhéle*
            And the ["more"] fatter the ["consequently more"] heavier
[VI : 1] *Avós', o Shibolét naródnïy*
            Mayhap, O national shibboleth
[VII : 1] *Avós' aréndï zabïváya*
            Mayhap, leases forgetting
[VIII : 1] *Sey múzh sud'bï, sey stránnik bránnïy*
            That man of destiny, that wanderer martial
[IX : 1] *Tryaslísya grózno Pirenéi*
            Shook ominously the Pyrenees
[X : 1]   *Ya vséh uymú s moím naródom*
            I everybody shall curb with the aid of my people

The next line, XI : 1, was accidentally omitted by Pushkin, and we shall see that in his next set he will also omit the second line of the same stanza. He will, however, remember to insert the rest of the quatrain in his third-line and fourth-line sets, but in compensation he will leave out the third and fourth lines of st. X.

[XII : 1] *Potéshnïy pólk Petrá Titána*
             Play regiment of Peter Titan
[XIII : 1] *RR [= Rossíya] snóva prism[iréla]*
             Russia again grew tame [or "inert"]

Our poet's attention had begun to flag by the end of st. X. He may have initially planned to do first a batch of ten stanzas, first lines, and then go on to the second lines. He decided, however, to go on with set 1—and made his first mistake, the omission of XI : 1. Now he makes another mistake. In this kind of task, especially when done from memory, as doubtlessly this was done, the mind tires easily because of the contrast between the percept of the material as live verses and the concept of it as mechanical itemization. The "flowing" tetrameter (i.e., with the scud on the third foot) always came to Pushkin more naturally than the "slow" tetrameter (scudded on the second foot), and, as he became bored with his coding, automatism turned the "slow" *Rossíya prismiréla snóva* into *Rossíya snóva prismiréla* (which, of course, abolished the rhyme). I think Pushkin noticed his mistake not at this first cryptogrammatic session, but at a later one, when glancing through the column to check if he had the first line of XI. The discovery of his mistake in XIII : 1 caused him to forget what he had wished to check. Now a curious thing happened: Pushkin's first movement was to cross out the two words (*snova prism*); his eye, however, was misled by the similarity of a word just beneath (*svoy*, "their") in the next line (XIV : 1), and it was through this and through the next word that he drew several rapid dashes. Then, noticing his error, he went one step up to the real offender, XIII : 1, improved its script by repeating more plainly the first letter (putting an additional *R* before the not very clear one already there), and, instead of rewriting the *snova prismirela*, scribbled a "2" above *snova*, meaning that it should follow *prismirela*.

[XIV : 1] *U níh ⟨svoí bïváli⟩ skhódki*
           They ⟨their own had⟩ forgatherings
  [XV : 1] *Vitíystvom rézkim znamenítï*
           For oratory trenchant famed
 [XVI : 1] *Drug Mársa, Vákha i Venéri*
           A friend of Mars, Bacchus, and Venus
[XVII : 1] ⟨*No t[am]*⟩ *Tak bílo nad Nevóyu l'dístoy*
           ⟨But t[here]⟩ Thus was it on the Neva icy

Here comes another mishap. Pushkin is already thinking of his second set of lines and, instead of XVII : 1, starts to write XVII : 2 (*No tám gdye ráne[e] vesná*, "but there where earlier the spring"). He notices his error and crosses out what he has already written, the first word of l. 2 and the first letter of its next word. Having now completed, as he thinks, set 1, he draws a line under XVII : 1, and launches upon the set of second lines. But after writing the first three letters (*Ple*) of the Russian for "bald," i.e., the beginning of I : 2, tedium (or some interruption) leads him to postpone set 2. When he resumes the task, he has a new pen, pen 2. The writing becomes smaller and finer; many words are now fused or not finished.

Right-hand page, pen 2

[1 : 2] *Pleshíviy shchyógol', vrág truda*
a baldish fop, a foe of toil

The switch from pen 1 to pen 2 takes place after *Ple* and is very clear in the script.

[II : 2] *Kogdá ne náshi povará*
when not our cooks

In this line, and in two further lines, one notices a feature that was absent from the first set—the merging of words: *nenashi* instead of *ne nashi*, *iskoro* instead of *i skoro*, and *yaodu* instead of *ya odu*.

[III : 2] *Nast[ála]—któ tut nám pomóg?*
took place—who here us helped?
[IV : 2] *I skóro sílo[yu] veshchéy*
and soon by the force of circumstances ["things"]
[V : 2] *O R[ússkiy] glúp[iy] násh na[ród]*
O our R[ussian] stup[id] na[tion]
[VI : 2] *Tebé b ya ódu posvyatíl*
to you I'd an ode dedicate
[VII : 2] *Hanzhá zapryóts[ya] v monastír'*
the bigot will shut himself up in a monastery
[VIII : 2] *Pred kém unízilis' Z [Tsarí]*
before whom groveled kings
[IX : 2] *Volkán Neápolya pilál*
the volcano of Naples was aflame

Here our poet, being cramped for space but wishing to have the whole of set 2 on the same page as set 1 (whicl up to here he had been continuing down the page), a' dressed himself to the left-hand margin and wrote ir   , at right angles to the central column, the following lines in two adjacent columns of their own.

Lower part of left-hand margin, right-hand page, pen 2

[x : 2] *Nash Z [Tsár'] v kongr[ésse] govoríl*
         our t[sar] in congr[ess] said

XI : 2 is omitted, probably in consequence of the accidental omission of XI : 1.

[XII : 2] *Druzhína stárïh usachéy*
           a bodyguard of old mustaches
[XIII : 2] *I púshche Z [Tsár'] poshyól kutít'*
            and with more zest the t[sar] went reveling
[XIV : 2] *Oní za chásheyu viná*
           they over a goblet of wine

Upper part of left-hand margin, right-hand page, pen 2

[xv : 2] *Sbirális' chlénï séy sem'í*
          assembled the members of this group ["family"]
[XVI : 2] *TUt ⟨bes⟩ L[únin] dérzko predlagál*
           here ⟨un-⟩ L[unin] daringly suggested

Here Pushkin makes another slip and again corrects himself. Instead of "Here Lunin," *Tut Lunin,* he starts with the beginning of xv : 3—"At unquiet Nikita's"; he writes *U bes,* intending *bespokoynogo,* and then, seeing his error, crosses out the *bez,* but uses the *U* for *TUt,* flanking it with the two *t*'s. It is characteristic that these slips occur toward the end of sets, with fatigue and a foresense of the next set mingling. It confirms me in the notion that Pushkin worked from memory. Subliminally, moreover, he might have been disturbed by the recollection of having committed the same kind of mis-

take in set 1 at a point where XVII : 1 got entangled with
the next line.

[XVII : 2] *No tám gde ráne[e] vesná*
      but there where earlier the spring

Left-hand page, left-hand column, pen 2, continued

[I : 3] *Necháyanno prigrétïy Slávoy*
      fortuitously befriended by Fame
[II : 3] *Orlá dvuglávogo shchipáli*
      the eagle two-headed [they] plucked
[III : 3] *Ostervenénie naróda*
      The infuriation of the nation
[IV : 3] *Mï ochutílisya v Pa[rízhe]*
      we found ourselves in Paris
[V : 3] *Skazhí zachém zhe v sámom [déle]*
      Say, why indeed
[VI : 3] *No stihoplyót Velikoródnïy*
      had not a poetaster Highborn
[VII : 3] *Avós' po mán'yu [Nikoláya]*
      Mayhap, by the command of [Nicholas]
[VIII : 3] *Sey vsádnik Pápoyu venchánnïy*
      that horseman by the Pope crowned
[IX : 3] *Bezrúkiy K[nyaz'] druz'yám Moréi*
      The one-armed prince to the friends of Morea

It is now l. 3 of st. x that Pushkin accidentally leaves out.

[XI : 3] *A pro tebyá i v ús ne dúet*
      and about you does not care a straw
[XII : 3] *Predávshih nékogda [tirána]*
      who betrayed formerly a tyrant
[XIII : 3] *No ískrï plámeni inógo*
      but the sparks of another flame
[XIV : 3] *Oní za ryúmkoy rússkoy vódki*
      they over a glass of Russian vodka
[XV : 3] *U bespokóynogo Nikítï*
      at unquiet Nikita's
[XVI : 3] *Svoí reshítel'nïe mérï*
      his decisive measures
[XVII : 3] *Blestít nad K[ámenkoy] tenístoy*
      gleams over Kamenka shady

[I : 4.] *Nad námi Z-val* [*tsárstvoval*] *togdá*
over us reigned then
[II : 4.] *U B*[*onapártova*] *shatrá*
near Bonaparte's tent
[III : 4.] *B*[*arkláy*], *zimá il' R*[*ússkiy*] *b*[*óg*]
Barclay? The winter? Or the Russian God?
[IV : 4.] *A R*[*ússkiy*] *Z* [*Tsár*] *glavóy Z* [*Tsaréy*]
and the Russian tsar was the head of kings

Pushkin accidentally left out v : 4.

[VI : 4.] *Menyá uzhé predupredíl*
me already anticipated
[VII : 4.] *Seméystvam vozvratít S*[*ibír'*]
to their families will give back S[iberia]
[VIII : 4.] *Izchéznuvshiy kak tén' zarí*
gone like a shadow of the dawn
[IX : 4.] *Iz K*[*ishinyóva*] *uzh migál*
from K[ishinev] already winked

x : 4 is omitted, probably in consequence of x : 3 having
been left out.

[XI : 4.] *Tï A*[*leksándrovskiy*] *holóp*
you, [or "you are"?] A[lexander's] slave
[XII : 4.] *Svirépoy sháyke palachéy*
to a ferocious gang of deathsmen
[XIII : 4.] *Uzhé izdávna mózhet bít'*
already a long time perhaps

Here Pushkin stopped. This is all we have of set 4. Some
time later, however, he added on the same page the fol-
lowing lines from set 5:

Right-hand column, left-hand page, pen 3

[IV : 5.] *Moryá dostális' Al'biónu*
The seas were apportioned to Albion
[VI : 5.] *Avós' dorógi nám ispr*[*ávyat*]
Mayhap, the roads for us they will rep[air]
[VIII : 5.] *Izmúchen kázniyu pokóya*
Exhausted by the torture of repose
[XI : 5.] *Kinzhál L*[*uvélya*] *tén' B*[*ertóna*]
The dagger of L[ouvel], the shadow of B[erton]

Pushkin's plan in scrambling the fifth lines was, I think, to make things more difficult by starting with st. IV, then going to the next, then leaving one out, then leaving two out, and so on (IV : 5; V : 5; VII : 5; X : 5). However, for the wretched cryptographer that our poet was, the carrying out of this plan proved disastrous. When he consulted his set of fourth lines, he failed to notice that he had left out sts. V and X, so that when he wrote down the fifth lines of what he thought were IV, V, VII, and X, these proved to be actually IV, VI, VIII, and XI. I also suggest that he soon noticed that something was very wrong with his cipher and in utter disgust gave up the whole matter.

In 1831, a year after the destruction of Chapter Ten, Pushkin excluded the "Travels" as a "Chapter Eight" and revised the "High-Life" Chapter, making it Chapter Eight. I do not think that he had completed any more stanzas of Chapter Ten in addition to those he ciphered, and I think he did not cipher st. XVIII for the simple reason that it was not finished. Aleksandr Turgenev's reference to an account of the "Insurrection" (*Vozmushchenie*) suggests to Tomashevski that Pushkin had actually described—in stanzas that had not reached us —the abortive *coup d'état* of Dec. 14, 1825. I think we should understand under *Vozmushchenie* the specific preparations and the general unrest depicted in the stanzas we have. When Pushkin jotted down the remark "burned X Canto," we need not assume that any more than one third of it had been written.

Tomashevski also asserts, in a footnote to his 1934 paper in *Lit. nasl.*, that the nature of the code our poet used "would absolutely preclude any possibility of writing from memory; in front of him there certainly lay a fair copy of the stanzas he was ciphering." Tomashevski probably had not tried out the procedure. Anyone with an average verbal retentiveness should be able to keep in mind seventeen stanzas (238 lines). I have experimented on such sequences in *Onegin* as I know by heart. The first and second lines, and generally the opening quatrains with their autonomic lilt, are easy to deal with; it is beginning with the fifth lines that a kind of woolly weariness sets in and errors accumulate. I maintain that Pushkin sat down to cipher his text not prior to his burning the completed stanzas of the Tenth Canto (Oct. 19, 1830), but soon after reciting them by heart to Aleksandr Turgenev (beginning of December, 1831)—that is, when he began to feel doubtful of being able to retain them any longer. Indeed, by the time he started to embalm them in his code, the stanzas might have already begun to fade out in their vulnerable middle parts. The strange fact that, in the few cases when his auditors quote him, variants occur suggests that Pushkin may have filled up slight gaps of oblivion with substitute words here and there in the uneven course of recitation. I maintain, finally, that only the absence of a written text before him can account for the blunders he committed. In this respect the transposition of words in XIII : 1 is especially characteristic and could hardly have occurred if he had been transcribing from a copy.

Translator's Epilogue

Pushkin put the last touches to *EO* in the beginning of October, 1831, at Tsarskoe Selo, and a complete edition of the novel came out in 1833. It is futile to discuss our poet's possible reasons (political, personal, utilitarian, artistic) for ending it as he did; but there is no doubt that *EO* was his favorite work, and the beautiful verses he composed upon completing the nine-canto version at the end of September, 1830, at Boldino (see last page of my commentary) reflect the difficulty he had in weaning himself away from *EO*.

Several times during the ensuing years he dallied with the idea of continuing the novel. Thus, in the course of his penultimate visit to Mihaylovskoe, soon after his arrival there on Sept. 7, 1835, he began a verse epistle to Pletnyov, who had urged him to continue *EO*. He began his epistle (Cahier 2384, f. 30^r; on the other side of the page there is the draft of *Mihaylovskoe Revisited*) in iambic pentameters (A), which turned into octaved Alexandrines (B), but then thought better of it and (about Sept. 16) switched to his old *EO* stanza (C): *

---

*I translate A, ll. 1–8, from Acad 1948, vol. III, 1, p. 395; A, ll. 9–12, from *Works* 1949, vol. III, pp. 991–92; B from Acad 1948, vol. III, 1, p. 356; and C from ibid., pp. 397–98.

A

You give me the advice, my dear [*lyubéznïy*] Pletnyov,
to go on writing ⟨our⟩ abandoned novel
⟨and⟩ to amuse ⟨this austere⟩ age, this iron
4 age of accounts, with empty narratives.
You think that with a profitable object
one can combine the restlessness of fame.
⟨Therefore your⟩ colleague ⟨you advise⟩ to take
8 a reasonable payment from the public . . .

For every line ten rubles, which would make
a hundred forty rubles for a stanza,
five rubles for each published part . . .
12 a trifling tax for people who can read.

B

. . . while he's alive, unmarried,
4 the novel is unfinished. 'Tis a treasure.
Into its free and ample frame insert
a set of pictures, start a diorama:
people will flock to it, and you will pocket
8 the entrance fee, thus gaining fame and profit.

C

During my days of autumn leisure—
those days when I so love to write—
you, friends, advise me to go on
4 with my forgotten tale.
You say—and you are right—
that it is odd, and even impolite,
to interrupt an uncompleted novel
8 and have it published as it is;
that one must marry off one's hero
in any case,
or kill him off at least, and, after having
12 disposed of the remaining characters
and made to them a friendly bow,
expel them from the labyrinth.

You say: thank God, while your Onegin
is still alive,

> the novel is not finished; forward go
> 4 little by little, don't be lazy.
> While heeding her appeal, from Fame
> collect a tax in praise and blame.
> ⟨Depict the dandies of the town,
> 8 your amiable misses,
> warfare and ball, palace and hut,
> cell . . . . and harem, meantime⟩
> take from our public
> 12 a reasonable payment—
> five rubles for each published part:
> really, 'tis not a heavy tax.

B : 6 / diorama: *Webster's* says: "A mode of scenic representation, invented by Daguerre and Bouton, in which a painting (partly translucent) is seen from a distance through an opening. By a combination of translucent and opaque painting, and of transmitted and reflected light, and by contrivances such as screens and shutters, much diversity of scenic effect is produced" (and this applies to *EO*, too).

Louis Jacques Mandé Daguerre (1789–1851) gave his first show in 1822, in Paris. A diorama was shown in St. Petersburg in November, 1829, hence the topicality of the verse. The spectator sat in a loge that slowly revolved, with a slight rumble, not drowned by soft music, and took him to Rome, Egypt, or Mt. Chimborazo, "the highest mountain in the world" (it is only 20,577 ft. high).

*

In vol. V of Acad 1948, Bondi, the editor of that tome (Long Poems, 1825–33), basing himself on the researches of M. Gofman ("Propushchennïe strofi") and B. Tomashevski (*Neizdannïy Pushkin* [St. Petersburg, 1922], pp. 89–91), publishes under an arbitrary title (*Ezerski*) a set of fifteen stanzas of the *Onegin* type, of which II–VI, fragments of VII, VIII, and IX (combined to form two stanzas), and x were published by Pushkin in *Sovremennik*, 1836, under the title *The Pedigree of My Hero* (*Rodoslovnaya moego geroya*), with the subtitle "Fragment of a Satirical Poem." This hero is Pushkin's contemporary, the scion of a thousand-year-old line of warriors and boyars, originating with the Norman chiefs who, according to tradition, invaded Russia in the ninth century and gave her her first princes. The poem is an absolutely stunning performance, one of Pushkin's greatest masterpieces, and reflects the historiographic interests of Pushkin's last years. It was begun at the very end of 1832 and was taken up again in 1835 and 1836. The fair copy is in a batch of autographs sewn by the police into a cahier, PB 2375, ff. 23^r–28^v, except four stanzas, which are in PD 194.

Ivan Ezerski's grandfather had 12,000 slaves, and his father had only one eighth of that number, and these "had long been mortgaged." Ezerski lives on a salary and is a *chinovnik* (official, functionary, civil servant, clerk) with a drab job as "collegiate registrar" (the fourteenth and lowest rank in the service) in some government bureau in St. Petersburg.

I
O'er the gloom-covered town of Peter
the autumn wind was driving clouds;
the sky was breathing humid chill,
4 the Neva boomed. The billow beat
against the trim embankment's wharf
like some restless petitioner
against the judge's door. The rain
8 tapped sadly on the windowpane.
'Twas darkling. At this time
Ivan Ezerski came, my neighbor,
into his narrow study [*tésniy kabinét*].
12 However, his forebears and tribe,
his rank, his office, and his age
you should know, gentlemen.

II

Let's start *ab ovo*: my Ezerski
was a descendant of those chiefs
whose spirit bellicose and savage
4 was once the terror of the seas.
The generator of the family,
Odulf "was a most awesome warlord"
—so says the Sophian chronograph.
8 In Olga's reign his son Varlaf
embraced the Gospel in Constantinople
together with the dot of a Greek princess.
Two sons were born to them, Yakub
12 and Dorofey; of these, in ambush
Yakub was slain; while Dorofey
fathered twelve sons.

III

Ondrey surnamed Ezerski, fathered
Ivan and Ilya, and took vows
in the Pecherskiy Monastery.
4 Thence the Ezerskis
derive their family name

.   .   .   .*

IV

In centuries of our old glory
as well as in unhappy times,
in gory days of riots and uprisings,
4 the names of the Ezerskis glitter.
They're in the army and in council,
they are the governors and envoys

.   .   .   .

V

But when from the majestic Council
Romanov had received his crown;
when under a pacific rule
4 at last Rus rested,
and our foes were subdued,
then the Ezerskis came
into great force at court
8 under the Emperor Peter

.   .   .   .

---

*I omit the rest of this stanza and the closing lines of the next
two stanzas.

[I omit translations of VI–XII and finally of XV.]

XIII
Why does the wind revolve in the ravine,
sweep up the leaves and bear the dust,
when avidly on stirless water
4 wait for his breath the galleon must?
From mountains and past towers, why
does the dread heavy eagle fly
to a sear stump? Inquire of him.
8 Why does young Desdemona love
her blackamoor as the moon loves
the gloom of night? Because
for wind and eagle
12 and maiden's heart no law is laid.
Poet, be proud: thus are you too:
neither is there a law for you.

XIV
Fulfilled with golden thoughts,
but understood by none,
before the crossroads of this world
4 you pass, morose and mute.
You share not with the crowd its wrath,
its needs, its mirth, its roar,
its wonder, or its toil.
8 The fool cries: "Whither? Whither?
This is the road!" You do not hear.
You go where you are urged
by golden dreams. Your secret work
12 is your reward; 'tis what you breathe.
Unto the crowd you throw its fruit
—unto the slaves of vain pursuit.

And here follows a comm. on the foregoing fragments.

I

This stanza is very close to the beginning of *The Bronze Horseman* (1833), which I quote in my n. to Eight: XXXIX : 7.

9 In the fair copy (PD 194) Pushkin, probably in the fall of 1835, started to change the name Ezerski to "Evgeniy" and "Onegin" (Acad 1948, vol. V, p. 419)—II : 1:

> Let's start *ab ovo*: my Evgeniy . . .

III : 4–5:

> Thence the Onegins
> derive their family name.

V : 6:

> then the Onegins came . . .

One wonders if Pushkin knew that the Ezerskis were existing Polish noble families, going back to the sixteenth century, with one branch stemming from Kiev.

II

2 / those chiefs: The Northmen; Russ. *Varyagi*, Varangians.

7 / the Sophian chronograph: The so-called *Sophian Annals* (*Sofiyskie letopisi*) of the fifteenth century, based on the records kept at the House of St. Sophia, headquarters of the bishop of Novgorod in the city of that name.

8 / Olga: Queen of Kiev in the middle of the tenth century (d. 969).

III

3 / Pecherskiy Monastery: Kievo-Pecherskaya Lavra in the southern part of Kiev, founded in the eleventh century.

V

2 / Romanov: Tsar Michael (r. 1613–45).

XIII–XIV

A different and inferior version of the same idea is expressed in a draft (Cahier 2384), which recent editors quite arbitrarily insert in the gap of Pushkin's unfinished novella *The Egyptian Nights* (autumn, 1835).

*

After completing st. XV, Pushkin attempted to continue this poem, and made the scion of the Northmen a poor *chinovnik* in "a green dress coat bleached by wear" (canceled draft, 2375, f. 36ʳ). One immediately recalls Gogol's Bashmachkin, created a few years later (and of humbler descent): "His regulation dress coat was no longer green but a sort of mealy hue tinged with russet." It is this seedy young man, Bashmachkin's precursor, whom Pushkin, on second thought, employed in *The Bronze Horseman*. The Evgeniy of *The Bronze Horseman*, pt. I, is described coming home thus (l. 28):

> threw off his carrick, undressed, went to bed.

In the draft of *The Bronze Horseman* (2374, f. 10ᵛ), the lines corresponding to 24–26 read:

> he was an impecunious ⟨clerk⟩ [*chinovnik*],
> kinless, a total ⟨orphan⟩,
> ⟨his face a little⟩ pockmarked [⟨*litsóm nemnógo*⟩ *ryabovátïy*] . . .

In Gogol's story *The Carrick* (*Shinel'*), begun not earlier than 1839, in Marienbad, and completed in 1840, in Rome (first edition 1842, in *Works*), Akakiy Bashmachkin is also "somewhat pockmarked" (*neskol'ko ryabovat*), besides being "somewhat on the carroty side" (*neskol'ko rïzhevat*).

THE WORK [TRUD]*

Come is the moment I craved: my work of
     long years is completed.
     Why then this strange sense of woe
     secretly harrowing me?
Having my high task performed, do I stand as
     a useless day laborer
     Stands, with his wages received, foreign
     to all other toil?
Or am I sorry to part with my work, night's
     silent companion,
     Golden Aurora's friend, friend of the
     household gods?

---

*Pushkin dated this poem: "Boldino, Sept. 25, 1830, 3:15."
Translated one hundred and twenty-six years later, in Ithaca,
New York.

INDEX

Index

All works are listed under the author's name, and Russian works are given by Russian title even when given only by English title or first line in the text. Titles of articles in collections and periodicals are listed only for those published before 1837. An attempt has been made to list certain subjects (such as "dueling" and "Gallicisms") and certain Russian words (such as *starina*, "ancientry," and *sen'*, "shelter") that the reader might want to look up. In long entries, a main discussion is indicated by boldface figures. The abbreviation "P." stands of course for Pushkin and "*EO*" for *Evgeniy Onegin*. Superscript figures represent the volume numbers; where there is none, the previous one applies.

—V. N.

Editorial note: Volume numbers refer to the 1975 four-volume edition, the pagination of which has been retained for the paperback edition. References to the omitted material (Correlative Lexicon and appendixes) have been retained in the index.

A

Aachen, [2]82

Abbadie, Antoine d': *Des Conquêtes faites en Abyssinie*, [3]442

Abbé, Monsieur l' (*EO*), [1]96, [2]40

Abélard, Pierre, [3]223

Abha, [3]401

Abington, Lord, [2]153; *see also* Arouet: *Guerre civile, La*

Abissiniya, see Olderogge

Abissinskie hroniki, see Turaev

Abora (amba), [3]441

Abora, Mt., [3]441

Abram arap / Petrov arap, *see* Gannibal, A. P.

Abydos, [2]457

Abyssinia / -ian (Ethiopia), [2]34, 38, 181, [3]324, 395–414, 415, 417n, 423, 424, 427, 432, 436, 437–41

Abyssinian Church, [3]408

Acacia dealbata, [3]12

Academic Dictionary, see *Slovar' Akademii*

Academy of Arts, *see* St. Petersburg

Academy of Sciences, *see* St. Petersburg

A Catilie, see Bertin

Account of the Life and Writings of James Beattie, see Forbes, Sir W.

Achilles, [3]111

Achilles, see Zhukovski: *Ahill*

Acis et Galathée, see Didelot

Acosta / Dekosta, Jan d', [3]426 & n

Acres, Bob, [3]54; *see also* Sheridan: *Rivals, The*

Acts of Peter the Great, see Golikov: *Deyaniya*

Adam, [3]479

Addison, Joseph, [2]378; *Spectator, The,* [2]47, 495, [3]75

Adeline, [3]147; *see also* Radcliffe: *Romance of the Forest, The*

Aderkas, Boris Antonovich, [2]398, [3]307

Adi Baro, [3]432

Adieu, see Byron: *Fare Thee Well*

Ad Manlium, see Catullus

Admiralty / -eyskiy, *see* St. Petersburg

Adolphe, [2]152, 157, 163, [3]17, 100–1; *see also* Constant: *Adolphe*

Adonais, see Shelley

Adowa, [3]439

Adriatic / Adria / Adriatika, [1]119, [2]182, 183, 185, 358

Advice to an Epic Poet, see Batyushkov: *Sovet*

Adyam, *see* Jesus I

Aegean Sea, [2]457

Aeneas, [2]53; *see also* Virgil: *Aeneid*

Aeneid, see Virgil

Aeschylus, [2]83

Affinités électives, see Goethe: *Wahlverwandtschaften*

Afghanistan, [2]255, [3]114

Africa / -an, [1]25, 26, 117, [2]187, 189, 190, 191, 192, 311, 515, [3]293, 294, 388, 389, 396, 397, 398, 412, 424, 436, 437, 438, 439, 440

After, see Browning

Agafokleya (*EO* var.), [2]280

Agafon (*EO*), [1]207, 315, [2]280, 499

Again I'm Yours, see P., WORKS: *Opyat' ya vash*

Agandecca, [3]52; *see also* Macpherson: *Fingal*

Agasfer / Agasver vechnïy zhid, see Kyuhel'beker

Agatha, [2]385; *see also* Weber: *Freischütz, Der*

Agatho / Agathon / Agathonicus, *see* Agafon

Age of Bronze, The, see Byron

Ahasuerus, the Wanderer, see Medwin

Index

Aumer, J. P.: *Cléopâtre,* [2]79–80
A une femme, see Bertin
Aureng-Zebe, see Dryden
Aurora, [1]139, 213, 215, 314, 318, [2]522
Ausonia, [1]334, [3]23, 300
Austen, Charles, [2]368
Austen, Jane: *Mansfield Park,* [2]222, 368, 393–4; *Pride and Prejudice,* [2]424; *Sense and Sensibility,* [2]393–4
Austerlitz, [3]320
Australia, [2]357
Austria, [2]406, [3]183, 299, 330, 416n, 418, 487
Automedon, [1]267, [3]111
Automne / Autonne / Russ. Oton, César, [1]333, [3]298
Autumn, see P., works: *Osen'*
Autumn Morning, see P., works: *Osennee utro*
Avdotia, [1]245
Aventures de Télémaque, Les, see Fénelon
Aveux au tombeau, see Lafontaine: *Bekenntniss am Grabe, Das*
Awakening, see Kyuhel'beker: *Probuzhdenie*
Ay / Aï, [1]196, 317, 333, [2]147, 148, **480–1**, 483, [3]331
Ayan, [2]212
Azov, [3]418, 422
Azov, Sea of, [3]285, 288

B

B., Marquise de, [2]65; *see also* Louvet de Couvrai
Bacchante, see Batyushkov: *Vakhanka*
Bacchus, [3]317, 369
Bacchus (character), [3]134-5; *see also* Maykov, V.: *Elisey*
Bachaumont, François le Coigneux de, [3]274
Bagnères, [3]284
bagryaniy ("porphyrous," "crimson"), [2]520–1

Bagshot Heath, [3]42
Bahafa, king of Abyssinia, [3]407
Bahchisaray / Bakhchisarai ("Garden Palace"), [1]329 [2]125, 212, [3]286–7, 302
Bahchisarayskiy fontan, see P., works
Bahrey / Bahri: *History of the Galla,* [3]442
Baïf, Jean Antoine: *Passetemps,* [3]70
Bailey / Baillie (governess), [2]39, 162
Bailey, John, [2]39
Bailey, L. H.: *Manual of Cultivated Plants,* [3]75
Bailey, Margery, [2]248
Bakunin, Ekaterina Pavlovna, [2]544, [3]138
Bal, see Baratïnski
Balaklava Road, [3]286
Baldy, Mt., *see* Lïsaya
Ball, The, see Baratïnski: *Bal*
Ballad, see Polezhaev: *Romans*
Ballantyne's Novelist's Library, [2]352, [3]402n
Ballet, Auguste, [3]335
Ballet, Hippolyte, [3]335
Baltaji, Mohammed, [3]418
Baltic Region / Sea, [1]105, 324, [2]99, 221, 398, 479, [3]166, 307, 434
Balzac, Honoré de, [2]354, [3]182, 335; *Femme de trente ans, La,* [2]277–8; *Scènes de la vie privée,* [2]278; *see also* Sanson: *Mémoires*
Bantïsh-Kamenski, D. N., [3]394; *Slovar' dostopamyatnïh lyudey Russkoy zemli* (Dictionary of Distinguished People of the Russian Land), [3]442
Barataria (in Cervantes), [3]425
Baratieri, Oreste, [3]404; *Mémoires d'Afrique,* [3]442
Baratïnski, Evgeniy Abramovich, [1]4, 35, 39, 42, 189, 249, 316, [2]20, 26, 27, 29, 376, **380–2, 383,** 445, 447, 450, 475,

Evgeniy Onegin

(Headings: COMMENTARIES; EDITIONS; TRANSLATIONS; CONTENTS.)

Evgeniy Onegin (opera), *see*
   Chaykovski
Evgeniy Vel'skiy (anon.), ³126
   & n
Ewige Jude, Der, see Schubart
Excursion, The, see Words-
   worth
"Exegi monumentum," *see*
   Derzhavin
"Exegi monumentum," *see* P.,
   WORKS
Ex Ponto, see Ovid
Extasie, The, see Donne
Extinguished Is the Orb of Day,
   see P., WORKS: *Pogaslo
   dnévnoe svetilo*
Extract from a Letter to Delvig,
   see P., WORKS: *Otrïvok*
Eylau, ³320
Eyo glaza, see P., WORKS
"Ezerski," *see* P., WORKS
Ezerski, Ilya Ondreevich, ³380;
   see also P., WORKS: *Rodoslov-
   naya moego geroya*
Ezerski, Ivan, ³232, 379, 380;
   see also P., WORKS: *Rodoslov-
   naya moego geroya*
Ezerski, Ivan (s. of Ondrey),
   ³308; *see also* P., WORKS:
   Rodoslovnaya moego geroya
Ezerski, Ondrey Dorofeevich,
   ³380; *see also* P., WORKS:
   Rodoslovnaya moego geroya
Ezerski family, ³382

F

Faber, H., ²352
Fables, see Fénelon; La Fon-
   taine; *see also* Dmitriev, I.:
   Basni; Izmaylov, A.: *Basni*;
   Krïlov: *Basni*
Fadeevna (*EO* var.), ²273–4,
   399
Fadey (Thaddeus), ²273
"Fairhill," *see* Krasnogorie
Fairy Tales, a Noël, see P.,
   WORKS: *Skazki, Noel'*
Fall, The, see Sedley
Fall of the Leaves, see Baratïn-
   ski: *Padenie list'ev*; Milonov:
   Padenie list'ev
False Demetrius, The, see Bul-
   garin: *Dmitriy Samozvanets*
Familie von Halden, Die, see
   Lafontaine, A.
Famille de Halden, La, see
   Lafontaine, A.: *Familie*
Famusov, Pavel, ²509, ³166;
   see also Griboedov: *Gore ot
   uma*
*Fanatisme, ou Mahomet, Le;
   see* Arouet
Fancies, see Zhukovski:
   Mechtï
Fancy, see Batyushkov:
   Mechta
Fancy, see Keats
Fani, Ode to, see Delvig, A. A.

Index

Index

Index

Index

Pushkin, Aleksandr Sergeevich

(Headings: LIFE; LETTERS; WORKS; PUSHKINIANA: SUBJECTS and TITLES.)

378, 446, see also *Evgeniy Onegin*, EDITIONS: ed. Tomashevski; (1960, 1962, ed.

Pushkin, Aleksey Fyodorovich, [3]391

Pushkin, Elizaveta (Lev Sergeevich's wife), [3]437

Pushkin, Fyodor Petrovich, [3]391

Pushkin, Grigoriy Aleksandrovich (P.'s son), [3]47

Pushkin, Konstantin (Grigoriy Pushka's son), [3]391

Pushkin, Lev Aleksandrovich (P.'s grandfather), [2]40, [3]391

Pushkin, Lev Sergeevich (P.'s brother), [1]69, 71, 74, [2]9, 10, 12, 19–20, 23, 81, 87, 133, 176, 208, 390, 443, 481, [3]282, 283, 285, 286, 307, 389, 437

Pushkin, Maria Aleksandrovna (P.'s daughter), [3]47

Pushkin, Maria Alekseevna (m. Osip Gannibal), see Gannibal, Maria

Pushkin, Nadezhda (Osip Gannibal's daughter, Sergey Pushkin's wife, P.'s mother), [1]60, [2]207, [3]307, 309, 391, 437

Pushkin, Natalia Aleksandrovna (P.'s daughter), [3]47

Pushkin, Natalia Nikolaevna (b. Goncharov, P.'s wife), [2]264, 280, 414, 429, [3]47, 48, 49, 200, 246

Pushkin, Olga Sergeevna (P.'s sister), [2]39, 162, 331, 362n, 452, [3]307

"Pushkin," Pavel (P.'s illegitimate son), see Ivanov, Pavel

Pushkin, Pyotr (descendant of Konstantin, ancestor of P.'s parents), [3]391

Pushkin, Sergey Lvovich (P.'s father), [1]61, 73, [2]396, 398, 524, [3]307, 391, 392

Blagoy, Bondi, Vinogradov, & Oksman), [1]84, [3]138, 209, 268, 306n

Pushkin, Vasiliy Lvovich (P.'s uncle), [1]44, 72, [2]20–1, 323, 524–6, [3]116, 172, 218; *Kapitan Hrabrov (Captain "Bold")*, [2]525–6; *Opasniy sosed* (The Dangerous Neighbor), [1]318, [2]20–1, 247, 524–6, [3]19, 134; *Stihotvoreniya* (Poems), [2]21

"Pushkin," *see* Tsarskoe Selo

Pushkin family, *see also* Gannibal

Pushkinskiy Don, *see* St. Petersburg

pustinya ("wilderness"), [1]369, [2]244, [3]237

Pustyakov (*EO*), [1]216, 228, [2]523–4, 525, 541, [3]4

Pustyakov, Mrs. (*EO*), [1]221

Puteshestvie iz Peterburga v Moskvu, see Radishchev

Puteshestvie NN v Parizh i London, see Dmitriev, I.

Puteshestvie z Arzrum, see P., WORKS

Pyatigorsk, [2]121, 159, 167, 174, 193, 429, [3]163, 283, 284, 302

Pyatnitski/-skaya Church, [3]424

Pygmalion, [2]415

Pylades, [1]327, [3]287

Pyotr (P.'s coachman), [2]329

Pyotr I, see Bogoslovski

Pyotr Velikiy, see Lomonosov; Shihmatov

Pyrenees, [3]316, 329–30, 368

Pyrénées, Les, see Fontanes

Pyrénées-Orientales, [3]433

Pythias, [2]233

Q

Quaker, [1]285, [3]160, 187, 261

Quartin-Dillon, R., [3]445

270, 272, 274, 275n, 282, 284, 285, 288, 289, 293, 302, 303, 305, 307, 309, 344, 351, 352, 355, 358, 359, 360, 362, 364, 378, 379, 389, 390, 421, 423, 426, 427 & n, 434, 435, 515;
Academy of Arts (Iskusstv), [3]207; Academy of Sciences (Nauk), [3]169, 365, 484; Admiralteyskiy Boulevard, [2]69; Admiralteystvo (Admiralty), [3]270; Admiralty Square, [3]269; Alexandrine Column / Aleksandrovski / -skaya Kolonna, [2]311–12; Bol'shoy Kamennïy Teatr, [1]xxiii, [2]76, 79, 87, 91; Chyornaya Rechka / Black River, [3]46, 47–8; Court Opera, [2]79; Demut's / Demuth's Hotel, [3]161, 269; Ekaterininskiy Kanal, [2]178; English Club, [3]118, 275; Ermitazh (Hermitage), [2]331, [3]182; Field of Mars, see Marsovo Pole;

Fontanka Canal / Quay, [2]68, [3]344, 351; Hôtel de Londres, [3]269, 270; Kamennïy Ostrov / Stone Island, [2]31, [3]242; Kokushkin Most / Bridge, [2]177; Kolomna, [2]76; Kolomyaki, [3]46; Komendantskaya Dacha, [3]50; Konyushennaya Street / Church, [3]354; Krestovskiy Ostrov / Island, [2]175, 181; Letniy Sad (Jardin d'-Eté), [1]96, [2]41, 177; Malïy Teatr, [2]79; Marsovo Pole / Field of Mars, [2]179; Mihailovskiy Dvorets / Palace / Inzhenernïy Zamok / Castle, [2]344; Mil'onnaya / Milyonnaya Street, [1]116, [2]179, [3]182; Morskaya Street, [1]xxiii, [3]269; Moyka Canal, [2]68, 69, [3]269; Neva River, [1]25, 27, 96, 115, 122, 160, 289, 294, 303, 315, [2]41, 70, 143, 174, 175, 176, 177, 180, 181, 192, 310, 312,

384, [3]46, 91, 92, 175, 176, 177, 204, 212n, 232, 233, 265, 317, 339, 347, 369, 379; Nevski Boulevard, [2]68–9; Nevski Prospect / Avenue, [1]xxiii, [2]68–9, 71, 79, [3]269, 270; Okhta / Ohta, [1]111, [2]143, [3]202;

Palace Quay / Dvortsovaya Naberezhnaya, [2]175, 176, [3]233 & n; Palace Square / Dvortsovaya Ploshchad', [2]179, 311; Pazheskiy Korpus / Corp-des-Pages, [2]380; Peterburgskiy Ostrov / Island, [2]176; Petropavlovskaya Krepost' / Peter-and-Paul Fortress, [2]176, 177, [3]347; Publichnaya Biblioteka / Imperatorskaya Publichnaya / Leningradskaya / imeni Saltïkova-Shchedrina (PB), [1]85, 86, 87, [2]5, 7, 38, 234, 318, 320, 326, 365, 366, 414, 488, 506, 507, 518, 527, [3]87, 88, 132, 135, 196, 207, 268, 270, 272, 275, 277, 278, 285, 289, 292, 300, 304, 307, 313, 379, 431;

Pushkinskiy Dom / Institute of Russian Literature (PD), [1]84, 85, 86, 87, 88, [2]5, 75, 145, 267, 280, 320, 364, 365, 457, 467, 493, 505, 511, 524n, [3]55, 72, 122, 216, 217, 267, 281, 282, 307, 312, 313, 314, 365, 366, 379, 382; Senatskaya Ploshchad', [3]345, 346; Srednyaya Pod'yacheskaya Street, [2]426; Talon's Restaurant, [2]69, 71, 73; University, [2]20; Volkov Field, [2]89; Winter Palace, see Zimniy Dvorets; Zimniy Dvorets, [3]205

St. Petersburg Gazette, [1]5

St. Petersburg Mercury, see Sankt-Peterburgskiy Merkuriy

St. Petersburg Spectator, see

Index

Tolstoy, Count Lyov / Lev
Nikolayevich, [2]92, 204, 327,
428, 440; *Anna Karenina*
(Anna Karenin), [2]6, 279, 298,
344, 504, [3]38, 298, 311;
Haji-Murad, [3]52; *Istoriya
vcherashnego dnya* (History of
Yesterday), [2]70
Tolstoy, Count Nikolay Ilyich
(Lyov's father), [2]428
Tolstoy, Count Pyotr Aleksan-
drovich, [3]200
Tolstoy, Count Pyotr Andree-
vich, [3]395, 417, **418–19**, 422
Tolstoy, Count Yakov Nikolae-
vich, [2]77, 146–7; [3]162; *Moyo
prazdnoe vremya* (My Spare
Time), [2]146; *Poslanie k Peter-
burgskomu zhitelyu* (Epistle to
an Inhabitant of St. Peters-
burg), [2]146
To Luck, see Krïlov: *K schastiyu*
Tomashevski, Boris Viktoro-
vich, [1]60, 83, 84, [2]49, 80, 81,
92, 126, 133, 141, 241, 244,
247, 261, 274, 309, 320, 334,
336, 349, 370, 416, 417, 483,
509, 528, [3]21, 64, 78, 81, 101,
108, 194, 201, 209, 216, 250,
268, 271, 277, 324, 356, 357,
358, 363, 365, 366, 374; see
also *Evgeniy Onegin*, EDI-
TIONS; P., PUSHKINIANA: *Un-
published Pushkin*
Tombeaux champêtres, see
Chateaubriand
Tomi, [2]61
tomlenie ("languishment") /
tomimïy ("oppressed"), [1]379,
[2]337, 360, 382–3, 420
tomnost' ("languor") / *tomnïy*
(adj.), [1]379, [2]163, 171, 365,
382, [3]71
To My Aristarch, see P.,
WORKS: *Moemu*
To Pushchin, see P., WORKS: *K
P[ushchinu]*
To Pushkin, see Delvig, A. A.:
Pushkinu; Venevitinov: *K*

Pushkinu; Yazïkov: *K Push-
kinu*
Torbin, Miss (*EO* var.?), [3]276
Torigny, [2]220
Torquato, *see* Tasso
Torzhok, [1]61, [3]4, 112, 252, 272,
273; Pozharski's Restaurant,
[3]273
Toscar, [2]255; *see also* Macpher-
son
toska ("boredom," "yearning,"
"nostalgia," "heartache,"
"dull anguish"; between *sku-
ka*, "ennui," and *muka*, "tor-
ment"), [1]25, 379, [2]141, 156,
170, 171, 337, 360, 383, 399;
see also ennui
To the Emperor, see Zhukov-
ski: *K Imperatoru*
To the Goddess of the Neva, see
Muravyov: *Bogine*
*To the Portrait of Zhukovski,
see* P., WORKS: *K portretu*
To the Slanderers of Russia, see
P., WORKS: *Klevetnikam*
To the Volga, see Dmitriev, I.:
K Volge
Towneley, John, [2]98
*Traité d'économie politique,
see* Say
*Traité des grandes opérations
militaires, see* Jomini
Transcaucasia, [3]246, 281
translation, problems of, [1]vii–
xi, xiii–xiv, 1, 7–10, 337–9,
[2]12–13, 18n, 28, 45, 55, 81,
85, 93–4, 102–3, 103–4, 116,
120, 138–9, 141–2, 145,
148, 163, 165–6, 175–6,
187–91, 194, 211–12, 213,
218–19, 220, 233, 234, 235–6,
241, 243, 244, 272, 278, 279,
285–6, 289, 290, 295, 303,
308, 323, 324–6, 329, 332–4,
337–8, 347, 359, 360, 371–2,
378–9, 384, 386–7, 392–3,
404–5, 420, 422, 460–6, 469–
70, 480, 484, 496, 502, 537,
540, [3]9–13, 19–20, 28, 54, 63,

Index

Index